'I didn't expect you to choose sex without love.

'I didn't expect you to settle for that,' Cage said caustically.

Melanie turned her head slowly to look at him. She'd given herself out of love and there was no shame in that.

She said with quiet defiance, 'I don't regret a minute of it.'

'I don't regret it either,' he snapped, glaring at her. 'I just wish there could have been more between us.'

Dear Reader

The arrival of the Mills & Boon Mothers' Day Pack means that Spring is just around the corner . . . so why not indulge in a little romantic Spring Fever, as you enjoy the four books specially chosen for you? Whether you received this Pack as a gift, or bought it for yourself, these stories will help you celebrate this very special time of year. So relax, put your feet up and allow our authors to entertain you!

The Editor

LEGEND OF LOVE

BY

MELINDA CROSS

MILLS & BOON LIMITED
ETON HOUSE   18-24 PARADISE ROAD
RICHMOND   SURREY   TW9 1SR

*First published in Great Britain 1992
by Mills & Boon Limited*

© Melinda Cross 1992

*Australian copyright 1992
Philippine copyright 1992
This edition 1992*

ISBN 0 263 77805 3

*Set in Times Roman 10½ on 12 pt.
91-9302-52709 C*

Made and printed in Great Britain

CHAPTER ONE

MELANIE ANNABELLE BROOKS stood at the window of Florida's Tallahassee airport, looking out at a small private jet that shimmered in the July heat waves rising from the tarmac even this early in the morning. She was a striking young woman who looked as out of place in the bland surroundings of the executive lounge as a tropical flower springing from the cement of a car park.

Long honey-blonde hair curved from a central parting to frame her face, then folded on her shoulders like the crest of a golden wave. She had the elegant features revered by a long-dead Southern aristocracy, and even motionless she seemed to exude that presence and bearing that only a life of privilege could impart. Her very stillness was somehow graceful, and there was a quiet elegance in her imperturbable blue-eyed gaze.

Had anyone looked beneath the composed exterior, beyond the carefully cultivated demeanour that often made her seem unapproachable, they might have detected a hint of sadness in the depths of those Southern sky eyes—a quiet longing so old and so vague that those close to her never saw it.

But no one looked that carefully at anyone, she was convinced; and that was part of the reason the world was such a lonely place.

She smiled at the morose turn her thoughts had taken and moved one shoulder, as if gloom were an unwanted passenger she could shrug off with a minimum of effort. There was no reason for such ponderous, depressing thoughts; not today. Today she would embark on an adventure, and, since she had never had one before, the prospect was exhilarating.

She'd dressed with even more care than usual, striving for a businesslike appearance with a sharply tailored, expensive white linen suit. Long, shapely legs tapered from beneath the skirt to soft white Italian pumps, and she carried a small matching leather clutch-bag in one hand.

There were several other people with her in the airport's executive lounge, but most were clustered around the bar in the rear, engaged in quiet conversation. For the moment she had the window, the view, and her thoughts to herself.

Her focus shifted slightly from the plane outside to her own reflection in the glass. She could barely make out the details of her face—a flawlessly beautiful face, everyone said, although Melanie often thought it just looked empty. At the moment her entire reflection was so bleached by the light from outside that she looked almost ghostlike.

Lately she'd begun to feel that way, too—like the sketch of a woman that hadn't been completed yet— and at those times she berated herself sternly for daring to feel the slightest discontent when life had been so good to her.

She closed her eyes briefly and forced herself to count her considerable blessings. With the single exception of her mother's death before Melanie's first birthday, every one of her twenty-four years had been the stuff of fairy-tales.

She'd been born to the wealth and rich tradition of a grand old Southern family, raised on a Georgia plantation by a doting father and a raft of loving servants, and last month, with a strange sort of helpless resignation, she'd finally become engaged to Beauregard Parker, a dashing Florida State congressman who'd been courting her extravagantly for over a year.

It even *sounds* like a fairy-tale, she thought with a trace of cynicism she couldn't seem to control, because in spite of all her blessings she was still troubled with the vague sense of something missing. Something important.

At times it seemed that her entire life had been preordained—as structured as the train ride from her home in Creek County, Georgia to the Tallahassee station. You got on at one end, and off at the other, and someone else had pre-scheduled all the stops in between.

Her engagement to a proper choice like Beau had been one of those fated stops, as expected of her as attending the right schools or maintaining a proper public decorum. Perhaps the sheer predictability of the event was what made her feel even more like merely a helpless passenger on the train of her own life.

Stop it, she scolded herself. Beau's a wonderful man, and there isn't a woman in the South who wouldn't give anything to be in your position. Besides, soon you'll be married, and then you'll have children, and surely children will banish that empty sense of something missing.

Or, she thought, tipping her head to one side, maybe it's as simple as a sense of purpose, and who knows? Maybe I'll find that on this trip.

She focused on the plane outside the window again, feeling a warming, pleasant flutter of pride that Beau had asked her, rather than one of his aides, to represent him on this congressional fact-finding tour. Almost as a reflex, she touched a lace hankie to the dampness in the hollow of her throat.

A tall man with the carefully manicured appearance of a magazine model stepped up to her side from the rear of the room, and she felt crowded all of a sudden, as if he'd trapped her against a wall.

'Uncomfortably warm, isn't it, darlin'?' Beau murmured close to her right ear. The slow, syrupy cadence of his drawl called to mind hot afternoons on the magnolia-scented porch of her Georgia home.

She looked up at him with a faint, automatic smile. 'A true Southern lady never feels the heat.'

'And you are nothin' if not a true Southern lady.' Beau's voice seemed to hum with pleasure, but his eyes betrayed his distraction by flicking repeatedly towards the lounge door as he watched for the arrival of the all-important Press. 'Did you read the society column this morning? They're calling Beauregard Parker's fiancée "the flower of Southern womanhood".'

Melanie winced at the time-worn label she didn't feel she deserved. It belonged to women of a different era: women who floated over marble floors in low-cut dresses with enormous hoop skirts—women like her own ancestral grandmother, whose sultry, distinctively Southern femininity seemed to sizzle from the old oil portrait that hung on Melanie's bedroom wall. 'There are no "flowers of Southern womanhood" any more, Beau.'

'Nonsense! Look at yourself.' He turned his head from the door long enough to beam at their dual reflection in the tinted glass. 'As a matter of fact, look at the both of us. I swear I don't know which one is prettier.'

She suppressed the giggle just in time. Giggling in public was unseemly behaviour, particularly for the fiancée of Florida's favourite young legislator. You could laugh quietly, demurely, and lord knew you could smile—you *had* to smile—but giggling was not permitted. Still, it was the one thing she had liked about Beau from the beginning—that, on occasion, he could actually make her want to laugh out loud.

'There's no contest, Beau.' Her drawl softened every word to a sultry lullaby. 'You're prettier by far.' She saw that famous million-dollar grin of his flash in the window, and wondered again if he had been elected for his political opinions or his looks. He had the tall, aristocratic bearing of old Southern gentry, softly waved brown hair, and hazel eyes that brightened when he turned on the charm. The trouble was, she could never quite tell when the charm was genuine, or merely expedient.

'You *are* beautiful, Mellie,' he whispered, his breath stirring her hair. 'I'm the envy of every man who sees you...' Someone from the back of the room called his name and his eyes darted away from her like two startled birds. 'Excuse me, darlin'. I'll be right back.'

She nodded absently, looking back at her reflection, imagining she saw in the glass not a faint image of herself, but of the woman she'd idolised since childhood; the woman whose portrait hung over her bed. Like that woman, she had a rosebud mouth, whose corners lifted now as she recalled the day she'd rescued the painting from the attic, nearly twenty years before.

It had been a gloomy Saturday in her fifth year, with a steady rain polishing the fat, glossy leaves of the eucalyptus trees that lined the drive. The family's antebellum mansion had been a vast, lonely place for an only child; but the warm, cavernous attic, cluttered with the memorabilia of generations, was a strangely comforting haven. Being surrounded by the carefully stored possessions of all the Brookses who had gone before had given Melanie a much-needed sense of family continuity—an important feeling for a motherless youngster.

She'd found the portrait jammed behind boxes in a dusty corner, and had immediately dragged her new-found treasure downstairs to show her father.

'By heaven, I never knew this was up there, Mellie,' he'd said with a quirky smile. 'Do you know who this woman was? She was my great-great-grandmother. You were named after her, honey.'

'I have that beautiful lady's name?'

'You do indeed. And her looks, too, I think.' He'd propped the painting up against a wall and backed away, shaking his head with a little smile. 'They say she was a bit of a black sheep, you know. Her own husband crossed her name out of the family Bible, although I never was told why...'

'What's a black sheep, Papa?'

He'd sighed with a helpless kind of fondness, then scooped her up in his arms. 'Just someone who's a little different, Mellie.'

'Will I be a black sheep like her?'

'Oh, my, no,' he'd laughed. 'You're going to be my perfect little Southern lady, aren't you, Mellie? Just as your mother was.'

But she hadn't grown up to look like the fading photographs of that gentle, acquiescent soul who had been her mother—she looked like the first Melanie Annabelle Brooks—the family's black sheep.

The air seemed to push against her as Beau breezed up to her side again, and she wondered if this was what it would always be like—Beau rushing in and out of her life and her thoughts like a fickle wind.

'Well, Mellie, it's almost time. Are you excited about your little trip?'

'Yes.' This time her smile was genuine. 'Thank you for trusting me with an assignment like this, Beau. It means a lot to me.'

He chuckled quietly. 'Don't get yourself too worked up, darlin'. It's not as if I'm sendin' you to negotiate world peace. It's just a goodwill trip, the kind of thing politicians' wives do all the time. And, since that's what you're going to be in another few months, I thought this might be good practice.'

Melanie's brow threatened to crease. 'You make it sound unimportant.'

'Why, Mellie!' He turned her gently by the shoulders to face him and looked down at her with a wounded expression. 'Of course it's not unimportant! Would I have chartered that jet if it were unimportant? Would I have called a Press conference if it were unimportant?'

His expression was so boyishly earnest that Melanie's lips twitched with amusement. 'You'd call a Press conference to announce the weather if you could get away with it,' she teased gently. 'You're a politician down to your bones, Beau Parker, and don't you try pretending you're not.'

Strong white teeth flashed sheepishly in the sun-bronzed face. 'Guilty. But there's more to this goodwill jaunt than meets the eye, Mellie, and I'm countin' on you. Don't think I'm not. Benjamin Cage is a power to be reckoned with in this state, and when he sends an invitation any politician who wants to stay a politician sends a representative.'

Melanie sighed again, basically indifferent to the convoluted workings of politics. It was confusing, tiresome, and somehow a little distasteful. 'It doesn't seem right, Beau, that one little businessman should have that kind of power...'

'He's a *big* businessman, darlin',' he corrected her. 'Half the country drinks orange juice from his groves every morning, and ever since he heard the Florida legislature intended to cut some of the funding for the Everglades, he's been plastering "Save the Everglades" all over every bottle and carton. Now if we were to ignore his little invitation to see what's happening down there first-hand he might just decide to use all that advertising against us...understand?'

Melanie made a little face. Beau might think this was all legitimate politics, but it sounded like blackmail to her. 'So how many other congressmen are sending representatives on this junket?'

Beau shrugged. 'Who knows how many he invited? But I imagine you'll be a veritable parade, tourin' Cage's little Everglades.'

'*His* Everglades?'

'The way he talks, you'd think it was his.'

Melanie's brow arched in disapproval. The Everglades comprised millions of acres of sawgrass plain and dark, watery mangrove forests—the entire southern section of Florida. Anyone who thought of land that vast as his own private property was too arrogant for her tastes.

'I'm not going to like this man,' she stated with conviction.

Beau chuckled at her expression. 'I don't doubt that for a moment, darlin'. You and Mr Cage are on opposite ends of the social scale, I'm afraid. Clawed his way to the top, from what I hear, and doesn't think much of anyone who didn't have to do the same thing.'

Melanie's nose wrinkled. She'd encountered prejudice against those born to wealth before, and in her opinion it was just as insensitive as prejudice against those born to poverty. If you were going to judge people at all, you should judge them by what they did with their lives, not the circumstances of their birth. Benjamin Cage was sounding more unlikeable by the minute.

'He's a loner, too,' Beau went on. 'No family, no social life to speak of—doesn't seem to care much for anything or anybody, except that big swamp, and you can't talk reason to the man about that. If he had his way he'd pump every tax dollar the state raised into the place. I suppose he's hoping a private tour will convince the lawmakers that the Everglades needs more money next year, not less.'

Melanie nodded soberly; professionally, she thought. 'I'll listen to everything he says, Beau, and I'll take meticulous notes. By the time I get back you'll have all the information you need to cast an informed vote.'

Beau chuckled and shook his head a little, his eyes darting back to the door before meeting hers. 'Darlin',

I already know how I'm goin' to vote. My advisers don't think pouring money into a swamp makes much sense, and, frankly, neither do I.'

Melanie blinked at him, stunned. 'You've already decided how to vote?'

He nodded distractedly.

'But . . . then why are you sending me down there?'

'Because, Mellie,' he said, a trace of impatience creeping into his voice, 'I wouldn't want Mr Cage tellin' the voters I'd made a decision without hearin' all sides of the issue first, now, would I?'

'But, Beau . . . isn't that just what you're doing . . . ?'

'Now, now,' he interrupted her. 'Don't you worry your pretty little head about it, darlin'. It's just politics. All you have to do is go on down there and look interested when Cage takes you all on his tour, and maybe use some of that Southern charm on the man so it won't sting so much when I vote against him.'

For a moment, all Melanie could do was stare at him in disbelief. The disappointment would come later. '*That's* why you're sending me on this trip instead of one of your aides?' she finally asked in a whisper. 'Because I'm more charming than some near-sighted clerk in a three-piece suit?'

His mouth twitched in an uncertain smile, then his eyes jerked with obvious relief to the sudden flurry of activity behind them. 'Oh, dear. Looks as if the Press is going to interrupt us again. Sorry, Mellie, but I'm afraid this will have to wait.' He gave her waist a quick squeeze, then turned to face his public with a brilliant smile that didn't look sorry at all.

Melanie was too well-bred, too well-trained for her destined role as this gentleman's lady to make a scene in front of the journalists and photographers who quickly surrounded them.

After a full ten minutes of questions and photos, Beau held up one hand with an apologetic gesture. 'I'm sorry, ladies, gentlemen, but that's all we have time for this morning...'

'How about a goodbye kiss for the front page, Congressman?' a reporter called out, grinning.

'I trust you're suggestin' I kiss this beautiful creature, and not you, sir,' Beau fired back with his own grin, eliciting hearty laughter. 'And in that case, I'm most happy to oblige.'

Melanie submitted to one of the dry, passionless kisses Beau always gave her in front of the cameras, wincing inwardly because it seemed so contrived. It was at moments like these that she felt more like a stage prop than the professed love of his life.

'That wasn't the way I wanted to kiss you,' he whispered in her ear, almost as if he'd sensed her disappointment, 'but the way I wanted to kiss you was absolutely not for the public eye.'

She stilled in his arms for a moment, struck by the thought that, pristine as the kiss had been, it wasn't really all that different from the ones they shared privately. He just breathed harder when they were alone, that was all. She leaned back in the circle of his arms and gazed up at him, and, although that was the loving picture that ultimately made the front page of the Tallahassee paper, the photographer didn't see that her smile was a little strained.

Less than an hour later her small jet touched down at a private airstrip near Florida's Gulf Coast, just a few miles north of where the land designated as the Everglades began. She got off the moment the metal

staircase unfolded from the door, relieved to be off
the plane where she had been the only passenger.

The airport itself was little more than a few metal
hangars clustered around a single-storey brick building
with a short tower. She was walking briskly towards
the double glass doors in that building when a deep-
throated shout stopped her.

'Hey! You!'

She turned and squinted against the glare of sunlight reflecting off one of the metal hangars. When
her eyes adjusted she saw the distant figure of a man
standing perfectly erect next to an open Jeep.

'Where's the congressman?' the man shouted, and
Melanie's brows arched slightly in disbelief. Surely this
couldn't be the driver sent to fetch her to her hotel?
In *that* vehicle? Even from this distance she could see
the battered, mud-covered fenders and the ominous-
looking rollbar.

'Are you addressing me?' she asked without raising
her voice, refusing to bellow across an airfield like a
common barker.

It surprised her a little that the man heard her at
all; surprised her more when he began to cover the
distance between them with impossibly long strides.

As he drew closer her first thought was that he must
be a military man, his posture was so erect, his gait
so measured. The thought faltered a bit as she noticed
the very unmilitary clothing—heavy canvas trousers
tucked sloppily into knee-high boots, and a mud-
coloured sleeveless T-shirt that left tanned, muscular
shoulders and arms bare. Any notion of a military
connection collapsed entirely when he got close
enough for her to see his face; the face of a man she

knew instinctively would never take orders from another.

He stopped directly in front of her. 'Yes, I'm "addressing" you.' His voice had the same powerful resonance at a conversational level as it had in a shout. Melanie blinked, as if the force of it had blown across her face like a strong wind. 'So where's the congressman? I take it that *is* his plane?'

Melanie nodded stupidly, mesmerised by one of the most exotic-looking men she had ever seen. His hair was swept straight back from a high brow, its colour so purely black that even under the morning sun there were no highlights; just an even, blinding gleam. His face was deeply bronzed and almost ageless, it was so free of character lines. There was a faint, lighter-coloured webbing at the corner of each eye that marked prolonged squinting in the sun, but, other than that, the face gave no hint that any emotion had ever found expression there. His nose was strong and straight, his cheekbones high and proud, his mouth wide and crisply carved. Brows as black as his hair made two slashes over equally black eyes. The general impression was one of fierce indomitability, and only fascination kept Melanie from turning instinctively and running the other way.

'So?' he asked impatiently.

'Um . . . I beg your pardon?'

'So, if that's the congressman's plane, where is he?'

'Oh.' She licked her lips, unaccountably nervous. 'He isn't coming. I'm his representative——'

'*What*?'

Melanie took a quick step backward. 'I said I'm Congressman Parker's rep——'

'I *heard* what you said, I just can't believe it!' He
spoke in the rapid, clipped speech of a northerner,
making his verbal attack sound all the more vicious.
'Parker isn't coming himself? He sent ... *you*?'

It was his contemptuous emphasis on the word 'you'
that finally succeeded in snapping Melanie out of her
trance. Her back straightened, her chin lifted, and
those Southern sky eyes sparked with indignation.
'Yes, if it's any of your business,' her voice crackled
with the haughtiness only a Southern drawl could
produce, 'he sent *me*. Now, if you'll stand aside, I'll
go inside and connect with my driver ...'

'You have connected with your driver,' he snapped.
'I'm Benjamin Cage.'

Melanie's eyes swept over him once with thinly
veiled disbelief. *This* was Benjamin Cage? A man so
powerful that his invitations couldn't be ignored, even
by legislators? 'You can't be,' she said without
thinking how foolish it would sound.

His face was stone, only a slight narrowing of the
black eyes revealing any life at all. 'Who the hell are
you?' he demanded.

She tried to match his emotionless stare with one
of her own, but it was hard to manage with her head
tipped back to look up into his face. Besides, if this
really was Benjamin Cage, she was supposed to be
charming him, not alienating him. She adjusted her
tone accordingly. 'Congressman Parker is very
interested in what you have to say about the State
budget for the Everglades, Mr Cage, but it just wasn't
possible for him to get away right now. That's why
he sent me.'

Cage arched one brow, but said nothing.

'Please be assured that I'll convey everything you say to the congressman, and he'll consider it carefully before the vote on the budget next month...'

Her voice trailed away under his hard stare, and she swallowed. Clearly he was furious that Beau hadn't come himself, and if Beau's political future really depended on this man, he was in trouble indeed. 'The legislature *is* in special session, Mr Cage. I'm sure none of the other congressmen could get away to come in person, either,' she finished lamely.

Cage stared at her for a moment longer, then turned his head and looked off into the distance. 'I didn't invite any other congressmen.'

A careful upbringing kept Melanie's mouth from falling open in surprise. No one else was coming? No great crowd of people to ask informed questions, to occupy Cage's attention so she could fade into the background?

He turned his head to look down at her, his eyes hooded. 'Your Congressman Parker is the one legislator really pushing for a budget cut. I thought if I had a chance to show him how disastrous that would be for the Everglades, he'd convince the rest of them.' He sighed and one corner of his mouth tightened. 'The plan was to have his undivided attention for a few days so I could show him—one-on-one, man-to-man—the way things were down here.'

Melanie hesitated for a moment. 'You can show me. I'll tell him,' she said quietly, meaning it. Beau might not have sent her here to bring back information, but that didn't mean she couldn't do it anyway.

His chest and shoulders moved in what might have been a silent laugh. 'And who's to say he'll listen to you?'

She made no response at all for a moment, almost wishing he'd get angry enough to send her back to Tallahassee. Damn Beau for letting her think she was being sent on a real fact-finding mission; damn him for weaving her into this net of half-truths, making her an unwilling participant in political manoeuvrings she couldn't begin to understand; and damn him in particular for placing his future in her hands, knowing that her loyalty, once given, was a point of honour she couldn't betray.

'He'll listen to me,' she finally said with more conviction than she felt, forcing herself to meet Cage's intrusive stare. When she did, she felt that sudden vacuum inside she associated with the downward plunge of a roller-coaster.

He studied her face for such a long time that she became uncomfortable, then his lips tightened. 'I guess I don't have much choice but to take you at your word, do I?' He looked off to one side and sighed, and she caught a glimpse of a profile that looked as if it had been carved from granite. 'All right. We might as well get started. Let's get your luggage in the Jeep.'

She waited until he'd turned his back before taking a deep, quiet breath of relief. All things considered, she thought she'd done very well so far, walking that fine line between loyalty to Beau and her own sense of right and wrong. Without lying, she'd managed to weather Cage's anger that Beau hadn't come himself; she'd convinced him she was an acceptable envoy... and, she reminded herself wryly, watching his long strides eat up the tarmac as he walked towards the Jeep, you've talked yourself right into three days alone in the world's biggest swamp with a man who wears sleeveless T-shirts and rubber boots.

She caught her breath at that, feeling a strange quiver she finally recognised as a sense of impending adventure. Part of her wished she were back in Tallahassee—but, with her eyes on Cage's broad back, another part wasn't wishing that at all.

CHAPTER TWO

MELANIE had ridden in a convertible once, back in college when she'd been Queen of the Magnolia Parade. Riding in Benjamin Cage's open Jeep was nothing like that.

From the smooth tarmac of the airfield, he turned on to a narrow dirt track with rocks the size of a man's fist jutting out of the packed sand, and that was when the fun began. Her heart in her throat, her right hand clutching the armrest in a white-knuckled grip, Melanie repeatedly bounced high off the passenger-seat in wide-eyed, terrified silence. Only her shoulder harness kept her inside the vehicle, and only the fear of biting off her tongue kept her from shouting at Cage to slow down.

I should have worn a hat, she told herself as they sped down the track through an open sawgrass plain. It was not yet noon, but already intolerably hot, and Melanie felt like a helpless titbit in an open skillet, sizzling under the merciless gaze of the Florida sun. Between the bone-jarring bumps that seemed to jam her spine up into her brain, she worried about sun-burning her face, then chided herself for worrying about such a little thing when she'd never survive the Jeep ride anyway.

'It's not the best road,' Cage hollered over the noise of the straining engine, and if she'd been able to open her mouth against the hot wind of their passage she would have laughed out loud at the understatement.

She risked a hasty sidelong glance at Cage's profile, and could have sworn she'd just missed seeing a wicked smile. Damn him, he was actually enjoying her discomfort, probably punishing her because she wasn't Beau.

After what seemed like an interminable ride through the open space of the sawgrass plain, the little car shot suddenly into a hole in a thick, seemingly impenetrable stand of enormous hardwoods. Melanie squeezed her eyes shut and prepared for the inevitable collision, never for a moment doubting the victor in a battle between one of the monstrous trees and the tiny car. A short time later the Jeep slammed to a halt, flinging her forward against the strap of her harness. She kept her eyes closed for a moment, listening to the tick of the cooling engine, stunned to realise none of her bones were broken.

'You bastard!' she wanted to shriek at Cage, but Southern ladies of Melanie's standing did not shriek, nor did they stoop to guttural name-calling. She satisfied herself by turning her head slowly and giving him one of her most contemptuous, haughty glares.

He had his head tipped towards her expectantly, waiting for her reaction. With some dismay she noted that, even expressionless, his face conveyed more pride, more haughtiness than hers could ever muster with a conscious effort of will.

'Next time,' she told him with a voice that would have melted butter and burned it black, 'I'll drive.'

The mechanics of Benjamin Cage's reluctant smile were fascinating to watch. The wide, sharply chiselled mouth elongated slightly as muscles contracted on only one side, as if smiling was too painful an expression to commit fully. 'Here we are,' he said shortly, turning to face front, his mouth working to control the smile.

Melanie squinted through the mud-splattered windscreen, then frowned. For all practical purposes, they were in the middle of a towering jungle, parked in front of a small house perched precariously on a number of stilts. 'Where, exactly, is here?'

'Home,' he replied, those black eyes fixed on the pathetic structure rising from the forest floor. 'Well, not home, exactly; more like a weekend cabin. I come here when I need to get away from everything else.'

Melanie eyed the deeply shaded tangle of jungle that pressed in from all sides, making the already small house appear even smaller. 'Really,' she said with forced politeness, wondering why on earth anyone would choose to spend time in the ominous shadow of such an alien landscape. 'You mean you actually stay here?'

'As often as I can, for as long as I can. It's about as far as I can get from the office.'

Her smile was small and tight. 'Well, I'm sure it's very nice.'

This time he did laugh out loud. 'I'm glad you think so, since it's where you'll be staying, too.'

Obviously it was a joke; another sadistic attempt to get a rise out of her, just like the wild Jeep ride. 'Indeed.' She tossed out the word with a light chuckle, refusing to give him the satisfaction of appearing *that* gullible. He couldn't possibly expect her to stay in a place like this . . .

'Of course, you'll have to leave your modesty at the front door. The place is too small to provide much privacy, and I wasn't counting on having a woman guest.'

Slowly, lips parted incredulously, Melanie turned and looked at him. 'You're not serious. You expect me to stay *here*?'

'Of course I'm serious. You've got to live in the Everglades to understand them, even if it's only for a few days. The motels are for tourists. You want to be Congressman Parker's representative? You want to see what I intended to show him? Then this is how we start.'

A weak, breathy laugh escaped her lips as she looked at the house, seeing it differently now that she knew she was expected to live in it. Was it actually teetering on those stilts? Didn't the stilts themselves look more like toothpicks than the massive beams they actually were? Her concentration on the house was so intent that she barely noticed when Cage got out of the Jeep and started hauling her luggage up the dozen rickety steps that climbed from the forest floor to a wrap-around screen porch.

'Coming?' he called down from the top step.

Frozen in her seat, she looked up, up, at where he towered above her like some primitive god on his wilderness throne. She took a long time fumbling with her shoulder harness, suddenly reluctant to leave the uncomfortable, terrifying Jeep, now that she'd seen the alternative.

She wouldn't stay here, of course. She couldn't. Even if she managed to climb those splintered steps in her slender heels; even if her extra weight didn't snap the stilts and send the house crashing to the ground; there was still propriety to be considered. Young Southern ladies didn't spend unchaperoned weekends alone in the wilderness with strange men; especially not when those young ladies were engaged to up-and-coming congressmen constantly in the public eye. But how to refuse graciously, without offending the man Beau thought so important to his political future?

She had to concentrate to keep her brow from furrowing as she worked her way through the dilemma. For all Cage's stoic demeanour, she'd sensed a certain pride in this awful place, like a young boy eagerly showing off a tree-house he'd built himself. Wounding that pride with an out-of-hand rejection certainly wouldn't do Beau any good. The least she could do was climb up and look at the place, and if she didn't kill herself on the steps he'd see the foolishness of the plan for himself once she got up there. It was perfectly preposterous, imagining that any lady could be housed in such surroundings.

She took a deep breath and stepped from the Jeep, trying to ignore the way her expensive heels sank into the soft silt. She hesitated at the bottom of the stairs. There was no railing.

'I can come down and carry you up, if you like.'

He was taunting her, or challenging her—she wasn't sure which. 'Thank you, no. I can manage.' She placed a foot on the bottom riser and the step, little more than a slab of hewn wood, sagged under her weight and she froze.

'You sure?'

Melanie swallowed. 'Quite sure.' She waited until she heard the screen door slam above her before continuing her terrified, stiff-legged climb.

Only when she reached the safety of the top landing did she release the breath she'd been holding and smile tremulously, inordinately proud of her accomplishment.

'Congratulations,' he said from the other side of the screen door, and Melanie bristled at the mockery in his tone. She stood rigid and quietly furious, glaring at him through the distortions of the screen, wondering how long it was going to take this Bohemian to open the door for a lady. She went immediately slack-jawed when he ignored her, turning to walk deeper into the dimness of the cabin. 'Come on in,' he called over his shoulder.

'You *could* open the door,' she snapped.

'So could you.'

She made an audible sound of exasperated disapproval, then jerked the door open, stepped inside, and let it slam shut behind her.

The entire cabin was a single square room. In size, it was close to the small formal parlour of Melanie's childhood home, but any similarity ended there.

'How...rustic,' she said, for lack of a better word. 'Rustic' seemed far too generous. Every visible surface—walls, floor, angled ceiling—was made of splintery, bare wood, with mud-coloured caulking filling in the chinks and spaces.

Large openings in three of the four walls opened directly on to the screened porch to catch the slightest breeze. Above each a fitted piece of plywood was hooked to the ceiling, and Melanie shuddered, imagining how ominously dark the place would look with those shutters down and latched against the weather. A rough-hewn slab of lumber stretched the full length of the fourth wall, serving, she imagined, as a countertop of sorts. There was a single bed in a far corner, a small wicker sofa and chair in the room's centre.

'Sit down,' he told her as he bent to drag a large cooler from beneath the makeshift counter. 'I'll get us something to drink.'

Melanie walked gingerly to the only chair and sat down on the vinyl cushion, making a crinkly sound. She sat with her back straight and her bag clutched in her lap, like a woman who wasn't planning to stay long. She caught herself watching as his brown, muscular arms wrestled with the heavy cooler, then looked down, a little embarrassed.

'Oh,' she said quietly, noticing the woven mat beneath her feet for the first time. It covered a large area of the floor, its bright blues and reds and yellows the only colour in an otherwise drab space. 'This is beautiful. Where did you get it?'

'Not far from here,' he replied, telling her nothing. The floor creaked as he walked over to sit on the sofa that faced her. He passed her one of two small glass bottles dripping condensation.

'Wine cooler?' she asked, covering her distaste for the carbonated wine so prevalent in the marketplace these days.

'Worse. It's a bottled rum drink. A little rum, a lot of fruit juices. Totally offensive.'

Suppressing the urge to ask for a glass, at least, Melanie took the bottle, relishing the sensation of anything cold and wet in her palm. 'Why do you drink it, if it's so offensive?'

He almost smiled. 'I meant it would be totally offensive to you. I kind of like it, myself. But then, I'm easy to please.'

'Implying that I'm not?' she asked, a little testily.

'Implying that, from the looks of you, I'd guess you were more the champagne type.'

While she was trying to decide whether that was a compliment or an insult she sipped from the bottle and was surprised to find the drink quite palatable. She took another sip, then licked her lips. 'Actually, it's very refreshing. I think I like it.'

'It's almost a hundred degrees out there, and you haven't had anything to drink since the plane. You'd probably drink beer out of a barrel and love it at this point.'

Melanie's eyes widened slightly at the crude image, and thought she saw him start to smile again.

'You should change clothes right away. You must be sweltering in that get-up.'

She plucked self-consciously at the front of her suit jacket, pulling it away from her body to let some air circulate. 'I'm quite comfortable for the time being, thank you. I can wait to change until I get to my...'

'Maybe I didn't make myself clear before. If you're really going to take Congressman Parker's place for this weekend you're going to see the Everglades the way I planned to show it to him. From here. No motel, or no tour, take your pick.'

Melanie hesitated, wondering which would be worse as far as Beau was concerned: going back to Tallahassee now, alienating Cage and thus failing in her assignment; or staying alone with him in this God-forsaken place...

'Well? What's it going to be? I have a schedule too, you know. It wasn't easy to carve out these three days. I'd like to know they aren't going to be wasted.' He was leaning forward on the sofa now, his bare arms braced on his thighs, nearly empty bottle dangling between his knees. His black eyes never left her face.

She cleared her throat and swallowed. 'Surely you can see the impossibility of the situation,' she said in her most cajoling, honeyed drawl. 'You said yourself you never expected a woman guest, and you obviously don't have the accommodation...'

'You can have the bed. I've got a sleeping-bag.' The short clip of his northern accent made his words sound more sensible than hers; more definite. 'Don't worry. I have no intention of raping you during the night.'

Only the startled look in her eyes conveyed her loss of composure. 'The thought never crossed my mind,' she said stiffly.

'Is that a fact?'

Melanie didn't know if he was mocking her, or trying to frighten her, but in either case a haughty glare seemed an appropriate response. 'I'm concerned about the lack of privacy, and the lack of propriety in staying here, Mr Cage—not whether or not you will behave like a gentleman.'

'Who told you I was a gentleman?'

She hesitated for an instant, caught off guard by the question. 'I was giving you the benefit of the doubt,' she said frostily. 'Perhaps that was a mistake.'

His laugh filled the cabin. 'Giving any man the benefit of the doubt is always a mistake for a woman who looks like you,' he smiled, and Melanie thought she had never seen such a wicked smile in her life. 'However, in deference to your obvious naïveté, I promise I'll try to behave like a gentleman for the duration of your visit.' His smile tilted a bit. 'I'm not promising I'll succeed in my efforts, you understand.'

Melanie narrowed her eyes at the thinly veiled threat, and finally decided that it had no substance. He was still trying to intimidate her, and he'd almost succeeded simply by saying things he knew perfectly well would shock a lady. The truth was, she was the one who had *him* over a barrel. If he really wanted his information on the Everglades to go back to Beau he was going to have to play by her rules, not the other way around. Finally she spoke with all the dignity she could muster. 'Your promise isn't necessary, Mr Cage, since I have no intention of staying here. I'll stay at a hotel, or I won't stay at all.'

She watched with satisfaction as one of his black brows shot upward. She wondered if anyone had ever said no to him before.

'All right,' he finally said with a little shrug. 'Have it your way.'

She tempered her victory with one of her loveliest smiles. 'You'll see, Mr Cage. Spending my nights at a motel won't at all limit what I can learn when we go touring during the day...' Her sentence trailed away as he stood abruptly, picked up her bags from beside the bed and walked to the door.

'Come on. I'll drive you back to the airfield.'

'The airfield? But I thought...'

Her bags hit the floor with a double thump and he turned to face her chair, his back ramrod-straight, his chin high, only his eyes looking down. Melanie felt as if she was growing smaller under his stare.

'I told you,' he said flatly, 'I made time for this weekend because I knew actually living in the 'Glades would show Congressman Parker the need for more State funding. A lot of what happens here happens after dark, and you don't see much of that from an air-conditioned motel-room. So, if a motel is your condition for staying, then staying is pointless.' He picked up the bags again and moved towards the door.

'Now just a minute!' Her call stopped him, but now that she had him stopped she didn't quite know what to do with him. She looked down at her bag, still clutched tightly in one hand, as if that piece of very expensive leather could somehow solve her problem. Perhaps it was time to try a different tack.

'I confess I don't know what to do. I'm not sure which would be worse: abandoning my assignment, or my better judgement.'

'Are the two mutually exclusive?'

She looked up at him, big blue eyes troubled. 'I don't know,' she said in absolute honestly. 'It would help if I could call Beau...'

'Beau?'

She nodded. 'Congressman Parker.'

He snorted derisively. 'How did you ever land a job as a congressional aide without being able to make decisions on your own?'

Her eyes flickered. 'You don't understand. I'm not his aide. If that's all I were I wouldn't have to worry so much about how my behaviour would reflect on his...'

'Wait a minute. What do you mean, you're not his aide? What are you, then?'

She collected herself, straightening in the chair. 'I'm his fiancée, of course; the closest personal representative he could send. That's why you can be sure that I'll relay whatever I learn here directly back...'

The bags hit the floor again, startling her into silence. She didn't like the way he was looking at her. For once there was open expression in the black eyes, and Melanie decided immediately that she'd liked it better when they were unreadable. As it was now, they were narrowed and strangely bright for all their dark colour, focused on her with a fury so evident that it was almost palpable. He muttered a violent oath under his breath, and she wisely decided now would not be the time to criticise his language. 'You're his *fiancée*? He sent his *fiancée* on a fact-finding tour? What the hell did he think qualified you to investigate something this important? That you're good in bed?'

Melanie's jaw dropped open. 'How *dare* you say such a thing to me . . .?'

'And how dare *you* try to pass yourself off as a qualified professional when all you really are is——?'

'I *didn't*!' The unintentional volume of her own voice astounded her. Oh, lord, what was happening to her? Melanie Annabelle Brooks, daughter of the South, a well-bred lady of refined sensibilities, and here she was, bellowing like a hog-caller.

Mortified, she closed her eyes briefly, then forced the music of quiet modulation into her voice. 'I did *not* try to pass myself off as any such thing. I said I was representing the congressman, and that's precisely what he sent me down here to do. He had the perfectly silly idea that I would be one of several representatives on this tour; that sending someone as close to him as I am . . . might tell you just how much importance he placed on this trip . . .' Her voice faltered, then faded at the uncomfortable memory of why Beau had really sent her down here.

Cage's eyes narrowed in contempt. 'Is that what he told you?' She looked up sharply, but couldn't meet his cold, hard stare. 'You know exactly why he sent you down here, don't you?' he demanded. 'You're the decoy; the "representative" that's supposed to convince me and the Press that he's willing to listen to both sides of the issue. But he has no intention of really listening, does he?'

Melanie felt slightly ill to hear Beau's motives stated so plainly. The deception had made her uncomfortable when she'd first learned about it at the airport; now she felt somehow soiled to be a part of it. 'I think... I think you're making an unjustified assumption...'

'Are you a liar, too?'

Her eyes flashed a more brilliant blue at the personal attack. 'No!' she sprang to her own defence automatically. Beau might have made her an unwitting partner in deception, but she wouldn't lie outright for him. And yet if you continue this deception for Beau's sake, she thought miserably, a liar is exactly what you'll be. 'I am not a liar,' she mumbled, slumping a little in the chair.

There was silence for a moment as she stared vacantly at the far wall, trying to sort through the muddle of her thoughts. 'Come on,' she heard him say at last, and it was the gentleness of his tone that disturbed her more than anything else. All of a sudden he was trying to be nice to her; maybe, heaven forbid, because he pitied her for being as much a helpless pawn in this situation as he was. His contempt would have been preferable. 'I'll take you back to the airfield, Miss... what the hell is your name, anyway?'

'Melanie,' she replied tonelessly. She was still staring at the wall. 'Melanie Annabelle Brooks.'

He grunted softly, almost as if someone had punched him gently in the stomach. 'Melanie *Annabelle* Brooks?' he repeated softly. 'From Creek County, Georgia?'

She nodded absently, used to people recognising her name. Lord knew it had been in the society columns enough lately.

'Good lord,' he murmured after a moment of stunned silence. 'Full circle. It comes full circle...'

Puzzled, she looked up and frowned at him. He was staring out through the screen, and there was something wild about the way the light from outside limned his profile, outlining the strong nose, the firm jaw, the slight jut of his chin. 'Melanie Annabelle Brooks...' He repeated her name tonelessly, like a litany. 'Maybe it's true after all, what the Indians say... that the destiny of the adult is written in the name of the child.' He turned his head slowly to look at her. 'That grand names mandate grand deeds.'

Melanie looked away, a little uncomfortable with her notoriety. Just because her family's name had been in the social register for generations, it didn't mean there were grand deeds written in her future. If she had a destiny at all, it was to take her proper place in society as the devoted wife of some fine Southern gentleman. That had been the role of all the Brooks women throughout history.

Still staring at the wall, she wondered what it would be like to have a greater purpose; to leave a mark on history more memorable than an oil portrait gathering dust in a forgotten corner of an attic. 'Mr Cage,' she said suddenly, struggling with a vague, barely formed thought she couldn't quite articulate yet, 'what if... what if I was to stay...?'

'It's pointless. We both know that. Why continue the charade?'

She frowned and pursed her lips, then turned abruptly to look at him. 'Perhaps it did begin as a

charade, Mr Cage; but it doesn't have to end as one.'
The only outward sign of her anxiety was her hand's
tightening on the purse in her lap. 'Aside from the
reports Beau gave me to read, I don't know a thing
about the Everglades. Frankly, I don't know much
beyond the front veranda of the Georgia plantation
where I grew up. But I'm not entirely without influence on Beau, and if you can convince me voting
for the cut in the budget is a mistake . . . maybe I can
convince him.'

The offer was genuine, but in the circumstances it
sounded feeble, even to her. Cage thought she'd been
in on the deception from the beginning; that she'd
always known the trip was a sham; so why should he
trust her now? She watched his face, but there was
no change in his flat, oddly emotionless gaze, and she
had already resigned herself to the angry refusal she
deserved when he said, 'All right.'

She blinked once, so startled by the reply that she
didn't know what to say.

'We'll give it a try.'

Her lips moved involuntarily into a tremulous smile,
and she caught herself wondering why on earth she
was suddenly so happy that he had agreed to let her
stay.

For a long moment, only the ratcheting sound of
insects from outside broke the silence. Finally the floor
beneath Cage squeaked as he shifted his weight and
looked down at her, those black eyes narrowed in the
bronzed face, fixed so intently on hers that she felt
almost physically violated. 'The first thing we have
to do is get you out of those ridiculous clothes . . .' he
let the words hang for a moment, enjoying her re-

action, then added '...into something cooler. You have a lot to see, and it's hot where we're going.'

Melanie smiled with nervous relief, unobtrusively pulling her jacket away from her damp skin. 'And it isn't here?' she asked wryly, rising from her chair and smoothing the wrinkles from her skirt as she looked around. 'I'll just wash first, if you don't mind...' The sentence trailed away into the hot silence of midday. 'Where's the bathroom, Mr Cage?' she asked after a moment.

He was smiling when she looked at him. 'What bathroom?'

CHAPTER THREE

No BATHROOM. The words loomed ridiculously large in Melanie's mind, blocking out all other thoughts. She'd already forgotten about the impropriety of spending three days alone in this Everglades cabin with Benjamin Cage. Such a minor thing paled in the shadow of that short, yet overwhelming phrase—no bathroom. She quelled the impulse to sink back down into her chair and instead turned to face Cage directly.

He was still standing by the door to the porch, his head turned slightly towards her, those black eyes watching, waiting for a reaction. He probably thought she was a spoiled, simpering fool—a woman totally incapable of living outside her own sheltered, pampered environment, even for three days. And he wasn't far from wrong. She'd balked at staying in this place even before she'd learned there was no bathroom...

'No running water,' he interrupted the silence. 'No electricity, either.' His eyes swept over her expensive suit and shoes, as if to emphasise the obvious point that she did not belong here. She clenched her jaw, thinking that he was doing this on purpose: goading her into leaving just because that was what he expected her to do.

A tiny seed of rebellion flickered to life deep inside. All her life she'd done what people had expected of her—men, in particular. For her father first, and then for Beau, she'd always been precisely what she'd been born and raised to be: perfectly mannered, perfectly feminine—perfectly predictable. Both men would be horrified to think of her in conditions such as these, and suddenly that had a strange sort of appeal.

'If there's no bathroom where I can wash,' she tried to force nonchalance into her voice, 'I suppose you'd better show me the alternative if I'm going to stay here.' She felt a peculiar, racing thrill when one of his brows arched. She'd never taken a man by surprise before, and surprising this particular man was eminently satisfying.

That brief flare of bravado dimmed rapidly as she followed him down the steps outside, eyes and ears tuned to the surroundings with a new, very personal interest.

After the noise of the Jeep, the forest had seemed deadly silent when they'd first arrived, but now a veritable cacophony of sounds assaulted her ears from the wet, brilliantly green world that surrounded the cabin. Unseen insects buzzed and chirped and whirred; birds squawked and warbled and even screeched as they soared over the canopy above them.

On the ground every frond of every fern seemed to quiver, as if with the passage of a large, invisible beast, and the spongy humus gave way beneath the points of her heels with little sucking sounds as they circled the stilted house. She followed Cage closely, trying to plant her feet in the large prints left by his boots.

'That's the outhouse.' He stopped and pointed to a small half-wood, half-screened structure set back into the trees.

Melanie nodded silently, imagining a thousand scurrying creatures chasing her down that narrow path in the dark of night.

'And over here is the shower.'

'The shower?' She followed him around the thick timbers that supported the right corner of the cabin, her eyes hopeful. They clouded with dismay when he picked up the spray nozzle of a hose that snaked downward from a small hole in the porch floor above.

'There's a barrel up there that collects rainwater. Open this nozzle——' he pushed the trigger and a brief spray of water emerged '—and you have a hand-held shower.'

Melanie pursed her lips and looked around worriedly. 'But . . . it's right out in the open. There aren't any walls . . . not even a curtain . . .'

'You won't need one.' He gestured at the seemingly impenetrable greenery surrounding them. 'The forest may have a thousand eyes, but none of them is human.'

She smiled thinly at that, finding it very small comfort; and then she thought how odd it was that he hadn't considered she might have been worried about *his* eyes.

In the dry, almost lecturing tone of a bored tour guide he continued to explain the archaic water system. 'We're in the middle of the wet season now, so water conservation isn't quite so critical, but we still have to be careful. Never, ever leave the hose open, or you'll drain all the drinking water. If all you need is a quick wash, for instance, just fill that basin over there.'

She followed his gaze, then blinked in stupefied disbelief. The 'basin' was a shallow depression chipped into a waist-high tree stump.

'Clever,' she mumbled, but 'primitive' was the word that first came to mind. Primitive, uncivilised, barbaric. From the corner of her eye she saw the glint of light on metal and looked up. 'What are those?' She pointed at the broad, saucer-like rings of metal circling each of the stilts halfway between the ground and the cabin floor above.

He followed her gaze and shrugged. 'They help keep some of the wildlife out of the cabin. The rodents can't climb over them, and the snakes don't like to. The edges are very sharp.'

Melanie literally felt the blood draining from her face. 'Snakes?' she said in a small voice. 'In the cabin?' She had an immediate vision of snakes writhing over her in bed, and for a moment thought she might prove that irritating old caricature of faint-hearted Southern belles by swooning dead away.

'Don't worry about it. Most of them are harmless anyway.'

'Really,' she smiled weakly. 'How reassuring.'

'Come on back upstairs. I'll show you how to get drinking water out of the barrel, how to run the oil lamps, and then you really should change into something cooler. You look a little pale.'

He thinks I look pale now, she thought numbly as she followed him back up the steps. Wait till he sees me after I've met my first snake.

She traipsed behind obediently as he showed her where things were in the cabin, but she only pretended interest, reasoning that he would always be here to do whatever needed done. While he showed her how to light the smelly oil lamps and trim the wicks so they wouldn't smoke, her mind wandered back to her pampered youth on the family plantation in Georgia. Whenever the power went out during a storm, the servants had always moved through the house like candle-lit wraiths, carrying oil lamps with

crystal teardrops that tinkled when they moved. She
drifted with the memory, feeling oddly sleepy. She
barely noticed when Cage stopped talking and narrowed his eyes at her.

'You're not paying attention,' he said sharply.

She started a bit, then focused on the unusual
prominence of his high cheekbones, mostly because
she didn't want to meet his eyes. It seemed exceed-
ingly hot and close all of a sudden, and she touched
the dampness in the hollow of her throat with her
fingers. When she blinked it was all she could do to
open her eyes again. Her lashes felt heavy and wet.
'Do you think I could have a glass of water?' she
asked, her voice breathy and shallow. 'It's very warm,
isn't it?'

Without warning he reached out to lay both hands
on her cheeks. Normally she would have jerked back
from such familiarity, but her reactions seemed abnormally slow, as if she were trying to move through
air that had suddenly become syrup.

'Damn,' he spat, scowling down at her. 'I should
have known. That fair skin, those blue eyes . . .'

Her head wobbled a little to one side and she
blinked at him stupidly. His face seemed to swim in
and out of focus, and oddly the blurring made some
things more clear—like his eyes. They weren't really
black; the brown was just so dark that it looked as if
they were. And they weren't cold, unfeeling eyes,
either. As a matter of fact, they looked positively hot,
like two dark points of fire burning in his face . . .

'I think . . .' she started to say, blinking hard to clear
her vision, wondering what was wrong with her. Was
this strange, disconnected wooziness the way people
felt when they were going to faint? 'I think I'm a little

dizzy...' Her knees buckled abruptly and Cage
grabbed her quickly by the upper arms.

Oh, look at that, Melanie thought, blinking up at
him. Look at the pucker between his brows; look at
how worried he is about me. Isn't that nice?

'Easy...' She heard him speak, but it sounded as
if he were very far away. 'Easy, now.' He spoke again,
and his voice was beautifully deep, like the distant
rumble of the night train she'd heard as a child from
her bedroom window. It was a pleasant, soothing
sound, and yet a haunting one, making her long for
places she'd never seen; things she'd never done...
'Here. Let me help you.' She felt his arm snug around
her waist, supporting her so that her feet barely
touched the ground, and then somehow she was in
the chair and he was bent over her, his hands pressed
against her cheeks, his eyes worriedly searching hers.
His hands felt rough, and very hot.

'Dammit,' he muttered. 'I'll be right back. Don't
move.'

She almost giggled at the order, it was so foolishly
unnecessary. Her legs were rubber, and even if they
could have supported her weight, her thoughts were
too fuzzy to engineer the movement.

He was back almost before she knew he was gone,
pressing a glass of cool water to her lips, a damp cloth
to her forehead. It was the most delicious water she'd
ever tasted, and she would have drained the glass if
he hadn't taken it away. When she looked up to ask
for more he shook his head before she could give voice
to the request. 'Not just yet.'

'I'm still thirsty...'

'I know you are. You can have more in a minute.
Are you feeling better?'

'Yes, I'm feeling better...' She looked down as he knelt in front of her chair and watched the deft movements of his hands as they unbuttoned her jacket. There was something wrong about his doing that, but whatever it was kept slipping away in the fog of her thoughts. Besides, the air felt deliciously cool against the skin of her chest.

She watched his face as he parted the jacket, pressing the damp cloth to the sides of her neck, and then to the hot flesh that rose above the lace of her bra. There was a strange tightness around his eyes and mouth, as if he was exerting great effort, and she wondered what could be so hard about holding a little washcloth to her chest. After a moment she shivered involuntarily, and Cage took the cloth away and stood up.

'Here.' He handed her the glass of water and she drank again. Her focus on the world seemed to sharpen a little, and she looked up at him. What she saw in his eyes made her cheeks redden and her hands fly to pull her jacket closed. His only response was a tight smile.

'Thank you. That's much better,' she said, a little too fast. 'The room isn't spinning any more. That must be magic water.'

His lips twitched a little. 'Any water is magic when you're courting heatstroke. That was too close a call. You mustn't have had much to drink on the plane...'

'I didn't have anything to drink on the plane.'

He frowned at her. 'When did you drink last?'

'You know... that rum thing you gave me...'

'Don't remind me. I mean before that.'

She frowned, trying to remember. 'Early this morning, I guess. I had orange juice for breakfast. Some of your orange juice, as a matter of fact.'

'Breakfast? That must have been hours ago. What're you trying to do? Kill yourself? You're fair-haired, fair-skinned—you should know that makes you twice as susceptible to heatstroke.'

'That's ridiculous.' She fluttered her hand impatiently. 'I've never, ever suffered from heatstroke, and I've lived in the South all my life...'

'Unless I miss my guess, you've lived in air-conditioning all your life.'

'So?' she grumbled, thinking of the vast air-conditioned spaces of the family mansion, the pleasantly shivery chill of the Tallahassee hotel-room she'd stayed in last night.

'So you don't know the first thing about staying healthy in this kind of heat and humidity,' he snapped. 'If you did, you would never have accepted alcohol when you were already thirsty. Nothing dehydrates you faster.'

Her mouth twitched petulantly. 'You gave it to me...'

'I know I did! I also gave you credit for having a little common sense!' He closed his eyes briefly and blew out a long, exasperated sigh; then dropped to a crouch at the side of her chair, putting his head directly on a level with hers.

'Listen, Ms Brooks. If you're really going to stay here, and I emphasise the word "if", you're going to have to learn some new rules very fast.'

Melanie looked into the depths of eyes that made her want to look away and eyes that made it impossible to look away, all at the same time. She frowned and tried to sound decisive. 'There's no "if" about it. I told you I would stay, and that's what I intend to do.'

'Only if I let you.' His eyes were fixed on hers, just inches away.

'You need me, remember? I'm the only chance you have to convince Beau to change his vote. You have to let me stay.' Her smile was just a little smug, and Melanie decided she was feeling much better indeed.

'I don't have to do anything.'

Her smile faltered, then faded entirely.

He was very close. So close that the sheen of his black hair was almost blinding; so close that his eyes seemed like dark doorways she could walk through into rooms she'd never seen before. She caught herself breathing deeply, discerning for the first time in her life the scent of another human being. His was sharply aromatic, like the floor of a pine forest after a rain. Did Beau have a scent? she wondered, and then realised immediately that he didn't. Not one of his own, anyway.

'But I want to stay,' she whispered, wondering why it was suddenly so important to her.

He regarded her steadily. 'Will you follow the rules I lay down? No questions, no arguments?'

'Yes.' The breath from her mouth stirred the short, fine strands of hair at his temple.

His eyes were still fastened on hers, but she couldn't read them. 'You'll have to drink a lot of fluids, even when you don't think you're thirsty—at least twice as much as I drink. Agreed?'

She nodded.

'No heavy exercise, no big meals, just lots of small ones, and wear a hat outside all the time... you did bring a sun hat, didn't you?' She shook her head and his mouth tightened impatiently. 'Never mind. We'll get you one. How about clothes? What do you have in that bag?'

'Another suit, a sundress, a cocktail dress . . .'

'A *cocktail* dress?' He straightened instantly to his full height and scowled down at her. 'You brought a cocktail dress for a tour of the Everglades?'

Melanie's eyes flashed at his tone. 'I thought I was going to be staying at a hotel!' she snapped up at him, her chin jutting defiantly. 'A hotel with a lounge and a restaurant and air-conditioning and maybe even running water!'

Even through her anger she had the sense that he was about to burst out laughing, and then she wondered where she had ever got such an idea. His stony expression hadn't altered a fraction. 'All right,' he said quietly, handing her the glass, watching her drink the rest of the water. 'I guess the first order of business is a shopping trip to Everglades City. We're not going into the 'Glades until we get you dressed decently.'

She arched one brow at his use of the word 'we', but made no comment. Wondering if staying here with this man was the biggest mistake of her life, or if she had even bigger ones to look forward to, she took his hand and let him help her from the chair.

'Still a little shaky?'

She wasn't, but she liked the feeling of his arm firmly circling her waist. A lady should always be able to count on the support of a man. That was the way it was meant to be. 'Yes. Just a little.'

CHAPTER FOUR

EVERGLADES CITY was a seemingly endless drive from
Benjamin Cage's isolated cabin. The roads were tor-
tuous, rocky paths when they could be called roads
at all, and Melanie was certain all her joints had been
dislocated by the time Cage finally pulled the Jeep on
to a smoothly tarred surface that promised civilisation just ahead.

'City' was a misnomer for the one-traffic-light
Florida town whose main attraction was its Gulf Coast
entrance to Everglades National Park. A few tourists
wandered the main street, and as the Jeep slowed
Melanie looked at their brief shorts and loose T-shirts
with envy. Her linen suit had lost its crispness and its
bright white colour long ago, and, aside from feeling
unkempt and wilted in the heat, she felt ridiculously
overdressed.

Cage pulled into the shady car park of a drive-in
restaurant and turned to speak briefly into the speaker.
Melanie stared at the back of his head, fascinated by
the unrelieved blackness of his hair, wondering what
ancestor had donated that particular recessive gene.

Suddenly he turned towards her and she caught her
breath at the overpowering masculinity of his face.
'Hungry?' he asked her.

She brushed nervously at the long tangles of wind-
blown blonde, tucking them behind her ears. 'Not a
bit.'

'Nevertheless, you're going to eat.'

She nodded without protest and he raised his brows. 'You're very good at taking orders, aren't you?'

'That was the agreement, wasn't it? You lay down the rules, I follow them.'

His brows lowered back to their original position. 'Yes, that was the agreement. I just didn't expect it to be this easy. Somehow I pegged you as the kind who'd fight me every step of the way.'

Melanie's laugh was cultured—cultivated, actually—as musical as wind chimes in a soft breeze. 'I've never been the kind of fool who balks at doing what's best for me, Mr Cage.'

He was silent for what seemed like a long time. 'So you always do what other people tell you is best for you?' he asked quietly.

She thought about that for a moment, searching her memory for a single instance of even minor rebellion, but finding none. What had there been to rebel against? Why would she ever have questioned the guidance of people like her father, like Beau, who had only her best interests at heart?

Besides, there was a certain security in always being told how to behave, what to wear, what schools to attend and what young men to date. You never made any mistakes that way.

Cage was still looking at her, waiting for an answer, but before she could reply a young waitress in shorts and a halter top brought a tray of covered dishes and fastened it to his door. Melanie couldn't help but notice the way the girl's heavily made-up eyes sparked when they saw Cage's face. She flashed him a brilliant smile as she pocketed a generous tip, then looked over her shapely shoulder twice as she walked away.

Brazen, Melanie thought. 'Do women always react to you that way?' she asked archly.

Cage cocked a brow in puzzlement. 'What way?' He looked after the waitress with the expression of a man who thought he might have missed something.

Melanie's lips flattened a little. 'Surely you're not going to tell me you didn't notice that.'

'Notice what?'

'Her reaction to you, of course,' she said a little more snidely than she'd meant to. 'For heaven's sake, she did everything but crawl into the car...'

His sudden smile was open, almost boyish, and Melanie couldn't decide if it was genuine or contrived. 'Really? How nice.' He looked over at where the young waitress was leaning on a serving counter that opened to the inside kitchen, her weight on one leg, the opposite hip cocked and straining against the brief shorts. 'I didn't notice,' he mused. 'Maybe you could give me an insider's insight on the nuances of female behaviour...' This time when he looked back at her there was a definite twinkle of amusement in those black eyes. Melanie scowled at him.

'Here.' He passed over a tall glass of some kind of juice and an oblong dish heavy with an assortment of freshly cut fruit and a small loaf of crisp bread. 'Eat it all.'

The tart-sweet aromas of cantaloupe, water-melon, pineapple, mango, grapes and a few other fruits Melanie didn't recognise assailed her nostrils. Suddenly she was ravenous. 'I couldn't possibly eat this much,' she said automatically, but within moments she'd proved herself a liar. Her dish was nearly empty by the time she realised Cage was watching her. She glanced up at him, then down at her plate, embarrassed. 'I must have been hungrier than I realised,' she mumbled.

'They say the enjoyment of food is a measure of sensuality.'

Melanie almost choked on the last piece of pineapple. She coughed, then swallowed. Even without looking she knew he was wearing that expression that looked as if it wanted to be a smile. 'Where to next?' she asked, still staring down at her plate.

'First to get you some decent clothes, then back to the cabin. Are you finished with that?'

She passed him her totally empty dish with a sheepish expression, appalled by her own bad manners. Ladies always left a few morsels on their plates, indicating a dainty, controlled appetite. She closed her eyes as Cage started the Jeep and pulled out of the car park, thinking that she'd only been away from her own environment for a few hours, and already she was shedding the lessons of her twenty-four years of gentility.

He bypassed the main street's stores and drove to a rather shabby shop on one of the back lanes. 'This is Hildy's,' he explained as they entered the door to the chiming of a little bell. 'The locals get almost everything they need right here. Main Street is for the tourists.'

Melanie looked around the small interior, so crammed with merchandise that there was barely room to walk sideways down the aisles. The predominant smell was rubber, and the predominant colour was a mud green.

Cage walked straight to a table of jumbled knee-high boots and started rummaging. 'Here we go.' He

held a pair of sickly brown rubber ones aloft. 'These
are about your size. Try them on.'

She eyed the cumbersome things sceptically. 'I really
don't think they'll be necessary...'

'We'll be doing a lot of walking through wetlands.'
He looked straight at her when she didn't move to
take the boots. 'Snake country,' he added softly.

Melanie tried on the boots.

Within five minutes Cage had managed to select
the most unattractive assortment of clothing Melanie
had ever seen in her life. There were baggy canvas
trousers, similar to what he wore; two long-sleeved
shirts in the same muddy green colour; two T-shirts,
a pair of tennis shoes, some walking shorts, and the
boots, of course. He dumped it all on the check-out
counter next to the cash register, then went back for
a broad-brimmed straw hat.

'Perfect,' Melanie muttered, staring at the tacky hat
with its attached black scarf, wondering what she'd
look like with it tied under her chin.

Cage snapped the folds out of one of the shirts.
'Here. Turn around and we'll see if this is too big.'

She sighed and turned, arms outstretched while he
held the shirt up to her shoulders.

He gazed critically at the fit at the shoulders, then
his eyes dropped to the generous swell of her breasts
and froze. Melanie caught her breath silently when
she saw him swallow. His eyes lifted slowly to meet
hers. 'We'll just check the length of the sleeves,' he
murmured, his lips barely moving. Melanie lowered
her arms and felt the cuffs of the sleeves brush against
her fingertips. His hands still held the shirt at her
shoulders; his eyes still stared into hers. 'How is it?'
His words ran together in a quick exhale.

'Fine,' she whispered, transfixed by his eyes.

Mindlessly his thumbs moved downward, drifting lightly over the lapels of her jacket just above the rise of her breasts. Melanie's eyes widened at the sensation of the jacket's silk lining being pressed against her skin. She saw the sudden tightening of the flesh at the corners of Cage's mouth, and without realising it responded by letting her head fall backwards ever so slightly. The movement was too imperceptible to be measured in anything but increased heartbeats.

The soft sound of the shirt crumpling to the floor made them both start. For a moment they stared at each other wide-eyed, like guilty children, then Cage ducked abruptly to retrieve the shirt.

Melanie blinked her way out of what had seemed like a dream, amazed to find him behaving as if nothing had happened. What was he doing, bent over the counter like that, scribbling on that tablet? And what had happened between them just a moment ago, and why wasn't he affected by it? 'What are you doing?' Her voice sounded husky.

His pencil froze for a moment, then he cleared his throat and started writing again. 'Listing everything we bought and the price.' *His* voice was normal; crisp, cool, distant.

Melanie licked her lips. Nothing had happened. He'd held up a shirt and it had dropped to the floor, that was all. Anything else had been simply the product of her imagination. She frowned hard and looked down at the scuffed wooden floor. 'Shouldn't we wait for someone . . . ?'

'Hildy'll put it on my bill. She's probably out fishing.'

'Fishing?' It pleased her that the huskiness in her
voice had disappeared, and she looked up. 'She went
fishing and left the store wide open?'

He signed his name with a flourish and straightened.
'Hildy fishes every day, and she always leaves the store
open in case someone needs something. It's a small
town. Here. You carry these.'

He handed her the boots, looked at her thoughtfully for a moment, then took them back. 'There's a
bathroom in the back,' he said with a half-smile,
handing her some of the clothes and the tennis shoes,
'the last real one you'll see in a while. Why don't you
take advantage of it while I take the rest of this out
to the Jeep?'

He was halfway to the door before the blush reached
Melanie's face.

While barely large enough to turn around in, the
bathroom was infinitely preferable to the outhouse
she'd seen at the cabin, and Melanie savoured the
small luxury. With a scrap of soap on the ancient,
pedestal sink she gave herself a cursory sponge bath
before donning the new clothes, then brushed her hair
back to its honey-blonde perfection and repaired her
make-up.

Five minutes later she walked back out to the Jeep,
carrying what felt like her identity in her arms. Her
slip and tights were neatly hidden within the folds of
the suit she carried on her arms; her expensive pumps
dangled from two fingers.

She wore a black T-shirt and, over that, one of the
muddy green shirts she'd left unbuttoned. The stiff
canvas trousers were rolled halfway up her calves so
she wouldn't trip on the too-long legs, and the blind-

ingly white new tennis shoes were surprisingly comfortable.

To her own eyes she looked ridiculous in the too-large clothes, but she knew that some men found that lost-waif look strangely appealing. She wondered what Cage would say.

He gave her a cursory glance as she crawled into the Jeep, but made no comment on her appearance. 'Ready?' he asked simply, and, when she nodded, he pulled away from the kerb with a short squeal of the tyres.

On the bone-jarring ride back to the cabin, Melanie caught herself scowling more than once, miffed that Cage hadn't said something—*anything*—about the way she looked. In a way, she had always depended on the comments of the men in her life as a barometer of her own appearance, and hearing no comment at all on such a marked change made her uncomfortable. Not that she needed constant complimenting, of course; she was just used to being noticed. Beau would have noticed. Beau would have taken one look at this outrageous outfit, chuckled in that throaty way of his, then told her she looked irresistible, like a little girl playing at dressing up. But then again, she thought snippily, Beau was a gentleman well-versed in the proper way to treat a lady.

If anything, the cabin looked worse on second sight.

'Take your things upstairs and put on your boots,' Cage told her perfunctorily when he'd turned off the engine. She was almost halfway up the steps when he added from below, 'And take off that bra while you're at it. You'll be hot enough without wearing more than you have to.'

Blushing furiously, she hurried up the rest of the stairs without looking back.

So. Cursory glance or not, he'd noticed a good deal more than she'd thought. A good deal more than he should have, she amended, her mouth twitching angrily once she was inside the cabin. How dared he make such a suggestion? And if he thought she was going to follow it, whatever his reasons, he had another think coming.

She was bent over the bed, laying her suit out, when Cage's voice came from behind her, making her jump. 'Do you have something to tie back your hair?' He hadn't made a sound coming up the steps or into the cabin, and that he could move so quietly frightened her. He was standing in the doorway watching her, the light from behind making it impossible to distinguish his features.

'A clip, somewhere,' she replied, a little breathless from surprise. She knelt to the floor and started rummaging through her case. 'Here it is.'

'Good. Pin it up, then put on your hat. I'll spray you downstairs.'

She frowned as she caught her hair on top of her head with the clip, then looked back over her shoulder. The doorway was already empty, as if he'd never been there.

After pulling on the tall, hot boots and snatching her new hat from the bed, she stomped down the steps to where he waited at the bottom.

He held a spray can of insect repellant in one hand like a weapon. 'Put on your hat, then close your eyes,' he ordered. She did as she was told, shivering when the cold spray hit the skin of her hands and neck, wrinkling her nose at the awful smell. When he was finished she backed away from the chemical cloud and coughed.

'That's disgusting,' she complained.

'Agreed. But you'll need it. The biting flies and mosquitoes around here have fantasies about fair-skinned blondes like you.'

She cocked her head and eyed his bare head and arms. 'Why do I have to wear a hat and a long-sleeved shirt when you don't?' she grumbled.

He snorted softly, then simply turned away without answering, making her feel stupid for asking in the first place.

'Come on,' he said over his shoulder, crossing the small cleared space around the cabin in just a few steps. Melanie caught her breath when he seemed to disappear into the wall of green, then hurried after him while the movement of ferns and leaves still marked his passage.

The greenery that had seemed solid was merely a narrow circle of underbrush around the cabin. Once on the other side, walking was easy between the monstrous oaks and mahogany trees whose leafy tops formed a canopy that blocked out the sky and kept the forest floor relatively free from undergrowth.

It was dim, cool, and surprisingly quiet in this cathedral-like stand of giants, and the ground felt firm and dry beneath Melanie's boots. Just when she was beginning to wonder why she'd had to wear them at all, her right foot sank into a small, sucking bog of mud. Cage stopped and turned back to look at her when she emitted a small sound of surprise.

'It's going to get a whole lot worse,' he warned her. 'We're coming to the end of this hammock. We'll be wading soon.'

Melanie swatted at a persistent mosquito less offended by the insect spray than she was. 'What's a
hammock?'

Cage smiled. 'An island of trees in a sea of water.
That's what the Everglades is, basically. A million tiny
islands in a vast sea.'

After walking a few more moments, they emerged
with startling suddenness from the dark forest into
the full light of the sun. Melanie squinted as her eyes
adjusted, then breathed a soft 'oh' at the sight.

For almost as far as she could see an ocean of tall
grass swayed in the gentle current of the unseen water
at its base. Sunlight sparkled off the lighter tips of
the tall sawgrass like millions of pin-point fireworks,
entrancing the unwary. Mesmerised, Melanie took a
few steps past Cage and promptly sank in water almost
up to the tops of her boots. Before she could even
open her mouth to cry out in surprise, she felt herself
lifted by the waist and swung back to relatively dry
ground.

Cage's face was expressionless when she looked up
at him, but he kept his hands firmly on her waist.
'Beside me, maybe,' he said. 'Behind me, preferably;
but never, ever walk ahead of me again.'

Blue eyes wide, as startled by the pressure of his
hands as she had been by the sudden plunge into the
water, she nodded without saying anything.

'I'm beginning to think you should be on a leash.'

She narrowed her eyes and twisted free of his hands,
placing her own on her hips as if that would erase the
memory of his touch. 'I'm quite capable of following
a few simple guide-lines,' she snapped, 'if you'd just
be responsible enough to lay them out for me.'

He stared at her so intently that she had to concentrate not to drop her eyes. 'Fair enough,' he said finally, looking off into the distance. 'You've already learned your most valuable lesson: there's water everywhere. In dry-down, during the northern winter, you can walk across this plain; but now, in the rainy season, most of the 'Glades is under water, even when it looks dry.'

'The River of Grass,' she murmured a description she'd read, following his eyes across the vast, unbroken stretch of sawgrass.

'Exactly. And if you don't know where to walk, follow in the footsteps of someone who does, or don't move at all. Otherwise you're going to get wet.'

Melanie sighed, then nodded. 'So how do we cross?'

'The same way you'd cross any stretch of water. We float.' He turned right and walked along the edge of the hammock, never checking to see if Melanie was following precisely in his footsteps, as ordered. She was, of course, but it would have been reassuring to know he was keeping an eye on her.

She stumbled along behind for what seemed like a long time, watching the careful placement of her feet, glancing up only occasionally at the broad muscles of his back moving beneath the thin cotton jersey of his T-shirt.

It pleased her to notice the fabric clinging damply to the indentation of his spine, just as her own shirt was. Somehow knowing that at least his body reacted to the heat and humidity made him seem more human.

There wasn't a breath of wind, and moving through the sauna-like air was like trying to walk through soggy cotton. After five minutes Melanie was breathing through her mouth and her boots felt like concrete blocks weighing her down. 'Where are we going?' she asked, plucking her shirt away from her breasts, angry because her bra was chafing her skin.

'We're there,' he announced, stopping suddenly.

When Melanie looked past him she saw a small lagoon biting into the island of trees. At its apex was a short wooden pier, incongruous in this wilderness of plants. More incongruous yet was the strange-looking craft tied to a mooring post.

'Oh, my,' Melanie murmured, recognising the odd shape of the common Everglades airboat. They were little more than platforms with huge fans twice the diameter of a man's height fastened on the back. She'd seen them on television, whizzing through shallow water at breakneck speeds, passengers strapped help-lessly to the chairs screwed into the deck, looking horribly exposed.

'Have you ever ridden on one of these?'

Melanie shook her head weakly, shuffling as he took her hand and pulled her out on to the dock, and then on to the airboat's platform. It rocked beneath their weight and Melanie spread her legs and locked her knees to keep her balance.

'You'll sit here, in the front,' Cage said, whisking a canvas cover from a chair fastened close to the front edge of the boat. With her peripheral vision Melanie noticed a sudden movement from the chair seat that made even Cage jump backwards into her. She cried out and would have fallen overboard if he hadn't spun in place, grabbed her arms and jerked her full-length against him. She froze in his arms, her fingers wrapped reflexively around his biceps, her heart thundering against his chest. She didn't breathe for a moment, her mind racing to process the sudden input of sensory data.

Surely she was imagining his hands moving on her back, pulling her almost imperceptibly closer; surely it was a sudden breeze and not his breath stirring the wisps of hair on her forehead beneath the brim of her hat. And of course there was no fire in those black eyes as they gazed down at her—it was only a reflection of the sun bouncing up from the water.

She caught in a quick breath at last, and as her lungs filled her breasts swelled and pressed against his chest. She felt him stiffen against her, then his brows twitched in a hard frown.

'Nothing to worry about.' His voice rasped like the low notes on a cello. 'We just startled it, that's all.'

'Startled what?' she whispered in confusion, following his gaze to the chair where she was supposed to sit. She went instantly rigid and her eyes snapped wide as she watched a long, mud-brown snake uncoil, slither down from the seat, then across the platform to slip silently into the water. 'Omigod,' she whispered, and then her knees gave way and she sagged against him.

'I thought I told you to take off that bra,' was the last thing she heard before blacking out.

CHAPTER FIVE

MUFFLED sounds lapped at the door of Melanie's consciousness—the sporadic rasp of a single insect; the muted caw of a distant bird; the gentle sigh of grass blades rubbing against one another. As if sounds had opened the door to all her other senses, she suddenly felt the heat and weight of the humid air; the insidious brightness of sunlight spearing through her closed eyelids. Her eyes fluttered open, squinted against the light, and finally focused on the strong planes and angles of Cage's face suspended above her. Good lord. She was lying in the man's lap.

'What happened?' she mumbled, scrambling to sit up.

'Apparently you don't like snakes,' he said, tucking his legs into a lotus position, his torso swaying slightly with the gentle motion of the airboat.

Melanie's eyes shot to the chair seat, then darted wildly around the platform.

'It's gone,' he reassured her, 'and it was harmless anyway. A simple banded water snake. Looks a lot like a water moccasin, but it's not poisonous. You didn't have to worry.'

Melanie suppressed the urge to giggle hysterically. She hadn't fainted because she'd thought the snake was poisonous; she'd fainted because it was a snake. Period. 'I hate snakes,' she shuddered.

He made a derisive sound of exasperation. 'Then what the hell are you doing in the Everglades? The place is full of them.'

'I'm not here to make pets out of the wildlife,' she defended herself hotly. 'I ought to be able to learn something about this place without sharing my chairs with reptiles.'

He looked at her for a moment, then turned and looked off across the waving sawgrass sea. Melanie studied the proud lines of his profile etched against the field of tall grass, and felt the anger slowly seep out of her. There was an inexplicable sadness in the way he stared off into the distance; something tragic that seemed to tremble just beneath the surface of his seemingly impervious face.

'I promise not to faint any more,' she said softly, not really understanding what had prompted her to say it.

He looked at her with mild surprise, as if he'd forgotten her presence entirely until she spoke. His lips compressed briefly, as if irritated at the reminder. 'What are you doing here?' he asked abruptly. 'How did Parker talk you into coming?'

Melanie frowned down at her lap, remembering how proud she'd been when Beau had first asked her to represent him on this trip...back when she'd still thought the trip had meaning.

'He didn't have to talk me into coming,' she said quietly. 'I wanted to. I thought I'd be doing something important, something worthwhile.'

He sighed noisily. 'And when did he tell you the truth?'

'This morning,' she mumbled. 'At the airport, just before I left.' She shrank from the emptiness of his stare, knowing what he was thinking. Getting on that plane after she knew about the deception made her part of it. 'The Press was there,' she added hurriedly, trying to defend her actions. 'I didn't want to make a scene...' She stammered to a halt, uncomfortable under his gaze. 'He's my *fiancé*,' she insisted, as if that would explain everything.

'Does that title carry a requirement that you agree with everything he does?'

Melanie bit down on her lower lip. 'Of course not. But questioning him in public would have been inexcusable. Especially about his political judgement. I don't know a thing about politics...'

'You don't have to know anything about politics to know what's right.'

'Knowing what's right and having the courage to act on that conviction are two very different things, Mr Cage. There are no rebels in the Brooks family.'

For a moment he looked at her as if she'd said something incredibly stupid, but then he turned away quickly, and Melanie wasn't sure she'd seen the expression at all.

'Let's get going,' he said gruffly. 'You have a lot to see, and three days isn't much time.'

She nodded and stood up, taking a wide stance to counter the slight movement of the deck beneath her feet.

'Strap yourself into the front chair,' he directed. 'This afternoon we'll take a short tour of the immediate area, just to give you the lie of the land.'

With ill-disguised nervousness, Melanie settled herself in the chair towards the front of the platform, tightened the lap belt, then grasped the armrests so tightly that her knuckles whitened. Cage slipped the casting ropes from cleats on the dock, then climbed up on to the pilot's platform that perched high above the main deck, directly behind Melanie. She watched over her shoulder as he checked gauges she couldn't see, then suddenly he looked down at her. She faced front quickly, feeling like a student caught staring at the teacher.

'We won't be able to talk much over the noise of the engine,' he said from behind her. 'But after we cross this stretch of sawgrass there's a slough where the alligators congregate. We'll stop the boat there so we can talk.'

Melanie's eyes widened at the mention of alligators, and her mouth opened to rattle off a series of questions. Did alligators eat people? Could they climb up on the boat? Could the boat tip over? The engine roared to deafening life before she could ask a single one, and the initial thrust forward pushed her back against her seat.

After a few moments—long enough for Melanie to decide that Cage was a capable pilot and the boat was more stable than it appeared—fear gave way reluctantly to fascination. She watched the river of grass flatten beneath their passage, then with childlike delight saw it spring upright behind them, as if they'd never been there. The hot wind was a blessed relief against her face, and Melanie lifted her head and let the funny straw hat slip down her back to hang by the scarf tails.

For a time it seemed that the sawgrass stretched to the horizon, that the distant clumps of trees were miles and miles away. But then suddenly the grass opened on to a corridor of deeper black water banked on either side with water-lilies; then just as suddenly the sawgrass disappeared entirely behind thick brush that crowded the water on both sides.

Cage throttled back the engine to a soft rumble, and they puttered down the watery aisle at walking speed while Melanie looked around with wonder. She laughed aloud when their passage disturbed a flock of odd, spindly-legged wading birds, sending them skywards, with a graceful rush that belied their ungainly appearance. The Everglades wasn't so bad, she was thinking. It wasn't the dark, sinister jungle she'd imagined, with monstrous reptiles jumping out at you from dank pools of stagnant water. It was open and light and golden in the sun, with lush, exotic plants and snowy birds that beat their wings against an endless expanse of blue sky.

And then suddenly it all changed. The boat followed an abrupt twist in the watery path, and it narrowed rapidly as the surrounding greenery seemed to close in, robbing the world of light.

They passed another flock of wading birds off to the side, smaller than the first, with rosy patches brightening their white plumage. 'Roseate spoonbills,' Cage informed her. Big wings flapped diffidently as the airboat passed their fishing hole, but they didn't take flight. When he cut the engine abruptly the sudden silence was eerie.

'We'll let the current take us from here,' he said quietly from behind her. 'This is the slough I told you about. Keep your eyes open, and you'll see a lot of the local residents. Like there.' He pointed to a sandy, lumpy cove set into the right bank, open to the sun.

'Where?' Melanie whispered, leaning in the direction he was pointing with a puzzled frown, looking for wildlife but seeing none. Her eyes widened when one of the well-camouflaged lumps opened jaws as long as her arm, exposing a row of sharp, pointed teeth that seemed to glitter in the sunlight. With a slow, quiet intake of breath she pushed herself back into the chair.

'It's huge,' she whispered, eyes travelling from the long, smiling snout with its protruding teeth back a full ten feet to the tip of its powerful tail. With its bulging eyes and thick, bumpy hide, it looked remarkably like one of the fairy-tale dragons in a book she'd had as a child.

'It's a good size,' Cage agreed, apparently unconcerned that the boat was drifting ever closer to the bank.

Another lump opened another long set of jaws and emitted a thunderous bellow that made Melanie grip the arms of her chair even tighter. 'I think we should leave,' she hissed urgently, never taking her eyes from the group on the bank. She counted seven alligators, each one more ferocious-looking than the last.

In an abrupt scramble of motion so fast that all Melanie really saw was flying dirt and the splash of water, one of the beasts plunged into the slough and headed towards the boat.

'I think you may want to come up here with me,' Cage said calmly.

He didn't have to tell her twice. With speed born of panic, Melanie released her lap strap and scrambled up to where Cage sat at the controls. His startled look barely registered as she scurried to the other side of his chair and grasped his shoulder. His bare skin was hot under her fingers. 'Are we safe up here?' she asked breathlessly, her eyes fixed in terror on the alligator moving steadily towards the boat, only its eyes and nostrils visible above the water, its powerful tail whipping back and forth just beneath the surface.

'Safe?' Cage looked up at her, puzzled. 'Of course we're safe. I just thought you'd get a better view of him in the water from up here, that's all.'

Melanie held her breath for a moment, then released it, shoulders sagging. 'Oh,' she said in a small voice. 'I thought ... I thought ...'

'You thought it was going to climb up on the boat and eat you whole, right?' He was almost smiling.

'Something like that.'

'Well, at least you didn't faint.'

She tightened her lips, but made no reply. She was too busy watching the huge reptile circling the boat, like a buzzard waiting for the inevitable feast.

'I won't tell you that Everglades 'gators are harmless. We've had a few attacks over the years, but they don't climb up on boats. Just stay out of the water, and you'll be fine.'

'Right,' Melanie murmured, unconsciously tightening her grip on his shoulder when the alligator came so close to the boat that she couldn't see it any more.

'You don't have to be afraid,' he said quietly. 'I won't let anything hurt you.'

She looked down at her hand, at the fragile white fingers pressed deep into the sun-burnished musculature of his shoulder. She relaxed her grip a little, but couldn't bring herself to let go entirely.

'You'll feel safer sitting up here with me.' He moved sideways in the broad seat of his chair, making room.

Her head moved in a jerky nod, relieved to be as far from the water as possible. 'I'll stay up here, but I can stand.'

He left hand tapped the vinyl space next to him. 'Sit. I'm going to start the engine again, and you'll lose your balance and fall into the water...'

Melanie sat instantly, eyes wide and fixed straight ahead. She perched uncomfortably on the side of the chair, one hip on, one hip off, careful to keep a space between their bodies. She caught her breath when Cage grabbed her around the waist and pulled her against him.

'Relax,' he told her as he started the engine. 'I'm one of the creatures in this swamp that doesn't bite.'

She smiled a little, then gasped and caught his arm as the boat jerked forward.

'Sorry,' he mumbled, steadying the boat to a slow crawl. After a moment Melanie remembered to release his arm.

They rode in silence for a while, the big fan behind them whirring softly at slow speed, pushing the boat down the twisted, watery corridor. Melanie was sharply aware of the body pressed against hers. Aside from Beau, she'd never been in such close contact with a man before. It embarrassed her to feel it so keenly when his thigh muscle contracted beneath the heavy canvas trousers; to feel every degree of heat emanating from the bare skin of his arm where it pressed against the sleeve of her shirt.

Peripherally, she could see his chest rise and fall with each breath, and for a time she almost imagined she could hear the beat of his heart over the hum of the fan blade. She stole a surreptitious glance at his face once, and found it strangely insulting that his expression was totally indifferent. He doesn't even know I'm here, she thought irritably. We're pressed together like sardines in a can, and he doesn't feel a thing.

She shifted her weight on the seat intentionally and pretended to look around with nonchalance. 'Where's the alligator?'

'We left him behind long ago, but there's a water moccasin, sunning on that rock over there. Remember what he looks like. You'll want to give those snakes a wide berth.'

Instantly distracted from the press of his body, Melanie leaned forward to look past him at the brown coil on the jutting rock to their right. Her concentration totally fixed on the snake, she was oblivious to her breast brushing his bicep; to the sudden, reflexive narrowing of his eyes. 'It looks just like the one on the chair,' she said worriedly. 'I'll never be able to tell the difference.'

'You can identify a water moccasin by the inside of its mouth. It's all white. Some people call it a cottonmouth.'

They'd passed the rock by this time, and Melanie sagged back in the seat, folding her arms in disgust. 'Wonderful. I'll just get every snake I meet to open its mouth before I ask it to dance.'

He turned his head to look at her, and Melanie's scowl dissolved into an expression of unabashed wonder. He was smiling—all the way up to his eyes— and the transformation in his face took her breath away. The strength was still there, and the power; but the stern, forbidding aspect had softened into something dark and warm and incredibly seductive.

With the innocence of a child who had never felt the full, strident surge of her own sexuality, Melanie parted her lips and they curved upwards.

As focused on her countenance as she was on his,
Cage relaxed his hand on the rudder and the airboat
headed for the bank. His face was so close, Melanie
thought in a daze; his mouth was so close; with just
the smallest motion she could reach up and touch that
sharp, chiselled line of his lower lip with her
finger...she caught her breath at that perfectly as-
tounding thought, and then felt herself flung forward
sharply as the blunt prow jammed into the weeds on
the bank. In the next instant she was flung sideways,
and then his arms shot out and jerked her against his
chest.

'Dammit,' he growled, leaning back far enough to
look down at her face. 'Are you all right?'

She swallowed hard and nodded, gazing up into his
eyes, more shaken by his closeness than she had been
by the boat's thudding into the bank. His arms felt
like searing bands around her; his chest felt rigid and
hot beneath the soft press of her breasts. 'What
happened?'

As if checking for injury, he touched her cheek with
the fingertips of one hand, but at that touch took a
sharp, shallow breath that flared his nostrils. His gaze
dropped to her mouth and his eyes narrowed. It was
only his eyes touching her lips, and yet to Melanie the
glance was as searing as the press of his mouth would
have been.

In a gesture as seductive as if she had consciously
engineered it, she touched the centre of her lower lip
with her tongue to moisten it. At that the burnished
skin across his high, proud cheekbones seemed to
tighten, and she felt the soft breath of an inaudible
sigh brush her face. His chest swelled even as the rest
of his body seemed to go rigid, and his hand tightened

slightly on her back, flattening her breasts between them. She felt her nipples pucker in response to the pressure.

Had she been capable of rational thought at that moment, Melanie would have realised that the strange, hot sensations she was feeling were dangerous; that her engagement to Beau should have precluded her body's reaction to the touch of this strange, exotic-looking man; but rational thought was as far from her mind as she was from the staid, air-conditioned life she led back in civilisation.

All she knew was that right now she was feeling what those gangly, spindly-legged water birds must feel at the soaring lift of air beneath their wings. This was the exhilaration of flight; the almost unbearable ecstasy of pure physical pleasure; and anything that felt like this had to be right.

His head dipped down towards hers, blocking the sun. Their mouths were so close that, if she had spoken but a single word, their lips would have touched. And then suddenly she felt herself thrust backwards, and held rigidly at arm's length. Cage's face was dark, angry, and the quivering of tensed muscles passed through his hands into the flesh of her upper arms.

'This is crazy,' he muttered, jerking away from her and glaring straight ahead. His hands gripped the control sticks so tightly that the muscles of his fore-arms bulged with tension. 'On second thoughts, maybe you'd be safer down in the other chair.'

She felt a quiver run all the way from the base of her spine up into the back of her neck. After a hard swallow she said, 'I'll stand behind you, and hold on to your chair.' She didn't want to go back down to the lower deck, and she told herself it was because she was afraid of alligators. 'I won't get in your way,' she added in a whisper.

After what seemed like a long time he nodded once without looking at her, then gave his full attention to the controls.

They covered countless miles of inland waterways that first afternoon, and for the entire time Melanie stood directly behind Cage, her hands clutching the back of his chair, her fingers a breath away from the broad, tanned shoulders. Again and again she found herself looking down with fascination at the black sheen of his hair. It looked so smooth, almost unreal in colour and gloss. She had to fight back the impulse to touch it.

When Cage called her attention to the world around her she saw turtles and snakes and alligators and a hundred thousand birds. She heard the sound of his voice more than his words as he described their passage across broad, shallow lakes, vast sawgrass plains, and down countless narrow, twisting ribbons of water. At some point during the afternoon she forgot Beau, forgot her Tallahassee hotel-room and the family plantation in Georgia; forgot the world of automobiles and air-conditioning and computers and politics. For this tiny, single moment of her life she immersed herself totally in the present, and all the present contained was a man called Benjamin Cage and the vastness of a savage wilderness.

CHAPTER SIX

THE LATE afternoon sunlight had just begun to soften when Cage eased back on the airboat's throttle and pointed to the isolated dock just ahead. Melanie smiled at the one landmark she could recognise in all the twisted waterways of the Everglades, anticipating a shower, a reasonably comfortable chair, and, above all, food. During the course of the afternoon they'd drunk enormous quantities of metallic-tasting water from the canteens Cage carried on his belt, and they'd snacked almost continually on some kind of trail mix he kept in a metal chest on the airboat, but Melanie was still hungry. She couldn't explain the sharp increase in her appetite—she supposed it had something to do with sun and fresh air and excitement, and maybe the latitude, for all she knew.

Cage eased the boat into its mooring and gestured towards the coils of rope lying on the main platform. 'Grab one of those lines and make her fast,' he told her.

Melanie blinked at the back of his head as if he'd spoken in a foreign language. 'What?'

'I said grab one of those...'

'I heard what you said. I don't know what it means.'

He frowned at her over his shoulder. 'It means tie up the boat.'

Melanie stepped down from the pilot's platform, gingerly picked up a coil of rope, then stared uncertainly at the narrow expanse of black water between the deck and the dock.

'It's less than a foot,' he spoke impatiently. 'You won't fall in. Hurry up. I can't hold her here forever.'

Holding the rope like a lifeline, Melanie took a deep breath, jumped on to the dock, then froze when the wooden planks wiggled beneath her.

'Now make her fast.'

She looked back at Cage. His lips tightened with exasperation.

'Wrap the rope around that cleat...that metal thing right next to your left foot.'

She did as she was told, but left too much slack in the line. It dipped into the water and the boat drifted another few feet from the dock. Cage shook his head and cut the engine. After replacing the covers on the chairs, he leaped easily to the dock with the second line and crouched over one of the cleats. 'Now *this* is how to tie these. Come here and watch.' His fingers whipped the rope into a tight knot, then he tugged on the line and the knot disappeared. 'See? That's a slip-knot. It's easy. Now you try it.'

She crouched down next to him and proceeded to tie the rope into a messy jumble. She handed it back with a hapless shrug. 'Apparently I wasn't cut out to be a deckhand.'

He ignored the proffered rope and stared at her. 'You'll learn. Try again.'

After three more pathetic attempts Cage braced his arms on his thighs and looked at her. 'I thought all Southern ladies were horsewomen. Don't you ride?'

'Of course I do. I've been riding since I was——'

'Well, this is the same knot you use to tie a horse when you're grooming, or saddling up.' He studied

her blank expression for a moment, then shook his
head. 'Don't tell me. You never groomed or saddled
your own horse, right? There were always other people
to do it for you.'

She bristled a bit at his tone. 'What's wrong with
that?'

'Nothing. Everything. Never mind.' He poked the
end of the rope towards her again. 'Try it again. We're
not leaving until you get it right.'

Melanie sighed, then attacked the rope again.
Finally she managed to duplicate his knot ... after a
fashion. He made her do it several times before he
was satisfied.

She cocked her head and examined her last effort,
foolishly pleased with the way the line hugged the
cleat, tightening when the boat pulled against it.
'That's good, isn't it?' She looked up to find him
watching her with an odd expression.

'Yes, Melanie,' he said quietly. 'It's very good.'

Her smile blossomed under his approval, and he
turned away from it, frowning. 'Come on,' he said
gruffly, shading his eyes as he looked towards the sun.
'We've only got a few hours before dark.' Without
another word he marched off the dock into the brush.

Melanie stared after him a moment in dumb surprise before scampering behind to keep him in sight.
He led her around the waterline back into the forest
while she trotted to match his long strides. He never
spoke, he never glanced over his shoulder to make
sure she was still behind him, and the pace he set was
so fast that she was exhausted after just a few
moments.

What does he think I am, she thought irritably—a
marathon runner? She followed doggedly, too

breathless to complain, scowling at his back as she dodged the enormous trunks of the ancient trees. It was cooler under their shade than it had been in the open, but the air was still heavy with humidity and before long her T-shirt clung damply to her skin. Without breaking stride she slipped off the heavy overshirt and tied the sleeves around her waist, leaving her arms bare.

Almost immediately a swarm of tiny, biting flies appeared from nowhere to light on her arms, and the forest silence was broken by the sound of her hands slapping at them.

'Put that back on.' He'd stopped and turned to face her, and Melanie was so intent on brushing the bugs from her arms that she nearly ran right into him.

'It's hot,' she complained, scowling at his bare arms. 'Why aren't the bugs landing on you?'

He shrugged and started untying the sleeves at her waist. 'I'm a businessman, not an entomologist. Maybe they like your perfume.' Still facing her, he held the shirt open behind her shoulders while she slipped her arms into the sleeves. His eyes dropped briefly to the dip of her cleavage rising above the low-cut T-shirt. 'They say insects are attracted to the female hormone.'

Melanie blushed and pulled the front panels of the shirt closed. Her hands froze when she saw how intently he watched her working the buttons. His eyes jerked upwards, met hers, then he spun on his heel and strode away.

They reached the cabin in another five minutes, and Melanie paused at the bottom of the steps to catch her breath. Thanks to the pace Cage had set, she was

hot, sweaty, and exhausted; a totally alien condition
for her.

'What's the matter? What are you waiting for?' He
had stepped aside to let her climb the stairs first.

'I have half a mind to make you carry me up these
steps after that work-out...' she started to grumble,
then gasped when he swept her effortlessly into his
arms and started trotting up the steps. 'Good lord,
put me down. What are you doing?'

'Stop wriggling.' He nudged the screen door open
with his shoulder and walked inside, like a groom
carrying his bride over the threshold.

'Very funny. You can put me down now.'

He turned his head slowly and looked directly into
her eyes. He didn't say anything, and he made no
move to release her.

'Uh...Mr Cage...'

'You shouldn't have taken off your hat.' His voice
seemed to rumble through his body into hers. 'Your
face is sunburned.' He set her down then jerked his
hands away, as if he'd suddenly remembered she was
too hot to touch. 'We'll want to shower before it gets
dark. You first.'

She nodded wordlessly and backed away towards
the bed and her suitcases. He remained motionless
where he stood, watching her.

'Soap and towels are in the chest at the foot of the
bed. You remember how to run the shower?'

'I remember.' She turned and started to rummage
through her suitcase, but she could feel his eyes on
her back. It was a relief when she heard him turn and
walk towards the makeshift counter-top on the far
wall.

With increasing dismay she sorted through and rejected almost every article of clothing she had brought. What did you wear for a night in a primitive cabin without running water or electricity? A beaded cocktail dress? That stupid sundress with the low bodice and full skirt that Beau said photographed so well? She finally pulled her silk summer robe out of the case and slung it over her arm. It was more of a caftan, really; a shapeless ankle-length garment with big sleeves and a loosely fitted scooped neckline. She'd never dreamed she'd wear such a thing in company— she'd brought it along for wearing around the hotel-room—but at least it was comfortable, and the peaches and blues of the big floral pattern were a bright, welcome change from the drab colours she'd worn all day.

Once downstairs she stood in the shelter of the porch and looked around for a long time. The daytime sounds of the Everglades were muted by late afternoon, and the quality of light filtering through the giant trees had changed, become almost golden.

Dragonflies as large as her hand dipped transparent wings into the fading sunlight as they soared past, and even the ugly bluebottle flies took on an iridescent beauty in the softer light.

Melanie blew out a long, quiet sigh. She'd never undressed outside before, and it wasn't mere modesty that made her reluctant now. There was an awful vulnerability about being naked without the security of walls around you. She shifted her shoulders nervously, felt the sweat-dampened shirt chafe her skin, and stripped quickly out of her clothes, tossing them into a pile.

She stood there for a moment before opening the nozzle of the hose, shivering in spite of the heat, goosebumps rising all over her body. And then she giggled. She *had* been naked outside once before— she remembered now. All of three or four years old, just out of the family pool, she'd run from her nanny's arms, peeled off her tiny swimsuit, and raced buck-naked across the expansive lawns, shrieking with delight at the sense of freedom; at the glorious feeling of absolutely nothing between her skin and the world outside. Unconsciously she rubbed her right buttock, remembering the gentle slap from her nanny's hand and the verbal rebuke that had shamed her for such unladylike behaviour. She'd never done such a thing again. Until now.

She smiled a little as she opened the hose nozzle and let the tepid water soak her hair and sluice over her body. She could hear Cage's footsteps in the cabin above when she turned off the hose to lather her hair and skin.

Attracted by the prism of sunlight through the bubbles, a dragonfly lighted on her forearm, and she touched the edge of one of its four wings delicately, marvelling when it didn't fly away. Entranced that such a fragile creature could be so fearless, she waited until it took flight again before opening the hose nozzle to rinse herself.

Cage looked up from something he was doing at the counter when she came back inside. His black eyes swept from the hem of the brightly coloured robe up to her dripping hair, then fixed on her face. 'You took a long time.'

'Sorry,' Melanie smiled sheepishly. 'A dragonfly landed on my arm—it actually landed on my arm . . .'

The childish excitement in her voice trailed away at his perplexed expression. 'Anyway, I didn't want to frighten it,' she finished in a mumble.

It nearly bowled her over when he smiled, and, as she gazed at that proud, rigid countenance suddenly softening with the gentle grin an adult reserved for a very young child, she thought that she had never really seen a genuine smile until she'd seen his.

'I won't be long.' He gathered a stack of clothing from a chair and passed close to her as he went outside. The air stirred at his passage, brushing Melanie's face like a whisper that smelled like sunlight. 'There's water in the jug and some snacks on the counter. Help yourself.'

He wasn't halfway down the outside steps when her stomach growled noisily. While he showered downstairs she stood at the counter and ate peanuts out of the bowl, then attacked a plate of cheese and some sort of crisp corn cracker. Everything was unbelievably delicious, and after a few moments she stopped and looked at the rapidly emptying dishes with dismay. If she didn't slow down there wouldn't be anything left for Cage.

She sighed, touched a finger to the bridge of her nose, then shrugged and drained the icy fruit drink in the tall glass next to the food. This time she heard the soft steps of his feet on the stairs, and wondered if she was becoming attuned to the sound.

'Good lord,' he said from the doorway, eyes on the empty glass in her hand. 'You drink like a longshoreman.'

'Salty food,' she said, staring at him openly. His hair was wet and shiny black, dripping water on to a thin white cotton shirt open at the neck. He was

wearing snug, faded blue jeans, and his brown feet
were bare.

He walked over and took her glass, staring at it as
if he couldn't believe it was empty. 'I thought we
covered this once today. You eat salty food here to
replace what you lose in perspiration, but drink *water*
to quench your thirst. Not this stuff.'

She blinked at him, confused. 'You said to help
myself...'

'To the water in the jug.' He pointed at a large
Thermos container next to some empty glasses. 'Not
to my drink.'

'Oh. Sorry I drank yours. It was good.' She smiled
up at him broadly. 'Water, fruit juice...what difference does it make? It's all liquid...' She frowned
hard, wondering why she suddenly felt so warm.

'That "fruit juice" was almost half vodka, and you
just drank it without taking a breath,' he informed
her. 'How do you feel?'

Her eyes widened slightly. 'Oh, dear. Vodka? Well.
I must have more of a tolerance for alcohol than I
thought, because I feel fine. Just fine.' She had the
sinking feeling she was grinning again. 'Why? Do I
look funny?' She couldn't imagine why she'd asked
him that, but for some reason her mind couldn't fix
on the question long enough to find an answer.

He pressed his lips together hard. 'You look...' His
black brows twitched towards one another in a pained
expression.

'Nevermind.' Melanie made a face when the words
ran together. 'Never *mind*,' she amended. 'I know how
I look. Bedraggled. No make-up, wet hair, good
heavens, it's hot, isn't it?' She plucked the bodice of

her robe away from her chest. 'I don't drink alcohol, as a rule,' she said importantly.

'Really?'

'No, really. I don't. Maybe a little wine with dinner, but never more than that, because . . .' She cocked her head, frowning hard, trying to remember why ladies never drank more than a little wine with dinner.

'Melanie.'

She looked up at him seriously. 'Benjamin.'

He rolled his eyes and tried to scowl at her. 'Go sit down,' he said firmly. 'Way over there. I'll bring you something to eat.'

With exaggerated care, Melanie walked obediently to the chair next to the sofa and sat down. 'Is this far enough?'

'Probably not,' he said without turning around from whatever he was doing at the counter. She smiled, thinking again how melodic his voice was; deep and rich and lulling, in spite of the hard northern accent.

'Where are you from?' she asked idly, lifting one foot to admire her red cloth slipper, wondering why she'd never noticed how pretty the colour was before.

'Right here. Florida.'

'You don't talk like a Southerner.'

He shrugged carelessly, still working at the counter. 'My mom left us when I was a kid, and I guess Dad went a little crazy. He said he couldn't stand living in the place they'd lived in together, so we moved north to Chicago.'

'Your mother just . . . left you?' Even through the pleasant fuzz cushioning her thoughts, Melanie was appalled. Her own experience had taught her the pain of being a motherless child; but to be motherless because the mother had simply walked away...? She couldn't imagine the kinds of scars that would leave on a young psyche. 'Did you ever see her again?'

Cage shrugged again, as if that were the only gesture he could remember how to perform. 'No. Never saw her, never heard from her, never wanted to.'

Melanie cringed at the bitterness in his voice. 'What about your father? Didn't he try to contact her...?'

'My father was a fool,' he snapped, and Melanie cringed at the contempt in his voice. 'He died years later, when I was fourteen, but the truth is he'd stopped living the day she walked out of his life.'

'When did you finally come back to Florida?' she asked carefully.

'I started hitch-hiking back down here the day I buried my father...'

'When you were *fourteen*?'

He sighed impatiently. 'I was old enough. I lied about my age, worked the groves during the day, and finished school at night. By the time I was eighteen I had my first orchard.'

Melanie blinked, finding such independence frightening, almost incomprehensible. She was twenty-four, and had trouble deciding what to wear in the morning. She remembered Beau's words about Cage clawing his way to the top on his own. No wonder he seemed so self-contained; so distant. 'You barely had a childhood,' she murmured.

He walked over and set a plate of food in her lap. 'That's enough ancient history. Here. Eat every bite. I'll start some coffee.'

She stared after him, struggling to keep her thoughts focused on the image of Cage as a young boy, living alone, forced to leap suddenly into adulthood...

He turned back and scowled at her. 'Eat!' he commanded, shattering her already weakened concentration.

She sighed and looked down at her plate, speared a piece of cold meat, eyed it sceptically, then placed it in her mouth. 'Good,' she said perfunctorily, happy for an excuse to change the subject. 'I hope it's not something you caught outside.'

He chuckled softly. 'It's chicken, marinated in a herb dressing, then roasted and chilled. I brought it from home for my first meal with the congressman.'

'Oh.' Melanie stared glumly at the colourful pile of baby carrots and bright green snap beans, unhappy at the reminder that she was not the guest of choice.

Cage brought his plate to the couch opposite her, and they finished the meal in silence while the aroma of coffee perking on the camp stove filled the cabin. After her second full cup, Melanie's mind was perfectly, painfully clear again. She hadn't realised how dark the room had become until Cage got up to light the oil lamps. They smoked for a moment, then cast a beautiful golden glow within their small circles of light. There was one on the counter next to the stack of dirty dishes, one on a small table between the couch and the chair, and another near the bed.

'How do you feel now?' he asked her, leaning over from the couch to fill her cup for the third time.

She looked across the small space between them. The lamp flickered in an unseen breath of wind, making shadows dance on his dark face. He sat with one knee cocked, foot on the couch cushion, his arm stretched over the back. 'Sober,' she replied, and then added in a small voice, 'unfortunately.'

He smiled a little at that. 'Why "unfortunately"?'

She looked down into her cup and sighed. 'I don't know. Maybe because, for a time, I forgot who I was and what I was doing here, and it all just seemed like some wonderful child's adventure.'

'The Everglades *is* an adventure.'

She smiled sadly. 'After a drink or two it's an adventure. Stone-cold sober, it's a terrifying, alien place to someone like me. The women in my family weren't bred to be very daring, I'm afraid.'

'That's the second time today you've said something like that. You're kidding, of course.'

Melanie's look was a question.

'What about the woman you were named for? They don't come much more daring than that.'

Melanie felt her whole body go still. 'I was named for my great-great-great-grandmother,' she said carefully.

'When you told me your full name I assumed you were one of her descendants. Still, it was a shock . . .' He shook his head with a funny little smile. 'Melanie Annabelle Brooks, wife of Henry Albert Brooks of Creek County, Georgia . . . do you have any idea what the odds must be against her namesake showing up down here?'

Melanie stared at him, blue eyes wide and mystified, wondering how he could possibly know the names of her ancestors.

'They still talk about her, naturally. It's part of——'

'They?' she interrupted sharply.

'The Seminole Indians, of course. Who did you think?'

Melanie couldn't stop staring at him, as if she could pull the knowledge she craved from the black depths of his eyes. She felt the strident pounding of her heart, the wild surge of anticipation coursing through her veins like a shot of adrenalin. All her life she'd been searching for a single scrap of information about the woman in the old oil portrait, and now, impossible as it seemed, a stranger was going to fill in the blanks in her own family history. She licked her lips and spoke carefully. 'You know about my great-great-great-grandmother?'

'Well, of course. She's a legend down here.'

The chirping of insects filled the silence that followed, and to Melanie the darkness outside seemed to be creeping into the cabin, trying to obliterate the tiny circles of light.

Slowly, balancing her cup on her lap, her eyes fixed on his face, she leaned forward in her chair. 'Tell me,' she whispered. 'Tell me what you know about her.'

'You want me to tell you about your own ancestor?' he asked, confused. 'I'm sure you know more...'

'No. I don't know anything about her, except what she looked like, and that her own husband crossed her name out of the family Bible.' She shuddered. 'I still hate to think about that. It's almost as if he tried to...erase her.'

Cage's expression hardened. 'He actually did that? Crossed out her name?'

Melanie nodded.

He sighed heavily and looked off to one side. 'I suppose that was to be expected back then...' he murmured, then looked at her, his gaze sharp. 'And you really don't know anything about her? No family stories? No journals?'

'Nothing. I found her portrait in the attic when I was a kid, but if it weren't for that, it would be as if she never existed at all.'

His eyes softened a little, reflecting the lamplight. 'What did she look like?'

Melanie glanced down at her lap. 'Like...me.' When she looked up again he was smiling.

'The legend says she gave shelter to one of Osceola's warriors when the government troops were hunting them down during the uprising of 1835...'

She frowned hard, scouring her memory for old school lessons in history. Osceola...who was Osceola? She shook her head, passing over the question for the time being. It would come to her eventually. 'Go on,' she encouraged him.

He studied her face silently for a moment. 'She was here, you know,' he said quietly.

'Here?'

'In the Everglades.'

'But that's crazy. It's hundreds of miles from Creek County. It would have taken days, maybe weeks to make that trip in a carriage, and why would she have come in the first place...?'

'That's the legend. Part of Seminole history, handed down by word of mouth from generation to generation.'

Melanie sagged against the back of her chair, her thoughts numb. Her eyes drifted to the blackness outside the screen, as if she could see the savage land encroaching on the cabin. 'It would have been even more wild then,' she murmured, more to herself than to Cage, entranced by the notion that she might not be the first Brooks woman to see this place; that the first would have worn full, floor-length dresses in this impossible heat; that her shoes would have been soled with thin leather that let the water seep in; that she would have slept on the ground with the snakes and chased insects with a silk fan. Suddenly she felt foolish and spoiled and unconscionably helpless.

'Why?' she whispered. 'Why would she come to the Everglades?'

Cage stared at her. 'If you're really interested, tomorrow I'll take you to someone who can answer that. Someone who knows all the old legends.'

She almost wrung her hands in frustration. Tomorrow was a million years away.

'It's dark, Melanie,' he said gently. 'You're going to have enough trouble finding your way to the out-house and back, let alone going deeper into the 'Glades.'

'Oh, dear.' She made a woeful face at the reminder of things a little more immediate than learning about her ancestor. Sun and sweat had taken care of the water they'd had during the afternoon, but all the liquid she'd drunk this evening was another matter. 'I forgot about the outhouse.'

He smiled at her. 'It's a long way in the dark your first time. You want an escort?'

It must be just a little bit wicked, Melanie thought later, spending the night with a man you'd just met. But it didn't feel wicked. As she lay in the only bed, arms crossed under her head, eyes staring up into the darkness, she felt as deliciously giddy as a young girl on her first trip to summer camp.

Within the short space of a single day the world had opened like a Christmas package filled with pos-sibilities. She'd done things she'd never dreamed of

doing; seen things she'd never expected to see; felt
things she hadn't known she was capable of
feeling ... her mind slammed shut abruptly on those
particular thoughts and she blushed in the dark.

And tomorrow—she tried to shift her mind's direction—tomorrow you'll have answers to questions
you've been asking for years. Who was the first
Melanie Annabelle Brooks? What had she been like?
What terrible thing had she done to cause her memory
to be nearly obliterated? And why had she come here?

She shivered with anticipation, listening to the
sounds of an insect symphony outside the screens,
syncopated by the throaty croaking of frogs. Occasionally there was a distant, muted bellow—alligators
talking, Cage had told her. He'd called it the night
music of the Everglades, making her smile at his poetic
phrasing.

He'd been a perfect gentleman on that first embarrassing trip to the outhouse, lighting the path with
his flashlight, then leaving it with her while he went
back to the cabin to give her privacy. She'd imagined
giant snakes and ravenous alligators lying in wait on
the path, and had scurried back to the cabin steps
with her heart thumping. The truth was she would
gladly have sacrificed privacy for the security of his
presence on the return trip, and she imagined that the
early pioneer women must have felt the same way
about their men.

He was asleep now in his sleeping-bag, over by the
sofa. She'd heard the sounds of clothing hitting the
floor in the dark, and couldn't help but wonder how
much he'd taken off, and how much he'd left on. For
herself, she'd been perfectly comfortable stripping out
of her robe and crawling into bed in only a short

cotton nightie. The utter blackness of a world away from city lights made her feel invisible, satisfying whatever sense of modesty that had survived the walk to the outhouse. Besides, it was still too hot and humid to wear anything but the barest necessity. Even the weight of the sheet on her bare limbs seemed stifling, but she didn't dare kick it off in case Cage woke first in the morning, before she had a chance to cover herself decently.

'Having trouble falling asleep?'

She started at the unexpected sound of his voice, like a kid caught up past her bedtime. 'A little,' she said after a beat. 'How did you know I was still awake?'

'Your breathing.'

She thought about that for a moment, her pulse quickening to know he'd been lying there all this time, listening to her breathe.

'Is the bed uncomfortable?'

'No, it's fine. I don't know what it is. Over-excitement, I suppose. It's been quite a day.'

They were both whispering, as if the camp counsellor would barge in any minute and scold them for talking past lights out.

'Cage?' she whispered, wondering why she'd automatically chosen his last name rather than his first. She decided it was because Benjamin didn't suit him. It was too... ordinary.

'What, Melanie?'

There was something magic about hearing her name spoken in the dark. It made her smile. 'This is... fun.'

Silence for a beat, and then softly, 'Fun?'

She sighed noisily. 'I know. It's a child's word, and it doesn't sound very professional ... but I just can't

think of another. I've never done anything like this,
you know. I never rode in one of those boats; I never
saw an alligator or used an outhouse or—good
heavens—I never even had too much to drink before.'
She paused and frowned up at the ceiling she couldn't
see. 'It's just been the most extraordinary day,' she
finished softly.

When he didn't say anything in response, she
thought he'd probably fallen asleep after all. She
turned her head and squinted through the blackness
at where he lay on the floor, but it was too dark and
too far away to see anything clearly. Surely it was only
her imagination that made her think she saw two spots
of light where his face might have been; the kind of
light that might come from the moist surfaces of eyes
held open, staring up at the ceiling.

She flopped on to her back with a sigh, and then
realised that at this moment, lying here in a pitch-
black primitive cabin in the middle of the wilderness,
she was happier than she'd ever been. The realisation
troubled her, and she rolled on to her side, resigned
to spending the entire night awake worrying about it.
Within moments she was sound asleep, and a short
time later her subconscious mind directed her foot to
kick the offending sheet off her body.

Cage turned his head silently at the sound and narrowed his eyes in the dark.

CHAPTER SEVEN

MELANIE was teased awake by the aroma of fresh coffee and the homy sound of sausages sizzling in a hot skillet. The smells and sounds conjured up the lazy weekend mornings of her childhood in Georgia, and she stretched and yawned with a child's sense of well-being.

'Good morning.'

Her eyes jerked and focused past her bare toes to where Benjamin Cage stood over the camp stove on the counter, creating the heavenly aromas that filled the cabin. He wore cut-off jeans and nothing else, and she looked away quickly from his broad, tanned back. Even after such a brief glance, the image of him remained etched in her mind. She still saw the shiny black hair swept back; the interlacing of muscle across the shoulders, sloping down to meet the indentation of his spine.

'Good morning,' she mumbled, thinking that the least he could have done was dress decently. It was unthinkable that a man who barely knew her should parade in her presence half-naked...

The thought had barely formed when she glanced down at her own body, and swallowed a horrified gasp. The sheet was in a tangle at the foot of the bed, and her cotton nightie was bunched up over her ribs, exposing a good deal of flesh above the matching scrap of panty.

She sat up quickly, jerked her nightie down, and grabbed for her robe.

'Too late,' Cage chuckled without turning around. 'I've already seen you in your nightgown. I suppose that means we'll have to get married.'

Melanie jammed her arms into the sleeves of her robe, blushing furiously.

He turned and smiled lazily over his shoulder at the clatter she made scrambling for her tennis shoes. 'You've got five minutes before breakfast if you want to wash first.'

She nodded brusquely, grabbed her cosmetic case and a flannel and headed for the outside steps. She froze on the top one and stared, caught off guard by the wild sensation of being so high in the middle of a forest. She'd forgotten as she'd slept, or perhaps she'd been too preoccupied yesterday to fully appreciate the view from this height.

It wasn't the kind of scenery that sold property—no mountain vistas, no golden plains stretching for the horizon—but there was something magical about looking straight into the leafy canopy that sheltered the forest floor. It *was* a tree-house, she mused, her eyes searching for the source of a raucous cawing, finally focusing on a nearby branch. A bright green bird perched there on the edge of her nest, ministering to scrawny, open-mouthed fledgelings. Melanie couldn't help but smile.

'That's a green jay,' Cage said from behind her as he walked out to join her on the porch. 'They make a terrible racket in the morning. I was surprised you slept through it.'

'They're beautiful,' Melanie murmured, pulling in a deep breath of the clean, golden morning air. 'Everything's beautiful from up here.'

She felt his eyes on her as he moved to her side, and wondered how she could be aware of that when she wasn't looking. She let her eyes fall closed, as if testing the limits of all her senses except sight. Curiously, she felt Cage's presence much as she would feel the weightless warmth of sunlight on her skin. She remembered feeling stifled sometimes when Beau came too close, and then frowned at the way she'd phrased her thoughts. Beau was her fiancé. She shouldn't ever think of him as 'too' close—and yet when he approached he seemed to push the air against her, like a strong wind battering a wall. It was so unlike Cage standing here, his bare arm a hair's breadth away, his nearness moving the air in a soft breath that seemed to circle her like the lovely tendrils of a warm mist.

She knew when his eyes left her to look out over the canopy; she felt the absence of his gaze as keenly as she had felt its touch. 'I think I love it here,' she murmured, before she even knew she was going to say it.

'Do you?' he asked quietly, but it was more confirmation than question, almost as if he had expected she would see the beauty here, if she only looked closely enough.

Like the carefully choreographed movement of two dancers, their heads turned and their eyes met. 'But only up here,' she added with a chagrined smile. 'I'm still afraid of almost everything on the ground in this place.'

She felt the protectiveness of his smile more than she saw it; felt it lifting her up until she wondered if her feet still touched the wooden floor. 'You're safer in the Everglades than you are on the streets of any major city in the world. The only really frightening thing here—or anywhere, for that matter—is man.' He turned his head to look out over the canopy again. 'Everything else here has been the same for centuries. Like this particular stand of trees. It's one of the old-growth forests that man hasn't touched yet, and it looks pretty much the same way it did hundreds of years ago. If your ancestral grandmother travelled this way, you're seeing what she saw.'

Melanie felt a flutter of excitement at the reminder that today she would learn something of her own history, and that, ironically, it was all part of this strange place she had always thought of as alien and frightening.

'Breakfast is almost ready,' Cage reminded her gently, and she heard in his voice a reluctance to have the moment end.

'I'll hurry,' she said quietly, but she moved slowly towards the door and the stairs, totally comfortable with his eyes on her back as she walked away. It occurred to her briefly that comfort was the last thing she should be feeling with Benjamin Cage. He wasn't supposed to be the kind of man that inspired comfort—he was supposed to be an unreasonable zealot; a radical; a man you simply couldn't talk to, Beau had said.

But Beau had lied. She stopped halfway down the steps as the words popped into her mind with the suddenness of a gunshot, threatening to shred the very fabric of the life that had been so carefully planned for her. She stood immobile for a moment, struggling with a dizzy sensation that had come out of nowhere. Suddenly the green jay squawked over her head, and thoughts of Beau and her dizziness vanished at the same instant. Neither belonged here.

She caught herself smiling as she walked back from the outhouse towards the hose that snaked down from the rain barrel—maybe because she hadn't been eaten by any ferocious reptilian monsters—or maybe because there was something energising about running around outside in your housecoat and washing your face in a hollowed-out log. Her face stung a bit as she splashed the soap away, and she remembered Cage telling her she was sunburned.

A circle of reflective tin was nailed to one of the cabin's support posts close to the hose, and she moved towards it, realising that she hadn't looked into a mirror since yesterday. Her appearance had always seemed such a crucial part of her life; how strange that within the space of a single day all that had changed. She thought about that as she peered into the shiny circle of tin while she brushed her long blonde hair back from her face. No make-up, no hairspray, no perfectly co-ordinated outfit, and yet somehow she didn't think she looked that bad. The sunburn was mild, making her appear flushed more than burned, and the added colour made her eyes rival the blue of the sky peeping through the treetops.

'Come on!' Cage called from overhead, and she gathered her things and hurried up the steps.

He'd brought folding chairs out to the porch and they ate there, plates balanced on their laps, coffee-mugs held in their free hands, eyes wandering the world around them. It was the first time Melanie could ever remember eating in her housecoat, and there was something wonderfully decadent about that.

'I could get used to your cooking,' she told him, spearing the last piece of fluffy scrambled egg with her fork and popping it into her mouth.

'You probably won't feel that way after supper tonight. The cooler is only good for a day or two of reliable refrigeration in this heat. I'm afraid we're down to canned goods now.'

She shrugged, unconcerned. 'It doesn't matter. Everything seems to taste wonderful here.' She felt his eyes on her in the silence that followed, and finally looked up to find him staring at her with the most peculiar, speculative expression.

'You don't look much like the woman who got off that plane yesterday,' he said quietly.

Melanie laughed. 'I'm quite sure of that...' She sobered suddenly. 'Was that an insult?'

'Definitely not.'

'Good.' She balanced her empty plate on her lap and cradled her mug in both hands, staring off into the forest canopy. 'I don't feel much like the woman who arrived here yesterday.'

'What's different?'

She glanced at him to see if the question was serious before answering with a chuckle, 'Everything. I feel like an impostor, pretending to be myself.'

He laughed at that.

'It's true. Yesterday I was prim and proper Melanie Brooks of the Creek County social register; today...' she shrugged eloquently '...today I'm some wild woman who showers with dragonflies and eats breakfast in her housecoat...stop laughing. You can't imagine how out of character I am.'

'Are you?' he asked quietly, and she turned to look at him, her face as serious as his tone had been. 'Maybe that woman in the social register was the one who was out of character.'

She was just starting to think about that when he smiled suddenly and leaned back in his chair, crossing his legs at the ankles. 'This is nice,' he said.

'What is?'

'This. Sharing breakfast. Sharing the morning here. I've never done that before. I didn't expect to enjoy it so much.'

'Neither did I,' she murmured, then caught her lower lip between her teeth. She shouldn't have said that; she probably shouldn't even have thought it. 'I mean I didn't expect to enjoy a fact-finding trip,' she tried to disguise the intimacy of what she had really meant. 'This isn't what I thought it would be like...' She frowned hard and let the sentence fade away.

'You expected cocktail parties and slide shows.'

'Yes,' she said with quick relief.

'And you didn't expect to like me.'

She hesitated. 'No. I didn't.' He smiled easily, lazily, somehow relieving the tension so that Melanie could smile, too. 'And I expected to be lectured,' she added. 'Shouldn't you be doing that? Itemising all the reasons the budget for Everglades protection shouldn't be cut?'

He shrugged. 'The idea is that, after you spend some time here, the reasons will become apparent. I'll answer your questions; I'll even volunteer some information; but, if I start to lecture, stop me. Seeing for yourself, doing for yourself—lectures can't compete with that kind of hands-on learning.'

'You should be a teacher.'

'That's the role I'm playing this weekend. I'm your teacher, and the Everglades is the lesson and the classroom, all rolled into one. You've already learned a lot. You just don't realise it yet.'

There was silence between them for a time; a comfortable, restful silence as they both absorbed the peace of their surroundings, and Melanie wondered what he thought she had learned. He might be surprised, she mused, because the lessons so far had taught her more about herself than about the Everglades.

'I've been trying to remember my old school lessons,' Melanie said at last. 'I don't think Osceola was much more than a paragraph in an American history text. He was a rogue warrior of the Seminole Indian tribe back in the 1800s, right?'

He turned his head to look at her, one brow arched. 'Some called him a rogue. Do you remember why?'

Her brow furrowed in concentration. 'I remember something about the government trying to move all the Seminoles out of Florida to a reservation somewhere, but Osceola refused to leave his home. He started a rebellion, didn't he?'

Cage looked at her steadily. 'A war, actually. Osceola and a small number of renegade warriors against the entire US Army.'

Melanie smiled sadly. 'Sounds as if the odds were a little uneven.'

'A little.'

She eyed him intently. 'Are you trying to tell me that my ancestral grandmother actually knew Osceola?'

'Maybe,' he shrugged. 'That's not clear in the legend. Only that she hid one of his wounded warriors from government troops.'

Melanie sighed hard and looked off into the distance, frowning. 'I find that very hard to believe. The Indians were killing settlers back then. They were savages.'

He looked at her for a long moment. 'The white men were also killing Indians. Perhaps the Indians thought *they* were savages.'

She pondered the logic of that for a moment, then conceded the possibility with a slight nod. 'With that kind of prejudice on both sides, it makes it even harder to imagine a white woman meeting a Seminole warrior, let alone hiding one from government troops...'

'Get dressed, Melanie,' he interrupted her gently. 'I think it's time I took you to meet the one person who can tell you the legend word for word, just as it was told to her.'

Melanie leaned forward in her chair. 'It's a woman?'

Cage nodded and smiled. 'A very old Seminole woman. Now go get ready. I'll clear up the dishes while you dress.'

Melanie dressed hurriedly, almost oblivious to Cage at the nearby counter, his back turned. If she'd thought about it she would have found her adjustment to the current circumstances quite amazing. Yesterday she couldn't imagine surviving without indoor plumbing and privacy; today she'd used an outhouse without a second thought, and was now dressing within a few feet of a man she'd known for less than twenty-four hours.

She pulled on a new pair of the heavy canvas trousers, then, after a token glance to ensure Cage's back was still turned, slipped her nightgown over her head and pulled on a fresh T-shirt. Back in Tallahassee, being seen in such a top would have been unthinkable; being seen in such a top without a bra beneath would have been downright indecent. It occurred to her then that Beau would be horrified to see her like this—but then Beau had never spent an afternoon trudging through a steamy rain forest with bra straps chafing his shoulders.

'Are you decent?' Cage said without turning around.

Melanie looked down with a wry expression at the clear outline of breast and nipple under the thin cotton. 'I suppose that would depend on whom you asked.'

'I'm asking you.'

She slipped her arms quickly into the long sleeves of a clean overshirt and pulled it closed over her breasts. 'Now I am.' She sat on the bed and started to put on the hot rubber boots. 'Do we really need boots today?'

'I'm afraid so.' He went to the chest at the foot of the bed and pulled clean clothing from beneath the towels. 'When we get to where we're going you can take them off and go barefoot.'

Melanie stifled a giggle at the perfectly preposterous image of Congressman Beau Parker's fiancée barefoot *and* braless.

'I don't know about that...' she started to say, glancing up at Cage. Her jaw dropped open at the same moment Cage dropped his cut-off jeans to the floor. Totally oblivious to her wide-eyed astonishment, clad only in black briefs, he stepped into a pair of canvas trousers like hers and hopped once as he pulled them up. He caught sight of her expression just as he was about to pull on a black T-shirt and froze.

'What's wrong?'

She blinked once and swallowed, gesturing mind-lessly with one hand at the crumpled cut-offs on the floor.

'What?' he whispered, still immobile, moving only his eyes to examine the floor. 'What?' he spat again, jerking his eyes up in a wary question.

Melanie cleared her throat, embarrassed. 'Well...you just...took off your pants. Right in front of me.'

'Oh, for crying out loud,' he muttered, his whole body sagging with a sigh of relief, then he finished jerking on the T-shirt and snapped at her, 'Dammit, don't ever do that again! I thought I was about to step on a snake.'

'Well, pardon me,' she snapped back. 'I just don't happen to be accustomed to men undressing right in front of me.'

'Really. And what does Congressman Parker do? Go to bed fully clothed?'

'I'm sure I wouldn't know,' she fired back haughtily. The moment the words were out of her mouth, she wished she hadn't revealed so much.

'*What*?'

Melanie ignored him, pretending to concentrate on buttoning her shirt. Even in the heavy rubber boots, he barely made a sound walking around the bed to stand in front of where she sat. She stared straight ahead at the mud-green of his trouser legs.

'Are you saying that you and the congressman don't...?'

Her head jerked up and her eyes flashed angrily. 'That's really none of your business, is it?'

Cage stared down at her, his black eyes sharp and intrusive. 'A little defensive, aren't you? Is that because you are sleeping with him, or because you aren't?'

It felt as if all the heat of all the Everglades summers had settled in Melanie's face. She swallowed hard and looked away, wondering why it bothered her so much for him to know she wasn't just inexperienced at tying knots—she was inexperienced at everything. 'Are we ready to go yet?'

He was silent for what seemed like a very long time. 'I'll fill the canteens.'

She closed her eyes and released an enormous sigh of relief when he turned away.

They walked away from the cabin in the opposite direction they had taken the day before, Cage leading the way through the dark hush of the cathedral-like pine forest. Melanie followed silently, her thoughts turned inwards.

Times have certainly changed, she thought miserably. In my mother's day, having sex before the wedding-day was one of those dark, humiliating secrets you prayed would never get out. And here I am, embarrassed to admit that it *hasn't* happened. Not that I think it's essential, of course. There's absolutely nothing wrong with saving yourself for marriage; in fact, there's something very pure and admirable about the virgin bride—but isn't holding on to your virginity supposed to be at least a little bit of a challenge? Aren't men supposed to be driven by their passion? Out of control most of the time, with only the strong will of the woman keeping them at bay?

She watched the steady placement of her feet on the forest path, frowning hard. Beau had *never* been out of control; as a matter of fact, *he* had been the one to take her shoulders and push her gently away when their kisses had become too prolonged. So what did that mean? That he didn't love her? Or simply that she wasn't the kind of woman who inspired men to passion?

She sighed heavily and glanced up at Cage's back a short distance ahead. Do I inspire him? she wondered, staring at where the thin material of his T-shirt was already clinging to the indentation of his spine. She recalled the moments of physical contact they'd had yesterday—on the airboat when they'd run into the bank; in the cabin after he'd carried her up the stairs. A dark, heavy flutter rippled from breast to stomach when she recalled the heat in his eyes; but then she remembered that each time he'd put her from him, almost as an afterthought. Her mouth twitched irritably, thinking that Cage didn't have any trouble keeping his hands off her, either. Maybe no man would.

'Melanie?'

'Hmm?'

'Come up here and walk next to me.'

She hung back sullenly. 'I'm following in your footsteps, just as I was directed yesterday. Have you forgotten? I'm the one who follows orders so well.'

He ignored the crack and slowed until she came alongside. 'There are no hidden bogs on this trail. It's safe to walk next to me.'

'If you say so.'

He suppressed a smile. 'You're very quiet. What are you thinking about?'

'I'm not thinking. I'm absorbing the environment. I'm fact-finding. That's why I'm here, remember?'

'I remember.'

They both stopped and looked up as their passage disturbed a flock of small, colourful birds roosting overhead.

'We're walking inland now,' he said, moving forward again, 'towards a small stream where I keep a canoe. The airboat's too big for the waterways we'll take today.'

'I thought all of the Everglades was under water; that you could take an airboat anywhere.'

'Not any more. They've drained a lot of it. Originally it was five times larger than it is today.'

Melanie looked down at the animal trail they were following and saw the one thing she'd never expected to see in the country's biggest freshwater marsh—little dust clouds rising around her boots. 'They're draining the Everglades?'

'They don't call it draining—they call it water management.'

'Oh, *that*. I read about the water-management programme. It's very scientifically controlled; very carefully monitored to minimise damage to the Everglades ecosystem,' she quoted some of the literature Beau had given her to read.

'Right,' he said drily. 'They very scientifically decide how much land to drain for housing developments, how much water they can get away with diverting to the big agricultural fields up north...'

'None of that is hurting the Everglades,' she said petulantly. 'They're about to complete a very extensive study that will prove that.'

He sighed noisily. 'The study was published a month ago, and what it proved was that the water-management programme—the very programme designed to protect the 'Glades—is killing it, acre by acre, year by year. Certain people would like that information kept quiet, or, at the very least, discredited.'

Melanie stopped dead and looked up at him, blue eyes quiet. 'I didn't read anything about the water-management programme hurting the Everglades . . .'

He turned and continued walking. 'Then you'd better do a little more reading.'

Melanie trotted to catch up with him, plucking at his arm like a child trying to get the attention of an adult. 'But I read everything Beau gave me . . .'

'Then he didn't give you everything.'

She scowled at the ground as she walked, wondering why Beau wouldn't have included such a vital study in the reading he gave her, and then finally her face cleared when the answer came to her. It was so obvious that she felt foolish for not realising it immediately. Beau hadn't read the study either; he probably didn't even have it.

'I'll get a copy of that study and read it just as soon as I get back to Tallahassee,' she said firmly.

'You can read it tonight. I've got a copy at the cabin.'

'Good. And, if what you say is true, I know Beau will work as hard as anyone against cutting the budget.'

'Oh, wonderful. I feel much better now.'

Melanie stopped walking and glared at him. 'He will,' she insisted, her lower lip creeping out a fraction. 'And if you doubt that, it's only because you don't know him.'

'And you do?' He stopped and turned to face her.

'Of course I do,' she said, trying to keep the doubt out of her voice. The truth was, she'd been shaken to learn the real reason Beau had wanted her to come here; it had made her wonder if she really knew the man she was going to marry at all. 'He's a good and honourable man, and I'm sure he thinks he's doing the right thing...' She recited the words as if they were a chant that would make them true.

Cage snorted derisively. 'If he's so sure voting to cut the Everglades budget is the right thing to do, why did he even bother going through the motions of sending someone down here?'

Melanie hesitated. 'He's... afraid of you. Afraid you could use your money and power to convince the voters he *wasn't* right, even if he was.'

Cage gave her a long-suffering look. 'If it were really the right thing to do, the facts would support him, and no one—not even me—could convince the voters otherwise.'

Melanie looked down and frowned hard at the strange, ugly boots on her feet.

'There is no honour without honesty, Melanie.'

Her head jerked up with a small remnant of her old defiance. 'I know that.'

'Parker hasn't been honest with any of us—not the voters, not me, not even you—so what is it that makes you think he's such an honourable man?'

Melanie sighed and bit down on her lip, trying to sort out the jumble of her thoughts.

'Were you supposed to sleep with me? Was that my consolation prize?'

She flinched hard, shifting her hair from her shoulders to tumble down her back. 'Dear lord, no!' she gasped. 'Is *that* what you think...?'

He shrugged idly. 'What am I supposed to think? I invite a congressman, and who does he send as his representative? An aide? A well-informed, experienced professional? No. He sends a woman who's never seen the Everglades; who's afraid of everything in them; a woman who doesn't know the first thing about a fact-finding expedition, but who sure as hell could make any man forget what he was trying to accomplish in the first place.'

Melanie just stared at him. She'd heard everything he said, but her mind had zeroed in on the last part and wouldn't let go.

'Weren't you a little suspicious yourself when you found out the trip was a ruse?' he asked innocently. 'Didn't you wonder just what it was you were supposed to do to pacify me?'

Her mouth quivered uncertainly. 'You don't understand. It wasn't like that. He told me to use some of my Southern charm...'

One side of his mouth moved slightly, and he arched one brow. 'Right.'

'And he meant *charm*,' she insisted, frowning now. 'Nothing else. Beau doesn't even *think* of me that way...'

'There isn't a man alive who could help but think of you that way.'

Her breath caught in her throat, and she had to swallow before she could continue. 'Southern gentlemen do not think of the future mothers of their children like that——' she started to say, and once again he interrupted her, leaving her with her lips parted and her thought barely begun.

'Who the hell told you that?'

Melanie swallowed hard, confused by the sudden twist in the conversation.

'Good lord,' Cage said quietly. 'That's why you think he's such a "good and honourable man", isn't it? Because he hasn't taken you yet.'

Her peripheral vision caught the motion of the canteens as he let them slide from his arms, but she was afraid to take her eyes from his, even when she felt his hands close around her upper arms. 'Hell, Melanie; haven't you wondered if there just wasn't something missing that was supposed to be there?'

She stilled under his hands, shocked to hear the thought that had troubled her most spoken aloud.

He looked deeply into her eyes, then frowned in genuine puzzlement. 'Why?' he whispered. 'Why would you choose a man like that?'

With that single question, all the tidy pieces of her life seemed to explode outward, and that train she'd always felt as if she were riding screeched to a halt, dropping her in the middle of nowhere, leaving her to find her own way. She hadn't really *chosen* Beau, any more than she'd chosen anything else in her life. He'd been...provided. 'I've arranged for you to meet a special man tonight, Mellie,' her father had said, 'the perfect man; the kind of man your mother and I always dreamed our baby girl would marry.'

'Why?' Cage was repeating again, and she became aware of his hands tightening on her arms. She blinked her way out of her confused thoughts, and for the first time saw the dark tightness of desire on a man's face.

'Honour and honesty,' he said, barely moving his lips, the total focus of his intention spearing her from the black centres of his eyes. 'They're inseparable. Seeing you and not wanting you is dishonest. Touching you...' his thumbs stroked through the fabric of her sleeves along the insides of her arms, making her shiver '...and not taking you is dishonest.'

With the sudden, thoughtless instinct of prey recognising predator, she started to scramble backwards—not necessarily because it was what she wanted to do, but because it was the only reaction that seemed proper.

'Oh, no, you don't,' he murmured, pulling her against his chest, one broad hand solid on her back, the other circling her neck with a thumb under her chin, holding her head still.

'Cage, no,' she whispered, feeling a rapid hammering against her chest that might have been her heartbeat or his. 'You can't do this. You have to let me go.' She searched his face for a remnant of reason, but all she saw was an intensity of purpose that narrowed the dark eyes and drew lines of determination at the corners.

'I'll make a deal with you,' he said in a voice so harsh that she barely recognised it as his. 'If you ask me to let you go again, I will.'

The statement so puzzled her that she was totally unprepared for the sudden, hard descent of his mouth on hers. She went rigid against the brace of his arm, feeling her lips flattened against her teeth. The first thought to leap into her mind was that she wasn't being kissed; she was being conquered. The next

thought was that Benjamin Cage tasted exactly the
way he smelled—tangy and sweet and musky and wild,
and very, very hot. As his fingers twined into her hair,
pulling her head back, his mouth worked against hers
expertly, making it strangely hard to draw breath.

It's the heat, she thought crazily. You simply can't
breathe properly in this kind of weather. But then she
felt the slick wetness of his tongue at the crease of her
lips, and knew that the steaming liquid rush she felt
in the pit of her stomach had nothing to do with ex-
ternal temperatures.

Nothing in her life had prepared her for this singular
moment when she would feel physical desire for the
first time. No one had taught her that it should be
resisted, that there was merit in exercising control over
the frantic demands of her own body—perhaps because no one had ever imagined that a well-bred, well-
raised daughter of the South would ever feel such
things.

As they stood staring into each other's eyes, his
hands slid down the generous rise of her breasts,
opening the buttons of her overshirt along the way.
He parted the shirt and looked down at the sharp
outline of her nipples against the thin cloth of the
T-shirt, and, just when she was sure she could feel his
gaze as strongly as she would have felt his hand, he
touched a forefinger lightly to one shuddering peak
and her knees threatened to buckle.

It was totally unlike the forceful, hasty press of
Beau's hands on those occasions when he'd done more
than kiss her. Once, and only once, she'd grabbed his
hand and held it to her breast, thinking that if the
moment could be prolonged it would eventually
mature into tenderness. He'd pulled back immedi-

ately, obviously disconcerted that the proper young
woman he was going to marry was capable of such
boldness. She'd seen the disappointment, maybe even
the wariness in his face, and knew instinctively that
taking the initiative had threatened him somehow.
He'd made her feel like a whore with that single
glance, and she'd been passive ever since.

But passiveness now was impossible, and blessedly
unnecessary. At Cage's touch she'd grabbed his arms
to hold herself erect, and the convulsive leap of his
biceps beneath her fingers told her that here was a
man who responded to passion, not submission.

She felt as if bonds that had chafed her spirit for
a lifetime had been suddenly cut, granting her a
freedom she'd never known existed. For this gift
alone, she knew she would love Benjamin Cage
forever, and the last remnant of the woman everyone
thought she was and should be disappeared forever.
She gazed up at Cage with clear, shining eyes, and
showed him the heart that had been hiding there.

There was an almost imperceptible narrowing of
his eyes, as if she'd uttered something profound, and
for a moment, his hands stilled on her breasts. Then
his lips moved silently to form her name and his hands
moved to her shoulders. He pushed the straps of her
sleeveless T-shirt and her shirt down to her elbows,
effectively pinning her arms, exposing her breasts.
They seemed to rise towards him with her startled
intake of breath. He stared at them, then released a
long, shaky exhalation and let his eyes fall closed.
Melanie saw the frantic beat of the pulse in his corded
neck, felt the trembling of his hands on her arms, and
then suddenly he was looking down at her again, his
eyes wide and clear and perfectly eloquent, as if an-

nouncing his intentions. When he reached out to fill
his hands with her breasts, when thumbs and fore-
fingers found her nipples and began to massage gently,
her own eyes fell closed and she sank helplessly to her
knees.

Following her down, he let his mouth find her neck,
then her collar-bone, and finally his lips closed around
the peak of her left breast. She moaned aloud, her
back arching, and then she felt tongue and teeth
tasting delicately at first, then sucking hard as her head
fell back on her shoulders. She reached for the back
of his head, whimpering when the prison of her own
clothes frustrated her. He sat back on his haunches
and tore the shirt from her arms, then rested there a
moment, breathing through his mouth, black hair
dangling over eyes hooded to gaze into hers.

'I've always taken what I wanted from life, and
made it mine.' He exhaled raggedly, then paused to
take a series of shaky breaths. 'But I've never wanted
anything so much.'

She didn't know if those were really the words she'd
always wanted to hear from a man. She only knew
that they made her feel like a woman for perhaps the
first time in her life. It didn't matter that he hadn't
mentioned love, because love and desire had to be
part of the same thing, or else the whole world was
upside-down.

When she reached for him, not wanting him to talk,
not wanting words that would remind her of that other
world and promises she had made there, he snatched
her wrists and held them, his eyes fierce. She met his
gaze fully, her eyes darkened by forest and passion to
a deeper, more complex blue, then she slowly drew
his hand back to her breast.

A brief shudder passed through him as he took her by the shoulders and lowered her gently to the forest floor. As his mouth travelled over her face and neck his hand loosened the waistband of the heavy canvas trousers, then slid beneath her lace panties to rest lightly on the softness of her stomach. She gasped quietly at his touch, then felt a great, peaceful stillness settle over her body, a powerful sense of certainty which she wanted to last for the rest of her life. This was what she wanted. *He* was what she wanted. Forever.

Trembling beneath him, clutching the back of his head, she felt his fingers slip down her stomach into the damp forest of hair, then further into the slick wetness of passion that throbbed under his touch. Her back arched involuntarily and she whimpered as he cupped her gently, then allowed his fingers to travel in tender exploration.

She was vaguely aware of the leafy canopy overhead, of filtered sunlight dappling her face. Her hair spread in a golden fan on the rich brown soil, and occasionally, when a leaf stirred above, a shard of sunlight found a lighter strand of blonde and seemed to set it on fire. In some distant part of her mind, Melanie savoured the sweet irony of first being touched by a man in a savagely beautiful wilderness as pristine and innocent of man's touch as she was.

Cage's dark eyes drank in the sight of her face as his hands caressed her, and Melanie was gazing up at him in wonderment when suddenly his eyes flickered, then froze on a point just past her head. She opened her mouth to speak, but he silenced her with a quick, urgent tightening of his eyes. Completely silent, his lips mouthed the words, 'Don't move.'

Less than a hand's breadth from the top of
Melanie's head, Cage's gaze was fixed on a blunt, cy-
lindrical head poised over the fan of blonde blocking
its path, its dark tongue flicking curiously.

His breath caught in his throat, his body painfully
rigid, Cage tried to keep the horror out of his eyes as
the small, deadly snake wove its black and yellow and
red body through the blonde strands.

Beneath him, Melanie lay perfectly still, watching
his eyes track slowly to the left. His fear was almost
palpable, and she sensed the rigid tension of muscles
prepared to react instantly and violently. She felt the
soft stir of something moving in her hair, and when
she saw his nostrils flare and his gaze sharpen, she
knew instinctively that her life depended on remaining motionless. And yet miraculously—foolishly, perhaps—she was not afraid. Cage would never
let anything hurt her. She knew that with a greater
certainty than she had ever known anything in her
life.

She watched as his eyes tracked so far to the left
that a great portion of the whites showed; and then
slowly, with a shudder that passed violently through
his entire body, his lids fell closed in relief.

In one quick, fluid motion he slipped his hand from
her pants, gathered his legs beneath him and rose to
his feet, pulling her with him. His embrace was so
fierce that it was painful.

'Dear lord,' he breathed raggedly into her ear, his
voice as tight as the arms that held her.

She leaned back against his arm and looked up at
him. His face was twisted, tortured by thoughts of
what might have been. 'What was it?' she whispered.

He swallowed hard. 'Snake,' was all he could manage to utter.

'I thought so.'

His eyes widened. 'You thought so?' he repeated numbly, and she nodded.

'I felt something in my hair, and I saw you staring, watching it move along the ground...it couldn't have been anything else.'

He shook his head as if to clear it, mystified by her reaction. 'But you're terrified of snakes. You fainted when you *saw* one...'

'I know. But I wasn't afraid this time. This time I knew you wouldn't let anything hurt me.'

He stared at her in dull disbelief for a moment, then his face darkened in anger she didn't understand. 'Dammit, it was a *coral* snake, Melanie. They're deadly. They make the cottonmouth seem like a household pet. One bite and...' His voice caught and he shuddered.

'I'm sorry,' she murmured, wanting to erase the anger from his face; wanting to make everything all right again.

'You're sorry,' he echoed dully. 'I let things get out of hand and nearly get you killed, and you're sorry.' He turned his head away, frowning hard, then took his hands from her and jammed them in his pockets. She started to lift her hand to reach for his arm, then looked at his face and knew that something was suddenly, terribly wrong. She let her hand fall back to her side. The crease between his brows had deepened with the intensity of his thoughts, and the muscle along his jaw stood out in sharp relief. He's going away, she thought, without realising where the thought had come from; but still her gaze remained riveted to his face, as if her whole future hung in the balance. She was afraid to speak.

Finally he released a long, sombre sigh and turned his head to look straight at her. 'This was all wrong. We're probably lucky that snake came along when it did.'

Melanie felt her heart still in her chest, and she had to concentrate fiercely to keep her voice steady. 'Why was it all wrong?'

His brows twitched once in a pained expression. It was the last visible sign of emotion he would give her. 'Because you want more than I can give you.'

She felt a prickle crawling up her spine, that prelude to an adrenalin surge the body sensed long before the mind directed the legs to run. 'I don't understand,' she whispered.

There was no more black fire in his eyes. The surfaces looked flat and impenetrable. 'You wanted love, and I can't give you that.'

She could sense her chest rising and falling, so she knew she was breathing, but she wondered how she could manage that with her heart lying so dead and still. 'But . . . we almost made love . . .'

'No. We almost had sex. I don't think you know what love is yet.'

She flinched at each word as if it were a blow, standing there stoically like a torture victim determined not to show pain. He didn't love her? What they'd felt together; what they'd shared together—that hadn't been love? After a time it occurred to her that she should say something. 'Really,' was all she could manage to utter, and for some reason that response seemed to amuse him. She felt the sharp, ironic twist of his mouth like a knife in her stomach.

'You would have hated yourself later, you know. Once you came to your senses and went back where you belong.'

Her eyes fell painfully closed at the 'came to your senses' remark. It made her sound the way... the way Beau had made her feel that one time she'd held his hand to her breast. Melanie the Wanton, she thought with a grim smile that never made it from her mind to her lips.

'You should cover yourself.' He was staring at her bare breasts, and, when she realised that, she felt the stirrings of shame where a moment before there had been none. It had been all right as long as he'd been holding her; as long as she'd been within the circle of his arms and his tender attention. But now she was just a half-naked woman being told to cover herself.

Her face started to colour slowly, as if humiliation was an afterthought—something she just remembered she was supposed to feel. It felt the same as it had all those years before when an appalled nanny had chased her naked across the lawn. She pushed arms she could barely feel through the straps of her T-shirt and pulled it up over her shoulders, keeping her eyes cast down. It wasn't necessary to see his face to feel the indifference of his gaze, and it was all she could do to keep her features rigidly aligned; to pretend it didn't matter; to maintain that level of control the human animal clung to as a shield against despair.

You can live through this, Melanie, she tried to tell herself. It isn't the end of the world, just because the first man you've ever wanted—the first man you've ever loved—doesn't want you...

She heard his voice like a pain coursing through every nerve. Dear lord, she thought, I'm falling apart at the sound of his voice; what will happen if I look at him again?

'Melanie?' he repeated. 'I asked if you wanted to go back.'

'Back?' she asked with forced lightness, hurriedly pulling on the shirt. 'Back where? To the cabin? To Tallahassee? Or all the way back home to Georgia?'

He was quiet for a time, and she felt his stare as she looked down, pretending to concentrate on her buttons. 'Wherever.'

She took a deep breath and looked around, anywhere but at him.

'Look at me, Melanie.'

And there it was. The command to bare soul and mind through the windows of her eyes. The insistence that she look again on what she couldn't have, and show her pain.

She turned her head very slowly and gazed upon the sheer masculine beauty of his face, her own features perfectly composed. 'What is it?' she asked calmly.

He didn't see the agony the gesture had cost her; he couldn't see that she wanted to double over with the pain of something absolutely essential being torn from deep inside. 'Do you want to go back?' he repeated.

'No,' she said firmly. She wasn't going back. Not empty-handed. If she couldn't have Benjamin Cage, the very least she was taking out of this miserable sticky place was a piece of her own family history. 'I want to meet the Seminole woman. I want to hear the legend. You promised me that.'

He was silent for what seemed like a very long time, and in the silence they stared at each other, proud blue eyes and proud brown ones each jealously guarding the private thoughts behind them.

'Let's go,' Cage said finally, turning and striding deeper into the forest that was part of his world, and as alien to Melanie as the far side of the moon.

It occurred to her as she followed him how much he belonged here, and how much she didn't. Hadn't she been foolish to imagine an affinity with such a man? They weren't the least bit alike...

In the distance she heard the mournful shriek of some wild, exotic bird, and thought it sounded like a woman screaming.

CHAPTER EIGHT

FOR the better part of an hour Cage paddled the oddly short aluminium canoe through a labyrinth of serpentine waterways. Melanie sat on the front bench, resisting the urge to look back at him. She barely noticed the green, brackish water slipping beneath the hull, the riotous colour of jumbo orchids peeking through the deeply shaded jungle around them, or even the feathery strands of moss dangling from overhead branches, sometimes brushing against her face like the dainty webs of spiders. She was too busy wrestling with her emotions, remembering what had happened between them back on the forest floor, and trying to forget what had been said afterwards.

Forever. That was what she had decided back there—that Cage was what she wanted for the rest of her life. That was love, wasn't it? But what did love become when it wasn't returned? Could it even exist at all?

She worried the questions in troubled silence, unaware of Cage's eyes on her from the back, flickering with something like pain whenever she lifted her head or moved her shoulders in a sigh.

After a time he spoke occasionally, but only to point out an unusual plant or bird, or to call her attention to once-lush areas now drained dry by the canals and choked with brush. It was doubly painful that he could speak so calmly of such inconsequential things, as if nothing at all had happened between them. Very little

of what he said registered, but she felt the sound of
his voice through every nerve in her body.

'There used to be thousands of snowy egrets nesting
right here,' he said at one point. 'Now the water is
gone, the fish are gone, and the egrets are gone, too.
That's our water-management system for you.'

Her only response was to nod absently as she rubbed
at her arms, trying to erase the memory of the way
his hands had felt on her skin.

At times the watery road they followed seemed to
disappear in a thick jumble of floating lilies, but Cage
just continued to paddle through the viney mass,
always finding a clear passage beyond.

Eventually he steered the canoe into a part of the
bank that looked exactly like every other part, and
tossed a line over an overhanging branch. 'We're here,'
he said perfunctorily, extending a hand to help her on
to the reedy shore.

Melanie clung to his hand until he pulled away and
pushed through the undergrowth to a hidden path.
Without a backward glance to make sure she could
follow through grasses and ferns taller than she was,
he stomped ahead into a stand of old-growth mahogany. For the first time in well over an hour she
felt the edge of her pain sharpen into resentment.

Beau would never do that, she thought bitterly,
hurrying to keep Cage in sight. Beau would never push
on ahead and leave me to find my own way. He'd be
right back here next to me, one hand on my elbow,
eyes watchful to make sure I didn't step wrong. And,
come to think of it, Beau wouldn't expect me to use
an outhouse, either, or to shower outside or tie up a
boat or trudge through a forest in a hundred-degree
heat. He wouldn't even think of asking such things.

He knows the limits of my experience, and doesn't fault me for it. Cage, damn him anyway, doesn't think I *have* any limits.

She froze suddenly, feeling as if she'd been hit in the stomach with a two-by-four, blinking at the sudden, faint glimmer of understanding that was almost like a visible spark in the air ahead. Her mind reached out, grasping for that elusive spark like a child chasing fireflies in the dark.

'Melanie, dammit! Hurry up!'

She jumped at Cage's impatient shout from somewhere up the trail, frustrated by the distraction. The bright glimmer her thoughts had been chasing seemed to disperse into a million pinpricks of light, and she cursed softly under her breath and trudged forward.

She found Cage a short distance ahead, looking up at a small palm-thatched hut rising amid the trees. A rickety flight of steps rose upward to what seemed little more than a roofed platform—no screens, no walls, just woven mats partially rolled up to admit the slightest breeze. 'There it is,' he said.

'Someone actually lives here?'

A figure suddenly appeared at the top of the steps. 'She does.'

As she drew close enough to see the woman clearly Melanie caught herself staring in disbelief. It seemed impossible that anyone who looked that old could even draw breath, let alone exude the vitality this woman did without moving a muscle. She was incredibly tall, thin, and totally without the stoop Melanie had come to expect from people of a great age. Her skin was nut-brown and deeply seamed; her full, brightly coloured skirt brushed her ankles, and a blazing red bandana was wrapped so tightly around her skull that Melanie wondered if she had any hair beneath it. 'Hurry up!' she called down to Cage in a strong, youthful voice, and he left Melanie behind, vaulting up the stairs to lift the old Seminole woman in an exuberant embrace.

Melanie gazed up at the pair, feeling for an old, barefoot Seminole woman one of the first pangs of envy she'd ever felt in her life. Cage's love for the old woman seemed to radiate like a miniature sun—she saw it in the way he held her, heard it in the mellow music of his laughter—and realised with a wrenching pain that, whatever Cage had felt for her back on that forest trail, it had not filled him with this kind of joy.

She dropped her eyes abruptly, feeling like an unwelcome intruder.

'Come up, Melanie.' His voice drifted down like early morning mist in the sudden silence.

She climbed reluctantly, her boots thumping noisily on the risers, as out of place on her feet as she was in the Everglades. She should never have come here, she thought as she climbed. She didn't belong here. Not in Cage's beloved swamp; not in this old woman's pathetic hut...

And then suddenly she was at the top of the stairs and the old woman turned from Cage and looked at her, and Melanie almost reeled under the sudden, stunning sense of finally coming home to a place and a face she had never seen before.

It was the woman, of course. She had that rare, magical gift of drawing you into the circle of her warmth with a glance. Perhaps it was simply the serenity of a very old soul; perhaps it was that kind of charisma politicians like Beau could only dream of;

but, whatever it was, Melanie felt herself tremble, humbled by it.

Strong, weathered hands grasped hers and black eyes bright as buttons seemed to peer into her soul. The old face seemed to dissolve in the hundred wrinkles of a smile, and Melanie felt as if the sun had just broken through the clouds to shine on her face. 'You are the first woman Asi has ever brought to me,' the old Seminole woman said quietly. Her voice was rich with the cadenced drawl of the South, her words slow and precise, as if English were her second language.

'It's an honour to meet you,' Melanie murmured, meaning it.

'I think he honours us both. What's your name, child?'

'Melanie.'

The old woman smiled and nodded. 'Call me Grandmother. Everyone does, even this fellow.' She chuckled and poked a bony finger at Cage's arm.

'You're . . . his grandmother?'

'Oh, my, no. He's not nearly lucky enough to have my blood in his veins.' She chuckled again, then tucked Melanie's hand into the crook of her elbow and led her into the full shade of the hut's roof. 'Come along. You, too, Asi. We'll rest while the sun is hot.'

They sat cross-legged in the nearly empty hut, drinking thick, sweet juice from hand-thrown pottery cups with no handles. While the old woman and Cage talked about people with strange names, Melanie absently stroked the woven mat beneath them, strikingly similar to the one on the floor of Cage's cabin.

'You like it?'

Melanie glanced up to find two sets of black eyes on her. 'It's very beautiful.'

The old woman smiled broadly. 'I'll make one for your wedding gift.'

Melanie smiled uncertainly, wondering how she could know about her wedding. She swiped at the damp tendrils clinging to her forehead, then moved her shoulders beneath the hot, heavy mass of her hair, wishing she'd brought a clip.

'I can braid that for you. I used to braid the hair of my daughters, and then my granddaughters, back when the water lapped at the posts below.'

Melanie started to protest automatically.

'Hush.' The old woman moved quickly, pulling a low stool behind Melanie and plunging her fingers into the tangles of her hair. 'This will be much cooler.' She hummed as she started to work, and Melanie felt the muscles in her neck and shoulders start to relax, almost against her will. 'I'm braiding sunlight, Asi,' she heard the old woman say over her head.

Cage smiled briefly. 'I've brought Melanie to hear one of the old legends, Grandmother.'

'Really? Well. I know them all. Which one should I tell?'

There was silence for a moment, then he said quietly, 'Her full name is Melanie Annabelle Brooks.'

The old fingers froze in the intricate weave they were creating, as if they had suddenly become part of it. Melanie thought she felt them tremble slightly.

'She wants to hear the legend about her great-great-great-grandmother,' Cage added.

After what seemed like a very long time the old woman sighed, as if she'd been holding her breath. Melanie imagined she could feel the whisper of that sigh pass through her hair to tickle her scalp. 'Is this true, child? Melanie Annabelle Brooks was your ancestor?'

Melanie nodded, puzzled by the crackle of tension in the air.

'How did you find her, Asi?' the old woman whispered.

'Actually, she found me.'

Melanie heard another sigh from behind her, this one almost musical. After what seemed like a very long time the fingers started their work again.

'All right, then.' The old woman cleared her throat and began to recite. 'Truth and legend weave together, like the mat we sit on, like the braid of your hair, and so this is the legend, and this is the truth.' Melanie felt the shivery thrill of a child hearing her first ghost story by an open camp-fire. Cage straightened slightly opposite her, fixing her with his eyes as they both listened.

'Once there was a young warrior who rode at the right side of Osceola, the greatest Seminole warrior of all. On a raid in a place called Creek County, the young warrior was wounded and separated from his band. He hid himself in a great forest, and there he saw a woman sitting on the bank of a creek. She had hair the colour of the sun . . . like yours, child . . . and the young warrior was blinded by her beauty. He remained hidden, watching her, until a doe and her fawn came to drink at the creek, and the woman became a tree . . .'

'She means she didn't move,' Cage interrupted, and the old woman clucked her tongue impatiently.

'She knows that,' she said sharply. 'There is a good mind beneath all this hair. I can see it.'

Cage looked down, properly chastised, but Melanie could see him suppressing a smile.

'The woman was so moved by the beauty of the deer that tears fell from her eyes, and the warrior knew then that her heart was good. He showed himself and they talked with their eyes, and fell in love before the first words were spoken.'

Melanie saw the story come to life in her mind, imagining a dark man with eyes like Cage first startling, then entrancing a young woman who had heard eloquence, but never seen it in a man's face.

'She took the warrior to a secret place to tend his wounds and kept him hidden from all eyes but hers. For the time it took him to heal they loved only with their eyes and hearts, because he was an Indian warrior and she was a great white man's wife, and only their spirits could join. And then one day she disappeared, and her husband thought she was dead, but she was only bringing her warrior home.'

The old woman paused a moment. 'Her name was Melanie Annabelle Brooks, and she stayed with the Seminole many days, learning the ways of the tribe and this place. The warrior's parents called her daughter, honouring her for saving the life of their son. Others called her the White Seminole. On the day she left to return to her home they say the sky looked down on the warrior and the white woman and wept, because you could see their hearts breaking in their eyes.'

Melanie felt the old hands drop from her hair, but remained motionless, connected to a woman who had died more than a century before; a woman who had also found love here in the Everglades, a love she couldn't keep.

Finally she reached up to wipe her cheeks with both hands, unashamed of her tears. Cage was looking at her, his lips pressed tightly together.

'That is your legend, child,' the old woman murmured.

Melanie turned to look at her, her eyes brimming again. A gnarled hand cupped her chin while the other wiped gently at her cheeks.

'You shouldn't cry,' she smiled tenderly. 'This is a great day. The circle is closing.'

'What do you mean?' Melanie sniffed.

The old woman's eyes speared Cage. 'Asi?'

'Why do you call him that?'

'Because it's his name.'

Cage scowled at her questioning glance, then grumbled, 'My full name is Benjamin Osceola Cage.'

'Benjamin *Asi-Vaholo* Cage,' the old woman corrected him sternly. 'That is the Seminole name, and that is your name.' She looked at Melanie and smiled. 'The descendants of that young warrior all carry the name of Asi-Vaholo, honouring the memory of that great chief...' Melanie's breath stopped in her throat. 'Asi is the great-great-great-grandson of the young warrior saved by your great-great-great-grandmother.'

Melanie blinked at the old woman, then turned to Cage, her blue eyes round with amazement. 'But this is incredible,' she whispered, wondering why he hadn't told her the legend himself, as soon as he'd found out who she was. She stared at him for a long time, trying to read his expression, then finally looked down at the mat beneath her crossed legs, her mind numb. 'You never said a thing,' she mumbled senselessly. 'I didn't even know you were Seminole . . .'

The old woman chuckled. 'The generations have diluted his blood, but the spirit is still strong. In his heart, he is Seminole. He carries the spirit of his ancestor, just as you carry the spirit of yours. And now the circle is closing and, in you, the hearts of your ancestors will join at last.'

She rocked back on the little stool, beaming. 'This is a great day. I am grateful I lived to see this day.'

'It's a coincidence, that's all, Grandmother,' Cage said in a voice so flatly indifferent that it made Melanie wince. 'Melanie doesn't belong here any more than her ancestor did. The circle is *not* closing.'

The old woman seemed unperturbed. 'You think not? Even you, Asi, are not strong enough to deny destiny. The circle *is* closing, and there's nothing you can do to stop it.'

Suddenly Cage leaped up and stomped from the hut, his feet beating angrily down the primitive stairs outside. The old woman never moved, never glanced after him, and her expression remained serene. 'Men always make such a noise when they're afraid, don't they?' she mused.

Melanie frowned up at her. 'I don't think Cage—Asi—is afraid of anything.'

For some reason that delighted the old woman, and she chuckled deep in her throat. 'He's afraid of you, child; can't you see that?'

Melanie just stared at her.

'You've made him want to love you, and that's a fearful thing for a man afraid to love.'

'Afraid to love?' Melanie echoed in a whisper.

The old woman looked away for a moment, her eyes troubled. 'Perhaps he thinks you will leave, as your ancestor did—as his own mother did. He's afraid to put his love, and therefore his life, in someone else's hands. His father did, and when she left it destroyed him. I think it was then that Asi decided it was easier not to love at all.' She turned back to Melanie with a warm smile, her face creasing like soft, buttery leather. 'I think only women understand that love and pain are also companions, just like truth and legend, and that the joy of one makes the agony of the other bearable. Asi may never be able to let himself love you, but is that really so important? You love him, and that love belongs to you forever. Not even Asi can take that away—unless you let him.'

CHAPTER NINE

THE circle is closing. The phrase repeated itself constantly in Melanie's mind as Cage hurried her back towards the canoe, away from the spartan hut, as if the old woman's ideas about destiny were a disease they might catch if they stayed too long.

Melanie moved mindlessly in the direction she was led, her eyes all but unseeing, her thoughts turned inward. Occasionally she blinked hard, as if the seeds of thought the old woman had planted were as dazzling as the light of the noonday sun.

For the first time Cage seemed uncomfortable with the silence between them. 'Grandmother's getting old,' he grumbled as he pushed the canoe away from the bank. 'Don't put too much stock in what she says. She's too wrapped up in the old legends . . .'

Melanie almost smiled, wondering what he'd think if he knew what had been said after he left the hut. 'You don't believe the legend?'

He shrugged irritably, biting deep into the water with the paddle. 'I believe it happened; but I don't believe that something that happened over a century ago has anything to do with what happens now. Turn around and get your hands inside the boat.'

Melanie jerked her hands to her lap and faced front, her eyes on the silvery prow as it sliced through the murky water. She was still a little shaken by the revelations of the afternoon. It had been surprising enough when Cage had told her her ancestral grand-

mother had actually been here; that she had loved
Cage's great-great-great-grandfather was one of those
unbelievable coincidences that left your sense of logic
reeling.

It must have shaken him too, when he first heard
my name, she thought, remembering his reaction. At
last she understood the things he'd said afterwards,
about grand names mandating grand deeds. If that
was true, they both had a lot to live up to.

She sighed deeply, watching the impenetrable wall
of green slide by the canoe, wondering what it would
be like to have the kind of courage her ancestral
grandmother had had. She'd sacrificed everything—
her reputation, her marriage, even her place in the
family history—for love of a man she knew she could
never have. No wonder she had become a legend.

Fingering the intricate weave of her hair, she caught
herself wondering if the first Melanie Brooks had worn
such a braid, and how she could have returned to one
man when she loved another.

She pondered that question for a very long time.

The sun had barely dipped to the treetops when they
arrived back at the cabin. As soon as they were inside
Cage peeled off his overshirt then sat down on the
chair and began taking off his boots. Melanie walked
over to sit on the bed, folded her hands in her lap,
and watched as he set his boots carefully to one side,
then leaned forward, his arms draped across his thighs.
'The old woman fell in love with you.'

Melanie felt her mind smile. At least someone had.

'Part of it was the legend, of course. The Seminole
put a lot of stock in legends . . .' He stopped abruptly,
frowning at her expression. 'You look . . . different.'
His black hair shifted slightly as he tipped his head.

'Do I? It must be the braid.'

He shook his head, dark eyes fixed on hers, his expression suddenly still, as if he were catching a mental breath. Melanie used the moment to memorise that exotic, implacable face with its stoic gaze and carved features, making a photograph her mind would carry with her forever.

Suddenly he looked down, breaking eye-contact, then braced his hands on his knees and stood. 'I'd better get us something to eat. It's going to be full dark soon. You light the lamps.'

She remained sitting for a moment, looking out at the deepening shadows of dusk with a faint, rueful smile. He actually thought she'd been paying attention when he showed her how to light the lamps. He actually expected her to do that without any help, just as he'd expected her to use an outdoor shower and tie a boat and keep pace with those impossibly long strides of his when he stomped through the forest . . . what a testament to fate's sense of mischief that helpless, coddled Melanie Brooks would fall in love with a man who expected more of her than anyone ever had . . .

She tensed on the bed suddenly, feeling her mind snatching at that same firefly glimmer of light she'd sensed on the path to the old woman's hut this morning. But she'd done all those things, hadn't she? She wasn't helpless, coddled Melanie Brooks with Cage, because he expected her to be more than that.

She felt the rush of epiphany like the pulse of wind stirred by a thousand wings. In her mind's eye she saw the bright, blinding essence of her love for Cage and realised it was not so much for the way he made her feel, as the way he made her feel about herself.

'You love him,' the old woman's words echoed in her mind, 'and that love belongs to you forever. Not even Asi can take that away—unless you let him.'

She raised her head and looked across the room to where Cage was busy at the counter, his back to her. Wasn't that what she'd been doing? Ever since the morning she'd been burying her feelings, hiding them like some shameful secret, just because they weren't reciprocated. She wasn't just letting love be taken from her—she was handing it over, like a bloody sacrifice on the altar of her pride.

Her mind felt exquisitely clear, like sunlight on the smooth surface of polished crystal. You may never belong to me, Benjamin Cage; but the love does. The love is mine.

There should have been bells, or fireworks, or a volley of cannon-fire—something to mark this extraordinary moment when Melanie Brooks first took her life into her own hands. From cradle to betrothal, everything had been given to her long before she would think to ask for it. It was time—past time—that she learned to take something for herself.

Cage was hunched over the counter lighting the camp stove when she rose quietly from the bed. He swept one hand back through his hair as he straightened. It was beautiful hair, Melanie thought, her hands quietly busy as she watched him from across the room; one of the many gifts of his Seminole heritage. The Indian blood might have been diluted, but the surviving genes were strong. The dark hair and eyes, the classic high cheekbones and the strong, sensual mouth—all these were part of the legacy of his ancestry, as much as his spirit.

When her hands had finished their work she stood rock-still, wondering why she wasn't terrified. She'd been afraid of almost everything all her life—afraid of the dark, afraid of snakes, afraid of making a move without someone telling her what to do—and yet at this moment she was leaping fearlessly into the unknown on the strength of no one's judgement but her own. She could almost feel the whistling rush of wind beneath wings she'd never had.

'Asi,' she murmured, her voice as light as the early evening breeze.

He spun at the sound of that name on her lips, his eyes flashing darkly...and then his mouth dropped open and he took a quick step backwards into the counter.

She was totally naked, the clothing she had so quietly shed lying in a crumpled heap at her bare feet.

She watched his eyes travel the full length of her body and then up to her face again, and for the first time in her life she felt as beautiful as people had always told her she was. Her mouth curved automatically in a smile, and she didn't have to see her reflection to know she had never looked more like her ancestor's portrait than she did at that moment. She'd often wondered at the reason behind that woman's enigmatic smile—even speculated that it might have been a secret, illicit love-affair—but she realised now that it had been more than that. Perhaps consummating a great love wasn't nearly as important as recognising it. Just recognising it was an enormous achievement. And it made you smile.

The smile deepened as she watched Benjamin's face darken and his throat move convulsively. She felt wonderfully strong, almost invincible; a feeling so

alien that she marvelled that it was hers. Maybe it
isn't, she mused. Maybe I've been possessed by that
part of the first Melanie Brooks's spirit that still lingers
here, in the Everglades—or maybe a part of that spirit
was alive in me all the time, and I just never knew it.

'What the hell do you think you're doing?' he
rasped.

She met his gaze fully, but felt her lower lip threaten
to quiver. She'd never seduced a man before, and she
didn't quite know what to do next. 'I'm ... finishing
what we started this morning.'

His eyes narrowed sharply and suddenly without
losing their focus on hers, and Melanie imagined that
she saw deep within them a reflection of that fear the
old woman had talked about. Fear of love, of trusting,
of commitment.

'You don't have to love me,' she tried to reassure
him, hoping he wouldn't notice how the words caught
in her throat. 'I don't expect that. This isn't forever.
It's just for now.'

In the deep silence that followed, while Cage stared
harshly, almost hatefully into her eyes, she started to
wonder what she would do if he simply turned his
back on her ...

She needn't have worried. In the next instant a
strangled sound rose from his throat, and he moved
so quickly that she barely saw him cover the distance
between them. One second he was across the room;
the next he was kneeling at her feet, his arms around
her bare hips, his mouth pressed into her stomach as
if to seal his voice inside.

She looked down at the tangle of his hair, violently
black against the white of her skin, and plunged her
fingers into it, pulling him against her. At the silken

touch of his tongue she sagged forward, and just when she thought her knees would collapse he rose to his feet, gathered her in his arms and laid her on the bed.

Standing over her, his eyes black and seething, he growled, 'I'll give you one last chance to think about what you're doing. Whatever your reasons, when you get back where you belong they aren't going to seem good enough.' He remained motionless next to the bed, only the crackle of his eyes and the strained lines around his mouth revealing emotion barely kept in check.

Melanie gazed up at him, blue eyes perfectly still, perfectly sad. How strange that he could wonder at her reasons, when she felt they must be shining from her eyes, as easily read as a neon sign flashing against a dark sky. Couldn't he see that for her, at least, making love was only the confirmation of loving? She wanted desperately to give her heart a voice, to be as unafraid to state her feelings aloud as she was to express them with her body... but the old woman had told the truth. Cage *was* afraid of love—he'd said as much this morning when he'd told her she'd wanted more than he could give. And, if he knew now that what she really wanted was forever, he might not let her have the single moment she was willing to settle for.

It was better, she thought, to say nothing at all. She lifted her arms and parted her lips and invited him home.

In the next few moments she forgot that he didn't love her, because such a thing seemed impossible. How could his touch and his eyes and his voice be so gentle, so cherishing, without love behind them? How could his breath come as rapidly as hers; his heart pound as frantically as his lips and tongue and hands explored her body and left a trail of fire?

Blue eyes dark and wide, she watched breathlessly as he straightened and stripped out of his clothes, then she held up one hand. 'Wait,' she said, her voice husky. 'I want to look at you.'

Surprise flickered across his dark face, but he stood obediently, proudly naked as she studied his body. Astonished innocence and fiery passion mingled in her face in an extraordinary combination. She reached out tentatively to let her fingers flutter over the hard muscles of his thigh, then up to tremble across the ridges of his stomach. Wonderfully intricate musculature convulsed under her hand as she stroked downwards, and she looked up at his face with a tiny, awestruck smile.

It was his face, more than the velvet beat now encased in her hand, that startled her with a molten rush that seemed to tug painfully from within.

'Melanie,' he murmured, coming down on her slowly, hesitantly, the bed reflecting the violent trembling of his restraint. The black fire of his eyes met the blue fire of hers as he braced himself over her, and in spite of the savage fierceness in his expression she knew that this last searching look was a question, a final offer for her to say no before it was too late. She loved him even more for that last supreme gift of choice, and thanked him by lifting her hips to meet his.

'Asi,' she breathed into his ear, because no other name could have belonged to him in this moment, when, whether he wanted it or not, the circle finally closed.

*   *   *

When Melanie awoke, the cabin was already shimmering in the diffused golden light of early morning. Outside, she could hear the raspy night music of insects just giving way to the sunrise chatter of birds.

She rolled on her side in the empty bed, expecting to see Cage somewhere in the cabin, then sat up with a start to find herself totally alone. 'Benjamin?' she whispered, a formless fear tightening in her stomach.

A hundred times during the night she'd wondered what the morning would bring; how Benjamin would relate to her in the cold light of day, after all that hot, passionate melding in the dark. Would he be tender? Cool? Or, heaven forbid, would he make light of it and suggest that they be friends? She hadn't known what to expect, but what she had expected least was to wake up and find him gone altogether.

Straining to sort out all the sounds of the Everglades coming to life, she finally heard the distant splash of the makeshift shower under the porch. Strangely relieved, she propped the pillow against the wall and sat up, tugging the sheet up over her breasts.

At the sound of the screen door her breath seemed to freeze in her throat and her heart turned over in her chest. She turned her head to look at him, and it felt as if all her emotions had suddenly raced to gather in her eyes, making them a liquid blue stream that could cross the room and touch him. 'Good morning,' she whispered.

He stood in the filtered sun of the doorway, jeans-clad legs spread, his bronzed chest and arms sparkling with jewels of water. A white towel dangled forgotten from his hand as he remained motionless, gazing across the room at her, as if he didn't know what to do next. 'Good morning,' he finally replied.

Melanie stared at him for an endless moment, praying he would cross the room and gather her up in his arms and end this terrible awkwardness between them, but he didn't move; he just continued to stand there, looking at her.

'How do you feel?' he asked.

Her mouth twitched in a poor excuse for a smile. 'Fine. I'm just fine.' Oh, hell. This was awful. They were making that dreadful kind of small talk people made when they met acquaintances on the street. Was this the way it was going to be? Were they just going to pretend that last night had never happened?

'No regrets?'

Her eyes flickered at that. 'None.'

The muscle in his jaw tightened briefly, then he dropped his eyes and frowned at the towel in his hand as if he couldn't remember how it had got there.

'When are you going home?' he asked without looking up.

She tensed under the sheet, wounded by his obvious eagerness to be rid of her. 'The plane comes for me tomorrow morning.' Unless you ask me to stay, she added to herself. That's all you'd have to do. Just ask. Please ask...

He nodded briskly, sending a cascade of water droplets flying from the thick, wet tousle of black hair that made him look almost boyish. 'Do you still intend to make a report to the congressman?'

Melanie frowned in momentary confusion. She'd almost forgotten what she'd come here to do, and that he should bring it up so quickly on the heels of last night seemed to negate everything that had happened between them—but that was what he wanted, she realised. 'Yes,' she managed to force out. 'I suppose . . .'

'Fine. Then there's still a lot you have to see. We should get started.'

She blinked at him, shaken by the chill in his voice and his manner. She held her breath, as if that would help hold all her emotions inside, too. You asked for it, she reminded herself. You knew that he couldn't give you love, and it didn't make any difference. All you wanted was a chance to give him yours. So what did you expect? Were you really harbouring some tiny, pathetic spark of hope that making love would make love happen?

She took a deep breath and licked her lips. 'I'd like a shower,' she said in a strange, constricted voice, looking down at where her feet made two tiny mountains under the sheet. It was so quiet in the cabin that she could hear the sound of her own breathing, but not her heart. Her heart, she decided, had probably stopped beating.

She didn't know how much time had passed when she heard him speak again. It seemed like an eternity, but when she looked at him he was still standing in exactly the same place, watching her with an animal-like alertness.

'I'll start breakfast,' he said coldly. 'It should be ready by the time you finish your shower.'

It seemed that she had to wait a very long time before he turned and walked over to the counter, giving her the privacy of his back, and then she fumbled for the clothes she'd shed the night before, crumpled into a colourless heap on the floor.

CHAPTER TEN

THIS time Melanie found no childlike pleasure in the primitive open-air shower; no smiling wonder at the bold dragonflies attracted to the spray of water. With impatient swipes of her hand she brushed them away and focused her attention on the mechanics of the business at hand.

She scrubbed herself brutally with the rough cloth, as if heartbreak were just another kind of soil that could be scoured away. The final rinse stung her pinkened, chafed skin, but she almost welcomed the distraction of pain. Even though she wanted to soap her hair, at the last minute her fingers refused to release the band that held the braid. It was her last fragile connection, if not to Cage, at least to the old woman, and, through her, to the first Melanie Brooks. In the end, she simply sprayed it thoroughly and squeezed it dry.

The floral robe was an unwelcome reminder of how light-hearted she had been the last time she'd worn it—she'd felt like a child on an innocent summer adventure then, less than two days ago—but it was all she had to slip on after her shower.

The aroma of sweet fried corncakes met her halfway up the stairs, and she wondered absently how Cage had made the batter without fresh eggs. He was waiting on the porch, holding two plates stacked with crisply browned discs. His gaze swept over her with studied indifference, flickering slightly when he saw her braid.

'I'm not very hungry,' she said, pleased that her voice sounded almost normal. It occurred to her that she was learning a lot about having the courage to love against the odds. The real test wasn't in loving enough to give yourself without hope of return; the real test was surviving the contempt of others on the morning after. And, if her ancestor had been able to survive the contempt of a husband so furious he had tried to erase her from memory, she could survive this.

'You have to eat something substantial now. We'll be out in the field all day.' He took a seat, balanced one plate on his lap and held the other out towards her.

She sighed and took it reluctantly, sitting in the chair next to him. He was already dressed, canvas trousers tucked into the high rubber boots, one of the heavy shirts open over a black T-shirt. It was demeaning, somehow, to sit there in robe and bare feet when he was fully clothed, but she supposed any pretence at modesty was pretty silly at this point.

'They're here again.'

'Who's here?'

He pointed to the family of green jays they'd watched yesterday morning. 'Our jays.'

She felt a sudden thrust of pain around her heart, just because he'd called them 'our jays'. He'd only meant it as a figure of speech, but it could have been so much more, and it was the could-have-been that hurt. Our jays. Two small words that conjured up the never-to-be image of a lifetime of mornings with Cage at her side.

'They're noisy things, aren't they?' The overly bright sound of her voice made her wince. Oh, please, please, she thought fervently; let me be strong, just for this one last day. If I have to be so hopelessly in love with a man who can't love me, at least let me keep my heartbreak to myself. A broken heart is such a private thing.

In what seemed to Melanie like a sick parody of companionship, they sat in silence for a time, both pretending interest in the raucous antics of the birds. Cage carved steadily at his stack of corncakes; Melanie merely picked at hers.

'You're not eating.'

She forced a small bite into her mouth, chewed, and swallowed. 'I told you I wasn't very hungry.'

He sighed audibly, and when he spoke again his voice was strained. 'We can't go through the whole day like this, Melanie. We have to talk about last night.'

She exhaled sharply in a wry, silent laugh. 'What is there to say about last night?'

'That it was wrong. That I shouldn't have let it happen.'

Her lower lip started to quiver, but she caught it before it became visible. 'You didn't let anything happen. I made it happen. It was my choice, not yours.'

'I didn't expect you to choose sex without love,' he said caustically. 'I didn't expect you to settle for that.'

Melanie turned her head slowly to look at him. Contempt was a funny thing, she was beginning to realise. It only hurt if you accepted it; if you thought you deserved it; and she didn't. She'd given herself out of love, and there was no shame in that.

'I don't regret it,' she said with quiet defiance. 'I don't regret a minute of it.'

'I don't regret it either,' he snapped, glaring at her, the muscle in his jaw standing out in sharp relief. 'I just wish...' he hesitated for a moment while something like a pained expression flickered across his face '...I just wish there could have been more between us.'

Oh, lord. She didn't know which was worse, his contempt, or his pity. Now he was apologising for not loving her. 'So do I,' she replied dully, staring off into the greenery, seeing nothing.

Oddly enough, as strained as the conversation had been, things seemed easier between them afterwards, as if having it all out in the open had relieved them both of the responsibility of their actions.

Cage seemed distant as he told her what he intended to show her on her last day, but then he had been distant from the beginning—until yesterday. As a matter of fact, she thought sadly, looking at the two of them now, you might think that yesterday had never happened at all; that she and Cage were simply two people who didn't know each other very well, a little uncomfortable with each other.

Men were basically a mystery, she decided as she was dressing in the ugly trousers and shirt. They were obviously capable of separating sex from love for their own purposes, and yet they thought less of a woman who was willing to accept them on those terms. What kind of sense did that make?

She stole a glance at Cage over at the counter, clearing up the breakfast dishes, and wondered if she would ever be able to look at him without feeling that painful tightening in her chest. This is pay day, she thought miserably; fate finally balancing the scales, exacting a payment for the fairy-tale life you've had so far.

They started her final tour in the canoe, although Cage had told her they'd ultimately end up in the airboat. Melanie felt even more useless than usual, sitting in front while Cage paddled from the stern. That was another thing she'd never done. Good lord. She was twenty-four years old, and she'd never even paddled a canoe. She was making a mental list of all the things she'd never done for herself, and its length was alarming.

They headed first in the same general direction they'd taken to get to the old woman's cabin yesterday, but veered west at the first discernible fork in the narrow waterway. After a short distance they entered a shadowy mangrove forest whose entire floor was under water, and, to Melanie, every direction looked the same.

'We're taking the long way around to the airboat,' Cage told her as he guided the canoe around aerial roots that lifted the reddish-brown trunks above the waterline. 'If we're lucky we might surprise some woodstorks at a fishing spot I found earlier this year.'

Melanie was gazing up through the spreading branches of glossy, oblong leaves, peppered with pale yellow flowers. 'Why lucky?' she asked absently. 'Is there something special about woodstorks?' She'd seen too many wading birds already to be impressed with any one in particular.

'You never know. On the rare occasions I see them I have to remind myself that I may never see them again. There used to be thousands here, not so many years ago. There are only a few hundred left now.'

'Oh.' A little chagrined, she turned sideways on her bench to look back at him. 'What happened to them? Disease? Poachers . . . ?'

'Preservation,' he replied drily. 'Misguided preservation. One of the many unexpected, unintentional side-effects of the infamous water-management system. Turns out it floods the woodstorks' fishing holes during drydown, letting the fish go too deep for the birds to reach. And like that of most species, their reproduction grinds to a halt when the food supply is gone. They haven't had a proper breeding season in almost a decade. Another year or two of this and the woodstork can take its place next to the dinosaur and the passenger pigeon.'

'I didn't know,' she murmured, troubled by the irony of a conservation effort gone awry, actually destroying the species it had hoped to save.

'It's all in the study you were going to read. You remember the study—the one that's going to make your fiancé fight the budget cut, instead of supporting it?'

She bit her lip in consternation and faced front again, remembering her promise to read the study last night. 'You never gave it to me,' she grumbled.

'I know. I got distracted.'

Her face coloured and she changed the subject quickly. 'I can't see how you know which way to go in here.' She pretended to look around at the watery forest. 'One tree looks just like another.' She heard the paddle lift from the water, spill its drops on the surface, then splash slightly as it entered again.

'See that arch up ahead?' he asked her.

She squinted through the shaded world, finally focusing on a distant arch formed by the branches of two trees coming together. It looked like a doorway to a brighter place.

'It opens on to the sawgrass plain just north of where I keep the airboat. The woodstorks' fishing hole is just beyond a stretch of deeper water, but it's snake and alligator country, so keep your hands in the boat.'

Melanie jerked her hands from the canoe's sides to her lap instantly, her eyes wide and busily scanning the water as they approached the archway.

The moment they passed through, the sunlight speared painfully at her eyes, and she pulled her hat on and tied the scarf under her chin. Even under the shade of the brim, she blinked repeatedly while her eyes adjusted to the brightness of open water after the dim light in the forest.

They had emerged on to a highway of water that separated the mangroves from the waving plain of sawgrass on the other side. The canoe veered left with the current and floated leisurely southwards. Cage used his paddle primarily as a rudder, to keep the small aluminium craft in the centre of the slow but steadily moving stream.

They'd drifted perhaps a mile when a hammock of land with a single mangrove tree jutted out from the sawgrass on their right, constricting the water's flow.

With a startled lurch of her stomach, Melanie saw the now unmistakable lumpy forms of alligators sunning themselves on the tiny patch of dry ground the mangrove had gathered around its roots like a skirt. She went rigid on the seat, hoping they could slip by without disturbing them.

On the way around the hammock, the current slowed to a sluggish trickle, forming a stagnant pool of greenish slime that brought the canoe to a halt directly opposite the alligators' beach.

'Snake,' Cage hissed from behind her, pointing over her shoulder at a wedge-shaped head slicing through the scum on the water, an arm's length from the front of the canoe. 'Cottonmouth, no less. This place is full of them.'

Melanie shuddered as she watched the sinewy movements of the loathsome thing, seeing malevolence rather than grace.

'Can we get through here?' she whispered urgently over her shoulder, worried about a bank of reeds that seemed to block their progress forward.

'Sure we can, but not just yet.' Cage dipped the paddle and steered across the pond, towards the forest on the left. 'We'll beach the canoe and stretch our legs a bit first. The woodstorks fish in a shallow spot just beyond those reeds, and, if they don't show, the alligators should keep us entertained for a while.'

'And the snakes,' she grumbled.

'Those, too.' The canoe made a squishing sound as it bumped into the mush of submerged land at the edge of the forest. 'Jump out and tie us to that big root—the way I showed you, remember?'

Melanie hesitated. 'Are you sure it's solid? When we came through it back there the whole forest was under water...'

'It's dry here,' he said with a trace of impatience, struggling to hold the canoe steady. 'Look at the trees, the plants... oak doesn't thrive in standing water; neither does holly.'

Lips pinched tight, fighting the urge to snap at him that she wasn't any damn botanist so how was she supposed to know which plants were which and

whether or not they grew in water, she stood gingerly
in the wobbly canoe. With the rope in her hand and
her heart in her throat, she leapt to what she hoped
was dry land and nearly kissed the ground when it
didn't swallow her up. Moving rapidly so he wouldn't
see how badly her hands were shaking, she tied the
rope to a root the size of a man's waist. It irritated
her a little that the unsteady craft barely wobbled as
Cage stepped lithely from the back to the front, then
to the shore. He carried a bulging pack under one
arm. 'Lunch, such as it is,' he explained, walking
inland a few feet and brushing a tangle of damp leaves
from the base of a giant tree with his foot. 'Come on.
Sit down. We'll eat, drink, and watch alligators.'

She moved carefully towards him, testing the
ground with each foot before putting her weight on
it, finally sagging to lean against the trunk next to
him. 'I don't feel very safe here,' she confessed, her
eyes glued to the reptiles sunning on the other side of
the narrow strip of green water. About twenty
swimming strokes, she thought. That was all it would
take for her to cross that deadly pond. A 'gator could
probably do it in a single whip of its powerful tail.
She jumped when one of them bellowed and snapped
at a companion before settling back into a sunning
stupor.

'The alligators aren't a threat as long as we keep
our distance,' he said mildly, digging into the pack.
'Besides, the shore on this side is a little too sheer for
them to climb comfortably.'

She accepted a Thermos lid brimming with cool
juice and drank gratefully. 'What about the snakes?
The cottonmouth we saw? *He* probably wouldn't have
any trouble crawling up that bank, would he?'

He handed her a corncake with a guarded expression. 'Relax, Melanie. I checked for snakes before we sat down.' She blanched, remembering him kicking away the leaves. Somehow the idea that a snake might have been there was more than enough to terrify her. 'And if one happens to come along we just sit perfectly still until it passes...' He hesitated, and she knew he was thinking of yesterday. 'They don't *hunt* humans, you know. Not even the cottonmouth.'

She sat motionless, filled with a sudden, overwhelming hatred of snakes, alligators, heat, biting flies, juice in plastic Thermos lids...of the Everglades in general. She understood for the first time the pioneers' obsession to chop down the primeval forests and burn off the grasslands; to destroy the habitat of the things you feared, so you wouldn't have to be afraid any more.

'You're shaking.' Cage's voice was as gentle as his touch on her arm, but she still jumped.

'I want to get out of here,' she whispered, her lips barely moving. Her eyes were fixed and intensely blue, her pupils tiny, panicked pinpricks. 'I want to get back in the canoe and leave this place—now.'

'There's nothing to be afraid of...'

'Please. You don't understand. This is your world, not mine.'

'It isn't mine, either,' he said quietly, his eyes drifting to the green water where deadly snakes swam, to the hideous beasts lazing on the other side, up to where a lone hawk painted predatory circles across the blue canvas of the sky. 'It's theirs. At least, it was.' He looked back at her calmly. 'But we'll leave if you like. You can see as much from the canoe, I suppose. All the other tourists do.'

Even softly spoken, she heard the recrimination in his tone. He wanted her to see more than the tourists saw; to experience and at least respect, if not appreciate, the savage beauty of this place as he did; but she couldn't. Fear kept clouding all her senses. The small reserve of her new-found courage had already been drained by the choices she'd made in the last twenty-four hours. She just didn't have any left.

He started to get up, then stopped and looked at her. 'You hate everything about the Everglades, don't you?'

'I'm afraid of it.'

'And fear translates into hate. It always does. It's why our ancestors hated each other, with a few notable exceptions.' He tipped his head and sighed quietly. 'It's ironic, isn't it? If this place is going to survive it's going to need a champion, and the only one available happens to be a woman who hates it, a woman so timid that she's afraid to chart the course of her own life.'

Melanie straightened and felt the bark of the tree trunk scrape her back. 'Yesterday I would have deserved that,' she said carefully. 'But not today.'

The level of the contempt in his face hit her like a physical blow. 'You lost your virginity last night, not your timidity,' he said tonelessly, rising slowly to his feet, glancing over at where the canoe was tied.

His face didn't even change expression to give her a warning of what was to come. One second he was standing there; the next he was gone, leaping down to the bank with a shouted curse, jumping into the water's edge, clinging to a stationary root with one hand while his other arm stretched through the slimy water, reaching desperately for the white rope that drifted maddeningly just beyond his fingertips.

Her expression sick with disbelief, Melanie scrambled to her feet and stared at the canoe drifting aimlessly away from their shore, across the scummy pond towards the alligators' bank, the rope trailing behind on the surface like a leisurely white snake. She knew in an instant that it was too late, that the rope was already beyond Cage's reach; but for an agonising moment more he refused to admit defeat, his arm still stretching through the water, the cords in his neck taut and bulging with the effort.

Finally he pulled himself back on to the bank and stood with his shoulders slumped and his chin on his chest, breathing hard, water dripping from his soaked shirt and trousers to puddle at his feet. 'Damn,' he muttered under his breath.

For a moment Melanie just stood there, unable to speak, her lips folded in on themselves, her hands pressed flat against her chest. It was all her fault. They were stranded in this terrifying place, and it was all because she was so stupid, so helpless, so damned incompetent that she couldn't even tie a simple knot.

She steeled herself as he started to raise his head to look at her, prepared for the onslaught of his justifiable rage, but when their eyes met he just shook his head tiredly. Melanie burst immediately into tears.

'Oh, for heaven's sake,' he grumbled, moving quickly to take her into his arms, and she didn't know which was making her cry all the harder—that his arms were around her again, albeit reluctantly, or that he wasn't yelling at her as she deserved. She buried her face in her hands and sobbed against his chest while the wet from his clothes soaked into hers.

'It's . . . all . . . my fault. Dammit, I can't . . . do anything right . . .'

His hands moved awkwardly on her back, trying to soothe her. 'It wasn't your fault,' he said gruffly. 'It was mine. I should have checked the rope.'

It wasn't true, of course, and they both knew it. The words were simply the gift of a kind heart, and because kindness was one thing she hadn't seen in Cage, and was the last thing she expected in the circumstances, she sobbed harder still.

He stood like a rock, silent and comforting, just holding and stroking her for a very long time. The worst part of the whole incident was that once again Melanie found herself leaning on him, depending on him, and once again she was devastated by the realisation that this was where she wanted to be forever, and where she would probably never be again.

Sheer exhaustion finally quieted her sobs to an occasional, almost comical hiccup. She pushed away from his chest and wiped her eyes on her shirt-tail. 'What are we going to do now?' she sniffed miserably.

He lifted her chin with one finger and almost smiled at her. 'We'll improvise. If we can't manage to snag that rope we'll just find a way to the airboat through the woods, and come back for the canoe later.'

She looked out at where the canoe rested in the middle of the water, its rope still floating just a few inches too far from their shoreline. 'It sounds too simple.'

'Everything's simple, once you know your choices. Are you all right now?'

She sniffed and nodded, avoiding his eyes. 'Can we really get to the airboat through the woods?'

'Eventually. We'd have to do some pretty innovative trail-blazing, I'm afraid. It's only about two or three miles downstream, but there's a lot of marshland between here and there we'd have to find a way around. It could take most of the day.' He pursed his lips thoughtfully, looking out towards the canoe. 'Let's see what we've got to help us drag that damn thing back to shore.'

The pack yielded several packets of trail mix, sweets, a tightly coiled rope, a flashlight, and a snake-bite kit that made Melanie's eyes go wide. The very fact that he carried such a thing with him made the possibility of snake bite all too real.

'Ah. This is what we need,' he said, pulling a loop of broad elastic from the kit.

'What is it?'

'With a twist of a stick, it can be a tourniquet,' he replied absently, attaching the length of rope to the elastic circle. 'But maybe, with a little luck, I can use it to snag the cleat on the bow of the canoe.'

Melanie felt the first stirrings of hope and watched anxiously as he stood on the very edge of the bank, tossing the rope again and again towards the canoe. The slapping noise it made on the water disturbed the alligators on the opposite shore, and a few growled irritably and slid into the green depths. His best effort, with the line fully extended, fell a foot short.

'Dammit, it's so close...' he muttered, gazing around as if he expected to find a longer rope hanging from a nearby tree. His eyes finally came to rest on a broad, gnarled branch that jutted a few feet out over the water. 'There's the extra distance we need. I'll try from up there.'

Melanie felt the hollow leap of fear in her stomach. 'Don't climb out there...' she started to say, but he was already scrambling over the aerial roots of the old tree, straddling the branch, shinnying cautiously along its length until his feet dangled over the water. Like a cowboy astride a horse, he straightened, swung the makeshift lasso in larger and larger arcs at his side, then flung it towards the canoe.

Mouth open, heart in her throat, Melanie watched the elastic loop sail across the water, hesitate in mid-air as if it were weightless, then drop in a perfect circle over the cleat. 'You did it!' she cried, jumping up and down, clapping her hands in excitement, startling every alligator left on the shore into a frantic thrashing that sent sand flying in clouds around them.

The sound of the crash was sudden and heart-stopping, and, when Melanie jerked her head to look at where Cage had been, for a moment all her frantic thoughts could piece together was that somehow he had just disappeared into thin air. For an eternal second she remained frozen, her breath caught in her throat, then she saw the ragged wound where the branch had broken and raced over to find Cage's limp form half in, half out of the water, his head flung back on a rock-hard knot of the limb that had given way beneath him.

'Cage!' she screamed, crouching on the bank, reaching to grab under his arms before he could slide totally into the water, pulling with a strength she didn't know she had.

Blood rushed in her ears and her heart pounded against her rib-cage as she grunted and heaved and wept and cursed and, through some miracle, finally managed to drag him up on to the bank. Oblivious

to the pain of pulled muscles in arms and shoulders
and back, she hovered over him, whispering his name
hysterically over and over again.

He looked almost peaceful, lying there with his eyes
closed, his expression as serene as hers was twisted
with terror; but there was a foreboding pallor beneath
the bronzed skin of his face, and the flattened grass
under his head began to turn red.

CHAPTER ELEVEN

NOTHING in Melanie's sheltered life had prepared her for what she faced now. In that first split-second when she saw the red stain spreading on the grass beneath Cage's head she felt her mind shatter like an exploding bomb, with a million pieces flying off in all directions, each piece representing a question there was no one there to answer. In their simplest form, they all boiled down to the biggest question of all, the one she felt like wailing to the emptiness around her. What am I going to *do*?

But that was in the first second. Before her racing heart had taken another beat she felt an extraordinary, totally unexpected wave of calm rise from somewhere deep inside. Within an instant her tears stopped, her pulse quieted, and her thoughts almost dazzled her with their clarity. She had to take care of Cage.

There was a visible pulse beating just beneath the line of his jaw. Encouraged by that, she began to explore the wet tangle of his hair, lifting his head ever so gently until her hand found the gash oozing blood. In seconds she had stripped down to her T-shirt and folded her overshirt into a thick, hard pillow of fabric she placed directly under the gash, hoping the weight of his head would create a crude pressure bandage. There was too much blood, she thought, terrified that the shirt wouldn't stop it, that he'd bleed to death while she watched . . .

Relax, relax, she commanded herself sternly. You aren't going to do him any good if you get hysterical now. Besides, didn't you read somewhere that even superficial head wounds bleed profusely? Just wait a minute; see if the bleeding slows down; and do what else you can in the meantime.

But what else was she supposed to do? Should she try to wake him up? What if he had a concussion? Didn't something terrible happen if you didn't wake concussion victims and keep them awake?

She bit down hard on her lower lip, racking her brain for the tiniest piece of buried information, feeling the thread of panic start to unravel again. She fought it with deep, hard breaths, clinging desperately to a thin edge of control.

Her eyes never left his face as she counted aloud to sixty with forced slowness, the terrified little girl inside hoping against all reason that he'd open his eyes and laugh at the way her voice was shaking; maybe pull her into his arms again and pat her back and tell her everything was going to be all right, not to worry, he'd take care of everything, just as someone had always taken care of everything for her.

By the time she got to sixty all those little-girl hopes for a last-minute reprieve had been dashed. Cage wasn't going to wake up and make everything all right. He was still lying there, deathly still, with only that tiny beat in his throat giving any promise of life at all.

She took a deep, shaky breath and eased his head up from the thick folds of her shirt, checked the wound, and thought the bleeding might have slowed. Next she ran her hands cautiously over his arms and legs, nearly sobbing with relief when she found no obvious broken bones.

'Cage.' Her hands braced on either side of him, she bent until her braid dangled on his chest. 'Benjamin Osceola Cage. Can you hear me?' She put her ear close to his mouth and held her breath, then tried again. 'Asi? Talk to me, Asi.'

The rasp of a grasshopper shattered the stillness, signal to all the creatures that had been frightened into silence when the branch broke. A red-winged blackbird trilled an answer from its wavering sawgrass perch; a small fish leaped from the water and came down with a splash of its tail; but Cage said nothing.

Still hovering over him, Melanie placed her hands on his cheeks, her lips folded in on one another. Even unconscious there was such pride in his face, such an aura of strength behind the sleeping features—but he was so pale beneath his tan now, so very pale.

Dammit, it just wasn't fair. This was all backwards and upside-down. The strong were always taking care of the weak—not the other way around. What kind of cruel, twisted fate would place the life of such a strong man in the hands of a stupid, helpless woman who couldn't even tie a simple knot?

She licked her lips, oddly dry in spite of the humidity, and looked down at the man who had broken her heart because he hadn't been able to love her. How pathetically unimportant that heartbreak seemed now. What did it matter that he couldn't return the love she felt? That didn't stop it from existing, and it didn't diminish her need to give it, either.

'I love you, Asi,' she murmured out loud, understanding for the first time what the words really meant. She'd always believed that love, like everything else in life, had to be an exercise in the art of give and take; but it wasn't like that at all. Giving was the important part—giving without reservation, without conviction, without promises and even without hope—that was love. The first Melanie Brooks had known that. It wasn't necessary for Cage to love her back to keep her love alive; it was only necessary that he continue to exist. For that, she was willing to give anything.

'I have to leave, Asi,' she said quietly. 'But I won't be gone long. Just stay here and rest, and before you know it I'll be back...'

She had to push herself to her feet with her hands, her legs were shaking so badly, and even once she'd managed to rise they nearly collapsed under her weight.

The trick is not to think about it, she told herself as she pulled off the heavy rubber boots and stripped out of her canvas trousers. Because if you let yourself think about it you're going to fall apart, and it's not like there's a line of stand-ins waiting to take your place.

She'd known the options the minute she'd seen the pallor of Cage's face. Even then, even before she'd finished hauling him up to the safety of the bank, she'd already made the only possible choice. What was it Cage had said? That everything was simple once you knew your choices? So she'd seen the choices, she'd picked one, and now she was going to act on it. Cage would be proud of her.

Overland through the forest, the airboat was hours away, if she was lucky enough to find it at all; but downstream, in the canoe, it was only a couple of miles. There really was no choice to be made, when you thought about it; just an unwavering certainty of what had to be done.

Clad in silly, lacy bikini panties and the awful mud-green T-shirt, Melanie paused on the edge of the bank and looked out at where the canoe floated, two ropes now trailing from its bow. It rested precisely halfway between her and the alligators. Ten strokes, she remembered as she stepped down into the water, the muddy bottom squishing between her toes; ten swimming strokes out, and ten back. That's all it will take. You're a good swimmer, a smooth swimmer; you can do that. Twenty strokes altogether. A child could do that.

The green scum lapped at her knees, then her thighs, then seeped into the brilliant white of her panties to stain them forever. She wasn't even looking at the water, because she knew if she did she'd see thousands of deadly cottonmouths and snapping turtles as big as she was and toothy alligators with hungry grins—whether they were there or not.

Instead she narrowed her vision to a single spot on the distant aluminum canoe where the sunlight reflected a metallic flash so bright that it nearly blinded her. Totally focused on that tiny square inch of brilliance, she took another step and felt the sucking pull of mud as the bottom reluctantly released her feet. The moment she felt herself suspended, supported by deep water, her arms started to move in slow, controlled strokes that barely rippled the surface.

She heard a faint splash to her right. Don't look! she told herself. Don't even think about it. Think about something else . . .

Reluctantly, her mind produced a vision of Cage on that first day, striding powerfully across the airfield towards her, eyes black and hot as boiling pitch, hair swept back from a lofty brow. Seven more strokes to go...

Something smooth and slithery brushed against her calf, then curled loosely around it, and she felt a jolt to her heart. Snake? Fish? Maybe just an underwater reed, it doesn't matter, as long as you don't think about it... they don't hunt humans, you know... but maybe you shouldn't kick your legs, just fight that instinct to kick as hard as you can and scream and only move your arms slowly, slowly, that's it, your legs will follow...

Whatever was down there slipped away as she moved forward through the water, trying not to think about the things that lurked in the depths of a greenish-black Everglades pond. Her lips pressed so tightly together that they hurt, she kept her eyes glued to that bright spot on the canoe, just five strokes away now, trying to call back an image of Cage's face— Asi's face—suspended over her in the golden light of late afternoon...

Her right hand sliced the air, tiny droplets catching the sun, then entered the water noiselessly directly on top of a thin, serpentine shape. She froze instantly, rounded eyes still fixed on the canoe just ahead, afraid to blink, afraid to look. The snake moved just a little under her hand and she swallowed a shrill scream of horror, then out of the corner of her eye she saw the white shape under her fingers. She had been so totally focused on the canoe, so intent on its being the ultimate goal, that she had forgotten the two white ropes that lay much closer. One of them now lay just under her hand.

Not a snake, not a snake, her mind babbled hysterically while her fingers closed around the rope and she started to turn back towards the shore. Halfway through her turn she caught a glimpse of movement from the opposite bank. Frozen by fear, she watched the alligator rise on its stubby legs and lift its pointed snout into the air. It was less than twenty feet away.

Oh, dear heaven, can it smell me? Can it hear me? Can it see me? her thoughts jittered frantically as she tried to tread water with as little motion as possible.

A brilliant, alien eye seemed to connect with hers across the water, reflecting, perhaps, on what she might taste like. The long toothy jaw opened, then clicked shut.

For the first time Melanie felt the chill of the water. It seeped through every pore into her bones. She wanted to finish her turn and race back to Cage, but her muscles wouldn't obey.

Move, dammit, move! her mind screamed inside her skull, but a force stronger than her fear kept her still, legs moving only enough to keep her afloat. The tension of waiting for the inevitable attack was so agonising that when the beast finally slid into the water she felt a perverse relief. At least she wouldn't have to wait any more. At least she wouldn't have to be afraid any more. In a minute it would all be over. Her eyes closed in a brief spasm of regret, then opened, as empty as the blue sky overhead.

With a gaze of dull resignation, she watched the alligator move towards her, wicked snout and bulging eyes barely visible above the surface. When it turned abruptly and headed downstream all she could do was blink in shock, barely able to register the reality of what had happened.

Her mouth sagged gradually in disbelief, her heart raced with renewed hope, and her eyes followed the alligator as his tail whipped him through the reed bank, into the clear water beyond. 'Thank you,' she whispered after him, as if the alligator had made her a conscious gift of her life. 'Thank you, thank you,' she kept repeating under her breath, over and over again, as she turned and swam woodenly back towards the bank. The canoe trailed obediently behind her, like a dog on a leash.

By the time she got back to Cage the gash in his head had stopped bleeding. As she knelt on the ground next to him, water still sheeting from her shivering body, she thought that his colour seemed better.

With the mechanical movements of an automaton she dressed as quickly as possible then started to lift Cage gently by the shoulders. She hadn't even stopped to consider the logistics of moving the dead weight of a strong, well-built man from the bank down to the waiting canoe, and in truth it never occurred to her that the feat might be beyond her. Whatever was left of her fading strength would be enough, simply because it had to be.

He stirred and groaned when she started to move him, and his eyes fluttered, then opened. 'Melanie? What the hell . . .?' He braced himself shakily on one forearm and reached for the back of his head. 'Hell, what happened?'

She caught his hand gently before he could disturb the wound, her own shaking so badly that it seemed a miracle she could control it at all. 'Don't touch it,' she warned him. 'You're hurt.'

'Tell me about it,' he said drily, his expression pained. 'I feel as if I just went ten rounds with a bull 'gator.'

She fought back the hysterical laughter bubbling in her throat, the tears rising in a tidal wave behind her eyes. 'The branch broke beneath you,' she told him in a choked voice, 'and you cracked your head. We have to get you to a hospital, Benjamin . . .'

'Hospital?' He scowled at her, but his eyes seemed a little unfocused. 'I don't need a hospital. What are you talking about . . . ?' He wobbled a bit on his arm and she reached out to steady him.

'Easy . . . you've lost a lot of blood. Do you think you can stand? We have to get you into the canoe.'

'Hell, yes, I can stand,' he grumbled, but the short distance to the canoe turned out to be an exercise in endurance for both of them. Melanie saw the blood drain from his face as she helped him to his feet; heard his teeth grinding with effort as he tried to take his own weight.

'Dammit, Cage, lean on me,' she ordered him, wrapping both arms around his waist, bracing herself to take his weight.

'I thought you'd never ask.' What started as a grin ended in a grimace as he draped his arm heavily over her shoulders.

Getting him down from the bank and into the canoe was the worst part. Melanie grunted at the sharp, sickening pull of muscles stretched too far in her back and shoulders, but at last he was lying in the bottom of the canoe, facing Melanie on the stern seat. Paddle in one hand, her other on the rope that tied them to the root on the bank, she eyed his face worriedly. He seemed to be having trouble keeping his eyes open,

and she was afraid he would drift back into unconsciousness at any moment.

'Cage. *Cage*. Don't fall asleep yet. Tell me how to
get to Everglades City.'

'Upstream ... about five miles ...' he grunted,
wincing. 'Or downstream ... a mile past the
airboat ... there's a ranger station ...'

'All right,' she said quickly, leaning forward to
brush his cheek with her fingers. 'We'll go downstream. Rest now. No more talking.'

She untied the rope quickly and pushed away from
the bank with one hand. The canoe was halfway into
the middle of the pond before she'd worked out how
to steer with the paddle.

'Melanie?'

'Hmm?' Her lips were thinned in concentration as
she made the turn back out into the main stream of
the waterway.

'How did the canoe get back to shore?'

The fickle craft was veering too far to the right,
towards the sawgrass, and she had to paddle hard to
correct it. 'I went and got it,' she murmured
distractedly.

He was very quiet. Too quiet, and Melanie felt a
flutter of panic in her stomach. 'Asi?' she whispered,
jerking her eyes quickly to his face, the paddle suspended over the water in mid-stroke.

His eyes seemed more focused now, quietly intent.
'I'm still here, Melanie,' he said softly, looking at her.

She closed her eyes briefly in relief and kept
paddling.

CHAPTER TWELVE

THE doctor nudged Melanie's shoulder gently, waking her. She sprang to immediate attention in the vinyl waiting-room chair, wincing at a hundred dull pains coming from muscles all over her body. The grey-haired man in the white coat smiled sympathetically.

'You look worse than Benjamin,' he said, not un-kindly. 'You sure I shouldn't be treating you instead?'

'How is he?' she asked breathlessly. 'Will he have to be flown to Miami?'

The park ranger, apparently a friend of Benjamin's and as concerned for his welfare as she was, had taken them by airboat to the closest clinic. It was staffed by the best, he assured her, equipped to handle anything short of major surgery, and, if Ben needed that, they'd airlift him to a Miami hospital.

'He'll be fine,' the doctor soothed her. 'Only took ten stitches to close that gash on his head, and the concussion is mild. We'll keep him here for a day or two, but the worst he'll be left with is a dandy headache for a week or so. Frankly, I'm more worried about you . . .'

'I'm fine,' Melanie insisted. 'Just tired.'

The doctor clucked his tongue sceptically and sighed. 'Well, get yourself home and to bed, then. You can see Benjamin tomorrow if you like. You have a ride?'

She nodded. 'The ranger that brought me here is waiting outside, down at the dock.' She hesitated,

frowning hard. 'Doctor...the thing is, I'm leaving
for Tallahassee early tomorrow morning...could you
tell Benjamin...?' The words, whatever they might
have been, wouldn't come. What could she say? She
took a deep breath and forced a tremulous smile.
'Could you tell him goodbye for me?'

The doctor cocked his head and raised one bushy
white brow. 'That's it? Just goodbye? From what he
was babbling in there when I was sewing up his head,
I thought...'

'Just goodbye,' she said hurriedly, pushing herself
up from the chair, commanding legs wobbly from fatigue to carry her just a little further to the exit. At
the last minute she turned and looked over her
shoulder. 'Thank you, Doctor. Thank you for taking
care of him.'

Just as she was about to push open the big glass
doors to the outside, she caught a glimpse of her reflection and started. Lord, no wonder the ranger had
looked at her askance when she'd first burst into the
station. No wonder the doctor had looked at her the
same way, convinced she had to be sick to look *that*
bad.

Her braid was a tangled mess; the T-shirt and canvas
trousers were filthy, and where her skin wasn't
smudged with mud it was coated with a dried film of
green from the pond. 'Behold the flower of Southern
womanhood,' she said wryly at her reflection, then
she pushed the door wide and walked out into the
muggy Florida evening.

The ranger's name was Tom, and a relieved smile
split his freckled, sunburned face when she told him
that Cage was going to be all right. 'Take more than
a little bump on the head to put old Ben out of com-

mission for long,' he said brusquely, but his voice gave
away just how worried he'd been. He took her back
to the park station by boat, then on to Cage's cabin
by Jeep. Melanie had slept for most of the trip. 'You
sure you want to stay here alone tonight?' he asked,
looking doubtfully out of his window at the dark
cabin. 'I could run you up to one of the motels...'

Melanie wanted to throw her arms around him and
give him a grateful kiss, but she decided that, the way
she looked and smelled, it might be more of a kindness
not to. 'I'm sure.' She managed a warm smile and
squeezed his hand. 'You could do me another favour,
though, if you're going to see Benjamin.'

'Sure I will. Thought I'd stop by the clinic tomorrow
and see how he's doing.'

'Would you tell him I borrowed his Jeep to get to
the airstrip? I have an early flight out tomorrow.'

'No problem. I'll pick him up when Doc says he
can go home, and we'll collect the Jeep then. Park it
on the north side of that big tin pole building. That's
where Ben always leaves it when he flies out.'

She nodded, peered once more at the darkness
outside, then took a breath and climbed out of the
Jeep. She closed the door, then bent to say a last
goodbye through the side-window. 'Thanks again,
Tom. For everything.'

'Here, Melanie. You take this with you.' He handed
her a heavy metal flashlight. 'You'll need that to find
the oil lamps, let alone light them.' He gave her a two-
fingered salute just before pulling away. 'You take
care, now. Hope to see you again soon.'

She watched his headlights bounce and flutter
through the black forest until she couldn't see them
any more. After a time the cicadas and frogs restarted

the night symphony interrupted by the noise of the Jeep. Melanie stood there for a while, listening, soothed by the sounds of nature's syncopation. Eventually her lips curved slowly into a smile, because she was all alone in a totally dark wilderness, and she wasn't afraid.

Beau was waiting on the tarmac when the little charter plane taxied to a halt the next morning. He looked crisp and elegant in a light linen suit, his omnipresent grin a white slash through the perfect tan of his face. Melanie saw him first from the plane window and wondered how he could look exactly the same when things were so different. She felt as if she was looking at someone she'd known only in passing, a very long time ago.

And I was going to marry him, she thought numbly. I would have married him, borne his children, and spent the rest of my life believing that was the way things were supposed to be. She shivered a little, chilled by the thought, and looked down at the thin booklet resting on her lap—a booklet that had taught her as much about Beauregard Parker as it had about the impact of the water-management system on the Everglades.

At the hiss of compressed air that announced the plane door's opening, she sighed heavily and rose to her feet, handbag clutched in one hand, the booklet in the other. She wondered if Cage would mind that she'd taken it from the cabin; if he'd approve of what she intended to do with it.

Aside from a slight sunburn she'd concealed under a dusting of powder, she looked exactly like the woman who had boarded this very plane just a few days before. Her navy suit with the white piping was classically elegant; her freshly washed hair gleamed on her shoulders in honey-blonde waves; and her blue eyes were as wide and bright as ever. But that was just the package, just the superficial window-dressing. She wondered if Beau would be able to see through that, to know immediately that the woman inside was very, very different.

'Mellie! Darling!'

He stood at the bottom of the short flight of aluminum steps, grinning up at her as she made the descent. A ripple of flashes from behind the terminal gate captured the moment. Melanie glanced over and saw the tight cluster of media people waiting, and felt her stomach roll.

'Hello, Beau.' She winced at the force of his closed, dry lips on hers.

'Mellie, darlin', are you ever a sight for sore eyes,' he drawled into her ear, wrapping her in an embrace that set off another round of camera flashes in the distance. 'Don't pay any attention to them,' he whispered, directing a dynamite smile towards the very people he was telling her to ignore. 'We'll dodge a few questions, then get out of here.'

'They'll want to know what I learned on my trip, Beau.'

'And I'll tell them, darlin', at my Press conference tomorrow. Don't you bother your pretty little head about it. Just tell them you had a nice time, honey.'

Gritting her teeth against his blatant conde- scension, wondering if he'd always treated her this way and she just hadn't noticed or minded, Melanie allowed herself to be led towards the mob of waiting reporters. Strobe lights clicked on as the video ca-

meras whirred to life, and half a dozen voices called
out half a dozen questions all at once. Most of the
questions were frivolous—had she seen an alligator?
Had she ridden in an airboat?—and for a moment
she despaired that she would even have a chance to
deliver the little speech she'd prepared; then one voice
sang out louder than the rest.

'Did Benjamin Cage present any real evidence that
this budget cut would do irreparable harm to the
Everglades?'

She turned towards the voice and looked into the
serious dark eyes of the man who owned it. Knowing
that her reply would change her life forever, she hesitated for a moment. 'As a matter of fact,' she finally
managed to reply, 'he presented some very convincing
evidence indeed.'

There was immediate, total silence, perhaps because the reporters were surprised to hear her speak
at all. It was obvious, Melanie thought ruefully, that
they weren't nearly as surprised as Beau. She felt his
fingers tighten convulsively on her shoulder, and his
entire body went rigid next to her. A glance at his face
showed that even his smile seemed frozen.

Thinking that swimming in snake- and alligator-
infested waters was a lot less dangerous than this, she
cleared her throat nervously. 'Some of you may not
realise that southern Florida's fresh water supply is
entirely dependent on the Everglades,' she began
softly. 'I know I didn't. I didn't know that the
Everglades made its own rain; that it acts like a giant
filter, cleaning the water that fills our wells. And I
didn't know that we were destroying that filter by
draining too much land—did you?' She paused and
looked over the audience, into each set of eyes that

would meet hers. 'Billions of gallons a day are diverted to irrigate the huge corporate farms to the north, and the chemical run-off from those farms is killing the Everglades, acre by acre. We have to stop them.' She heard Beau's sharp intake of breath next to her, and went on quickly, her words coming so fast that they almost ran together. 'If we don't stop them we won't just be destroying the Everglades; we'll be destroying our own supply of fresh water. It's all in here.'

She held up the booklet, turning to give every camera a full shot. She heard the steady whirr of the video cameras, the distant rumble of a small jet coming in for a landing, but other than that there was utter silence. 'I'm certain that once Congressman Parker has read this study,' she added, 'he'll want every one of you to read it, too.'

The silence stretched for another interminable moment, then, as if responding to some unseen, unheard signal, the crowd came to immediate, noisy life. The air was pummelled with a dozen different questions, shouted all at once. Where could reporters get a copy of the study? Why hadn't it been released to the public? What did Beau intend to do with this new information?

Beau's smile wavered as he blinked uncertainly, holding a hand palm-out as if to deflect the clamour. 'That's all for now, folks. Miss Brooks needs to rest after her tiring trip. Excuse us, excuse us...' He smiled good-naturedly, guiding Melanie through the crowd, his hand uncharacteristically tight on her upper arm as he steered her expertly to a waiting limousine and slid into the plush interior beside her. 'Miss Brooks's hotel,' he told the driver, still waving at the Press through the side-window.

Once the big car was on the highway, he pushed savagely at the button that closed the privacy window behind the driver and turned sideways on the seat to face her. His face was incredibly red, and Melanie noticed the cords standing out on the side of his neck. 'Where the *hell* did you get a copy of that report?' he snapped at her.

Melanie stared at him, a little saddened by her first look at the man who had been hiding beneath that glorious smile and those courtly manners all along. 'Cage gave it to me . . . or, rather, I took it. I told him I was sure you hadn't seen it, but you have, haven't you, Beau? You've read it already.' It wasn't really a question.

'Yes, I've read it! And it's garbage!' He snatched the booklet from her hand and flung it across the seat.

She folded her hands in her lap, noticing that her fingers felt strangely cold. 'Then you know that there's a list in there of all the men who own those corporate farms—the ones killing the Everglades.' Her expression was as flat as her tone. 'They were all at our engagement party, Beau. Every one of them. They were the men who financed your campaign; the men who paid to get you elected. And, in exchange, you agreed to fight for this budget cut, didn't you? To make sure there wouldn't be money for any more research studies like this one; to make sure no one ever found out that the life was being drained from the Everglades to line the pockets of a few very rich men.'

Something shifted under the handsome, aristocratic features; something hard and unpleasant and ugly. 'Don't meddle in things you don't understand,' he said evenly, his gaze frighteningly cold. 'I don't know what happened to you down in that God-forsaken swamp, but whatever it was apparently made you forget your place. I'm not going to have any wife of mine speaking her mind in front of the media the way you did back there, and——'

'I liked speaking my mind, Beau,' she interrupted with a strange smile. 'I didn't think I would, but I did, and who knows? I just may do a whole lot more of it in the future.'

'Not as *my* wife, you won't . . .'

It was the smile that disconcerted him most. 'No, not as your wife,' she agreed.

A short time later the limousine pulled up in front of Melanie's hotel. Nothing further had been said between them, but somehow they both understood that there was nothing more to say. As passionless in death as it had been in life, their relationship simply fizzled.

Ever the gentleman, Beau walked around the outside of the car to open her door personally. While she waited Melanie took the copy of the study from where it had fallen between the seats and slipped it into her bag.

By sunset that evening, every television and newspaper reporter in the city of Tallahassee had a copy of their own, covered with a note that said simply, 'Courtesy of Melanie Annabelle Brooks.' She signed each note personally with a grand flourish; proud, at last, of her own name.

CHAPTER THIRTEEN

THAT night the local television stations and newspapers all did lengthy reports on the newly discovered study of the Everglades water-management system. Watching the coverage on her hotel-room television, Melanie saw the film of her speech at the airport again and again. Ironically, Congressman Beauregard Parker was credited for bringing this critical information to the public's attention, and reporters praised him lavishly for 'sending his own fiancée to ferret out information others had tried to suppress'.

Melanie shuddered to see how adroitly Beau donned the sudden, undeserved mantle of hero when he found himself in the rather awkward position of receiving accolades for the very act he had tried to prevent. Yes, he told one reporter, the corporate farms attacked in the study had indeed been large contributors to his campaign; and yes, he was certainly going to lose their support after making the study public; but he'd felt a moral imperative to sacrifice his own career, if necessary, to bring the voters the truth.

She rolled her eyes at that and turned off the set.

Part of her wanted to expose Beau for the deceptive, self-serving creature he really was; but for the moment she just didn't have the stomach for it. Perhaps some day she'd have the strength to speak out against Beau, and politicians like him; hell, maybe some day she'd really get involved in politics and run for public office herself; but not just yet. It was all

she could do now to get from moment to moment
without stumbling over her own pain.

Anticipating the luxury of a long soak, she slipped
into a tub filled with fragrant, bubbly water. The
moment she leaned back and closed her eyes she saw
Cage's bronzed face, eyes dark and blistering, sunlight glancing off the sharp line of those exotic cheekbones. She sat up quickly, sloshing water over the rim,
suddenly deciding that a shower would be better than
a bath anyway. With the last of the bubbles swirling
around the drain and hot water beating on her
shoulders, she imagined she saw the flicker of a
dragonfly's wings in the spray sheeting off her body.
'Oh, damn,' she murmured softly, covering her face
with her hands, closing her eyes—but then she saw
Cage's face again on the insides of her eyelids, the
dark eyes softer and deeper now, haunting her. As if
she could escape the image inside her head, she backed
into the wet tile wall, then slid down to sit on the hard
porcelain, hugging her knees, letting the water pummel
her body for a very long time.

Much, much later, with the world outside her
window shimmering with that first hesitant glow of
pre-dawn, she huddled on her bed and placed a call
to the clinic. Mr Cage was resting comfortably, a
sleepy night nurse told her. Any message?

Melanie hung up and fell back on to a pile of
pillows, seeing a wavering image of a broad back in
a black T-shirt walking away. She didn't know if her
eyes were open or closed.

She was ready to leave Tallahassee by sunset of the
next day. She'd woken deep into the afternoon, groggy
and exhausted, her eyes swollen from crying in her
sleep. After forcing down a room-service luncheon

plate, she packed with a kind of frenzied care, concentrating furiously on stupid little things, like the way she folded her clothes, to keep the aching emptiness at bay. She had no master plan, no foreseeable purpose for her life, only a driving need to leave this city and all the memories it held of the woman she used to be. An image of the family mansion in Creek County wavered in the fog of her thoughts like a secret haven seen through a spring mist, but it wasn't where she wanted to be—it was just the only place she had to go.

At last she was standing over her suitcase on the bed, ready to close and snap the lid. In it were all the clothes Cage had bought her at Hildy's store, washed, pressed, and neatly folded by the hotel's laundry.

She smiled ruefully at the crease they'd ironed into the ugly canvas trousers; at the rounded toes of the ungainly rubber boots poking out from beneath them. She wondered what her own descendants would think when they found these things in the next century, carefully, lovingly stored in the family attic.

Her fingers trailed lightly over the shirt top—the one she'd worn the last day—then started when she caught a glimpse of herself in the dresser mirror across the room. She'd packed every item of clothing she'd brought, completely forgetting that all she was wearing was the peach and blue robe she'd worn at Cage's cabin.

With a forced, wry smile at her own absent-mindedness, she stripped down to her underwear, then dressed in the canvas trousers and one of the bulky overshirts. It didn't matter what she wore for travelling. She'd rented a car for the drive up to Georgia, and no one would see her anyway. Come to think of it, it didn't matter if she *was* seen. She stared at her reflection as she pulled her long blonde hair back into a pony-tail, thinking that she liked the way she looked in these clothes. They reminded her of who she really was; they reminded her of three precious days she would hold in a cherished part of her memory forever. Maybe she'd never take them off.

She closed the suitcase and called down for a bellman to come to collect her bags.

A few moments later he banged on the door, so hard that it made her jump. Up until now the employees of the hotel had been so deferential that it had almost bordered on the absurd, but this sounded as if the bellman had actually used the side of his fist on the door. Irritated, she hurried to jerk it open. The sharp reprimand she intended to deliver died on her lips.

Cage stood painfully erect in the doorway, backlit by the golden glow of the hallway lights. He wore a starkly white dress shirt open at the collar and a pair of snug, faded jeans, as if he'd started to dress formally and had changed his mind at the last moment.

A single band of white gauze rode just over his black brows, circling his forehead. The black hair was ruffled by wind and finger tracks, and a few strands spilled over the white gauze strip. His eyes were dark and hot and steady.

Melanie blinked once, hard, as if she didn't trust the evidence of her eyes. 'You're at the clinic,' she said foolishly. 'You're supposed to be there for another day or two at least. Why did they release you?'

'They didn't.'

'But...'

'I saw you on television. They keep replaying that little speech you gave at the airport.'

She stared at him mindlessly, lips slightly parted, blue gaze wide and unblinking.

'You threw it all away, Melanie.'

Her pale brows twitched in confusion and her head tipped until her pony-tail dangled off to one side.

'Beau,' he explained. 'Your marriage; the life you'd planned ... everything. You threw it all away.'

Melanie's brow cleared. 'Oh. That.'

He almost smiled. 'Yes. *That*.'

Peripherally Melanie saw the uniformed figure of the bellman appear behind Cage, but she never took her eyes from his, nor he from hers.

'Your bags, miss?' the bellman asked politely.

'Later,' Cage growled without turning his head, and the man disappeared. Cage continued looking at her for a moment longer, then sighed. 'You might as well ask me in, Melanie. I'm not leaving until I say what I came here to say.'

She glanced down at where her hand still clung tightly to the doorknob, as if that were all that was holding her upright. She knew what was coming. He'd come all the way up here to thank her for what she'd done for his Everglades, and, although his motives were noble enough, she didn't know if she could bear it.

What was she supposed to do? Smile graciously while he told her what a fine thing she'd done? Stand within touching distance of a man who would forever be out of reach, and pretend it didn't matter? Wouldn't it be easier to ask him to leave; to never, ever have to look on his face again and feel that agonising pain around her heart?

'Melanie?'

'Come in,' she mumbled, standing aside, closing her eyes as he walked by into the room, feeling the slight movement of the air he displaced like a hurricane-force wind against her body.

Oh, lord, she thought, maybe I can get a job in his orange groves or his factory, so that once in a great while he might walk past me on his way to somewhere else, and I can feel the air that touched him touching me. That would be enough, wouldn't it? That would be enough to make life worth living...

'Come here, Melanie.'

Her eyes flew open and she turned her head to look at him. He was already over by the easy chairs in the sitting-room, and here she was still standing by the door, holding it open as if she expected someone else to walk in. She licked her lips, swallowed, then released her death grip on the door. It swung closed with a quiet click, and she moved woodenly to within a few feet of him.

His eyes swept over her as she approached, brows twitching at the bulky shirt and comically creased canvas trousers. 'You're leaving Tallahassee?'

She gripped the back of a chair and wondered if she looked normal; if it only felt as if she was falling apart at the seams. 'Yes. I'm going back home. Back to Creek County.'

Just like my great-great-great-grandmother, she added to herself. We Brooks women just keep going around and around that same circle, never really closing it, and we all end up back in Creek County.

He nodded once, then turned to look out the picture window. It was almost full dark now, and the lights of the cityscape stitched a random pattern of sparks across the black void beyond the glass. Melanie's gaze shifted to the thick bandage on the back of his head, held in place by the gauze band.

'How's your head, Benjamin?' she asked quietly.

'My head's fine.'

She frowned at the sudden chill in his voice. 'You shouldn't have left the clinic...'

The impact of his eyes almost pushed her backwards. 'And you shouldn't have jumped into that pond!' The sheer volume of his shout was like a hard slap across her face. 'You could have died in that water! Why the hell did you do that? Why the hell didn't you go overland to the ranger station? Why the *hell* didn't you just wait until I——?'

'Because!' she shouted back helplessly, because shouting was the only way she could keep from bursting into tears. 'Because you were hurt! Because I thought you were...' her voice broke and she had to swallow hard before continuing '...I thought you were dying.'

His head jerked convulsively, sending his hair flying across his brow. 'Dammit, what if *you* had died? Did you think I'd want to live in a world without you?'

Melanie felt the breath stop in her throat like a wad of dry cotton; felt every muscle in her body freeze. She was afraid to move, afraid to speak, afraid that even a breath might shatter this single bright bubble of hope that had suddenly, magically appeared.

He was facing her like a coiled beast caught in a trap, eyes narrowed, shoulders hunched, fists clenched at his sides. 'I didn't want to love you.' His voice crackled deeply, and Melanie felt its electricity shooting through the nerves of her body like a live current. 'I didn't ever want to love a woman so much that my life would be over if she left . . .' his gaze grew distant and he looked past her, back in time '. . . and then I saw you get off that plane and I knew that you were the woman I would love like that, and I also knew that you could never belong to me; that eventually you would leave.' He shoved his hands in his pockets, looked at the floor, then up into her eyes with a sad little smile. 'And, even knowing all that, I couldn't help myself. I tried telling you love was the one thing I couldn't give you, but the truth was, I'd already given it by then. The morning after we made love I was crazy enough to hope you'd say you wanted to stay—it nearly killed me when you didn't.'

Melanie took the quick, desperate breath of a drowning person who suddenly, miraculously found her head above water in the clean, sweet air. Her heart took a giant leap in her chest and she opened her mouth to speak, but he shook his head.

'You don't have to say anything. I knew from the start we were as different as two people could be; as star-crossed as our ancestors. I was just part of your first adventure, that's all.' He tipped his head with a self-deprecating smile. 'It's funny, isn't it? You were supposed to be one of those old-fashioned, helpless, dependent Southern ladies; but, underneath, you were the strong one—strong enough to throw away your future to do what you thought was right; strong enough to risk your life to save someone else's . . .' He took a breath, then straightened to deliver the highest accolade Melanie would ever receive in her life. 'She'd be proud of you, you know. The first Melanie Annabelle Brooks would be so proud that you carry her name.'

She was so stunned by the wonder of the things he was saying that her lips seemed frozen in place. Besides, even if she could speak, what would she say? How could she twist and compress the things she was feeling into something as pathetic as mere words? What did you say when someone reached across the vacuum of your existence and handed you love, handed you the reason for being...?

'Cage!' He had crossed the room and his hand was on the doorknob before she finally found her voice. 'I'll find out where you live,' she said in a choked voice, and then she almost laughed out loud, because she was hopelessly in love with this man and didn't even know his address. 'If you walk out that door, I'll find you somehow. If I have to I'll camp out in that cabin of yours and just wait until you come back.'

His hand still frozen on the knob, he turned his head slowly to look at her. She couldn't read whatever lay behind his eyes, not from this distance; but she didn't have to. She already knew what was in his mind and his heart and his spirit; she felt as if she'd known it for a hundred years.

'What?' he asked softly.

'I'll find you,' she promised, her voice stronger now, but tears were streaming unchecked down her cheeks. Benjamin gazed at them in wonder. 'I'll find you because I *am* an old-fashioned Southern lady; the kind who wants to be married, to have children playing in her attic, and...oh, Asi...I want them to be yours.'

He took a few steps towards her, then hesitated, and for the first time she saw naked emotion in that proud, stoic face, the tortured expression of a man afraid to believe what he most wanted to believe; afraid to love because love was the only thing that could hurt him. And then she saw a strange sort of peace settle on his face, and knew that he had cast the fear aside.

He stood motionless, gazing at her across the short distance that separated them, as if he would never again have a chance to see her from this far away. Melanie felt as if she was being drawn into those black eyes; being *absorbed* by them, committed to a memory that would endure long past the short span of one man's lifetime.

'We'll have your portrait done,' he murmured, 'just the way you look now, and we'll hang it next to hers, where our grandchildren can always see them ...' He paused and smiled crookedly at the baggy trousers and shirt. 'Why are you wearing those clothes, Melanie?'

She smiled through her tears. 'I love these clothes. I might never take them off.'

His eyes touched hers, a new light shining from their depths. 'Want to bet?'

Melanie felt her chest rise beneath her shirt, felt her heart rise beneath her breast, and imagined she heard the fluttery thunder of a thousand birds taking flight. She lifted her right arm as he lifted his left, and with the profound silence of love too old, too great to be spoken aloud, their fingers touched like phantom tendrils of history linking one century to another.

'I love you, Asi,' Melanie sighed as he pulled her into his arms, not quite sure if she had spoken or only merely thought the phrase. Ear pressed to his chest, she heard the rapid thunder of his heart like an Indian drum.

Outside, from a seemingly cloudless, starry night, a gentle, smiling rain began to fall as the sky wept.

Next Month's Romances

Each month you can choose from a wide variety of romance with Mills & Boon. Below are the new titles to look out for next month, why not ask either Mills & Boon Reader Service or your Newsagent to reserve you a copy of the titles you want to buy — just tick the titles you would like and either post to Reader Service or take it to any Newsagent and ask them to order your books.

Please save me the following titles:	Please tick	√
BREAKING POINT	Emma Darcy	
SUCH DARK MAGIC	Robyn Donald	
AFTER THE BALL	Catherine George	
TWO-TIMING MAN	Roberta Leigh	
HOST OF RICHES	Elizabeth Power	
MASK OF DECEPTION	Sara Wood	
A SOLITARY HEART	Amanda Carpenter	
AFTER THE FIRE	Kay Gregory	
BITTERSWEET YESTERDAYS	Kate Proctor	
YESTERDAY'S PASSION	Catherine O'Connor	
NIGHT OF THE SCORPION	Rosemary Carter	
NO ESCAPING LOVE	Sharon Kendrick	
OUTBACK LEGACY	Elizabeth Duke	
RANSACKED HEART	Jayne Bauling	
STORMY REUNION	Sandra K. Rhoades	
A POINT OF PRIDE	Liz Fielding	

If you would like to order these books in addition to your regular subscription from Mills & Boon Reader Service please send £1.70 per title to: Mills & Boon Reader Service, P.O. Box 236, Croydon, Surrey, CR9 3RU, quote your Subscriber No:.......................................
(If applicable) and complete the name and address details below. Alternatively, these books are available from many local Newsagents including W.H.Smith, J.Menzies, Martins and other paperback stockists from 12th March 1993.

Name:...

Address:...

....Post Code:........................

To Retailer: If you would like to stock M&B books please contact your regular book/magazine wholesaler for details.

You may be mailed with offers from other reputable companies as a result of this application. If you would rather not take advantage of these opportunities please tick box ☐

Another Face . . .
Another Identity . . .
Another Chance . . .

When her teenage love turns to hate, Geraldine Frances vows to even the score. After arranging her own "death", she embarks on a dramatic transformation emerging as *Silver,* a hauntingly beautiful and mysterious woman few men would be able to resist.

With a new face and a new identity, she is now ready to destroy the man responsible for her tragic past.

Silver – a life ruled by one all-consuming passion, is Penny Jordan at her very best.

W◑RLDWIDE

4 FREE

Romances and 2 FREE gifts just for you!

You can enjoy all the heartwarming emotion of true love for FREE! Discover the heartbreak and the happiness, the emotion and the tenderness of the modern relationships in Mills & Boon Romances.

We'll send you 4 captivating Romances as a special offer from Mills & Boon Reader Service, along with the chance to have 6 Romances delivered to your door each month.

Claim your FREE books and gifts overleaf...

An irresistible offer from Mills & Boon

Here's a personal invitation from Mills & Boon Reader Service, to become a regular reader of Romances. To welcome you, we'd like you to have 4 books, a CUDDLY TEDDY and a special MYSTERY GIFT absolutely FREE.

Then you could look forward each month to receiving 6 brand new Romances, delivered to your door, postage and packing free! Plus our free Newsletter featuring author news, competitions, special offers and much more.

This invitation comes with no strings attached. You may cancel or suspend your subscription at any time, and still keep your free books and gifts.

It's so easy. Send no money now. Simply fill in the coupon below and post it to -
**Reader Service, FREEPOST,
PO Box 236, Croydon, Surrey CR9 9EL.**

------------------------------- **NO STAMP REQUIRED** -------------

Free Books Coupon

Yes! Please rush me 4 free Romances and 2 free gifts! Please also reserve me a Reader Service subscription. If I decide to subscribe I can look forward to receiving 6 brand new Romances each month for just £10.20, postage and packing free. If I choose not to subscribe I shall write to you within 10 days - I can keep the books and gifts whatever I decide. I may cancel or suspend my subscription at any time. I am over 18 years of age.

Ms/Mrs/Miss/Mr_____ EP31R

Address_____

_____

Postcode_____Signature _____

'You have needs, Verity. Be honest and admit you want the same as me, some warmth, some human contact, some bloody body-bonding!'

She swung back, her eyes wide with defiance. 'But that isn't enough for you, is it, Rupert? You want the whole package, my body! Well, you'll just have to go stuff that chicken because that's the nearest you'll get to any body-bonding while we share this house!'

Dear Reader

The arrival of the Mills & Boon Mothers' Day Pack means that Spring is just around the corner . . . so why not indulge in a little romantic Spring Fever, as you enjoy the four books specially chosen for you? Whether you received this Pack as a gift, or bought it for yourself, these stories will help you celebrate this very special time of year. So relax, put your feet up and allow our authors to entertain you!

The Editor

AN IMPERFECT AFFAIR

BY

NATALIE FOX

MILLS & BOON LIMITED
ETON HOUSE   18-24 PARADISE ROAD
RICHMOND   SURREY   TW9 1SR

First published in Great Britain 1992
by Mills & Boon Limited

© Natalie Fox 1992

Australian copyright 1992
Philippine copyright 1993
This edition 1993

ISBN 0 263 77806 1

Set in Times Roman 11 on 12 pt.
91-9302-48869 C

Made and printed in Great Britain

CHAPTER ONE

'YOU!'

The very male figure seated at a desk by the bedroom window of the old Spanish mill house had turned as Verity opened the door. Their mutual shock at the sight of each other, the stunned disbelief in both their eyes, had erupted with that simultaneous 'You'.

Shocked, Verity gripped the iron handle of the door till her fingers went white, but it was red that flamed through her in a fiery second of realisation. This wasn't some freak coincidence. This had been *arranged*!

Her violet eyes flashed round the bedroom and in a split second took everything in. Rupert Scott was living here, and working too. A lap-top computer was on the desk and papers were strewn everywhere; on the floor, on the bed.

They had met twice before, under awkward and embarrassing circumstances, and now this. Verity couldn't believe the man was here in this remote Andalucian mill house. El Molino, the house her cousin, Stuart, had arranged for her to work in for a month. She'd kill Stuart for this when she got back to England, slowly and painfully.

Rupert Scott found his voice before Verity could summon hers. A deep voice she remembered well— it had haunted her enough times since first they had met.

'What the hell are you doing here?' he growled.

Nothing had changed. His tone was as derisive as ever. He was as good-looking as ever too, though she'd never seen him like this before, so very laid-back in his mode of dress.

Verity's voice came back in a spluttering rush with a not very original exclamation. 'I could ask you the same question!'

She had a ghastly feeling that he probably thought this was her idea, as he probably thought their other meetings had been engineered by her. After all, Rupert Scott could be considered quite a catch, in a monetary sense; his personality wasn't such a snip. The man was cool, aloof, and wretchedly moody. But at least they had one thing in common: neither liked being matchmade by her cousin. Oh, yes, if Stuart was to step into the room now she would happily garrotte him for this, and she had a feeling Rupert Scott would readily assist her.

'This is beginning to get boring,' Rupert grated through tight lips. 'First the dinner party your cousin arranged for us, then that "accidental" meeting in a Knightsbridge restaurant, and now this. Can't you and your persistent cousin take a hint?'

Verity burned with embarrassment. She didn't want to be reminded about that awful match-making dinner party and that excruciating incident in the restaurant when Stuart had hovered over Rupert as he had dined alone, clutching her to his side as if she were a sacrificial offering. Of course he had asked them to join him—what else could he have done?—but he had made it quite obvious that he wasn't impressed with Stuart Bolton's cousin, who was being so determinedly pressed on him at every opportunity.

'Why are *you* here?' she blurted to cover her shock and embarrassment.

The 'arranged' theory swelled by the second. Stuart and her editor, Alan Sargeant, had set this up for her. A month in a converted mill house in Andalucia. Not a holiday, not in January, for she was here to work, but a change of scene after a bout of flu that had laid her out over Christmas and, as Alan had reiterated, she'd had a rough time after her boyfriend's death and needed some space and time on her own. This wasn't on her own, though. Rupert Scott was here and Verity was inflamed.

'To work; what does it look like?' was his sharp retort, which sliced into her fury.

'Yes, I can see that! I'm not blind!' she huffed impatiently. 'But why here of all places? Andalucia, in a remote mill house, miles from anywhere. Why did you have to pick this place?'

'Because it's quiet and peaceful—at least, it *was*.' His barbed sarcasm left no doubt he thought her a disruptive nuisance, just as he had at that dinner party and the restaurant. The man didn't like her and she didn't like him, and finding each other in the same house was incredibly awful.

'Is this your house?' she blurted.

'Is it yours?' he countered coldly.

'Well, this is getting us a long way, isn't it?' she spiked back. 'At least we've established this place belongs to someone else.'

'A friend of your cousin's, I was led to believe,' he drawled and stood up as he did so. Verity thought he was going to come towards her and bodily throw her out, but he folded his arms across his chest and leaned back on the desk. 'So perhaps you'd better explain your presence here,' he added.

'I'm here to work!' Verity exploded and then suddenly the fizz went out of her as sheer embarrassment swamped her once again. This must look dreadful to him. She actually felt more sorry for him than herself. She dragged a fretful hand through her pale blonde hair. 'Look, this is ridiculous,' she said levelly. 'Stuart arranged for me to come here for a break——'

'Did he, now?' he interrupted disbelievingly. 'Am I supposed to swallow that?' Before she could answer he went on, 'I don't, not for a minute. I know why you're here and so do you, so shall we stop pussyfooting?'

Verity's eyes widened and her mouth opened and shut as if she'd forgotten how to work it.

He gave her a grim smile. 'And don't come on as if you haven't a clue what I'm getting at. You're here to work your sexy charms on me. You're here to seduce me, aren't you?' Rupert Scott accused drily, his eyes glinting with what Verity could only assume to be disgust.

She matched his outrage and worked her mouth into a cry of horror. 'What?' The very thought, the very idea... She realised that her hand was still fused to the door handle and was aching badly. She let it go and pumped her fist at her side to get the blood flowing again.

Slowly, almost wearily, as if boredom had suddenly hit him, he said, 'Look, dear, you're a sweet kid but absolutely not my type...'

'Don't sweet kid or dear me!' Verity bit back. 'You're light years from my type too, I assure you. I thought you would have got the message on our previous meetings. As for seducing you, heaven forbid! Some hyper-imagination you have!'

His grey eyes darkened threateningly. 'Look, I don't believe for a minute this meeting is pure coincidence. I know exactly why you're here but you can forget it. No sale!'

No sale! Verity gaped at him, gazing at his shabby black tracksuit. He had a long red scarf draped several times round his throat for warmth, and heavy army-type boots on his feet. At Stuart's dinner party he'd been dressed formally in a black evening suit and he'd looked strikingly handsome; not handsome enough to impress her, though, and now he didn't impress her either, just made her so flaming mad that she wanted to bite his knees. His eyes were too grey, his mouth too mean, his hair too damned black and long, and 'no sale' went for her too.

She pushed her long golden hair from her face and steeled herself. 'I'm here to work,' she told him defiantly, 'not to mess with you. My cousin arranged for me to stay here——'

'And me too,' he interrupted icily. 'And, though I admire your cousin's ambition, I can't say I'm enamoured by his methods. I thought I made it quite obvious that night and at the restaurant that I take exception to being manipulated. I don't do blind dates and I don't do business in bed. Tell your cousin that when you get back.'

'Business in bed?' Verity echoed with horror. She dredged her memory pool to recall what he did for a living. And it was some living she remembered. Airline company, state-of-the-art recording studio, film company, so what had all that to do with bed?

His mean mouth broke into a cynical smile. 'Don't look so innocent, treasure. You know exactly what I'm getting at.'

Verity actually stepped further into the room, though her senses told her she ought to be thinking of getting out, back down that twisty mountain road to the coast, back to the airport and home to give her cousin a stripping-down for this. But she was curious, madly curious to know what all this was about. 'I wouldn't look so innocent if I had a clue what you were getting at.'

'Wouldn't you? Blondes have always struck me as being a contradiction of the old adage, dumb.'

Folding her arms across her scarlet sweat-shirt, Verity told him haughtily, 'I'm certainly not dumb but at the moment you are talking in riddles I find difficult to comprehend. If that's dumb, I'm it! So could you repeat what you just said and enlarge on it? I would like to know what my cousin and I are being accused of.'

'Frankly I don't think there's a name for it, and frankly I don't believe you don't know why this ridiculous charade has been set up.'

And it was a set-up, Verity inwardly agreed, a matchmaking set-up, though she failed to understand why this man needed someone to organise his love-life—he looked very capable of doing that for

himself. She didn't fancy him but she could imagine other women tripping over their hormones to
get to him. He had a certain bile-churning attraction—to sows!

'I want more than that!' she told him bitterly. 'I
want a full explanation and a damned apology for
thinking I'm here to bed you.'

He actually smiled. 'An apology for the truth you
won't get from me, and if there's any explaining to
do there's a phone in the village. Call your cousin
on the way back to the airport and tell him his
scheme won't work. I can't be bought with sexual
favours.'

He sat down and swung back to his work and
started tapping away at his computer. Verity's blood
started to overheat. Sexual favours! The man was
crazy *and* he expected her to go—and now!

'You expect me to go? Just as if I lived round
the corner?' She took a deep defiant breath when
he made no attempt to answer. He owed her an
explanation and an apology and she was going to
get both before she left.

'I've endured a delay at Heathrow Airport, a two-
and-a-half-hour flight with a plastic lunch and an
hour and a half of cross-country rallying to get
here,' she rattled on crossly. 'I arrive here expecting the same peace and quiet you did, and what
do I find when I'm exploring the rooms? A
nightmare in the form of you. I'm tired, thirsty and
hungry and I'm damned well going to satisfy my
needs before *you* dictate to me what I should do!
So stick that up your jumper, Mr Rupert Un-
Bearable, and incubate it!'

She stormed from the room and slammed the door after her and tore down the stone stairs to the kitchen. When she got there, breathless with fury and exertion, she slumped into a kitchen chair and held her head in her hands.

This was *awful*! So awful that she just didn't know what to do. She looked up, out of the window. The sun had gone, dipping down over some distant hill. It was suddenly colder than ever in this cavernous house, and exhaustion claimed her. She would have to drive down that fearful, twisty, narrow road back to the airport in the dark. Her return flight was a month from now and she'd have to mess around trying to get another flight back, struggling with her luggage, all alone... She covered her face and very nearly burst into tears.

She felt a hand on her shoulder. 'Beryl, I'm——'

'The name's Verity, Verity Brooks!' she snapped, swatting at his hand as if it were a disease-carrying mosquito. 'Get your hands off me!' Damn him! He hadn't even remembered her name!

She felt the warmth recede, heard him moving across the room to the sink.

'I'm sorry, Verity. It's a bit unfair of me to expect you to go immediately. The morning will do.'

'Oh, how very considerate of you!' she blazed sarcastically. 'Why don't *you* go? I've as much right here as you have!' She wasn't going to go without a fight—hell! She wasn't going to go at *all*!

He didn't answer till he'd filled a kettle and plugged it in. 'Squatters' rights, I'm afraid. I've been here a week already and have no intention of packing up and getting out to please the whims of you. I'm in the middle of an important pro-ject——'

'I don't care if you're in the middle of a mid-life crisis!'

'Too young. Now will you stop hissing at me like a she-cat and listen to some good down-to-earth reasoning?'

Her eyes flashed warningly at him when she realised he was quite angry now. Well, she was mad too, and she had more reason to be than him!

'Only if it's constructive,' she iced back. 'This situation is quite intolerable and you are making it worse. I arrived here in all innocence, not knowing you were here, but you seem to think it's some sort of scheme to get us together. I promise you, I wouldn't have come if I'd thought you'd be here. You talk of seduction and business in bed and I don't know what the blazes is going on!'

'I don't know you well enough to believe you're not in on this,' he insisted darkly. 'So perhaps you'd better start by explaining exactly why you *think* you are here.'

He held her warring eyes with those of steely fire and Verity felt the heat scorch through her. Now she knew what it felt like to be interrogated. So this was the famed Spanish Inquisition, was it?

'Why I *think* I'm here?' she flamed. 'I know *exactly* why I'm here... to work. Nothing more sinister than that, whatever your corrupted mind wishes to deceive you with!'

She didn't know if he believed her or not; he simply asked if she wanted tea or coffee.

Surprised, she uttered, 'Tea, please, decaf-feinated if there is any.' She ignored his intake of resigned breath at that. 'You don't believe me; you don't believe I'm here to work, do you?'

'I'm getting a little tired of this game,' he told her brittly as he measured tea into a metal teapot. 'Were you or were you not despatched here to lower my resistance with a seduction attempt?'

Verity laughed, incredulously. 'Don't take this as a compliment but you hardly appear to be an easy push-over, and I'm certainly no *femme fatale.*'

He smiled, and it was the first indication that he believed her, though Verity wished it wasn't because of that *femme fatale* remark. Blonde and innocent she might look, but she was streetwise enough to cope with his brash arrogance.

'So what were your intended tactics if they weren't to bed me into compliance?'

Compliance with what, for heaven's sake?' she croaked back in shocked disbelief. This conversation was getting ridiculous and her patience was running dry.

Her strangled reply had him looking at her with sudden doubt, as if he just might be beginning to believe her. 'Have you any idea what I'm talking about?' he murmured.

'None whatsoever, but no doubt some time this century you'll get around to speaking without a forked tongue.'

She watched and waited while he made the tea, and she remembered the sour milk she'd found in the fridge while she was exploring on her arrival.

'No milk,' she told him quickly.

She should have known then that the old mill was already occupied. There were enough signs lying around: the dirty dishes in the sink, keys on

the kitchen table, the back door unlocked. She had
stepped into the house, naïvely thinking that the
maid who came with the property was here preparing for her stay. No maid, just his arrogant self.
Goldilocks, discovering the grumpy grizzly bear.

He poured two cups of black tea and brought
them to the table, setting one down in front of her
and one across from her. He sat and faced her,
leaned back and gazed directly into her eyes.

'Tell me, Verity Brooks, tell me why you are
here?'

God, how she hated his supercilious tone and the
penetrating way he looked at her. 'I've already told
you! I'm here to work.'

'What work? Scrubbing floors, plumbing——'

'Don't try getting funny with me,' she cut in
quickly. 'There's nothing funny about this situation whatsoever.'

She had the power to annoy him. She felt satisfaction at that as his eyes glowered and his facial
muscles pulsed. 'I wasn't trying to be funny, and
will you quit fancy-footing around every question
I drop in your lap? Let's resolve this before I lose
my patience.'

Verity leaned forward. 'Well, I have a patience
too and at the moment it's full of holes. If you just
shut up for five minutes and let me have my say
neither of us needs lose our cool.'

He didn't like that, being spoken to as if he were
five. So what? Oh, boy, did he irritate her. So badly
that her skin fizzed with it. She analysed that irritation and found that it stemmed from his forgetting her name. She hadn't forgotten his, or

anything about him, but nightmares had that effect on her!

'Well?' he prompted when she added nothing.

She leaned back in her chair and tried to relax. Hard when a nightmare faced you across the table. So, if he hadn't remembered her name she doubted he'd remembered her occupation. 'I'm features editor of a health and beauty magazine. *Looks Healthy*,' she told him, wondering if she was jogging any memory cells. 'I had the flu over Christmas and I'd just returned to work and my editor, Alan——'

'Alan Sargeant?' he exclaimed, and his brow furrowed threateningly.

'Yes . . . yes,' Verity murmured in puzzlement. 'You know him?' If he did he didn't look too happy about it.

Rupert nodded as if something was suddenly dawning on him, 'Go on.'

'Alan thought I needed a break,' Verity went on, masking off the apprehension that was suddenly misting her thoughts. Was Alan involved in this supposed conspiracy too? 'We'd planned a book, a spin-off from the magazine I work for. We've done them before. This one's a book for brides-to-be, how to get fit for the big day. Diets and exercise regimes, that sort of thing. Most of the groundwork has been done by one of the other editors and now it just needs putting together, and Alan thought it a good idea to pack me off here for a month to do it.' She wasn't going to tell him about Mike's death; that was no concern of his.

'And?'

'And what?'

'And that's it?'

Verity wrapped her hands round her cup to warm her fingers. She was getting colder by the minute. Stuart had warned her that it might be chilly in the hills, but she hadn't been prepared for this cavernous house with its solid stone walls, seemingly to be hewn out of the very rock it was built against.

'Yes, that's it,' she murmured, her jaw aching from fighting to stop her teeth from chattering. 'Nothing more, nothing less.'

'What a very considerate boss you have. A month in Spain, all expenses paid, no doubt. Sounds too good to be true, and what has your cousin to do with this?'

The edge to his voice added to her apprehension. 'A...a friend of his owns this place and it was vacant——'

'But it wasn't,' he cut in. 'I'm here and Stuart knew that—it was he who offered me the place. What connection has he with your boss, Alan Sargeant?'

'Questions, questions,' she couldn't help retorting. 'In spite of the dinner party and the restaurant and the fact that Stuart loaned you this place, you really don't know him very well at all, do you?'

'And after this little mystery I don't think I want to. Now are you going to tell me the connection or not?'

'They met at university and have been close friends ever since; in fact, they're related too. Stuart's wife, Angie, is Alan's sister, so they're brothers-in-law,' Verity efficiently informed him, though what difference it would make to this situation she couldn't imagine.

'Aha, the plot thickens!' Rupert gave a cynical smile and lifted his cup to his mouth.

'What plot?' Verity husked. She didn't know it, but her eyes had widened innocently.

'Is that an act?'

'What?'

'That innocent look in your eyes.'

Verity slammed her cup down on the table. 'A Thespian I'm not, impatient I am. Will you kindly tell me what is going through your mind?'

'Don't you think this all rather a little odd?' he suggested darkly. 'First the dinner party to bring us together, then that contrived meeting in the restaurant, and now this.'

Verity lowered her lashes. At the time she had been mad with Stuart for trying to pair her off with this man. But later she had forgiven him. She understood that he'd done it out of love and concern for her. She had lost Mike but she didn't want another man in her life so soon after their rocky relationship had ended so tragically. She wanted time and space to pick up the pieces and try to forget and had thought she had got her point through to her cousin. Apparently not. Stuart was convinced that she needed a new man in her life and it was this one sitting across from her. Rupert Scott.

'I like it even less than you,' she husked and then bravely raised her eyes to his. 'Listen. I've no interest in you whatsoever,' she told him earnestly. 'I'm sure Stuart's intentions were . . . were . . .'

'Don't say honourable or thoughtful or kind,' he warned sardonically, his eyes sheet-metal grey and hard. 'I loathe these sort of manipulative tactics and I dread to think what nonsense they've stuffed your pretty little head with——'

'Will you stop this and tell me what is going on?' she pleaded.

His lips tightened and she thought she would never prise the truth from them. Why were they both here? It certainly wasn't a coincidence. It had been plotted and planned, she was convinced of that now, but why was he so reluctant to tell her the truth?

He stood up suddenly and gathered up the dirty cups. If she knew him better she might be led to believe that he didn't want to face her. He spoke at last, almost kindly but verging on patronisingly.

'I believe you now. You really don't know what is going on, do you?'

Verity could only shake her head.

'Perhaps your cousin is cleverer than I thought, or maybe subtler is a more accurate description.'

'I still don't know what you are getting at,' Verity murmured.

'Why do you think we are both here?'

Verity swept her hair from her face and shifted uncomfortably in her seat. 'I . . . I presume it was another of Stuart's matchmaking attempts.'

He laughed and shook his head. 'I can find my own women when I want them, and you're a pretty snappy-looking girl yourself—I shouldn't think you have any problems picking up a man. No, treasure, this is far more devious than it appears.'

'And you know precisely how devious, don't you?' Her heart was beginning to thud dangerously. It was a ridiculous situation. The dinner party was excusable on reflection, but not the restaurant and this third attempt? Teaming the two of them in an isolated mill house in Andalucia was...was determined, to say the least. 'Stuart and Alan are in this together, aren't they?' she breathed heavily.

'I'm afraid so,' Rupert grated, drawing a hand through his thick black hair. 'At first I thought you were a part of the scheme, but I don't think you're that good a liar.' His eyes narrowed at her sharp intake of breath, but he didn't apologise. 'It doesn't change anything. We are here together and what they expected to happen isn't difficult to imagine. But bedding you won't change my mind.'

Bedding? Verity shook her head, not believing what she was hearing. An affair with this man? Was that what her two so-called friends wanted and expected? But for what, she couldn't imagine. No, the idea was impossible. The chill inside her froze to the depths of her soul. They were chalk and cheese, as compatible as fire and water, even less likely of making a perfect match than her and Mike. And Mike was dead, but this man was very much alive, and if she stayed...

She suppressed a shudder of dread and opened her mouth to speak, and when the words came out they were very determined and strong.

'I think you'd better tell me everything you suspect,' she directed at him coolly, 'but before you do let's get one thing straight. You're right. I'm not a part of this and I'm not a liar. If there is a plot I know nothing about it. I came here in innocence and I plan to leave here in innocence too. I think you know what I mean.'

His lips tightened and his smoky grey eyes held hers. 'I know exactly what you mean,' he smoothed silkily.

Suddenly he stepped towards her and she flinched as he lifted a tendril of her long, silky fair hair from her shoulder. Surprised and confused, Verity closed her eyes for an instant as he rolled the pale golden tendril between his fingers and thumb as if testing its quality and strength, and when she opened her eyes and looked up at him with wide-eyed innocence he gave her a lazy smile that tightened her stomach muscles into a knot of apprehension.

Very quietly, very suggestively, he husked, 'Innocence, huh? I wonder just how innocent you are, Verity Brooks. You look it, you breathe it, but I wonder.'

'Well, wonder no longer and take my word for it, Rupert Scott,' she breathed defiantly. 'I don't do business in bed either.'

'Business might not come into it,' he told her, his voice so softly timbred that she was more afraid than ever. 'Let's not make promises we can't keep because that would be an added complication. Instead, let's both keep our options open on that innocence statement of yours, shall we?'

She didn't answer; she *couldn't* answer. That apprehension knotted inside her balled to something bigger and far more worrying. All the same, she held his grey eyes as defiantly and as determinedly as he held hers.

She wondered just how far he would push her with shrouded threats like that, for at this moment he was a far cry from that aloof, sophisticated man who had shown so little interest in her in the company of others. But they weren't in the company of others now, they were isolated together in so-called romantic Andalucia, where you could reach out and kiss the moon and clasp a handful of stars to your heart. And Rupert Scott wasn't half so daunting here, and yet he was, and suddenly he seemed very interested indeed in her and she wondered if she hated him as much as she had hyped herself up to.

That was a very perturbing conclusion to come to, one that warranted more tentative thought—later.

CHAPTER TWO

'So...so what's going on here?' Verity asked when
Rupert had sat down again. She nervously
smoothed her hand over her hair where he had
touched it. It was soft and silky and she wondered
what had gone through his mind when he had felt
it, though, given time, it wouldn't have taken much
guessing. It had been an intimate gesture and unexpected, and she wasn't at all sure about the feeling
that it had pulsed in her veins. She was beginning
to feel a bit soft in the head and dangerously
vulnerable.

'Your cousin runs an advertising agency and Alan
Sargeant is an ambitious editor, and——'

'And what's that got to do with us?' she
interrupted.

'Let me finish and you'll find out.'

Verity clutched her numb fingers in her lap. 'I'm
sorry. Carry on.'

'I have various companies that put out a lot of
advertising. In a year I spend on promotion what
some companies pay their staff. At the moment I'm
considering adding a cable-television franchise to
my corporation, increasing my Atlantic fleet of aircraft, restructuring the film company and ex-
panding the recording outfit.'

Verity nearly laughed out loud at that verbal
scrolling of his business interests. There he was,
sitting across from her, looking like a latent hippie

in his tracksuit and boots and hardly the pecunious man he had appeared at the dinner party. She bet he was warm, though. She shivered and concentrated her thoughts on what he was getting at.

'And Stuart is pitching for all your advertising,' she suggested.

Rupert nodded. 'He's too small, though. I've already told him that. We met last year and I like and admire him, but I can't use him. The agency I use is the biggest in Europe.'

'Spencers?'

He frowned. 'So you *do* know more about this than you're letting on.'

She shook her head. 'No, I don't, but I'm in the publishing business and know they're the biggest and the best.' Her eyes widened painfully as she looked at him. 'You thought that I was here to seduce you for your advertising account?' Her stomach constricted at the thought.

'I'm afraid so.'

Verity's eyes narrowed in disbelief. She was beginning to feel very bitter about this, with Stuart for exposing her to such humiliation and Rupert Scott for believing she was capable of such a despicable action.

'If I were the Delilah you thought I was when I arrived I'd be in on this—and I'm not.' She glared at him. 'You do believe me, don't you?'

He nodded his very dark head. 'I've already told you that I do. If I didn't you wouldn't be sitting there shivering now, you'd be well on your way back to the airport with a flea in your ear.' He stood up. 'I'll do something about warming this place up.'

Verity stood up with him, her legs wobbling a bit with fatigue. 'But we haven't finished yet.'

She rubbed her forehead fretfully. It wasn't as simple as that. There was more, much more. So she wasn't here to seduce him but she was here nevertheless, and so was he, and Stuart and Alan had arranged it all.

'You suggested that Stuart put me up to this, but you were wrong. I knew nothing about it and, besides . . . besides, he wouldn't do that sort of thing.' Hurt suddenly filled her. 'Stuart is my cousin; he cares about me. He wouldn't use me this way.'

He held her eyes steadily. 'Who knows what slimy depths a man will sink to if his back's against the wall?'

'And what exactly do you mean by that?' Verity asked fiercely. She loved her cousin and no one would put him down behind his back, least of all *this* man.

Rupert let out a disgruntled sigh. 'Look, Verity, I'm not into causing family rifts. If you want answers, go home and ferret them out of your cousin.' He turned away to go through to the vaulted sitting-room, and Verity caught at his arm as he went past her.

'No, you don't,' she exploded. 'You started all this, so you finish it. You've made sickening accusations since I've arrived, and for all I know they're a pack of wicked lies.'

He prised her white fingers from the sleeve of his tracksuit and his metallic grey eyes penetrated hers deeply. 'I'm not a liar, Verity, and I have precious little time to waste on arguing the toss with you. Tell me something: do you love your cousin?'

'Of course I do!' she retorted indignantly. 'We're more like brother and sister than cousins. What has that got to do with all this?'

'Everything,' he replied tightly. 'Families are renowned for closing ranks to outsiders in times of trouble and anxiety. I'm that outsider at the moment and you wouldn't believe a word said against Stuart, so this conversation is going precisely nowhere. I came here to work, not to get involved with family problems.'

Verity followed him through to the sitting-room and stood behind him as he knelt to rake the dead ashes in the huge grate.

'That's not fair to me,' she told the back of his head. 'What do you mean by trouble and anxiety? You seem to know more about my cousin's business affairs than I do at the moment. I came here in all innocence to work too. This is equally if not more unpleasant for me. You've hinted at——'

'At too much already,' he grated over his shoulder as he made a pile of kindling in the grate.

'And you're not prepared to tell me more?'

He swivelled on his haunches to look up at her. 'Look, Verity, this has nothing to do with me. I can't be expected to take on family hassles. I'm a busy man——'

'Oh, to hell with you!' Verity cried in frustration, and swung away and headed back to the kitchen.

'Where are you going?' he called after her.

'Home, of course. Back to England. I'm not staying to have obscure accusations made of my family. You're right, we close ranks to outsiders.' She stopped and glared across the room at him. 'I sincerely hope we don't ever meet again. If we do, it will be my pleasure to sock you in the jaw for your damned arrogance!' She swung round and carried on.

'Haven't you forgotten something?' he called after her.

She stopped once again. 'Yes, of course, my manners. Thanks for the tea!'

'I meant your luggage,' he sighed irritably.

'I didn't bring it in. I must have had a premonition of impending doom!' she bit back icily, and strode purposefully on.

She wrenched open the kitchen door and flew out into fresh air. Cold fresh air and it was dark too, and the bastard wasn't even going to try to stop her!

She hurried down the steps to the pink driveway. The thought of finding her way back down to the coast with just the lights of her car to guide her was terrifying. Some gentleman he was! He might have suggested she stay the night at least. She recalled that he had and then things had got a bit sticky... Damn him and damn her silly pride. If she weren't so stubborn she could have got a good night's sleep before leaving. But her stubbornness was nothing to his. He should have told her what was going on. But in one way he was right—she probably wouldn't have believed him. He could have tried, though, instead of taking that damned secretive attitude.

Lights suddenly blazed across the driveway. That was something at least. He'd put the outside lights on so that she could see to load the car up. When she'd arrived in her hired car from the airport she had unloaded everything on to the drive, and then she had run up the steps to the terrace where Stuart had told her the key would be under a flowerpot. She had found no key and had wandered round to the side of the house and found the back door open, and the rest had been a nightmare discovery: Rupert Scott, here in this house and as awful as ever.

The groceries she'd bought on the coast had toppled and were strewn across the driveway. She squatted down to gather them together when a hand hauled her up.

'Get back inside the house. I'll see to this.'

Her first reaction was to lash out at him for touching her again, but he seemed to know how she felt and his grip tightened on her arm.

'Don't argue, Verity. I'm not the heartless monster you think I am. Get back up to the house and find a bedroom and bathroom—there are enough of them—and we'll talk about this later.'

She didn't argue. Not one word of protest passed her lips. Wearily she left him to it, climbing back up the stone steps and thanking God that he had a heart after all. She'd never have made that drive back to the airport in the dark, and she was too exhausted to even argue with that awful man.

The massive studded front door was open now and she stepped directly into that cavernous main room which gave her the shivers. Stone steps rose to a gallery above the room and then more steps to the bedrooms. Verity took them wearily, forking left on a stone landing. His room was right. She wanted to be as far away from him as possible. She picked the smallest of the two bedrooms available, the one with twin beds and its own small bathroom opening off from it. She sat on her hands on one of the beds and waited for him to bring her case up. Her thoughts went to Stuart and Alan. What on earth were they up to? She knew her cousin wanted to expand his agency, but surely not at the price of her honour? No, Rupert Scott was very wrong.

'Thank you,' she murmured as Rupert put her case down at the foot of the bed. He placed her computer carefully next to it.

'Have you switched on the water heater?' he asked and went to the bathroom to check if she had.

'No. I didn't know there was one.' She stood up and followed him to the small bathroom and stood in the doorway.

He flicked a switch behind the door. 'It will take a while to heat up, so if you're desperate for a bath or shower you're welcome to use my bathroom.'

His bedroom had been none too tidy and she could anticipate the disarray in his bathroom, and declined the offer abruptly. 'I'll wait, thanks.'

'Suit yourself,' he muttered equally shortly, and brushed past her to step back into the bedroom.

Verity stiffened at the closeness of his body as he moved past her. He'd felt warm and smelled of soap and maleness. She couldn't believe she'd noticed that.

He turned at the door. 'I'll light the fire downstairs—you look perished. You must be hungry too. I can't promise a feast; I don't cook, but I'll rustle something up for us.'

'Thanks,' she murmured and then wondered what she was thanking him for. He *owed* her.

Verity unpacked only what she'd need for the night after he'd gone: her toiletries and nightdress and a change of clothes. She slid into the warmest clothes she had, ribbed leggings and a baggy chenille sweater in a deep mulberry shade. She was glad she'd heeded Stuart's warning that the nights could be cold in the foothills and packed warm things. She slid her feet back into her trainers, flicked a comb through her straight, glossy hair and rubbed at a trace of smudged mascara under her eyes. Except it wasn't mascara but shadows of weariness, and she wasn't surprised. What a day! She longed for a bath and bed, but she longed for food more.

She ran downstairs. A fire was blazing in the grate and as yet it hadn't taken the chill off the huge room; nevertheless, it was a welcome sight. She stopped to warm her hands on it and then went through to the kitchen, hoping that Rupert Scott wasn't trying to give the kiss of life to that limp salad she'd seen in the fridge earlier. It was on the table when she walked in.

'I hope we're not eating that,' she said disdainfully.

'No, I was about to throw it out, but now you're here you can.' He was bent over a pan of soup on the hob, stirring it intently.

Verity looked round the room for a pedal bin but only found a brimming plastic carrier-bag in the corner by the larder.

'How often does the maid come in?'

'Never,' he told her. 'I paid her off when I arrived.'

'That accounts for the state the place is in,' she mumbled as she shook the salad out into the carrier-bag and added the dirty bowl to the pile in the sink.

'You could do that washing-up while you're there,' he suggested.

'I'll do nothing of the sort,' she retorted. 'You shouldn't have got rid of the maid. Why did you? You're obviously not house-trained.' She thought she saw a flicker of a smile at the corner of his mouth.

'I came here for solitude, not female chatter.'

'So what happens about the chores?'

'Well, you're here now, so it doesn't present a problem.'

'I'm not clearing up after you!'

'But I'm making supper for both of us. The least you can do is help,' he reasoned, quite pleasantly.

She could have argued that clearing up his dirty crocks—probably a week's worth, by the look of the pile—was hardly a fair exchange for a measly tin of soup, but she went to it none the less.

'I packed your groceries away for you.'

'You can have them. I can't take them with me when I go.'

'So you're going, are you?'

She was so fascinated at the sight of him hacking at a loaf of bread that she took a while to answer. She'd never seen anything quite like it. The slices were wedge-shaped, and she supposed he had hordes of minions to look after him at home.

'First thing in the morning, that's if you don't mind me staying the night.' She turned back to the sink and scrubbed at a cereal bowl and wondered what she would say to Alan when she got back so soon—which reminded her.

'What interest would Alan have in sending me here?' she asked him, aware that that was almost an admittance that there had been a conspiracy.

'I'm thinking of starting a few magazines of my own. In-flight magazines, music and film publications. Sargeant has already approached me for editorship.'

'Hmm, I'm not unduly surprised at that,' she murmured. 'Alan always has some new scheme simmering away in his mind.' Yes, he was ambitious, but that had nothing to do with her. She wouldn't be able to sway Rupert Scott his way even if she succeeded in seducing him. Though she hardly knew the man, she believed him when he said he didn't do business in bed—he didn't need to! Furiously she wrung the cloth out and viciously wiped down the tiled work-surface. She was getting as bad as him with her wayward speculations.

'Do you want to eat here or by the fire?'

'By the fire, it's more . . .' She stopped suddenly, stunned by what she had nearly said. She'd been about to say 'romantic', which was quite ridiculous—moonlight and roses wouldn't be romantic with him. She was overtired, that was her excuse for such a silly thought. 'More warmer,' she finished as she hastily scooped the bread into a basket to carry through to the sitting room.

'More warmer,' he mused as he picked up the two bowls of soup. 'Are you sure you're features editor of a magazine?'

Verity was glad he went ahead of her and couldn't see her burning cheeks. It was as if he knew what she had nearly said.

The soup warmed and helped to relax her. Rupert had pushed one of the massive black leather sofas closer to the fire, and it was big enough for them to keep a healthy distance between them. Just in case he thought of putting that options remark to the test.

He tossed her an orange from a bowl on the sideboard and sat down again, peeling his and tossing the skin into the blazing fire.

'Dessert. I'm not much of a cook, so I'm afraid you'll have to fend for yourself while you're here.'

While you're here, his voice echoed inside her. 'Wh...what do you mean?' It sounded as if he was expecting her to stay, and not just for the night.

'What I say. I came here for solitude, but if you keep yourself to yourself we shouldn't have a problem. I can't be doing with worrying about when and what you eat.' He turned and his eyes, smoky grey now, raked her up and down. 'Though you look as if someone should be worrying about your health.'

Verity shifted uncomfortably. She was slim, probably thin after that bout of flu, but healthwise she was A-OK.

'It's only for tonight,' she told him, 'so you don't have to worry.' Worry—who did he think he was fooling? He wouldn't even put her mind at ease over Stuart, let alone show genuine concern for her health.

'You don't have to go.'

The suggestion was so unexpected that she swivelled to look at him. He'd finished his orange and his arm had crept along the back of the sofa, not nearly close enough to have her worried but something certainly had stirred her awareness. She was being over-dramatic. So he'd touched her hair, teased her with that options remark, certainly nothing she couldn't handle, so why was she so wary of him?

'No, I can't stay. I want to find out what's going on, and you're not going to tell me, are you?'

He shook his dark head and the absurd thought passed through her mind that if she did stay she might be able to persuade him to be a bit more forthcoming. Little chance, though. He seemed a pretty determined sort of specimen.

'I know you don't want to talk about it,' she went on, 'but at least you could tell me what you meant by Stuart being perhaps more subtle than you expected.'

He seemed to mull that over in his mind as he stared into the flaming fire, and then he turned his face back to her. 'It just occurred to me that if you weren't in on this scheme then perhaps Stuart was trying the softly-softly approach.'

'What do you mean?' Verity hoped she wasn't sounding too naïve, but she really didn't get the point.

'The dinner party didn't work, nor did that contrived meeting in the restaurant. I know how desperate your cousin is to get us together. This was his last resort. Put two people of the opposite sex together in an isolated environment, far enough from home for both of them to think twice about flight, and the inevitable will happen—an affair.'

Verity wanted to laugh hysterically. 'Are you out of your mind? We didn't get on before, so we're hardly going to indulge in a raging affair just because we're away from home!' She tore at the peel of the orange she had nearly squeezed the life from as they had talked. 'That's a ridiculous suggestion!'

'So how do you explain both of us being here at the same time, and this place just happening to belong to a friend of Stuart's? No coincidence, Verity. It was his belief that we'd get together intimately, and I don't mean sharing the household chores.'

Horrified, she tossed the uneaten orange into the pit of the fire and shakily stood up.

'Said like that, it's an appalling suggestion.'

'I fear it's the truth,' he told her calmly.

'I fear it's not!' she husked heatedly. 'And how dare you believe that I'm capable of that? You might have shaky morals, but mine are intact.'

'Somebody obviously thinks yours are unstable enough for an affair, otherwise why pitch us together this way?'

Verity's blood was swiftly coming to the boil. Not normally prone to violence, she felt very inclined to slap his head.

'Sit down, Verity,' he calmly ordered. 'And don't be mad with me. *I'm* not suggesting your morals are weak——'

'But you're suggesting Stuart thinks they are?'

'I don't know what he was thinking for sure. I'm only offering up some suppositions. You know him better. What do you believe?'

Verity slumped back down on to the sofa and covered her face with her hands. 'I don't know; I don't know what to believe any more. All the time I thought he was being kind and thoughtful and caring towards me because of Mike's death——'

'Who's Mike?'

Verity uncovered her face and stared into the fire. 'He was my boyfriend, and it was a complex affair and I won't bore you with the details, but he died tragically in a car crash about six months ago. We'd had a row just before he'd driven off and I suppose people felt sorry for me and believed I blamed myself, which I didn't,' she added quickly. 'Stuart thought it his duty to pair me off with a replacement as quick as possible. I thought that was the idea with the dinner party and then the restaurant, just a matchmaking attempt to get me back on my feet.' She faced him and looked into his eyes. 'But... but you seem to think it something more sinister.'

He didn't speak for a long while, and then he said softly, 'I'm sorry, this must be very painful for you.'

'I can cope,' she murmured bravely, tilting her chin defiantly.

'Prove it, then,' he suggested with intrigue.

The flames from the fire were reflected in his eyes and they didn't look half so cold and penetrating, just smoky and mysterious now.

'How?' she asked, her eyes violet and bright with curiosity.

'Stay.'

'For... for what reason?'

'To get on with your work and to prove to your cousin that you aren't the easily seduced woman he thinks you are.'

'He doesn't think that!' Verity shot back hotly. 'He knows me better than that. If he thought I was willing to bed you so easily he would have told me why, got me to go along with this so-called seduction plan to get your damned advertising for him you so hotly believe in.'

'Then the man is an even bigger bastard than I thought,' he drawled dangerously.

Flame burned in Verity's eyes and it had nothing to do with the fire. 'I've had just about enough of this! What the hell have you got against him?'

'Until today, not a lot. Now I see him for the greedy, grasping, selfish bastard that he undoubtedly is.'

Verity tried to get up again, but this time Rupert clasped her tightly by the wrist and held her in place. 'Think about it, just sit still for a couple of minutes and think about it. Your boyfriend is dead. I don't know how deeply you cared about him and I don't want to know, but whatever, it was a relationship and he's gone and it's left you vulnerable. Your loving cousin is very likely working on that vulnerability.'

'How can he be?' she protested.

'He's arranged for us to spend a considerable time together. You're here for a month, me much the same time: long enough for something to develop between us, long enough for temptation to bite into us, long enough to fall in love.'

His voice was soft and low as he spoke, and Verity's heart raced so painfully that it hurt. She couldn't imagine for a minute being in love with him. They were poles apart.

'Love?' she croaked in disbelief. 'We don't even like each other!'

'It's a good start, so the romantics would have us believe.'

'Fantasy with no bearing on true life,' she retorted, 'but that isn't the point. Speaking hypothetically, of course, supposing for a mad moment we were to succumb to temptation and have this affair you seem so ridiculously preoccupied with. How would that help my cousin and my boss?'

'I'm not familiar with the workings of the demented mind,' he grated sardonically, 'but there are two possibilities: blackmail after the event, not for money but for my advertising, although in this day and age not really worth the consideration. The other possibility is even more ludicrous: marriage.'

'Marriage!' Verity exhaled. She shook her head in wonderment at this man's soaring imagination.

'You and I married would be a very acceptable situation for the two of them.'

Verity was speechless. Her mouth dropped open and she stared at him blindly.

'Indeed, the more I think about it, the more I come to believe that that is your cousin's very intention.' His lips tightened. 'Don't look so shocked. I would be a part of your family if we were to be married and I'd be a heel if I didn't give my cousin-in-law my business. It would snowball too. Alan Sargeant is part of the family as well; he would undoubtedly expect some favours.'

Verity remembered an odd remark Alan had made when he had suggested this trip. She had protested at first, claiming that she was well now and didn't need a change of scene, especially not so far away, but Alan had been so persuausive, and when eventually she had capitulated and told him she could get the wedding book together in that time he had said he was sure she could perform miracles and mysteriously added 'For everyone's sake'. She'd thought little of it at the time. Was this indeed a conspiracy? Did those two creeps expect her and Rupert to fall in love, possibly marry...? It was too despicable...too horrible for words!

'That's only your interpretation of things,' she bit out. 'They wouldn't do that to me, they just wouldn't!'

He said slowly and levelly, 'I'm just offering you a reason for this, Verity, the only one I can come up with, I'm afraid. The only way you'll find out the truth is by asking your cousin and hoping he gives you an honest answer. But don't be too harsh on him——'

'Harsh!' Verity flamed. 'This is embarrassing and unforgivable! That's if it's true, of course!' She had a feeling it was, though. It was fantastic, but the only explanation for such subterfuge.

'You said your boyfriend had died; perhaps your cousin genuinely wants to see you settled with someone else.'

'And do himself some good too!' she retorted bitterly. She raked her fingers through her hair and let out a ragged moan. Stuart had known that her and Mike's relationship was breaking up but he cared for her and had tried so hard to make it all right for her after Mike's death, but this...this went beyond the boundaries of caring. This would benefit him more than anyone. Of course, it wasn't going to happen, but it left a very sour taste in her mouth.

'I'm sorry,' she said, 'sorry to have subjected you to all this. You're right, this is a family matter and it has nothing to do with you.' She raised her chin proudly. 'I couldn't possibly stay now. I'll leave first thing in the morning.'

'I thought you came here to work.'

'Work!' she spluttered. 'I'm beginning to think the wedding book was just a thin excuse to get me out here. It's been hanging around long enough. To hell with it! I won't do it!'

'You might lose your job over it,' Rupert suggested.

'Job? I won't have a job by the time I've finished telling Alan Sargeant exactly what I think of him.'

'Do you think all this is worth falling out with him over?'

Verity gazed at him incredulously. 'I have some pride, you know!'

'Pride doesn't pay the bills; nor does stubbornness.'

'This has nothing to do with being stubborn. I don't like being used——'

'You haven't been yet,' he interjected reasonably. 'Nothing has happened and it won't if you don't want it to.' He held her eyes, and as she stared at him she realised that he was trying to make it easier for her—and himself of course. He wanted no involvement with her and she wanted even less with him, but he was certainly trying to make her feel better about it.

'What are you trying to say? That I should brave it out?'

He gave a nonchalant shrug. 'I'm willing to.'

'What, stay here together, live together?' she breathed.

'We wouldn't be living together in the sense that your cousin and your boss hope. We'd be living under the same roof, that's all. Providing you keep yourself to yourself, I don't see a problem arising. We both have enough to occupy ourselves with; in fact, we could get away with not catching sight of each other for a month. This place is big enough for that. Are you big enough to give it a try?'

Verity slumped back into the sofa. She wasn't sure, she wasn't at all sure it would work, but for the life of her she didn't know why she had any doubts.

'Stuart and Alan would be sick as parrots if their plan didn't work,' she murmured at last, staring into the fire.

'That's one way of looking at it.'

She gave him a very small smile. 'Revenge, you mean? Stick it out and show that neither of us can be manipulated? I'll go back with my wedding book completed——'

'And your honour intact,' he added with a wry look.

Her smile widened. 'My honour intact,' she echoed. 'Yours too.'

He smiled with her and stretched and then got up. 'While you mull that over I'll make us some coffee, but rest assured, it will be the last I make for you. If this is going to work we each do our own thing.'

'Perhaps we ought to start tonight instead of to-morrow.' As soon as she said it she realised that it was almost an agreement that she would stay.

'No, stay where you are, you're tired. Sugar in your coffee?'

She nodded, and as he moved away she closed her eyes. Yes, she was tired, too tired to make a decision. At this very moment in time she never wanted to see her cousin or Alan again for as long as she lived. She would give in her notice, of course. No way could she work for *Looks Healthy* any more. But Rupert Scott had a point—why give those bastards the satisfaction that their plot might work? And, besides, her job was a good one. Damn, she didn't know what to think, but Rupert was being surprisingly civilised about it all. Perhaps he felt sorry for her; she was certainly the innocent party in all this. She sighed. It could work; it *might* work ...

She opened her eyes suddenly and he was sitting next to her, closer than before, sipping his coffee and gazing into the dying embers of the fire. She must have dropped off for five minutes and hadn't heard him come back. Her coffee was on the stone-tiled floor next to her and she reached down to pick it up.

'Verity, there is something I think you ought to know about me before we go any further.' He turned to her, and she looked at him with slumbrous eyes. She was so tired, and if he wanted to tell her that he had some strange habits that might disturb her work she would rather hear them to-morrow or, better, not at all.

'Go ahead,' she told him sleepily. 'If you snore and grind your teeth in your sleep, I can survive it. My room is far enough away from yours for it not to keep me awake.'

He didn't smile at that but somehow, without much effort, his face seemed to darken. She remembered that her sort of humour had gone down like a lead balloon at the dinner party. He didn't find her faintly amusing. If this was to work she would have to button her lip if they came into contact at all.

He spoke at last, after draining his coffee and standing up to tower over her. 'I have a lady in my life, Verity,' he told her sombrely.

She looked up at him and for a crazy second didn't think much of his humour either. But this wasn't a joke and she wondered why she had thought it was. She also wondered why he had told her in that warning tone of voice. Was it to put her off or remind himself that he had a commitment to someone else—just in case he was tempted, as the options remark had suggested?

'So? I can live with that,' she returned coldly, surprised at the coolness of her own voice.

'Good. I'm glad,' he said flatly. 'I just thought you should know. Goodnight, Verity. Sleep well.' He turned and walked away, and she stared at the last dying embers of the fire, hearing his tread on the stone steps, the hollow sound of his bedroom door closing behind him.

Verity slowly stood up and shivered. Of course she could live with that; in fact, now she understood why he had made the suggestion that she stay. There was no fear of their having an affair here because he was already in love with someone else. Pity Stuart and Alan hadn't checked that out before arranging all this. But why, then, had he caressed her hair that way, made that very suggestive remark which had unnerved her so? She didn't know and hoped she never would. Attractive he might be; undoubtedly dangerous, though.

Sleep well, he'd said; she doubted that. Too much had happened, far too much for her to sleep at all well.

CHAPTER THREE

'TURN that damned thing off!'

Verity scrambled up from the rug on the floor where she was doing her callisthenics and pulled nervously at her pink leotard, horribly embarrassed at being caught so scantily dressed.

Rupert strode into her bedroom and snapped off the ghetto-blaster she'd found downstairs. She'd brought her exercise tapes and Walkman just in case but, finding the blaster, she'd opted to use that for ease.

'I can't have that raucous din when I'm trying to work!' he stormed furiously.

'It's not loud!' Verity protested hotly. 'How can you possibly hear it across your side of the house?'

'Because this damned house is solid stone and every sound ricochets off the walls like bullets. If you must do that ridiculous stuff, have the consideration to do it outside!'

'Outside! It's blowing a gale out there and if we're talking consideration here,' Verity fired back, 'how about you clearing up your breakfast debris after you? The kitchen looked as if a missile had hit when I went down this morning!'

Crikey! Her first morning with him and it had started with him storming into her room in that baggy old tracksuit and attacking her so unfairly. She'd had a bad night, waking at every strange sound of the night. The wind had howled, vixens had screamed, an owl had hooted on the roof and she'd been sure someone had been scraping chains across the stone floors downstairs. The place spooked her and she had been glad Rupert Scott had been within screaming distance. Now this. It wasn't going to work if he was going to be such a slob and so touchy about a little bit of noise.

His grey eyes narrowed warningly. 'Look, we agreed to do our own thing——'

'Within reason!'

'That infernal row in the morning,' he flung his hand out to the blaster, 'isn't within reason!'

'And nor is your dirty dishes littering the kitchen table!'

'That's the way I live when I'm working! Now if you don't like it, clear out and leave me in peace!' He raked his fingers through his already unruly hair and Verity wondered what work he was doing that was causing him such frustration, for if all was going well he wouldn't notice the sounds she was making.

'No way! I'm staying. If you don't like it, *you* clear out!'

They stood glaring at each other, defying each other. He was being totally unreasonable, Verity inwardly flamed. She had purposefully kept the cassette low, but how was she to know that the house acoustics were so bad? Well, she wasn't going to apologise unless he did and if he didn't do something about his washing-up...fat chance! He wasn't the sort of man to stoop to such lowly tasks.

'We'll have to compromise,' she suggested raggedly. It was the only way. Work out some sort of system.

'I'll compromise over nothing!'

'Go hang yourself, then!' Verity shouted furiously at his stubborn arrogance. 'If you're not prepared to bend a little nor am I, apart from my exercise routine, that is!' she added pointedly. With one smart, calculated movement she sprang towards the blaster to snap it back on.

Rupert Scott's reactions were so quick that Verity recoiled back in horror. He grasped her wrist and swung it away from the blaster and pulled her unexpectedly into his arms.

His mouth locked over hers and she was so stunned that she couldn't stop what followed, his lips crushing hers, his tongue easing between her clenched teeth, his arms folding around her body so tightly that she could scarcely catch her breath. She was shocked, too shocked to resist or begin to understand the fierceness of his body hard against hers. She felt his every muscle mould against her, and as his arms slid down to her hips to grasp her into him she was flooded with a searing rush of sexual awareness. Her breasts fought the restricting fabric of her leotard and her pelvis melted against him. His mouth softened as if he knew what his kisses were capable of, as if he knew that the very next step was inevitable.

Verity's mouth parted to emit a small sob of protest under his lips as his hand came up to her breast and caressed the small firm mound. His fingers hardened over her aroused nipple and a sound came from deep in his throat, a terrifying sound of desire.

Verity's heart thundered at what was happening, but her head wouldn't clear enough to reason what to do about it. It simply buzzed out a need, a need that was so fierce and had been aroused so frighteningly easily. And then suddenly it was over. The contact, initially so unexpected, eased away from her, leaving her breathless, frightened and... and oddly empty.

Rupert Scott held her at arm's length and his breath came quickly, as if holding her away from him was causing him pain. His eyelids were heavy and his eyes brittle with anger. His voice was thick when he spoke. 'That wasn't very clever, was it?'

She shook her head in bewilderment. No words came to her lips because her mind was full of only one thought: the unexpected passion he had aroused in her. It had been coaxed so easily by a man she didn't even like very much. At that moment she couldn't help but think of Mike, though she didn't know why.

'Haven't you anything to say for yourself?' he said, his voice in control now.

'It wasn't my fault,' she uttered feebly, lowering her eyes so as not to meet his. She was ashamed of succumbing to that kiss when she should have known better and kicked him in the shins for taking it so daringly.

'Wasn't it?'

She shook her head. 'Don't start that again.' She pulled away from him and snatched up her robe from the bed to slide into it to cover her revealing leotard.

He stood back and watched her. 'The kiss or what?' he teased. How quickly he had regained control when she was still trembling with the shock of what had happened.

'Forget the kiss,' she husked back, 'you know what I mean. I suppose you think I did all this on purpose. Played my cassette at full blast so you would come to my bedroom and I would tempt you into seducing me for that wretched advertising contract for my cousin.'

'I didn't suppose anything of the sort but, now that you mention it, it could be a possibility.' There was mockery in his tone, a teasing mockery that irritated her.

'It isn't! I do this every morning and it isn't a sexual invitation to any passing male.' She looked across to him then, her eyes bright with determination. 'You shouldn't have stormed into my bedroom like that. I refuse to take the blame for what just happened. You were angry with me and that was my punishment, wasn't it?'

'Something like that. If I hadn't kissed you I might have killed you,' he drawled lazily.

'Huh, kiss or kill. I believe you. There are a hell of a lot of men like you around,' Verity sliced back disdainfully.

He frowned. 'Like what? Wanting to appease their frustration and anger with sex?'

Now she knew why her thoughts had spun to Mike. That kiss had reminded her of when their relationship had begun to go wrong. When she had realised she was being used.

'It's obvious your work isn't going well; that's why you're so touchy, and then you switch to punishing me for it,' she husked morosely.

'Was the kiss a punishment? I thought it was just one of those unavoidable accidents.'

'Huh, like slipping on a banana skin!' Verity retorted sarcastically. 'You don't fool me. My last boyfriend used me the same way,' she told Rupert Scott quite openly. 'When life wasn't going easy for him he turned on the sex, his way of blaming me for his own inadequacies. I think you suffer from the same syndrome. He didn't make love to me because he loved me, he just had to prove he was good at something.'

'Was he good?'

The question rattled her. The man had nearly succeeded in making love to her and now he was asking impertinent questions of her as intimately as if it had happened and they were now fully fledged lovers opening up their hearts and their pasts to each other. Well, they weren't and never would be, but she had rather asked for it by mentioning Mike that way.

'I wouldn't know,' she told him defensively. 'I'm not a whore and I don't have a vigorous sex life——'

'So you don't have anyone else to compare him with?'

She held his mocking grey eyes. 'Exactly, and if you've any ideas on supplying me with any comparisons, forget it!' she retorted hotly.

He smiled. 'I wouldn't dream of it. *If* we make love I'd like to be sure it's for the right reasons, not for tallying up the scoreboard.'

'Well, you'll never know, will you?'

'Meaning, you believe we won't make love?'

'Meaning, *if* we did you'd never know if I was chalking up a score for your performance or not!' This was the only way to handle him. Give as good as he expected her to receive. He was pushing her, mocking her, and two could play that duet.

'We might get so desperate that we wouldn't care,' he suggested in that same mocking drawl.

'Speak for yourself! I haven't any problems in that way.'

'Implying I have?'

Verity smiled sweetly at him. 'I'd say you have. You can't keep your hands off me and yet last night you felt the need to tell me you have a lady in your life. I'd say your hormones are niggling at your conscience. Well, I'm no sex therapist, so don't even think about taking what happened just now any further.'

He didn't let up on the teasing smile. 'You could be very right in your pyschoanalysis. My lady doesn't give me any ear drill any more and I find yours sexually stimulating. Keep it up, treasure, and we just might fall into the trap that's been set for us.' With that he turned and left the room.

Verity stared at the back of the door he'd closed after him. So that was a warning, was it? Keep your mouth shut and I won't make any more advances towards you! Or, keep it up and I will! What a choice! She would have to vet every word that came to her lips, and that was going to be quite a strain. But the consequences if she didn't were certainly a deterrent. No problem. She'd just keep out of his way. It was as simple as that!

Verity was cold. Even with a blanket tucked round her legs, she couldn't generate much warmth, nor could the oil-filled electric radiator she'd found in one of the other bedrooms. She'd chosen to work

in her bedroom to keep her distance from Rupert
Scott, and had set up her computer on the dressing-
table. Candice's diets and exercise routines were
spread out all over the spare bed. It wasn't the ideal
environment to work in but there was no other
choice. Downstairs was even colder.

She wondered how he was keeping warm. Better
than her, no doubt, in his cosy tracksuit and ex-
army boots.

Verity wriggled her toes to get the circulation
going and glanced at her watch. Four in the
afternoon and so far the day had not been very
productive. This morning he had ranted that he
couldn't work with the din from her cassette; now
she was finding the deathly silence equally irritating. Trouble was, she was listening out for every
sound from his quarters. Not that she was remotely
interested in what he was doing, she just hadn't
wanted to bump into him when she popped downstairs to make lunch or a cup of tea.

She slipped on a jacket and went downstairs. It
was a lot warmer outside then in, she discovered
when she let herself out of the old mill house. She
bared her face to the warmth of the sun and let out
a deep breath. She felt better already. Who was she
fooling? She sighed deeply. She didn't feel right at
all and she knew why she hadn't achieved much all
day: her thoughts had wandered down too many
leafy lanes of speculation with wretched Rupert
Scott for a companion.

That kiss hadn't been too surprising. He might
have a lady in his life but she wasn't here, and all
men were the same: the first opportunity and they
would try it on. Stuart and Alan would have known

that, being men themselves. How clever they
thought they had been, but she wasn't feeling so
clever. That kiss had shaken her for more than one
reason. Last night Rupert Scott had convinced her
they could handle the situation. Twelve hours later
he obviously couldn't, and she wondered about
herself. If he hadn't stopped, would she?

Funny, but his mouth hadn't been mean when
he had kissed her. It had turned her on. She shivered
at the memory of it and turned back from the dirt-
track lane she had been wandering aimlessly down
and headed back to the mill house.

It was then that she saw him at his bedroom
window. Tall, dark, powerfully built and very
slightly sinister in the frame of the window. He was
watching her. She lowered her violet eyes and
carried on back to the house.

'I'm going out tonight. I'll be late. Will you be
all right on your own?'

They met on the lower stairs, Verity going up to
her room with a scalding mug of tea in her hands,
and he coming down, dressed in jeans and a chunky
dark green sweater. He was freshly shaved and his
hair gleamed in some order and he smelt of cologne.

Verity stood back to let him pass. 'I'd planned
on being alone here for a month, don't forget, and
don't feel obliged to tell me you're going out for
the night. You can manifest yourself into a werewolf
and howl through the hills all night, for all I care.'
She hadn't intended to sound quite so barbed, but
nevertheless it had come out that way.

'I wasn't suggesting you did care, Verity,' he said
solemnly. 'I just wanted to know if you'll be all

right on your own. The house is probably more isolated than you expected and——'

'And I'm not an easily scared child,' she told him sweetly. 'I'm not afraid of the dark or things that go bump in the night, so off you go.'

She carried on up the stairs, thinking what a little liar she was. Last night, with a hulk in the house, she'd been scared. Tonight could be worse; she would be totally alone. She hoped he didn't plan on staying out all the night.

Later she lay in bed, waiting, listening to every creak and groan of the old house. She knew she wouldn't sleep till he was home. The evening had been long and unnerving *and* annoying. So they had agreed to do their own thing, but he might have lit the fire for her before he'd gone out. She'd struggled for what seemed like hours to get the kindling going, and then the big olive logs had refused to ignite and in a temper she had abandoned it and retired to her room to work. Cold had driven her into bed at around eleven, and now at twelve he still wasn't home!

'You're beginning to think like a wife,' she murmured to herself. She rolled on to her stomach and buried her face in the pillow. Was his lady his wife? No, he would have said. A wife would have been an even bigger deterrent, but perhaps that lady was going to be his wife and that wouldn't have stopped him kissing her this morning. He'd been here a week already and a man had needs . . . Stop it!

Verity sat up, a cold sweat misting her brow, one of the after-effects of that bout of flu. A cup of hot tea usually put her to rights. She swung her long legs out of the bed and reached for the bedside light. Nothing happened when she flicked the switch. Nothing happened when she tried the main light by the door. Mild panic built up to mania as she lurched across the pitch-dark room and hauled open the curtains at the window. No moon. No light; nothing but the terrifying darkness.

'Don't panic!' she breathed, taking great gulps of air to calm herself. 'There are matches down by the fireplace and candles in the kitchen larder. All you have to do is get downstairs without breaking your neck and find them. Easy.'

Verity lost her footing on the uneven steps the last flight into the sitting-room. She grazed her knees as she pitched forward on to the cold stone floor and bit back tears of frustration at her own stupidity. She should have stayed in bed till day-light—any sensible person would have done that instead of risking life and limb in an unfamiliar setting. She struggled to her feet and touched her knees and let out a cry of pain.

'What the...?'

Verity stiffened in fright, heard the squeak of leather and was aware of movement close by. Someone was in the room!

'Rupert?' Her cry reached the volume of a hysterical scream and echoed terrifyingly loudly in the vast room.

'I'm here; it's OK, I'm here.'

She heard a muffled curse as his foot came in painful contact with the edge of the sofa and then she felt him grip her shoulders, and another cry, this time of relief, tore from her throat as she threw herself into his arms.

Her fingers clawed at his warm, comforting sweater and then wrapped frantically around his neck. Her whole body went into a spasm of violent shaking and, teetering on her toes, she pressed her cold wet cheek to his for comfort.

He held her tightly, securely, his warm mouth brushing her forehead. 'It's all right. There's nothing to be afraid of,' he soothed.

'There's no light,' she whimpered like a small child.

He laughed softly against her. 'I know. The whole village is out. I came back right away. You're terrified.' His hand came up to touch her cheek. She was hot now. 'You've a fever. How old are you?'

Her brow puckered into a frown. 'Twenty-four.'

'Not the menopause, then?'

His attempt at humour brought her down to earth with a bump. He was still holding her tightly with one arm, and she ... she was still clinging to him like some poor demented soul.

'No, just the after-effects of some antibiotics I've been taking.' She pulled out of his arms in embarrassment. Thank God he couldn't see her face; it was probably scarlet and blotchy, with little to do with the fever. She had thrown herself at him in sheer relief, and he probably thought the worst.

'I'm sorry,' she blurted, 'sorry for throwing myself at you. I was a bit scared and then I fell down the steps.'

'Are you hurt?' He didn't give her a chance to answer but swept her up into his arms and deposited her on to the leather sofa in front of the fireplace. It felt warm through the thin satin of her nightdress, and she supposed he had been lying here in the darkness. The thought unsettled her, more so when he scooped a fleecy blanket round her, and that was warm too. Had he been sleeping here?

'I didn't hear you come in.' She bit her lip; that sounded as if she had been listening out for him. She had, but... 'Rupert?'

His voice called back from the kitchen. 'I'm just getting some candles and firelighters.'

Seconds later he was back with both. 'You must have cat's eyes to see your way around,' Verity remarked.

He lit the candle and placed it on the stone hearth. The small flame momentarily highlighted fatigue in his face. 'I've been here longer than you; I'm used to the place—used to power cuts too.'

'Why didn't you go up to your room, then? You were sleeping down here, weren't you?'

'Does it matter where I sleep?' He gave his attention to the fire.

'Not really, but you look shattered, and bed is the place to sleep.'

'And a place to make love.'

'Sofas make good substitutes too.' She didn't know why she'd said that.

'Is that an offer?'

She gave a small nervous laugh and wished she'd thought before speaking. She tightened the blanket around her. 'No, it wasn't and you know it.'

'I know nothing of the sort. I hardly know you enough to hazard a guess at what's going through your mind.'

'I can see that in future I'll have to be very careful what I say to you.'

'Your energies would be better employed with keeping out of my way altogether,' he said drily.

'Yeah, not so easy when you burst into my bedroom and lurk around down here, waiting for me to fall downstairs.' She tried to inject some light-heartedness into that statement. He really could be quite a sombre and humourless man when he wanted to be, which she thought on reflection was probably most of the time.

'It seems to me you put yourself into these situations on purpose, and I wasn't lurking down here like a crazed psychopath waiting to pounce on you. What were you doing down here anyway?'

The fire suddenly blazed brightly and he sat back on his haunches, staring into the flames. Verity watched him, suppressing yet another sigh. Would he ever believe she wasn't after his body?

'I couldn't sleep, and don't read anything into that. I decided to make some tea, but when I tried the lights there was nothing. I remembered there were candles down here and, well, you know the rest.'

He turned suddenly and looked at her. 'When you threw yourself into my arms you were terrified.'

'Well, wouldn't you be?' she retorted hotly. 'I thought I was alone in the house with no power, and I'd just fallen down the stairs and then I heard this sound. You could have been that crazed psychopath, for all I knew.'

'And you were so relieved it was me——'

'I threw myself into your arms,' she finished for him. 'Very understandable in the circumstances, I'd say—after all, I am a woman.'

'Yes, I suppose so,' he conceded.

'What, suppose I'm a woman?'

He half smiled. 'No doubt in my mind about that, but I meant I suppose it's understandable that you threw yourself into my arms.'

'Oh, I suppose you're well used to it!'

'Thanks for the compliment.'

'I was being sarcastic.'

He turned back to the fire. 'So was I,' he murmured.

Verity's lips thinned with annoyance. 'You're quite a cool cookie, aren't you? I can't imagine you having a lady in your life. I get the distinct impression you don't like them very much.'

'I don't, not since...' He positioned more logs on the fire and she wondered why he didn't finish what he was saying. 'I usually manage quite successfully to ward off preying females,' he went on, 'but some are more persistent then others.'

His words were so loaded that she knew instinctively that he wasn't referring to *his* lady but her!

'May I remind you that I'm not interested in you in any shape, size or form? I've already had a disastrous relationship with one of your species, and I'm not looking for trouble a second time around.'

'Man-hater, are you? That really surprises me.'

From here she could quite easily place her foot between his shoulder-blades and pitch him head first into the fire, but he really wasn't worth the trouble and the mess.

'I must admit to a certain loathing for a certain type—yours. You remind me of my deceased boy-friend, as it happens. He was a miserable, sarcastic moody too.'

He took that, right in the back of the head, and didn't even flinch at her insult, though she had a strong feeling it had hit home. Remorse seized her. He wasn't Mike and to compare the two had been unjust.

'I'm sorry,' she said. 'I shouldn't have said that.'

'Apology accepted,' he said quietly.

He stood up and turned towards her and she wondered if he *had* accepted it. His eyes were un-fathomable, his jawline surprisingly tense. She *had* hurt him.

'Any injuries?' he asked.

Her thoughts were diverted by his enquiry and she pulled the blanket off her legs and was dis-mayed to see that her nightie had risen up over her thighs. She pulled it down quickly but not quick enough for him not to have had a good eyeful of most of her long slim legs. The expression on his face gave nothing away, but nevertheless Verity felt hot with shame.

'Only my knees,' she husked. Both were grazed and one quite swollen and already blue. They didn't hurt any more, so she supposed that there was no structural damage.

'They need bathing,' Rupert told her quietly. 'The floor here isn't too clean.'

He went back to the kitchen before Verity could retaliate by retorting, 'Whose fault's that?'

She leaned back and waited for his return and wished with all her heart she hadn't ventured out of bed—in fact, she wished she'd never come to Spain in the first place. It wasn't working out well at all. But what were her prospects of going back, say, tomorrow? She'd have no job, and a fiery row with her cousin was on the cards, not that she couldn't handle that. They'd practically grown up together and she knew his weaknesses—money and Angie. Though she didn't dislike Angie, she didn't exactly like her either. Angie was a name-dropper, a social climber, the sort of woman who would push her husband to his limits to get the material acquisitions she seemed to thrive on—their enormous house in Barnet, the Porsche, the holidays in Mexico. Verity was beginning to think this very situation was probably engineered by her! She would have to find out.

'You said there's a phone in the village; is it easy to find?' she asked him when he came back with a first-aid kit and a couple of glasses. She wondered what the glasses were for.

'There's a public call box in the plaza, but I'd advise you to use the phone in the Bar Especho. It's metred, so you can pay for it after. There's nothing more offputting than feeding a coin box. I presume you want to phone home.'

'No one at home to call,' she told him, watching as he went to the sideboard and took out a bottle of dubious-looking Spanish brandy. 'I live alone in London. My parents are divorced. My mother lives in Canada with her new husband and my father's a doctor in South Africa and lives with his stethoscope.'

He looked grim. 'I get the picture. I suppose that contributed to the break-up of the marriage.'

'My father's a workaholic and always has been. I don't even know how they got together long enough to produce me.'

He smiled at that and Verity thought he ought to do it more often: it suited him, creased his face in an endearing way. He poured two brandies, put them down on the floor by the sofa, knelt in front of her and clicked open the first-aid box.

'I couldn't boil any water, I'm afraid, no electricity, but there's antiseptic lotion in here. Can you suffer the pain?' He took out cotton wool and up-ended the bottle to soak it.

Verity realised that he intended to deal with it himself. Her heart contracted at the thought. If she let him he might think it another come-on; if she didn't he'd think any physical contact would be disturbing to her. Strange, but it would. Already she was tensing in anticipation. He dabbed at the graze.

'Ouch,' she cried, 'that stings!'

'Don't be such a baby, it's hardly a scratch. Have a sip of brandy if you're so squeamish.' He reached down to the glass and handed it to her.

'So that's what it's for, to deaden the pain.' She took a sip and shuddered and took another sip.

'Partly. I also thought it might knock you out for the night and we both might get some peace,' he told her drily.

'Very funny!' She gritted her teeth as he dabbed at the other graze, then she gritted every nerve-ending in her body as he gripped her thigh above her knee to hold her still. The effect on her senses was electrifying. She forgot the stinging pain of her knee and the stinging pain of the brandy on her throat. There was only one sensation hurtling through her: his touch on her warm thigh. It was more of a grip than a touch, but the thought of it softening to a sensuous caress had her temperature soaring. No, that's not possible, she reasoned. I must be in shock!

'I think that's good enough,' he murmured, and looked up at her. 'Verity, are you all right?' He took the glass from her clenched fingers and put it down on the floor.

She swallowed, hard. No, she wasn't. She felt sick at what her body was screaming out to her, that she *wanted* his touch to soften, she *wanted* him to caress her intimately. So this morning hadn't been a temporary aberration of her mind. He had aroused her and could so easily do so again, and she didn't really know what she would do if he did.

She held his eyes painfully, and because he didn't take his hand away she knew he knew what she was thinking. His eyes were impenetrable but that mean mouth had softened.

The touch lightened and she thought he was going to pull away, and then very slowly he lowered his head to her thigh. His lips brushed her silky flesh causing a rush of fiery blood to her head, so overwhelmingly that she nearly cried out. His lips lingered, sensuously, then moved higher up her thighs.

'No,' she breathed raggedly, and her hands went jerkily to his head. His hair was soft and unexpectedly silky under her fingers and she wanted to tear at it to hurt him, but instead they coiled into its thickness, drawing him into her. A low groan of pain came to his throat and his hands slid her satin nightie higher and higher, trailing warm, sensuous kisses over her newly exposed skin.

'Rupert, please, don't...'

His head came up at her strangled plea, and as their eyes locked she saw such deep anger that her heart thudded furiously at the injustice of it all.

'Don't look at me like that,' she breathed, pulling her nightie down and trying to get up. 'I'm the one who should be damned furious. How dare you do that to me?'

'Arouse you?' he cried, standing up. 'Have the bloody decency to admit your sexuality instead of trying to hide it with soft, puritanical pleas of no! You want me as much as I want you, so quit the baby-talk.'

She struggled to her feet and faced him angrily. 'Well, our good resolutions didn't last long, did they? How long have we been together in this house...twenty-four, thirty-six, forty-eight hours— oh, who the devil is counting?' Her mind seemed to snap, and furiously she started to unbutton the tiny glass buttons at her breast. 'Let's get it over with now, then perhaps we can both get on with our lives!'

His hands locked over hers, so fiercely that she bit her lower lip. Tears welled in her eyes, blinding her to the sudden softening of his. Her head suddenly cleared and she realised what she had done, and her whole body stiffened with horror and shame. Slowly he drew her into his arms and held her tenderly.

'You didn't mean that, did you?' he breathed into her hair.

'Of course not, you bastard,' she sobbed, so deeply ashamed that she wanted to die. 'Brandy makes me mad as Hades!'

She felt him laugh in her hair and slowly he lifted her chin and lowered his lips to hers. No kiss of passion but one of sweet tenderness, and when it was over he said poignantly, 'Go to bed, Verity, the time isn't right for us yet.'

She didn't question that remark but simply drew away from him without looking at him. As she bent down to pick up the candle to light her way up to bed she knew that something had started, something that might be hard to stop.

Upstairs, confused and weary, she slid back into bed and lay with her eyes wide open. That *something* loomed black and menacing in her mind, blinding her to any sort of coherent thinking. Rupert Scott's lady wasn't much of a deterrent to either of them at the moment, and that was a dangerous thought, even more dangerous than the idea that that awful man was having a devastating effect on her emotional needs. Tonight she had wanted him to love her, or did she just want him to make love to her?

Verity pulled the sheet around her face and bit her lip to stop the tears. She had never felt more lonely and desolate in her life before.

CHAPTER FOUR

So now Verity knew why Stuart was so desperate for Rupert Scott's advertising package.

She had let a week pass before making the call to her cousin and probably wouldn't have made it at all if her work had been going well, but it wasn't, and she thought her concern for her cousin was causing the block. It certainly wasn't anything to do with Rupert Scott. She'd convinced herself that vulnerability was a great deceiver of true feelings. She didn't want him—the idea was ridiculous. She was lonely and probably a bit depressed after her illness and that accounted for her silly behaviour on the night of the power cut. Rupert was coping; why couldn't she?

He was being very considerate. No more dirty dishes left lying around; no more sexual overtures; in fact, no contact whatsoever. It it weren't for the diminishing pile of tins in the larder Verity would swear she was the only person occupying El Molino.

For that she should be grateful, but she wasn't. Trying to keep out of his way was getting her down and she was going to have it out with him—that and what Stuart had just told her on the phone.

He was in the kitchen making himself a coffee when she returned from the village, and for that she *was* grateful. He would undoubtedly take it the wrong way if she'd burst into his bedroom.

She plonked the shopping on the table and faced him. 'I've just been to the village and spoken to Stuart on the phone.'

'Was that the first time?' he asked, taking another mug from the cupboard. 'Coffee?'

She nodded. He looked drained and she wondered what he was working on that had kept him locked away for so long. 'Yes. To be honest, I was afraid too call sooner but...well, my work's not going very well and I think I was too preoccupied with wondering at all you had hinted at. Now I know and...and I'm begging you to reconsider, Rupert...'

His eyes blazed suddenly. 'Did he put you up to this?'

'No, he didn't, and after I'd finished with him he wouldn't have dared.' She hadn't gone for the jugular straight away but it was a measure of her cousin's despair when he had broken down almost as soon as she had mentioned Rupert Scott. *Then* she had let rip.

'He's going broke, Rupert, as well you know. His agency is struggling and the banks are calling in his loans and he'll lose his house——'

'Tell his wife to cut down on her silk stockings, then!' he interrupted brutally.

Verity slumped down into a chair and took the coffee he offered. She knew he was right. Angie and her extravagances were bleeding Stuart dry.

'It's not as simple as that,' she murmured. 'He's heavily in debt and your advertising would——' His grip on her shoulder stilled her.

'Listen to me, Verity, because I'm not going to repeat myself.' His voice was low and deliberately pitched so sternly that she knew he meant every word. 'I'm not responsible for your cousin's debts or for the high standard of living that's led him into so much trouble. I've already told you he's not capable of handling my work and nothing you say will change my mind. I don't want him. I don't want Alan Sargeant and I don't want you here if you are going to hassle me every five minutes!'

'I haven't seen you for a week!' she blurted, tempted to sink her teeth into his hand, which was brushing her neck. 'I've only just found out about it and I'm just asking you to give him a chance. Let him do a projection for you... What the hell are you doing?' Suddenly she was being hauled to her feet.

'I'm projecting *you* up to your bedroom, and don't get any fancy ideas that I'm going to bed you. You're going to pack——'

'All right! All right!' Verity cried, twisting so violently in his grip that he let go. 'I won't mention it again!'

He waved a threatening forefinger at her. 'If you do, beware! Remember what happened last time I nearly lost my temper.'

'Kiss or kill,' she murmured, watching him through thick lashes, hating herself for the heat that pulsed through her at the reminder. She rubbed her shoulders where he had gripped them so ferociously.

'Did I hurt you?'

'Some chance! But, seeing as you think you're some sort of commando, do something about this.' She pulled a chicken out from the bag on the table. A *whole* chicken. 'I didn't know how to ask them to top and tail it, and for all I know its insides are still intact.'

He stared at it, lying white and lifeless on the kitchen table, its head to one side, its feet stiff and pointing skyward. 'You want *me* to disembowel it?' He was so aghast that she thought he might have a phobia about such things, but it was more than likely that it was because he thought it beneath him.

'I...I can't,' she murmured. She *did* have a phobia.

'Why buy the damned thing, then?' he shot back.

'I...' Verity shrugged and sat down to drink her coffee. 'I thought I'd cook it—for us,' she added tentatively. 'And don't take that the wrong way,' she blurted quickly as his brow furrowed. 'It isn't an attempt to win you over, it's just that...'

'What?' he urged when she didn't go on.

She stared into her coffee, wishing she hadn't started this. Then she braved herself to look up at him. 'It's just that...I think this is all ridiculous. Us, living like this, avoiding each other. You've been very good this week, clearing up after yourself, making an effort for me. I thought...I thought I'd make an effort too. Cook us a meal——'

'Very dangerous,' he breathed raggedly.

'I'm not that bad a cook,' she tried to joke, and he actually smiled, if thinly.

'You know what I mean,' he said before going to the kitchen drawer and taking out a lethal-looking knife. Verity closed her eyes as he tackled the head and feet of the chicken. She opened them when it was all over.

'Yes, I do know what you mean,' she murmured, 'and I've given it a lot of thought.'

'Have you, now?' he drawled sarcastically, and plunged his hand into the dark interior of the corpse on the table.

'Yes, and I think that we're both being very silly about the whole thing.'

'And what exactly is "the whole thing"?'

'You're not making it very easy for me,' she bleated, studying her coffee once again as he cleaned out the chicken and deposited it into a roasting dish. She waited till he'd washed his hands before going on. 'You've been avoiding me all week.'

'That was the original plan,' he told her drily, leaning back against the work-surface to drink his coffee.

'Well, I think it's silly and childish. We are adults——'

'Precisely.'

Verity let out a long sigh. She wasn't making much headway. She was trying to clear the air and he wasn't helping one bit. 'I didn't like the way you said that,' she told him, 'as if you thought being adults was the whole problem.'

'Isn't it? If we were both children we could handle this situation quite easily. Children don't have the sort of needs we've already displayed to each other. What exactly do you want of me, Verity?'

'Nothing!' Her eyes widened plaintively. 'It's just that I'm not working very well and . . . and I think it's because . . .'

'Because you want me?' he suggested with such devastating honesty that Verity recoiled with the shock of it.

'No!' she cried, gripping the mug of coffee so tightly that she nearly crushed it. 'I don't want you! I'm just finding avoiding you a bloody nuisance!' she flamed. 'If I want a cup of coffee or something to eat I'm having to creep around like some damned fugitive. Oh, to hell with you!' She stood up and went to leave the kitchen, but he caught her arm and swung her back.

He held her at arm's length but not far enough for her not to be shaken by every *frisson* of awareness that sizzled between them. She had made a mistake, a terrible mistake in bringing this up, because he was misinterpreting her motives.

'You're taking this all the wrong way,' she told him stiffly. 'I just wanted to make my life easier. I can't work with this tension between us and it has nothing to do with what you're thinking.'

'Funny that it took you a week to come to that conclusion,' he bit out. 'Funny that you should bring it up after talking to your cousin.'

Verity wrenched her arms from his grasp. 'I could have put money on you thinking that!' she cried furiously. 'Let's get one thing straight: I'm looking after number one, *my* needs, *my* feelings. Yes, I'm concerned about my cousin's well-being, but whatever you think I'm not trying to soften you up for his sake. I'm doing it for *me*! I can't work because I'm terrified of bumping in to you and rubbing you up the wrong way. I bought that chicken for us because I'm fed up with eating alone ... not having anyone to talk to ...'

He gripped her arms again but not half so fiercely. 'When you first came here you expected to be alone.'

'But I'm not!' she sparked back. 'It's different now. I could have coped with being alone somehow but the fact is, you *are* here!'

'That doesn't make sense.'

'Nothing makes sense,' she breathed dramatically. 'I'm just trying to make the best of a bad situation.'

'And your best is cooking chicken for me tonight, knowing what that might lead to?' The depth of meaning in his eyes said it all but she made out that she didn't know anyway.

'Like what?'

'Don't sound so damned naïve. Any enforced intimacy, even over a meal, is very dangerous, Verity, as well you know.'

'No, no, I didn't mean——'

'Like hell you didn't mean,' he grated angrily, his grip tightening. 'Don't be so damned selfish, Verity. All I've heard from you so far is *your* needs, *your* feelings. What about mine?'

'Yours?' she uttered in a hushed whisper.

'Yes, mine!'

He suddenly lowered his head and took her mouth, pulling her so firmly against him that escape was impossible. The pressure of his mouth was crushing, so fierce that her heart leapt with fear, and then slowly, slowly the fear evaporated, exposing all her raw nerve-endings, exposing them to that pressing need deep inside her. The need for someone to hold her and make her forget, someone to love her and make her feel whole again.

The kiss softened into a tempting caress of her sensitive lips, easing away her resistance till she wanted more and more. His arms eased around her, drawing her into his power, running down her body and then crushing her into his sexuality. There was no doubt in her mind of his need at that moment, and how easy to admit to her own. How easy to make love with him, here, now, for the duration of their stay together. And then, after, to return to her empty life and him to return to his lady.

She pulled out from his arms, turned her face up to his and was shocked at the smoky depths of desire in his eyes.

'I don't...don't understand,' she breathed raggedly. 'You want me——'

'Yes, I want you. Why is that so difficult to understand?' he husked, letting his hands drop to his sides.

'You call me selfish,' she whispered defensively, 'but what you are doing is doubly selfish and cruel. Not to me—I'm nothing in your life but a prospective fill-in while you're away from your lady——'

'You object to that?'

Verity's eyes narrowed angrily. 'With every defence in my body,' she breathed heatedly. 'You're despicable, a user——'

'So we're two of a kind!' His voice was terse and punishing.

Verity's mouth dropped open with shock and then snapped shut, only long enough for her wits to rampage wildly. 'Back to Stuart again, eh? You just don't give up, do you?'

'That's where you're very wrong, treasure. You're the one to keep ramming your damned cousin down my throat. At this moment in time Stuart doesn't warrant a mention, because this is between *us* from now on. Don't accuse me of being a user when you're doing the same thing.'

'Oh, yeah, and how do you make that out?'

'Quite simply!' That damned accusing finger of his came up again and Verity wanted to snap it off in fury. 'You have needs, as you so rightly stated, and for God's sake don't come on with that lonely tack again. A cosy dinner for two and a cosy chat, like hell, Verity. Be honest and admit you want the same as me, some warmth, some human contact, some bloody body-bonding!'

'No——'

'Yes!' Rupert insisted so decisively that Verity shuddered with the force of it. She couldn't take his blatant honesty and turned her back on it.

'And that's no way out,' he grated impatiently. 'Face me, Verity, and be honest with me and yourself.'

She swung back at that, her eyes wide with defiance. 'I was being honest with you. I admitted that I'm fed up with having no one to talk to and eating alone, but that isn't enough for you, is it? You want the whole package, my body!'

'What did you expect? Do you really believe it possible that we could live together this way and not end up making love to each other?'

'You said we could.'

'I thought we might, but circumstances change.'

'Nothing's changed!'

'Everything's changed. We want each other——'

Verity shook her head. 'No, you want me! That's the difference!'

'Hypocrite!'

Her anger welled inside her. 'You're being the damned hypocrite. You're the one with someone in your life and you're willing to risk that relationship with a bit on the side—me!'

'And you're trying to lay ghosts. Don't think you fool me with all that rubbish about wanting someone to talk to and being civilised enough to cope with this situation. We want the same thing, Verity: each other. I don't know what you went through with your former boyfriend but whatever it is it's left you with a yawning gap in your life——'

'A gap you think you can fill by making love to me?' she exploded. 'Don't kid yourself, Rupert Scott, you can't do anything for me that another man couldn't!'

'But there isn't any other man available at the moment,' he told her drily.

'And there isn't another woman available for you at the moment either,' she retorted venomously. 'That's why you're so despicable and such a user. I don't have anyone in my life but you have and she isn't here, and you only want me because you miss her!'

Tears burned feverishly in her eyes, tears of anger and dismay at his brutality. But why shed tears over him? And then it hit her why she so desperately wanted to cry: that old vulnerability again, the feeling of loss and failure and insecurity that Mike had endowed her with. He had always made her feel that it was all her fault, undermined her till she had begun to believe that he was right and the reason their relationship had foundered was because she hadn't tried hard enough. This man standing so powerful and strong in front of her was of the same ilk. Well, Mike had nearly destroyed her, but this man wouldn't.

'If you had an ounce of decency in you you'd pack up and get out of here,' she told him flintily.

'And so would you!' he slammed back. 'The fact that you have put up with this all week is a fair indication that you're hanging around waiting for the inevitable to happen!'

Her hand came up to give him that sock in the jaw she had promised, but he caught her wrist and deflected the blow.

'Don't make me mad again, Verity; you know what will happen, or is that the intention? To make me so bloody furious that I'll whip you upstairs and do what we both ache for!'

She twisted her wrist out of his hand and her eyes shot pure poison right between his.

'Go stuff that chicken, because that's the nearest you'll get to any body-bonding while we share this house!'

Verity slammed her bedroom door hard after her and leaned back against it, taking deep breaths to cool herself. She had tried, God only knew how she had tried. All she wanted was some cool, civilised living between them and all he wanted was his own satisfaction! And he had had the audacity to accuse of her of wanting likewise!

She tried to work, stared helplessly at the mountain of sickening diets and boring exercise regimes Candice had prepared for her. Did the bride-to-be really need all this rubbish to make the biggest day of her life worthwhile? Surely the sheer joy of marrying the man she truly loved was enough to bring a glow of radiance to her cheeks, a tingle of sweet anticipation of the wedding-night to hone her body to perfection?

Verity stared at the blank screen of the computer, hugging her shoulders for strength and warmth. She needed something to fire her, needed something to give her inspiration to get on with a job she had no heart for. She tried to project herself as that bride-to-be, to imagine she was preparing to marry, to marry Rupert Scott maybe. Impossible! She didn't even like him, but . . . there was something there. What on earth was it? A sexual attraction? She wasn't even sure of that. So his kisses turned her on, but his openness shocked her, or maybe it excited her. Maybe he was right and she was still here, hanging around waiting for the inevitable to happen. Oh, God, she didn't know anything any more!

Hunger and cold drove her downstairs when it was dark. She was exhausted but too hungry to take advantage of an early night. She hadn't had a good night's sleep since she had come to El Molino, and those restless nights were taking their toll.

A huge fire blazed in the grate of the sitting-room and there was a delicious smell of roasting chicken coming from the kitchen.

'So you do cook after all,' she said as she stepped into the kitchen. Rupert had just taken the chicken out of the oven, golden roasted chicken surrounded by crispy golden potatoes.

'When I have to,' he murmured, turning to attend to the vegetables bubbling on the hob.

Verity watched him and something inside her softened. He was clumsy and unused to this sort of thing, but he had made an effort and she appreciated that. He'd made an effort with his appearance too. He was dressed in clean jeans and a black roll-necked sweater, and his hair was well groomed. She almost felt guilty for not changing from her warm leggings and purple sweat-shirt to something more soft and feminine. But that would have been dangerous.

'Move over,' she murmured and took the pan from his hands. He didn't object and moved to the cupboard for plates. He'd already set the kitchen table with cutlery. She was glad he'd only done that—a candle, with its soft intimate glow, would have meant trouble.

She jumped when she heard the squeak of a wine cork being drawn and bit her lip.

'Don't panic, this is for me, not you.'

Defiantly she took another wine glass from the shelf and held it out to him. 'I believe in a fair distribution of wealth,' she told him; 'my chicken, your wine, share and share alike.'

He smiled and poured wine into her glass. 'You're not afraid, then?'

She knew what he meant. 'Wine doesn't lower my resistance, just makes me snore, as you'll probably find out in due course.'

He laughed. 'I just might settle for that tonight...' and just when she thought it was going to be all right he added mockingly '...but I won't make any promises.'

Surprisingly, that remark didn't rock her as much as she thought it might. She wondered if she pushed him far enough he might not funk out before she inevitably would.

'This chicken is gorgeous,' she enthused as they sat down to eat.

'Nothing to do with me,' he said modestly. 'It's just a decent chicken.'

'Thank you for cooking it. It was nice of you. Tomorrow it's my turn.'

'So this is going to be a regular routine, is it?' He spooned potatoes on to her plate.

'Why not? We've gone this far——'

'We might as well go all the way,' he finished for her.

Verity sipped more of the wine and decided not to bite back at that. 'Don't put words into my mouth. We've made a start and there's no reason to back down now. I can't see why we can't eat together every night. We both work hard all day and deserve some relaxation. Not the sort that's obviously on your mind morning noon and night, but just a meal and some talk. I'd like to know what you're working on.'

'It wouldn't interest you.'

Verity raised a brow. 'Try me.'

'No way, treasure. It's top secret——'

'And I can't be trusted?'

'It has nothing to do with trust. My emotions are running high enough with you in this house, Verity Brooks, without you putting a witch's curse on my work.'

'Hmm, now you really have whet my appetite. I just might creep into your bedroom while you're otherwise occupied and take a peek.'

'If I catch you in my bedroom I'll make the obvious presumption and act accordingly,' he warned with just a glimmer of humour in his eyes.

'I'll heed that warning,' she told him brightly to show she could take it. 'So if we don't talk about your work, what will we while away the hours with—mine?'

'Remind me; I've forgotten what you said you were here for.'

Verity was inexplicably hurt by that. She watched him eat before saying anything. He was an impenetrable man. She'd thought that the first time she had met him. Hidden depths, a poor excuse for moodiness. So the man had quite an empire to run but was there no room for relaxation in his life? She was forgetting. His mode of relaxation was bedding. She could just imagine the sort of lover he would be—wham-bam-thank-you-ma'am, excuse me while I get up and make another million while you're recovering!

'The wedding book,' she told him offhandedly to cover her hurt. 'Diets and exercises to prepare the bride for a life of wedded bliss.'

'Ah, yes, I remember now. What some people will do for a buck, I thought at the time you mentioned it,' he said derisively.

'It wasn't my idea,' Verity retaliated. 'It's one of Alan's money-spinning ventures. It's giving me some trouble, though,' she admitted. 'It's dragging its weary train up the aisle at snail's pace.'

'I'm afraid I can't help you there. I'm not very successful at the wedded-bliss game,' he told her with such coldness that Verity nearly dropped her fork with surprise. For some reason a cold chill ran up and down her spine. The lady in his life—was she his wife? Dear God, he was married! Not successfully, though, by the sound of it.

'You sound cynical about marriage,' she ventured, too afraid to ask him outright if he was or wasn't married.

'And what do you think of it?' he asked, cleverly getting out of giving her an answer, though it had hardly been a direct question.

'I believe in it. If two people truly love each other it's inevitable.'

'Did you expect to marry your boyfriend?'

Verity's eyes levelled with his. She had asked for this, wanting to shift their relationship to a more convivial level, and this was the result. Oh, well, if she opened up he might. She was madly curious to hear about his wife.

'I didn't love him,' she answered truthfully.

'Yet you were having sex with him, and there was I, thinking you were a little puritan at heart.'

Verity dammed a blush before it flooded her face. So he hadn't remembered much about the book she was working on, but there was nothing wrong with his memory where her sex life was concerned!

'I liked him a lot when we started going out with each other. You don't have to love a person to want to go to bed with them.'

His dark brow went up at that. He said nothing but she sensed what was going through his mind. If those were her views and morals, why hadn't she leapt into bed with him?

'I hoped it would lead to love,' she went on hurriedly. 'I cared enough for him to want him to make love to me. I thought that once we were actually lovers it might prove that I actually was in love with him but if I wasn't it might deepen into love. I made a wrong calculation, a mistake. I ended up being used.'

'And you're still very bitter about that?' He leaned back in his chair, the meal finished, the dessert, her confessions, making her squirm in her seat.

'Yes,' she whispered. 'With myself more than anyone. I made a mess of the whole affair.' She levelled her eyes at his and he held them and she thought he would understand. 'I made mistakes and then couldn't rectify them. I didn't know how to handle him or how to get out of it. He was a graphic artist and in the wrong job and he wasn't happy. I couldn't help him and he made me think it was my fault. When he died it was as if he had done it to punish me.'

'He committed suicide?'

Verity shrugged her narrow shoulders. 'I'll never know. We had rowed for the umpteenth time and he went out drinking and headed up north. There was a motorway pile-up...and...and he died. It was foggy——'

'So it was more than likely just an accident,' Rupert volunteered quietly.

Verity shrugged. 'I try to convince myself that it was an accident, but there will always be a doubt.'

'You can't go on living like that, though. You've to get on with your life.' He didn't sound as if he was very convinced of that advice himself, and Verity frowned slightly.

'Oh, I have,' she insisted. 'I can't change what's happened but...well, it's made me wary, unsure of myself where personal relationships are concerned.'

'And you don't want to make the same mistake twice?'

'Something like that.'

'It might surprise you to hear that I wholly endorse that.'

So he did have a murky past he was trying to live with. Perhaps a painful divorce, or possibly one coming up!

Verity gave him a watery smile. 'If there is ever a next time for me I want to be absolutely sure the man is as committed to me as I would be to him. A good, honest, down-to-earth relationship with no holds barred.'

'Equal partners in the love game,' he mused with a cynical laugh. 'Asking a bit much, aren't you?'

He grated his chair back and got up to put the kettle on, and Verity watched him through narrowed eyes. He looked so sombre that she wondered what had happened in his life for him to be such a cynic. That painful-divorce theory loomed larger than life now.

'I don't think so,' she told him warily. 'At least I'm looking on the positive side of marriage.'

'You're seeking perfection, which is totally unrealistic in this day and age.'

Verity bridled. 'And you're preoccupied with the imperfect side of it. Just because yours didn't work, it doesn't mean——'

'My what didn't work?' he questioned stonily, turning to face her.

'Your... your marriage.'

'I don't recall mentioning I was married.'

'You didn't but you said you had a lady in your life and... and you're pretty cynical about marriage *and* you just said you weren't very successful at wedded bliss.'

'All very true,' he admitted in an unforthcoming manner, and turned back to making the coffee.

'Now who's turning their back,' she said pointedly. 'Face me, Rupert,' she mimicked, 'and be honest with me and yourself.'

He swung round then, so ablaze with anger, his eyes so threatening and intense with rage that she nearly ran for her life.

'Just what the hell do you want from me?' he rasped furiously.

In that moment Verity wasn't at all sure why she was doing this, pushing him to reveal something of himself, something he was loath to open up to. Her mind flash-fired everything she knew about him, and one thought flamed above all others: the picture of him dining alone in that Knightsbridge restaurant; a lonely man. She hadn't seen it before, not till now.

'I'm sorry,' she murmured, lowering her lashes. 'I...I don't want anything from you...I just thought...' She took a deep breath and looked up at him, her violet eyes wide open. 'It helps to talk,' she murmured.

'It hasn't helped you much, has it?' he said frostily. 'You're still carrying your boyfriend's death around like spare emotional baggage.'

Shakily Verity got to her feet. 'I've tried,' she told him levelly. 'Which is more than you're doing. I don't know what your problem is but I know what you think the answer is—to bury yourself out here and hope when you surface the nasty gremlins will have run away. Life ain't that predictable,' she spiked bitterly. 'If I were you I'd go back to this lady of yours and bed her instead of me! I'm no damned substitute for the real thing!'

He caught her as she reached the archway to the sitting-room. He pinned her to the wall, holding her wrists above her head. She smelt the wine on his breath and his cologne and in that instant wondered why he had bothered, and then knew, knew what the whole evening was about, cooking for her, making an effort with his appearance: he wanted her and fully intended it to be tonight.

'You are the real thing,' he rapped urgently. 'Flesh and blood——'

'For the moment!' she grazed back bitterly. 'A warm body to take the place of your lady till you get back and pick up your flagging wedded bliss!' She tried to twist her wrists free but they burned painfully.

'They do say that an affair can sometimes resurrect an ailing relationship,' he mocked.

'So that's what all this is about, is it? By seducing me it might make you realise what a little *treasure* you have at home.'

'I know precisely what I have at home: fifteen empty rooms with the lingering scent of my lady's perfume . . .'

Verity's whole body stiffened. So he was married and she'd left him! She didn't want to hear any more, she just didn't.

'Let go of me!'

'When I'm good and ready.' His lips were hot and angry on hers, punishing her for that wife of his who'd left him. Verity boiled with rage and the injustice of it all. She squirmed and battled under the assault of his desire but the pressure of his mouth softened, with deadly expertise, the fight that blazed inside her. Slowly, fatally, he worked on her lips till she felt the well of her own desire rise inside her. He let go of her wrists and her arms dropped weakly to her sides and she clenched her fists tightly in a desperate attempt to hate him.

His mouth moved from hers, fluttered across her jawline and down to the small hollow of her throat. His hands moved round her hips, moulding her into him, then, satisfied that she wouldn't struggle any more, he slid them under her sweat-shirt, beaming up to her naked breasts, so smoothly as if they were programmed for that very purpose.

To her shock, his fingers trembled on her nipples, only for an instant, as if he was unsure, and then he was in control again, circling her breasts, teasing her nipples till her whole body flamed with liquid heat.

But it was that small unsure tremble that had the deepest effect on Verity. He didn't even care for her. Just like Mike, he was trying to prove a point. Rupert loved his wife and she had left him, and she, Verity Brooks, was the woman who would prove that he wasn't the failure he thought he was.

She brought her hands up then and pressed them hard against his chest. He didn't take much persuading to pull back from her. He stepped back and those smoky grey eyes were unfathomable again.

Verity's brimmed with unshed tears, for in that moment she knew that she wanted him. She wasn't sure how deeply or intense the need for him was, but what she did know was that if it were a different place in different circumstances she would want this man in her life. To love her, to make love to her, to give her all she lacked in her life. But it was an impossible dream, as impossible as speculating for sure what had been in Mike's mind when he had taken off for that foggy motorway.

Without a word, a look, a gesture, she turned away from Rupert Scott and walked resolutely away from him.

CHAPTER FIVE

VERITY'S work took off with a vengeance the next day. She worked feverishly, determinedly. It was the only way. Rupert was married, not happily; he still loved his wife; she'd left him; he wasn't coping... A knock on her bedroom door had her jerking with fright.

'Come in.' She turned from the computer as Rupert stepped into the room. 'How very civilised, knocking now. What happened to the SAS approach?'

'Sarcasm is the lowest form of wit,' he drawled. 'Can I borrow your car?'

'Why?'

'It's raining and I don't want to get wet.'

She turned back to the computer. 'Why haven't you got a car of your own?'

She heard a rasp of impatience come from deep in his throat. 'I wanted total isolation. I took a taxi from the airport and I'll take a taxi back. I need to go to the village to make some phone calls; now do I get the car or do I get wet?'

She was tempted to shoot back 'Get wet' but didn't. 'The keys are downstairs on the shelf next to the glasses.' Without turning, she said, 'While you're out, get some fresh bread and some salad, and I think we're out of milk.'

'What did your last slave die of, battle fatigue?'

'Sarcasm is the lowest form of wit,' she echoed brightly as he slammed the door after him.

She stared at the window after he'd gone. She hadn't noticed the rain and the wind howling and rattling the ill-fitting grilles on the windows. She saw it now, felt the chill of the room close in around her. She hated it when he wasn't here, though this was only the second time it had happened. But it was daylight and she wasn't afraid, just sort of... She shrugged; she really didn't know.

An hour later he still wasn't back. She hadn't done much in that time. He'd distracted her by coming into her bedroom, and since then she'd been too preoccupied with him and all that had happened last night. She got up from the computer and moved restlessly out of her room, across the landing and into his.

It was tidy, although she wasn't checking up on him. But what was she doing in his bedroom? She didn't know, but she was here and standing in front of his computer. She wondered at her nerve as she loaded it and then slid in the nearest disk to hand.

'Surprise, surprise,' she murmured after a while, and picked up the book he was working from. She flicked through it, put it down and picked up his notes.

'You surprise *me*,' a cold voice came from the door.

Shakily Verity turned to the door, scarlet in the face by the time she faced Rupert fully. He stood in the doorway, watching her, his hair wet and his features tense.

Though his voice was cold and his words mild, she knew he was red mad with her. His narrowed, steely eyes indicated the intensity of his control over that fury.

'I'm sorry. I didn't mean to snoop.'

He came towards her and ejected the disk from his machine. 'And this loaded itself, did it?' he grazed sarcastically.

'Of course it didn't,' she retaliated quickly. There was no defence, none at all, and she didn't attempt it. 'I was curious to see what you were working on.'

'You could have asked me——'

'I did. You wouldn't tell me.'

'So you just waited till I was out and then sneaked in here and invaded my privacy.' His voice was so thick with contempt that Verity wished she had kept away. 'That does surprise me, Verity; I was beginning to think you weren't a typical female.'

Her colour had returned to normal and she drew her chin up. 'Well, I suppose this proves I am. I'm not denying it. I was crazy with curiosity.'

'And you know what happened to the cat who was too curious?' He slid his notes and the book into the top drawer, out of her way.

'Are you going to kill me?' she murmured, half teasingly.

He held her eyes and she knew her attempt at humour wasn't going to abate his anger.

'Perhaps you're angling for the alternative.' His eyes seemed to darken more, if that was possible. 'Remember what I said about catching you in my room?'

Verity bit her lip. She had forgotten his threat and what he would assume if he did find her here.

'I didn't, I honestly didn't come here ... for ...'

'For sex?' His black brows winged. 'Hardly—I wasn't here. But now I am,' he added meaningfully.

Verity took a step back and then another. 'Don't make threats like that, Rupert,' she murmured.

He didn't say anything, which surprised her. She would have thought something mocking would have tripped from his lips.

'I'm sorry,' she offered once again. 'I didn't mean to invade your privacy...' She let out a small sigh. 'That's silly; yes, I did, I suppose, but...but I didn't expect to get caught.'

Rupert leaned back agains the desk. 'Well, that's honest,' he grated, 'but doesn't alter the fact that you did it and I'm not very pleased about it.'

'Why?' Verity asked. She knew she ought to be high-tailing it out of here but that wretched curiosity of hers was pinning her to the spot. The contents of that disk she had loaded had hooked her.

'It's personal.'

'What is? *Molly Shaw*? There's nothing personal about that. The book is a classic.'

'You really have been snooping pretty hard, haven't you? Did you sneak in here as soon as I'd left?'

'No!' Verity exclaimed. Her hand went up to rake her hair from her face. 'Look, I didn't meant to. I was just restless, waiting for you to come back, and I wandered in here and honestly, I don't know why I did it. I just loaded your machine up and read a bit of your work. I mean, I don't even know what it's about...what exactly you are doing...'

'A screenplay, an adaption of *Molly Shaw* for the big screen.'

'Oh,' Verity breathed. She hadn't been sure, she had suspected it was something like that, but, 'I...I didn't know you were a writer,' she said.

'I'm not.'

'Oh,' she breathed again, trying to understand, and then suddenly she did. She smiled. 'I do understand, you know. Childhood ambitions and all that. I used to want to be a ballet dancer but I didn't have what it takes...'

'This isn't a childhood amibition,' he told her curtly.

'Oh——'

'And will you stop breathing "Oh" like that?'

Verity shrugged. 'I'm sorry. It's just that I'm surprised. I thought you were a businessman and presumed you were working on some accounting or something. A screenplay,' she murmured, fishing for more. 'I'm very impressed.'

'I doubt that,' he grated. 'Now would you like to leave so that I can get on with it in peace?'

'Why doubt that I'm impressed?' Verity urged. She didn't want to go yet.

His eyes locked into hers. 'Are you really interested or are you just making conversation? In my bedroom?' he added meaningfully.

Verity shifted her feet but held her ground. 'I'm not interested in what you think I'm here for because it isn't true, but I'm very interested in your work. I'm loosely a writer too, nothing as impressive as a screenplay, but you never know what the wedding book could lead to.'

He smiled at that but offered no more and went over to the bathroom to get a towel for his wet hair.

'Is it still raining?' she asked. Silly question when it was obvious it was, but she was making conversation because she wanted to hear more about his work.

He stopped rubbing his head and looked at her coolly. 'Get out, Verity.'

The tone of his voice and the way the words were delivered with such deep warning affected her. She felt it as sharply as if he had pricked her with a hot needle. Suddenly something sheered off the walls, nothing you could put a name to, just a charged feeling of awareness of each other. Nervously Verity stepped back, not taking her eyes off him for an instant. He didn't move, just stood poised with his hands stilled on the towel and his damp hair, watching her, testing her, daring her.

Verity turned and fled.

She was making tea when he joined her in the kitchen, and probably because it was the kitchen there wasn't a repetition of that buzzy sexual awareness.

'I got the shopping you asked for,' he told her.

'Yes, thank you. It's my turn to cook tonight. Do you like spaghetti?'

'Fine by me.'

He sat down at the kitchen table and she made the tea without speaking. She wondered why he was sitting there when he had lost a good part of the working day already.

'Is it easy to adapt a book for the screen?' she asked.

'Depends.'

'On what? How good you are?'

He smiled and took the cup of tea she offered. 'You really are intent on getting it out of me, aren't you?'

Verity sat at the table. 'It interests me, really it does. You have your own film company. Are you intending to produce it yourself?'

He nodded. 'And direct it.'

'And star in it?' Verity teased.

'Hardly. I'm not into drag. It's the story of a mother who raised seven daughters single-handed during the industrial revolution.'

'I know,' Verity smiled. 'I have read it.'

'Do you think it will make a good film?'

Verity was flattered that he wanted her opinion. 'I'm surprised it hasn't been done before and surprised you're tackling it personally.'

'I didn't intend to. I mean I intended to produce it but the team of writers I hired were hopeless.'

'So you thought you'd have a go yourself?'

He nodded. 'My father was a writer—Alex Scott; heard of him?'

'*The Shardfords* and the *Cumbrian Trilogy*.' Verity was impressed.

'I thought some of his talent might have rubbed off.'

'From what I read on your disk, I believe it has, and I'm not just saying that to make up for snooping on you.'

'Thanks,' Rupert murmured, and smiled. 'I'm sorry if I was a bit cross with you for intruding, but I must admit to a certain reservation with this part of my work. Sarah was very derisive——'

'Sarah?' Verity interjected quietly. Her fingers coiled round her cup. 'Your wife?'

'The lady that was nearly my wife. We lived together for two years. She walked out six months ago.'

Desperately Verity tried to appreciate the fact that he wasn't married but it wasn't easy. Sarah might not have been his wife, but Verity could read in Rupert's eyes the depth of his loss.

'Didn't she like the thought of you being a writer?' Verity realised she had forced that out, striving for some sort of normality though she wondered why the need. What did it matter, his ex-lover's opinions?

'She didn't like anything that took up my time. A very possessive lady.' He grated his chair back and the sound matched his voice. 'What time's dinner?'

'About eight.'

He went back upstairs and Verity was left alone with her thoughts. She cleared up the dirty cups and wondered why Sarah had left him if she was such a 'possessive lady'. Suddenly she smiled to herself. A week ago she wouldn't have had any doubt in her mind why any woman would want to walk out on such a morose, arrogant swine, but now . . . She shrugged. What had changed? He was still a morose, arrogant swine. Sexy with it, though, she conceded.

She went back upstairs to her bedroom. She had another couple of hours of working time but it was colder than ever. She peered down at the radiator and turned the setting up to maximum. It was then that the lights blew, and there was a flash from where the radiator was plugged in.

Verity screeched so loudly that she thought Rupert must surely hear. She rushed to her door to shout that she was all right, but he was already bearing down on her.

'What the hell have you done?' He thrust past her and wrenched the radiator plug from its socket. 'You've blown all the electrics!'

'*I've* blown all the electrics? How do you make that out?'

'You've got the damned thing plugged into a lamp socket.' He pointed to another plug-point across the room. 'You should have used that one, a heavy-duty plug-point.'

'Well, I'm not a damned electrician. How was I supposed to know the workings of Spanish electricity? It's been working perfectly on that,' Verity protested, waving her hands at the connector. 'There's something wrong with the radiator, there must be. I turned it up——'

'And overloaded the circuit,' he growled at her.

'But I might have been killed!' she wailed, distressed that he wasn't concerned for her safety.

'But you weren't and I've lost precious work on my computer because of the loss of power!' he slammed back at her.

Verity's shoulders sagged. 'I'm sorry,' she murmured. Oh, God, she knew how she would feel if it had happened to her.

'Like hell you are!'

'I am!' she screamed. 'Just remember my name's Verity, not bloody Sarah!' As soon as it was out she wished it was in. Her teeth clamped over her bottom lip in remorse.

'I can live without you, Verity Brooks,' he grated harshly after freezing her to the spot with the blackest of looks. 'I can live very well without you!'

He slammed her door after him. It was minutes before Verity moved and then only because the lights had flashed back on. Whatever he'd done, he'd fixed it. She wheeled the radiator across the room and plugged it into the socket he had suggested. It didn't work, but at least the lights hadn't blown again.

She didn't knock on his bedroom door but marched straight in. 'I'm truly sorry about what happened. It wasn't done intentionally.'

'I know,' he drawled, and turned from his computer to face her.

'And I'm sorry about what I said about Sarah. It was awful of me.'

'It was,' he agreed.

She stepped towards him. 'Did you lose much?'

He turned back to the computer. 'Not much, but enough to make me as mad as hell.'

Verity smiled and reached out and touched his shoulder, and the touch turned to a caress and she was amazed at her own audacity in touching him so intimately.

'Don't do that, Verity,' he warned without turning. 'I won't be responsible.'

Verity stilled her hand but didn't remove it. She knew then that she didn't want him to be responsible at all. She wanted him to turn and take her in his arms and forget Sarah and have only Verity Brooks in his heart.

Did he read minds too? He turned and slid his arms around her waist and she bent her head and buried her mouth in his thick hair.

'I'm sorry too,' he rasped. 'I should have shown more concern for you. Did you get a shock from the radiator?'

'Only one of fright,' she whispered back, but she was more afraid now. He slid her sweat-shirt up and grazed his mouth tantalisingly across her bare midriff. Verity let out a small gasp of sheer pleasure. Her mind accelerated, taking her further and further in her sea of imagination. She was naked with him and he was loving her, kissing her, about to consummate what she so longed for. He was loving her, making love to her, entering her and... mouthing the name Sarah as he did it.

Her body stiffened, her heated flesh cooled desperately quickly. She tried to pull away, but he held her.

'Don't tease, Verity. I don't like that,' he husked achingly.

He stood up as she tore herself away. He reached her at the door, swung her back and kicked shut the door.

'I said I don't like that, Verity. Don't start something you don't intend to finish.'

'I shouldn't have come. I just wanted to say I was sorry,' she uttered weakly as his hands pinned her to the door by her shoulders.

'And offer your body in payment and then draw back when you had second thoughts?'

She didn't answer, just stared at him, stupefied. Why had she come? She knew; deep in her heart, she knew.

'It . . . it wasn't second thoughts.'

'What, then?'

'You're clever at reading my thoughts. I'd thought it was obvious.'

He graced her with a cynical smile. 'The lady in my life?'

Again she offered nothing. Again he smiled cynically. 'And what about the lost lover in your heart, Verity?'

She shook her head. 'I never loved him, and he's dead now anyway. You loved your lady and she's still with you, you said that; you said she was in your life . . . so you must still love her.'

'And what the hell has love to do with us? Don't tell me it's a consideration here?'

Her whole body burned in his grasp. She squirmed, but it was useless to try to free herself.

'No, it's not a consideration!' she breathed heatedly. 'But I'm no substitute for your lost lover and that's what I would be if we did make love. You've never shown any feelings for me before——'

'And I'm sure the feeling is damned mutual!'

'My God,' Verity gasped. 'Stuart was right—put two people in an isolated situation and sex will rear its ugly head.'

'Sex is ugly to you, is it?' he asked derisively.

'I didn't say that . . . but yes . . . yes, it damn well is when it's used this way!'

He lowered his lips and let them brush dazedly across hers. 'This is ugly, is it?' His body, warm and inviting and very aroused, was crushed against hers.

Dear God, but it was the opposite. Beautiful and tempting.

'Don't——'

'Don't,' he echoed against the paleness of her throat. 'That's all I ever get from you, Verity Brooks. Why don't you try "do" for size and see how you like it.'

'Not this way!' she cried, struggling in his grip, but when his mouth took hers again the struggle faded away. There were tears in her eyes because this was all so reminiscent of what she had been through before. Mike punishing her for his inadequecies, and now Rupert punishing her for Sarah's.

She wanted him to stop this assault on her tender emotions. She wasn't ready for this, to just give herself to him in the heat of the moment, just because she was so desperately lonely and so was he.

With a mammoth effort she was out of his arms and wrenching at the door-handle. To her surprise, he stood back and opened the door for her. His eyes locked her out, staring down at her as she hesitated in the doorway. They were cold and hostile and she returned that hostility with her own cool violet eyes.

'I came here to apologise and it stands. I haven't changed my mind.'

'Will you ever change your mind?' he husked.

She didn't even question about what, because she knew. She didn't answer yes or no either, but that was because she didn't know.

She tried to work but it was impossible, so she went downstairs and struggled with the fire till she had it blazing. She sat back on her heels and watched the flames fiercely gather momentum. She presumed Rupert was still upstairs working. It was getting dark and she ought to be thinking of getting the dinner on, but she was loath to leave the fire and loath to make that final decision. Did she want to let go and allow this affair to happen? She liked him enough to, but she had been hurt and used before and so had he, and was just liking enough? She bit her lip and realised that that was just the decision she'd had to make with Mike. She hadn't loved Mike but had hoped the intimate side of their relationship would develop that liking into love.

'What are you thinking?' Rupert asked as he came down the stone steps into the sitting-room.

Verity didn't get up and Rupert came and sat behind her on the sofa. He reached out and loosened her long blonde hair from where it was caught in the collar of her sweater.

'I was thinking about relationships,' she told him quietly, staring into the fire.

He laughed softly. 'Your honesty is one of the things I like about you. Any other woman would have said something inane like "nothing in particular". There isn't a second of your life when you think of "nothing in particular".'

'Would Sarah have said that?'

'Yes. She wasn't honest like you.'

'Why did she leave you?' She turned then to look at him. His eyes were dark and broody and she sensed he might not tell her. Men were worse than women for hiding their true feelings.

'I didn't give her enough of my time. Sarah was a very demanding lady.'

She sounded like Mike, Verity mused. 'You loved her very much, didn't you?'

To her surprise, he shook his head and the corners of his mouth turned up. 'Not enough. If I'd loved her more I wouldn't have left her alone so much, would I?'

Verity shrugged. 'I don't know. Maybe you didn't realise quite how much you loved her till after she'd gone.'

'Maybe.'

That wasn't what Verity wanted to hear. She looked away from him and stared into the fire again. 'I got the impression you were choked off with her leaving you.'

She heard a soft laugh behind her and swung round again. 'What's so amusing?'

'You. You're determined to get it all out of me, aren't you?'

Verity coloured and lowered her lashes. 'I'm just curious.'

'You are,' he agreed, 'but I wonder for what reason.'

Her eyes widened. She wondered herself, but not for long. Of course she wanted to know his feelings before letting herself go. She didn't want to be hurt again.

She scrambled to her feet. 'I'll get on with the dinner.' She hurried out of the room and he didn't follow her. She worked feverishly on the meal, amazed at the thoughts that swept in and out of her mind. She was actually considering having an affair with that man and wanting to get the clutter of his past relationship with Sarah, a woman she didn't know or want to, out of the way. She was mad, quite mad, because what difference would it make? An affair was an affair and didn't spell anything more.

She had to go through and get him when he didn't respond to her call that dinner was ready.

He was asleep, stretched out on the sofa. The fire was dying down and she jammed a couple more logs on the embers. Then she turned and studied him. He was tempting. So strong and powerful and very good-looking. His hair was in need of a cut and somehow that made him more appealing than when she had first met him. Then he had been suave and sophisticated and quite aloof; now he was human. Sarah had been a fool. To be living with this man and to have lost him. She should have stood her ground and fought for his attention.

'That's what I would have done,' Verity murmured as she reached down and touched his shoulder.

'What was that?' he muttered, opening his eyes fully.

'Supper's ready.' She smiled and flicked a wisp of hair from his brow in a playful gesture, and he caught her wrist and pulled her down on top of him.

'How much longer are you going to hold me off?' he drawled against her silky hair.

'I wasn't aware I was,' she murmured back.

'That sounds very interesting, very interesting indeed.'

'And so is my spaghetti,' she teased. 'I improvised a bit but I'm sure you'll like it.'

'Do you improvise in bed too?'

'You'll probably never know.'

'Only probably, so there is still hope,' he teased, running his hand up and down her back.

'Very little,' she murmured, and suddenly knew that to be true. She did want him and there was no doubt he wanted her, but only while they were here in this isolated mill house. Then the affair would be over and they would return to their lives. So what more did she want? Disturbed by that thought, she tried to get up from his lap.

'Not so fast.' His hand locked around the back of her neck and he pulled her down to him. The kiss was incredible. Powerful and promising, and the temptation surged urgently inside her. She responded because she could do little else. Her lips parted, her hands slid over his shoulders. His warmth and smell engulfed her, tempting her further and further down into his sexuality.

He moved and swivelled her round so she was lying on the sofa and he was straddled across her. His head was above hers and he gazed down into her eyes.

'Do you mean that, that we have little chance of coming together?'

She bit her lip and couldn't answer. How did she know? Today was today, tomorrow tomorrow. If he kept up those kisses, who knew where it would lead?

He smiled as if knowing her hesitation. 'It will have to be your choice——'

'That's not fair!'

His brows rose darkly. 'I think it's very fair. You know I want you, so you're not going to get a fight from me. But I'm not going to force myself on you,' he grinned suddenly, 'unless, of course, that's what you want.'

'Violence?' she husked, aghast. 'You wouldn't?'

'I wouldn't,' he smiled, 'but you do rather tempt me at times. Now it's my turn to be honest with you. I want to make love to you. I want an affair with you, but I warn you, I'm not very good at relationships.'

Verity smiled cynically. 'So you're offering an imperfect affair, no strings, no pain. Straight sex and when our time is up——'

'We more than likely go our separate ways,' he finished for her.

She started to laugh then, and her body shook under his. 'Well, I've had some propositions in my time but that takes the biscuit. Sarah did the right thing by walking away from such blatant chauvinism.'

He stiffened against her and then sat up. Verity swung her legs over the sofa and stood up.

'I suppose you thought you were being very nineties by making a statement like that?' she asked him, though it was more of a statement than a question.

His dark eyes held hers. 'I said it, Verity, because it's how I feel. I've had one sour relationship which I don't want to repeat——'

'So you're afraid? Well, so am I,' she told him levelly. 'But that gets you nowhere in life. Some time you'll have to take the plunge with another woman, but with that dour warning at the beginning of things I'll doubt you'll ever get further than a one-night stand.'

'So you are a typical female after all. Making demands and expecting hearts and roses and wedding bells from the off.'

'I didn't say that. I'd be quite willing to live with a man if I cared for him enough, and I'd have an affair if I cared and wanted enough.'

'So why this argument? Do you care enough for me to take on an affair with me?'

'I . . . I . . .'

'You don't know, do you? You're putting up barriers before you even know what's going on in your own mind. You do want me, you do want an affair, but you're as scared as I am.'

'Of course I am. I've already said I am. I've had a rotten relationship too and I'm wary, but at least my heart is open to offers. Yours isn't. Sarah still lies bleeding in yours and not because you really cared for her but because your bloody pride was stung because she walked out on you!'

She went to skirt the sofa and he reached for her, tenderly, which surprised her. His hands smoothed down her upper arms.

'You're very right,' he said quietly. 'I failed in a relationship and that isn't anything to be proud of. I can't offer you anything more than I could offer Sarah. I can make love to you, I can provide for you——'

'But you can't give your time and your heart?' she offered quietly.

He didn't say a word, not one, just held her eyes tenderly. She didn't understand him; how could he be so certain of that? A challenge stirred inside her, a very odd one. Did she have a chance of persuading him otherwise? That it was possible for him to love and give his time and his heart? And was that what she truly wanted? Those thoughts frightened her.

'I think we'd better eat before the food spoils,' she suggested, and turned away from him.

'Verity?'

She turned.

'It doesn't end here, you know,' he told her bluntly.

She nodded and this time knew the truth when it was put to her. She said after only a moment's consideration, 'I know. It's only the beginning.'

CHAPTER SIX

HER body burned. Verity flung the bedclothes from her and sat up. The bedroom was cool but she burned, an inward heat that pulsed through her.

They had talked all evening. The spaghetti had been good and the wine heady and she had fully expected Rupert to try to make love to her in front of the fire.

But he hadn't and she knew why. It had been an evening of exorcism. They had talked about their ex-lovers as if they needed to clear a path through their emotions before taking their own course.

Now she burned. She held her head in her hands. She burned with need, the need for Rupert Scott to hold and love her.

'Verity?'

Her hand shot to the bedside lamp and she snapped it on.

'Can't you sleep?' he asked in little more than a husky whisper. He stood in the doorway, wrapped in a white towelling robe. His hair was damp as if he'd just stepped from the shower. Verity glanced at her travelling clock.

'It's three o'clock. What are you doing up?'

He stepped into the room. 'I've been working. Come, I want to show you something.'

Verity scrambled out of bed and slid into her satin robe. He took her to his bedroom and she fully expected his computer to be glaring and the final page of his screenplay displayed to be read.

'What?'

He slid his arm around her shoulders and led her to the window. A full moon hung moodily in the black sky, and Verity exhaled a small gasp at the huge moonbow that caressed it.

'They say it's a sign of rain,' he murmured behind her and slid his arms down and around her waist. She felt his warm breath on the top of her head and his heart pulsing in her back.

This was the beginning and she was ready for it. The end she didn't even want to try to foresee. It was the moment, the time. She leaned back into him and clasped her hands across his. 'I didn't think you were romantic,' she murmured. The heat was already building up inside her, the heat and need that had woken her.

'There's a lot you don't know about me and a lot you're going to find out very shortly.'

He turned her into his arms and she went willingly, her mouth seeking his as urgently as he sought hers. The kiss was wild and frenetic, as if the world had only minutes to live its last. Verity coiled her fingers into his damp hair, almost clawed at him with the passion that rose so desperately inside her. Rupert ran his hands down her back, pressing his thumbs into her hips and grinding her against him.

Suddenly he lifted her and lay her down on his bed.

'I think you arranged that moon just to get me into your room,' she murmured as he lay beside her, gathering her into his arms to hold her against his body.

'I can't make love to you in a single bed.'

'So you're not romantic after all,' she laughed softly into his cheek.

'I arranged the moon for you, didn't I?'

She didn't answer because her mouth was too busy, grazing across his jawline, seeking his mouth once again.

He groaned under the pressure and then he parted her lips and explored the soft silkiness of her inner lips with his tongue. Verity's heart and senses spun with the depth of her passion for him. She slid her hand into his robe and smoothed her fingers over his chest, caressing the hair and the muscled flesh beneath.

His exploration was equally heated. He pushed her robe aside and smoothed her nightie up over her thighs and then lowered his head to kiss the smooth planes of her stomach. Verity arched against him, feverishly pulling at his robe to completely release his body from any confinement.

At last she felt his heated flesh on hers and, drugged with the intoxication of it, she gasped out his name and rushed her hands down over his hips.

She marvelled at the sheer splendour and power of his body. It was taut and power-packed, hot and hard, yet yielding under her every caress.

He lowered his head and drew on her creamy breasts as her hands made contact with his arousal. The power that charged through them both was catastrophic. Verity cried out and he steadied her with his mouth, desperately trying to cool the heat with small, soothing kisses on her face and neck that did little but heighten her need to the point of explosion.

His legs entwined with hers as he crushed her to him, moving restlessly, urgently against her perfumed flesh. And then his mouth crushed hers once again, his tongue fierce in its deep exploration.

There was just one small tremor of his hand as he parted her thighs, as if even now he was unsure of her. With a single smooth, elongated caress of his arousal Verity soothed his uncertainty and, gauging her need, his fingers parted her silky womanhood and began his seductive prelude.

Oh, God, he was beautiful, his tantalising thrusts so skilled and sensuous. Her orgasm rose and hovered and hung suspended in the web of her ecstasy. She desperately wanted to please him before wallowing in her own pleasure but her caresses weren't enough. She wanted to give every part of herself, to give him everything. Her most intimate love.

'Dear God, Verity,' he moaned. 'Don't do that.'

She did. Unashamedly she lowered her head and kissed him tenderly, caressed him with her tongue and lips, drew deeply on his lust till he shuddered deeply with the intimate pleasure she was giving him. And then he would allow her no more but lifted her away from him and rolled her over.

He entered her immediately, his breathing heavy and harsh. And she was ready for him, curling her arms around him possessively and drawing him deeply into her suppliant body. They moved awkwardly for a fraction of a second, but then the rhythm was set and their urgency unleashed as they rose higher and higher into that red vortex of liquid pleasure and hedonism.

Verity cried out as she came and then cried again as his orgasm swelled inside her. He let out a shuddering groan, so deep and primeval that her heart raced excitedly at the power she had over him at that moment. But she didn't feel triumph at that power, more a pride and a fantastic thrill that she had excited him so deeply.

They lay in each other's arms for a long while before raising the strength to speak. And when they did they spoke soft intimate praises to each other.

They slept at last and, when Verity awoke in the morning, Rupert was still there, coiled into her back, holding her as if never to let her go.

And so it began. The affair she had fought against and lost and didn't regret for a minute.

Verity loaded the washing-machine and stood back, watching her underwear tumbling with his, and smiled.

'What are you grinning at?' Rupert came up behind her and slid his arms around her waist.

'That.' She grinned happily, and nodded at the machine. 'Our washing, sloshing around so intimately.'

'Hmm. What's it supposed to mean?'

Verity shrugged. To her it meant everything. That very special closeness, somehow more intimate than anything else they shared, apart from bed, of course. It might be an imperfect affair but their lovemaking was perfect enough.

'It's a woman's thing that men wouldn't understand,' she murmured, leaning her head back so he could graze his lips down the side of her face.

'I'll leave it alone, then,' he laughed, and spun her round and kissed her lips. When they parted he flicked her hair behind her ears. 'I'm going to the village—what do we need?'

He'd got into the habit of going to the village most mornings and he never offered to take her, not that she wanted to go. She had far too much to do. They'd slid into a very domestic routine. While Rupert shopped she did the housework. They lunched together, mostly outside on the sunny terrace, as the weather had turned so good, and then parted company for the afternoon to work. Though that didn't always pan out. Sometimes Rupert would come to her room and they would make love, unhurriedly, as if they were on a permanent honeymoon and had all the time in the world to indulge themselves.

Verity moved away from him and picked up a pencil and paper and made a list. When he'd gone she stood staring at the washing-machine. It was all so unreal. This old mill house, her love for Rupert Scott, his insatiable appetite for her.

She loved him, had known it for days now, but deep in her aching heart she sensed he didn't love her. He made love to her beautifully, sometimes very erotically, anywhere he pleased and always satisfactorily, but there was never any talk about their feelings for each other or of their future or what would happen when they both had to return to England.

Sometimes she suspected he called Sarah from the village because when he came back he was quiet and morose, and sometimes she suspected he was thinking of her when he was making love to her.

She wished she didn't have these suspicions because they were without foundation, but they were there nevertheless and added to her insecurity.

'I've brought you a present.'

In surprise Verity turned to him from the computer. He tossed her a plastic bag.

'Market-ware, but it comes from the heart.' He grinned as she pulled the garish T-shirt from the bag.

'I don't believe it!' she screeched. 'It's perfectly hid...' She stopped and bit her lip. Perhaps he thought it was fantastic. It was huge, bright red with a lurid appliquéd parrot on the front. It sparkled with gold and silver sequins, not her style at all.

'It's a bit of fun, Verity,' Rupert assured her, noting the look of horror on her face.

Verity smiled up at him, but there was a deep sadness in her heart. Yes, it was a bit of fun, but the parrot reminded her of her remark about her cousin and her boss being sick as parrots if their plan didn't work. Part of it had worked. She had fallen in love with Rupert and that was the only part, nothing else. The T-shirt was also a painful reminder that their time together was nearly up. Another week and it would all be over.

'It's lovely,' Verity croaked. 'No, I mean it.' Her eyes twinkled mischievously. 'It's just what I need to clean out the bath.'

He was upon her in a second, laughing and sweeping her up into his arms and crushing him to her.

'For that, you'll wear it as a penance,' and he added throatily, 'now.'

'You want me to actually *wear* it?' she giggled.

And when he held her away from him she knew the look in his eyes and her heart hammered out her acceptance.

'Turn your back,' she murmured coyly and he did, with a smile of resignation.

'OK,' she said. 'You can look now.'

It was made for an Amazon and hung limply from her narrow shoulders and skimmed her thighs. But he looked at her as if she were swathed in the most sensuous of eastern silks, his grey, moody eyes eating her hungrily.

He held his hands out to her and she stepped into his embrace and buried her face in his sweater so he wouldn't see the tears in her eyes. His arms enfolded her and held her tightly and then he lowered his mouth to hers, crushing her lips so desperately that she stemmed a cry of pain.

Their lovemaking was different this time. He insisted she keep the T-shirt on; he thought it sexy and arousing and slid his hands under it to caress and arouse her. For Verity it was heartbreaking. She quickly went under his spell but her heart ached at all the gift meant to her. Losing him, having to face Stuart and Alan. It was a life she didn't want any more. She wanted Rupert's life, not his working empire and that fifteen-roomed house with the lingering perfume of his ex-mistress, but this life, eating and working together and sprawling in front of the olive-wood fire at the end of the day.

She blotted it all away as Rupert made love to her, feverishly, as if he too was aware of the time slipping away from them. His thrusts were deep and penetrating, his kisses executed with that same urgency, and when at last there was no more energy and strength left they allowed their orgasm to swell and burst till there was nothing left but their hot breath, their skin raw and aching, their muted kisses and weak caresses fading as the afternoon sun faded over the distant hill.

Later they cooked a meal together and tried to recapture something of their passion over the last few days. But something had changed, and neither knew what it was, and neither spoke of it.

'Did you manage to finish it?' Rupert asked.

Verity was exhausted. Time had been running out, but the book was finished now. She peered into the casserole Rupert was stirring on the kitchen table.

'Yes, and I can't say I'm sorry.' She poured two glasses of wine and sat down while Rupert dished up the food. 'Towards the end I was beginning to think the whole idea of the wedding book a waste of time and effort. Thank goodness it's fact not fiction. It must be awful to be writing something you haven't any heart for. It must show.'

'I'm sure it'll be a success, though. The bride-to-be market must be quite a lucrative one. And, talking of weddings...'

Verity held her breath and her heart stilled. She watched his eyes, searching, searching.

'...how would you like to go to one?'

Her heart, already overworked and flagging, began to pulse feebly. 'Whose?' she murmured, trying to keep the hope out of her voice.

'The guy who owns the bar in the village. He's getting married tomorrow and has invited us both.'

'He doesn't know me!' Verity protested. Her heart was back to normal and so were her wits. Had she really expected a proposal?

'The whole village is invited. Shall we go?'

She didn't want to, absolutely not. It would be painful. But she wanted to get out of the old mill house. Apart from a few walks when the weather had been good, they had never ventured out together. They'd been cocooned for almost a month, living and loving together and not seeing another living soul. Perhaps too much of a good thing.

'Why not?' she answered coolly.

The wedding-day dawned bright and beautiful. Verity lay next to Rupert, her arm across his chest, and gazed out of the window. Their last full day together and they were going to a wedding. Her heart ached for it to be their own, but that was a hopeless dream. Yet she would settle for just one declaration of love from Rupert. She didn't need marriage but she needed him in her life to love her; perhaps that was a hopeless dream too.

They had their breakfast on the terrace, laughing and joking, but there was a void already opening up between them, stilting that humour.

'When will you be coming back to England?' she asked him as she sat back and sipped her coffee. The sky was so blue it made her ache inside. There was the sweet scent of pine in the air and she wanted to remember this forever.

'I don't know, maybe next week. I'll see how I survive without you.' He was grinning as he said it and for once Verity didn't appreciate the smile.

'You'll have to make your own bed and do your own washing-up from now on.' She kept her voice light. She didn't want him to know how desperate she felt about leaving.

'I managed before.' This time there was no accompanying grin.

And you'll manage without me forever because there isn't anything there, Verity mournfully thought. He'd made it clear from the start that he wasn't promising anything, and if she had fallen in love with him she only had herself to blame. She had been warned.

'We'd better get ready,' she said brightly and stood up to clear the dishes. Rupert was still sitting there after she had washed up, distant and morose and gazing into space.

The village church was packed and cold, and Rupert slid his arm around her to keep her warm.

'The bride is quite fat,' Rupert whispered, 'she obviously hasn't read your book.'

'It wouldn't have done her much good—she's pregnant!'

They discussed this on their way home, after the reception, which was held in the local bar and spilled out on to the plaza. Rupert drove and Verity sat next to him, clutching a piece of the bridegroom's tie in her hand. At the reception the groom's tie had been cut into small pieces and each guest had bought a piece, and the money collected was part of the couple's dowry. Verity was enthralled by the custom, amazed how sensible and practical it was.

'Must have been a shotgun wedding,' was Rupert's cynical contribution to the discussion.

'Not necessarily,' Verity argued. 'They were obviously very much in love.'

'They had no choice but to put a brave face on.
An abortion in a Catholic village like this was
probably out of the question.'

'The question probably didn't even arise!' Verity
snapped back. 'They were in love and wanted that
child; their timing was just a bit out, that's all. Why
do men always think abortion is the answer?'

'I didn't say that, Verity,' Rupert insisted darkly
as they turned into the pink driveway.

'OK, let's drop it,' she suggested flintily, and was
the first out of the car and into the house.

She left Rupert to lay the fire and ran upstairs
to her bedroom to change her clothes. It had been
a long day and she was tired and her suitcase was
staring at her as she opened her bedroom door. Oh,
God, this was their last night together. She slumped
down on to the bed and held her head in her hands.

How would they leave it? Would he want to see
her in England? It would be different in England.
Both returning to such a very different life from
the one they had shared here.

'I'll drive you to the airport tomorrow,' he told
her when she came downstairs. So their parting had
been on his mind too.

'It's not necessary,' she told him quietly as she
passed him to go to the kitchen.

He caught her wrist and pulled her to him, but
not into his arms, just in front of him so he could
pressure her shoulders and keep her still.

'It is necessary,' he insisted. 'It's a long drive
and...'

'And you'll have to get a taxi back——'

'It isn't a problem.'

'I don't *want* you to drive me to the airport!' Her voice rose dramatically and she swallowed hard. 'I'd much rather go on my own,' she said more levelly.

'Do you hate airport goodbyes?'

Her heart iced. And it would be goodbye. He'd said it and he meant it.

'They don't bother me,' she told him dismissively and tried to shift away from him.

It seemed to irritate him and his fingers tightened on her shoulders.

'I warned you, Verity. I warned you I couldn't make any promises——'

'About what?' she stormed, angry now because of her disappointment. 'Us? I knew the score, Rupert. I don't expect anything from you, so don't waste your breath offering me excuses.'

'I'm offering you nothing of the sort. I didn't want any of this to happen——'

'But it did, and whatever you say it won't right a wrong.'

'It was wrong, was it?'

He obviously didn't think it had been, but then he wasn't suffering and she wasn't going to show him she was.

'No, it wasn't,' she offered on a sigh. She looked into his eyes but they were as unreadable as when first they had met. For a short time, since she had loved him, she had seen those eyes soften, but no more. 'I have no regrets, Rupert, but tomorrow I go home and I have a life and a job to pick up on and that's all I need.'

His fingers bit into her fiercely. 'That's all you've ever needed, isn't it? Someone to ease your way back into life after Mike's death.'

'Well, we did each other a favour, didn't we?'

'Meaning?'

'You filled a few gaps in my life and I filled a few in yours. We're quits, so let's leave the score even, shall we?'

'So this was all a game to you——'

'Some game, some damned rules! You started all this, Rupert,' she cried. 'If you had just kept yourself to yourself, just as we had arranged——'

'Stop it, Verity,' he growled. 'You sound like one of those typical females I despise so much.'

'Oh, the Sarah sort? You know, I can sympathise with her. Life with you must have been a miserable tirade. I bet the poor girl didn't know where she was with you from one day to the next.'

He said nothing but his eyes darkened so threateningly that she felt fear rattle its chains. She pulled herself away from him and rubbed her shoulders.

'I'm sorry——'

'Don't apologise for the truth,' he rasped. 'Sarah too was quite inept at voicing her opinions till she walked out on me. Now she just sends me bills, but I don't fall into those traps so easily now——'

'How dare you? How dare you insinuate that I would do the same?'

'I didn't. You took it that way. Now listen, Verity,' he ordered blackly, 'I told you from the off that I'm not into the wedded-bliss game——'

'Who mentioned marriage?' she stormed, her eyes wide and raging.

'No one, but before you get any ideas——'

'I haven't any ideas, Rupert bloody Scott. And that is your big problem. You think that every female that comes on to you wants marriage. So Sarah gave you a hard time—tough. I won't. I've enjoyed our affair but if I never saw you again it would be too soon!'

She swung from him then and powered out to the kitchen. She wanted to power up to her bedroom but that would show she cared and was ready for a good sulk. Well, she'd get on with the dinner and just show him she didn't care a damn about leaving him tomorrow.

Later, when they were in bed and making love for the last time, Verity behaved badly. She knew what she was doing and her only excuse was that she was hurting so badly inside that it seemed the only way. She was demanding; not verbally, she didn't have to speak; her hungry body said it all. But at the same time she gave as good as she demanded, wanting to store away every caress, every kiss, every hungry thrust of his manhood in her memory banks.

Deep into the night when he slept beside her she coiled herself into him and cried quietly to herself, ashamed and remorseful for demanding so much of him. She smoothed her hands over his exhausted body and kissed his lips softly and let her tears dry on his face. It was all she had to leave him, tears of sorrow and regret for their very imperfect affair.

CHAPTER SEVEN

'HAVE you got everything?'

How banal, how damned unoriginal! Verity wanted to scream it but didn't. It would show her bitterness and Rupert would read it as sadness, and she had her pride.

'Yes, everything,' she told him brightly.

He settled her lap-top computer on the back seat of the hired car and slammed shut the door.

'I can still drive you down to the airport.'

'Forget it,' Verity told him with a forced smile. 'It's a lovely day. I'll enjoy it better on my own.'

She thought she saw hurt in his eyes but she had thought she'd seen much more this morning when he had woken her with soft tempting kisses. But she was wrong, of course, just hopefully seeking something that wasn't there.

'I'll phone you,' he murmured as he took her in his arms for the last time.

'Yes, that would be nice,' she murmured back and as his mouth closed over hers she wondered how he would do that, for he didn't know her number or where she lived or very much about her at all. She wondered that because she was forcing herself to think of anything but what was really on her mind—the terrible feeling of loss.

She didn't look back, not even a glance in the rear-view mirror, not even a perfunctory wave out of the open window as she rattled down the dirt-track road and out of his life.

'Who sent the roses?' Alan asked a few weeks later. They'd arrived that morning. Delivered to the office because that was the only place he knew where to find her.

'A secret admirer, probably,' Verity told him and nothing more. The card with no message, simply Rupert's name on it, was ripped and in the bin. If only he'd written something ...

'A bit late for Valentine's Day.'

'Is it?'

Verity didn't even bother to look up from her work. She was still frosty with Alan. On her first day back to work she had coldly told him exactly what she thought of him, as she had done her cousin Stuart. She had also told them that absolutely nothing had come of their disgusting plan and she didn't want to hear another word mentioned about Rupert Scott. The subject was closed.

'Still mad with us?' Alan asked quietly, determined to reopen it. He sounded repentant and Verity wavered.

She looked up then. They would never know how much. She was mad with everyone, even herself. How could she have been so stupid and let all this happen? Now she was going to pay for that disastrous affair, more than she could ever have anticipated.

'I feel sorry for you both more than anything, not that you deserve my sympathy,' she retorted loftily. 'You and your warped ambition, willing to sacrifice my honour for your own ends, and as for

Stuart, poor soul, my heart bleeds for him, he's getting his come-uppance all right, at the hands of his greedy grabbing wife, your sister Angie.'

'It was her idea, you know,' Alan told her, ignoring the slur on his sister and perching on her desk as if ready for a good old heart-to-heart.

Verity shuffled papers. She really didn't need this. She sighed. 'I'm not surprised by anything that Angie does, but what does surprise me is the way you both went along with it. I really believed you cared about me.'

'We do, and we thought we were helping.'

'Helping yourself!' Verity cried. Her hand came up and kneaded her feverish brow. She didn't feel well and hadn't felt well since she had realised ...

'That was an afterthought.'

Verity's eyes widened. 'An afterthought?'

'It was true that Stuart arranged that dinner party to get you two together, thinking that it might help you and us, but the rest was all to do with Angie.'

'Yes, I can imagine! You two amaze me, grown men as well, manipulated by little Angie,' she gibed sarcastically.

'She didn't manipulate us, Verity,' Alan said calmly, 'just made us see something we missed. She saw the look in Rupert Scott's eyes every time he looked at you.'

'Oh, yes.' Verity smiled cynically. She didn't believe the look could have been anything but derisive. 'Contempt, was it?'

'Far from it,' Alan smiled. 'Women are far more astute than us poor blind males. Angie saw the interest, the attraction, the lust, if you like.'

Verity shook her head in disbelief. 'Rubbish. Shall I tell you something? He didn't even remember my name when I turned up at El Molino. Hardly the reaction you'd expect from a man champing at the bit. No, Angie saw what she'd hoped to see, Alan. She *wanted* Rupert to be interested in me, for her own ends!'

Why, she'd done the very same thing herself. Imagined that Rupert had cared for her when she had caught him looking at her in a certain way. But looks were deceptive and, besides, they weren't enough, nor were bouquets of red roses with no message!

'That's unfair, Verity. We all care very deeply for you. Do you honestly believe we would have arranged for the pair of you to spend such an intimate time together if we didn't think some sort of happiness for you would come out of it?'

Verity lost her temper then. She stood up and angrily faced her boss. 'You wanted to get us together for his advertising and his magazines——'

'OK, what we did was out of order but worse things have been done in the name of business; nevertheless, we all hoped you would get some happiness out of it,' Alan insisted.

'Well, I didn't!' Verity cried, trying to hide the hurt from him. The opposite, the very opposite. Even the good times had soured now. How could she have even thought she'd been happy in that old mill house when her love hadn't been returned?

'I'm sorry about that,' Alan offered at last after studying her intently. 'But I know it all looks black to you and our intentions not particularly honourable, but when Angie saw the way he looked at you . . . well . . . we just thought no harm would be done.'

No harm done, she mused ironically after Alan had left. If only they all knew how deeply the damage went. She stared at the deep red roses. Moonlight and roses, she had never thought it possible from him. And if only this hadn't happened . . . her hand strayed to her stomach . . . she could appreciate that he might, he just might care a tiny bit. But she had to force herself to think otherwise, that the moonlight had been a prelude to the affair and the roses the grand finale.

'I . . . I didn't expect you so early.'

Verity stood back from the door of her first-floor flat. Her heart was pounding erratically but Rupert stood as still as a statue in front of her. The Rupert Scott she had first known; sophisticated, cool and aloof. She knew then that Angie had been very wrong and hadn't seen any sign of interest in those cool grey eyes. They weren't capable of showing or feeling *any* emotion.

'Aren't you going to ask me in?' were his first stiff words.

She stood back further and let him step into the small hallway. He turned to her as she closed the door after him.

'Why the coolness on the phone, Verity?'

She led him through to her small sitting-room. She'd made it as comfortable as possible for him, lit the gas log fire, bought fresh flowers that very morning, plumped up the cushions. She wanted to show him that she had a life without him and a pleasant one too.

'I was just surprised you'd called. How did you know my telephone number?'

'Don't be absurd. I looked in the telephone book, of course.' His voice was brittle.

Of course. She hadn't thought. The call and his request to see her had been such a surprise that she hadn't wondered till now how he had known her number.

'Sit down,' she offered nervously.

He did, in her favourite armchair. He looked so very different from the Rupert she had loved in Andalucia. His hair had been cut since then and was stylishly blow-dried. He looked good in his formal grey suit, almost the same colour as his eyes. She still loved him; how could she stop?

'Did you get the flowers?'

'Yes, thank you.'

There was a long, long silence in which Rupert stared at the floor and Verity watched him staring at the floor. They had shared so much and now suddenly there was an unbridgeable gulf between them.

'The cold farewell at El Molino, the frosty phone call, and now this bleak reception,' he said at last. 'Are you trying to tell me something, Verity?' He looked up at her then, his jawline stretched taut as if he was gritting his teeth.

Verity stood by the fire, leaning one arm on the stripped-pine mantelpiece. She felt at an advantage standing and she needed to be at an advantage with him, but all the same her insides twisted painfully.

'It depends on what you want to hear,' she said coldly.

Another awkward silence before he spoke. 'When you left El Molino so breezily I hoped you were just putting on a brave face. I'd like to believe you didn't give me a backward glance because your eyes were filled with tears.'

She couldn't believe his cruelty. Had he come here to turn the knife? 'I...I can't believe we are discussing something so very unimportant——'

He stood up suddenly, taking her by surprise and grasping her arm. 'Well, it is important, damned important. I want to know what's going on in that unemotional mind of yours. Tell me, Verity, were you crying?'

'The hell I was!' she snapped sarcastically. 'I had my eyes on that dirt track and there were no tears in them, I assure you!' She shook his hand from her arm. Why was he doing this to her, rubbing her face in the mud? 'Why did you bother phoning, Rupert, why did you bother coming here?'

'Because I thought we had something going——'

'Something going,' she echoed. Suddenly she understood and she had to fight back the tears and the pain. He was here because he *did* care, but the timing, just like that of the loving bride and groom in Andalucia, was way out. Oh, God, if only...

'We had an affair,' she cut in, 'a very imperfect affair.' She laced her voice with contempt because that was the way it had to be. 'And I can't see it going any further.'

'I told you in Spain that I wasn't in a position to offer you anything more.'

'I'm not asking for anything more, Rupert. I never have done. But I don't want it to go on.' How it tore at her heart to say that. 'Andalucia was ... well, it was different ...'

'A holiday romance?' he blazed contemptuously.

'Hardly a holiday,' she spluttered. 'We were both working our socks off.'

'In and out of bed.'

Verity flushed. 'Don't bring it down to that level,' she breathed huskily.

'Gutter-level? You brought it down, Verity, by your dismissive attitude on that last day. As if you'd had your fun and it was over and you were quite happy to be going home ...' He stopped, unable to go on, and Verity gazed at him in dismay.

How could he think that? How could he? Surely he must have known how badly she was hurting and that she was putting on a front to hide her hurt? If only he had said he loved her and wanted to see her back in England because he couldn't live without her. But he hadn't, and now it was too late. Minutes ago she had thought he might care, but all he'd come for was to ressurrect that Spanish affair.

Verity braced herself to be hard and resolute. 'In that case, why suggest I might have been crying as I left? A bit of a contradiction ... Look, this is getting us nowhere,' she breathed sensibly. 'Now, why are you here? To say that maybe we had something going——'

'I came here to talk to you, over dinner—out, not in——'

'I don't want to go out——'

'Well, out it's going to be,' he rasped thickly, 'because if we stay here a minute longer I'm going to take you to bed and positively remind you of just what we had going in Andalucia.' His eyes were smoked dark grey as he issued that warning and Verity didn't doubt he would do just that.

'Sex,' Verity hissed in harsh defence, 'that's what we had, Rupert, and a lot of it. Too much, because now there isn't any more left.'

'So damned sure of that, are you?' He lifted her chin with burning fingers and lowered his lips to hers. Not in a gesture of love or even passion but a gesture of punishment and revenge and to prove a point.

Verity tore her mouth away, shocked at how cold and unfeeling she could be. But she had to be because now there was no hope. Later would come the remorse and more suffering because he was trying, and she recognised that even if he wasn't offering her some sort of permanency in their relationship... he nevertheless wanted it to continue. But she couldn't, not now that she was... was carrying his child. Because at some stage he would have to know and the trap would close around them both.

His burning fingers cooled and he grazed them over her jaw. His eyes softened and Verity felt her strength dangerously weaken. Don't let him say something nice, she prayed.

'Verity. Things have changed since Spain. I'm freer now to offer——'

'I don't want anything,' she interrupted painfully. Oh, she did, she wanted it all, his life and love twinned with hers. But now there was a barrier between them that neither of them could have dreamed of.

'I can't believe that,' he breathed and his lips came to hers again, and this time there was no anger but for Verity the punishment was worse. His mouth was warm and sensuous, pleading, demanding, seeking her submission.

And she felt her resolution slipping from her and she was blindly clawing in the dark for something to hold on to.

'Rupert,' she implored when he eased his lips from hers. She had to try to stop this. 'You ... you wanted to talk ... so tell me ... what do you mean, freer?'

It had heatedly crossed her mind that he might have lied about his relationship with Sarah and that they had been married and perhaps now a divorce was imminent. But what difference, what difference?

He held her gently in his arms now, confident that he had broken down her reserve. 'I've sorted out a few things in my life and my mind,' he whispered against her pale blonde hair. 'I want you to come and live with me, Verity.'

She pulled away from him slightly to look into his face. Her eyes were violet orbs of surprise. 'Live with you?' she husked. She hadn't expected that, not at all.

He smiled and smoothed a wisp of hair from her temple. 'Don't sound so aghast, it's not a sin, and you said——'

'Yes, I said, didn't I?' she murmured, remembering and regretting it now. If two people cared about each other, why not live together? But now she was in love and feeling very different. Surely marriage, that definite, wonderful commitment, was the only way. But Rupert didn't love her because if he did he would want that as much as she did. But he did want her by his side, so surely that was a caring start? But now, how wrong the timing.

'I . . . I don't think that's a very good idea.' She lowered her eyes so he couldn't see her pain.

'Why? It's no different from us living together in the old mill house.'

Couldn't he see that it was? She shook her head and he stilled it with his hands clasped each side of her face. He tilted her face up. 'Don't argue with me, Verity,' he said earnestly. 'It's what I want and I believe it's what you want.'

Her lashes flickered over her eyes and she bit her lip. 'I don't think you're ready for another relationship so soon after Sarah,' she husked.

He laughed softly. 'That's my affair and not your problem.'

'But . . . but it is,' Verity insisted. All her insecurities flew to the defence of her aching emotions. Sarah, bloody Sarah; he claimed he was free of her but she couldn't accept that he was. There was something blocking it for her but she didn't know what.

Rupert's eyes darkened. 'It isn't, Verity. Leave it alone. It's history, so forget it. I don't keep harping on about your affair with Mike, do I?'

'Mike is dead and no threat; Sarah is alive, and you know that's different.'

He sighed deeply, slightly edgily. 'And it always will be in your eyes. Forget it, Verity, forget them. I want you with me and I want to provide for you——'

'And you want to make love to me every night?'

He missed the aggrieved tone in her voice and gathered her into his arms again. His charisma and sensuality overpowered her as his mouth crushed hers, parting her lips with the insistence of his probing tongue, giving her his answer in the impassioned kiss.

She felt it all slip out of her grasp, the fight, the reasoning she had thought she had already coped with. How easy to love him, how easy to let him have his way and go and live with him in the hope that he might learn to love her, not just care for her. But the... the baby? So very wrong and out of place in this relationship that was already so unstable.

His hands slid under her silk shirt and her breasts were ready for him. Engorged and heated and so desperate for his touch. He moaned passionately against her throat and trailed searing kisses down to the opening of her shirt. Easily he released the small pearl buttons and then, so easily and swiftly, he lowered his head to draw from her nipples every last vestige of rebellion.

She clawed at his hair, closed her eyes and threw her head back to let out a silent mouthed moan of submission. He had such power, such demanding insatiable power over her, and she couldn't fight it and in that moment didn't want to. Already his hands were at the zipper of her jeans and her hand came down and helped him.

Their clothes were discarded with almost indecent rapidity and Rupert with one deep persuasive kiss lowered her to the rug in front of the fire. He straddled her, gently and tenderly caressing her breast and watching the flush of desire rise and deepen the colour of her cheeks.

'You feel different,' he murmured throatily.

Surely he couldn't have noticed the subtle difference in her body? It was only weeks, not months. The pain of having to tell him knifed through her. But not now, she couldn't tell him now.

'Do I feel different?' he asked and there was no mistaking the suggestion in his tone.

She gave herself to him then, smiled up at him and lifted her hands to caress him. As she stroked and smoothed his beautiful muscled arousal she blanked off everything but the pleasure of giving and receiving. She loved him so very much and for the time being it was enough that he wanted her so strongly and passionately.

His first thrust was tentative, as if afraid to hurt her, as if he knew that a tiny life was blossoming inside her, but he couldn't know, of course. His life, she mouthed to herself as she urged against him, her body telling him in its frenzy that she wanted him so very deeply inside her. She smoothed his hips and pulled him into her and he responded with such passion that she was suddenly afraid. And then there was no more fear but the dizzy need that couldn't be held back any longer. Harder and faster and somehow more penetrating than their lovemaking before, and then that last desperate sprint in case that miraculous feeling slipped out of reach and Rupert steadying her, gripping her hips in that last shuddering penetration as their orgasm spun their hearts and their bodies through space and time.

Later his kisses soothed her wet brow and his fingers teased the moist silken flesh of her inner thighs.

'You *do* feel different,' he whispered.

She wondered at the heightened awareness of her body. Every sense and nerve pulse seemed crazily near the surface of her skin. Was it because of that tiny bud of life forming deeply within her? Or was it that she had missed him so desperately?

Rupert moved his hand higher and she felt the heat rise so rapidly that even he was surprised. He laughed, softly against her breast, and as his hand started a pulsing rhythm between her legs his mouth closed over her nipple and in the instant he drew on it Verity arched her back and cried out.

Minutes later she was still trembling in his arms, shocked at the intensity of what had just happened.

'I don't know what came over me,' she whispered.

'Whatever, I'm glad.' He leaned on one elbow and gazed down at her. 'You have an incredible sexuality.'

Verity blushed. 'Don't you mean insatiability?' She was embarrassed now.

'That as well,' he murmured. 'Parting obviously makes the heart grow fonder.'

'Or needier,' she responded cryptically, and tried to get up from the rug.

Rupert pulled her back and his voice was harsh when he spoke. 'I didn't like that remark——'

'I didn't like you making me come like that!'

'For God's sake, Verity, what's got into you? We've never been this way before.'

She sat up and buried her head in her knees. 'I...I don't understand.' She really didn't. They had been so close and uninhibited before, but now... 'I...I don't like the power you have over me.'

'What power, for heaven's sake?' He tried to prise her head from her knees but she wouldn't let him. 'Verity,' he tried to soothe, 'we know each other well enough not be shy with each other.'

'Sexually, you mean?' She raised her head and looked at him. 'It seems this relationship is all about sex. OK, so we're good together in bed or on the floor or wherever, but is it good enough for us to live together? You came here tonight with all your demands off pat, but what about me?'

'What about you?' he asked incredulously.

'Yeah, what about me?' she drawled sarcastically. She struggled up and reached down for her shirt and slid it round her shoulders. 'You demand too much, Rupert, you expect too much. *You* insist I go and live with you; well, perhaps I don't want to. Perhaps I want——'

'Marriage?' he rasped bitterly.

Oh, no, suddenly this wasn't about marriage. It was about loving and caring, and Rupert Scott had shown none of that. But by the very mention of marriage he must assume that she loved him enough to want that. Well, she wouldn't let him have the satisfaction of knowing she cared that deeply for him.

'I don't care a mouldy fig for marriage.' Her eyes were very vivid when she added with a challenge, 'You want me to live with you? OK, I will, but I live my own life——'

'Don't start bargaining with me!'

'No bargaining, Rupert, take it or leave it, I'll live with you but I go my own way and I don't mean with men. I mean with my career and what I do with it, and my time. Yes, my time——'

'Forget it, then,' he slammed back brutally. He got up and started to throw his clothes on, far more determinedly than he had discarded them. 'I want you in my life but I don't want a repeat of what I've been through before—life with conditions.'

'You wouldn't get it because I'm not the jealous, possessive type. I wouldn't grizzle if you stayed out all night. I wouldn't be another Sarah in your life,' she flamed. She would, though; she was lying through her teeth, because she'd be exactly like Sarah, wanting him to spend time with her, hating every minute he was out of her life.

'I repeat, forget it. I've just got rid of one helluva bitch and I don't need another!'

Verity realised she had been backtracking with her last remark. Dizzily she rubbed at her forehead. She didn't know what she was doing or saying any more. She'd actually agreed to go and live with him and she didn't know why she'd said it. Desperation perhaps. Suddenly her head cleared.

'Wait, Rupert,' she murmured as he slid into his suit jacket and turned away as if to leave.

He stopped and looked at her warily.

'Let me make some coffee and let's talk some more.' Suddenly she desperately wanted him to stay. She *did* want to talk. She wanted to find out what he truly wanted and if there was a remote chance of making something of this crazy relationship.

'You mean bargain some more?' His mouth twisted wryly. 'No sale, Verity. I've made my offer and *you* take it or leave it.'

What was the use? It was all one way with him, his way. 'You selfish bastard!' she grazed spitefully at him.

'Substitute bitch for bastard and you have a perfect description of yourself,' he retorted with deathly calm. 'You're up and down like a Yo-Yo and I'm not even going to question what you really want, Verity, because I don't think you know yourself——'

'But I know what you want, Rupert,' she flamed back. 'You want what you came here for tonight, sex on demand, and to make it easier for yourself you want me on an intravenous drip in your own house so you don't even have to go out for it——'

She thought he was going to be the first man to strike her. Her head reeled as he crunched her shoulders up round her ears.

'What the hell has got into you since you got back from Andalucia? You're different, a rotten little spoiled brat!'

'And what are you but a spoiled brat too?' she cried. 'All I hear from you is self, self, self. My life isn't a consideration. I said if I came to live with you I'd want my own life, but you're not even willing to...' Her voice trailed away on a sea of realisation. It swirled around her, spinning her crazily. She had made it clear to him that she wanted a life but he didn't want her to have one. Love or mere possessiveness? There could be a thin line between the two or a yawning gap. She didn't know which, but if she lived with him she would surely find out. Did she want to go that far?

Oh, God, she did. She loved him and she was desperate for him to love her, so she had to give him a chance but...but there was so much that frightened her. She didn't want to be another Sarah.

'Rupert,' she went on, and because her voice wasn't so shrill he eased the pressure on her shoulders. 'I have to say this and please don't tell me to forget it. It's something I need to know...'

'Dear God, not Sarah again?' His eyes were black with suppressed fury but suddenly they softened. 'Look, get it out of your system because it's obviously blocking your reasoning.'

'It isn't,' she insisted and then bit her lip because she knew it was. 'It's nothing major. But you said...you implied tonight that you'd just got rid of her and I...I thought you'd said she'd left six months before.'

His grip turned to a gentle caress. 'Darling, she did. I didn't lie to you and it's what I meant when I said I was freer now, freer to offer you more. Since Sarah left I've been maintaining her, paying her bills...'

'Guilt money?' Verity ventured in a tight whisper.

He nodded. 'Partly; I mistreated her and I was sorry for that. She got her vengeance, though, but all that's in the past now and I want you to forget, as I've done. She's well and truly out of my life now.'

'And you want me in now?'

A hand spurred through his hair in frustration. 'Not the way you make it sound, Verity, as if I'm

exchanging one for the other. It isn't like that. I
want you in my life and I intend to have you.'

'And ... and when you've finished with me, will
you pay me off the same way?'

She didn't know why she was doing this, pushing
him, pushing him. Then she knew: if she shoved
hard enough he might tell her exactly why he wanted
her in his life, because up until now she had only
her own feeble hopes to hang on to.

'I'm going to treat that remark with the contempt it deserves,' he told her darkly, 'and ignore
it.' His thumbs dug into her shirt. 'Get dressed,
Verity. We're going out to dinner to discuss how
quickly you can move in with me, because I'm not
taking no for an answer.'

She went to the bathroom to shower and dress
and wondered at her sudden timidity in standing
up to him. She had every reason to refuse his request. She didn't like being manipulated, for one
thing; she didn't like his out-and-out insistence that
she go and live with him. But three things had
swayed her reasoning. Sarah was indeed out of his
life now, that was the first; the second was that
silly, silly word, darling. He had never said it before
and it gave her hope that he might care for her more
deeply than he could admit. The third was her own
deep love for him. If she lived with him and showed
it he might learn to love her ...

'You look beautiful,' he breathed when she came
out of the bedroom in amethyst silk. He took her
hands and raised them to his lips and kissed them
tenderly.

Verity smiled up at him and would have been
filled with happiness at the look in his soft grey

eyes but she still had so many doubts and insecurities to overcome. She would need to know he truly loved her before telling him about his baby, and that could take time that she didn't have. And if she found he didn't love her she would never be able to tell him, and that was one reason why he wasn't going to get all his own way and reason enough for her to be very firm with him. He said he didn't bargain but he would have to, because she had to think of herself and the baby in the event that the novelty of his having her in his life wore off the way it obviously had with his last lover.

CHAPTER EIGHT

'I WANT to carry on working, Rupert. It's the only way for me.' It was imperative to have something to fall back on if it didn't work out.

Verity leaned back and let the waiter serve her with gingered prawns. It was a lovely restaurant in Holland Park. One of Rupert's favourites, of course, one she couldn't afford to frequent if she scrimped for a month.

She leaned forward when the waiter had left but not before she had seen that tell-tale darkening of Rupert's eyes.

'And don't argue,' she went on, 'because it will be useless. I like my job and want to keep it.'

'What are you trying to prove—your independence, your feminism, or are you just thinking that I'm the sort to take you over, body and soul?'

'Well, you haven't done a bad job so far. You've insisted on taking me out to dinner.'

He smiled. 'Surely not against your will?'

'No, I was starving, as it happens, and quite willing to be manipulated that far, but I want my independence, Rupert, you must understand that.'

'So why agree to live with me?'

'I haven't yet.'

His eyes softened. 'You might not have said the words but you will, won't you?'

'Depends.' She was still playing cat and mouse, more with herself than him. One minute she was

143

convinced it would work, the next she was mortally afraid it wouldn't.

'Terms again?'

'All agreements state terms, Rupert, even marriage. To love, honour and obey and all that.'

He grinned suddenly. 'That sounds like my sort of terms. Marry me, then.'

Verity raised a cynical brow. She didn't take that proposal seriously, as she knew it wasn't meant that way.

'With the emphasis on the obey bit, no doubt?' She shook her head. 'Marriage wouldn't make any difference to what I want, Rupert. I want to keep my job because for one thing I enjoy it, and another is that if this cohabiting doesn't work I don't want to be left high and dry.'

His eyes glinted and she knew he was losing his cool. 'With that attitude it doesn't stand much of a chance from the off.'

'What attitude?'

'Think positive, not negative, Verity. Think it's going to work and it will.'

'Fairyland,' she countered drily. 'Do you know the divorce rate?'

'We're not getting married, are we?'

It was a rhetorical question and she was glad she hadn't taken that silly proposal seriously in the first place.

'Definitely not, and I'm not sure our living together would work.'

'Well, it will have to, because I'm insisting on it,' he told her firmly.

'Such macho treatment,' she sighed theatrically. 'You really scare me. I can see I'm going to have to take a course in subservience.'

There was a weighty pause before he said very seriously, 'Why are you doing this, Verity, why are you being so flippant and cynical about it all?'

Seriousness suddenly hit her too. 'I'm sorry,' she offered quietly. She didn't know why she was being so offhand about it all—defence possibly, that fear of being left high and dry. Rupert wanted her to live with him, wasn't it enough for her?

Panic suddenly clawed at her. She couldn't do it and it was because of this baby. It wasn't fair to him. A life with conditions he'd led with Sarah; well, there would be conditions with her as well when she told him about the baby. Not ones imposed by her, but emotional bonds he'd feel duty-bound to uphold. No, not that way.

'Do I get time to think it over?' she murmured at last.

'Not one second,' he told her firmly. 'I want you in my life, here and now——'

'I can't just up and move in——'

'Why? You don't own your flat; just give in your notice and move out.'

Her eyes narrowed. 'How did you know I don't own my own flat?'

He smiled secretively. 'What a short memory you have. You told me at Stuart's dinner party.'

Verity tilted her head. 'Funny you should remember that and not my name when I first arrived at El Molino. You called me Beryl.'

'It was a slip of the tongue,' he said and she didn't know whether to believe him or not but there was one way of finding out.

'Were you attracted to me the first time you met me at Stuart's and Angie's dinner party?'

He looked at her in surprise. 'You've never asked me that before.'

'No, and I've never asked you if you like your porridge made with sugar or salt but it's one of the things I'll find out if I agree to live with you.'

'And is that question relevant to your decision?'

'Not really. I don't suppose I'll ever cook you porridge—— '

'The first question,' he interrupted tersely.

'Silly me. No, it isn't relevant, but I'd just like to know.'

Rupert leaned across the table and his eyes were suddenly teasing. 'Yes, I was attracted to you, so strongly that I wanted to drag you away from the party and make love to you in the back of my car. Happy?'

Verity held his eyes, searching for the truth and finding it without any trouble. Of course he'd been attracted—sex again. No, she wasn't happy.

'Why didn't you, then?' she asked brazenly.

'Because I knew why we were both there. You were bait and I wasn't biting.'

'Because you were still involved with Sarah?'

His eyes darkened. 'No, I just like to pick my own women and not have them thrust upon me. Now, if this is question-and-answer time, it's my turn. Would you have come with me to the back of my car?'

'No, I damned well wouldn't!'

'Why not?'

'Because . . . because I'm not that sort of girl.'

'But you are.' His voice was low and very pointed as he said that.

Verity shifted uncomfortably in her seat. 'I'm not,' she insisted faintly.

'But you are, Verity. I don't mean it in the way that you'd jump into the back of a car with anybody, but we have a strong sexual attraction and it was there from that first night, and that's why you will never accuse me again of wanting you for sex on tap. Look to yourself before passing judgement on me.'

Oh, that statement was so loaded, and she couldn't respond to it because if she did the only answer would be that love was her excuse for her desire for him. She must really have got to him earlier for him to have made such a cutting remark.

'So why do you want me to come and live with you? Upgrading me from back-seat sex?' she asked.

'I upgraded you long ago, but don't get too smart, Verity, there's more to life than bedding. Apart from the fact that we are good together in bed, I happen to like you around.'

'That's something,' she breathed exaggeratedly, as if it were a weight off her mind. 'But we'll hardly see each other. We'll both be out all day.'

He smiled. 'Not me. I've decided to work from home. The screenplay turned out well and I want to do more.'

'What about your companies?'

'I keep slaves. So are you really determined to carry on your work when you come and live with me?'

So he'd given in. Her terms. She felt no triumph, was only slightly galled by the fact that he'd said when not if.

'Yes, I do want to carry on until...'

'Until when?' he urged when she didn't go on.

She wondered what he would say or do if she told him the truth—that she would work as far into her pregnancy as was possible.

'Until I change my mind,' she went on. Or until you fall in love with me, she added to herself, knowing she'd give a limb to have that happen.

'So, it's up to me to change it for you,' he said softly and raised his wine glass to hers, and somehow she knew that that was it, confirmation that they would live together.

Verity loved his riverside house at Kew. It was elegant and comfortable and she lacked for nothing, but happiness eluded her.

Their first few days together had been wonderful, with Rupert trying to please her in every way and she him, but the transition from her cosy flat to this elegant home in Kew wasn't easy to adapt to and it was beginning to show. There were staff hovering, for one thing, and she didn't like that because she wasn't used to it and it made her feel uncomfortable.

'I can't help the way I feel,' she told Rupert one morning as she was dressing for work. 'I'd like to get up one morning and go downstairs for my breakfast and not trip over an assortment of grovelling serfs.'

'Dismiss them and serf yourself, then. Fifteen rooms——'

'OK, OK, bloody point taken!' she retorted.

He used every opportunity to get her to give up her job but she was defiant. And work; it wasn't the same. She couldn't admit it to Rupert, or anyone, for that matter, but she was losing interest in it. She had her love and the thoughts of the baby to fill her mind, and somehow that was suddenly more important than her career, a startling discovery but none the less true.

She hadn't told anyone she had moved in with Rupert, and keeping that secret was proving to be a strain as well. In fact, *everything* was a strain and she sensed that Rupert was feeling it too.

'Darling, you look exhausted. If this goes on I'm going to insist you give up your job,' Rupert declared one evening as they were having a drink before dinner.

Here we go again, she grumbled to herself as she sat by the window, gazing out at the grey river. The weather was struggling through spring and she wasn't seeing much of it. It was usually dusk by the time she got home after work.

'Career, not job,' she corrected stiffly, 'and you insist on far too much, Rupert.'

She held the gin and tonic he had handed her but didn't touch it. She couldn't drink it, the doctor had said not to. He'd also said to ease up; she was stressed, and that wasn't healthy for the baby. She was only two and a half months pregnant and it felt like ten, and the thought of the rest wasn't particularly enthralling.

'I want you to be happy,' he murmured.

Love me, then, she wanted to cry, make it easy for me to have to tell you about our baby. She looked up at him and smiled faintly. 'I'm sorry,' she breathed regrettably. 'I am trying, but...but...'

Greta, the housekeeper, came in to tell them dinner was ready. Resentfully and without another word Verity got to her feet, and Rupert frowned at her as she walked towards the door. He caught her arm.

'What's wrong now?' he asked impatiently.

She snatched her arm away. 'Nothing. I'm just tired, and for God's sake don't tell me to give up work again—you've pushed that one to death and back!'

She walked away from him, knowing in her heart that it was all her fault. The gulf was widening and she wasn't doing anything to stop it.

That night he didn't come to bed till two in the morning and when he did he didn't make love to her. Verity lay awake all night and stared into the darkness and listened to the night sounds.

She had everything and nothing. Rupert was always there for her and yet he wasn't. She felt that these last few days he'd had something on his mind but she hadn't asked what, and that was her failing, not his.

The next morning she didn't go to work. She was tired and felt slightly sick, and worry was beginning to take its toll. Rupert would notice her condition before long and she wasn't ready for that yet.

'I've a few days' leave,' she told him when he queried why she wasn't rushing around at the last minute as she usually was every morning.

It was partly true. She had some leave coming and would phone Alan later and tell him she wanted it now.

'Good. I'll take a break with you——'

'No!' Verity sat up in bed, her heart hammering. She had a doctor's appointment later. 'No, it isn't necessary, and didn't you say you had a lot of work on this week?'

'It can wait. Why don't we go out for the day?'

Verity smiled. 'No, it would put you behind, Rupert. I've masses to do and...and I'll keep popping into the study to see you.'

He seemed placated but she noticed the slight frown on his brow and later she thought she knew why.

It was that phone call. Verity was down in the sitting-room overlooking the river and reading the morning's papers, and the phone was ringing incessantly. Normally she didn't answer the phone because it was never for her and usually there was someone else to pick it up anyway. She remembered that Greta was out shopping. She reached out and picked up the receiver just as Rupert picked up the extension in his study. She was about to put it down when she heard Rupert's voice.

'Sarah, we've been through all this before. You're wasting your time... I'm sorry...'

Slowly, silently and desperately Verity put down the receiver. There was a cold sweat on her brow and her legs would hardly carry her weight as she rushed to the cloakroom.

She was sick and then sick again, and then she leaned her hot forehead against the mirror over the sink. She had known... all along she had known that Sarah was still with Rupert, in his mind and his heart. They were still in touch with each other and perhaps they were still seeing each other and...and... Her anguish took her tormented thoughts further. Rupert had suggested they go out for the day because he knew Sarah would ring him and there was a chance she would find out... Verity didn't know what to do. To tackle him or...or what?

'Verity!'

She jerked herself away from the mirror and stared at her reflection. She couldn't tackle it yet; no, not yet. Oh, God, she looked awful and felt it; she was pale and colourless.

'Verity, I have to go out,' he told her briskly as she met him on the curving stairway, she going up and he coming down. There was no eye contact, just Rupert rushing past her, pulling his leather jacket on.

He was going to see her, that woman. She just had to pick up the phone and he went running!

'What time will you be back?' She hadn't intended to sound so demanding but it came out that way.

'When I'm ready,' he told her shortly and went out of the front door.

Half an hour later Verity went out herself after calling a mini-cab. She just had to get out of that house, *his* house with Sarah's lingering perfume. She hated him for this, demanding that she live with him and then carrying on with his ex-lover, except she might not be his ex-lover; they might never have stopped seeing each other!

'Verity!' Rupert called out as soon as she returned, five hours later and so tired that she was fit to drop.

He came out into the hall. 'Where have you been? I've been worried... Verity, what the devil have you done?'

Her hand went instinctively up to her new shorter-length hair. She'd had it cut and restyled and she'd had a facial and a manicure, because that was what kept mistresses did. She looked at Rupert and burst into tears.

'Darling...'

'Don't darling me!' she sobbed, and dived for the stairs. She'd had a horribly stressful day, spending his money, trying to make herself into something she wasn't, and then that painful blood test at the doctor's and another warning to ease up. She had gone back to her flat—contrary to what Rupert had believed, she had kept it on—and it was cold and empty without her personal things there. She had felt homesick on top of everything else and so so lonely.

'Darling, what's wrong?' Rupert asked, sitting on the edge of the huge double bed she had thrown herself on.

He eased her up into his arms and held her tightly. 'Did you think I'd be mad at you for having your lovely hair cut off? I'm not, treasure, I adore it.'

'I hate it!' she sobbed. Her hand came up and rubbed at the new eyeshadow that widened and deepened and added allure to her eyes—so the assistant had told her. 'I... I wish I hadn't had it done.'

'It's lovely, makes you look sixteen and incredibly desirable.' His hand slid into the bouncy curves and it so painfully reminded her of the time he had first touched her hair at El Molino. She wished they were back there, where life had no outside interferences. Just the two of them, cocooned so intimately together.

'Verity,' he breathed huskily and moved her face so he could kiss her lips. And she let him because the day had been so awful and she wanted his comfort and his lovemaking. He kissed away her tears and slowly started to undress her. All the grim questions she wanted grim answers for lay buried under the avalanche of the sensations he was rushing her with. His hands were so warm and tantalising on her rounded breasts, and his lips blazed a trail of white heat as they ran over her stomach. His breathing quickened and was roughened by his rising desire and it all gathered up to swamp all else from her heart and mind.

She didn't know why she thought this time was different from the other times they had made love. She imagined that Rupert was more tender and that his kisses were more ardent and he was more gentle with her when he entered her. He was a beautiful lover, always surprising her with a touch, a caress, and this time was no different in that way. She thought he had discovered every secret part of her, but there was always one more delight.

She was crying as she reached her climax, silent tears that he would never see. He didn't come with her but stilled himself as her muscles spasmed around him, enhancing her pleasure and then moving slowly inside her once again, his breathing now more ragged and drugged with sensation. When he came she clasped him to her, raking her hands in his hair, urging her hips into his, silently saying the words she so longed to speak, that she loved him and always would and would give years of her life to hear him speak the same to her.

Later they went down to dinner, and Verity watched him across the table. She was searching again, for some sign of what made him tick. She wondered if he had made love to Sarah today and bit her lip at the sordidness of such a thought.

'Where did you go today?' she asked after Greta had dished up delicious marinated lamb and rice.

He looked up from his food and she thought she saw guilt in his eyes; no, she was *certain* she'd seen guilt.

'You going out to work every day certainly has its advantages,' he told her teasingly. 'If you were home all day you could be one of those possessive wives questioning every move I make.'

'But I'm not your wife. Was that another of your slips of the tongue or a Freudian slip?' Dear God, but she was sailing close to the wind.

'It could have been a disguised proposal,' he suggested pointedly.

Her stomach tightened. 'Was it?' she murmured, hope rising and falling and swishing around inside her till she felt sick and disorientated

'Do you want it to be?' he asked, those eyes of his offering no such promise.

Her heart spasmed defensively. What game were they playing here? Russian roulette? Someone was going to get the bullet and it wasn't going to be her.

'I've told you before, I don't care a fig for marriage.' She carried on eating, not wanting to look into those eyes and read relief.

'I have to go away for a couple of days,' he said at last, and Verity felt the awful day crowd in on her with more awfulness. First the phone call and then his rushing out, and her despair over Sarah, resulting in that childish display of attention-seeking with her hair and face and nails and then . . . then his beautiful, poignant lovemaking, making up in advance for this bombshell, no doubt.

'Where?' she asked, as if she didn't really care, except she did and life was getting worse by the minute.

'New York. I'd take you with me, but I'm only staying overnight and you'd be bored with the meetings I have to attend.'

Don't even give me the option to refuse, she dismally thought.

She didn't even get the chance to pack for him— Greta did that. She didn't even get the chance to drive him to the airport—he had a chauffeur for that. So what was her damned role in his life—to buffet his ego, to warm his bed?

She was desolate when he left the next morning after kissing her goodbye. She tried to make conversation with Greta in the kitchen but Greta was Austrian and, though her English was good, they were continents apart in conversation. But she learned how to make apple strudel, Vienna-style, so at least that was something.

The phone rang at midday and Verity rushed to it before Greta. Concorde was supersonic, but surely not even with a tail-wind behind it . . .

'Hello; hello.' There was silence the other end and Verity's heart iced, and when the receiver clicked down she instinctively knew that the caller had been Sarah. Then realisation surged through her: well, at least she wasn't on her way to New York with Rupert. She forced herself to feel happy at that thought but when the next call came five minutes later her heart chilled frighteningly.

'Look, who is this? Just say what you want...'

There was faint breathing from the other end and Verity's fist tightened around the receiver.

'He's not here,' she cried. 'Rupert isn't here. He's away...'

The line went dead and Verity was trembling as she put the receiver down. That had been a dumb thing to say. The caller could have been a burglar checking to see if anyone was at home. For once she was glad there were staff around.

Later Greta announced that she was going out for a couple of hours and had left her a cold lunch in the fridge. The two cleaners had already left, and suddenly Verity was alone in the house, alone and very nervous. There were more unproductive calls till Verity was nearly tearing her hair out with anguish by the time Greta returned. She said nothing about the calls, though, after deciding that she was over-reacting, but nevertheless her stomach somersaulted when the next one came.

'Mr Scott on the phone for you,' Greta told her later, popping her head round the door. 'I'll make you some tea and the strudel, yes?'

Verity thanked her and dived to the phone, her pulses racing with relief.

'Rupert!' she wailed.

'What's wrong, darling?'

She'd planned on being angry with him; had even rehearsed her words and her accusations, but it all drained from her lips as she heard his voice.

'Nothing,' she breathed softly, clutching at her chest. 'I'm just relieved you got there safely.'

He laughed and then he said words she had so longed to hear.

'Verity, I'm missing you like crazy. I wish I'd brought you with me.' His voice was low and very slightly unsteady.

'I wish too,' she murmured.

'Are you happy, darling?'

Verity nodded and bit her lip. 'Yes, just a bit worried about you arriving.'

Where were the accusations and the demands for the truth? But what truth? Perhaps there wasn't any, perhaps she was being silly, her nerves so taut and stressed that she was willing to believe any-thing—that he was still seeing Sarah.

'I meant long-term happy, Verity. You've seemed so preoccupied these last few days. I only want your happiness, you know.'

'Oh, Rupert,' she breathed. Suddenly her eyes filled with tears and she wanted to tell him about the phone calls and her fears, but it was painful, too painful, and the words just wouldn't come.

'Verity...' He went silent and she could almost hear his inward struggle, as if he wanted to say so much, but it just wouldn't come out. She helped him.

'I'm missing you too, Rupert,' she breathed huskily. 'Listen, I've ... I've decided I don't want to work any more.' Her statement was as much a surprise to herself as it was to Rupert.

His laughter was soft and relieved. 'I'm glad to hear that and I look forward to hearing a lot more from you when I get back.'

'Oh, Rupert, I wish you were here. There's so much I need to know and so much I want to say.'

'It won't be long, darling,' he soothed. 'I'll be back with you tomorrow.'

They were an ocean apart, but somehow that gulf between them was narrowing. Verity didn't know why. After those phone calls she should be desperate, but hearing his voice like this, soft and warm and tender, as if that flight across the Atlantic had made him realise what he had, filled her with hope.

'Hurry back,' she urged. 'The house is bleak without you.'

'You have the staff for company,' he laughed.

She made a snorting sound and he laughed again, and then his voice turned mysterious. 'After you've put the phone down, go to my desk, and in the top drawer you'll find something I bought for you a couple of days ago. I wasn't going to give it to you till I got back, but you sound as if you need a bit of an upper.'

'A present?' she breathed.

'More like a promise,' he told her quietly, and then added, 'I have to go, Verity; I'll call you later.'

'I'll wait up,' she said quickly.

'I'd rather you took the call in bed and then I can imagine . . . well, you know.'

'Yes, I know,' she grinned.

She hugged herself as she went to the study after putting the phone down. Something had happened in the relationship, something too subtle for analysis at the moment. It was odd, but after hearing his voice so very far away she felt reassured rather than anything. Those calls she'd presumed had come from Sarah could have been wrong numbers or someone messing around, a troubled person who got a thrill from worrying the life out of people.

'Oh, Rupert,' she breathed, staring down into the black suede box with its black silk lining. Carefully she lifted out the platinum chain with its solitaire diamond pendant and held it up to the light.

It was beautiful, simple and yet quite exquisite. Shakily Verity pressed it to her lips. Diamonds were forever. He'd said a promise...

'I'm sorry, Miss Verity...'

Verity swung to the door, shocked at the sudden commotion and Greta's apologetic outburst. The pendant slid from her fingers and plopped to the floor.

'So, you're the new bed warmer,' came a silky drawl from behind Greta.

Verity knew right away who she was. Tall, elegant, stunningly beautiful with jet hair that moved as she walked. She came straight up to Verity and would have done an inspection circuit if it weren't for Rupert's leather chair blocking her way.

'It's all right, Greta,' Verity assured the nervous housekeeper. Verity clenched her fists at her side as Greta gave her an apologetic look and backed out of the room.

'What do you want?' Verity bravely asked.

'Do you know who I am?' The woman asked with a cynical smile on her lovely face.

'Yes, you're Sarah,' Verity said.

The beautiful Sarah gave a knowing smile. 'So he talks about me to you, does he?'

'Not really,' Verity told her coolly. 'But when you live with someone you find out about their past.' She laid emphasis on the past and Sarah was on to it straight away.

'I'll never be his past, dear——'

'Don't call me dear,' Verity cut in sharply. 'The name is Verity.'

There was a long pause as Sarah eyed her up and down again. 'Well, Verity,' she drawled at last, 'you and your presence here surprise me. Rupert doesn't go for blondes, and frankly I didn't think he'd enter into another affair so quickly after me.'

Verity held her temper because to let rip at this woman would be playing into her hands.

'What did you come here for?' she asked, feigning uninterest.

'I came to see Rupert, but it's obvious he isn't here.'

'You knew that. I told you when you phoned.' She watched her reaction to that and in an instant knew by the darkening of her eyes that the calls had come from her, and now she was here because curiosity had spurred her.

Sarah didn't like being caught out and her eyes narrowed angrily. 'Well, much as it galls me to have to ask, when will he be back?'

'Tomorrow, but perhaps I can help you in the meantime.' Verity's fingernails were almost imbedded in her palms. She wished she would go because she was afraid she wouldn't be able to contain herself much longer.

'You could help yourself by getting out from where you don't belong.'

Verity forced a confident smile, though she didn't feel it. 'What I do is nothing to do with you, and what Rupert does is no longer a concern of yours, Sarah.'

'You have half a point. You are none of my business because you won't be around for long, but Rupert will always be of concern to me, as I am to him. I'm a part of his life and no one can change that.'

'I think he already has. He's told me you're nothing——'

'Then he's a liar!' Sarah suddenly stormed. 'And you're a fool to think you can take my place. Rupert and I have ties that can never be broken. Oh, he's tried, but I'm not having any of that——'

'What do you want, more money?' Verity's eyes blazed now. She wasn't going to take all this garbage from this woman.

'Money!' Sarah laughed spitefully. 'No money in the world will compensate for what that bastard's done to me and our child . . .'

Verity's stomach tipped and she gripped the edge of the desk to steady herself.

'Child?' she croaked.

Sarah suddenly looked so triumphant that she seemed to swell with it.

'I can see that's shocked you. A small part of his life he failed to tell you about?' she simpered cruelly.

Verity just stared blindly at her. 'He . . . he didn't say,' she whispered.

'We have a baby daughter, a daughter he doesn't want to know about, never did want to know about. He told me to get out when I was five months pregnant, when it was too late for an abortion. He didn't want to know about fatherhood or even being a husband; all he lives for is his damned business empire...'

Verity swayed and righted herself and closed herself off from the outside world. She was only vaguely aware of the rest of what Sarah was screaming at her. She remembered her own cold indifference as she asked Sarah to leave, and she remembered thinking as Sarah stormed out of the house that she felt desperately sorry for the poor woman; the rest was a red mist of anguish. Sarah loved Rupert and was desperate to get him back. She had a child to cope with, Rupert's child, and he hadn't wanted to know, and that mist thickened and engulfed her.

Slowly Verity went upstairs to the bedroom she shared with Rupert and shakily pulled her clothes from the wardrobe.

Funny, but she was glad Sarah had come, because now she knew that Rupert would never marry her or love her or care two hoots for the child she was carrying. And deep down hadn't she known this all along? Some sixth sense must have warned her to keep her flat on, and her job. Thank God. For once in her life uncertainty had paid off.

'Are there being dramatic, a detail of the drama a
brand as brand about, alone, etc. next to I now about.
He told me to put with matures was five months
maturing, whatever you notifier for go the retiring. He
Areas work to top be to be more of the neighbouring
or hand special ten very which in the desired framed,

CHAPTER NINE

'WHAT'S wrong?' Alan asked as Verity shakily put
down the telephone receiver. 'Bad news?'

Dazedly Verity looked up at him hovering over
her desk. 'No...no, just something a bit unexpected has cropped up. Personal, I'm afraid, so
don't waste your breath asking me what.'

She pushed her trembling fingers through her hair
and stood up. 'I'm sorry, Alan, I've got to ask for
this afternoon off as well.' If he objected she was
going to have to give in her notice, because if her
worst fears were realised there would be a lot more
of these missed working hours.

'No problem. I didn't expect you in this morning
anyway. I thought you said you wanted a few days
of your leave; you only had two.'

'I was bored.' Verity told him, crossing to the
window and desperately wanting to be alone to get
her thoughts together. She'd slept badly, as the flat
had taken ages to heat up, and there was only one
place to go when she had got up and that was work.
She wanted to carry on as before, and calling the
doctor for the results of her blood test was part of
her normality plan. The doctor wanted to see her
today. She had a rare blood group and, though there
was no cause for alarm, they wanted to keep a close
eye on her throughout her pregnancy...and there
would be tests on the unborn baby.

'Are you sure there's nothing wrong? You haven't been right for ages,' Alan persisted.

Verity moved back to her desk. 'Just tired.'

'Can you untire yourself for tonight? Stuart and Angie are having a dinner party. Stuart's phoned you at home every night, but you're never there.' He grinned knowingly as he added, 'Perhaps that's why you're looking so washed out. Who's the new man in your life, or is it men?'

'Shut up, Alan,' Verity ordered scathingly. 'You can ring Stuart for me and tell him what to do with his dinner parties.' She suddenly smiled over-sweetly. 'No, don't bother; why should you have all the fun? I'll tell him myself.'

'You're not still holding a grudge over that Scott business, are you?' he laughed.

Verity paralysed him with a fast-freeze look. 'How is my cousin, by the way?' she asked, lifting a file from her desk and flicking it open. She really didn't want to know, having troubles enough of her own, but he was still her cousin.

'He's fine. Business picking up and it looks as if he might get Scott's advertising after all——'

Verity tensed and lifted her head to look at Alan. 'What the hell do you mean?' she blurted sharply.

Alan frowned at her sudden outburst but didn't remark on it. 'Scott's put a new man in as his advertising director, and Stuart's approached him and it's looking good.'

Verity desensitised herself. For a moment she thought Rupert might have given Stuart the advertising because of her, but highly unlikely from a man who was insensitive enough not to want his own child.

She didn't go back to work after the doctor's appointment. She was too tired and stunned. She'd never known about her rare blood group, but that wasn't surprising. She'd never had an accident or a serious illness that warranted a blood test. It wasn't serious but could be for the baby if the father's blood wasn't compatible. Somehow she had fluffed her way out of that question—what was the father's blood group? She'd said she'd find out, but how? Short of cutting his throat and taking her own sample . . .

She sighed heavily as she drove home, taking it easy in the rush-hour traffic, as the warning the doctor had issued her with had rather worried her. She was verging on anaemia and had a pile of vitamins to take, and she'd been told to ease up. Some chance of that, she thought ruefully as she parked in the square outside the flat. She was going to be a single parent and would have to support this child.

As she stepped into her hallway the phone started ringing. It was Alan.

'Verity, Rupert Scott has been in the office and practically blew a gasket when I told him you weren't here but at home.'

Oh, God. Verity flopped down on a chair and held her head in her free hand. She should have left a note, something to prepare him for this. But why? He didn't deserve any consideration for anything!

'What did he want?' she uttered weakly, considering that it was a rather stupid question.

'I might ask you the same thing. He didn't say, but he was livid. What the hell is going on? Did you walk out of El Molino with his Snoopy toothbrush?'

Oh, more than that!

'I have to go, Alan. I'll tell you all about it tomorrow.' She put the phone down and her hand was shaking as she did it. And she probably would tell him all about it. She had no one else to turn to and over the next few months she would need his support.

Rupert would come here, she knew that for certain. You couldn't just walk out on Rupert Scott. She was prepared, or thought she was, when she heard him leaning on the doorbell.

She opened the door and in that second lost her nerve completely, and all she had practised in her head went out of it like a puff of wind.

He stepped into the hallway, half-bull, half-man, grasped her arm and pushed her into the small sitting-room. When they got there he swivelled her to face him. His eyes were black and thunderous and his facial muscles were contorted with fury.

'This is a kick where it hurts, Verity Brooks!' His hand waved around the room. 'Why, Verity, why keep this place on? You had no damned intention of making a life with me, did you? Oh, no, milk me for what I could offer and——'

'Rupert!' Verity cried so harshly that he stopped mid-sentence. 'Stop this, it's doing no good——'

'It's a bloody release,' Rupert blazed, 'because I could kill you for this!'

'Go ahead!' she cried. 'Worse things could happen!'

His eyes locked with hers in a painful look that tore at Verity's heart. There was sorrow there in his eyes with the fury but she wasn't going to be fooled by that. She thought of Sarah, and an image of her and their child rose so vividly within her that she wasn't afraid any more.

'Why?' Rupert pleaded, his voice hoarse. 'Why are you here and not waiting at home for me?'

'What home?' she questioned defensively, her eyes wide and clear. 'Your home maybe, but certainly not mine. *This* is my home.'

'My home is yours; I never thought of offering you anything less, but when you agreed to come and live with me I didn't dream for a minute you'd be so chillingly deceptive. How could you have kept this place on, and why?'

Now she was the guilty party. Where was the justice in this world?

'I kept it on because...' She faltered. She had been wrong to do it. She should have loved and trusted him more and had faith enough that it would work out, but she hadn't, and on reflection it was one of her better decisions; otherwise, where could she have gone after Sarah's revelations?

'Because what? You were so unsure of my feelings for you?' he questioned dully.

She forced the answer through her burning lips. 'Yes, Rupert,' she whispered truthfully. 'I was so unsure of your feelings. You've never given me reason to think there were any.'

He stepped back from her as if she had shot him. He turned away and stood by the window and stared out at the small green opposite, raking his fingers through his hair.

'You didn't look hard enough, Verity.' He sighed raggedly. 'And you couldn't have had any intention of looking because you kept this place on. So why are you here now, why now, of all times?' he asked quietly, his anger seeming to have evaporated.

'Because...because it didn't work out.'

'I thought it was working out,' he grated, half turning towards her. 'I understood your insecurities at first. Didn't I do enough to make you feel happy and secure?'

She nodded bleakly. 'Yes, but...but it wasn't enough.'

'Living a life of luxury isn't enough? You had everything with me. I could give you everything.'

Love was all I wanted, Verity whispered inwardly.

He suddenly reached into his pocket and drew out the diamond pendant and held it up. 'Wasn't this enough?'

The pain was indescribable as she stared at the beautiful jewel. Rupert Scott bought people and paid them off when he'd finished with them, just as he had done with Sarah.

Her eyes were iceberg-cold as she glared at him. 'I'm not to be bought, Rupert.'

'Bought!' he raged. 'What the hell did you think I was buying, your bloody body?'

She shook her head miserably. She felt so weak and insignificant against his anger. And the pain in her heart prevented her from spilling out what she should. That he was a liar and a bastard for what he'd done to Sarah, and what hope had she with him when she was in the same position as his unfortunate ex-mistress had been? Carrying his child, a child he wouldn't want?

When she didn't fight back he suddenly came to her, gently took her upper arms and pressed his thumbs into her sensitive flesh. 'Is that why you took flight, because you thought the gift was...was some sort of payment for your services?'

'Oh, God, no!' she breathed hotly, her eyes filling with tears. 'I didn't think that, not that . . . and you shouldn't have suggested it, Rupert, you shouldn't have.'

His grip tightened. 'What am I to think, then? I get home and find your clothes gone, none of the staff knowing where you are, the pendant discarded on the floor of the study. I drove to your office, only to learn you are here. What the hell have I done to deserve this?'

Verity hung her head. Why did he make her feel so guilty when he was the one who was wicked and evil?

'I...I had to come here. I didn't...I didn't want to be with you any more.' She looked up at him then and it was the bravest thing she had ever done. She held his eyes. 'It wasn't working, Rupert——'

He shook her. 'It was, you know damned well it was. When I phoned you from New York it was good. I felt that something had changed and when I got back you would care as much for me as I care for you.'

The tears spilled from Verity's eyes then and Rupert smeared them away with the backs of his fingers.

'You do care, don't you, Verity? I know it. I feel it, but something has happened; tell me what?'

At last he had made an admittance of his deep feeling for her but it was too late, and she couldn't tell him why because it had all happened in his life before and no good had come out of it. She could imagine this very scenario happening between him and Sarah, and Sarah's saying that there was a baby and his going cold and thrusting her away...

Verity tore herself from his grasp and stood in front of the fireplace, staring down at the unlit fire. She felt as cold and dismal as the dormant coals.

'I'm...I'm sorry I left in such a hurry, without a proper explanation,' she murmured. 'But put it down to cowardice. I didn't want to face you.' She stared bleakly at the mantelpiece and couldn't face him now. 'I want it to end, this affair. I don't want to live with you any more. I want my own life, not yours. I'm sorry if I hurt you by keeping this flat on, but I suppose I must have known all the time that it wouldn't work.' She swallowed hard and wondered how she had ever got that out without completely breaking down.

She flinched as he came up behind her and touched her neck. 'I don't want it to finish this way, darling. I want you to come back with me now and we'll talk it over——'

'There's nothing to talk over,' she husked, wishing he wouldn't stroke the back of her neck like that. 'I won't change my mind. I want to stay here and live my life, not yours.'

Dear God, she prayed he wouldn't feel the tremor of despair that threaded through her and the tremor of reluctant desire that rose as he caressed her neck. She couldn't hate him. She could hate what he did, but he was still the man she loved and the father of the child within her.

She felt something cold around her neck, and her hand came up and she felt the beautiful single diamond in the hollow of her throat. Rupert was fastening the clasp at the back of her neck. Verity's fingers closed over the pendant and she closed her eyes in pain. The necklace seemed to sear her flesh. She wanted to tear it away but couldn't. Her whole body seemed to be paralysed in agony.

Slowly Rupert turned her to him. 'Wear this, Verity. I want you to have it, and please don't think of it as some sort of payment. I bought it because I love you...'

Verity's heart stopped and her legs melted. Oh, God, why was life so cruel and why was he? He loved her and she loved him, but he had done something so unforgivable to Sarah and he'd do the same to her if she allowed it.

He lowered his mouth to hers and kissed her lips so tenderly that she nearly allowed herself to clasp him to her and tell him all she had always wanted to say to him. That she loved him and only wanted him in her life. The kiss intensified and his body was pressed so hard to hers that she felt every beat of his heart twinned with hers. This was all she had ever wanted, his admission of love, but it was impossible now, impossible because of what Sarah had told her. He might love her but he wouldn't love another child forced upon him. He didn't want the one he had.

'A promise,' he murmured, 'it was a promise, Verity. To love, honour and obey——'

'Oh, no!' She tore herself away then and faced him bitterly. 'Don't say things like that!' she cried painfully. 'Don't say things you don't mean.'

He grasped her again, tightly. 'I do mean it!' he grated. 'I love you and I want to marry you——'

'You'd make any sort of promise to save your face, wouldn't you?' she flamed, her anger spurred by the pain within her breast. 'You say you love me but it's just a sham and nothing more. You just can't bear the thought that I chose to walk out on you. You didn't throw me out the way you threw Sarah out, and that's really got to your insufferable pride, hasn't it?'

'I have no damned pride where you're concerned,' he grated through his clenched teeth, 'but my God I had some where she was concerned. That's why she's out and you were in——'

'Like trading in a car for a more up-to-date model!' Verity cried back. 'You haven't any feelings, Rupert. If you had you would have been more compassionate to Sarah, you would...' Her voice trailed away and the silence that stepped into its place was heavy and ponderous.

Seconds later Rupert spoke heavily. 'I didn't come here to discuss Sarah, and you had no right to bring something up that is no concern of yours. I came here to take you back home with me——'

'No!' Verity cried.

It was the most final no in the world, and Rupert recognised it as such.

'Is that your last word?' he breathed heavily.

She nodded, because she couldn't speak.

His expressionless grey eyes lingered for only another fleeting second, and then he turned on his heel and walked out.

* * *

Verity stretched out her hand and turned the alarm clock to face her. Only midnight; she'd thought it was much later. She lay back on her pillows. This was how life was going to be in future—one long drag.

She sat up suddenly as the doorbell went, persistently. She'd know that ring anywhere.

'I've nothing more to say to you,' she called through the door. 'Go away and leave me alone.'

'Don't make me angry, Verity; open this door before I kick it in.'

She did because she had neighbours. Rupert brushed past her and went straight to the bedroom.

'Where is it?'

'What? *My* new trade-in?'

She leaned in the doorway, surprisingly calm as she watched him, surprisingly uncalm, searching her wardrobe.

'Your sense of humour is sick. I'm the only man in your life and you'd better believe it.'

Verity's stomach tightened. 'That's what you think.'

'It's what I know.' He hauled an overnight bag from the wardrobe and tossed it on the bed. 'Take what you need for your immediate needs and I'll send someone over for the rest of your stuff tomorrow.'

'Is this a kidnap?' she drawled sarcastically.

'No, this is reclamation of what is rightly mine— you!'

'I belong to myself——'

'Quit it, Verity,' he snapped, 'and don't give me all that "I'm my own person" rubbish. You're coming back with me because it's where you belong.' He wrenched open a drawer of her dressing-table and started pulling out her underwear.

Verity lurched across the room and her hand tightened over his.

'How dare you dominate me this way, bursting in here and being so bloody bolshie? Leave my knickers alone!'

'Would that I could!' His eyes softened and glinted with humour, and if her heart weren't tearing so badly she would have laughed with him.

'Why are you doing this?' she blurted; pulling her hand away from his.

'Because now I know what's driving you so crazy.'

Her pulses accelerated. He couldn't know. Nobody knew.

'What?' she uttered huskily.

'Sarah. When I came here earlier I didn't know she had paid you a visit. When I got back to Kew Greta told me she'd called.'

'So?'

'So now I understand.'

'You understand nothing, Rupert!'

'I understand jealousy when I'm faced with it.'

'Jealousy?' Verity screeched.

'Yes, jealousy, and don't try to deny it. You left because——'

'Because she's still a very important part of your life——'

'A part of my past, and not so very important,' he corrected, resuming what he was doing, stuffing her underwear into the hold-all.

'Past, present, future!' Verity stormed. 'And always will be. She still rings you up——'

He straightened himself up and glared at her. 'What are you talking about?'

'Oh, don't deny it. I overheard you talking to her one day and... and then you rushed out to meet her and no doubt you made love to her and——'

He gripped her arms. 'Dear God, but I wish I had half as much fun in real life as I have in your imagination!'

'My imagination? I haven't any. It's all fact! I picked up the phone at the same time you did and heard her voice, so don't you even think about denying it.'

'I'm not,' he grated harshly. 'A day doesn't pass when she doesn't call me, making more demands.'

'And you meet them, don't you? You couldn't wait to rush out to her. You tore down the stairs and went tearing out to meet her.'

He looked bemused for a second, as if dredging his memory, and then his face cleared. 'I dashed out to the jewellers to pick up the pendant I was having made for you. I'd called them after speaking with Sarah and it was ready, and I couldn't wait to collect it.'

Paling with shock, Verity gazed up at him and knew by the openness of his eyes that he was telling the truth. But she wasn't elated; somehow to her tortured senses it was worse than ever. Poor Sarah, calling him in another desperate attempt to win back his love for her and her child, and him preoccupied with a gift for the next lady in line.

Verity couldn't bear it and turned away.

'Where are you going?'

She didn't know, just as far from him as was possible. But, while she was clad only in a satin nightie and robe, out into the night wasn't a proposition. She flew to the kitchen and shakily poured a glass of water. She turned when he followed her into the small room.

'Believe me, Verity, I know what you're going through——'

'You don't!' she cried. 'You couldn't possibly know.'

'But I do,' he insisted. 'I understand it all, why you kept this flat on, why you felt so insecure with me. My relationship with Sarah was hanging over you like the sword of Damocles, ever a threat to our love.'

'*Our* love?' she spat. 'Aren't you taking a bit too much for granted? As always!'

He smiled, and that shocked her. 'Are you going to deny you love me? Because forget it if you are. You can only be jealous if you care, Verity, and you care, and that's why you ran away from me. You thought I was still involved with Sarah.'

'And you are and always will be.'

'Only in your mind, certainly not mine.'

How could he be so cruelly dismissive? She shook her head in dismay.

'You bastard,' she breathed raggedly. 'You're the biggest bastard I've ever met.'

He looked shocked at her statement and she was glad. He'd come here tonight to force her back into his home with promises of love and marriage that he couldn't hope to tempt her with because she knew him, knew exactly how hard and cruel he was.

'You'd better go,' she said quietly. 'Because if you don't I might be sorely tempted to kill you.'

He stepped towards her and her body stiffened in defence. He stopped in front of her and lifted her chin.

'Kiss or kill; I wonder which you mean.'

A reminder like that cut painfully into her heart. She tried to step back out of his way but her back was already hard up against the work-surface.

'Don't ... don't touch me.' It was then that she wanted to cry, for all the past and the dreadful future that lay ahead of her. To love a man like this was a punishment for her sins surely?

He lowered his mouth and his lips skimmed hers, lightly, lovingly and far too late.

She moved her head aside as he threatened to kiss her properly. It angered him and he gripped her by the shoulders.

'What games now, Verity? I love you and want to marry you; what else do you want from me?'

It was all she had ever wanted, but it was all out of sync and too much had happened for her to trust him.

'I ... can't trust you.' Her eyes filled with tears. 'And I can't give my love ... my love to a man who ...' She couldn't finish. The tears choked her nose and her throat.

'A man who what?' he pressed urgently, his eyes searching hers and not understanding.

Somehow she found the strength to tear herself away from him. She couldn't face him and tell him the truth, that she hated him for denying his own daughter and the mother who had borne her.

He caught her at the bedroom door and swung her round so viciously that she feared for her life and that of the baby within her. That fear manifested itself with an angry explosion.

'I hate you, Rupert Scott. You are a cruel, wicked man. You have a daughter...'

She thought he was going to kill her. His eyes hardened to shards of cold metal and his grip was so fierce that her blood stopped coursing.

'A daughter!' he growled, and then his whole body slackened. His face was suddenly grey and then he did something so totally unexpected that it threw her completely.

He gathered her into his arms and held her head against his shoulder. His breathing was heavy and his heart beat loud, and a deep tremor seemed to reverberate through his whole body.

'Dear God, am I going to pay for this for the rest of my life?' he whispered against her.

A great sickness rose inside Verity, so fiercely that she felt dizzy and weak with it. Even now he couldn't face his responsibility; even now he felt he was the wronged one.

She was crushed against him and unable to move, and when he spoke again the dizziness sped upwards and outwards.

'She told you, didn't she?' he whispered. 'But I bet she didn't tell you the child isn't mine——'

Verity came round. Slowly and swimmingly. She was flat out on her bed and someone was sitting on the edge of the bed, bathing her hot brow. The sickness was fading and life was seeping back into her bones.

'Rupert,' she whispered, and blinked open her exhausted eyes. She wished she felt stronger.

'I'm here, darling. I think you fainted, but I've never seen anyone faint before.'

'I fainted,' she murmured. Hadn't the doctor warned her to ease up? She licked her dry lips. 'Tell me it's true, Rupert.'

He smiled down at her. 'It's true, darling; you just went white and slid down and I caught you.'

She tried to laugh but it gurgled in her throat. She felt as if she'd swallowed a hammer.

'I didn't mean that. You said...just before I went silly and feminine...you said the...the child wasn't...' Perhaps she hadn't heard it at all; perhaps wishful thinking had spurred those words to her ears.

Rupert took both her hands and clasped them in his. 'The child isn't mine, darling. Did she tell you it was?'

Verity nodded. 'I couldn't bear it, Rupert, the thought that you didn't want to know your own daughter.' She bit her lip because she had shown no trust in him. 'I...hated you for it. I believed her, you see, and now I hate myself.' The tears welled again and she gulped. 'Oh, Rupert, I believed her, a woman I'd never met before, a woman so screwed up with revenge...'

'Stop it, darling,' he ordered softly. 'Don't torture yourself.'

'But Rupert, why didn't you tell me?' She searched his handsome, drawn face for an answer but didn't find it. He spoke it instead.

'I couldn't talk about it, Verity; maybe in time I would have told you, but the trauma was so deep-seated and she was still putting on such pressure. I've had two years of hell with her and at times I thought it would never be over.'

'You thought it was over when you asked me to come and live with you, though.'

He nodded his dark head. 'After El Molino I knew I wanted you in my life forever, but I wanted the past debris of my life cleared out of the way to be able to offer you all that I wanted to. Even when I knew I was in love with you there, I wasn't emotionally free to offer you anything. When Sarah left——'

'She said you threw her out.'

He gave her a thin smile. 'How could she say anything else? A woman scorned and all that. When she left I supported her, and when the child was born I supported her too, but I wasn't prepared to do that indefinitely. She claimed the child was mine but I knew it wasn't. The relationship had soured long before and I was away at the time she must have conceived.' He shrugged. 'In spite of everything, I felt sorry for her, and for a long time I blamed myself. If I'd given her more of my time and love she wouldn't have sought solace elsewhere, but the feeling wasn't there, you see.'

'I understand,' Verity murmured. 'You felt responsible.'

'And paid for my weakness.'

'It wasn't weakness, Rupert. You must have cared for her at one time and you just couldn't cut off that caring because she had done wrong. And there was a child to be considered, even if it wasn't yours, you wouldn't have seen it suffer.'

'No, it was an innocent being in all this.'

'But when you asked me to live with you you said you were freer.'

'I thought I was. I told Sarah I wasn't prepared to keep her forever and the father should take some responsibility. She then told me who who it was—my advertising director. I sacked him—— '

'Oh.' It hurt her to think he'd done that.

Rupert smiled. 'Don't take that the wrong way, but the bastard was encouraging her to squeeze more money out of me.'

'They were conspiring together?'

He nodded. 'Not a very pleasant discovery,' he husked, and she suddenly realised all that he must have been through. No wonder he had seemed distanced from her at times. And she had actually felt sorry for poor Sarah.

She smiled suddenly at a new realisation.

'What are you smiling at?' Rupert asked, smoothing her hands, which were still clasped in his.

'Well, you've put in a new advertising director and he's having talks with my cousin, Stuart.'

Rupert threw his head back and laughed out loud. 'It's an ill wind...'

She grinned and pinched the back of his hand. 'When I heard, I thought you'd done it for me.'

'And I would have done in time, darling,' he told her, still laughing. 'But the other way is best—let Stuart earn the favours, not try to buy them with his beautiful cousin.' He bent down and kissed her lips then, and Verity responded by throwing her arms around his neck. They broke off at last and Rupert spoke huskily. 'It's all over now, my dearest love. We are free, and you do love me, don't you?'

'I've never told you, have I?'

'Not in words.'

'Oh, I love you, Rupert. So very, very much. I always have.'

'Have you?'

She wrinkled her nose. 'Well, not at the dinner party or the restaurant. I thought you were pretty grim and moody.'

'You were attracted to me, though,' he persisted hopefully.

She had been, although she had buried it, not wanting to get involved so soon after her other disastrous relationship, but this wasn't the time to thrash that out in her mind—there were other more pressing needs.

She struggled up from the pillows and struggled with the words to tell him. They wouldn't come and her tongue felt swollen and unable to form them. Would he be angry or pleased? He loved her and wanted to marry her, but...

'Darling, what's wrong?'

She shook her head and wouldn't look at him. He lifted her chin and her eyes swam as she focused on his face.

'You...you said we were free,' she started nervously.

'We are, darling. Once we're married Sarah won't give me any more trouble.'

'It's not that, but...but something more. I shouldn't have left you when she told me all those things. I should have trusted you.'

'I understand, treasure. I really do. You were confused and upset and...'

She shook her head. 'It was more, Rupert——'

'There's nothing more.'

She had to be honest with him but she was so afraid. 'Rupert, please, please listen to me, and I'll understand if you don't want me.'

'Not want you! I'll always want you.'

She bit her lip and swallowed. 'I ran from El Molino because I loved you so very much and I thought you didn't love me. I was hurting so badly that that was why I was offhand, and I was even cross when you sent the roses without a message——'

'Red roses speak for themselves, Verity,' he told her earnestly. 'So does the moon.'

She nodded vigorously. 'I should have known, but I was so afraid.'

'And you're afraid now, aren't you?'

'Yes,' she whispered and tried to smile, but it wouldn't come. 'And...and I was even more afraid when you asked me to come and live with you because...because something had happened.'

His brow creased and she was even more afraid then, but she hid it because it was no good. She had to tell him, even at the risk of losing him.

'Rupert, when Sarah came to your house——'

'Our house,' he interjected as if to reassure her.

She couldn't repeat 'our house' because it wasn't yet. 'When she told me her child was yours and how you didn't want to know and how you only lived for your work I thought...I thought it would be the same for me, that...that you would reject me too.'

'I decided to work from home for that very reason, Verity. I never wanted the whole commitment with Sarah; if I had I wouldn't have left her alone so much. My love for you is whole and complete, and I want to be with you every minute of the day. It's why I've given you such a hard time over your job. I can't tell you what it meant to me when I called from New York and you said you were giving it up. It's all I've ever wanted. Just the two of us.'

Painfully she widened her violet eyes at him. 'That's just it, Rupert,' she said quietly. 'There isn't going to be just the two of us.'

He smiled. 'The serfs? You'll have to live with——'

'No, Rupert. I didn't mean...' She couldn't finish. She lowered her head and stared at her fingers, entwined in her lap.

There was silence in her tiny bedroom, a deathly silence and then a sound that filled it, every corner of it. Laughter, deep, deep, amazed laughter.

Her head jerked up as Rupert got to his feet and lifted her to him. The room spun and she realised it wasn't the room but her, round and round, clasped in his arms.

'A baby, dear God, a baby!'

The laughter was infectious and when her head stopped spinning she joined him.

'You don't mind?' she cried breathlessly.

'Mind? I'm crazy about the idea.' He held her away from him so that he could drink in her happiness. 'Oh, Verity Brooks Scott, what a clever girl you are. I love you so very much.' His mouth closed over hers and she knew it was going to be all right, and why had she ever doubted it?

She laughed one more time as he lowered her to the bed. 'I thought you didn't like making love in a single bed,' she giggled as she shifted over to make room for him.

'There's always the back seat of my car.'

She linked her arms around his warm neck and pulled him down to her. 'We'll save that for when the baby keeps us awake at night.'

'No baby is going to keep me from what I love doing most in the world,' he rasped as he shifted her robe out of the way, 'making love to my wife.'

'I suppose that means another addition to the staff, namely a nanny,' she teased, and he nipped her ear.

'We'll argue about that at another time,' he told her as his mouth closed over hers, blotting out the very argument that was already forming on her lips.

'Don't be such a baby,' Verity teased as they stepped out into brilliant sunshine in Harley Street.

Rupert slumped back against the railings, holding his arm and looking as if he was going to faint.

'It was only a fingernailful,' she laughed.

He pulled her against him as he supported himself against the railings. 'An armful,' he protested. 'How do you expect me to live and love without my full quota of blood?'

Verity laughed and kissed him on the mouth. 'That arm is already making a full recovery. It's acting as if it doesn't know this is broad daylight and there are hundreds of people milling up and down.'

Rupert glanced up and down the almost deserted street and then slid the arm in question under her coat to slide over her very slightly swollen stomach.

'Happy?' he grinned.

'Ecstatic,' she smiled. 'So we are compatible after all. Your blood is in tune with mine and we're going to have a beautiful healthy baby with violet——'

'Grey eyes,' he finished for her. 'The dominant streak always prevails.'

Those violet eyes twinkled. 'We'll see,' she murmured as she pulled out of his arms and stepped into the back of the car.

'Knightsbridge, Eric,' Verity instructed the chauffeur as Rupert slid in beside her. 'I want a wedding dress that fits before I get too fat,' she whispered in Rupert's ear.

'Then you'll need this to stop the sales assistant's tongue from wagging.' He plunged his hand into his pocket and took out a small, very interesting leather-bound box. He flicked it open, never taking his eyes from Verity's wide violet eyes in case he missed her ecstatic reaction.

'Rupert!' she exclaimed in a rush of excitement. 'Oh, it's ... it's totally beautiful.'

'Like you,' he murmured as he took the solitaire diamond ring and slipped it on to the third finger of her left hand. 'It's the perfect twin to the pendant, to seal the promise forever.'

Verity's eyes filled with tears of joy and sparkled brighter than the diamond on her finger. 'So ... so this is it. Babies, wedding dresses, engagement rings——'

'Just a minute,' laughed Rupert. 'Where have all these plurals come from? One wedding dress, one engagement ring——'

'One baby?' she murmured, wrapping her arms around his neck and nearly squeezing the life from him in her happiness.

He turned his head and his mouth claimed hers in a deep, deep kiss that promised nothing of the sort. When he finally drew away from her he told her throatily, 'And one official honeymoon.'

'Oh,' Verity uttered, feigning disappointment. 'There was I, thinking life with you would be one long honeymoon.'

'Oh, it will be, and that's another promise, but I did say an *official* honeymoon—you know, the one that generally follows the ceremony, after the champagne and rice throwing——'

'And the cutting up of your tie and auctioning it for our dowry,' she reminded him with a giggle.

'Ah, yes,' he laughed, remembering. 'So that's where you want to go for your honeymoon, is it? El Molino?'

She gazed deep into his eyes, almost afraid that it wouldn't be his choice, but she knew as soon as she saw his grey eyes mist with memories that he wouldn't disagree. They had fought there, and fallen desperately in love there, and their child had been conceived there. It was the only place in the world for a honeymoon.

'Yes,' she whispered dreamily, raising her hand to caress his chin lovingly. 'A honeymoon in Andalucia would be the perfect end to an imperfect affair.'

'And a perfect start to the rest of our lives,' he told her, holding her firmly against him and pressing his warm loving mouth to hers to seal yet another promise.

Next Month's Romances

Each month you can choose from a wide variety of romance with Mills & Boon. Below are the new titles to look out for next month, why not ask either Mills & Boon Reader Service or your Newsagent to reserve you a copy of the titles you want to buy — just tick the titles you would like and either post to Reader Service or take it to any Newsagent and ask them to order your books.

Please save me the following titles:	Please tick	✓
BREAKING POINT	Emma Darcy	
SUCH DARK MAGIC	Robyn Donald	
AFTER THE BALL	Catherine George	
TWO-TIMING MAN	Roberta Leigh	
HOST OF RICHES	Elizabeth Power	
MASK OF DECEPTION	Sara Wood	
A SOLITARY HEART	Amanda Carpenter	
AFTER THE FIRE	Kay Gregory	
BITTERSWEET YESTERDAYS	Kate Proctor	
YESTERDAY'S PASSION	Catherine O'Connor	
NIGHT OF THE SCORPION	Rosemary Carter	
NO ESCAPING LOVE	Sharon Kendrick	
OUTBACK LEGACY	Elizabeth Duke	
RANSACKED HEART	Jayne Bauling	
STORMY REUNION	Sandra K. Rhoades	
A POINT OF PRIDE	Liz Fielding	

If you would like to order these books in addition to your regular subscription from Mills & Boon Reader Service please send £1.70 per title to: Mills & Boon Reader Service, P.O. Box 236, Croydon, Surrey, CR9 3RU, quote your Subscriber No:...
(If applicable) and complete the name and address details below. Alternatively, these books are available from many local Newsagents including W.H.Smith, J.Menzies, Martins and other paperback stockists from 12th March 1993.

Name:..

Address:...

....Post Code:...........................

To Retailer: If you would like to stock M&B books please contact your regular book/magazine wholesaler for details.

You may be mailed with offers from other reputable companies as a result of this application.
If you would rather not take advantage of these opportunities please tick box ☐

Rico allowed his gaze to dwell on the gap between the edges of Merle's blouse with deliberate impertinence. 'I thought I'd made it quite clear that, despite what I may once have imagined I felt for you, I am no longer tempted by anything you have to offer—however charmingly it is displayed.'

She was mad to taunt him, but his air of self-righteousness was infuriating to her.

'From the way you acted a few minutes ago I could be forgiven for questioning that statement!' Her eyes spat fire at him.

'You mean because I kissed you?' Eyebrows arched in elegant disbelief. 'But my dear Merle, surely you realised that was merely an experiment to discover how you would react to me after such a long absence? Put it down to research rather than the pursuit of pleasure. I wanted to know just how fickle you could be.'

'Then I hope you were satisfied!'

Books you will enjoy
by ANGELA WELLS

RASH CONTRACT

After several years had passed Karis had managed to forget her tragic past—until Nik Christianides appeared to reawaken all her old memories. But he had a way of replacing what she had lost...

RASH INTRUDER

Autocratic, short-tempered and demanding was how Tamar summed up her new boss, Dagan Carmichael. He was also incredibly attractive; but Tamar knew all about the pitfalls inherent in office relationships. So why was it so difficult to keep him at arm's length?

SUMMER'S
PRIDE

BY

ANGELA WELLS

MILLS & BOON LIMITED
ETON HOUSE   18-24 PARADISE ROAD
RICHMOND   SURREY   TW9 1SR

*First published in Great Britain 1990
by Mills & Boon Limited*

© Angela Wells 1990

*Australian copyright 1990
Philippine copyright 1990
This edition 1990*

ISBN 0 263 76775 2

*Set in Times Roman 10 on 11½ pt.
01-9008-57257 C*

Made and printed in Great Britain

O Summer's Pride!
I loved thee from the first,
And, like a martyr,
I was blest and curst.

'The Lover's Missal'
Eric Mackay

CHAPTER ONE

'*GRACIAS.*'

Merle paid off the taxi, adding a fair tip, and stood watching its tail-lights disappear down the narrow unmade road before inhaling a deep refreshing breath of air tinged with the scent and taste of spring blossoms and the unmistakable tang of the sea.

Waiting while her eyes grew accustomed to the darkness of the Spanish evening, she listened to the soft sounds of the night creatures and the hissing roll of the Atlantic, clearly audible as it licked the expansive stretch of beach a few yards in the distance.

She was back once more on Spain's Costa de la Luz, and it was if the intervening months of sorrow and anxiety had never been. Except this time David wasn't with her.

It was a pity her flight from Gatwick had been delayed. She'd been looking forward to her first real sight of the Villa Paraiso ever since she had signed the contract for its purchase. Fortunately she had no doubts but that she would locate it easily enough even at night! Having studied the ex-owner's photographs of the attractive two-storey villa with its white-painted walls and dramatic wrought-iron railings, its large windows and flower-laden balconies and the attractive garden surrounding it, plus the fact that it had its name boldly printed on a stone plate at its entrance, she could hardly miss it, could she?

Congratulating herself on her forethought in bringing a torch, she searched in her shoulder-bag, producing it with a smile of satisfaction, before stooping to pick up her suitcase and making her way towards the footpath down which the taxi driver had indicated her destination lay.

Not being a total stranger to the area was a great advantage in the circumstances, and she was grateful that this wouldn't be her first sight of the small haven of half a dozen or so holiday homes sprinkled in their luxurious setting, far enough apart to give each occupant complete privacy, yet near enough to allow one to feel one was part of a community.

Walking easily in her flat-heeled shoes, comfortable in her cotton trousers and light edge-to-edge jacket over a long-sleeved blouse, Merle recalled her pleasure at that first sighting of the settlement nearly a year ago, the sense of appreciation linked to an odd sense of *déjà vu*, as if she had known even then that one day she would return to possess a part of it. That was why she hadn't hesitated when, back in England, she'd seen the Villa Paraiso offered for sale in a quality Sunday newspaper, and realised instantly where it was located. At other times she might have been more cautious, but this had to be Fate!

'It's very expensive!' her sister Barbara had temporised, when with a glowing excitement Merle had declared her intentions. 'Are you sure you can afford it?'

'I don't see why not.' Merle had met her worried glance with shining eyes. 'It'll be a marvellous holiday home for you and Grant and Natalie as well as me and Laurie, and when we're not using it we can let it out through an owners' villa service.' She had paused before adding softly, 'Besides, David would have approved. He loved the place. That's why we went back last year.'

'Yes, my love, I know.' Barbara had squeezed her arm in sisterly affection. 'It's just that I don't want you to be disappointed if it doesn't come off. I understand it's not always easy buying property abroad.'

Darling Barbie! Merle thought lovingly of her elder sister as she carefully negotiated the rough path. She owed the other girl so much, and now at last she had found a way in which she could repay just a tiny part of that debt. Fortunately Barbara's reservations had proved unfounded. The villa had been owned by an English couple who, having enjoyed its facilities for a number of years, had decided to join their married children in Canada, and therefore had no further use for it. Negotiations had been straightforward. The key was in Merle's handbag and at some time during the coming week she would go into Seville and collect the deeds from the Spanish solicitor who had acted for the vendor.

How often during the past weeks she had envisaged herself in this situation! Only then, of course, she had imagined the sun would be shining as she took possession of her new domain, not that she would be navigating by the stars! In her mind's eye the location was still quite clear. Turn right by the Villa Rosa... Yes! Merle's torch enabled her to spell out that tiled name on the wall now at her side—this was the silent unilluminated building she had sought... then a hundred yards further along and left... and there it was!

She stopped, as the playful night breeze teased the ebony softness of her hair against her shoulders, placing her suitcase on the ground at her side to enable her to drink in the beauty of her newly acquired Spanish home, a thrill of pure happiness surging through her at the prospect of ownership.

Beneath the starlit sky the white walls of the Villa Paraiso glowed, their smooth surface reflecting every particle of available light. In the darkness Merle's shapely mouth curled into a smile of satisfaction. It was beautiful—just perfect.

Basic furniture had been included in the purchase price, so at least she'd have a bed for the night and some bedclothes to put on it, according to the inventory! Then tomorrow she could start looking around, discover what else she needed to put her own stamp on the villa, arrange for a maid service, find out where the local shops were—all the hundred and one things she had come over by herself to do before sending for Barbara and the others to join her.

A few more steps and she was at the double wrought-iron gates, her fingers on the latch, pressing it down. Nothing happened. Bother the darkness! she thought crossly, juggling with the torch as a cloud momentarily obscured the sickle moon. Her searching fingers found a chain, followed its length and discovered a large padlock, firmly fastened. Ah, well, she sighed, security was good. She supposed she should be pleased about that, although she wished she'd been warned!

Standing back, she surveyed the rough stone walls on either side of the gates, relieved to discover that, although they were about six feet high, with a bit of luck they should be negotiable, though her suitcase would have to wait until she had gained access to the villa and could find some tool or other to break the chain. With a sigh of resignation she found a toe-hold and managed to drag herself towards the top. From there she jumped towards the ground, landing on hands and knees the other side, rubbing one knee ruefully as she rose to her feet. Thank heavens the trousers she was wearing had seen better days. She wouldn't have liked to have ruined a new pair, and her fingers told her these had sustained a ragged tear where they had come off worse in an encounter with a sharp stone. Still, she mustn't complain. In truth she should be grateful that her natural athletic ability hadn't diminished with her twenty-three years and had been sufficient to gain her access to her own property!

Without the suitcase her progress along the garden path was swift, her hand already groping in her shoulder-bag for the purse which contained the key to the Villa Paraiso. 'The Key to Paradise,' she translated in a soft whisper, resolving that she would take steps to improve her tourist Spanish into something worthwhile at the earliest opportunity.

She was still making plans for the immediate future when she inserted the key in the lock of the front door and attempted to turn it. Nothing happened. Damn! This was all she needed—for the lock to have rusted! Visions of having to spend the night sleeping in the garden filled her mind. But hadn't she been assured that the villa was being maintained by a gardener/handyman on a long-term contract? Agitatedly she tried to twist the key once more as her unease increased—again without result. There was only one other possible explanation. She'd been sent the wrong key! Hardly able to believe her bad fortune, Merle stared down at the useless piece of metal in her hand. Perhaps she could get in through a window?

A tour of the outside of the villa proved it impossible. Every window was barred and shuttered. Thoughtfully she stared at the white stone steps leading from ground level to the first-floor balcony, as her heart pounded in sudden anxiety. In the photograph she had they had carried open access from the ground, yet now they were shut off by six-feet-high iron gates with spikes on top— an addition of which she had received no notification and one she certainly hadn't authorised!

A cool breeze shivered across the warm skin of Merle's neck, as for the first time she felt fear stiffen her limbs. The animal sounds she had greeted with pleasure now seemed to have a hostile echo to them, and was this dampness she felt in the wind that blew her hair across her cheek with contemptuous disregard for her comfort? If she'd been Lucifer himself she could hardly have been less welcome in paradise, she thought wryly.

Obviously unless she meant to stretch out in the open she had to find someone to help her. If she could gain access to a phone she could get a taxi to take her further up the coast where the tourist hotels lined the beach. The season here, so far south, was a long one, so even in early June they would be open, and surely there would be a bed somewhere for her? Then in the morning she would locate the estate agent responsible and obtain the right key.

Now she had found her solution Merle's pulse quietened. It was unlike her to panic, but the events of the past year had weakened her, she admitted reluctantly. Only those who fought losing battles would ever guess how much her spirit had been drained in the long months of caring and waiting, how much she needed the peace and solitude this short break had promised her.

Resolutely she pulled herself together, gathering her energy to make a further assault on the wall. She succeeded, but not without incident. Ruefully she brushed down her soiled blouse, grimacing at the way it gaped open across her breasts, two buttons lost forever. As for her broken fingernails—well, they would grow again. Somehow she'd got a sharp stone in her shoe though. That would have to be removed before she took another step.

As she propped herself up against the wall, her hand encountered a piece of light card which had been fixed there and which had previously escaped her notice. Forgetting the pain in her foot, curiously Merle turned her torch on to the printed words ... *'Prohibido el paso'* ...

Even her limited Spanish could cope with that, as a sense of foreboding filled her. Entry forbidden!

As the small hairs at the back of her neck rose to attention she wondered if it had been meant for her, and if so—why? A qualm of apprehension brought goosepimples to her skin. Here she was in a foreign country, alone at night without transport or means of communication, and entrance to her own property denied! Anger and frustration mixed in equal amounts as she vigorously emptied her shoe of grit.

Vainly she cast her eyes about, hoping to discern a glimmer of light which would suggest habitation. Without some guide she had no way of knowing in which direction to walk to find an occupied villa, neither, she realised miserably, could she guarantee that anyone would understand her request to use their phone or let her over their threshold, especially in the disreputable state she was now in.

It was then that the Villa Jazmin forced itself into the forefront of her mind. Hadn't Rico told her that the Montillas made regular use of it not only for themselves and their friends but also for the workers on their estate? It was just possible that someone would be staying there. Perhaps even Rico de Montilla himself! For a few weeks last year they had struck up a casual fellowship, meeting by chance on the beach, finding an instant rapport... A warm glow of comfort renewed Merle's courage. It might be a long shot, but one worth trying. If Rico was there he would be bound to help her!

Until that moment she hadn't even admitted to herself that part of the attraction of returning to the Costa de la Luz had been the prospect that she might see Rico again and be able to renew their acquaintanceship. How much easier her acceptance into a foreign community would be if she was already known to one of its existing

summer visitors! Now the thought of his possible
presence brought a tingle of excitement with it.

As if it were only yesterday she could recall exactly
how to reach the Villa Jazmin. Not part of the holiday
complex, it was more isolated, much older, he'd told
her, going back in time to his grandmother's day when
it had been part of his family's large estate. He had described it to her so vividly that she'd had no difficulty
in picturing it in her mind's eye, as she had wondered
a little wistfully if he would ever suggest that she walked
with him along the twisting sandy track to see it in all
its summer glory. Perhaps in time he would have done
so as their acquaintanceship deepened into the friendship
it had promised to become, but something—she still
didn't know what—had prevented that from happening.

It had been two weeks before her planned return to
England when Merle had taken her customary stroll
along the long silver beach to their usual meeting place
to find it deserted. Even now she could remember the
hollow feeling of disappointment she'd experienced as
she had gazed fruitlessly along the beach. It had been
irrational in its intensity, but she had cast it aside, con-
soling herself that Rico's absence must be temporary. If
he'd had to leave he would have told her. His courtesy
had been one of the most charming qualities about him,
and she was sure he had enjoyed their quiet encounters
as much as she!

When three days had passed and there had still been
no sign of him she had been filled with apprehension,
experiencing a feeling of desolation beneath the shel-
tering pines where once she had found contentment.
Suppose he was ill? Or had had an accident and had
been unable to call for help? Panic had seized her and
she had forsaken any qualms about not wishing to in-

trude, finding her way easily to the villa. It had been locked and deserted.

Merle's disappointment had been a tangible pain. Some sudden summons back to Seville? she had wondered. The remaining days of her holiday had passed without any indication of Rico's whereabouts or the reason for his unexpected departure. At the time she had felt cheated. She had hoped so much to bid him a formal farewell, perhaps even telling him just how much she had appreciated his company for those few hours each afternoon....

Over the turbulent months which had followed her return to her home she had allowed him to fade from her mind. Now his image returned with remarkable clarity, as did the location of the Villa Jazmin.

Her mind was made up. Leaving her suitcase by the wall without a second glance, she began to retrace her steps towards the main track.

Fifteen minutes later she reached her destination, pausing in the archway that confirmed that her memory had not misled her. Pushing aside the thatch of bougainvillaea that covered its perpendicular sides, she was able to make out the small plaque that proclaimed it the entrance to the Villa Jazmin. Better still, she could detect a gleam of light behind the closed shutters!

Merle sent a quick prayer of thanks to her guardian angel. Whoever it was in residence, the very fact that she knew the owner should prove her veracity and enable her to use the phone to summon transport to take her to a hotel for the night! In the morning things were bound to look better.

Resolutely she walked up the low flight of stone stairs leading to the villa and pushed the bell.

A few seconds passed, then light flooded the interior, blazing out from the window above the sturdy olivewood

door. Instinctively Merle held her breath, aware that her
heart was thumping painfully behind her ribs. Then the
door was opened and Rico de Montilla was staring at
her.

He looked hard and sure of himself, a blue open-
necked sports shirt tucked into dark closely tailored
leather-belted trousers, his black hair thick and well
shaped against his proudly sculpted head. Only his eyes
were different from the last time she had seen him.
Darkly cold and hard as granite, they stared at her with
no welcome in their sable depths, while his mouth, which
in her memories had been so mobile and tender, was
now drawn into a forbidding line.

He had recognised her without doubt, she realised as
her insides seemed to wither beneath the coldness of his
gaze—and it was painfully clear he wished her a thousand
miles away!

'You!' His greeting was terse, his mouth snapping shut
into a grim line after the utterance of the monosyllable.

'I'm sorry it's so late,' Merle blurted out unhappily,
a wave of embarrassment bringing a flush to her pale
skin as she searched for a reason for the iciness of his
greeting. Had she interrupted a clandestine lovers'
meeting—or even a honeymoon? The months between
their last meeting were a blank calendar—anything might
have happened in his personal life! 'Or if I'm inter-
rupting anything,' she rushed on awkwardly, 'but I've
only just got here from the airport and I'm in a spot of
trouble. If I could just use your phone?' Her dark blue
eyes met the Spaniard's unfriendly regard pleadingly. It
was humiliating to beg a favour in the circumstances,
but the alternative was even less to her taste.

For a moment Merle thought she would be denied
access, then Rico's dark head dipped in acknowledgement of her request as he stepped backwards a pace mo-

tioning her to cross the threshold. *'Mi casa es su casa,'* he told her softly.

Merle felt her cheeks burning as she looked away, painfully aware of the sarcasm behind his apparent courtesy. Either she'd come at a grossly inconvenient time or he harboured some grudge against her of which she was totally unaware. His whole attitude was so opposed to what she had expected.... It would have been much easier to accept that he didn't remember her at all rather than that he remembered her with such evident dislike! It was clear from the unspoken message in his sombre eyes that she was as welcome in his house as a plague of locusts! In the midst of her distress about her own predicament she still wished she could erase the icy veneer which had transfigured what she recalled as being a warmly attractive face, and had no idea what she should do.

'You are alone?' he asked coldly as she obeyed his gesture to enter.

'Yes,' Merle nodded, rushing into speech, in an effort to lighten the atmosphere. 'You see, I've bought this holiday villa on the Playa Estate, and I've come here by myself to look it over: see what decorations it needs before the summer starts...' She gestured with her slim hands. 'To organise things generally. Unfortunately my flight was delayed and it was dark when I arrived, and——' she gulped as a wave of self-pity engulfed her '—it looks as if I've been given the wrong key, so I can't get in!'

'You intend to make a home here?' Rico's gaze drifted over her with scant regard, a frown creasing his smooth forehead as she became embarrassingly aware of her ragged appearance.

'A holiday home,' she agreed, grabbing at the edges of her blouse and drawing them together as his eyes lingered thoughtfully on her exposed skin. 'We—I—it's such a lovely, unspoiled spot, and I thought when neither I nor my family were here I could let it out.'

'Only now you find yourself unwelcome, *no*?'

'It would appear so, yes.'

Merle didn't like the way he said it, sensing his personal animosity. Dear lord, what had she expected? A year ago, from a chance meeting, an unusual relationship had sprung up between them, almost what one could call a melding of spirits. A strangely satisfying, comforting yet compulsive association—or so, in her innocence, she had imagined! On several occasions she had even sensed a strong pull of physical attraction towards her attractive companion, though she had resolutely denied it.

Each of them had been vulnerable in those balmy summer days, at turning-points in their lives, and each had indulged in a warm, escapist world of sea, sand, sun and philosophical conversation which had exercised and expanded her mind, freeing it momentarily from the weight of sorrow it had borne.

An idea seized her. Did Rico see her return as some kind of threat? Surely he didn't suppose she had any idea of intruding into his life when he was committed elsewhere? The idea was ludicrous, and not worth challenging! She just wished she had a better understanding of men in general—arrogant Spaniards in particular!

She wished, too, that her eyes had been able to deny his attractiveness, her heart been able to control its unexpected agitation, her mind been able to obliterate the memories of the lazy afternoons they had shared together on the beach. Instead she was shocked to admit that their magic had been reawakened at the mere sight of her former companion. Obviously Rico had not been affected in a similar way!

Drawing herself up to her full five feet five inches, Merle regretted her lack of high heels which would at least have brought her eyes to the level of his straight chiselled nose.

'I apologise again for my intrusion. If I could just phone for a taxi to take me to a hotel I needn't bother you any more.'

'A taxi at this time of night?' Straight brows furled in amazement. 'You are very optimistic, *querida*. You're not at the airport now, and as for staying at a hotel, I doubt you'd be welcome without some luggage!'

'But I have luggage!' she assured him eagerly, deciding to ignore his sarcastic endearment. 'I left my case outside the Villa Paraiso.'

'And who is going to retrieve it at this hour, in the dark?' He smiled without humour, his enigmatic eyes boring into her startled gaze. 'You or the taxi driver— or did you suppose *I* would be only too eager to act as your porter?'

This wasn't the charming, tender Rico Merle remembered. She was staring at a man without compassion or understanding. Gone was any semblance of the friendship and liking she had imagined had once existed between them. With every exchange of words between them she was forced to accept that, far from being willing to help her, Rico de Montilla was regarding her with barely restrained hostility.

'I'm sorry, I should never have come here...' She turned abruptly, reaching for the door, wanting only to escape from him. Sleeping on the ground would be preferable to exposing herself one moment longer to the frost of his cool reception. Tears of frustration clouded her vision. She had travelled with such high hopes. Was nothing going to go right for her?

'Wait!' A capable hand closed on her arm and she shuddered at the power of his touch. 'Perhaps you're right. But now you *are* here you must stay. There is a spare room and ample bedclothes available. In the morning you'll tell me where your estate agent is, and I will drive you to him. Doubtless he'll be able to provide you with the correct key. Tonight there's nothing to be done.'

'I can't stay here!' The chilliness of his reception had excluded that solution. She might be destitute, but her pride was the equal of his any day!

'You prefer to insult me by refusing my hospitality?'

'If it was genuinely offered I'd accept it,' Merle returned haughtily. 'But you've made it abundantly clear that, for some reason I don't even begin to understand, you find my presence offensive, and I'm afraid I'm too tired to ask you to explain, so it's best that I leave.'

For a few seconds their gazes clashed, then the man's face relaxed, the long curve of his beautiful mouth twisting into a rueful smile.

'I stand suitably rebuked, Merle.' The sound of her name on his tongue for the first time that night was strangely sweet, recalling memories best forgotten. 'Surprise deprived me of my manners. I thought that either my mind was playing me tricks or you were a ghost returned to haunt me!' The hand that had seized her arm relaxed its hold to travel slowly upwards so that the sensitive skilful fingers could touch her cheek.

'Rico...' Astonished, for the first time she mouthed his name, her senses sharpening as she heard the small hiss of satisfaction that escaped his lips. He was so close to her that she could feel his body warmth, sense the aroma of his skin. With an effort she controlled the mad impulse to raise her hands to his head and drag her fingers through the thick straight ebony of his lustrous hair. What fantasy—half dream, half nightmare—was possessing her?

A year ago she had taken temporary refuge in an illusory world. It would be a terrible mistake to recreate it. Now she had passed through her proverbial vale of tears she must face up to reality—whatever it was and wherever she would find it, but logic told her it could never be here, or with this clever, brooding Spaniard whose aura had fleetingly touched and brightened her life, even if he were to show any desire to re-cultivate their acquaintanceship. They had been platonic friends, that was all. Against all the evidence of her racing senses—that had been all! Tiredness and apprehension were taking their toll of her, that was the obvious explanation.

Parting her lips, gazing up pleadingly into the dark pools of Rico's eyes, she begged silently to be released, not only from his grasp but from the spell he held her in.

'Ah, Merle...' It was no more than a sigh as, incredibly, his mouth covered hers, homing on its soft, trembling outline with a purpose that stupefied her into immobility. It was a lover's kiss, deeply penetrating, ruthlessly possessing. Bewildered by this first ever intimate contact with Rico's body, Merle was left stunned and shaking, gasping when he released her, her hands scrabbling at his chest, trying to push him away, alerted to the anger simmering behind his unwarranted action and the threat it posed her: but worse than that, frightened by the perverse response of her own body to the male assault upon it.

'Ah, Merle...' An intense whisper this time as her hands were pushed aside and his fingers fleetingly touched the pale swell of her breasts, visible between the edges of her tattered blouse as she fought to regain control over her feelings. 'There was a time when I would have given you everything I possessed for the pleasure of taking you to my bed and loving you, losing my body in your heated depths, taking you and binding myself to you. I was entranced by you... and you knew that, didn't you, my dark angel?'

Astounded by the passion echoing in his velvet tones, and the hard glitter of his narrowed eyes, Merle stood silent, her breathing light and shallow as her pulse raced. Of course she had known he liked her, found her a compatible companion, but she had never guessed the depth of the desire he was admitting, the agony his tortured voice was laying claim to.

'No, it's not true...' she protested faintly, but he brushed her words aside, continuing as if she had never interrupted.

'Did you guess it all, *querida*? Did some instinct warn you that day by day, hour by hour I was falling into your trap? That you had created an illusion I would not be able to resist?'

He took a pace backwards from her, thrusting his hands into the pockets of his closely tailored black trousers, his face shuttered, his eyes veiled by the sweep of jet lashes. 'I was going to ask you to be my *enamorada, mi amante*—you understand?'

'Rico, please... that can't be true! I'd only just met you. We were little more than strangers! You'd never touched me...' Her widened eyes beseeched him to tell her he was exaggerating, but her protest was waved away with an impatient gesture.

'What is time but a passage of the sun? I thought I knew you: fooled myself that what your lips didn't say I could read in your eyes—in your actions.' He was flailing himself with his own scorn, laughing at his own gullibility. 'I'd convinced myself that you were innocent, untouched, something rare and beautiful...' His mouth turned in self-mocking humour. 'But you are right—we were strangers with nothing in common other than shared tastes in unimportant things, our ethics as totally distanced as the poles!'

'I had no idea...' White-faced, Merle shook her head, shocked at her own blindness, but it was as if he had never heard her murmured interruption as, scalpel-sharp, his deep voice continued,

'Forgive me if I choose not to believe you, *querida*! Your act was too carefully planned and played not to be convincing and too cruel not to deserve punishment. And as you see, it worked. Too well, in fact, because, fired with enthusiasm and the thought of conquest, I broke my own rules of seeking seclusion. I left the solitude of this place and went to the hotel where you'd told me you were staying with your friends...'

'Oh, no!' The nerves of Merle's stomach clenched, precipitating her into a state of nausea, as she realised with an icy dread what must have happened. At last she knew why Rico had disappeared from her life without a word.

'Oh, yes, *querida*!' Contempt sharpened his gaze and turned his strong jawline into steel, as he continued remorselessly, 'I'd decided the time had come to put our relationship on a more intimate footing. Afternoons were no longer enough. Damn your friends—my need for your company was greater than theirs! I intended to ask you not to return at your usual time that day, but to come back here with me. We would have dinner together—I'd bought the food and wine, everything was prepared...and afterwards...' He paused, his eyes blazing pools of accusation in his taut face.

If only she dared speak, but what could she say? Merle fought a sudden faintness that made the room grow darker. Rico was systematically and painfully exposing his own weaknesses, lacerating his own pride in front of her in an act of self-immolation as courageous as it was heartbreaking, and there was no comfort she dared offer.

As if from a great distance she heard his voice continue, deep, husky with emotion, as she closed her eyes, unable to bear the scorn that had turned his face into a mask of condemnation.

'I went to Reception and asked if you were still in the hotel. The Señorita Merle Costain…that's whom I asked for—and do you know what I was told?'

Merle's ashen face told him that she did, as relentlessly he concluded without waiting for her to comment— even if she had been able to find the ability to do so.

'I was told that the *Señora* David Costain was outside on the hotel patio enjoying the delights of the swimming-pool—in the company of her husband and baby daughter!'

CHAPTER TWO

'YOU'RE not laughing...' Rico's eyebrows lifted in mocking invitation. 'I thought it was a good joke, one that would appeal to your sense of humour—*no*? A young woman, married to a much older man, confined to domesticity by the arrival of a child, is taken on holiday, and while her less active husband is resting in the afternoons with their toddler she seeks her own diversion on the beach, regardless of the damage her irresponsibility could cause.'

Merle winced as the cold words hit her like slaps. This was the last way she would ever have wished him to discover her background. There was too much truth in his angry accusation for her to deny it, but there *had* been extenuating circumstances for the silence she had kept.

Meeting Rico's baleful regard, she knew with a sinking heart that this was no time to tell him the kind of marriage she and David had shared. Not only would such an explanation take time, but she would have to be in the right mood and the atmosphere would have to be sympathetic for her to be able to unburden herself. With Rico regarding her with such deeply ingrained contempt she would never find the words which, if they didn't exonerate her actions, might at least make them understandable...

'And there I was....' he continued softly, bitterness cloaking every word '...convinced that you were as virtuous as you were beautiful, behaving like some gauche teenager, fooling myself that heaven itself had planned our meeting—when all the time you belonged to another man!' He shrugged expressive shoulders, not waiting for her reply as his cruel gaze glinted over her. 'Absurd, isn't it? I suppose I should be grateful that I discovered what you were up to in time to deny you the opportunity of giving your husband the horns of the cuckold to wear!' His fingers stabbed at his forehead in a gesture that was frighteningly evocative before he rammed his hands in his pockets and glared at her, his body tall and forbidding, his face as stern as any inquisitor's.

There was a short strained silence as Merle hesitated, her lips parted slightly from the shock of his indictment, guilt washing over her like a wave of pain. She just hadn't been prepared for this confrontation and in her present emotionally drained state she was finding it hard to cope with.

'I thought there was no harm in seeing you in the afternoons,' she said awkwardly at last, wishing desperately that his cold stare wasn't making her feel unclean. It wasn't as if David had ever monitored her actions. As far as he was concerned she had been a free agent. He had trusted her discretion absolutely, and she had never abused that trust, despite Rico's angry accusations!

With a muffled curse Rico moved away from her. 'Heaven help you if you'd been my wife! Day or night I would have demanded your loyalty.' His dark eyes narrowed calculatingly. 'What kind of wife ignores the existence of her husband and her child? *Dios*, you didn't even wear a wedding-ring, did you, you little *coqueta*?'

Despite her lack of Spanish Merle could see from Rico's expression that his description wasn't intended to be flattering, and she had no difficulty in guessing its meaning. There was little point in trying to defend herself, since it was obvious she had been judged and found guilty. And the truth was, she *was* culpable in having given a corner of her heart to this angry foreigner, although at the time she hadn't even realised it.

Faced now with Rico's disdain, how could she explain that she had never deliberately intended to flirt with anyone and that her ring had been discarded because of a sand abrasion beneath it? Besides, the likelihood of his believing her was negligible, and the thought of his calling her a liar as well as a cheat was more than she could bear in her heightened mood of tension.

Instead she swallowed the lump of chagrin that had risen to her throat and made a show of moving her shoulders in a poor display of sang-froid. 'If anything I did misled you, then I'm sorry,' she said quietly.

'Sorry!' he echoed sharply, taking a step towards her and seizing her shoulders in a relentless grip. 'What for, Merlita? For all your sins of omission? For letting me believe you were on holiday with friends? Friends!' He gave a harsh laugh, his breath rasping as he pulled away to stare into her upraised face. 'A husband and a child! *Por Dios!* At first I didn't believe it. I went outside to see for myself—and there you were. The three of you. You, a man old enough to be your grandfather and the child!'

Merle shuddered. David had been in his late fifties, but his illness had aged him beyond his years. 'I would have told you, if I'd had any idea...' she began miserably, her assumed air of insouciance unable to prevail against the sharpness of his assault as she wondered how she could possibly expect him to understand how she had felt. How part of the joy of being with him had been the opportunity of leaving all her pain and anxiety behind her for those few magic hours each day.

'What stopped you, then?' Rico asked sharply, his fingers achingly tight on her flesh. 'Was it because you sensed that if I'd suspected for one moment that you belonged to another man I would never have willingly set eyes on you again?' He shook her gently, insisting on a reply. 'Did you enjoy making a fool out of me? Is playing dangerous games the way you get your kicks, and was I just one more scalp you intended to hang on your belt of holiday romances?'

How could he be so cruel? For a few seconds Merle closed her eyes, blotting out the image of his censorious face, frighteningly aware that behind the anger there lay a fine line of unwilling sexual tension, and that her own nervous system was responding to it.

'Well?' Rico prompted softly. 'I'm waiting for your answer, Merle. Are you unfaithful by nature—or was I an exception?'

'Does it matter?' She faced up to him coolly. 'Whatever my reasons for not being entirely frank with you, you discovered my secret. Isn't that enough for you?'

'Not if you and your family are going to spend part of the summer here in future,' he told her grimly. 'I have every man's sense of self-preservation. Apart from anything else, I want to know if your husband ever found out about your afternoon excursions.'

'For heaven's sake, you make it sound as if I was spending my time in a lover's bed, instead of sitting on a beach!' Merle had hoped to ridicule him, but failed to disturb his cool countenance. With a sigh of exasperation she told him what he wanted to know. 'I can assure you you've no need to worry on that account!' Her lips twisted in a wry grimace; Rico could hardly guess how ironic such a question was. 'David had no idea I was seeing you. I didn't consider our meetings important enough to mention.' She paused, aware that his eyes had darkened with disbelief. 'I enjoyed your

company. It was as simple as that. I thought we were
just friends. I had no idea you...' She stopped, confused.

'Desired you?' he finished caustically. 'You surprise
me, Merle. I'd assumed you realised that although my
body was scarred its virility remained intact.'

Stunned by the bitterness in the words, Merle felt the
strength of argument drain away from her, as Rico made
a small sound of disgust and allowed his hands to drop
from her arms.

'I suppose I should be grateful for the lesson you
taught me,' he added dourly. 'Never again shall I mistake
a passing physical attraction, a basic chemical reaction,
for something of greater significance. So perhaps I
should be thanking you for the experience instead of
berating you!'

'Perhaps you should!' His dismissal of any true feeling
for her was strangely hurtful, prompting Merle to utter
a more spirited reply. 'To be honest, I find your reaction
a little naïve. Just because a woman is married it doesn't
mean she can't enjoy the company of other men, surely?'
Her small rounded chin rose defiantly. 'I can assure you
I never had any intention of being unfaithful to my
husband, just because I chose not to disclose his existence. It seems to me your responses to a casual female
contact were triggered a little too easily!' As a threatening glint narrowed the dark eyes glowering at her, she
went on hurriedly, 'Obviously it was a mistake, my
coming here for help, so I'll say *adios*...'

'*Hasta la vista*, don't you mean?' Rico smiled without
humour. 'Since you and your husband are to be my
neighbours we're bound to meet again from time to time.'

Merle nodded curtly. The sooner she left the Villa
Jazmin the better. Let Rico de Montilla continue to believe for the time being that David would be joining her
later. With her reputation in his eyes sunk to rock-

bottom, this was no time to tell him that David had died a few months after their return to England, that she had always known his time was limited and that her grief at his loss was total and genuine, although she had never loved him—nor he her.

To her annoyance tears sprang to her eyes as she reached for the doorknob. Surreptitiously she dabbed at them with the back of her hand, knowing they were as much due to tiredness and frustration as they were to David's death. If what she had been brought up to believe was right, her late husband was reunited with the only woman he had truly loved, while her own problems were still manifold!

'Wait!' Rico's peremptory order stopped her. Turning, Merle saw that his face was now devoid of expression, not even a flicker of his previous scorn etched on the pleasant features with their trace of Moorish heritage.

'Now that we understand each other I propose we act in a civilised way. I've offered you a room. I suggest you take it.'

Merle felt her pulse quicken alarmingly. 'That's quite impossible after what you've been saying to me!'

'Indeed not!' He allowed his gaze to dwell on the gap between the edges of her blouse with deliberate impertinence. 'I thought I'd made it quite clear that, despite what I may once have imagined I felt for you, I am no longer tempted by anything you have to offer—however charmingly it is displayed.' His mouth curved in a slight smile as her hands rose to conceal the exposed cleavage with a quick angry movement. 'I've made many mistakes in my life, but one I will never repeat is to have an affair with a married woman! So you'll be able to rest easily in your bed.'

Merle's blue eyes, still bright with unshed tears, met and held Rico's steady gaze. His offer had been made in the most humiliating terms, yet what real option did she have? It was all very well standing on her dignity and rushing out into the night, but the beach wasn't the most comfortable place to sleep, Neither could she be certain of finding help elsewhere. On the other hand, her mouth still tingled from Rico's angry salute when both her mind and body had been forcibly reminded of his hard strength. Without conscious thought her tongue touched the full lower sweep of her lips, as she remembered the intensity of his unwanted tribute.

Even while she stared back at him, her eyes dazed with the need to make the right decision, she saw his expression sharpen with recognition of her dilemma, feeling the colour flood her face as he pre-empted her protest.

'Don't be alarmed, Merlita... I have no intention of poaching on another man's property. As far as I'm concerned the grass on the other side of the fence is trampled and unattractive.'

She was mad to taunt him, but his air of self-righteousness, however justified it might be, was as infuriating to her as was his scornful action of turning her name into the Spanish affectionate diminutive as he looked down his beautiful Andalusian nose at her. 'From the way you acted a few minutes ago I could be forgiven for questioning that statement!' Her eyes spat fire at him.

'You mean because I kissed you?' Eyebrows arched in elegant disbelief. 'But my dear Merle, surely you realised that was merely an experiment to discover how you would react to me after such a long absence? Put it down to research rather than the pursuit of pleasure. I wanted to know just how fickle you could be.'

'Then I hope you were satisfied!' For the life of her she couldn't remember how she had reacted to his sudden assault. On top of everything else it had been just too much. A cold shiver of trepidation travelled down her spine. For all she knew his declaration of a past desire for her was total fabrication, his sole purpose being to discomfit her, to punish her in his own coin for the actions he saw as breaking his own strict code of morality.

His glance raked over her, missing nothing, from the challenging tilt of her head to the way her fingers trembled slightly against her breast.

He nodded. 'Enough to repeat my assurances that you will be as safe under my roof as you would be in a nunnery. And now we understand each other may I offer you some refreshment before we start getting your room ready?'

Wary and uncomfortable, Merle allowed him to lead her through an archway into what appeared to be the main sitting-room. On two levels joined by two further archways, it was a large, pleasant room with a polished flagstone floor, simple olivewood furniture and two splendidly opulent leather couches. A large stone fireplace was occupied by a metallic urn amply filled with fresh flowers, while the alcoves in the white stone walls contained a selection of elegant bric-à-brac.

At Rico's invitation she sank gratefully down on one of the couches, murmuring her acceptance of a cup of coffee but refusing anything to eat. The meal served on the flight had been adequate in the circumstances—any resurging appetite having abated as a result of the heated confrontation with her host.

The coffee when he brought it was accompanied by a large brandy.

'Oh, I don't think...' Merle began doubtfully.

'Drink it.' Rico drew out the smallest from a nest of tables, placing it before her and resting the glass and cup on it. 'One glass of Fundador never hurt anyone, and you look as if you need it.'

'All right, thank you.' She gave him a tentative smile. 'Doctor's orders?'

'If you like.' He regarded her solemnly before reaching in his pocket and holding out his lean-fingered hand, palm up towards her. 'I thought you might like to have this, to effect running repairs.' Nestling on the smooth masculine skin was a slim gold tie-pin with a hooped head of seed pearls and tiny sapphires.

His eyes, a dark oloroso now in the subdued light of the wall-lit room, rested for a moment on where one of Merle's hands still held the torn edge of her blouse in place.

'Thank you.' She was touched by his thoughtfulness, although a plain safety-pin would have been more suitable for the purpose of retaining her modesty! 'I'll let you have it back as soon as I can get my case and change.'

'There's no hurry.' Rico waved aside her thanks, choosing to sit opposite her, holding his own glass of brandy and stretching long muscled legs out into the space between them, as she slid the pin into the gaping cotton edges at her breasts, before shrugging off the jacket which had been inadequate to cover her revealed skin.

He'd changed in the last twelve months, she thought, her task completed, sipping the heady spirit in her glass. There seemed to be a new maturity, a greater serenity and less strain in the face which she remembered as being more than usually attractive even then. She wondered if life had been good to him and found herself unexpectedly hoping that it had.

'Did you get the position you were after last year at the clinic in Cadiz? she asked hesitantly, half afraid that he wouldn't be prepared to discuss his personal life with her, yet strangely anxious to know if he had been successful.

To her relief, he nodded. 'So you remember that, do you?'

'That you were hoping to join them as an orthopaedic surgeon?' Merle was momentarily hurt that he could think her interest in him had been so shallow that she could possibly have forgotten what had been so obviously important to him. 'Of course I remember. I often wondered if your application had been successful and how it worked out.'

'I was lucky,' he admitted, his broad frame appearing to lose some of its previous tension. 'The board considered my experience in the field more than compensated for my lack of years.'

Merle shivered, remembering how Rico's field experience had nearly cost him his life in Nicaragua when he had been caught in crossfire between two groups of combatants, while trying to save an injured woman. The machine-gun bullets which had splayed within a hair's breadth of his spine had left a diagonal tracing óf angry seared flesh from his left shoulder-blade to just above the right side of his lean waist, as a lasting memento.

That first day she'd met him she had wandered far along the seemingly endless stretch of silver beach, leaving the hotels in the distance, deeply immersed in her thoughts, enjoying the rush of the cool Atlantic against her feet, when she had realised how hot the sun had become on the top of her uncovered head. Shade in that part was at a premium, but she had espied a cluster of pine trees way back where the beach met with scrubland and what appeared to be the beginning of a path.

Thankfully she had ploughed her way through the soft sand, only realising when she was a few yards away that the area wasn't deserted as she'd believed but that a man was seated there, back against one of the trees, reading: long tanned legs emerging in beautiful male musculature from short white shorts and a flimsy short-sleeved cotton shirt hinting at an equally well-developed torso between its open edges knotted at his lean waist.

As Merle had approached he had looked up and in response to her uncertain smile had invited her to share his shade, speaking first in Spanish and then, as he saw her struggling to translate the words, doing the job for her and repeating them again in flawless English.

She hadn't been too surprised he had discerned her nationality. When foreigners realised that her dark hair had Gaelic red rather than Latin blue undertones it seldom took them long to work out that her flawless magnolia skin owed its perfection to the notoriously damp air of the British Isles!

Thus Rico de Montilla had entered her life at one of its lowest ebbs. There had been something about him which had drawn her back time and again, something she hadn't wanted to stop and analyse, as each day when David and Laurie took their long afternoon siestas together she had traced her footsteps back to the welcoming shade of the pine trees and the pleasure of Rico's company.

It was two weeks after their first meeting that she had been delayed because Laurie had been fretful and she had stayed to soothe her, despite David's assurances that he could perfectly well cope with his three-year-old daughter. The space beneath the trees had been deserted as Merle's heart had plummeted painfully, a real sense of loss spreading through every cell of her body at Rico's absence. It was then she should have been warned how dangerously warm her feelings for this engaging Andalusian had become, but somehow the knowledge had eluded her. She had always imagined that love for her would be a slow process as liking grew into love over many months. She'd never expected it to be born and mature like a may-fly in a matter of hours!

Sinking down on the soft sand, using the full turquoise seersucker skirt she wore over her one-piece swimsuit as a barrier against the sand, she had barely settled herself down when, turning her attention to the sea, she saw a figure emerging from it. Her heart had seemed to perform impossible acrobatics as a weird yawning ache spread uncertain tentacles through her nervous system to touch every muscle of her body.

She'd told herself her reaction was due to mild heatstroke, but watching Rico come lazily towards her, his strong graceful body so aggressively balanced, his shirt hooked over one shoulder, she knew *he* was responsible for this inexplicable thing that was happening to her...

'I thought you weren't coming!' His pleasure at seeing her had been so intense she could almost feel it warming her skin. Laughingly she had risen to her feet, going towards him as he had held out his hands to her. The next moment she'd been in his arms, his flesh cold and damp but incredibly exciting against her, her hands reaching for his back, touching his naked skin, feeling the raised pattern of scarred tissue that marred the oilskin smoothness of the surrounding tissue.

She had heard his intake of breath and let her hands fall, terrified that she had hurt him, but the pain in his dark searching eyes had not been physical as he had asked her tautly, 'You find my *cicatriz* repulsive, Merlita? To be honest, I had wished to hide it from you for a while longer.'

He had swung round, presenting to her eyes the sight of which only her fingers had knowledge. Merle had gazed her fill, absorbing with every sense of her body the splendid mature frame before her, her eyes registering the smoothly developed muscles of his shoulders, the sleekly sculptured line of his ribs, the faintest trace of dark hair at the narrowest part of his torso where the golden skin disappeared into his dark bathing trunks.

The scars weren't disfiguring—even if she hadn't felt her heart swell with sympathy for him she would have been able to look at them without flinching. Like a primitive tribal decoration their half-hoop served to highlight the smooth perfection of their background. For a fleeting moment Merle marvelled at his self-consciousness, then her natural compassion took over from her inherent shyness.

'Repulsive?' she had heard her own voice crack a little. 'How could anything about you ever be repulsive?' It had been the point where things had begun to go badly wrong, only then in her innocence she truly hadn't realised it. Rico de Montilla had been a fully mature man approaching his thirtieth birthday, and every fibre of her mind and body had been forced to recognise that fact!

Somehow she had managed to blank the realisation from her consciousness, making an effort to drain the tension from the charged atmosphere by encouraging Rico to confide his experiences in South America, listening with rapt attention as he had told her how on a visit to see his mother in Argentina he had met relief workers from Nicaragua and learned from them the need for skilled medical help.

'It was a challenge,' he had explained quietly. 'I'd qualified and specialised in Spain as an orthopaedic surgeon and had every intention of returning there—but first...' He had opened his palms upward in a gesture of despair. 'It was a call I couldn't refuse. I'd been there just over a year when I got caught in crossfire—and this was the result.'

Looking back, Merle could see how her own confused feelings had deceived Rico, yet at the time she had truly thought his interest in her had been compounded of curiosity, the pleasure he took in perfecting his English and the loneliness his chosen isolation during convalescence had visited on him.

Merle's hand shook slightly as she drained the glass of brandy, placing it on the table beside the now empty coffee-cup, aware that during the past few moments of silence Rico's eyes had been fastened to her face. He looked thoughtful rather than haughty now, and she wondered what he had read there; she hoped it was her regret that she had ever given him cause to condemn her!

When a few minutes later he suggested that she might like to go to her room, she followed him up the open-plan staircase to a small room containing a single bed with an intricately carved olivewood headboard, a low dressing table in similar wood and a free-standing wardrobe which was obviously part of the suite.

'The bathroom's next door.' Rico indicated the direction with a brief nod of his dark head, leaving her alone to accustom herself to her surroundings before returning with an armful of white linen.

'I've got an apartment in Cadiz,' he told her conversationally, shaking a sheet over the mattress with a show of domestic skill which surprised her. 'Actually it's in the grounds of the clinic itself, but I find this place very convenient for a relaxing break, especially as it's equidistant from my work and my brother's *cortijo*. One of the local women comes in on a daily basis while I'm here and keeps the place tidy and the fridge stocked as well as doing the laundry, so I'm quite prepared for the unexpected guest.'

'So I see.' Glad that their conversation had achieved an impersonal civility, Merle reached for one of the pillows Rico had placed on the dressing-table, slipping it inside the cover he had provided. 'I still feel dreadful, imposing on you like this. If I could have thought of any alternative....' She stopped, aware that her implication was scarcely flattering, yet not meaning to be offensive.

'Not at all.' His dark regard showed no emotion. 'You were in an unfortunate predicament. Whatever our differences I should have felt more offended by your decision not to come here than by your arrival—although I admit I was more shaken to see you than I had supposed would be the case.' It was a smooth statement and just for a moment Merle wondered how seriously he had considered the possibility of meeting her again, before he asked politely, 'Will you be warm enough with just this cover over the sheet?'

It was a thick blue and white woven spread which he had draped across the bed. Beneath it Merle knew she would find the warmth and comfort her body craved.

'Thank you. That will be ample.'

Rico made her a stiff formal bow, eyes shuttered, long lashes a fan against his high Andalusian cheekbones. 'In that case I'll wish you *buenas noches*.' For a moment she saw the shadow of a smile soften his firm masculine mouth. 'I regret I'm unable to provide you with night attire. My guests usually bring their own—should they require it.' He paused fractionally as if inviting her to consider the kind of guests he might invite who would consider nightwear extraneous to their needs. It wasn't a difficult vision to conjure up. Rico de Montilla was a highly charged male animal. In the past David's existence as her husband had acted as a screen between that knowledge and the full realisation of its potency. With that screen removed her perception had sharpened to a painful and unwelcome intensity.

She watched him leave the room, waiting for the sound of his footsteps to fade as he went downstairs before leaving the room to enter the bathroom, glad that she had a small selection of toilet things in her shoulder-bag. At least she could wash and clean her teeth in an effort to restore her morale!

The sheets were cool to her naked body as she slid beneath them, their crispness scented with a heady perfume that owed nothing to modern washing powders but everything to the way they had been aired in the hot Spanish sunlight. An evocative mixture of myrtle and sweet basil that was as effective as any soporific prescribed by a doctor.

Tomorrow would see things back to normal, Merle thought as with her own body heat trapped beneath the traditional cover she felt sleep overtake her. Tomorrow she would get the right key from the estate agent and take possession of her new domain. Then, apart from the formal greeting decreed by custom when their paths crossed on their day-to-day business, she need never speak to Rico de Montilla again! They would become the strangers he so obviously wished they were!

CHAPTER THREE

A SHARP rapping at her door accompanied by the delicious smell of freshly brewed coffee awakened Merle the following morning. Stretching luxuriously, she hauled herself upright on the comfortable mattress, instantly aware of her surroundings.

'Come in!' Hastily she arranged the sheet to shield her nakedness as Rico obeyed her summons.

'Did you sleep well?' The question was courteously asked as he placed a cup of coffee on the small table at her side, with nothing in his voice to remind her of the previous day's abrasiveness. Standing back, he appraised her sleep-flushed face, politely awaiting her response.

'Like a baby!' Merle smiled her gratitude stiffly, acknowledging the tenuous armistice between them. 'Last night I was beginning to feel I couldn't cope with the situation, but this morning I feel refreshed enough to face anything.'

'*Bueno* ... Let us hope the problem is easily solved.' Rico turned away from her before she could question what she had detected as a note of reservation in his comment. 'In the meantime I've brought you something you'll be needing.'

He was out of the door, returning in seconds with her suitcase and putting it down at the foot of the bed.

'Oh, marvellous!' Her face lit up with pleasure. 'But how did you find it? I mean, I didn't tell you where my villa was, did I? And I certainly didn't expect you to go out so early in the morning on my behalf.'

Rico shrugged broad shoulders clad this morning in a navy T-shirt above white cotton trousers which seemed to emphasise the lean power of his lower body. 'I know the Playa Estate. It's not that large, and since only one of the villas had a suitcase outside its walls there was no need for supernormal detective powers. As for the time . . .' he raised lazy shoulders ' . . . it seemed prudent to go early before someone else saw it and interfered. Besides, it's not unusual for me to go for a swim first thing.'

'Oh, I wish I'd known—I would have . . .' Confused, Merle stopped. For a moment she had forgotten the harsh exchanges of yesterday. Probably the last thing Rico had wanted was her company on an early morning beach outing, despite the present aura of truce he exuded.

'I thought you needed your sleep.' To her relief he ignored the opportunity of embarrassing her by overt rejection. 'No doubt there'll be many opportunities for you to swim before breakfast in the coming days.'

Had there been an odd inflexion in his voice, or had she imagined the note of doubt in what should have been a reassuring statement? For the second time she felt a strange sense of foreboding. Perhaps he thought her interest in the property was less genuine than she was claiming. In which case he was in for a disappointment.

'Yes, of course I shall,' she retorted firmly. 'Once I've got this matter of the key sorted out it'll only be a matter of days before my family join me here and we can all enjoy the sunshine and sea.'

Rico glanced down at his watch. 'Then the sooner we obtain the right key for you the better. Where exactly do we find this estate agent of yours?'

'Seville.' Leaning out of the bed, Merle drew up her shoulder-bag from its position on the floor, searching in its depths for her purse with one hand while the other anchored the sheet firmly between her breasts, uncomfortably aware of the amusement lurking in the depths of Rico's dark eyes at the contortions necessary to retain her modesty. Let him laugh at her! Yesterday he had called her a *coqueta*. Today she'd give him no cause to repeat the insult.

'Here...' A few seconds later she had retrieved the business card from her purse and offered it to the patiently waiting man at her bedside. 'Perhaps you could phone him on my behalf?' Her azure eyes darkened in supplication. 'As it's his mistake he may be prepared to send someone over here with the right key.'

'Possibly.' Rico took the card from her, casting a cursory glance at it. 'On the other hand, there are one or two things I need in Seville myself, and I always feel a face-to-face confrontation is the best way of solving a problem.'

'Well, if it's not inconveniencing you too much...' If there had been an alternative solution Merle would have taken it, rather than throw herself on Rico's generosity, but it wasn't just for her own peace of mind, she consoled herself: Barbie's family and Laurie were depending on her to deliver the glorious holiday she had promised them. For their sakes she must learn to swallow her pride and to take the easiest way of achieving her purpose.

'Not at all,' Rico informed her gravely. 'A couple of hours by road will see us there, and we can start immediately after breakfast. An acquaintance of mine is one of the chefs at the Majestic Palace, so I called in on my way back along the beach and collected some freshly baked rolls still hot from the oven, so if you like them warm don't be too long in coming down.'

'The Majestic Palace!' Merle's voice echoed her surprise. 'But that's a couple of miles along the beach from here, isn't it? You must have taken a long walk!'

'About five kilometres, I believe.' His dark eyes dwelt on the soft fair skin of her attractive face. 'Let's just say that I was up very early this morning, not having enjoyed the blessing of a long night's sleep, hmm?' He left the room before she could respond.

Thankfully Merle allowed the sheet to drop as she reached for her coffee, drinking it with real pleasure. Had that last remark been loaded? Had her presence irritated Rico to the extent of depriving him of sleep? She replaced her cup and with unaccustomed annoyance thumped her pillow. Damn that stupid estate agent for sending her the wrong key! If it hadn't been for his inefficiency she would have been spared this embarrassment!

Thankful at least that her small but adequate wardrobe had been returned to her, she scrambled out of bed, unlocked the case and extracted the pink satin sleeveless nightshirt she'd packed. Clad in this, she gained the bathroom, returning a few minutes later showered and lightly made-up, her dark hair brushed away from her smooth forehead and held in place by a white chiffon scarf. Selecting the briefest of cotton underclothes on her return, she replaced the nightshirt with these, topping them with a pastel print skirt and matching short-sleeved bolero over a strapless white top. It was an easy outfit to wear, cool and formal enough for town but easily transformed into a sun-dress should the opportunity arise.

Despite the edginess she felt in Rico's presence she was filled with a joyous anticipation at the prospect of seeing Seville. Last year David had been too weak to travel far from the hotel, and although he had encouraged her to go by herself on some of the organised tours she had always refused, not wanting to leave him alone for too long. It was ironical that the few hours she had stolen, with his blessing, when he had been resting, had resulted in her being branded a *femme fatale* by a man whose respect she would have welcomed but which had now been irretrievably lost to her!

Sighing, Merle removed a pair of smart new wedge-heeled peep-toe shoes from her case and slid her elegant slender feet into their cushioned comfort. In retrospect she couldn't blame her unwilling host for his scornful judgement on her past behaviour. If she could have the time again she would have been more cautious, but then she was looking at events with the hindsight of experience. There was little doubt she had changed in the months since David had died. The responsibility of being alone, of dealing with the large estate bequeathed to her, of trying desperately to discern and meet the needs of the baby daughter denied the fond affection of a loving father... they had all made their mark on her, ageing her mentally if not physically. No, she was no longer the timorous naïve girl whose heart had warmed so innocently to the charisma of the youngest Montilla brother...

Somewhere she had packed a large, squashy white bag, ideal to complete her outfit. Diligently she searched for it, unwilling to disturb the contents of the case too radically. On her return from Seville she would be transporting it back to the Playa Estate and the Villa Paraiso where it could be completely unpacked. As she felt through the layers of clothes with sensitive fingers her train of thought continued. Undoubtedly Rico, too, had changed. She had met him at a time when he was convalescing physically and emotionally from the horrors of war, the scars on his mind less obvious but potentially more serious than those on his body.

Still uncertain as to whether his confession of having experienced desire for her had been genuine or a means of attacking her, Merle decided that if he had spoken the truth then it had been because he too had been caught in an emotional vacuum—haunted by tragedies that the human mind refused to rationalise. In that state it was only too easy to imagine feelings which had no roots in reality. . . .

She gave a small murmur of satisfaction as her seeking hand closed on the bag and she was able to withdraw it. Yes, Rico had changed. A year ago he had been living the life of a hermit, refusing to stray more than a few yards from the quiet sanctuary of the Villa Jazmin and the nearby beach. Now he had secured an important and worthwhile job and clearly enjoyed the healthiest of minds in the healthiest of bodies.

Leaving the bedroom and making her way downstairs, her mouth watering as the smell of fresh bread titillated her senses, Merle was certain of one thing. However much Rico de Montilla might despise her, she was delighted that he had made a complete recovery from his South American ordeal. Not that for one moment she had ever doubted his ability to do so . . .

His attitude towards her as they shared the Continental breakfast was beyond reproach. He was polite in the extreme, treating her as an honoured guest with none of the previous evening's hostility apparent. Watching him covertly as he raised his cup to his lips, Merle found it difficult to believe that he had kissed her with such punitive intent or used such evocative words to describe the desire he once claimed to have harboured towards her. There was nothing now in his bearing to suggest that he felt anything other than the need to extend hospitality to a visitor to his country. Aware of his disdain, though, she resented being obligated to him, but maybe that state of affairs would soon be ended!

Leaving the Villa Jazmin immediately after breakfast as he had suggested, they entered the environs of Seville in Rico's small dark Seat, shortly after eleven.

'Not very luxurious, I'm afraid,' he had admitted on opening the passenger door for her at the commencement of their journey. 'But she's ideal for the country roads and easy to park in the city.'

'She looks fine to me!' Merle had been only too grateful for the door-to-door transport, and indeed the journey had been smooth and comfortable as Rico's precision touch on the controls sped them quickly and safely towards their destination.

Her first sight of Seville was disappointing as they entered the city through the hot and dusty industrial outskirts, but as they drew nearer to the centre she cried out in delight as she caught sight of the famous and beautiful landmarks.

'You've never been here before?' Curiously Rico questioned her.

'No.' She was too excited to attempt to hide her happiness. 'Last year was the first time I'd ever come to Spain, and we didn't go far from the beach.' She paused, then added, 'But David, my husband, had been here before. He wanted me to go on one of the tours to Seville, but...' She stopped, unwilling to plunge into the reasons David hadn't taken her, and hoping her unfinished sentence would be allowed to die without comment.

'But you found the pleasures of sea and sand more to your liking, hmm?' A dark eyebrow lifted in her direction. 'That doesn't make you unusual among your compatriots. In fact many of them appear to prefer the inside of bars to the attractions of nature, let alone culture.'

'You don't care for the tourists?' A slight edge to her voice challenged him.

'I try not to generalise.' Rico steered the car neatly into a side-road. 'Their advent has brought prosperity and disaster hand in hand to this country, a state of affairs for which they are not entirely to blame. It is a sad fact of mass tourism that by its very nature it tends to destroy that which it most desires to enjoy. En masse it would be fair to say I resent them. Individually,' he slid her a sideways glance, 'individually I find some compatible.' He made another turn, this time steering the car neatly into a private forecourt and bringing it to a halt. 'This is the address you gave me.'

The estate agent's was in a small modern block of buildings, its large window filled with colourful photographs of villas. Obviously a company which catered for the influx of tourists rather than the domestic market, Merle thought wryly. In which case she should have no difficulty in making her complaint known.

'I can manage now, thank you.' She turned to Rico as he came to join her at the window. 'I'm sure someone there will speak English if you want to go and do your own business.'

'There's no hurry.' To her surprise he placed a firm hand beneath her elbow, preparing to shepherd her into the office. 'I have to collect a watch that's in for repair, that's all, so we'll get this problem settled first. It's always possible you may need my help.'

He couldn't have spoken a truer word, Merle ruefully agreed some ten minutes later when the young woman to whom she had put her complaint continued to insist that there had been no mistake.

'We sent you the key to the Villa Paraiso,' she said positively, her dark eyes showing annoyance at Merle's persistence. 'I can assure you, *señora*, there has been no mistake!'

'But it doesn't fit!' Merle felt as if she were losing her reason. In exasperation she turned to bring a silently watchful Rico into the battle. 'You tell her, please, Rico! You know I couldn't have made a mistake!'

Opening her bag, she seized her purse, intent on thrusting the evidence before the girl.

'The *señora* is correct,' Rico confirmed calmly. 'I tried the key myself. There is no way it fits.' His hand slid into the pocket of his close-fitting trousers, reappearing with the key between his fingers and pushing it across the counter towards the clerk.

So he hadn't trusted her judgement! This morning when he had gone to collect her case he must have taken her key and tried the lock himself, which meant he had come into her bedroom while she slept... It had been warm in the early hours of the morning and she had allowed the covers to drift down her body... Had Rico looked at her half-naked body—or had he been too involved in his purpose to have spared her a glance? A wave of embarrassment flowed through her. Stoically she ignored it, dwelling rather on the fact that at least he was in a position to corroborate her declaration.

'Then the lock must have been changed!' The clerk's liquid eyes dwelt on Rico's face, their impatience masked with a new kind of respect. 'I do assure you, *señora*——'

'I think you may be right.' Tersely he interrupted her, as Merle asked in shocked surprise,

'Changed? How could it have been changed? No one had the authority to change it——'

'Hush! There is nothing to be obtained by arguing the point here.' Rico's arm fastened securely on her own, guiding her from the premises as he murmured a polite farewell to the intrigued clerk.

'What do I do now?' Furiously Merle detached her arm from his grasp, turning to face him beneath the blazing sunshine of the street.

'You tell me who has the deeds of the property.'

'The solicitor who acted for the vendors.' Fighting to control the way her fingers were shaking, Merle took her purse from her bag, extracting a business card. 'Here it is—Señor Juan Montero. We arranged that I should collect them from his office here in Seville on my arrival.'

'Let me see.' Rico took the card from her hand, perusing it thoughtfully. 'How very convenient! His office is quite close to where we are. We'll find a phone and I'll see if I can make an appointment to see him.'

'You think he may have the right key?' Merle asked eagerly, a ray of hope illuminating the gloom that had descended on her.

But she was to receive no answer as Rico discerned a phone available for public use and moved swiftly from her side. Minutes later he was back, his expression quietly triumphant.

'He'll see us at four o'clock.'

'Not until then?' Dismay was mirrored in her widened eyes, as Rico greeted her protest with a wry twist of his mouth.

'Consider yourself lucky. We Andalusians, more than anyone else in Spain, use the philosophy of *mañana*. In truth, he originally suggested some time the week after next.'

Rebuked, Merle had the grace to feel ashamed. 'Forgive me, I wasn't complaining on my own behalf, but you'll be wanting to get back to the coast.'

'Not at all.' He glanced at the thin gold watch on his wrist. 'I intend to stay with you until we get this matter clear. In the meantime I suggest we stroll through the streets towards the Jardines del Alcázar. On the way I can collect my other watch. We should then have time to visit the Cathedral and the Giralda Tower, by which time we should be ready for lunch.' He shrugged his shoulders. 'By the time we've eaten, our appointment will be due.' His quizzical look invited her approval of his plan.

There was nothing she could do but nod her acceptance, although his generosity put her even further under his obligation.

'This way, then.' Acknowledging her rather subdued agreement, Rico guided her gently across the road, one hand lightly on her arm, moving with a positive masculine grace which suggested he had never considered her disputing his plans.

Later, walking through the ancient quarter of the city, Merle was glad she had raised no objection to the sightseeing tour. This was the Andalusia of her dreams: the Spain that David had enthused about. In the midst of an urban city here was an enclave of haunting beauty— a glistening maze of white houses and narrow alleys, where a myriad flowers spilled from wrought-iron balconies in a riot of colour and perfume. It was dramatic and beautiful, a picture painted in bold tones of white and scarlet and black where the deep shadows contrasted against the glare of the whitewashed walls.

'I feel as if I'm on a stage set,' she confided, her lingering concern about the coming interview temporarily diverted by her surroundings.

'It struck me that way too, when I first came here.' Rico smiled slightly, turning his head to meet her sparkling eyes. 'Even now I can never take it for granted like the people who were born here. I still see it with the admiring eyes of a stranger.'

'Of course,' Merle remembered what he had once told her in the days when they had enjoyed each other's company, 'you were born in Argentina, weren't you?'

'Uh-huh, but my father was Andalusian. I lived over there until I was seventeen, then I came back to Spain to live with my brother Armando and study for the medical profession. So you see, although I have the blood of Andalusia in me, I still see her through the eyes of a visitor.'

'Is that good or bad?' There'd been something behind the coolness of his expression that prompted her enquiry.

'Who knows?' Rico made a careless gesture with both hands. 'It means I perceive her beauty more sharply but by the same criterion am less inured to her ugliness. It's not always a comfortable relationship.'

There was a flash of anger in the dark eyes which met her own, a return of the previous hostility with which he had first greeted her, as if it was she to whom he was referring rather than the city; then it was gone, leaving her feeling oddly bereft, and he was leading her towards a gracious forecourt where canopied tables invited the hot and weary traveller to rest.

Sipping gratefully at a fresh iced orange juice, Merle leaned back against the padded headrest of her wrought-iron chair, her eyes fastening on Rico's lean handsome face. There was, she thought, a special quality about him that didn't depend on the almost classical beauty of his features with their obvious debt to his Moorish ancestry, a mingling of composure and authority in his bearing that gave maturity to a face of hard bones and cleanly cut sweeping curves. If it came to a fight he was a man she would want on her side, despite the disquieting air of antagonism which was never far below the surface of his stylised courtesy.

Last year she had seen the handsome Spaniard as a fellow spirit: someone with whom she could relax and discuss shared likes and interests. Now, because of his denunciation of what he saw as her wilful deceit and betrayal of her husband's trust, he seemed tougher, more formidable. Oh, how she resented his arbitrary judgement! Was she fated to be the victim of men with shining, rigid consciences? First her stepfather and now Rico? She stole a quick look at her companion's face, knowing she should hate him for his cursory condemnation. And what about his own motives? What was particularly honourable in planning to seduce a woman for a quick, casual summer affair? For that was all it had been.

Suppose she told Rico the truth about her marriage with David—and how it had ended? Would it make him regard her in a kindlier light—make him feel any shame for the way he had treated her yesterday?

She stretched out her legs, turning her closed eyes towards where the sun filtered down between the tables, and decided to hold her peace. Try as she might, it was impossible to forget the passionate persuasion of the contemptuous kiss Rico had inflicted on her the previous evening or her spontaneous response to it. The continued presence of a husband in her life was the best protection she could imagine against Rico's undoubted ability to trample on her bruised emotions.

Inhaling the mingled aromas of deeply scented carnations and the delicious smells from a Spanish kitchen, Merle sighed deeply. Yes, the longer she could pretend she was still a married woman the easier it would be for her to remain aloof from Rico's very personal blend of Latin charm and male machismo. As a guide around Seville he had been both attentive and informative, she reflected wryly, and on the occasions he had taken her

arm or clasped her hand to guide her across the thronging
roads, she'd had to remind herself that his actions were
all a part of his inherent courtesy: that there had been
nothing personal about it. Yet it would have been all
too easy in those magical hours to have fooled herself
into believing she could regain his friendship.

In the circumstances, she reflected, her peace of mind
depended on the preservation of her own pride, rather
than attempting to resurrect the camaraderie which had
been built on such a fragile and specious base!

'What will you eat, Merle?' Her eyes flicked open as
Rico's deep voice penetrated her thoughts.

'I'm really not very hungry...' She took the menu he
offered her, scanning its contents. 'I'm afraid tension
always affects my appetite.' She cast him an apologetic
look, adding for good measure lest he should assume it
was his presence which was disturbing her metabolism,
'And this business about the villa has wound me up.'

'Like an alarm clock.' Dark eyes set in deeply cut
sockets beneath thick straight brows regarded her speculatively while the vestige of a smile dimpled the corner
of his sensuous mouth, as he acknowledged his understanding of her colloquialism. 'Let us hope you are not
about to explode with a shattering peal to disturb the
tranquillity of the afternoon. Since you intend to take
up residence here you will have to learn to live at the
tempo which surrounds you, or you'll end up a very
frustrated young woman.'

'You're talking about the cult of *mañana*.' Merle made
a moue of resignation, irritated by the light mockery of
his tone.

'Ah, you Anglo-Saxons!' The lines at each side of
Rico's mouth deepened in amusement. 'It is you who
waste time, by abusing rather than using it. What is one
day more or less in the scheme of things?'

'A philosophical hypothesis, but one which won't help to get a roof over my head!' Merle decided against pointing out that she was Gaelic rather than Anglo-Saxon, fancying that to a Spaniard it was a moot difference.

'Relax!' He sounded more amused than contrite at her tart retort. 'Since you can't fight the inevitable you may just as well enjoy a leisurely lunch. If it's something light you fancy why not try the *gambas* with a salad? And to drink, tell me, which do you prefer, wine or *sangría*?'

Bowing to the inevitable as recommended, Merle sighed, accepting his suggestion of the large grilled prawns marinated in seasoned oil and served with lemon wedges with a side dish of lettuce, tomatoes, cucumber and olives.

It was then, just as she was beginning to relax beneath the sun's hot caress, that Rico brought her sharply back to reality. Leaning forward to fill her tall glass with the iced *sangría* she had chosen in preference to wine, he said calmly, 'So your husband has chosen to stay at home and look after your daughter?'

His voice had lifted slightly at the end of the sentence, turning it into a question as his eyes caught and held her shocked gaze.

CHAPTER FOUR

MERLE stared back at him, blindingly aware that her bluff was being called. Staunch to her previously determined resolution, she searched her mind for an explanation which would not be entirely untrue.

'He—no——' she stumbled, aware of Rico's keen penetrating brown eyes regarding her with interest. 'David is away—out of the country—that's why I'm handling the business.' That at least was true. David was away in a place not plagued by the sorrows and problems of this life, if what the churches taught was true, she comforted herself, swallowing a sudden surge of unhappiness at the memory of a gentle and compassionate man no longer able to enjoy the sights and sounds that surrounded her at that moment.

'Ah!' Rico sat back in his chair, lifting a prawn from his plate and neatly extricating it from its shell. 'Then your daughter—I don't believe I know her name—your daughter will be staying with your own parents, no doubt.'

'Laurie. Her name is Laurie.' His sudden interest in her family was unexpected and unwelcome. Presumably it was his way of passing the time while they ate. In view of his assistance it would be churlish to resent his questions. She would just have to tread carefully if she were to preserve the myth of her married status! She took a long draught from her glass before completing her reply. 'As a matter of fact she's being looked after by my sister Barbara. She and her husband Grant have a daughter just a year older than Laurie. As soon as I've got the villa organised they'll all be coming over here for a holiday.'

Rico nodded. 'You and your sister are perhaps orphans?'

'No, not at all.' Merle was quick to correct him, feeling on safer ground now David himself had been dropped as a subject. 'My mother and stepfather live in Scotland.'

'Then they will also enjoy a holiday in the Spanish sun, *no*?'

'I'm afraid not.' Merle couldn't keep the regret from her voice. 'I'm sure my mother would love to come over here, but my stepfather never goes on holiday.'

'Perhaps you'll be able to persuade her to come over by herself, then.'

'He'd never allow it!' The bitter words were out before Merle could control them. As usual whenever she thought of her mother, dominated by the man who had married her after she had become a widow and whose possessiveness towards her had made the lives of his stepdaughters a misery, she felt a burning resentment. Latent fury darkened her eyes to ultramarine as she added disparagingly, 'But then you wouldn't find that kind of dictatorial attitude in a man as appalling as I do!'

Rico didn't deny it, but the flash of anger that flickered across his lean features had its origin in another source. 'You consider you know me so well you can forecast my opinions?' he demanded silkily.

Once that would have been true. Now he was a stranger, as potentially explosive as a stick of dynamite.

'If I prejudged you, I'm sorry...' Merle stared down at her plate, knowing her reactions were born of the long-held animosity she had nursed against her stepfather. 'I did assume that, your being Andalusian, your attitude towards women would be one of absolute sovereignty.

But not without evidence, surely?' Her beautiful sweep of dark-winged brows lifted slightly above innocently wide eyes. 'It was only yesterday that you told me you would demand loyalty day or night from your wife!'

'True.' His dark eyes gleamed with a breathtaking arrogance. 'Although I'm not sure that being Andalusian has anything to do with it. Far from being parochial, I consider myself cosmopolitan. You seem to forget that the early part of my life was spent in the environs of Buenos Aires, and while I was doing my medical training I lived in Madrid. Because I would demand fidelity from my own wife it doesn't mean that I hold the creed of the Dark Ages or that I would be unsympathetic towards her visiting a close relative without me.'

'But you would prefer she didn't?' Merle refused to back down. Cosmopolitan or not, Rico was Latin and male. She didn't need a crystal ball to understand the temperament that dwelt in his lean hard body, the complex character formed by a culture where harsh moral strictures reflected on one's own virtue, for hadn't she already received ample evidence of his intolerance? Only Rico hadn't always been virtuous, had he? she reminded herself. Hadn't he hinted at some affair he had once had with a married woman? She was looking at a convert, and they were notoriously rigid in their views—everyone knew that!

Rico was regarding her closely as if his clear eyes could read her innermost thoughts. 'Let us just say that any feeling of indifference towards her holiday destination would undoubtedly be compensated for by the pleasure of sharing her company,' he replied smoothly. 'Perhaps you judge your stepfather too harshly?'

He was leaning back in his chair now, half turned so that she was the full object of his concentration. One of his bare tanned arms lay languidly along the arm of the

chair, fingers lightly cupping its end, the other was bent
on the other arm so that one thumb and forefinger rested
against his cheek. Only the intensity of his stare belied
the casual laziness of his lounging body.

Afterwards she was never sure why she confided in
him. Perhaps it had been the effect of the shimmering
heat, the headiness of the wine cup or her repeated
awareness of his potent charisma that had caught her in
its charm so long ago and was now reaching out to entrap
her once more. Perhaps it was just because she felt the
need to release some of the miserable pent-up memories
of her earlier life or simply because she felt the need to
justify to her condescending companion the antipathy
she felt for the man her mother had married.

'Is it possible to find an excuse for a man who marries
a widow with two young daughters and then shows every
evidence of hating them?'

'It's even difficult to find a reason, Merlita.' Rico's
response was gentle, as if he were aware of the tightly
battened emotions that threatened to burst free whenever
she thought of the kind of life they had been forced to
lead.

'He was jealous because she loved us—I realise that
now, but I can't forgive him. He wanted all her attention
all the time, resenting our need for her.' She paused as
the waiter placed more bread on the table, waiting until
he was out of earshot before continuing dully, 'I was
five, my sister Barbara eight when she remarried. Too
young to understand that whatever we did, however we
behaved, we would always be in the wrong...' She
stopped speaking, swallowing the lump in her throat.

'Was he cruel to you, Merle?' There was a deep pity
in Rico's voice as his hand left the arm of the chair to
cover her straining fingers.

'Not physically,' she whispered, remembering the cold silences, the harsh instructions, the icy discipline which had denied both Barbara and herself any contact with friends or amusements outside of school. Even when they had left school and found work, Barbara as a clerk in a local supermarket and she as an assistant in a chain store, their social life had been non-existent.

'I see.' Rico nodded as if he understood all the things she couldn't tell him, reading the truth in the unhappiness that darkened her eyes. 'But you managed to leave home eventually?'

'When I was eighteen, yes. Barbara fell in love with one of the mechanics who serviced the supermarket's fleet of vans. Grant is a super person, not the kind of man to be cowed by anyone, but even he couldn't persuade my stepfather to agree to their getting married.' Merle shivered, reliving the past. 'There was a dreadful row, and I think if it hadn't been for Grant's determination Barbara would have given in and refused to see him again. As it was, he persuaded her to elope with him. It wasn't as if they needed anyone's permission—just that Barbara so wanted a family blessing at the start of a new life.'

'That must have made matters much worse for you and your mother.' With unerring accuracy Rico homed in on what had happened.

'It was awful.' Merle spoke so softly he had to lean towards her to catch her answer. 'Barbara and Grant moved down south to the London suburbs and as soon as they were settled they offered me and Mother a home. Mother refused, but she begged me to go. I didn't want to leave her, but eventually she persuaded me that if she were alone with my stepfather things would improve, that it was seeing us—the fruits of her love for our real father—that was making him so unreasonable. She felt that if they were on their own matters would improve.'

'And did they?' Rico prompted gently as she paused.

'I don't know.' Merle shook her head, staring out into the bright sunlight and seeing nothing but the internal images of a dark cheerless house in the Scottish country-side. 'That was five years ago. Barbara and I write to her regularly and her replies are always cheerful, but we know it could only worsen matters if we ever went back there, and Mum won't agree to meet us outside the house—so...' She left the sentence in mid-air.

There was no need to finish it for Rico to gather how desperately she prayed for her mother's happiness; her love and concern were mirrored on her expressive face.

'So perhaps now you understand why my judgement of my mother's husband is so harsh!' Pride tightened the line of her jaw as she challenged Rico to question her reactions.

'Indeed, I now understand many things.' He signalled for a passing waiter to serve them with coffee, remaining silent while their cups were filled. 'And it was while you were living with your sister and her husband that you met David?'

Merle nodded. She'd been desperate for work. Barbara and Grant had been living on a council estate near the factory where Grant had found work. It was a two-bedroomed house and Barbara had already been expecting Natalie. With little experience Merle had anticipated difficulty in finding work, so when she had seen an advertisement for a live-in home help she'd rushed to apply. That was where she had met David and his wife Rosemary in their beautiful house in its acres of ground only two miles away from the industrial settlement where her sister lived. Two miles—but it could have been in another world!

'And he was kind and wealthy and he wanted you?' There was no edge to Rico's voice, just the polite enquiry.

'Yes.' Both David and Rosemary had warmed to her immediately. The latter had explained that at the age of thirty-nine and after fifteen years of marriage she was unexpectedly and delightfully expecting a baby. David, fifteen years her senior, was also thrilled, but concerned because of her age.

'It's absurd, my dear,' she had confided with a grin. 'I'm as fit as a fiddle, and after all, it's fashionable now to wait until you're in your thirties before starting a family, but David's insisting I give up work and have help around the house, and I'm not going to argue with him!'

'So you exchanged your youth and your beauty for his protection and his patronage.' It was a statement, not a question. It was also a condemnation that brought the blood surging to Merle's pale cheeks. He knew nothing, nothing! How dared he stand in judgement on her? For a few moments she had been deceived by what she had misread as his compassion. His pity had been skin-deep, beneath the surface his condemnation of her burnt as fiercely as ever!

'I married David because he wanted me to and because I loved and respected him!' It was not entirely a lie. Pity, after all, was said to be akin to love, and when Rosemary had suffered a fatal brain haemorrhage six months after Laurie's birth her heart had overfilled with pity for the dazed and shocked widower.

Not that marriage had entered either of their heads at that time. No, it had been two years later that David had proposed to her—and only then because he knew he was dying and Laurie would be left destitute. Once she was the little girl's stepmother no one could challenge her authority to continue bestowing the love and care she was already lavishing on her!

It had been no sacrifice. She and Rosemary had learned together about looking after babies, both as ignorant and enthusiastic as each other at the start! Far from being merely employer and employee they had become firm friends in their limited time together, each devoted to Laurie and cognisant of her needs. After the trauma of Rosemary's unexpected death Merle had automatically taken over full care for the child, loving her as if she'd been her own, and David, inconsolable in his grief, had been only too relieved for her to do so...

None of which she was about to explain to the man tossing down his coffee at her side with complete disregard for its heat. She owed him nothing, least of all the exposure of her soul!

As he replaced the cup in its saucer Rico reached for her left hand, running his forefinger over the band of gold that encircled her ring finger.

'Not because he could afford to buy you villas in Spain?' His mouth stretched in a humourless smile. 'Then I suggest that out of the respect you claim for him you always remember to keep his ring on your finger.'

After the empathy she had been tricked into believing they'd shared his remark was like a slap round the face and it was all Merle could do not to gasp. Abruptly she removed her hand from his hold, not deigning to answer. There was a sober truth in his advice. David had entrusted Laurie to her with a blind faith that she would always do what was best for his daughter. It was a trusteeship she intended to honour, regardless of the consequences it might have on her own future!

'Finish your coffee.' Rico's curt nod in the direction of her cup signified the end of the subject. 'It's time we were leaving, if you want to try and claim Paraiso tonight.'

'Señora Costain!' Juan Montero advanced across the floor of his pleasant first-floor office in one of Seville's modern blocks to greet them, hand extended, eyes flicking swiftly from Merle to the man who accompanied her.

There was something about his manner—a kind of defensiveness which immediately alerted her. Despite the festering indignation she was still harbouring against him, Merle was suddenly very glad to have Rico at her side.

'May I introduce Señor de Montilla?' Deliberately she didn't define Rico's role, not that she was sure of it herself! But it wouldn't hurt the dapper little lawyer to see she wasn't on her own if he was going to make any difficulties about handing over the deeds of her property. Maybe he would even be fooled by Rico's professional bearing into believing she had brought her own legal counsel with her.

As the two men gravely shook hands Merle subsided in the seat offered to her. 'I've come to collect the deeds of the Villa Paraiso,' she began without preamble as Rico took the seat beside her. 'I understood from the Bennets that they'd be ready for me as soon as I arrived?' she smiled brightly, her heart beginning to increase its beat as Juan Montero's brows drew together in a puzzled frown.'

'You didn't receive my letter, then, *señora*?' he questioned.

'What letter?' Merle leaned forward towards the desk.

'The letter where I explained about the court case.'

'What court case?' The sense of doom she had felt began to increase. 'I've received no letter and I know nothing about any court case. All I'm asking for is the deeds to the property I've bought and paid for!'

'I'm afraid that's not possible any longer, *señora*...' The Spanish solicitor was obviously ill at ease, his accented English thickening a little, his glance darting from her face to linger momentarily on Rico's quietly perceptive features. 'It is a matter of law, you see. Unfortunately the Bennets weren't the original owners—they purchased the property from a speculator. Before he sold it to them he had certain alterations effected by a local tradesman—and unfortunately these were never paid for. For ten years this builder has waited for payment. When he heard the villa was changing hands yet again he took his claim to court....' Heavy shoulders beneath the smart grey suit shrugged philosophically. 'The bad debt was proved and the judge awarded him the villa in compensation. There is nothing to be done.... *lo siento mucho, señora*....'

'But the villa cost me over six million pesetas! This is madness!' There was a pain in Merle's chest and she could actually feel the blood pounding in her ears, as her voice soared out of control. It wasn't possible that she'd lost tens of thousands of pounds of her dead husband's legacy—the legacy she'd vowed to guard and tend for Laurie's future.

The villa had been intended not only as a memorial to David but as an investment as well as a personal haven of holiday enjoyment. Nausea made her swallow violently as her eyes flamed at the discomfited Montero.

'Relax, Merle.' The calmly spoken words bounced meaninglessly off her ears as Rico moved at last to place his arm firmly round her shoulders. 'Whatever has happened, Señor Montero is not to blame.'

Relief was mirrored in the older man's eyes as he launched into a rapid exposition in his native tongue, gesticulating with his hands, apparently soliciting Rico's understanding. Still dazed, Merle allowed the fast exchange of Spanish to continue without interruption. Thank goodness Rico had been with her! Clearly there had been some absurd misunderstanding. She would raise the amount required to pay off the debt and her villa would be returned to her. She breathed deeply, feeling her nerves begin to steady. She'd been stupid to panic.

'*Entiendo, entiendo....*' Rico smiled pleasantly, accepting a slip of paper from the other man, as their conversation appeared to reach a satisfactory conclusion. '*Gracias, señor.*'

Following Rico's example, Merle found herself shaking hands with the lawyer, before allowing herself to be led from the office and escorted outside into the heat of the street.

'But this is monstrous! If that's the law then it should be changed!' Outside on the pavement she blazed her protest into Rico's set face.

'I agree.' His calm acceptance of her scorn did nothing to placate her, as memories rushed back to alert her.

'You knew, didn't you?' she accused breathlessly. 'Yesterday, when I told you what had happened...you knew!'

'I suspected the possibility,' he admitted gravely. 'It's not the first time it's happened, and all the signs were there.'

'And you didn't even warn me!' She didn't stop to consider that he might have done her a favour by letting her have a night's sleep devoid of anxiety as her fury gathered force. 'I suppose you're glad! You never really wanted me here, did you? What was it you called me— a *coqueta*? I guess you're glad I've lost everything, that I won't be around to lower the tone of the place...' Her voice shook with anger. 'What a sadistic pleasure you

must have been enjoying all this time at my expense!'
Taking a deep breath, she fought to gain control of her
emotions. Unless she was careful she was going to burst
into tears of frustration, and that would never do!

Raising one dark eyebrow in a gesture she was beginning to recognise, Rico waited patiently for her to
calm down with an attitude of laboured courtesy that
made her blood run cold. How he must detest her! The
dreadful thing was, she *needed* his advice. The shock of
events had annihilated her usual reserves of mental
strength. She felt stunned, unable to make any kind of
rational decision as to what her next move must be.

'What—what do I do now?' she whispered, drained
of every vestige of pride, as she raised beseeching eyes
to his austere countenance.

'There is obviously only one thing you can do.' Rico
paused meaningfully. 'You must get in touch with your
husband, wherever he is, without delay, and let him know
what has occurred. The final responsibility, after all, is
surely his.'

This was it, then. The final crunch. No longer was
she going to be able to protect herself with the power of
another man's presence in her life—however distant. 'I—
I can't.' Her reply was little more than a murmur, as her
eyes closed in spontaneous pain. 'David and I are no
longer—together.'

'You're divorced!' Rico's voice was sharp with
amazement. 'No, no, I don't believe that! There has not
been sufficient time for divorce, even under your liberal
laws. Legally separated, then? Your wealthy husband has
grown tired of your little games, hmm?' He took her by
the shoulders, hauling her so close to his own body that
she could feel the warmth of his flesh radiating through
the flimsy covering of her dress. 'Have I guessed right,
Merle? You bought the villa with the settlement he made

on you, and now you've lost everything? The egg from
the golden goose has been snatched from your predatory little hands, never to be regained?'

'Stop it!' Merle had had enough. On top of the shock
she had just received Rico's determination to attribute
to her the lowest possible motives was more than she
could bear. 'How dare you judge my reasons for marrying David or criticise our relationship?' Tears blinding
her eyes, she tried to detach herself from his predatory
hold, digging her nails into the hard strength of his upper
arms in an effort to obtain her release.

'*Basta!* Enough!' Her struggles were useless as he ignored the pain she was inflicting on the taut muscles at
the mercy of her fingertips, and the musky exciting scent
of his displeasure invaded her heightened senses. Suddenly she felt energy draining from her as she half collapsed against his vibrant strength, her hands
relinquishing their attack to clutch at his imprisoning
arms to save herself from falling.

'I demand an answer.' Rico's voice was low and intense, close to her ear. 'This is no business for a woman.
If your ex-husband's involved in this transaction he
should be here with you now! So you're going to tell me
exactly where he is at this moment!'

He wasn't going to let her go, allow her to merge into
the colourful crowds, as she desired, and suddenly it
didn't matter what she told him. She'd been financially
raped with the connivance of the law. She was wounded,
angry and totally vulnerable, excruciatingly aware that
she could no longer shelter beneath the cover of her
mythical marriage.

Flinging back her head, she said clearly, 'My husband
is dead. He died six months ago.' When she actually
spoke the words she felt relief, even a moment of triumph
as the blank shock wiped Rico's expression clear.

Time seemed to stand still as her words died to silence and neither of them moved a muscle. It was Rico who broke the frozen tableau, taking her cold hand in his own.

'Come, this is no place to discuss our next move. We cannot stay here in the street forever gazing into each other's eyes with such intensity or we will be suspected of having a lovers' quarrel!'

He was right. Latin curiosity was already making them the centre of attraction—besides, like it as little as she did, Rico remained her only link with sanity! As if in a dream Merle allowed herself to be led silently through the crowded streets back to the place where the car had been parked.

It was only when they were once more on the road out of Seville that Rico broke the silence between them.

'Your husband's death was sudden?' His eyes on the road, he presented his cool profile to her quick glance.

'Not really. He'd been ill for some time.' She wasn't going to tell him her shock of learning that David had Hodgkin's Disease or her dismay when it was clear that unlike the vast majority of cases which were curable David's was diagnosed as terminal. She wouldn't divulge how much greater her distress had been than David's, the latter having accepted the news with a resignation that had much to do with his adamantine faith that he would be reunited with his beloved wife, only the thought of leaving alone the little girl who had been the fruit of their love torturing him.

She sighed reminiscently. It had been an easy decision for her to make a marriage of convenience to ensure that Laurie's young life would have some degree of continuity. She would have done it, whatever David's circumstances had been, out of love for the child and her affection for Rosemary, but for his part David had been quick to point out that he wouldn't have considered such a possibility unless he'd known she would be comfortably off after his death, assured of an income not only from his investments but by the regular royalties she would receive from his publishers. As he was a compiler of scientific textbooks which were sold to schools and universities all over the world, David's income from this source had been as healthy as any popular fiction writer's—probably more healthy than most!

It had been Barbara who had been more impressed with this aspect of the future when Merle had confided her intentions, pointing out that with a dependent child her sister's chances of finding future happiness for herself would be much improved if she had a private income.

'There aren't many men who can afford to take on another man's child, even if emotionally they're prepared to do so,' she had told Merle soberly. 'Especially when they find out that you're not Laurie's real mother. Are you quite sure you know what you're doing?'

'Quite sure.' Merle had had no doubts. 'Laurie needs me. As far as marriage is concerned I've never even thought about it.' She'd laughed. 'Perhaps I'm a natural spinster!'

'Or perhaps you've never been in love.'

Her sister's clear voice echoed in her memory. Of course Barbie knew she'd never been in love. Never even had a boyfriend. Even seeing Barbie and Grant so happy in each other's company and the warmth between David and Rosemary so evident, Merle had never imagined herself falling in love. Her contact with the opposite sex had been so limited she supposed she was just unawakened.

She must try to keep her problems in perspective. Even if she had lost a large sum of money she wasn't by any standards broke. It was just that she felt so unworthy of the trust David had invested in her.

Beside her Rico sat silent, concentrating on driving, and she was glad that he wasn't going to pursue the state of David's health at their last meeting. The illness had been in a period of remission when her husband had expressed a wish to return for the last time to the Costa de la Luz, and she had willingly agreed. For those few weeks in the sun he had appeared contented with no signs of distress except extreme tiredness. On their return his condition had deteriorated rapidly and fatally. Watching the passing landscape, Merle decided that Rico had formed his own opinion once more, and whatever it was, it would almost certainly be to her own detriment.

CHAPTER FIVE

ARRIVING at the Villa Jazmin, Merle allowed Rico to usher her into the pleasant living-room, sinking wearily on to one of the couches. His silence during the drive had given her plenty of time to appraise her situation, and, although she still couldn't come to terms with it, she had formed a plan of action.

'I hate to trouble you further,' she told him stiffly as he stood looking down at her, 'but I'd be very grateful if you could drive me to one of the hotels on the beach. I think the best thing I can do is get a room somewhere while I try to arrange a flight back to England.'

'Running away?' he asked smoothly.

'Cutting my losses.' Her chin came up defiantly at his tone. 'Since I've been assured on such good authority that I can't fight the law, there's no point in my staying here, is there?'

'Probably not,' Rico agreed calmly, standing a few feet in front of her and gazing down at her, 'but, on the other hand, you should explore all avenues before surrendering. For instance, I obtained from Montero the name and address of the man who now owns the Villa Paraiso.' He withdrew from his pocket the slip of paper she had seen him place there in Montero's office. 'His name is Sanchez and he lives on the outskirts of Seville. I understand he's already put the villa back on the market, but he might be amenable to reason.'

'Appeal to his sense of chivalry, you mean?' Her eyes flashed scornfully. 'I thought you said his name was Sanchez, not Quixote!'

A glimmer in Rico's dark eyes appreciated her acidity. 'Sometimes calm talk can prevail over anger. Señor Sanchez has waited ten years for repayment, he has a right to be angry. However, he may not be a man of great greed. Having been compensated more than justly he may be open to reason.' There was a gleam behind his dark eyes she couldn't put a name to. 'We Andalusians are quickly aroused to passion, but we are generous too if our sensibilities are honoured!'

'You think I should approach him personally?' she asked doubtfully, willing to clutch at any straw, however slender.

'If all else fails that might be the solution.' Rico appraised her upturned face with deep interest. 'Depending on the kind of man Sanchez is and the type of price you are prepared to pay, it might be possible to come to an agreement.'

He couldn't mean——? Merle felt the blood rise from her neck to scald to her forehead, but before she could put her thoughts into words he was continuing unhurriedly, 'The best thing to do is to hire a local lawyer with real-estate experience and have him act as an intermediary between yourself and Sanchez or Sanchez's own legal representative. That way you will learn exactly what you're up against and determine if there is any way to mitigate your loss.'

'Is it really worth it?' Professional help never came cheap, and every penny she spent was robbing Laurie.

'I think so,' Rico nodded firmly. 'Not all faith in human nature is misplaced. A compromise solution might still be possible.' His broad shoulders moved lazily beneath their covering. 'The payment of the outstanding debt plus accrued interest charges, for instance. That would be acceptable to you, yes?'

'Yes! Yes, of course!' It seemed such a vain hope, but one she couldn't afford to turn her back on.

'Good! I know just the very man to act on your behalf. He manages all the real-estate deals my brother Armando makes. He's trustworthy and ultra-efficient. If anyone can find a means of negotiation Fidelio Diaz can!'

Merle felt as if her brain were overflowing like some malfunctioning computer: the only stable thing in her life appearing to be the tall, powerful figure of the man staring down at her awaiting her response. Why would he want to help her? Had his discovery of her widowhood softened his attitude towards her? Was it pure altruism born from compassion—or was there some ulterior motive in this sudden offer of assistance? Clearly if David had been alive she would have been offered no such advice!

Briefly she closed her eyes, envisaging the Villa Paraiso—her and Laurie's villa—bought from the savings David had accrued and entrusted to her. Of course she had no option. She must take every possible step open to her, even though it meant putting herself under obligation to a man who had made no attempt to conceal his contempt for her.

'Then I agree we should try, if Señor Diaz is prepared to handle the problem,' she decided firmly, adding softly, 'And thank you for suggesting it.'

'Oh, he'll accept it.' Rico's smile was only slightly malicious. 'When he knows it's Montilla business!'

'But it's not!' Merle protested as he sat down nonchalantly on the arm of the couch where she rested.

'You're my guest—therefore it's my business.' He waved a dismissive hand.

'But I'm not going to be your guest any longer,' Merle said quickly. 'That's why I asked you to take me to a hotel. I can't possibly stay here another night—you must realise that.'

'Why?' The blank question forced her frankness.

'Because yesterday was different. It was too late to get a taxi and—and...' She paused, her eyes pleading him to understand but not comment on what he must know were her reservations.

She was to be disappointed. 'Because last night I thought you were married and tonight I know that to be untrue?'

'Something like that.' Merle couldn't meet the cool assessment of his brilliant eyes, glancing away as his hand rose to take her chin, but there was to be no gentle acceptance of her scruples.

'And because I told you that I once desired you, and even now—although that adolescent yearning has evaporated like the morning dew in midsummer—you must be aware that I am still enchanted by your false projection of unworldliness and your undeniable physical beauty?'

Her face was swung gently but firmly so her eyes could meet his level gaze, as she gasped at his frankness. His words affected her even more than the feel of his hand on her skin. To hear herself described as beautiful in a voice of such deep enthralling timbre was as erotic as a caress, although it had been no compliment.

'You're afraid to stay under my roof because you think I still desire you enough to creep into your room in the middle of the night and claim the treasure you promised me now I know you have no male protector? Is that your reason, Merlita?'

'I only know you regard me as mercenary and immoral.' Merle forced herself to speak calmly with a supreme effort, unable to deny her awareness of his desire for her, a desire coupled with disgust both for herself and himself for harbouring it. The tension between them was like static electricity. Even now, Rico's fingers on her chin were sending thrills of feeling down her nervous system, unwelcome and unsettling, like nothing she had ever experienced before.

He gave a short laugh, his fingers moving from her chin to stroke her cheek, while she sat transfixed. 'My feelings may be ambivalent where you are concerned, but I would never transgress the rules of hospitality. You are as safe here as you would be in a nunnery, I promise you—if that is what you want.'

If it was what she wanted! How dared he even suggest anything different?

'There's no lock on my door,' she said crisply. 'If I did accept your offer I would require your word that you wouldn't come in without knocking first.'

Remembering how he must have seen her spread out on the bed when he had taken her key earlier, Merle felt the colour rise to her cheeks. How wanton she must have looked, her breasts bare, her hair tumbled against the white pillow! She saw the frown crease his brow as he observed the change in her complexion.

'You're suggesting that you didn't hear my knock this morning and invite me in?' He regarded her coldly. 'Your memory appears unusually short.'

Merle met his stony gaze unflinchingly. 'I'm referring to earlier on when you took the key of the Villa Paraiso from my purse while I was still asleep.'

'You misjudge me.' Rico considered her outraged expression thoughtfully, his mouth drawn into a grim line. 'Although from your blushes I almost wish I had committed such an indelicate intrusion. I obviously missed a delightful sight!' The glitter behind his dark eyes could have been amusement or anger as he continued. 'The truth is, you left your jacket downstairs last night and when I went to hang it up in the lobby for you the key fell out of the pocket. To borrow it was a liberty I felt justified in taking in your own interests.'

'Oh!' Both hands rose to her burning cheeks, as she remembered thrusting the key in her pocket after having made her decision to go to the Villa Jazmin. Relief and remorse flooded through her. 'I'm sorry, Rico.' In her embarrassment she couldn't meet his haughty appraisal, staring down at her own hands as she made her apology.

'*Gracias.*' He rose to his feet, extending a hand to her so that she too rose to stand facing him. 'There's one thing you should know about me, Merle. I'm no saint and I've crossed thresholds that many would condemn me for—but never uninvited. Never! And I'm not so insensitive as not to realise that there is a great difference between a married woman seeking extra-marital amusement and a widow who has to replan her future on a long-term basis.' Blithely he ignored her hiss of indrawn breath as he continued without a pause, 'So, tonight you stay here. We will spend a pleasant evening listening to music and taking refreshment, enjoy an early night in our separate rooms and face tomorrow and its problems when it comes.'

Merle was really too tired to argue, and there was a remarkable degree of comfort in having Rico concern himself so deeply with her affairs, whatever his motives. Her sense of isolation had been banished. Even if nothing came of it she would have the satisfaction of knowing her lack of language had not prejudiced her chances of beating the system.

He was still watching her intently and she realised he was waiting for her agreement. Taking a deep breath, she made her mind up, deciding that despite his tendency to place himself next to God when it came to judging his fellow human beings—perhaps even because of it—Rico de Montilla was very much a man of his word.

'Then I gratefully accept your invitation.'

'Good!'

Then before she realised his intention he dipped his dark head and kissed her briefly but firmly on her mouth.

'Just remember not to issue any of your own, won't you?'

Merle slept badly that night, her slumber beset by dreams in which she relived the stress of the previous months when she'd been forced to carry on her domestic duties as if nothing were wrong both for David's and Laurie's sakes.

Barbie had been wonderful, her original qualms stilled when she had seen how devoted the little girl and her sister were. It hadn't only been moral support her older sister had offered either, Merle accorded the next morning, pulling a face at her image in the bathroom mirror as she saw the heavy shadows beneath her eyes. Barbie and Grant had kept an open house for both herself and Laurie, often having the latter to stay with them so that Merle could spend hours at a time at David's bedside during the final few days.

It had been a great comfort knowing that Laurie enjoyed staying with her auntie Barbie and playing with Natalie. It was one of the reasons Merle had reluctantly left her behind in England while she made a preliminary inspection of the villa, rather than submit her to an uncertain routine. She missed her dreadfully already, but in the circumstances it was just as well! Today she'd phone England to check that everything was all right and to break the bad news to her sister.

Sighing, she applied a light covering of pink lipstick to her mouth in order to add a little colour to her face, trying to lessen the effect of lack of sleep. If she were honest it wasn't only the dreams that had disturbed her. It had been several hours before she had even lost consciousness, lying there with her mind full of Rico. Dear heavens, how she hated to be in his debt when he so obviously despised her! But what reasonable alternative had she had? She shuddered, recalling the pressure of his mouth against her own as he'd warned her not to issue any invitations.

Did he really think she was so promiscuous and lacking in pride that she would offer herself to him when he had attacked her so scathingly? And that remark about promising him treasure! She supposed she should have denied it at the time, but what was the point? In his eyes she was the original scarlet woman... And as for re-planning her future on a long-term basis...the only plan she had in mind was that of providing Laurie with love and security...

Dressing herself in pale lilac trousers topped with a darker mauve sleeveless shirt knotted at the waist, she admitted grimly to herself that in Rico's eyes her virtue was certainly suspect! An opinion that made his charity even more difficult to bear.

For a moment last night her hand had tensed, the muscles of her arm knotting as she had fought the impulse to smack his autocratic face as he had stepped back from embracing her. To have done so would have forfeited his help, logic had argued with her, and she needed that help if she was to do the best for Laurie.

She sighed. If she were honest with herself, there'd been more to it than that. On a purely physical level Rico's nearness to her, the caress of his hard silky mouth, the touch of his hands on her arms had not been unpleasant. Confusing, disturbing, insulting—yes, but although she had felt the contempt in his dismissal she had been aware of an underlying tug of attraction, the same magnetism that had drawn her to him in the first place when she had been so dazed with the pressure of her unhappiness she had responded automatically to his warmth and tenderness.

Returning to the bed, she smoothed the covers back into place. What warmth and tenderness, she asked herself bitterly, and how long would Rico expect her to stay? Another day perhaps, while he contacted his brother's lawyer? More than that would be an impossible imposition, she determined fiercely. Rico de Montilla wasn't the only one around with unmitigated pride. She had her fair share too, and it wouldn't allow her to accept his hospitality a day longer than necessary.

Firmly she quashed the idle thought that she could explain to her censorious host about the terms of her marriage. In the first place it was none of his business. In the second place it would be ridiculous to expect him to find the circumstances mitigating. He was too endowed with that Latin pride that saw marriage, any kind of marriage, as sacred and binding.

Angrily Merle thumped one of the pillows. For that matter, she shared the same belief—it had been David who had insisted that she was perfectly free to live her own kind of life, form her own attachments even while she was still nominally his wife. In fact he had positively encouraged her to do so, which was why she had felt no guilt in seeking Rico out each afternoon. The latter had been a friend, a like spirit—or that was what, in her innocence, she had imagined at the time!

So, she decided, it was far better to keep silent, maintaining the uneasy peace that existed between them. She was being childish and unrealistic in wanting to regain his approbation. All that mattered now was trying to retrieve something from the fiasco into which she'd plunged herself.

Casually dressed in pale grey trousers and a white open-necked shirt, Rico was in the living-room, a cup of coffee in his hand.

'*Buenos días,*' he greeted her formally, rising lazily to his full height. 'To avoid any misunderstanding I waited for you to come down before offering you breakfast.'

Merle's cheeks heated under the light flick of his eyes as she ignored his sarcasm.

'Good morning,' she returned stiffly, as he bent to the elegant coffee-table before the couch and filled a waiting cup, offering it to her.

'Thank you.' Seating herself opposite him, perching on the edge of the couch, she wondered why the sight of him so relaxed and in command filled her with such mixed feelings of fierce antagonism and equally vivid attraction, as she waved away his offer of croissants. 'Thank you, I'm not hungry this morning.'

'A bad night?' His sympathy was accompanied by a close scrutiny of her wan face. 'I'm afraid you suffered a very traumatic experience yesterday, and staying here alone with me can hardly have added to your peace of mind.'

Meeting his ironic expression, Merle lifted a casual shoulder. 'I worried about the villa, yes, of course I did, but as far as you were concerned I accepted your undertaking at face-value.' It was true. It had never occurred to her that he would break his word.

'I'm flattered.' His coolly cynical gaze lingered on her face. 'Nevertheless, your original misgivings were justified. It isn't suitable for you and me to be living under the same roof without a chaperon, so I have arranged alternative accommodation for you as you originally requested.'

'Oh, but that's marvellous!' Merle smiled her relief, delighted that she was going to be released from the strange tension of the atmosphere surrounding her. 'I was afraid all the hotels might be fully booked. Which one is it, and for how long have you booked a room?'

'It's an open-ended reservation.' Rico took a casual sip of his coffee. 'These things can't be hurried.'

His cool, level gaze was somehow unnerving, causing the small pulse at the base of her throat to hammer in sudden apprehension. 'But I have to get home to Laurie——'

'Or arrange for her to come out here to you?'

'Well, that was the original plan. Once the villa was cleaned up and sufficiently furnished Grant and Barbie were coming over with Natalie and Laurie and all four of them were going to stay.'

'So you must have allowed yourself a week to get things in order?'

'Yes, I did—but in the circumstances...'

'In the circumstances you still have a few days left. You can phone your sister and let her know what's happening. If at the end of the week...' Rico paused, shrugging his shoulders, his action needing no explanation.

It was patently clear that if nothing had been resolved in seven days she would never set eyes on the Villa Paraiso again unless she was prepared to repurchase it. Desire it as she did, she would never be able to justify putting good money after bad.

'I guess you're right,' she sighed with resignation. 'I'm grateful for your finding me a hotel. Where is it?'

Watching the corners of his mouth deepen into what could only be a suppressed smile, and the sudden challenging sparkle at the back of his dark eyes, Merle was filled with instant foreboding.

'As you so rightly surmised, all the hotels along the coast are fully booked. The place where you'll be staying is called the Cortijo del Rey—and it's not a hotel. It's my brother's farm,' Rico announced serenely.

'Oh, but I can't!' Horrified, Merle sprang to her feet. 'How could you suggest a thing? You can't inflict a stranger's company on them!'

'Hardly a stranger, surely?' he baited her softly. 'Have you forgotten all the good moments we shared last year?'

It was a question Merle refused to answer. She might not have forgotten them, but Rico's present attitude had besmirched their memory. How she wished she could put their lingering sweetness out of her mind forever!

'I'm sorry.' She shook her head, full of determination. 'For one thing, I've only brought casual clothes with me, I should feel out of place and miserable. I'd— I'd rather stay here.'

Who would have thought she would ever make such an admission? And the low laugh which greeted it brought a flood of colour to her face.

'You may have no need to preserve your good name, but for me it's imperative.' Rico's dark eyes mocked her embarrassment and for a moment she thought he must be joking. 'It's perfectly true.' He'd caught her wide-eyed disbelief and proceeded to demolish it. 'The clinic which employs me is supported by many Christian charities. In return for their generosity they expect the highest level of ethics to be demonstrated by their practitioners—both professional and moral. To have you stay for two nights in an emergency——' he made a careless gesture with one beautiful long-fingered hand '—that would be acceptable. But to keep you under my roof for a week—ah——' the dark head shook chidingly '—that would make the idle tongues gossip—and bring me into certain confrontation with my employers' benefactors.'

'You mean they would demand you were dismissed?' she asked incredulously.

'Or married, to regularise the situation.' A cynical sparkle brought a golden gleam to his dark regard. 'Take your choice.' His eyes rested on her, alive with cool speculation, indolently awaiting her reaction.

He'd deliberately set out to infuriate her, and she wasn't going to rise to his bait. A disdainful shrug was intended to demonstrate her indifference.

'A good doctor can always find work. You'd soon be re-employed.'

'But I enjoy the job I have and intend to keep it, or at least,' Rico amended smoothly, 'to sacrifice it for far greater rewards than your continued presence here.' He rose to stand over her. 'Neither, like you, do I find the alternative appealing, so I'm afraid if the matter of your property is to be contended you'll have to do as I've arranged . . . and stay at the *cortijo*.'

An angry tautness held Merle immobile as she felt her tenuous grasp on events slipping away. It was too much of an imposition on people she didn't know, yet the only real alternative was to get a flight back to England as soon as possible and forsake even this last forlorn hope of regaining Paraiso.

'Don't be foolhardy, Merle.' Unexpectedly Rico's hand came to rest on her shoulder. 'To be honest, you'd be doing my sister-in-law a great favour. My brother Armando is in Madrid on business at the moment, and Pavane would dearly love company. Of course, she's got the children and the household staff, but it's not the same as having a fellow-countrywoman to talk to, is it? This morning when I phoned her she was absolutely thrilled with the idea and looking forward to hearing all the news from England.'

'Your brother's wife is English?' Startled, Merle wasn't aware how her expression lightened with interest and pleasure.

'Indeed yes. I've already explained your predicament to her, and she'll be a staunch ally on your behalf, I can assure you. In fact, at my request she's already alerted Señor Diaz of the problem and is trying to arrange a meeting between the three of us at the *cortijo* tomorrow.'

'But—but I hadn't accepted her invitation...'

'She assumed you would, since I suggested it.' Rico paused slightly before adding, 'I explained how I met you—and your family—last year and your present circumstances. A white lie, I believe you call it? Preferable, I'm sure you will agree, to the absolute truth.'

'Which is?' Shock mingled with indignant anger as Merle stared at Rico's grim face, daring him to put his reservations into words.

'That last year I was crazy enough to become attracted to you, only to discover that you were a married woman looking for a fling. And that now the only thing that makes me act on your behalf is compassion for the little girl who has lost a father and whose mother is incapable of managing the estate her misguided husband left to her.'

So that was his motive. A form of reparation to the child he had seen so briefly and after whose mother he had fleetingly lusted. Yes, that was the word, Merle thought bitterly. All Rico had felt for her that brief summer had been the natural desire of a young and virile man for what he had assumed to be an available female. While she...she in her naïveté had believed his interest had been rooted in something far less physical. Biting her lip, too weary to defend herself, she looked away.

'So you'll come? Good!' Rico took her silence as tacit agreement, removing his hand from her shoulder with every sign of triumph written on his imposing face. 'We're expected for lunch, so we can leave as soon as you've finished breakfast. It won't take me long to pack.' He moved towards the staircase as the impact of his words struck her.

'You mean you'll be staying at the *cortijo* too? But I thought...'

'That I'd stay here?' He regarded her as if she were abnormally simple. 'When Fidelio Diaz is going to call at the *cortijo* that would seem a very unrealistic situation, unless you feel confident enough to brief him yourself?'

'I thought you just wanted to get rid of me,' Merle mumbled, letting her eyes drop from his derisive gaze. 'You could have briefed him by phone—and besides, what about your work?'

'I've a few days to spare,' came the lazy answer. 'The clinic is undergoing renovation work and only emergency cases are being admitted. If I'm needed I'll make sure I can be contacted.'

Merle glanced back at him uncertainly, trying to assimilate the import of this new development. 'It's very good of you to put yourself out on my behalf like this. It makes me feel very guilty.'

'*Verdad?*' A cynical sparkle illuminated his charismatic eyes. 'Then I feel myself well rewarded. Guilt, Merle? That must be a very strange emotion for you to experience. Savour it while it lasts. I doubt it will often be repeated!'

CHAPTER SIX

As a Parthian shot it was unanswerable. All Merle could do was grit her teeth in frustration as she watched Rico's lean powerful frame move purposefully towards the stairs while she nursed the sudden ache in her heart his cruel condemnation had evoked. A year of trauma and tragedy had passed from which she had emerged a stronger more positive person. How was it then that Rico de Montilla still had the power to incite a perverse excitement in her despite the lash of his sarcasm?

It was a question she didn't want to think about, let alone answer. Resolutely she poured herself another cup of coffee from the percolater. The only reason she had even considered his invitation had been for Laurie. If it hadn't been for David's enchanting daughter and the obligation she felt towards her, she'd be on her way home now rather than share a roof with this dominating Spaniard for even one more night!

Despite her strong reservations about the wisdom of her decision, the first sight of the Cortijo del Rey caused Merle to cry out in delight, when they arrived a few hours later.

'It's beautiful!' she exclaimed.

Rico nodded his agreement. 'Mainly because of the work Armando's put into it these past twenty years. When he came here from Argentina on our father's death, I understand it was badly dilapidated. He's restored it from an old crumbling ruin into something like its former glory, modernising it without spoiling its intrinsic beauty.'

Parking his car outside the entrance gates, he continued idly, 'Legend has it that one of the caliphs of Cordoba had it specially built so he could entertain his favourite mistress here. Of course, being Muslim, he had wives and probably a harem as well, but this particular lady was of a noble Spanish family. It seems he was so infatuated with her that he would have given her anything she wanted, but she refused to join his harem. In the event he gave her a son and this farm. The story goes that he would have taken the child and recognised him as his son, but the lady was adamantly opposed to it, so the boy remained with her and took her name.'

'Montilla, you mean?' Merle was fascinated.

'Montilla y Cabra, to be precise.' Rico alighted from the car with swift grace to open the passenger door for her. 'Yes, it seems I can claim an Arab prince among my forebears.' A firm hand supported her elbow as Merle stepped from the car into the blazing sunshine, breathing in the air perfumed with herbs and flowers, closing her eyes in delight as she savoured the warm breeze on her skin.

How easy it was to imagine Rico as a descendant of some Moorish princeling! Dress him in Arab robes, cover his crisp dark hair with a flowing headdress banded with the traditional *'iqal*, boot and spur him and mount him on an Arab stallion and he'd be a match for Saladin himself!

Unpredictably a heady feeling of anticipation thrummed through her nervous system. Rico would not lightly abandon any cause he took up. If anyone could retrieve the Villa Paraiso for her it would be he!

It was with a much lighter heart that she allowed herself to be guided towards the imposing entrance of the *cortijo*, only to see a flutter of colour in the open doorway as a young woman emerged carrying a blonde-haired little girl in her arms and followed by a dark-haired boy a few years older.

'Rico and Merle!' The smile on her exquisitely pretty face was natural and welcoming. 'I'm delighted you could both come—though I wish the circumstances had been happier!' She cast a sympathetic glance towards Merle. 'Both Armando and Rico know how I feel about some of the laws in this part of the world, and, although they tell me that British justice isn't perfect either, I know that in this case they'll both agree it's appalling you should be made to suffer.' She smiled down at the toddler in her arms. 'The children have been so excited ever since they heard you were coming. This is Elena, she's just two, and this——' she reached down to the solemn-eyed little boy at her side '—this is my son, Nacio.'

'How do you do?' Nacio greeted her solemnly in excellent English, extending a small hand.

Smiling, Merle shook it, replying formally, 'How do you do?'

In the next second the solemnity had disappeared completely as Rico stepped forward and lifted the child up in his arms. 'And how about a welcome for your *tío* Rico?' he demanded.

'Put me down!' Nacio squealed happily. 'I'm not a baby any more. I'm five!'

'My, my, how time flies!' Rico pressed his hard cheek against the boy's soft face before flinging him upwards so the child sat astride his shoulders, falling into step beside Merle as their hostess led them into the house.

Pavane was absolutely lovely, Merle accorded admiringly to herself with the simple generosity of one woman acknowledging another's beauty. Probably no more than half a dozen years older than herself,

Armando's wife had the slim but curvaceous figure of a teenager. Soft short blonde hair curled appealingly round a face in which the eyes were the dominant feature, only just marginally more remarkable than the short classic nose and the soft full mouth with its ready smile.

How like her her daughter was, and how different the son. Nacio obviously resembled his father, which meant Armando and Rico must share the same dark handsomeness. His face relaxed, head turned towards the child on his shoulders, strong mouth curved as he teased him in his native tongue, Rico had fleetingly become the person she had met on the beach. The sensitive, humorous man she had believed could be her friend. But her emotions had been blunted by pain, her judgement warped by inexperience, she thought sadly.

Banishing the unwelcome memories from her mind, she followed her hostess into the *cortijo* and up the wide staircase, along a corridor until they reached a heavy wooden door.

'This the room I've prepared for you.' Pavane flicked a quick gaze round as if checking that everything was in order. 'The bathroom's through there,' she indicated a closed door on the left-hand wall, 'and, as you can see, through the archway there's a sitting-room. Pedro will have your case up here in just a few minutes. When you're ready perhaps you'll join us outside on the terrace—I'm sure you're gasping for some refreshment after that drive.'

'Yes, thank you.' Merle returned the other girl's smile, sinking down on the comfortable double bed as the door closed gently behind her hostess. It was the kind of accommodation she imagined one would find in luxury hotels. The room was vast, bisected by an arched opening through which she could see a low coffee-table, two armchairs and an emerald-green velvet chaise-longue.

Shaking her head in bemusement, she absorbed the plain white walls, their bareness relieved by framed prints, the polished wood floor with its soft blue rugs, the exquisite bedroom suite hand-turned in the natural olivewood of the region. Her eyes lingered on the bedside table, the small vase of carnations, the English magazines, a small pile of paperbacks... With a sigh she rose to her feet, making for the window, drawing back the heavy sun-resisting curtains, delighted to find that behind slatted blinds a large double-glazed area included a sliding door which led on to a wrought-iron balcony, from which she could overlook the terraced area and the large expanse of land which formed part of the Montilla estate.

From below came the sound of voices speaking Spanish. It was easy to recognise Pavane's light voice, her tone quick and amused as she responded to the deeper, more vibrant timbre of her brother-in-law. It wasn't necessary to understand what they were saying to be aware of the warmth and friendship that underlined every word.

Feeling as if she were eavesdropping, Merle stepped back into the room, at the same time as a knock on the door heralded the arrival of her suitcase. Since she had travelled lightly, it took her little time to unpack her belongings, smiling wryly to herself as she admitted they were hardly the wardrobe she would have packed if she'd had any idea she might have ended up in such stylish surroundings.

It was over a delicious lunch of gazpacho, followed by grilled lamb cutlets in orange sauce with savoury rice, that Merle felt some of her earlier tension draining away as she found an instant rapport with Rico's sister-in-law.

'You'll have to bring me up to date with what's happening in England,' Pavane smiled across the table at her. 'As a matter of fact my sister's over there at the moment with her husband and young son. Rodrigo had to go over there to a vintners' conference and it was the ideal opportunity for Melody to revisit some of our old haunts.'

'Your sister's married to a Spaniard too?' Merle couldn't keep the surprise from her voice.

'Why so shocked, Merle?' It was Rico whose lazy voice answered her. 'Surely you've discovered by now that we hot-blooded Andalusians have a penchant for cold-blooded Anglo-Saxons? Some say it's the attraction of opposites, others that deep into the Andalusian nature is built a masochistic streak that makes us seek out that which has the power to destroy us.'

'Oh...' For a moment Merle was lost for words as Rico calmly reached for his wine glass and drained the last few drops. 'I hope you don't include your sister-in-law in that racial castigation?' Her eyes regarded his dark face, the ironic expression, refusing to quail before him.

'Of course not,' he denied easily, flashing a smile of undeniable sweetness towards Pavane who was regarding him with a slight frown marring the smooth expanse of her forehead. 'Pavane knows I'm one of her greatest admirers.'

'You must forgive him.' Pavane shot a conspiratorial glance towards Merle. 'Rico's idiomatic English is generally excellent, but I imagine he means "cool-blooded" rather than "cold-blooded".'

'Do I?' he asked. Merle flushed as his contemplative gaze raked her face. 'Is there a difference, then?'

It was Pavane who answered, with a light laugh.

'I take it you were referring to calmness and composure. "Cold-blooded" means barbaric, ruthless, stony-hearted... It's not the same thing at all.'

'Then I apologise, of course.' His voice was as expressionless as his face as he dipped his dark head in assumed contrition.

Frustrated by his cool arrogance, Merle felt an untypical anger uncurl inside her. Was it his intention to bait her at every opportunity under the guise of being pleasant? If so, she'd have to learn to combat his sly digs or her stay at the *cortijo* would be untenable.

'But I didn't take your remarks personally.' The smile she conjured up was a masterpiece of sweetness. 'My genes are more Gaelic than Anglo-Saxon, and the former aren't noted either for their coolness or their coldness.' She paused slightly, aware that her hostess was regarding her thoughtfully, and glad that the children were taking their lunch in the nursery and not a part of this delicate emotional fencing, then added softly, 'Particularly when it comes to a fight.'

'That's excellent news!' The other girl neatly bridged the developing tension. 'Because I'm afraid you're in for a hard one as far as trying to gain repossession of your villa is concerned.' She cast a sympathetic look at Merle, waiting until the maid who had served the meal had departed with the empty plates. 'Señor Diaz is coming over here tomorrow morning, but, to be honest, he holds out little hope. The only possibility is that he and the present owner's lawyer can prevail on Sanchez to exercise compassion on your behalf and agree to a compromise.'

'Perhaps I was silly to allow Rico to persuade me to come here. It's obviously a lost cause...' Merle swallowed the sudden lump in her throat, unable to meet Pavane's pitying gaze.

'No cause is lost until it's been fought!' Rico intervened roughly. 'So just relax and enjoy your surroundings and let me work out the strategy!'

'Rico's right.' Pavane reached across the table to touch Merle's hand where it lay clenched on the table. 'Ever since he told me about you, I've been so looking forward to meeting you.

'While he's fighting it out with the lawyers you and I can go sightseeing and shopping, so at least whatever happens you won't return to England with totally unhappy memories, and this coming Sunday Armando will be back and my other brother-in-law Ramón and his family are visiting us from the Argentine, so we're throwing a big reunion party. You simply must be here for that!'

'Oh, but I don't think…' Unwilling to offend the other girl, whose genuine enthusiasm warmed her spirit, Merle hesitated, torn between her desire to fight for Paraiso to the bitter end and her longing to hold Laurie in her arms again. Besides, with the harsh feelings between herself and Rico so lightly veiled, to meet the rest of his family would be an impossible ordeal.

'Of course she'll stay.' Rico rose smoothly from the table, pushing back his chair, to come and stand behind her, resting his hands on her shoulders, automatically conjuring her troubled gaze to meet his own. 'Nothing could please me better than to introduce her to Armando. My brother has always been a superb judge of character and I'm sure he'll be enchanted with her.'

To Merle's shocked surprise his fingers lifted the heavy fall of bronze-black hair that splayed on her shoulders and came to rest on the nape of her neck, moving sinuously to caress the soft line of her throat. 'So let's say that's a definite appointment, eh, *querida mia*?'

It was a decision, although it had been voiced as a question, but as Merle's body tightened in defiance of his tyranny as much as against the liberties of his fingers, all thought of protest was banished from her mind as he dipped his sable head with elegant slowness to bestow a light kiss on her surprised mouth.

She sat speechless, embarrassed that he had touched her in front of his sister-in-law, giving such a wrong impression of the emotions that churned between them, yet unable to put the matter right. She knew only one thing: she was swimming well out of her depth in a pool the dangers and darknesses of which were well beyond her experience.

The shiver which traversed her spine had started on its unwelcome journey seconds before she heard Rico's voice, oozing with self-satisfaction, announcing smugly, 'Well, that's settled, then.'

It was with trepidation that Merle shook hands with Fidelio Diaz the following morning, her natural anxiety surfacing after a surprisingly restful sleep. She had been made so welcome at the *cortijo* the previous day, by the time night fell she had felt as if she had known and liked Pavane all her life! The presence of Elena and Nacio during the afternoon had probably accounted for Rico's relaxed attitude, she decided. He had been marvellous with them, demonstrating a limitless patience as they had clambered over him and involved him in their games. As with most Spanish men his affection for children was openly displayed, as was his pride in the fact that they were his brother's offspring, and heirs to the Montilla name.

Watching his gentleness, the sweetness of his smile, the power allied to the delicacy of his adroit hands, Merle had felt her heart lurch with the heady yet alarming emotion which had first assailed her a year earlier.

Lying in bed later, watching the pattern of moon-beams on the walls, she had realised with a shock that

she had just spent one of the happiest days of her life
since Rosemary's tragic and sudden death.

Rico's affability had still been in evidence at breakfast
as he courteously enquired about her night's rest as if
he really cared whether she had lain awake all night or
found some respite in slumber.

Now, as the lawyer seated himself, Rico drew her down
beside himself on the couch, taking the correspondence
she had fortunately brought with her to Spain and
passing it over to the older man.

'Is there anything you can do?' Her anxiety brought
a tremor to her voice.

'It's a difficult situation, *señora—muy difícil*...' His
face was stern, promising her no easy solution. No solution at all really, Merle recognised with painful per-
spicacity, as Rico's arm tightened supportively round her
shoulders, before he addressed the other man in clipped
Spanish.

There was no way Merle could understand the following exchange, neither did either man's businesslike
tones convey anything to her. For all the use she was she
might just as well have stayed in her room, she thought
wearily.

At last it was over, Fidelio Diaz rising to shake her
hand with studied courtesy, addressing her in her own
language.

'I can promise you nothing, *señora*, apart from the
fact that I will do my utmost on your behalf.'

She was grateful, of course, but it wasn't much to hold
on to. Why on earth had she allowed herself to be talked
into this diversion, she wondered miserably, when she
could have been home with Laurie? Although she didn't
question her decision to leave the little girl, especially in
the present circumstances, it was the first time she had
been parted from David's daughter since Rosemary had

triumphantly brought her home from the maternity hospital. A wave of loneliness swamped her, destroying her composure, as she closed her eyes in an unsuccessful attempt to prevent her tears from spilling.

'*Fortaleza, mi amor* . . . our lawyer friend is too professionally reserved to raise your hopes, but I can assure you his best is very good indeed, and remember, the war isn't over until the last battle has been fought and won!'

Merle hadn't heard Rico re-enter the room after escorting their visitor to the front door, and she gave a little start of shock as his hand fell lightly on her shoulder as an accompaniment to his sympathetic words. It seemed he was exhorting her to show fortitude, although she was surprised he should address her as 'my love' in tones which showed compassion rather than the sarcasm to which she had grown accustomed.

Hastily she brushed the moisture from her cheeks, deciding there was little point in confessing that her tears had been because she missed Laurie rather than for the potential loss of Paraiso.

'In the meantime,' he was continuing briskly, 'the best thing you can do is to stop dwelling on your problems and try to enjoy yourself instead.' His gaze lingered speculatively on the plain pink cotton button-through dress she had chosen to wear for the morning's confrontation. 'So why don't you go and change into trousers and trainers and I'll take you for a ride through the estate?'

'You're very kind, but you don't have to entertain me.' Stiffly Merle refused his offer, not at all sure that being in his contentious presence would amount to much enjoyment! 'I want to phone my sister this morning, and afterwards I thought I'd help Pavane.'

'Phone by all means,' a dark brow rose in what she thought was faint amusement, 'since the advent of international subscriber dialling that will hardly take up much of your time, but as for helping Pavane, I can assure you my brother keeps an adequate staff for that purpose.'

'I thought you said she'd appreciate my company,' Merle challenged coolly.

'I don't deny it, but not this morning. Wednesdays are when she gives piano lessons to some of the children from the nearby village.'

'She's a music teacher!' It was impossible to hide her surprise. Somehow she hadn't expected Armando's wife to have a job.

Rico nodded. 'It was to be her career before she met and married Armando. Now it's her hobby, a way of passing on her talents to those less fortunate than herself. Rather than let her cancel her arrangements and disappoint the children, I've assured her that you and I will find plenty with which to amuse ourselves.'

'But what about Nacio and Elena...?' Some inner turmoil insisted she continued to oppose his suggestion, although reason prompted her that a tour of the estate in one of the *cortijo's* Jeeps would be instructive as well as enjoyable and she was being churlish to contend the suggestion.

Rico sighed impatiently. 'They have a perfectly good nurserymaid in Conchita. Today is one of the days she takes them to the village play-school. Now, are there any more obstacles you wish to erect? You want to write a letter, read a book, perhaps?'

His unqualified sarcasm brought the colour to her cheeks, aware as she was of her own ungraciousness. For a split second she even considered taking him up on one of his alternatives, but how could she concentrate on reading while the future of her investment lay in the balance? Besides, a breath of fresh air would do her a power of good.

'I wouldn't want to interfere with any plans you'd already made for yourself,' she returned stiffly.

'Good, that's settled it, then,' triumphantly Rico answered her querulous regard with a brilliant smile which lacked nothing but humour, 'since the only plan I had in mind for this morning was to pay a visit to an old friend of mine who's just got married, and has brought his wife here to introduce her to his family. As Esteban is staying with his father, who is Armando's farm manager and who has property on the estate, there's no problem.'

It was only because he disliked being thwarted rather than because her company was of paramount importance to him that Rico had been so adamant, Merle decided as a few minutes later she dragged on a pair of old blue denims, and topped them with a crisp shirt of blue checked cotton. Briskly she rolled the sleeves up above her elbows before brushing her thick hair and gathering it into a workmanlike ponytail. She didn't possess trainers, but she supposed an old pair of tennis shoes which were blissfully comfortable would suffice, although what had been wrong with her previous mode of dress she couldn't guess.

Rico was waiting for her in the hall as she moved lithely down the stairs, and she noted with some surprise that he, too, had changed, the light cotton trousers he had worn previously exchanged for black denims which highlighted the powerful musculature of his long legs. His broad shoulders now stretched the black cotton of a T-shirt, the rib of its short sleeves tightly encompassing the smooth bulge of his upper arms.

Her quickening pulse made her grab for the handrail as he stood, hands in his pockets, watching her descent.

Like an echo from the past a throbbing excitement held her in its thrall, as she experienced for a fleeting second the type of response she had once felt in his presence. How stupid and untutored she'd been not to realise that she had already been caught in a mire of dangerous emotions, and flee from them before Rico had gone in search of her that morning a year ago...

Meeting him again, she knew with a quiet desperation that she had left it too late to raise defences against him. She could only escape now when he chose to release her, but he was proud and unforgiving, and unintentionally she had aroused his antipathy. Too sensitive not to discern that under the guise of helping her Rico's motives were mixed, she knew that until that time came she would have to pay the price of her foolishness in whatever coin he demanded.

Almost unbearably conscious of the way Rico's dark eyes glittered, sensually alive as they surveyed her chosen outfit, Merle was determined he wouldn't guess the effect he had on her. To offset the sudden weakness in her legs and the unwelcome constriction in her throat she held her head proudly high, refusing to enquire whether she met with his approval as she reached ground level.

'That's much better!' He gave it to her anyway as if it was of primary importance to her, continuing smoothly, 'I've written out the international dialling code for you on the phone pad. All you have to do is add your sister's number.' He indicated the telephone ensconced on its own unit at one side of the expansive entrance hall. 'Take your time. I'll be waiting for you in the *sala* when you've finished.'

Without waiting for her answer he turned on his heel and strolled away. For a moment Merle paused, watching his retreat, fighting down unbidden speculations: was his body as marvellously tanned as it had been last year?

Was the smooth flesh of his back still seared with the brand of war? Was it just the awareness of his contempt that made his physical presence so actively disturbing to her?

From upstairs came the sound of children's laughter interspersed with Pavane's light tones—a sound that tugged at her heartstrings. What would Laurie be doing now? she wondered. She hoped she was not missing her as much as she missed her little stepdaughter. Resolutely she made her way to the phone and dialled Barbie's number.

Twenty minutes later she replaced the receiver, making a mental note to check how much she owed Pavane for the call. Barbara had been horrified at her news and intrigued by Rico's intervention. Not surprising, since she had told her sister very little about her previous encounter with the imperious Andalusian. Abruptly she had put an end to Barbie's speculations of romance, advising her sister that Rico was only acting out of a natural sense of justice and a wish that foreigners should see his country in a good light.

She smiled wryly to herself, imagining Barbie's reaction if she had told her Rico regarded her as a woman on the make—avaricious, disloyal and promiscuous! The only good news was that Laurie was well and happy. It had been wonderful to listen to the four-year-old bubbling on about the lovely time she was having with Natalie and how they'd been to a theme park and were looking forward to visiting a local zoo.

Rico was gazing out of the large windows at a terrace aglow with the colour of potted plants when Merle entered the *sala*. A slight lift of his dark brows demanded to know if her domestic affairs were in order and full explanations given and accepted. On her confirmation that everything was as settled as could be expected, he gave a satisfied nod and led her briskly outside.

Matching his stride, Merle followed in silence, too intent on enjoying the warmth of the sun on her bare arms and the spicy sweet scent of the atmosphere to pay much attention to their destination. It was with something of a shock that she came to a halt as Rico announced their arrival at the stables.

Stables! She had assumed they'd been walking towards a garage! Any hope that motorised transport awaited them was immediately dispelled as Rico continued forward across the cobbled yard, greeting the stablehand who hurried towards them.

'I'll take Zarina and Relámpago for a bit of exercise if they're fit.'

'*Por cierto*, Don Rico!'

Merle watched aghast as the lad moved towards some open stalls to return leading a horse by the bridle in each hand, a flush of mortification burning in her cheeks, more because of her misinterpretation of the word 'ride' than her lack of equestrian skills. How stupid she'd been not to put two and two together and realise the reason Rico had insisted she changed her dress!

'Rico...' she began.

'Mmm?' He had already thrown a blanket across the chestnut's back and stopped in the process of settling the saddle, to pay attention to her, his eyes narrowed against the glare of the sun. 'You've no objection to my choosing your mount, have you?'

'No...yes...' His impatient frown told her to be brief and specific. 'The thing is—I misunderstood you. I thought we were going by Jeep.' She took a deep breath. 'You see—I don't ride horseback!'

CHAPTER SEVEN

MERLE wasn't sure what reaction she had expected—irritation, disbelief, even annoyance that she'd spiked Rico's plans. What she hadn't anticipated was the careless shrug with which her statement was received as Rico returned to the task of tightening the girths.

'Then this is a marvellous opportunity for you to learn,' she was told calmly. 'Zarina is the most sweet-tempered mare that ever lived. She's sixteen years old and wise as befits her age. Believe me, she'll look after you with as much devotion as if you were her own foal!'

Merle swallowed unhappily. Sweet-tempered Zarina might be, but she was also large.

'Here...' Rico held out an imperious hand as, finishing his task, he rose to his full height and stroked the chestnut's copper nose. 'Come and make friends with her.' He paused as Merle hesitated. 'You're not afraid of horses, are you?'

'No, of course not!' Only of being astride their backs and out of contact with the ground, she might have added, but refrained from doing so. She moved forward boldly, allowing the mare to blow softly into her hand as she enquired doubtfully, 'But doesn't it take a long time to learn to ride?'

'If you wish to compete in the Olympics, undoubtedly. If you merely wish to ride around the *cortijo*, no time at all. The rules are simple. Here, let me help you mount and you'll see.'

She could refuse and risk his lifting her bodily into the saddle, or she could comply with good grace and

hope for the best. The determination on his prepos-
sessing face informed her that they were the only options open to her.

With as much dignity as she could muster Merle
walked to Zarina's side and under Rico's instruction put
her left foot in the stirrup.

'Fine,' he encouraged. 'Now grab the pommel on the
saddle and swing your right leg up and over!'

It sounded easy, but Merle found herself lacking the
confidence to put her full weight on the stirrup. Suppose
Zarina moved? It was on her third attempt that Rico
assisted her, placing his hands each side of her hips and
thrusting her upwards so that she arrived on the saddle
with a little gasp of surprise, as much at the feel of his
firm hands placed so intimately on her body as from her
sudden successful elevation. Comforted that beneath her
Zarina remained as solid and stationary as a rock, she
felt for the other stirrup, sighing with relief as her foot
entered it effortlessly.

Beside her Rico mounted the large bay Relámpago with
effortless athletic grace, reaching across to take Merle's
reins, twist them into a circle and hand them back to
her.

'A touch on the left rein and she'll go left, a touch
on the right, right. Both together gently and she'll stop.
To make her start press your heels in. The harder and
more frequently you press the faster she'll go.'

'And that's all?' Merle asked faintly.

'For the moment.' Rico's beautiful mouth parted in
a genuine smile as his eyes took in her rigid posture.
'The rest is common sense. You and the horse are a
partnership and have to aid each other. When you go
uphill lean your weight forward to distribute it. When
you go downhill, lean backwards to balance the strain—

and, above all, relax. You're meant to be enjoying yourself!'

Fifteen minutes later Merle admitted she was. With Rico riding at her side and Zarina's sure-footed walk beneath her she had gradually gained confidence, her tight grip on the reins had loosened, her leg muscles had lost their tenseness and she was finding the leisurely transport through the leafy woods at the *cortijo*'s perimeter a stimulating experience.

'Am I going too slowly for you?' She turned concerned eyes to her companion, who was moving at the same pace, holding the reins loosely against Relámpago's back with one hand while the other rested lazily on one firmly muscled black-denim-covered thigh.

Rico's shapely mouth slanted her a mischievous grin for her solicitude.

'Do I take that enquiry to mean that you understand the translation of Relámpago's name?'

'No?' Merle raised enquiring brows.

Rico laughed, a natural expression of easy amusement that lightened her heart. 'He's called "Lightning", but that's because he was born in a thunderstorm rather than a reflection of the speed he can travel. But I'm quite content with our present pace. I can assure you I'm long past the wild days of my youth when I believed the only way to ride a horse or drive a car was at breakneck speed!'

The note of self-deprecation brought Merle's eyes back to his face, where she surprised a grimness of expression that made her heart beat a little faster. She knew so little about his early life, just the scant facts he had told her at their first meetings. A sudden need to gain his confidence prompted her to follow up his lead.

'You mean when you were still in the Argentine?'

'And afterwards.' Rico gave a short humourless laugh. 'I'm afraid I caused a certain amount of havoc when I arrived at the *cortijo*. In retrospect I'm amazed that Armando was as tolerant of my behaviour as he was!'

'It must have been a traumatic experience for you,' Merle pondered aloud. 'How old did you say you were— seventeen? Wouldn't it have been possible for you to study medicine in Argentina?'

'Theoretically, yes, of course.' He shrugged his shoulders, drawing her attention to the movement of their broad expanse beneath the dark shirt. 'In practice the truth was that my mother had just announced her plans to remarry and I didn't see eye to eye with her second husband-to-be. I was jealous that Mama had taken her attention from me to bestow on him and I resented his trying to take my father's place. As far as he was concerned, I was a thankless, selfish tearaway who had been thoroughly spoiled by a widow whose two eldest sons had returned to Spain, one to reclaim the heritage his father had neglected and the other to seek his fortune in Europe.'

'And were you?' Merle dared to ask, casting a sidelong glance at the stern profile beside her.

'Oh, yes indeed. The criticism was well merited, although naturally I didn't appreciate it at the time!' Dark eyes glowed with mocking self-knowledge and a hint of amusement, perhaps even pride, as Rico recalled his youthful exploits. 'Armando had always been very close to my father. I think Papa always regretted having neglected his Spanish property, but Mama would never dream of leaving South America, so Papa instilled in Armando the necessity of his reclaiming his inheritance one day and restoring it to its former glory. When Papa died, Armando would have stayed to look after Mama, but when she made it quite clear she preferred to return to her own family he felt free to leave her. My second brother, Ramón, decided to go with him. At the time Armando was just twenty and Ramón a year younger.'

'So you stayed with your mother?'

'Uh-huh. I was twelve, and for the next five years every whim I had was indulged. In Mama's eyes I could do no wrong, and I'm afraid I took every advantage of her complaisance! By the time I was seventeen and Mama broke the news to me that she was about to remarry, I'd become the leader of a small gang of youths whose sole aim in life was to live daringly. We rode too fast and drove too fast and boasted among ourselves of the conquests we'd made amongst feminine hearts!'

'I can imagine!' Merle interposed drily, finding no difficulty in envisaging a teenage Rico, blessed with fortune and good looks, idolised by his remaining parent and with no male control to guide his youthful exuberance. In all probability it wasn't only the female hearts he had captured but their bodies too, and it was only out of a courteous deference to herself that he had avoided making the point!

'In that case you can imagine too that I wasn't going to give up my lifestyle without a fight!'

'So what did you do? Challenge your prospective stepfather to a duel?' Merle wouldn't have put it past him. Rico aroused, she assessed, would stop at nothing to get what he wanted.

'No.' He offered her a contrite smile. 'I would feel prouder of my youthful self if I had. That, at least, would have been an honest action. Instead I was vain enough and stupid enough to try and force Mama to choose between the two of us. For some time, before I turned into a young savage, I'd been drawn to medicine as a profession and fortunately I'd done well enough in the sciences at school to make the possibility of medical school realistic. I told her that unless she gave up this idea of replacing Papa in her life I would follow Armando back to Spain and qualify there.' He gave a nonchalant shrug of his shoulders. 'You have a saying in English, I believe, about being hoist with one's own petard?' He invited her amusement with a lift of his dark brows.

Strangely Merle felt no delight at his humiliation. It was too easy to visualise Rico at seventeen, very proud and terribly vulnerable. His bluff called, he would have no recourse but to carry out his threat: leave his home and his doting mother to travel from one continent to another and place his future in the care of an older brother he hadn't seen for five years. The shock of his mother's decision must have hit him hard. How else could he have seen it but total rejection?

'It must have been a difficult time for you.' Merle's blue eyes darkened with sympathy as they dwelled on the lean face of the man riding beside her.

'Nothing more than I deserved.' He brushed aside her pity. 'My dislike of my stepfather was based on pure selfishness and an infantile possessiveness I felt towards Mama. There was no way we could have co-existed in the same house and he knew it. The truth is, he's a great guy, *muy hombre*, we would say, and he's made my mother very happy. After I'd qualified I went back to Argentina and made my peace with them—both of them.'

'I'm glad!' Merle spoke from her heart. What wouldn't she have given to be able to let bygones be bygones, but she hadn't needed her mother's warnings not to attempt a reconciliation. Her own intuition told her that neither she nor Barbie would ever be welcomed across the threshold of their own home while her stepfather still ruled it.

How hard it must have been for Rico to apologise for his youthful rashness, and how much she admired him for his action, guessing it couldn't have been without personal cost to his pride.

'Not as much as you undoubtedly will be to learn that we've arrived at our destination and you can dismount!' Rico cast her an amused look.

'Oh!' Merle had been so intent on her own thoughts, she hadn't realised that they had left the bridle path and were approaching an attractive white-painted hacienda, set in a fenced-off garden. 'As a matter of fact, I've enjoyed every moment of it!'

'Then it's my turn to say "I'm glad",' Rico nodded approvingly. 'You have a natural grace and carriage on horseback, a symbiosis with the animal which is very gratifying to watch. Within a few weeks you will be riding as well as I.'

'Except that I probably won't be here in a few weeks,' Merle returned sadly. 'In any case, even if miracles do happen I certainly won't be at the *cortijo*.'

'Oh, I don't know,' he contradicted her coolly. 'I'm sure my family would be only too delighted to meet yours. It occurs to me that your daughter must be about Nacio's age.'

'Laurie's four.' Even to her own ears Merle's voice sounded breathless, as her heart beat rhythmically faster. It had to be because of the graceful compliment he had paid her and the challenge of guiding Zarina towards the hitching post Rico was indicating to her. It couldn't be because of the way he'd looked at her just now, could it? She must have imagined the sudden unsullied glow of pure male appreciation in the slumbrous glance he'd levied at her.

Yet watching his casual dismount she felt every nerve in her body tingle with inexplicable anticipation. He made it look so easy, one hand steadying himself on the pommel as he swung the other high and wide across Relámpago's broad back.

For a split second it seemed that every muscle in the taut line of shoulder, buttock, thigh and calf was outlined beneath his clothes in splendid definition. Merle caught her breath in sheer admiration at the pure line of masculine beauty before her, the strength and resilience of God's ultimate creation casually displayed to heart-stopping effect. Dear heavens! What was happening to her? Her mouth dry, the perspiration breaking out on her forehead, she tried to forestall the sudden warm rise of blood to her face.

'It's not so difficult!' Rico had tied Relámpago to the post before coming to stand at her side, laughing up at her, his teeth a flash of white against the tanned darkness of his skin. 'Come, have confidence. You watched the way I did it, and I'll be here to catch you!'

Merle swallowed resolutely. Yes, she had watched him, but she had been thinking of other things than his technique. Gratefully she realised he had no idea her discomfort could be caused by anything other than her fear of leaving Zarina's back successfully.

Carefully she transferred her weight to the left stirrup, freeing her other leg. Gaining confidence as the mare stayed quietly in place, she swung her right leg up, but either she had misjudged the distance, or lacked Rico's athletic swing, because her heel dragged across the mare's back and, when she managed to get it clear, the ground seemed to be much further away than she'd judged. Her right leg buckled as it reached the ground and her hands fell from the pommel, leaving her left foot still in its stirrup.

'Careful!' She would have fallen if Rico hadn't held her firmly, his hands steadying her hips so she could disengage her foot.

'Well, I managed—after a way!' Triumphantly she turned in his arms to smile widely up into his dark eyes, the humour leaving her face as she read his purpose.

'Merle...' As his hands skimmed up her body to fasten around her shoulders, his words were little more than a sigh. 'Oh, Merle, how can I resist you?'

He didn't give her an opportunity of replying, as his arms tightened round her, pulling her hard against him, drawing her into his muscled frame. They were locked into a contact so intimate that their body heat mingled, and he bent his head to part the softness of her surprised mouth with his firm lips in a deep, searchingly ardent act of possession.

In his embrace Merle forgot everything—pride, self-respect, her resolution to keep their contact businesslike. Suddenly, with Rico's intimate caress on her lips, the passage of his hands branding her body even through the crisp cotton of her blouse, it was as if she had been transfixed by a magic spell, unable to do anything but respond to the invasion of her privacy with a delight that shocked her as much as it thrilled.

Even while her mind fought what was happening to her, her body was unashamedly glorying in the feel of Rico's powerful bones against her own, the sweet taste of his kiss, the highly erotic smell of clean sweat mingled with the lighter, tangier scent of some cologne and the aura of parched earth and grass beneath their feet.

She had never lain in a man's arms, or satisfied a man's lust. She had never been aroused by a man's touch or ached for fulfilment. For the first time in her life Merle was aware of her body's awakening; the stirring of desire; a muted hunger the pangs of which were painfully increasing; an unsuspected appetite that longed to feed from the grace and style of the clever, sensitive man who held her captive.

It was impossible! To give herself in a casual affair was utterly beyond everything she believed in, even if Rico had cared for her as a person. One day she might meet a man prepared to accept Laurie as his own child, a man she could respect as well as care for, a man who would like her as much as he desired her. In fact she hoped very much that she would. Ideally a child should have two parents, and Laurie had been most cruelly deprived. She owed this shadowy figure of her imagination her loyalty and her chastity. To indulge her own frailty with a man who saw her simply as a summer's pastime was unthinkable!

She opened her mouth in an attempt to put her thoughts into words when she saw Rico's glance flick behind her and felt his shoulders stiffen slightly.

The next moment he had taken her unresisting hands in his own and turned her so that she stood in front of him facing in the same direction. Instantly she realised why he had been distracted. Walking swiftly towards them was a man, probably a year or so younger than Rico himself, his face showing every sign of pleasure as he approached.

'Rico!' His hand went out in greeting. *'Estoy muy contento de verle!'*

'Esteban!' If there was a slight tinge of disappointment in Rico's voice Merle was the only one who heard it. *'Mi amigo!'*

The two men exchanged an arm clasp as Rico added in English, 'I'd like you to meet Merle, who is doing me the honour of staying with me at the *cortijo* for a few days.'

'I am delighted, *señorita*.' Esteban moved smoothly into barely accented English.

'Actually it's *"señora"*,' Merle corrected him awkwardly. 'My husband—that is...I'm a widow. But I'd really prefer you to call me Merle.'

'Con su permiso?' Dark eyebrows rose enquiringly as Esteban addressed Rico, a mocking smile on his lips.

The latter's mouth twisted in a wry grin. 'Certainly you have my permission, my friend, provided I am allowed to address your wife by her Christian name.'

'Ah, Isadora——' A shadow passed over Esteban's pleasant face. 'As a matter of fact I'm afraid she's not with me at the moment.'

'No?' Rico looked troubled. 'She's not unwell, I trust? I understood your purpose in coming here was to introduce her to your family.'

'Indeed it was, but things haven't worked out that way.' Esteban shrugged his shoulders. 'But allow me to explain over some refreshment in the house. My mother's very lonely now since the recent death of my grandmother, and with my father spending so many hours at the *cortijo*, she'll be delighted to see you—although,' he added with an apologetic glance at Merle, 'she has very little English.'

'Oh, please don't exclude her from the conversation on my behalf!' Merle interposed quickly. 'I shall be very happy listening to the three of you speaking in Spanish. It's a beautiful language and I have every intention of learning it when I—that is, if I ever come back here again.'

She was rewarded by a swift smile of thanks. 'You are *muy simpática*, Merle. My friend is a lucky man to have your companionship.'

'Indeed, yes,' Rico agreed suavely. 'Merle has been a constant delight to me since our first meeting a year ago.'

He placed a proprietorial arm around her waist as Esteban led the way to the hacienda, tightening his hold slightly as he felt her flinch involuntarily. Uneasily Merle glanced up at his strong profile, silently cursing her previous inability to repulse to him. It was clear from his whole bearing that he assumed she had welcomed his surrender to his baser nature. Well, she'd no one to blame but herself.

She could hardly envisage herself slapping his handsome face—the gesture would have been far too histrionic for her normally peaceable nature—but if she'd been able to gather her wits in time she could have told him in no uncertain terms that he would have to learn to resist her since she was definitely not available! It was an omission she would have to repair as soon as possible, she determined. In the meantime she must behave as distantly as she could without appearing too churlish.

In the event, it wasn't too difficult, as Esteban's mother Mariana made them welcome with a jug of *sangría* and a plateful of delicious *tapas*. Since the conversation was mostly in Spanish she accepted the fact of Rico's sitting beside her and holding her free hand, or occasionally putting his arm round her shoulders, with a good grace. Obviously he was ensuring that their hostess did not feel embarrassed by one of her guests being excluded.

In fact Merle found she was enjoying herself. The assortment of snacks was delicious and the wine cup cold and marvellously refreshing, so that she was surprised how quickly the time passed.

It was two hours later when Mariana excused herself to see to some household duties, and Esteban raised once more the question of his wife.

'We were all set to come here when Isadora heard from a friend of hers in Granada that she'd just given birth to her first child. As we were in this part of Spain she took the opportunity of visiting her and seeing the baby for herself.'

He didn't look too happy about the decision, Merle saw, and she could hardly blame him. Surely meeting one's in-laws was a greater priority than visiting a friend?

'Doubtless she'll be joining you soon?' asked Rico, sparing his friend a quizzical look.

'Certainly!' Esteban's reply was just a little too quick and to Merle's sensitive ear held an unnatural light-heartedness. 'I'm expecting her any day, and of course she'll be here in time for the party Pavane and Armando are throwing for Ramón's return!'

'Then I shall have to hold my curiosity in rein until then,' Rico said lightly. 'I must admit I'm intrigued to meet the woman who persuaded my old friend to give up his bachelorhood. I'd begun to believe you were finding the single life too full of opportunities to tie yourself to one woman.'

'We're not all as self-sufficient as you, my friend,' the younger man pointed out with a slight smile. 'And, while you no doubt spend many of your evenings reading learned medical journals, when I leave my office I leave my business worries in it.'

'Esteban runs a very successful company based in Barcelona designing and marketing ceramic tiles,' Rico advised Merle, before addressing the other man. 'Pavane mentioned something about your meeting Isadora through business, I believe?'

'She's a freelance interior-decorating consultant,' Esteban nodded, the pride in his wife's achievements clearly audible in his voice. 'We had to fit our wedding in between her commitments, which is why we didn't make a big fuss about it.' His pleasant face darkened as he rose to his feet and moved towards the window. 'I'm afraid that's something my parents find very hard to forgive, but, apart from having so little time to spare, Isadora hasn't any close family and she saw no reason to have anything other than a quiet ceremony.'

'I'm sure they'll forgive you both when they meet your wife,' Merle interposed sympathetically, addressing the young man's back. 'After all, it's the bride's prerogative to choose the kind of ceremony she wants on the day, isn't it?'

'Not if it takes place in Spain and excludes her husband-to-be's parents,' Rico commented drily. 'But Merle is right. I'm sure your wife is as charming and intelligent as she is undoubtedly beautiful. One look at her and she'll have Mariana and Enrico eating out of her talented hand!'

'I sincerely hope so!' There was heartfelt emphasis in Esteban's retort as he turned from the window. 'In fact, I'll drink to it! Pass the *sangría*, will you?'

It was just past midday when Merle remounted Zarina, delighted when she discovered she could do so without assistance, so much had her confidence increased.

'I thought we'd have a short ride through the fodder and grain fields before we turned for home,' Rico announced, having satisfied himself that she was securely and comfortably mounted. 'It's very pleasant up there and it'll give you some idea of the crops the farm produces. That is, unless you're stiffening up at all? I wouldn't want you to overtax yourself on your first ride.'

'No, I'm fine—honestly!' Merle turned eyes shining with happiness on him. She would never have believed the triumph she felt at accomplishing such a simple task as sitting on a horse while it ambled along beneath her. Of course, one couldn't call it riding as such, but it was a beginning. More to the point, she didn't feel at all stiff or tired. Probably because she had always been active her muscles were easily adaptable to new exercise.

The ride, as Rico had promised, was well worth taking, and she listened with interest as he explained that the farmland stretched over twelve thousand acres and was divided into different areas for different purposes, naming the various crops as they passed them.

It was about half an hour later that the cultivated parcels of land came to an end, to be replaced with open tree-dotted grassland.

'We can stop here and give our animals a breather,' Rico decided, narrowing his eyes to look at the broad clear expanse of azure sky over their heads. 'A little shade won't do us any harm either.'

He was right about that, Merle agreed silently, feeling the sun scorching her fair skin beneath the cotton of her blouse, and gratefully guiding Zarina in Relámpago's hoofmarks. She felt oddly lethargic—probably a combination of sunshine and *sangría* and the somnolent effect of her mount's gentle movement. Whatever the cause, when she tried to emulate Rico's clean dismount she found it impossible, hearing his soft laugh behind her as she struggled to clear Zarina's back with her plim-solled foot. A final effort had her making the same error she had made at the hacienda, stumbling back into Rico's arms.

For a few minutes she had forgotten the threat his presence posed her, the implications latent in that brief, interrupted embrace they had shared. Now they came sharply to the forefront of her mind, so that her whole body stiffened in his light hold.

CHAPTER EIGHT

'COME and sit down.' To Merle's relief Rico made no attempt to carry on where Esteban's appearance had interrupted them. Instead he led her towards the shade of a large tree, indicating where she should rest. 'Give me a few moments while I unsaddle the horses and lead them to some other shade, and I'll join you.'

Sprawling down on the surprisingly green turf, Merle watched Rico suit his actions to his words. There was a painful joy in watching the smooth muscular action of his body as he lifted the saddles off, placing them with the blankets in a neat pile beneath an adjacent tree.

Had she been a fool to allow him to bring her out here, so far away from the *cortijo*? Her mouth, dry already from the heat of the day and the mild alcohol of the *sangría*, became suddenly parched.

'What's the matter, Merle?' Every line of his intent face portrayed concern for her well-being as he approached her, a flask in his hand. 'Is the heat affecting you? *Dios*, I should have known better than to let you ride in the heat of the day without a hat!' He passed one hand through his own thick thatch of hair. 'I forget you're accustomed to colder climates. Here, have a drink from this. It's iced water Mariana gave me before we left.'

'Thank you.' Gratefully Merle accepted the flask, holding it to her lips and swallowing a couple of mouthfuls. 'I'm quite all right, really. Is it—is it safe to leave the horses like that without tying them up?' she pointed to where Zarina and Relámpago stood shoulder

to shoulder, heads down nibbling at the grass, glad to
have an opportunity to defer the reckoning of her un-
predictable capitulation.

'Quite safe.' His tone teased her. 'You'll see I've pulled
the reins down in front of them. They understand that
means they are to stay where they are.'

'And they wouldn't dare to disobey you, I suppose?'
An element of tartness had crept into her voice at his
sublime faith in the creatures' behaviour.

'Not many people do,' Rico agreed easily. 'And they're
both well trained and very contented where they are. Why
should they wish to gallop away?'

'As long as you're happy...' Merle handed back the
flask, watching as Rico lifted it to his own mouth,
standing before her, head thrown back, the golden
column of his throat strong and beautiful in the filtered
sunlight.

'Oh, yes, I'm happy, Merle,' he answered her softly,
dropping swiftly to her side to stretch out beside her in
the welcome shade. 'Happier than I've been for a long
while. Nearly as happy as I was last year before I found
out that you didn't consider a husband an obstacle to
enjoying yourself.'

'Oh!' For a moment she had forgotten the recrimination that lurked beneath the surface of his pleasantries.

'No, don't be upset, *mi amor*,' he instructed swiftly.
'Oh, I don't deny I was hurt and angry when I found
out you were married. And when I saw your husband
was so much older than you all I could think of was
that you could only have married him because of the
material things he could give you.' His mouth twisted in
a wry smile that lacked humour. 'Not that I've anything
against that in principle. All marriages are basically for
selfish reasons, even if they're based on "the exchange
of your true love for mine"!' He turned a thoughtful

look on her distressed face. 'I just happen to believe that all contracts should be honoured, not just those concerning bricks and mortar.'

'I can't—I won't listen to this!' However much she might be in his debt, she wouldn't sit through these cruel aspersions against her character. 'There's no point in repeating what you thought——'

'Oh, but there is!' As she tried to rise Rico turned towards her, pinning her back on to the ground with swift motion. 'Because I think I understand now. It was security you were looking for. *Dios*, Merle! Ever since you told me about your childhood, the way that love was withheld from you, it's been becoming clearer and clearer in my mind. You weren't just looking for a rich husband, you were looking for a father figure to give you the love you were deprived of when you were young. But you'd never known what it was like to love and be loved. You didn't know what you would be missing, did you, *querida*?'

'You're wrong,' she interjected harshly, trying unsuccessfully to escape Rico's impassioned hold. How dared he try and evaluate her motives in an attempt to rationalise his own behaviour—whitewashing what he still despised to justify his own desire for the imperfect? Her voice shook. 'What gives you the right to try and analyse me? I thought you were a bone surgeon, not a psychiatrist!' Angrily Merle sprang to her own defence, pleased when she saw his jaw tighten at her indictment and knew her barb had met its mark.

'I'm the man who wants to become your *amante*—your lover: the man whose dreams you've haunted for the past year.' Rico drew in a harsh breath. 'Whatever happened in the past, you're free now: free to take and enjoy what you desire...'

'And you think that's you?' His face was so close to her she could see the texture of his skin and feel his breath on her cheek, perceive the tingling of her nerve-ends below the surface of her skin, as she recognised with an aching desperation that his audacity would have been more bearable if it had been less well founded!

'Isn't it?' he asked gently, dark eyes soft with beguilement as they surveyed her hostile face. 'When I hold you in my arms and taste your sweet kiss I believe it is.'

'Then you're fooling yourself!' Gathering her strength, Merle pushed herself up on her arms, relieved when Rico allowed her to rise to her feet. She brushed fragments of grass off her jeans, not prepared to meet his pensive gaze as she told him shakily, 'The fact is you've taken me by surprise once or twice and I've . . . I've responded automatically.'

'Oh, delicious automation!' Cynicism burned in the deep timbre of his quick retort. 'Oh, faithless Merle who will give her favours at any man's touch!'

'You're deliberately misinterpreting what I mean!' she flared back angrily. 'Ever since we met again you've been teasing me for your own pleasure . . .'

'You do me an injustice, *mi amor*. Although I find the prospect of doing so an entrancing one, I can assure you I haven't even started yet—and when I do you won't be in any doubt about it.' Rico rose easily to his feet.

'You speak as if I won't have any say in the matter.' Her blue gaze flicked contemptuously over his gracefully lounging figure, her voice low and well controlled despite the increased beat of her heart. 'Where I come from a man who forces his attentions on an unwilling woman is considered a criminal at the most, a lout at the least!'

Merle saw his expression harden and wondered if she'd gone too far, stepping back as he moved forward and caught her roughly by the arm.

'Here too, *querida*,' he clipped out softly but vehemently, 'we have a great respect for virtuous women, women who honour themselves and their men! But by the same token we are not always averse to indulging the passions of the flesh when they are freely offered outside the bounds of matrimony!'

'And when they're refused?' she challenged boldly, feeling her blood change to water as his fingers moved gently on her upper arm.

'Why do you deny the attraction between us, Merle?' Rico had chosen to ignore her question, asking his own instead. 'Last year you were ready to flirt with me, encourage me to believe you wanted me as badly as I wanted you. Now suddenly you're denying it with your lips, yet when I'm close to you I can feel you tremble. Am I to believe it's fear and not desire, hmm?' His other hand moved to trace a line down her cheek, while she stood mesmerised by his dark intensity. 'Ah, no. You know too well I'd never hurt you deliberately. Why go on punishing me, then? Is it because I left you so suddenly?'

Wordlessly Merle shook her head. More than anything else in the world at that moment she wanted to take him in her arms, cradle his head against her breast and feel his strong heart beating against her own. Still some remnants of self-respect held her back. In Rico's eyes she was 'easy' and available. To go to him on those terms would cheapen both of them, and she knew she must fight the growing temptation that was threatening her resolve.

She heard him sigh, felt its aftermath pass through his frame. 'Do you think it was easy for me to go like that? To pack my bags and disappear without seeing you once more, without feasting my eyes on your lustrous eyes and smoky hair, without hearing your soft voice and seeing your tremulous smile again. Do you Merle?'

The soft words flowed over her, caressing her with compliments, attacking her already weakening resolve. Somehow she had to find the strength to hold to her convictions, and the best way was in attack!

'Easy?' she echoed the word, lifting her delicate eyebrows and allowing the niggling pain caused by his disparagement to surface. 'Yes, since you ask, I would think you found it very easy. With such a well developed sense of morality I imagine you drove away on a cloud of virtue that cushioned you against any temporary disappointment.'

'Devastation,' he corrected softly. 'Devastation, not disappointment, and certainly not temporary. The discovery of your *desenfreno*——' He saw her frown of puzzlement at the Spanish word and sought for a translation with an impatient exhalation of breath. 'You would say "wildness—lack of restraint", I believe. The discovery of it has burned in my memory since I saw the evidence of it with my own eyes.' His voice deepened, developed a husky note. 'It wasn't the first time, you see. Once before I'd had the misfortune to imagine myself in love with a married woman, but on that occasion I'd known she had a husband before we became lovers...'

'Rico...' Shocked by the pain on his face, Merle made an involuntary movement towards him. 'You don't have to tell me...'

'I think I do.' He spoke with a quiet emphasis, brushing her protest away with a sharp movement of his hands. 'If only to stop you regarding me as some pious celibate who has never known the fires of the flesh!' He paused, swallowing before continuing matter-of-factly, 'It happened many years ago, shortly after I arrived in Spain. I could try to make excuses—tell you I was lonely and unhappy, that I was finding medical school hard work and it didn't help my confidence when the other students laughed at my South American accent.' He smiled deprecatingly, a soft turn of his lips that made Merle's heart seem to turn over. 'I could confess I missed my mother's adoration and the plaudits of my old friends. As I told you earlier, I was a typically spoiled young man feeling that the world owed me a living... None of which exonerates me for what I did. *She*...' he paused again as if collecting his thoughts, while Merle watched sadness shadow the clear sparkle of his eyes, '...she was going through a bad patch in her marriage. She needed help and understanding, and she came to me for them because she didn't want to talk to a priest, and as a trainee doctor I was the next best thing in her estimation.'

'And you took comfort from each other,' Merle said softly, compassion for his obvious distress lending her tone a husky depth.

'Yes.' His dark head dipped in acknowledgement. 'To my eternal shame, we did. I betrayed her confidences and her trust. Instead of being strong I acted like a weak simpleton...and then...her husband became suspicious...'

'Dear heaven!'

Merle didn't need the danger of that situation being spelled out to her, her fingers automatically curling into her palms in fearful expectation, as Rico continued roughly. 'If the true facts had been found out so many lives could have been ruined. Her husband's, hers, my family's...'

'And yours...'

'Mine, too.' He gave a poor imitation of a smile, the agony still sharp behind his eyes. 'In the event I paid a painful enough price for my indiscretion, but nothing more than I deserved—and of course I lost the girl . . . It was only thanks to some speedy action by Armando and Pavane that the true facts were never made public, and her husband was eventually persuaded to believe that my lover was another woman who couldn't be hurt by the scandal.'

'Her husband—he avenged himself on you before your brother intervened?' The reference to a painful price could surely only refer to physical retribution, and the thought made Merle shudder as she found herself unable to refrain from asking the question.

'Does the thought please or concern you, I wonder?' Rico cast her a speculative glance from sombre eyes. 'If the former then you can be assured he spared no effort in making his displeasure felt, and, since I had no heart to defend myself against his righteous wrath, I was lucky to escape with all my faculties intact.' He paused as if trying to read her expression, then went on equably, 'If the latter, then I can promise you I suffered no lasting physical harm.'

'Did you love her very much?' An unaccountable pang of jealousy lanced through Merle as painful as a rapier thrust.

'At the time I believed so.' Rico shrugged his shoulders. 'I was very young and very impressionable. You might say that the experience made me grow up overnight. Particularly when I saw my ex-lover's marriage begin to thrive again and realised I'd only been used as a substitute for the husband she had truly loved all along!'

'I'm sorry.' They were plain little words to explain how deeply she understood and sympathised with his suffering.

Again that barely perceptible movement of his broad shoulders. 'Perhaps you'll understand now why I reacted so strongly when I discovered that for the second time in my life I'd been travelling down a forbidden path, and this time, unknowingly! You set me up, Merlita, with your innocent eyes and breathy sighs, your smiling lips and gentle hands.' The dark gleam of his eyes was intense through the narrowed lids. 'I believed you were offering me the only pleasure in the world I craved——'

'No!' It was a cry of anguish wrung from her dry throat, as guilt tortured her. He would never believe she had been stupid rather than wanton! 'I wanted——'

'The best of both worlds—I know!' Rico reached for her, drawing her unresisting body against his own, staring down into her pale face. '*Santa madre de Dios*, and who am I to judge you? There is nothing, no one now to stand between you and your need for love.' He lowered his head, but she jerked her face away so that his seeking lips brushed against her cheek.

'You're not talking about love—what you mean is carnal appetite—animal desire...' she accused angrily.

'Do I?' There was a breath of laughter in his voice, a wicked promise in his expression that had her pulling away from him, only to find herself backed up against the wide trunk of the tree which had been her protector from the sun.

Immediately Rico's arms left her body to rest palm outward against the tree, effectively imprisoning her. With his body still in such close contact a wave of desire flooded through her system. Horrified at her own weakness, she recognised a desperate ache to pull him even closer, an impulsive urge to wind her fingers through the glossy hair on his formidable head, to seek and return his soft kisses with an ardour which should both shock and delight him, as his dark-pupilled eyes rested on her face, drowsy with supplication.

It wasn't fair. She was having to fight both of them. If only she was able to ignore the persistent murmur from her subconscious mind which was telling her over and over again that, although pity might be akin to love and her compassionate nature had responded to Rico's story of forbidden romance, it wasn't pity which held her enthralled in his company! It wasn't sympathy which had set her pulse into overdrive, sent the blood thrumming through her veins and weakened the muscles of her legs so greatly that it was all she could do not to throw herself against the strong body which prevented her escape and beg for support. She loved Rico de Montilla.

She had never gone through the throes of calf-love, never been infatuated by pop stars of TV actors. All her life until now her heart had been encased in ice where the opposite sex had been concerned. It had taken the heat of Andalusia and the stunning presence of the man in front of her to reach through that frigid barrier and begin to show her the depth of her own sensuality. Wearily she recognised that the process had started a year ago, only she had been too blinded by her immediate problems to acknowledge it.

Only her pride now stood between Rico and her unconditional surrender, and she would make every effort to preserve it.

As if guessing her inner turmoil, Rico slackened the rigid length of his restraining arms, allowing himself to seek her soft cheek with his questing lips. The sensation was devastating, generating a response she could barely understand and only control with enormous difficulty.

Inhaling sharply, Merle closed her eyes, making no attempt to repulse him. He was reading her as experienced and disillusioned, ripe for picking and enjoying, so that the physical pleasure of his touch was sullied, contaminated by his poor opinion of her.

'Merle, oh, Merle...' He had sought and found her trembling mouth, whispering her name against soft lips. 'It was Fate that brought us together again...'

It was then Merle knew what she must do. She must become the mercenary, heartless woman whose ethics he deplored while he still hungered for the relief and comfort of her body. Raising her hands to his face, she gently pushed him away, mutely praying for the confidence to carry her plan through.

'Tell me, Rico,' she asked softly, 'why did you bring me here? Do you really have any intention of getting Paraiso back for me, or did you intend all the time to seduce me?'

'I don't regard the two things as mutually exclusive.' Rico regarded her quizzically. 'I can assure you Fidelio Diaz will be working on the problem, if that's what's worrying you.'

'Mmm...' Merle raised her hands to his shoulders fending him off as he would have moved closer to her. 'I seem to remember you recently told me you found the grass on the other side trampled and unattractive?'

To her utter astonishment he actually had the grace to blush, a dull tide of colour climbing his jaw to confirm his embarrassment.

'A remark that was ungallant and uncalled-for... and untrue. Since then I've not only discovered that you are no longer married, but I can understand better your reasons for acting as you did. The truth is I——'

'The truth is your first estimation of my motives for marrying David was perfectly accurate.' Commanding every last gram of her courage, she met his regard without blinking, lying in the cause of self-preservation. 'He was a wealthy man and I was tired of being poor. You seem to think I'm the kind of woman who'll tumble into bed with anyone who asks her. Well, you're wrong! I don't deny you're attractive, but if I had an affair with every good-looking man who asked me then I would deserve your contempt!'

'Merle!'

The laughter had left Rico's face as she ignored his protest, continuing doggedly, 'I don't give anything away for nothing—I never have.' She paused, her breasts rising and falling rapidly in her agitation. 'I'm quite happy for us to become lovers...' she glimpsed and momentarily enjoyed the triumph that blazed across his face before adding '...the day you give me the key to Paraiso.'

'I see.' He smiled slowly, his gaze travelling over her in a way that sent the warm blood pouring into her face. 'No pleasure without business—that's the message, is it?

Merle nodded, not trusting herself to speak. The odds against Fidelio Diaz's accomplishing anything constructive had always been long. In a day or so when he reported back the failure of his undertaking she would be able to return to England, if not heart-whole at least without the agonising memory of the knowledge of Rico's magnificent body to torment her. And if Diaz succeeded? a tiny inner voice demanded. Why, then she would keep her word and Rico would never know she had given him her heart as well as her body. That way she could hold her head high when she left. They would have met and loved as equals, and he would never dream how absolutely he had conquered her.

'So...' He stepped away from her, his composure apparently undisturbed by her revelation of her supposedly mercenary heart—but then she'd only confirmed what he'd already suspected, hadn't she? 'You certainly put a high price on your favours, or can it be you doubt the success of my mission? I do hope it's not the latter, because I don't give up anything easily, *querida*, and I regard a bargain as a bargain.'

'Good.' Merle was proud of her bearing as she moved past him, her head high. 'Now we understand each other so well, perhaps we should be returning to the *cortijo*?'

'*Por cierto.*' He followed her lead, moving towards the blankets and saddles and beginning methodically to resaddle their mounts while she watched him, her heart heavy with despair. She allowed her eyes to linger on Rico's elegantly muscular body as he tightened the girths on Zarina with brisk efficiency. He might feel frustrated now, but he wouldn't be without female company for long, she was sure.

She sensed that she was the first person Rico had opened his heart to so fully, expunging the guilt and bitterness of the past. With luck it would leave him purged of remorse, enabling him to discover true love instead of mere sensual satisfaction. Doggedly she ignored the pang of grief which accompanied the belief.

'Shall we go?' His voice was as expressionless as his face as he offered her his help to remount.

'Thank you.' His hands had stayed in contact with her only as long as necessary to see her safely in the saddle.

At the very least she had earned herself a respite from his provocation, she consoled herself reading the coldness that hardened his profile as he turned away. It was a pity the realisation didn't fill her with the exultation she had expected.

After the silence of the ride back to the *cortijo* Merle was relieved when they reached the farm and she was able to relax temporarily in the sanctuary of her room.

Pavane had met them on their return to say that lunch would be ready as soon as they wished on the terrace surrounding the swimming-pool. A tepid bath would have been a pleasant way of indulging herself, but rather than keep her hostess waiting Merle settled for a shower before surveying her wardrobe. Something cool was called for, and a little sun on her pale skin wouldn't do much harm if she applied sun milk lavishly.

Quickly she decided on rose-pink cuffed shorts with a matching print vest top, grimacing slightly as she caught sight of her pale legs in the long mirror. At least they were long and shapely, which did something to offset their winter pallor, she supposed, smiling inwardly at her own vanity.

Sliding her bare feet into a pair of white wedge-heeled mules and with her hair cascading softly to her shoulders—a sure protection on the tender nape of her neck against the burning kiss of the early afternoon sun—she hurried down the superb staircase and out on to the patio.

Pavane and Rico were already seated at a long table beneath a flowered canopy when she arrived beside the pool, having made her way round the side of the *cortijo*. There were two pools, one kidney-shaped, the other a circular child's pool with a small fountain in the centre.

'Have I kept you waiting? I'm so sorry!' She hurried forward.

'Of course not.' Rico rose leisurely to his feet, the epitome of elegant courtesy. 'Our time's entirely our own and the meal's a cold one.' He pulled the remaining wrought-iron, sumptuously padded chair away from the table with the practised ease of a head waiter, as Merle murmured her thanks.

As he bent considerately over her, easing the chair back into place as she took her seat, Merle caught the citrus-fresh tang of his still-damp hair. He too had changed his clothes, she saw. Of course it had to be coincidence, but she could have sworn he was wearing the identical outfit he had had on when she had first set eyes on him.

Whether he had intended it or not, she felt an almost unbearable twinge of sweet remembrance at the sight of his unclad legs, muscularly golden beneath the short white shorts, and the expensively thin short-sleeved shirt worn casually open to display the firm unblemished skin of his chest and diaphragm. Finding herself wondering if the marks of war that laced his back had faded with the passing months, she made a conscious effort to drag her mind away from such disturbing contemplation, to concentrate on the present.

The table was laden with covered dishes which were opened to reveal an assortment of cold meats and exotic mixed salads. One wicker basket contained chunks of delicious French-style baguette while a large silver tureen encased in a bowl of ice cubes was filled with a luscious gazpacho.

Merle felt her appetite reviving just at the sight of the simple but beautifully prepared and served food, helping herself eagerly as invited and accepting a glass of ice-cool Spanish champagne from Rico.

'To us and the success of our endeavour!' He smiled across the table at her, lifting his champagne flute towards her so she had no option but to clink her glass against his, intensely aware that his bold dark eyes were toasting something quite different from the obvious.

'I'll drink to that!' Pavane touched her own glass against her brother-in-law's and her guest's before taking

a deep sip and leaning earnestly across the table towards
Merle. 'We've had a marvellous idea!' Her blue eyes
sparkled with enthusiasm. 'After lunch you must phone
your sister and invite her to bring your little girl and her
own family over here for the holiday they've been looking
forward to. They can stay in the Villa Jazmin for as long
as they like as our guests!'

'Oh, but——' Sheer surprise struck Merle dumb.

'It's perfect, don't you see?' Pavane enthused happily.
'Everyone gains. You'll be reunited with Laurie—and I
know how you must be feeling. Armando insisted I went
into a maternity hospital for Elena's birth in case there
were complications, and I couldn't wait to get back to
Nacio. Your sister and her family won't be deprived of
a holiday I'm sure they've been looking forward to, and
you yourself will be able to stay here until we know
something definite about Paraiso without eating your
heart out for Laurie!'

'But what about Rico?' Too stunned to know exactly
how she felt, Merle turned questioning eyes to the sombre
face of the man opposite her. 'It's your summer retreat.
I couldn't expect you to move out.'

'On the contrary, if you cast your mind back you'll
remember that Jazmin belongs to the estate and is in my
brother's gift.' There was no indication in Rico's bland
expression as to how he had received Pavane's suggestion, but any doubt Merle might have harboured regarding his approval of the plan was immediately
dispersed by his sister-in-law's interjection.

'Actually it was Rico's idea, though why I didn't think
of it myself I'll never know. Oh, you must agree, Merle!
There can't possibly be any reason for refusing, can
there? It comes with an excellent maid service. The whole
place can be restocked with food, cleaned and made
ready in a matter of hours. Just think of it, this time

the day after tomorrow you could all be on the beach together just as you'd originally planned. Even if, heaven forbid, Rico and Diaz can't do anything about Paraiso at least you'll all have had the holiday you planned.'

Playing for time, Merle drank a deep draught of champagne. How ironical that she should receive such an invitation when she'd just been considering escaping from the heady atmosphere of Rico's presence by returning home!

'How about Armando?' she asked, carefully replacing her glass on the table. 'Will he be prepared to let the villa out to strangers?'

'Rest assured, my brother's a total slave to his wife's desires, though neither would publicly admit the fact.' Rico exchanged a look of deep affection with his lovely sister-in-law as she contented herself with a soft smile and a tiny shake of her head. 'But I can assure you of two things, the first is that neither Pavane nor myself regard you as a stranger, the second is that Armando would never "let" Jazmin. It's there for the benefit of his friends and employees, and as far as he's concerned, my friends are his.'

'I don't know...' Merle began a little desperately. It would mean another two weeks of leaving herself open to the disquieting effect Rico had on her... On the other hand, would it? Perhaps with her family occupying Jazmin he would return to Cadiz. In any case, if he spent time at the *cortijo* he would be well away from the coast. He could hardly harass her from that distance, could he? And Barbie and Grant deserved a holiday. All her sister's sympathy had been for her, Merle, when she had broken the news to her, but she didn't need to be psychic to know how disappointed Barbie must have been on her own account. For weeks now she had been shopping around compiling what she called 'a hot-weather wardrobe'. How could she turn down such an opportunity to give Barbie the pleasure she'd promised?

CHAPTER NINE

'WHAT'S the problem, Merle?' Rico's soft question interrupted her deliberations. 'Is it that you find our hospitality lacking in some respect?'

'Of course not!' His carping words spurred her to speech. 'I can't begin to thank Pavane for allowing me to come here, and as for you . . .' She paused, drawing in her breath, trying to salvage something from the morass of emotions she was experiencing for the taunting Andalusian who continued to regard her with barely veiled irony.

'As for me . . .?' he prompted gently.

In front of Pavane Merle could hardly say anything uncomplimentary, and in truth she had to acknowledge a debt to Rico. Without his help she would already be back in England, sadder, wiser and poorer, without even the faintest glimmer of hope.

'As for you,' she continued smoothly, 'I hope I can find some way of recompensing you for all the trouble you've already taken on my behalf,' and dared him with sparkling eyes to say one word out of place.

'Your continued presence here is reward enough,' he told her gallantly, but the chivalry in his soft tone was belied by the sudden flash of naked warfare that dilated his pupils. 'Do you wish me to beg you to stay?'

'No, of course not.' The thought of Rico prostrate at her feet was more than she could bear, and she wouldn't put it past him to subject her to such an embarrassment. 'I'll phone Barbie after lunch.'

'Splendid!' Rico refilled her glass. 'Finish your salad and I'll go and tell Ana that we're ready for dessert and coffee.'

He pushed his chair away from the table, suiting his actions to his words, striding with lazy power towards the kitchen.

'I'm so glad you're staying.' Genuine warmth echoed in Pavane's soft tones. 'And I know Rico is delighted!'

It wasn't the word Merle would have chosen herself, but certainly Rico was at his most charming for the remainder of the meal, which consisted of crunchy meringue and cherries laced with kirsch with a dressing of whipped cream and aromatic coffee served in a *cafetière*. For those relaxing, blissful moments she could almost imagine he was once more the man she had met and been entranced by on a lonely beach on the Costa de la Luz so many months before.

An hour later, after an excited exchange of news with Laurie—who, fortunately, didn't appear to be missing her at all!—she was listening to Barbie's squeal of joy echoing over the phone wires. 'Merle darling! Oh, how marvellous! Of course we'd love to come. Grant's working until Saturday because we weren't sure what was happening, but if we can get a flight we could be with you this coming Sunday, would that be OK?'

'Sunday?' Merle repeated the word, turning raised eyebrows for approval towards Pavane, who was waiting beside her in the hallway.

'Lovely!' Armando's wife nodded. 'Ask her to let you know in advance which airport she'll be using and we'll arrange for her to be picked up and brought directly here. That way you can all meet Armando and be at Ramón's welcome home party, stay the night and we'll take you over to Jazmin the next day.'

'Oh, but surely...' Clapping her hand over the mouthpiece, Merle demurred. 'There'll be five of us altogether. You can't cope with all that extra work!'

'Merle, are you still there?' Barbie's voice sounded querulously in her ear.

'Here—let me.' Pavane held out a slim hand for the phone. With a despairing shrug of her shoulders Merle handed it over, standing by helplessly as arrangements were neatly taken out of her hands.

'That's settled,' Pavane said with satisfaction, re-placing the receiver after a ten-minute conversation. 'Believe me, it's entirely in my own interests. If your sister arrives on Sunday and goes straight to Jazmin you'll go with her, and Rico will never forgive me for allowing you to go without meeting Armando first. They may have had their disagreements in the past, but these last few years they've grown a lot closer, finding a mutual respect for each other.'

Love for her husband endowed Pavane's face with an inner radiance, the source of which was unmistakable, causing Merle's breath to catch in her throat.

'Are they very much alike—Rico and your husband?' she asked with a sudden desperate need to know what it was Armando possessed to capture and hold a woman as lovely as the one who now turned eyes bright with emotion to survey her.

'Yes.' The reply was without prevarication. 'Both are proud and handsome, idealistic and charming, hard as steel when the mood takes them, yet soft as the hair on Elena's pretty head when the moment's right.' Pavane looked thoughtfully at her guest. 'Someone once said to me "never fall in love with an Andalusian! They're vol-atile, graceful, charming and ardent lovers—but they make deadly enemies and they can break a woman's heart

with impossible cruelty," all of which is true, but...'
her smile was secret, turned inwards towards her own
memories '... but that same quality which makes them
so rigid and unbending can also, when they fall in love,
turn them into devoted husbands whose generous and
passionate love can make every day into a celebration
of life! But there, I admit it. I'm prejudiced!'

Prejudiced she might be, but there was no doubt that
Pavane's marriage was idyllic. Lying on her soft bed,
the blinds half shuttered so that the slanting rays of the
sun fell in zebra-like stripes across her half-naked body,
Merle felt an aching envy for her hostess's glowing
happiness.

She had chosen to rest rather than join Rico in the
pool after lunch, making the excuse that her legs were
beginning to ache after the morning's exercise. The truth
was that the ambivalent feelings she was experiencing in
Rico's company were becoming difficult to bear with
equanimity. Distance, she had told herself firmly, would
lend enchantment to her present position. Today was
only Wednesday and it would be another four days before
she could escape the effects of the electrically charged
aura he seemed to generate around her.

Suppose she had been single when they had met? That
she had never known David or Laurie? Would the same
attraction have blazed between them? And if so, what
would have been the outcome? She stirred languidly as
the breeze through the shutters fanned her warm cheeks,
and her imagination wandered freely, still continuing to
function long after sleep had claimed her, weaving its
fantasies into her dreams.

A light tap on the door brought her back to wakefulness. Quickly holding the bedcover to her chest, she
bade the visitor enter.

'I thought you might be able to use a cup of tea.' It was Pavane who came in, putting a cup and saucer on the bedside table.

'Lovely!' Gratefully Merle took a sip, allowing the bedcover to drop into her lap. 'What time is it?'

'Six.' Pavane smiled at her guest's horrified face. 'You've had quite a long siesta.'

'Heavens!' She should have realised that sunshine and champagne mixed could have a super-tranquillising effect. 'You must think me awfully rude.'

'Of course not, you're entirely free to do as you wish.' Any embarrassment Merle felt was dispersed by the other woman's friendly denial. 'I just came to tell you that dinner will be at eight tonight. Rico's gone over to see Esteban and I've invited him to join us this evening. I imagine he's feeling a bit depressed with Isadora still away.' For a moment the smile died from her face, to be replaced with a thoughtful frown before she brightened again. 'Come down whenever you're ready, I'll be on the patio with the children. It's lovely out there now, not too hot, and we can have a chat over pre-dinner sherry.'

Left alone, Merle sipped the tea while bringing herself slowly back to a state of complete wakefulness. Taking her time in getting ready, she applied a light foundation to her creamy skin, touching it with a puff of powder sufficient to remove any shine, before turning her attention to her eyes. She used eyeshadow sparingly, applying neutral shades to highlight the lid and deepen the socket area. In the soft light of the bedroom her eyes seemed enormous, the lashes already dark, but discreetly thickened with mascara forming a silkily lush frame around them.

From somewhere outside on the patio came the sound of light classical music as Merle traced the perfect outline of her mouth with a soft pink lipstick, deciding at the last moment to seal it with a coat of gloss. What to wear? Thoughtfully she surveyed the choice available, eventually selecting a full-skirted dress of emerald silk, simply cut with a boat-shaped neckline and tiny cap sleeves which just covered her shoulder-bones. Lastly she slipped her feet into high-heeled black sandals, pausing to survey her reflection in the mirror on her way to the door. Yes, she decided critically, she looked as good as she could reasonably hope to, and the added sparkle in her eyes and lift to her walk was undoubtedly due to the expectation of her imminent reunion with Laurie...

'What a lovely dress!' Pavane cast admiring eyes over Merle as she joined mother and children. 'I remember I wore one just the same colour shortly after I married Armando.' The compliment was obviously genuine, the memory apparently reawakening some tender emotion from the past, if the other girl's reminiscent smile was anything to go by.

'Thank you.' Merle sank gracefully down on the swinging hammock, to be immediately approached by Elena demanding to sit on her lap. The time passed so quickly after that, what with amusing the children and exchanging news and views with Pavane, the arrival of Rico and Esteban took her by surprise.

Dinner was served in the *sala*—a pleasant meal accompanied by fine Spanish wines, which Merle partook of with caution, not wishing to fall asleep before the evening was over. Pavane proved a charming and accomplished hostess, the conversation flowing easily among the four of them, although to Merle's perceptive eye Esteban's gaiety seemed rather forced and his appreciation of the wine somewhat indiscreet.

Although Elena had gone to bed before the meal began, Nacio had been allowed to join the adults for the first hour, behaving himself with a maturity far beyond his years and winning Merle's unqualified admiration.

Relaxing afterwards on one of the luxurious leather couches, Merle, having turned down the offer of brandy or liqueur with her coffee, was only too pleased to indulge herself with one or two *petits fours*, as Pavane, in answer to Rico's request, seated herself at the grand piano at the far end of the room and played Beethoven's Pathétique Sonata. Beside her on the couch, Esteban stared down unblinkingly into the depths of his brandy glass as if it held the answer to some insurmountable problem, while Rico, sprawled in an easy chair with his eyes closed, absorbed the beauty and technique of his brother's wife's performance as the music sprang to life beneath her able fingers.

'I'm sorry to interrupt, Doña Pavane, but the baby is restless. She's crying for Mama. I thought you'd want to know...' The last chords had only just faded as the young Spanish nurserymaid stood uncomfortably in the doorway, her worried gaze fastened on her employer. 'I've tried to comfort her, but...'

'Of course, Conchita, I'll come immediately.' Instantly Pavane rose from the piano stool. 'You'll all forgive me, won't you? She's having some trouble cutting a tooth at the moment and it makes her a little fractious. We've got a gel to rub on, but it doesn't always work, and a kiss and a cuddle will do wonders!'

'A universal panacea for a great number of ills,' Rico remarked drily as his sister-in-law followed Conchita from the room.

'But not always so instantly available on demand!' Esteban rose a trifle unsteadily to his feet and advanced towards the decanter of brandy on the nearby table. 'You permit, *amigo*?'

'*Por cierto*—what is mine is yours, *amigo*.' A lazy wave of Rico's hand invited Esteban to help himself, as the sudden high-pitched beep of a telephone broke into the warm stillness of the night.

Rico hauled himself to his feet with a sigh. 'Probably my brother, unable to settle down for the night without assuring himself of the safety and happiness of his dependants.' Mockery tinged his comment. 'I'd better put his mind at rest.'

'Lucky Armando!' Esteban's voice was thick with alcohol and something more which might have been misery, as Rico left the room. 'Not many marriages are as ideal as his!' To Merle's consternation he drained the remainder of his drink and rose to refill his glass.

It was none of her business, but something was very wrong with Rico's friend and, whatever the problem, his unrestricted intake of alcohol wasn't going to mitigate it, that was for sure!

'It must be difficult being separated from your wife so soon after your marriage,' she hazarded experimentally. 'But I expect she'll soon be here, won't she?'

'Huh!' Esteban sat down heavily beside her, placing his refilled glass on the table, much to her relief, rather than sampling its contents. 'The truth of the matter is that Isadora has left me, abandoned me. She refuses to speak to me, let alone come here to meet my parents and friends. She says it's all over between us.'

'Oh!' Merle felt totally out of her depth. Obviously Esteban needed counselling, and urgently, but not from her. Such a job needed qualifications she certainly didn't possess.

'What should I do?' Clearly Esteban didn't share her opinion of her capabilities as he turned pleading eyes on her startled face. 'Perhaps you can tell me what's gone wrong? You're both about the same age and probably share the same outlook on life. She's very independent and sure of herself, but she's been putting off meeting my parents, and now she's chosen to visit her friend rather than join me here.' His voice deepened to a growl. 'Yesterday I phoned her and ordered her to come here immediately if she wanted to remain my wife...'

'And she said she didn't?' Merle asked softly as he nodded glumly.

'I've phoned her since and she refuses to speak to me. She just left a message saying it was all over between us. *Dios*, Merle, what the hell do I do now?'

'Go and see her?' she suggested gently.

'Crawl, you mean?' All the arrogance of Andalusia sharpened his tone as Merle suppressed a smile.

'Actually all I meant was talk to her face to face. Had you considered she might be afraid of meeting your parents? After all, they were excluded from the wedding, and, independent though she may be in her job, you told me earlier today that she had no close family ties herself. It may be much more of an ordeal for her than you can possibly imagine.'

'Mmm.' He didn't look particularly convinced, but at least he was turning the idea over in his mind.

'Ordering her back would only have aggravated the situation,' Merle continued quickly, warming to her theme. 'She may feel she can never make you understand. If I'm right she needs your support, not your condemnation.'

'So what should I say?' If it hadn't been so serious for Esteban, Merle would have seen the funny side of the situation, but she was too sensitive to allow even the glimmer of a smile to touch her eyes as she met his anxious gaze.

'Just that you love her, I guess,' she told him simply. 'And that you're so proud of her that you can't wait to show her off to your family, who will be bound to care for her as much as you do...and...and that you've come over to escort her back home and give her all the loving support she needs.'

For a few moments Esteban stared back at her silently before leaning forward to take her hands in his own. 'Do you really think that will do it?'

He was bemused by brandy and showing an indecision Merle was sure he would regret when he sobered up, but she had taken on the burden of advising him, however foolhardily, and she was bound to follow it through. Even if she had misread the situation surely no harm could be done by Esteban telling his wife he loved her? At least it would get them on speaking terms again. It was entirely possible that Isadora was just as miserable as her estranged husband. Merle had no doubt but that it had been a love match originally, and the odds must be in favour of a reconciliation if the two protagonists could meet.

'I think it's the only thing you *can* do,' she told him honestly, adding for good measure, 'Remember it takes a strong man to make the first move, and Isadora will appreciate that, I'm sure.'

'Yes, I think you're right.' The dark eyes filled with warmth as his hands tightened around hers. 'I think you're marvellous Merle, so...so...*perspicaz*!'

He was gazing avidly into her earnest face when Rico re-entered the room, his countenance hard and unsmiling.

'That was the clinic,' he said without preamble. 'There's been a bad accident on the Cordoba road and they're transferring a patient to the clinic tomorrow morning for treatment.' His stern gaze flickered over Merle to rest on Esteban. 'I'm sure you'll understand that I need a good night's sleep in the circumstances, so if you're ready, I'll drive you back to the hacienda.' His appraisal was scathing as it lingered on his friend's flushed face. 'For certain you're in no fit state to drive yourself in the Jeep. One unexpected operation to re-build a human body is enough to be going on with!'

'Oh, Esteban can stay here.' Pavane came in hur-riedly, having overheard Rico's last speech. 'There's always a spare room ready...'

'Thank you, but I think I'd better go back.' Esteban pulled himself to his feet. 'I can't begin to tell you how much I've enjoyed the evening...'

'Good, then we'll be going!' Curtly Rico truncated the other man's appreciation and led the way from the *sala* with an urgent stride.

Pavane made a little gesture of despair as they heard the front door close behind the two men. 'It's probably a child who's been injured. Rico's too professional to be a prey to emotion usually—it's just sometimes that it gets to him.'

Merle nodded understandingly, refusing her hostess's next offer of more coffee or a further drink and stating her own intention of going to bed.

It had been a strange evening, she brooded several minutes later, stepping out of the shower and patting herself dry. Rico had behaved with impeccable manners until that last moment, when he had seemed to lose the patina of politeness to reveal a more basic side to his nature.

Merle reached for the aerosol container which con-tained the matching body foam to her favourite perfume and began to massage the creamy mixture into her warm skin, inhaling pleasurably the delicate aroma it released. Rico had almost kicked Esteban out, and it wasn't even as if it had been his own house. Correctly speaking, as

Pavane was mistress of the house, Esteban had been her guest...

The tap at the door, which could only be Pavane—for who else was there to disturb her at this hour?—interrupted her musings. Hastily donning her pink satin nightshirt, she didn't bother to button its neck as her skin still glowed from the warmth of the shower and the lingering warmth of the Andalusian night.

'Come in—I was just having a shower...' The words stilled in her throat as she opened the door and found herself facing Rico. Without conscious volition her fingers tightened their grasp on the polished olivewood knob of the door. 'I thought you were Pavane,' she accused, flushing involuntarily and praying he would attribute her risen colour to the warmth of the shower rather than to his own unexpected appearance.

Unprepared for him to accept the invitation she had meant for Pavane, she stepped back, shocked, as he crossed the threshold, closing the door behind him and leaning against it while his dark eyes swept over her.

'Leave Esteban alone, Merle. He's a married man.'

'What?' A tremor of fear mingled with the horror that drained the blood from her face.

'You heard me.' His quiet tone was more alarming than if he had shouted at her, robbing her of words. 'He's vulnerable because Isadora's away and he's missing her badly, but he doesn't need you as a substitute, however willing you are to console him. Do you understand what I'm saying?'

'I *hear* you.' Her voice was shaking so badly she had to pause and gather herself together before continuing. 'But I don't *understand* you. There's nothing between your friend and me.'

'And there isn't going to be.' His brilliant gaze pinned her, intimate, deliberately caustic. 'I won't let you make the same mistakes I did. There can never be any joy in coming between two people who love each other—and Esteban's marriage deserves a chance, whatever the reason for Isadora's prolonged absence—and however overheated our Spanish climate has made your cool Gaelic blood.'

'Get out of my room!' If Rico had slapped her round the face Merle couldn't have felt more hurt and humiliated. She wouldn't stoop to defending herself—not that he would have believed her if she'd told him the truth!

'Not before I have your undertaking to keep your distance.' He moved towards her, every inch of his body threatening as she backed further away, determined not to surrender to his absurd demand. 'How do you think I felt when I came back from answering the phone and found you gazing into each other's eyes, your fingers entwined?' He gave a brief sarcastic bark of laughter. 'When I told Esteban that what was mine was also his, I was being polite.' His beautiful white teeth showed briefly as his lips curled sneeringly. 'I hardly expected him to take me at my word where you were concerned, but I might have guessed he wouldn't be able to resist the invitation to drown in your beautiful eyes!'

'I was never yours!' Merle seized on the most hurtful point, her accusing eyes mirroring her intensity, her fast shallow breathing a witness to her agitation.

'That could so easily be remedied.' Rico's contemplative gaze travelled slowly over her body, making her horribly aware of the shortness of the pink satin which clung damply to her tense breasts, the length of naked leg revealed to his encompassing stare. She felt her whole body glow with an inner heat as his words burned into her brain.

'You know my terms!' Pride lent her the courage to taunt him, but his quick aggressive movement towards her had her stepping backwards once again, only to catch her calf against the soft edge of the chaise-longue, and to be forced to sit down abruptly on its velvet softness.

'And what was Esteban prepared to pay for the privilege of taking you to bed, eh, *dulzura mia*?' Firm hands reached to grasp her wrists in an implacable hold as he dragged her to her feet. Only inches divided them as he glowered down at her. 'Or was the challenge of taking another woman's husband satisfaction enough for you?'

Goose-pimples caused by the scorn in his voice rose on the exposed skin of her upper arms, while her pulse beat in a wild rhythm to augment the gathering heat of her temper. 'Who better than you to answer a question like that?' Bitterly angry, she returned his furious stare, delighted when her retort had his breath hissing in as if he had been stung.

Every cell in her body was vibrating as its warmth liberated the exotic aura of her perfume to surround them. Fear? No. Although she half expected Rico to punish her, if not with the flat of his hand, then with the angry contemptuous pressure of his mouth against her own, the emotion building in her was a tumultuous sense of expectation and excitement rather than terror, a force that was spiralling to a vortex in which anything would be possible.

With a sick sense of shock Merle recognised that her body was immune to the insults being levelled at her ego and that if Rico took her in his arms at that moment she would be like putty in his hands, moulding herself to the strong lines of his body and accepting any pleasure or punishment he thought fit to administer with a deep resignation to the inevitable.

Never in her life had every nerve in her body screamed in a torment born of injustice and a wild physical attraction that answered to no logic.

Painfully aware of the heightened tension of her breasts beneath their satin covering, the ache of her engorged nipples against the soft rub of material, and the yawning need streaming through her being, she could do nothing but watch the strange mingling of hauteur and pain on Rico's dark countenance.

'*Es verdad*...' He spoke softly, with none of the overt fury she had anticipated, yet she could feel the sheer force of his personality reaching out to her, weakening her justifiable bitterness. 'Which is why I don't intend for you to abuse my brother's hospitality while you are living under his roof.'

'And you don't consider you're doing just that by forcing yourself into my room and maligning me?' Try as she might she couldn't prevent her breath catching in a half-sob in her throat.

'You invited me in, Merle,' he told her quietly, only the muscle that twitched beneath his cheekbone betraying his calmness as being the result of iron self-control rather than indifference. 'Believe me, I'm well aware of the obligations of hospitality... besides...' his smile was cruel rather than humorous '... it's not in my nature to take anything unless it's freely offered,' again a tiny pause before he added, 'or it's been bought and paid for. Look at me!'

The last instruction was rapped out with such power that Merle responded obediently, raising eyes that had momentarily strayed, to focus on his face. Silently absorbing the beautiful bones, the strongly rounded chin with its dark shadow advertising both his heritage and the lateness of the hour, the sweet curve of his mouth now hardened to a line of condemnation, she waited for him to speak again.

'Stay away from Esteban, or you'll live to regret it.'

'You dare to threaten me?' Some last remnant of pride forced her to challenge him as he released her wrists, her eyes flashing a sapphire fire as she lifted her chin haughtily.

'Only to warn you. We have a proverb in Spain: "Take what you want," said God. "Take what you want—and pay for it." The point being that invariably the price is more than the desire is worth, and believe me—Esteban is not for you.'

He turned abruptly, leaving the room without a backward glance, closing the door firmly behind him, abandoning her shaken and trembling to face the lonely hours of the night before sleep claimed her, shamed by his baseless accusation and mortified by the knowledge that, although only her wrists had known his touch, every cell of her body had responded to the latent power of his arrant masculinity with an abandonment which had been entirely beyond her conscious control.

CHAPTER TEN

ARRIVING at breakfast the following morning to find only Pavane, Nacio and Elena present, Merle felt absolute relief.

'Rico left first thing this morning,' her hostess told her, offering a basket of warm croissants across the table. 'He never discusses the work he does, but I can't help feeling he's concerned about the outcome of this particular operation. He's not usually so taciturn, and he did say not to expect him back for a couple of nights. I do hope his absence won't spoil your stay too much.'

'No, not at all,' Merle hastened to assure her valiantly, wondering how Pavane would react if she knew just how pleased her unexpected guest was to be deserted by her apparent patron. In fact she had spent a good part of the previous night frustrated beyond belief because Barbie's proposed visit had effectively prevented her from pleading a need to see Laurie again as an excuse to return immediately to England and leave Rico to savour his nasty suspicions in isolation!

'I'm sure we can keep you amused,' Pavane was continuing cheerfully. 'Nacio wants to show you how well he can swim and Elena wants you to see her doll's house.' She cast a loving eye on her two offspring, intent on enjoying their breakfasts. 'And to be honest, I could do with some help in planning the menu for Sunday's party! Ana, our housekeeper, will be organising all the catering once I've decided on a buffet menu, but I'd like to do something a little different. Do you know, I haven't seen my brother-in-law Ramón since my wedding day over nine years ago! And Pablo, his son, must be eighteen now...' Her eyes sparkled with laughter. 'I looked after Pablo for a short while after I was first married and before he joined his parents in Brazil, and I must admit I can't wait to see what he looks like now. Even at nine he had all the embryo qualities of looks and charm that make the Montilla men so compelling.'

'Rico...' Even his name on her tongue was difficult for Merle to handle without betraying herself. 'Rico is certainly compelling—perhaps overpowering would be a better description!' Despite her efforts the comment lacked the light-heartedness she had hoped to convey, drawing towards herself a sharp look from Pavane.

'As a matter of fact Rico is a very compassionate man, much more vulnerable than most people would ever guess. Not that he'd thank me for telling you! I'm afraid he sets himself impossibly high standards and is his own severest judge when he fails to meet the criterion he has set out to attain. If he were less harsh with himself I'm sure he'd get more pleasure out of life...' Pavane sighed. 'But enough of the Montillas—you'll have your fill of them on Sunday! In the meantime we've got to arrange a programme for you so that you get the best out of the coming days.'

Breakfast passed pleasantly as Pavane chattered on happily, telling Merle about her early girlhood in England and how her great-aunt's death had brought her to Spain to stay with her sister Melody, who had already married a Spanish landowner. Without prying she encouraged Merle to confide some of her earlier life. Merle kept the information she divulged light and general, feeling under no pressure. More and more she was finding herself drawn to the pretty blonde who had offered her such a warm welcome.

Certainly the day flew past, divided between swimming and sunbathing and playing with the children in the morning and a tour of the outer regions of the estate in the afternoon, undertaken in a Jeep driven by the farm manager.

By the time evening came Merle was feeling much more relaxed, her skin warmly blushed from careful exposure to the sun, her spirits high because Barbie had phoned to say their flight was booked for Sunday and they would be arriving at Seville at six in the evening after a short stop-over at Barcelona. The older girl had greeted the idea of the party with great enthusiasm, declaring herself thrilled to be able to participate in a real piece of Spanish life and promising to pack her best party dress for the occasion.

At least, Merle thought, brushing her hair with thoughtful strokes that night, Rico's absence had given her time to breathe and recollect her senses, and to remind herself that whatever she felt for him there wasn't a snowball's chance in hell of the attractive Andalusian ever forgiving her for what he saw as a wilful deception—whatever other feelings he might harbour towards her.

Tomorrow, Friday, Pavane had suggested a trip into Seville, something Merle was really looking forward to, especially since her last visit had been so full of unresolved trauma. This time she determined she would relax and enjoy the experience. Perhaps she'd even lash out on a new dress for Sunday's celebration!

In all probability it would be the last day she would ever set eyes on Rico de Montilla. Some perverse pride dictated that she should go out of his life in style. He had set himself up as a knight on a white charger for motives she couldn't begin to analyse, but such figures belonged to fairy-tales. The reality was that she had lost

Paraiso for all time, and with it any hope of time re-
kindling the camaraderie she had once shared with him.
It was the last thought she had before falling to sleep.

True to her expectations, the following day's shopping
expedition proved a great success, Pavane clapping her
hands in unrestrained approval as Merle paraded in the
dress she had seen in a boutique and fallen in love with.
In royal-blue georgette with a low-scooped neck and long
filmy sleeves, it had a full swirling skirt beneath a nipped-
in waist which emphasised her curvaceous figure, moving
seductively against her calves as she twisted around for
her companion's benefit.

It was late afternoon before the two girls returned to
the *cortijo*, having enjoyed a leisurely meal in one of the
delightful outdoor restaurants, and Merle was content
to spend the rest of the day at leisure in the grounds of
the estate.

The following morning she sang softly to herself as
she stepped from the shower. Tomorrow she would see
Laurie again and be freed from the oppressive power of
the man whose presence in her life earlier on was causing
her such anguish. Rico... Resolutely she forced her mind
away from him, telling herself that hungering after forbidden fruit had been the cause of Eve's downfall. It
wasn't a precedent she wanted to follow!

Thoughtfully she selected tiny cotton briefs and a
strapless bra to wear: the latter kinder to her sun-kissed
shoulders. Even though it was so early in the season the
day promised to be another scorcher, she determined,
reaching for the pretty print skirt she had worn on her
first visit to Seville. The matching bolero neatly covered
the bra, tying loosely just above her waist so that the
fresh air could circulate freely against her warm skin.

Hadn't Pavane said something about their going down to Jazmin to make sure that everything was in order before Barbie and Co arrived tomorrow? Thrusting her feet into her favourite wedge-heeled sandals, Merle gave herself one last cursory look in the mirror, twisting her hair into a loose knot on top of her head and securing it with hairgrips masked with a small white chiffon bow.

'*Buenos diás!*' Delighted with the progress she had been making under Pavane's willing tuition, she uttered her usual morning greeting as she stepped out on to the patio.

'*Buenos diás*, Merle.' There was no mistaking the leanly elegant figure that rose to greet her from his place at the table.

'Oh, you're back!' It was an inane remark as Merle felt a slow tide of colour flow into her cheeks. For some reason she had imagined he would stay in Cadiz until tomorrow's party.

'Evidently.' His amused glance fed on her discomfort. 'And none too welcome, by appearances.'

'I—I...' As quickly as it had come the colour ebbed from her face. Goodness knew what feelings she was betraying to the discerning eye of the man whose gaze concentrated on her. To think she'd almost persuaded herself she had become immune to him in his absence! With the blood hammering in her veins and a hollow sickness silently torturing her midriff, she admitted the enormity of her error. 'I just wasn't expecting to see you today,' she finished weakly, adding quickly, 'Was the operation successful?'

'Fortunately, yes.' Rico's quick smile was absolutely genuine, lending his saturnine face a wicked charm that made the breath catch in her throat. 'There was fear at first that we might have to amputate. Fortunately that has been avoided. There will be scars...' he shrugged

'... but we hope not too unsightly, and the main thing is that mobility should be nearly a hundred per cent in time.' He pulled out a chair. 'Won't you join me, Merle? Pavane and the children had breakfast early this morning. My sister-in-law's busy discussing tomorrow with Ana, and the children are in the nursery ensuring that Conchita earns her wages.'

'Thank you—*gracias*!' Her resolve was paying off as her confidence began to return, nourished by the growing realisation that Rico appeared to have forgotten the way they had parted. If he was going to play the perfect host for the rest of the day it was just possible she would be able to relax, even begin to enjoy his company as she had in those far-off days, she thought wistfully, wondering which would cause her most pain—Rico unjustifiably furious or Rico unexpectedly tender.

Breakfast was always the same: rolls and croissants, butter, black cherry jam or Pavane's home-made Sevillan marmalade which Rico assured her with unstinted admiration had become something of a cult among the estate workers. Coffee was supplied in an enormous silver coffee-pot with tea available on request.

With a small dip of her head acknowledging his invitation, Merle seated herself, accepting a roll and spreading it with the delicious tart marmalade provided.

'Coffee?' Rico barely waited for her nod of acquiescence before filling her cup. 'Pavane's asked me to apologise to you, but there's been some drama in the kitchen—nothing serious, but something which demands her attention——' A lofty hand waved away his interest in further details of a domestic problem. 'But it seems she won't be able to drive over to the coast with you to make sure everything in the villa's up to standard, so I've offered my services instead.'

'That's very kind of you.' Even to her own ears the words seemed cold and formal. Rather that than he should guess how her heart seemed to do acrobatics at the very thought of an enforced journey in his company.

'De nada.' He matched her politeness, very Latin in his rebuttal of her gratitude.

Too conscious of his eyes resting on her every action, Merle felt her hand shake as she offered a small piece of roll to her mouth, feeling his penetrating gaze watching every movement of her lips as she swallowed the mouthful and washed it down with a long draught of coffee.

'I've one or two things to do before we leave, so I thought we'd aim to arrive at the villa in time to take an inventory and then have lunch there—I understand there's plenty of food laid in. The main things we need to check are cutlery and crockery, and of course you'll be able to tell me if there's anything missing that your sister would require. That way we can arrange for the deficiencies to be made good first thing Monday morning before she takes possession.'

Merle abandoned the remains of her roll, pushing her plate away, too unnerved by Rico's steady appraisal to continue eating. 'I don't know why you're doing all this for me,' she told him honestly.

'Don't you?' His smile was enigmatic, his eyes behind the dark flare of lashes echoing the amusement in his voice. 'Let's just say, for the time being, that it's because of what might have been. Does that satisfy you?

Fortunately he didn't wait for her answer, because she had none to give him. Instead he rose lazily to his feet. 'I'll be ready to leave in about two hours.'

Watching his departure, her gaze feasting on the breadth of his shoulders beneath the thin cambric shirt, drifting downwards to encompass the line of his leather belt above the hip-hugging Levis that emphasised his muscular leanness, Merle felt her mouth go dry. How bitter the pain to long so avidly for his favour when she had forfeited it so completely from the moment she had cast her first tremulous, innocent smile on his compelling features.

In fact it was about fifteen minutes short of two hours when Rico sought her out to enquire if she was ready to depart.

'Of course.' Merle rose to her feet and accompanied him to where the car waited for them. 'I do hope that having to do this isn't interfering with any other plans you might have made.' She slid gracefully into the passenger seat as he closed the door behind her.

'Not at all.' He was all suave politeness as he took his seat beside her and turned the key in the ignition. 'As a matter of fact, I can't think of a more pleasant way of spending the day.'

She cast a quick suspicious look at the strong profile presented to her. No, there was no suspicion of sarcasm marring its classic lines. Had he come to the conclusion that he had misjudged her intentions towards Esteban? Or perhaps he had ascertained from Pavane that Enrico's son had been nowhere near the *cortijo* during his absence. If that was the case she would very much like to receive her short-tempered host's humble apology. An expression of contrition would sit strangely on Rico's arrogant features and would have given her much pleasure! Unfortunately, to demand it might necessitate her relating Esteban's confidences, and that would be unforgivable.

On the other hand, Rico's observation probably applied to the prospect of going down to the coast rather than spending the time in her company. At least it appeared he wasn't going to be boringly disparaging, and that was something for which Merle was extremely grateful. She had greeted his announcement at breakfast with some trepidation. Now it seemed it had been unmerited. The day might prove to be enjoyable after all.

The sun was high in the sky when the Seat turned into the road leading to the Villa Jazmin—and continued right past it.

'Where are we going?' Surprised, even wondering if Rico had been thinking of other things, Merle half turned in her seat towards him, eyebrows raised enquiringly.

'I thought we'd take a look at the Villa Paraiso.' A few hundred yards further on he parked the Seat off the road. 'Make sure that no one's vandalised it.'

'Oh, surely they wouldn't!' she protested, nevertheless obeying his unspoken command and alighting into the shimmering heat of mid-morning, not at all sure that she wanted to set eyes on the villa again. 'Must we?'

Rico shrugged indifferently, winding up the windows of the car before locking the door. 'It won't do any harm to have a look and it'll do us good to stretch our legs and feel the wind on our faces.'

Well, that was reasonable enough, Merle concurred, stretching her limbs with a feline grace and enjoying the caress of the salt-laden Atlantic breeze as it played with the escaped tendrils of dark hair that curled round her face, as she prepared to follow in Rico's footsteps.

'Oh, no!' Minutes later a wounded cry of protest burst from her lips. She had prepared herself for seeing her dream home turned into an impregnable fortress—but the reality was far worse. Gone were the chains and notices, the bars at the windows and the spiked gates barring access to the upper storey. The white stone gleamed, the natural wood shutters were immaculate against their purity, the revealed windows shielded by internal blinds. Flowers tumbled down in brilliant array from the first-floor balcony and she could see the top of a dark blue sun-umbrella fringed with white flexing as the light wind caught it.

All the time she had known she was fighting a useless battle. She had no reason to feel so totally devastated, but disappointment struck her like a blow to her stomach so that she had to swallow several times in quick succession to relieve the wave of nausea she experienced.

'He's already sold it!' She turned anguished eyes to Rico, making a valiant effort to hold back the tears that were already too near the surface.

He couldn't have heard her, because after casting an appraising look over the villa he opened the gates and strolled into the garden.

'Rico, we can't!' Hurriedly she moved after him, catching him by the arm as he reached the front door. 'It's too late to do anything now. Obviously your lawyer was unsuccessful. It's already been sold to someone else!'

'It's possible.' Rico turned to face her, lifting her hand from his arm, searching her troubled face with every sign of compassion. 'On the other hand, Merlita...' he thrust his right hand deep into the pocket of his Levis '...it may have been restored to its rightful owner.'

She stood stock-still, unable to believe what she saw as Rico produced a key, fitted it with leisurely ease into the lock and opened the door.

'Welcome home, Merle.'

'I don't understand...' Was this some kind of obscene joke at her expense? No—instinctively she knew Rico would never stoop to such cruelty, but still her eyes pleaded for reassurance as she fought down the swelling knot of excitement which threatened to disrupt her nervous system, in case it should prove premature.

'What more is there to understand?' His smile flipped her heart. 'I told you Fidelio Diaz was a man of many parts and that human nature has more virtue in it than most people suspect. It seems our Señor Sanchez had no wish to steal the widow's mite when the facts were explained to him. He agreed to accept the settlement of the debt plus the accrued interest.'

'How long have you known?' No longer could Merle contain the joy she felt as, half laughing, half crying, she crossed the threshold.

'Since yesterday morning,' Rico acknowledged, closing the door behind them. 'I hope you'll forgive the liberty I took, but I wanted you to see your Paraiso in the best possible light. I arranged for it to be cleaned and prepared for you.'

'Oh, Rico!' The eyes she turned on him were swimming with tears. 'I can't believe it! You must have had an army of people working on it!'

'Quite a few,' he agreed equably. 'The name of Montilla y Cabra carries a lot of weight in this part of the world—a benefit for which my brother deserves full credit.'

He was being unduly modest, she was sure, as she sped from room to room, delightedly surveying everything that had been accomplished, her elation increasing with each perfect revelation.

'I thought we'd eat on the balcony,' Rico smiled at her flushed face, the enthusiasm she wouldn't have hidden from him even if she'd been able to do so. 'Everything should have been provided to order, so by the time you've checked upstairs, luncheon will be served.'

'Yes, fine!' Delightedly Merle ran up the open-plan staircase. Here again everything sparkled. Three bedrooms, each with a double bed made up for use, a large bathroom with shining tiles complete with lemon verbena soap and thick fluffy towels that matched the pale lemon walls... Catching sight of her face in the mirror, Merle raised her palms to its warm surface. She was almost drunk with pleasure—the adrenalin flowing through her veins lifting her to a state bordering on ecstasy. Calm down! she apostrophised herself, thrilled when the cold tap duly delivered clear cool water. Splashing it on her face, she tried to get her elation under control. Rico deserved someone better than a half-crazed woman as a companion for his meal!

It was in a more composed state of mind that she eventually walked through the door at the end of the first-floor corridor leading to the balcony, to find the table laid and a bottle of champagne nestled in an ice bucket awaiting her arrival.

'Well?' Rico rose to greet her. 'Is everything satisfactory?'

She swallowed in an attempt to keep her voice steady. 'I don't know how I'll ever be able to thank you...'

'No?' With the unerring courtesy he had always showed at the table Rico pulled out a soft-cushioned chair for her to sit down upon. 'Surely you haven't forgotten our arrangement?'

For a micro-second she didn't understand him, and then realisation burst upon her with shattering effect. She had been too overjoyed to remember what she had said to him. Now the words came back to her, echoing with an appalling clarity—'I'm quite happy for us to become lovers...the day you give me the key to Paraiso.'

'I hope the menu pleases you.' Rico, having delivered his bombshell, was continuing the conversation as if nothing had changed. 'The first course is honey-glazed quail, followed by scampi cacciatore and a side salad with lemon sorbet to clear the palate before profiteroles and cream, with champagne, of course, to ease its passage.'

He didn't seem to expect an answer, which was just as well, because what could she say? She had made a statement and, unlikely though it had been that she would be called on to honour it, she had known then— as she did now—that she would; and although the knowledge shamed her she admitted to herself that it would not be under duress.

'A truly international menu, I believe.' The muscle in Rico's arms tensed as he thumbed the champagne cork, sending it exploding into the air. 'To the repossession of Paraiso...' He filled her glass, indicating that she join him in the toast.

'To Paraiso,' she murmured faintly, swallowing the liquid sparkle with more enthusiasm than good sense. 'You must let me know how much I owe you, plus Señor Diaz's fee, of course.'

'Call it a house-warming present.' Neatly Rico uncovered the foil-wrapped dishes, exposing the golden-brown quail garnished with shredded salad.

'Oh, no! I couldn't possibly do that!' Horror made her voice rise. 'The cost must be several thousand pesetas, and I can well afford it!'

'So can I.' There was no laughter now on the beautiful male face which dared her to contest his will. 'And since it's Fidelio Diaz who has done all the work and I who will reap the benefits of his endeavour I feel it's the very least I can do. More champagne?'

Her glass was empty, and she lacked the bravura to prevent his filling it to the brim. She could have expected no more, yet to find herself treated as a woman who sold her favours was the most humiliating ordeal she had ever faced in her life. Presumably Rico was used to such encounters, for he seemed totally unperturbed by her sudden lapse into silence.

Merle ate like an automaton as one delicious course followed another, allowing Rico to pour her one further glass of champagne. She wasn't going to make the situation worse by being too inebriated to know what she was doing. Suppose she reneged on her bargain? Told Rico it had been a spur-of-the-moment retort never intended seriously? No, that was impossible. Her pride was equal to his any day, and she would never have made the offer if it had gone totally against the grain. That was the hardest part to admit to herself: that she *wanted* Rico as a lover, that she wanted the one last glorious memory of him held in her arms...

'Shall we?' Panic caught at her throat as she realised she could prolong the duration of the meal no longer, the dregs of her second cup of black coffee grown cold in the cup.

Stiffly she rose to her feet, allowing Rico to propel her gently into the comparative dimness of the villa. At the door of the main bedroom she hesitated.

'Rico, I...'

'Yes?' He was patience personified, courteously waiting for her to continue. The embryo protest died on her tongue. If he had been impatient or even excessively ardent she might have been able to dredge up the indignation she needed to repulse him. This quiet businesslike manner defeated her utterly. 'Nothing,' she whispered.

'Ah, Merle...' He took her hand, drawing her towards the bed, sitting down on it and pulling her on to his lap. *'Mi mujer bella...'* Suddenly he was no longer the cool, slightly superior man whose indifference had taunted her for the past hour, as one hand slid beneath her bolero to discover and remove with indolent ease the simple bra it discovered. As his fingers forked beneath her swelling breasts, raising them to his lips, and he bent his ebony

head the better to caress their tumid apexes, Merle felt
her mind spin in helpless agony, her body blossoming
into a hitherto unknown arousal, passion surging like a
storm through every cell of her being.

With a moan, half pain, half pleasure she lifted her
hand to latch her fingers through the dark glory of his
hair, burying her face in its softness as the rising golden
tide of ecstasy coursing through her veins demanded.

At last his soft warm mouth left her flesh as he eased
himself a few inches away, his voice hoarse, to stare down
into her flushed face, her wide blue eyes luminous with
emotion. 'I'm not going to release you from your
promise... If that's what you're waiting for, Merlita,
then it's not going to happen...unless...'
He heaved in a deep breath and his hands tightened
around her while she stared back into his grim face, her
lips parted in unconscious invitation. 'Unless,' he continued harshly, 'you tell me you've had a change of heart.
No explanations necessary—just one word. Just "no",
Merle, and we'll leave now—get into the car and drive
back to the *cortijo*...'

Suddenly he was the man she had met on the beach,
compassionate, caring and tender, and her heart swelled
with the love which had always lain dormant there.

'No...' She would deny him nothing—no, that wasn't
right, she would deny *them* nothing. With a certainty
she knew it was her destiny to be joined with this man,
however brief the union, however transient the joy; it
had been written in her stars.

When Rico eased her off his lap and rose to his feet
she turned towards him with starry eyes, eager for him
to lead her into unknown pleasure, certain he was about
to help her discard the few items of clothing that kept
her hidden from his gaze. It was several painful seconds,
during which she saw but didn't comprehend the stark

tautness of his face and discerned the way his fingers trembled as he smoothed down his shirt as if fighting to regain control over himself, before she realised he had misunderstood her sharp ejaculation.

'Rico!' She was off the bed, flinging her arms around him, totally unselfconscious in her need to reassure him, her heart thumping painfully as she felt his whole body tense against her. 'I meant—no, I haven't had a change of heart!'

'Are you sure?' The words were torn out of him, then as she nodded he found her mouth with a passion and purpose that had her gasping as he swept her up into his arms.

'I've dreamed of this for so long...' He laid her gently on the bed, and his words were as gentle as the soft caressing movements of his able hands as he paid homage to her beauty, untying and discarding the light bolero, fondling her pale breasts with sensitive fingers, deliberately controlling his own urgency to incite a wondrous pleasure that sent sensuous shivers trembling up and down her spine, as he murmured soft endearments in his native tongue with a thrilling huskiness.

Merle was quivering with anticipation before he left her side to strip off the few garments which clothed his own magnificent body. In the stillness of the room shadowed by half-closed shutters she watched his powerful silhouette, feeling a poignant stab of longing as her eyes dwelt on the raised weals that decorated the satin smoothness of his back.

If he had rushed it, the experience could never have been so good, so satisfying for her. Even as her body shed the sweet musky tears of love Merle's heart leapt with joy at the solicitude shown by the strong man who had both captured and become her captive.

Rico loved her with infinite forbearance, marvellously aware of her desires and doubts. She wanted nothing from him but the satisfaction of knowing she had been the instrument of his pleasure. It wasn't the thought of a liberated woman, just an instinctive emotion which she need never publicly acknowledge or apologise for; but he gave her so much more than that, wreaking an awesome magic on her untutored body, until in her need she whimpered for release, lifting her hips to receive him and hold him completely and tightly with an expertise which owed nothing to experience and everything to instinct and the love she bore him.

There was no pain or discomfort as she had half feared. Nothing to detract from the glory of taking him and finding herself possessed by him in a mutual agony of sensation. Belonging to him in that fierce act of dominion where power always replaced persuasion, Merle moved with and against Rico's vital male body in perfect harmony until the pleasure became too intense to contain, spiralling into a plane of ecstasy before stilling into a shining peace.

All her life she would remember this afternoon, the harsh beauty of Rico's face, the dark ebony of his hair on the pale cover, the slumbrous heavily lashed eyes closing as his sharp cry of exultation pierced the silence and she felt his weight grow heavy on her for a few seconds before he rolled away.

Carefully, quietly, she swung her legs off the bed, gathering her clothes together before making her way to the en-suite bathroom. It wasn't unusual for a man to sleep in such circumstances, she knew. Methodically she showered, re-dressed and brushed out her hair, which had become impossibly tumbled. When she re-entered the bedroom Rico was still stretched out on his face, his sable head buried into the pillow, the lean muscularity of his virile body simply stunning.

Quite unable to resist the temptation, Merle approached the bed, bending to place her lips, as soft as the touch of the breeze, in swift salutation on the raised tissue of his back which evidenced his resolve and his bravery.

Briskly she collected her senses, walking out on to the balcony to clear the table. Downstairs she filled the sink with warm water, delighted at the efficiency of the solar panels in the roof and, finding some liquid in the cupboard, began to wash up.

Filled with a quiet satisfaction, she was aware that nothing would ever be quite the same again after what had occurred between Rico and herself. She felt stronger for the experience—as if she had taken some of his power. He had imprinted his body on her, and although the physical sensation of his possession, which still lingered, would fade, the memory of his power and purpose would live with her forever, sustaining her.

CHAPTER ELEVEN

MERLE was smiling to herself as she turned her attention to the task in hand. She had been too caught up in events before to examine the plates and glasses. Now she realised she was handling the finest porcelain and lead crystal. Carefully she rinsed and dried them. These were certainly not part of Paraiso's inventory!

A sound behind her made her turn as Rico entered the room, fully dressed and groomed to perfection.

One thing she did know. It wasn't the done thing to hold a post-mortem after a casual relationship. The smart thing was to ignore what had happened, relegating it to 'just one of those things' rather than an event which had revolutionised her life.

'Hi,' she greeted him cheerfully. 'You're just too late to dry for me. Did you provide the china and glass from Jazmin—it certainly didn't come with the fittings!'

'Yes, they're mine.' Rico moved forward to lift a glass, holding it towards the window so that the sun reflected baubles of light from it to dance across the ceiling. 'I supplied them as well as the food and wine—everything was identical with the plans I made last year when I went to your hotel to invite you to have dinner with me.'

A quick glance at his profile, eyes narrowed as he observed the glinting crystal in his hand, told her nothing—but there had been something in his tone which was curiously disturbing.

'Oh, you mean when you were going to ask me to become your lover?' she asked lightly.

'When I intended to ask you to be my wife.' The glass was abandoned on the table as he moved forward, removing the space between them to seize Merle by the shoulders.

'Wife?' Her voice cracked. 'But you said...'

'The only thing I could to protect my own pride! The truth was when we met it was *flechazo*, what you would call an arrow through the heart.'

'Love at first sight?' Unbelievably she saw him nod.

'You don't believe in it? Ah, Merle, it happens. Ask Armando—he saw Pavane across the aisle of a church and was lost. Nearly a decade later he is still entranced.' Rico smiled a little grimly. 'In the first few hours of meeting you I too was lost. I didn't need time. I knew everything I needed to know—it was written in your eyes, your voice, the way you walked, the way you smiled...'

Sensing what must follow, Merle took the initiative, uncertain where this conversation could possibly lead. 'Everything about me—except that I was married,' she whispered, looking away so that she didn't have to meet the accusation in his eyes.

'Yes...' It was almost a sigh as he released his grip to walk away from her, thrusting his hands deep into his pockets and staring moodily out of the window. 'It was like the end of the world—a judgement—a divine punishment, as if despite my contrition I still hadn't expiated my sins.'

'I'm sorry...' Merle's heart ached for him. If she had had any idea at all about the way he had felt...

'It wasn't your fault—I realise that now. It was my own wishful thinking that convinced my ego that you felt the same way about me. I mistook your natural compassion for a much deeper, more personal emotion; but at the time all I could think of was that you had deliberately used me for amusement. *Dios*, how that hurt!'

'Rico—I——' Merle licked lips grown unnaturally dry as adrenalin pumped through her veins in answer to the tension that simmered in the atmosphere between them.

He brushed aside her interruption, his voice harsh and deep. 'Then just when I thought I'd got you right out of my system you turned up on my doorstep and I knew I'd been fooling myself, that I would never be truly free of you. When I still believed you to be married I found the strength to fight my own weakness, but when you told me you were a widow... *Santa madre de Dios!* I kept telling myself that last year you'd been prepared to deceive your husband, deliberately alienating myself to avoid becoming involved with you again.'

Sadly Merle shook her head as he turned to face her, his features contorted with fervour. 'That was never true. I was reaching out for something, someone I needed, but I had no idea what I was doing! I can't explain in simple terms!' Her voice rose in anguish as she considered the complications of her life.

'Hush, *querida*, you don't have to.' Again she was in his arms, nestling her head against his chest as he soothed her. 'Eventually I had to face the facts. Without you my life would always lack meaning. I had to keep you here in Spain for as long as I could and try to persuade you to give me a chance to show how much I wanted you.' He sighed and she felt his whole body tremble with release. 'But you didn't want to know—and who could blame you after the way I treated you?—and then you offered yourself to me in exchange for the key to Paraiso and I dared to hope that once we had lain in each other's arms, touched intimately as man and woman, joined our bodies together in nature's most powerful union, you would give me the chance to share your life for more than one brief hour... give me the opportunity to prove how much I love you!'

Her heart clenching painfully as she fought down every instinct to agree to continuing their affair over the coming weeks, Merle raised one hand to touch Rico's cheek, feeling the muscle tighten beneath her fingertips. 'I—I can't. I have to think of Laurie. I can't consider any irregular relationship for her sake.' Wide-eyed, she begged his understanding.

'And marriage is irregular?' Rico pushed her gently away from him so that he could gaze quizzically into her astonished face. 'Nothing's changed, Merlita. I want you to be my wife. I want Laurie to be my daughter, to take her into my home and into my life, to give her the things her own father would have wanted for her. I want both of you, *mi corazón*. Is it such an impossible thing to ask? After what has just happened between us I dare to hope not.' His smile was heartbreakingly tender. 'I was lying on the bed a few minutes ago wondering if I stood any chance of ever winning your love—and then I felt your lips on my skin—and I dared to hope.' He paused for a long second. 'Was I wrong, Merle?'

For ten seconds Merle was silent, savouring the idea as if there was the slightest possibility of accepting it, and knowing it was totally impossible.

'Well?' he prompted her gently, forcing her out of her daydreams.

'There's something I have to tell you. Laurie's not my own child,' she said painfully. 'David was a fine man, but I never loved him. We never lived together as man and wife. I married him to give his daughter a stable home and preserve her inheritance...' She paused fearfully, as Rico exhaled his breath in a low hiss of shock.

'I didn't imagine it, then! I was the first man who has ever loved you!'

If the pain in her heart had been any less Merle would have laughed at his astounded face. 'I thought you hadn't realised.'

He shrugged, his expression still bemused. 'I thought it was so good, so incredibly perfect because I loved you so much, and because, despite the way I'd constantly misjudged you, you didn't detest me as much as I deserved.'

'Oh, Rico...' Tears flooded her eyes. 'I fell in love with you a long time ago, but I never realised it until I saw you again.' She saw joy illuminate his face and hurried on before he could speak, her voice trembling with misery, 'But you still don't understand!'

As briefly as she could she told him about David and Rosemary and their lovely child that she had brought up as her own.

He listened intently without interruption, waiting for her to finish before lacing his fingers through her dark hair and turning her face upwards to receive his kiss. For several seconds his mouth possessed hers with a proprietorial adoration that left her gasping.

'Do you think I should love Laurie any less because of this?' he asked tenderly. 'Is this why you hesitate to give me the answer I want?'

'No, it's not that,' she hastened to assure him, confident that he would have welcomed Laurie with the same open-hearted affection he bestowed on his brother's children. 'But I can't possibly marry you, Rico. I have to go on living in England. It's why I married David! Oh, don't you see!' She searched his still face with eyes luminous with tears as she rejected the promise of earthly paradise. 'David left me everything he owned on the understanding that it would be used for Laurie's future. It's a trust, a sacred duty, something I can never turn my back on. I have to raise her in England as David and

Rosemary would have done, provide the house and environment that's rightly hers. If I uproot her I'll have betrayed the two people who befriended me when I most needed it as well as a young child entrusted to my care!'

The ensuing silence was broken by a solitary cicada perched somewhere in the garden, before Rico spoke again.

'I can't leave Spain, Merle. My life, my future are here at the clinic. There's no way I could live in England.'

'I never expected you to.' She winced at the harshness of his tone. Not for a single moment had she considered he would make such a sacrifice. There would always be another woman available, and Rico de Montilla belonged to Spain, to the warmth and beauty of Andalusia and the eminent career he was carving out for himself. It was something she had always recognised and respected.

'But I can't let you disappear from my life!' He gathered her even closer, running his hands down her trembling back, finding her mouth again with his own, easing her away so that his seeking hand could find the swelling mound of her breast, closing his fingers over it as his kiss became deeper and more urgent.

For several seconds Merle savoured his embrace, enjoying the sensual responses of her own body. Then he was holding her away from him, staring down at her dazed face, her pleasure-swollen mouth, with haunted eyes.

'We'll see each other when I come here on holiday. We can still be friends.' Even as she said it she knew the futility of such a suggestion.

'Friends!' he grated. 'After what has just happened between us? Do you really imagine I could be in the same room, on the same beach, sitting at the same table, without wanting to take you to my bed and love you until you cried for mercy?'

She stared at him, blindingly aware that he spoke the truth, sharing his feelings.

'I tried to stop this happening,' she told him through parched lips. 'I wanted you to go on despising me so that the temptation never arose. That's why I didn't tell you I was a widow or that David and I had never been lovers. I wanted you to go on thinking I was meretricious and wanton...'

'Stop it, Merle!' His hand rose to silence her mouth with a velvet touch. 'I tried to believe those things because I was hurt and jealous, but it was impossible. The attraction between us was always more than physical, a mixture of chemistry and spirit. When you stood on my doorstep that first night I tried to persuade myself that I hated you, but I always knew it was a lie. If you were in trouble I had to help you, and heaven forgive me, I wanted to savour the pleasure of sharing my house with you even if it was for such a brief time. I thought you were forbidden fruit and I swore not to repeat Adam's sin a second time, but I could look, couldn't I—and fantasise a little without incurring damnation?'

'There'll be another girl in your life, someone who will love you as much as I do. A girl who shares your background and whom you find irresistible.' Merle tried to console him, although unreasonable jealousy tortured her at the very idea.

'Not second best—I'll never settle for that. If I can't have you, then I shall never marry!' The white torment on his face shocked her to the core of her being, but she could only shake her head, denying him hope.

'Then there's nothing more to be said. We have reached a *callejón sin salida*—a road with no exit, no?'

'Yes.' It was as much as Merle could do to speak as her throat muscles knotted in a lump large enough to choke her.

'Then we may as well be leaving.'

Rico didn't wait for her answer but turned on his heel and made for the door. Merle lingered in the sunny kitchen for a few more seconds, fighting and winning the battle to avoid breaking down completely. That would come later when she was in the privacy of her own room. Having Rico detest her had been pain enough. Having him love her was an agony against which she needed every shred of her courage if she were to survive the coming days.

'When am I going to meet this mysterious benefactor I've heard so much about?' Barbara twisted in front of the long mirror, admiring herself in a black off-the-shoulder blouse and long floral cotton skirt.

'Rico?' Merle looked up from filing her nails, casting an approving glance at her sister. 'You look gorgeous in that, Barbie.'

'Of course Rico.' Barbara refused to be side-tracked. 'I must have met the entire Montilla clan this afternoon, with the exception of the guy who rescued our holiday home.'

'It *was* rather like Victoria Station, wasn't it?' Merle remembered, her eyes lighting with laughter. 'As a matter of fact, Armando, Ramón and his family had only just arrived back after a tour of the *cortijo* when Enrico delivered you from the airport.'

'Do you know, that's the first time I've seen you laugh since I arrived?' The older girl studied her sister reflectively. 'I thought you looked a bit strained when I first saw you, but I wasn't going to say anything in front of

Grant and the children, but now we're alone I hope you're going to confide in me.'

'There's nothing to confide.' Merle smoothed the last nail, before discarding the file and rising to her feet. For a zombie she was coping extraordinarily well with events, she flattered herself. 'Come on, it's time we went and joined the party. We've been talking so much I didn't realise how late it was getting. Pavane will think we've deserted her.'

'No, not yet, love.' Barbara spun round from the mirror, barring her exit. 'We may have been talking all afternoon, but not about anything meaningful. Something's upset you—and you still haven't told me when I'm going to meet this Rico. I've got a feeling the two things may be connected!'

Merle hesitated for a moment, faced with her sister's concerned expression—and was lost. Too many times Barbara had been her friend and protector, her confidante.

'Oh, Barbie, it's awful! I love him so much, and it's hopeless!' She bit her lip, determined not to give way to the threatening tears that she felt gathering. She had drained herself dry during the hours of darkness, surely? Tonight was a celebration, not a wake, and she was determined to join in the fun.

Her sister's face became serious. 'You mean he's married?'

'No—oh, no. In fact he asked me to be his wife, but of course it's impossible.'

'Impossible—why?' Barbara's brow wrinkled in puzzlement. 'If you love each other...'

'How can you ask?' Astonished at her sister's reaction, Merle regarded her with amazed eyes. 'It's Laurie.'

'You mean he doesn't want her?' Barbara's soft eyes filled with compassion.

'It's not that.' Eagerly Merle denied her sister's suspicions. 'But you more than anyone know the promises I made to David. Rico's working as an orthopaedic surgeon in Cadiz. His life is here, and I, of course, have to stay in England with Laurie. You know the only reason David and I married was to ensure that she wouldn't have to go into a foster-home, that she'd continue to live in the house where she was born...' Despite her resolution Merle's voice broke. 'Please, Barbie, I don't want to discuss it. I'll get over it in time, you'll see.' She made a determined effort to reach the door. 'Listen, I can hear music outside on the terrace, and I'm dying to have a dance with Grant...'

'You're wrong, Merle!' To her dismay Barbara refused to move. 'You have to listen to me. You're too near to the problem to be seeing it clearly. Yes, sure, David married you for Laurie's sake, we all know that. But it had nothing to do with the house.'

'Barbie—please...' Near to breaking-point, Merle tried to prevent the older girl from continuing, gasping when, instead of allowing her to pass, Barbie took her by the shoulders and shook her gently.

'Merle, you little fool! If all David had wanted was to ensure that Laurie had the house and was financially well provided for, he could have appointed trustees, instructed a solicitor. When he married you he was getting for her the one thing he couldn't arrange legally. He was ensuring that she would be loved and cared for by someone who loved her as much as he did, as Rosemary did! If Rico loves you and wants to care for both you and Laurie, then does it really matter where it happens?'

'But the house...?' A wild tumultuous joy was building inside Merle as she stared into her sister's face.

Barbara had never lied to her or tried to protect her from reality. Was it really possible that she could bring Laurie here and not betray David's trust? Her sister's strong assertion had had the ring of truth to it, and Barbara had been a constant and sympathetic audience at the domestic drama in which she, Merle, had starred.

'Rent it out,' Barbie answered her question succinctly. 'Bank the money for her. Let her inherit it when she's old enough to decide whether she wants to live there or not. It's a beautiful house, I agree, but it's only bricks and mortar. If that's the only reason you've turned Rico down, you're not thinking straight!'

'If I dared believe it...' Her heart beating faster as a seed of hope began to grow, Merle clutched at Barbara's arm. 'I've never thought of it like that before.' Had she really been blind to David's real intentions? She pushed her dark hair away from her brow as if it would clear the mist from her mind.

'If you're convinced of this man's love for you and his willingness to take Laurie into his heart and home— then believe it,' Barbara encouraged softly. 'David would have wanted both of you to be happy. You can't be in any doubt about that.'

'I don't know...' But the pall of misery which had dampened her spirits was lifting. Barbie was right, she had been too close to the problem to see it clearly. Suddenly hope was streaming through her, bringing in its wake a golden stream of happiness, but she mustn't make any rash decisions. 'I'll have to think about it.'

'Then don't take too long,' Barbara hugged her, touching cheeks with her in a sisterly embrace. 'I haven't met your Rico yet, but if he's anything like his brothers I can't wait to welcome him to the family!' She grinned conspiratorially. 'You look beautiful, Merle.' Her soft eyes assessed the floating georgette. 'That's the prettiest dress you've ever had, and, now the smile's come back to your face, I don't think I've ever seen you looking lovelier. Heaven knows, if anyone deserves to find true happiness, it's you! The moon's bright, the music's sweet and everyone's celebrating—I may be a romantic, but it seems a perfect night to rethink your decision and put your young man out of his misery.'

The party was in full swing as Merle stepped out on to the terrace. Unable to resist taking another peep at Laurie in the nursery, she had let Barbie go downstairs by herself, confident Grant would be impatiently awaiting her appearance.

Looking at the sleeping child, her dark curls splayed on the pillow, she had tossed over in her mind her sister's advice, for the first time allowing herself to recollect the way David had broached the subject of marriage when he had received his negative prognosis.

As if a veil had been torn from her eyes, the more she thought about it the more she became convinced Barbara was indeed right. It hadn't been only material goods Laurie's father had wanted to preserve for his daughter, it had been *her* love—and that would never alter wherever she was or with whomever she shared her life!

Now, her eyes sparkling with new-found elation, she searched the terrace for Rico. He had disappeared from the *cortijo* before she had dragged herself down to breakfast that morning, but he had promised Pavane to be at the party—and, knowing Rico, she was sure he wouldn't break his word.

Anxiously she smoothed down her dress, her fingers shaking with anticipation. Suppose he had changed his mind about wanting to marry her? Suppose the proposal of marriage had been made in the heat of the moment? A cold shiver trickled down her spine.

'Señora Costain...' A deep voice behind her had her spinning round to meet the friendly smile of Fidelio Diaz. 'Doña Pavane tells me you wished to speak to me?'

'Ah, Señor Diaz.' Forcing a smile on her face, Merle held out her hand, wishing the meeting could have been postponed. Suppose Rico simply put in a courtesy visit and disappeared again before she could speak to him? 'I just wanted to thank you for acting on my behalf with Señor Sanchez. You did a marvellous job.'

'You flatter me, *señora*. All I did was to locate the man. If it hadn't been for Don Rico nothing could have changed his mind.' He sighed as Merle looked bewildered. 'He is not an avaricious man, you understand. He had long since decided not to pursue the debt, but when he learned the extent of his granddaughter's disablement and the cost of the only operations which could help her, he realised he had the means of paying for them by taking the matter to court.'

'I'm not sure I understand,' Merle searched the lawyer's face for enlightenment. 'What operations?'

Fidelio Diaz looked surprised. 'Perhaps I do not explain myself so well in English. Sanchez's granddaughter was born with a badly deformed leg. The doctors suggested amputation, but there was an alternative, a series of bone implants over a number of years, but the cost would run into many millions of pesetas, so when Don Rico offered his professional services free plus accommodation at the clinic in Cadiz Sanchez agreed to release the deeds to him, taking in full settlement only the original debt and the accrued interest.' He paused to study Merle's shocked face. 'But surely you knew this, *señora*?'

'No—no, I didn't.' Rico had made this fantastic gesture for her? Her heart seemed to somersault at the sheer enormity of his sacrifice.

'Perhaps I shouldn't have mentioned it...?' The lawyer appeared discomfited. 'I wouldn't want to be considered indiscreet.'

'No, I'm glad you did. What you've just told me confirms a decision I made a few minutes ago.' Merle flashed him a dazzling smile. 'Now if you'll forgive me, I have to find someone...'

Just when disappointment was a hard knot in her chest and she was about to return to the *sala* to question Pavane about Rico's intentions, Merle saw his tall figure standing alone in the shadows, apart from the crowd, beneath the cluster of the lemon trees that edged the patio.

From a distance of a few yards their eyes met, his darkly courteous, hers sparkling with anticipation mixed with apprehension. Her heart was thumping like that of a trapped animal as she weaved her way through the dancing couples towards him. How magnificent he looked, wearing a light jacket over dark trousers, his face starkly handsome in the filtered light of the decorative lanterns.

'Merle...' He acknowledged her presence with a slight bow of his head as if she were a stranger, and she couldn't help but notice the lines of pain etched round his beautifully sensuous mouth as he let his eyes travel over her with a restrained yet hungry appreciation. 'You look more beautiful every time I see you.'

'Thank you,' she said breathlessly, her eyes glowing with the love it was impossible to hide. 'Rico, I've just spoken to Señor Diaz. He told me about Sanchez's granddaughter—how you purchased Paraiso with your time and your skill.'

'He should have been more discreet.' Anger tightened his jaw. 'The matter is entirely between Sanchez and myself.' He paused, his dark gaze travelling over her face

as if he would imprint it on his memory for ever.
'However, since you've discovered it, you'll understand
why it was impossible for me to consider living in
England. The surgery is complicated and protracted. The
child will need careful monitoring every month over a
period of at least five years.'

'You mean—if it hadn't been for your promise you
would actually have considered giving up your home and
your job to start afresh in England?' Merle stared at him
aghast. In her wildest dreams she had never thought to
ask for so great a renunciation.

'Why not?' he asked tightly. 'If, unlike you, I hadn't
been bound by a moral tie I wouldn't have let any frontier
stand between us. Ironical, isn't it?' He smiled without
amusement. 'I was determined to get Paraiso back for
you, yet its attainment devastated all my dreams. It was
to have been my wedding gift to you—as it is, I must
ask you to accept it as a farewell present.'

'No, that's impossible.' Firmly she shook her head,
adding before he could remonstrate, 'You see, I'm not
going anywhere...but I will accept it as a wedding
present.' She smiled up into his startled face, seeing a
dawning hope bring fire to his sombre eyes. 'That is—
unless you've changed your mind.'

'What are you saying, Merle?' Rico reached out his
hands and she slid between them, nestling up against his
tautly held body, alerted by the hoarseness of his voice
to the extent of his reaction.

'That Barbara's made me see things in a different light.
I've thought things over and I realise that David would
never have entrusted Laurie to me unless he'd had absolute faith in my judgement,' she confessed simply. 'He
knew I'd never contemplate marriage unless I believed
my future husband would treat her as his own child.

Barbie made me see that it's not where we live that matters but with whom...'

She would have said more, gone on to explain that since speaking to Barbara she had decided to offer the rental of the house to her sister and Grant, for who else would make better custodians of Laurie's property? But Rico stopped her mouth by the most effectual means possible, his lips warm and erotically persuasive as they moved on hers, causing a sigh of pleasure to shudder through her.

She was trembling as he released her, her senses filled with the taste and touch of him, the erotic scents of fresh linen, subtle cologne and the indefinable essence that was Rico himself. She shuddered in delight as he buried his mouth in the perfumed skin at the curve of her neck and shoulder, moving it downward to discover the tender swell of her breast within the soft georgette neckline of her dress. She gasped with delight, and her hands rose to hold his head, her fingers tangling in the dark softness of his hair, her body aflame with desire.

'I thought I should never hold you again, never kiss you...' he whispered huskily. 'The hours since we've been apart have been a torment I wouldn't wish my worst enemy to share. I couldn't let you go, yet because I loved you I dared not try to force you against your own judgement, in case you grew to hate me.'

'I could never hate you.' Merle strained against the eager strength of his body, delighting in the knowledge that he was aroused by her softness and the perfume of her hair and skin.

'*Por Dios*, Merlita...!' His breath rasped as he pulled away from her to gaze into her expressive face. 'If we stay here we shall become a spectacle to rival the flamenco dancers whose performance begins soon. We should tell Armando, I think, that there is yet one more event to celebrate tonight and that he'd better prepare the family chapel for a wedding.'

'But not too soon...' Merle's blue eyes pleaded for his understanding. 'Not before Laurie's got to know you—and like you.'

'You mean to make me wait a week?' Laughter lent a boyish charm to his splendid features. 'Agreed, *mi corazón*, on one condition—you allow me my own private celebration before we break the news to our family and friends.'

'You mean now?' she asked tremulously, knowing perfectly well that he did.

He didn't disappoint her, letting his eyes roam over her parted lips, the classic line of her throat and shoulders, his eyes flaring with passion beneath his lowered lashes, 'I mean now, *mi corazón*,' he agreed softly, 'and afterwards we shall seek out Esteban, who has been demanding quite imperiously that I shall summon you forth to be introduced to Isadora.'

'She's here with him?' Delightedly Merle saw his nod of assent. 'That evening when you saw him holding my hands...'

'Yes, I know,' he smiled shamefacedly. 'He told me when I drove him back to the hacienda.'

'And you still came to my room!' If she had been less happy her indignation would have been greater.

'I needed an excuse to see you, *amada mia*, and I was mad with frustration and self-doubt. Even if you didn't want him—you'd made it clear you didn't want me either unless I gave you something more valuable than myself alone, and that was a hurt that still smarted!'

'It wasn't true,' pleaded Merle, searching his expression with troubled eyes. 'I only said it because I thought to admit that I wanted you too would only lower me further in your estimation—if that were possible.'

'And that was never true either, *dulzura mia*.' The power of his gaze transfixed her as he swallowed with effort. 'Sometimes pride acts like a poison which corrupts the mind, but love proved a powerful antidote. Prove to me that you are as compassionate as you are desirable and tell me you forgive me.'

'Perhaps...' But her smile told him what her lips withheld, as the tension left his shoulders. 'When you've made a perfect apology.'

In the soft dimness of her bedroom Rico smoothed away the flimsy georgette from her unresisting body until it lay in a crumpled heap on the floor, before lifting her and carrying her towards the bed. As she relaxed on its softness Merle watched him discard his own clothing with a joyous anticipation of the pleasures ahead.

There was no doubt left in her mind now but that she had made the right decision. She thought briefly of Barbie and Grant enjoying the house in England for a token rent until they had saved enough money to buy their own property; of the possibility of persuading her mother to come to Spain for her wedding; of Laurie having new cousins to play with and perhaps, in time, a brother or sister—then Rico joined her, drawing her into his arms, and she held him closely, her fingers playing lightly on his back as she recalled that moment long ago when she had first felt the unwitting pangs of love for him, and after that there was no thought of anything but the splendour of the moment and the fulfilment of her dreams.

Mills & Boon

Accept 4 Free Romances and 2 Free gifts

• FROM MILLS & BOON •

An irresistible invitation from Mills & Boon Reader Service. Please accept our offer of 4 free romances, a CUDDLY TEDDY and a special MYSTERY GIFT... Then, if you choose, go on to enjoy 6 more exciting Romances every month for just £1.45 each postage and packaging free. Plus our FREE newsletter with author news, competitions and much more.

**Send the coupon below at once to:
Reader Service, FREEPOST, P.O. Box 236, Croydon, Surrey CR9 9EL**

— — — — — NO STAMP NEEDED — — —

YES! Please rush me my 4 Free Romances and 2 FREE Gifts! Please also reserve me a Reader Service Subscription so I can look forward to receiving 6 Brand New Romances each month for just £8.70, post and packing free. If I choose not to subscribe I shall write to you within 10 days. I understand I can keep the free books and gifts whatever I decide. I can cancel or suspend my subscription at any time. I am over 18 years of age.

Name Mr/Mrs/Miss _____ EP86R

Address _____

_____

_____ Postcode _____

Signature _____

The right is reserved to refuse an application and change the terms of this offer. Offer expires May 31st 1991. Readers in Southern Africa write to Independent Book Services Pty., Post Bag X3010, Randburg 2125, South Africa. Other Overseas and Eire send for details. You may be mailed with other offers as a result of this application. If you would prefer not to share in this opportunity please tick box ☐

Zodiac Wordsearch
Competition

How would you like a years supply of Mills & Boon Romances ABSOLUTELY FREE?

Well, you can win them! All you have to do is complete the word puzzle below and send it into us by Dec 31st 1990. The first five correct entries picked out of the bag after this date will each win a years supply of Mills & Boon Romances (Six books every month - worth over £100!) What could be easier?

S	E	C	S	I	P	R	I	A	M	F
I	U	L	C	A	N	C	E	R	L	I
S	A	I	N	I	M	E	G	N	S	R
C	A	P	R	I	C	O	R	N	U	E
S	E	I	R	A	N	G	I	S	I	O
Z	O	D	W	A	T	E	R	B	R	I
O	G	A	H	M	A	T	O	O	A	P
D	R	R	T	O	U	N	I	R	U	R
I	I	B	R	O	R	O	M	G	Q	O
A	V	I	A	N	U	A	N	C	A	C
C	E	L	E	O	S	T	A	R	S	S

Pisces	Aries	Leo	Earth
Cancer	Gemini	Virgo	Star
Scorpio	Taurus	Fire	Sign
Aquarius	Libra	Water	Moon
Capricorn	Sagittarius	Zodiac	Air

Please turn over for entry details

How to enter

All the words listed overleaf, below the word puzzle, are hidden
in the grid. You can can find them by reading the letters
forwards, backwards, up and down, or diagonally. When you find
a word, circle it, or put a line through it. After you have found all
the words, the left-over letters will spell a secret message that
you can read from left to right, from the top of the puzzle
through to the bottom.

Don't forget to fill in your name and address in the space provided
and pop this page in an envelope (you don't need a stamp) and
post it today.   Competition closes Dec 31st 1990.

Only one entry
per household
(more than one
will render the
entry invalid).

Mills & Boon Competition
Freepost
P.O. Box 236
Croydon
Surrey CR9 9EL

Hidden message _____

_____

Are you a Reader Service subscriber.   Yes ☐   No ☐

Name_____

Address_____

_____

_____

_____ **Postcode**_____

'You . . . you've just assaulted me!'

'It is hardly an assault if a man should decide to kiss his wife,' Zarco told her dismissively. 'And maybe it is something I should have done a long time ago, hmm?'

'But I'm *not* your wife!' she cried huskily.

'*Cale-se*. Be quiet!' he rasped, his temper almost flaring up out of control, once more.

'My name is Tiffany Harris—and this is all a t-terrible, *terrible* m-mistake!'

Dear Reader

The arrival of the Mills & Boon Mothers' Day Pack
means that Spring is just around the corner . . . so why
not indulge in a little romantic Spring Fever, as you
enjoy the four books specially chosen for you?
Whether you received this Pack as a gift, or bought it
for yourself, these stories will help you celebrate this
very special time of year. So relax, put your feet up and
allow our authors to entertain you!

The Editor

LOVE IS
THE KEY

BY

MARY LYONS

MILLS & BOON LIMITED
ETON HOUSE   18-24 PARADISE ROAD
RICHMOND   SURREY   TW9 1SR

*First published in Great Britain 1992
by Mills & Boon Limited*

© Mary Lyons 1992

*Australian copyright 1992
Philippine copyright 1993
This edition 1993*

ISBN 0 263 77807 X

*Set in Times Roman 10½ on 11½ pt.
91-9302-54651 C*

Made and printed in Great Britain

CHAPTER ONE

How could she have been so foolish?

Sitting on a slatted pine bench amid the dense, steamy atmosphere of the dimly lit sauna, Tiffany glumly wiped the perspiration from her face.

If only she'd had the sense to check the date with some of her Portuguese friends, she would never have made the elementary mistake of arriving in Lisbon on the eve of a national holiday. Not that it was a total disaster, of course. But, having only a weekend to explore the old city before continuing her journey to England, she now had to face the fact that most of the important museums and palaces would be closed during Liberation Day—when the citizens of the country celebrated their release from a dictatorship which had ruled Portugal for many years.

To compound her mistake, she hadn't even bothered to book a hotel room. So, it probably served her right, Tiffany told herself gloomily, that all she'd been able to find, on her arrival late yesterday afternoon, had been a very small ground-floor room in a shabby hotel, tucked away in a side-street off one of the main avenues.

Since the whole city seemed to be preparing for the grand processions tomorrow, and with no conducted tours available, the opportunity to have a swim and a sauna in this glamorous health club next door to her hotel had proved to be irresistible.

However, despite looking forward to all the festivities tomorrow, she couldn't shake off her feelings of

deep disappointment and depression. She had hoped
that this trip would mark the beginning of a fresh new
life, but it seemed to Tiffany as if she was still being
hounded by forces beyond her control; the unhappy
trials and tribulations which had dogged her life for
the past few years.

Unfortunately, she couldn't blame anyone for her
first serious error. By running away from home to
marry Brian Harris she had, quite frankly, cooked
her own goose. And when her hasty marriage had
quickly disintegrated—as all her friends and relatives
had accurately forecast that it would—she'd been far
too proud to admit that she'd made a disastrous
mistake.

'When it all goes wrong, don't bother to come
running home,' the elder of her two aunts had told
her sternly. 'Because, as far as we're concerned, you
no longer exist!'

Tiffany had barely listened to the dire warning of
her only relatives. Especially since it was her lonely
'existence' in her elderly aunts' gloomy Victorian
house in Eastbourne—where she had lived since the
death of her parents in an air crash, when she was ten
years of age—which had been the main impetus
behind her decision to run away from home.

As always, when thinking of the death of her
mother and father, Tiffany felt a pang of deep sadness.
In the fourteen years since she'd been left an orphan,
she had never ceased to mourn the loss of her parents'
love and laughter—both so conspicuously absent from
her aunts' austere, harshly controlled way of life. The
boarding-school to which they sent her had been an
equally unfriendly, ugly pile of Victorian archi-
tecture—but at least she'd been able to make some
friends, although none of them had been welcome to

visit her during the holidays. So, was it any wonder that she'd fallen madly and hopelessly in love with the very first glamorous man she'd ever met?

An emotionally starved eighteen-year-old, Tiffany had thought Brian Harris—a minor tennis star, who'd been making a promotional visit to her local town—to be the hero of all her young dreams. Far too young and innocent to see beneath the handsome tanned face and long mahogany legs, so graphically displayed beneath his whiter-than-white tennis shorts, she'd thrown all caution to the winds and followed Brian to London.

The only amazing fact of the whole miserable affair had been why Brian should have taken any notice of the star-struck, foolish young girl. Maybe he'd rather liked being idolised, and treated as though he were a divine being? Whatever the reason, it was now clear to Tiffany that her adoring, naked worship must have acted like soothing ointment to his bruised ego. Because, completely unbeknown to her, Brian's inability to resist the temptations of wine, women and song meant that he was already slipping down the ranks of the world tennis ratings.

However, wildly in love with the man of her dreams, she wouldn't listen to any good advice—not even from her schoolfriends, who were quite capable of seeing through Brian Harris's glamorous façade to the weak, shallow personality beneath.

And, of course, everyone had been quite right. Life on the American tennis circuit was very hard at the best of times—and there had been very little 'best times' about her marriage to Brian. With no permanent home, and always living out of suitcases in second-class hotels, which rapidly became third- and fourth-class hotels as his career continued to decline, their marriage had clearly never stood a chance.

Possibly, if she'd been older and more experienced, Tiffany might have been able to make a success of such a turbulent life. But it was, unfortunately, her total ignorance of sexual matters which had caused the first immediate rift, and from which their relationship had never recovered. Bored by her frightened rigidity and lack of response—and not even prepared to make any allowances for her youth and innocence—Brian had quickly grown tired of his new wife, returning to his old bachelor habits of swift sexual conquests with sophisticated women who, as he'd told her, 'knew how to enjoy a good time'.

How matters would have turned out, or whether Tiffany would have eventually found the strength of will necessary to leave her husband, she never knew.

Two years after their marriage—which was by now well into injury time—Brian had left her alone in a shabby hotel room in the Algarve, in Portugal, to go to a party given by some old friends of his. Deaf to her pleas that it wasn't a good idea—especially before a match due to be played the next day—Brian had been obviously drunk when, returning to the hotel late at night, he'd driven his hired car off the road. Contacted by a local hospital, Tiffany had learned that her husband was in a coma—and not expected to survive the night.

However, for almost a year, Brian had survived. Never regaining consciousness, he had remained a pale, silent figure in the hospital bed, whom Tiffany had visited as often as she could. It wasn't always possible, because the mounting hospital bills meant that she had to take any job she could find. Which meant working in local hotels and cafés to pay the medical expenses, and to keep a temporary roof over her own head.

With the memory of her aunts' last words still ringing in her ears, Tiffany had been far too proud to ask them for any financial help. And when Brian had eventually died without regaining consciousness, she'd barely had time to mourn the tragic loss of her young husband. With no other source of income, she was forced to keep on working, to save enough money for her eventual return to England, where she hoped to train for some form of career.

After a great deal of effort, she had managed to accumulate a small nest-egg. It was just about enough, if she was *very* careful, to enable her to exist for some months before she found a job. However, she hadn't been able to resist dipping into her small savings, and breaking her journey in Lisbon—a city she'd been longing to visit—before taking the plane on to London.

The loud, hissing crackle of cold water being tossed on to hot coals suddenly broke into Tiffany's thoughts. Raising her head and peering through the dense, heavy cloud of steam, she became aware of a shadowy female figure regarding her with a puzzled expression.

Tiffany was sure that she'd never seen the other person before, and yet there was definitely *something* familiar about the woman's face and figure. However, only later, when sitting in front of the mirror in the changing-room, did she discover the answer to her question.

'I always find saunas so *fearfully* exhausting—don't you?' a towel-robed figure drawled some moments later, as she sat down in an adjoining chair.

'Yes, they can be rather tiring,' Tiffany murmured, surprised and relieved to come across someone speaking English, especially as she only knew a few words of Portuguese. 'In fact, I . . .'

But, whatever it was she might have been going to say was instantly forgotten—driven totally from her mind as she raised her head to look at the other girl in the mirror. Like Tiffany, she too was wearing only a towel wrapped around her body with another short white towel swathed about her head.

Open-mouthed with astonishment, Tiffany could only stare bemusedly at the other person who, as far as she could see, might well have been her own twin sister. No wonder the other girl had seemed so familiar—it was virtually the same face she saw every day in her own mirror! The very same wide forehead over arched, fly-away eyebrows; the same clear, translucent blue eyes set in a heart-shaped face.

It was a moment or two before Tiffany realised that the stranger was also rigid with shock, and staring at her with an equally amazed expression. However, the other girl was clearly able to pull herself together faster than Tiffany, as she threw back her head and gave a peal of shrill laughter.

'My God—I simply *don't* believe it!'

'N-no—er—no, neither do I,' Tiffany muttered, shaking her head and closing her eyes for a minute. However, when she opened them again, she could see that there was no escaping the truth: she and this total stranger looked as alike as two peas in a pod!

'I guess the odds against this sort of thing happening must be about a million to one . . . ?' the other girl said slowly, pulling the towel from her head. 'But maybe you've got black hair—or you're a redhead . . . ?'

'No...' Tiffany murmured, still feeling stunned and not really able to believe the evidence of her own eyes as she, too, removed her towel.

'It's difficult to tell when our hair is so wet—but it looks as if yours is only a shade or two darker, and a bit longer than mine!' The girl gave another incredulous laugh. 'They say everyone has a double, somewhere in the world, but I *certainly* never expected to meet her—and in a Portuguese sauna, of all places!'

'No...I...I'm sorry, you must think me a complete fool,' Tiffany mumbled with a helpless shrug. 'I...I can't get over the amazing coincidence. It feels so extraordinarily weird to meet one's double, if you see what I mean...?' she added lamely.

The other girl gave a snort of wry laughter. 'I know *just* what you mean! After all, it's happening to me too—right?'

Tiffany nodded, and made a determined effort to pull herself together. It wasn't an easy task, since she and this stranger didn't just bear such a startling resemblance to one another—she was also considerably shaken to note that their voices sounded quite alike, as well. Although the other girl was obviously English, it seemed as if she also must have spent some time in the United States, since they both had a very slight American drawl overlying their basic British accent.

Quite frankly, this whole affair was beginning to feel definitely spooky! Unless, of course, she was going to wake up in a minute and find that it had all been a bizarre, unnatural dream...?

However, when the other girl put out a hand and suggested that they introduce themselves, there was nothing dreamlike or unearthly about the firm clasp

of her long, slim fingers as she announced that she
was Maxine dos Santos.

'I'm—er—Tiffany Harris,' she replied, almost
sagging with relief at the discovery that their names
were so dissimilar. It would have been just *too much*
for them to have also shared the same name! Slowly
beginning to recover from the shock, Tiffany began
to think that she might be guilty of over-reacting to
the admittedly strange situation.

There was, of course, no question about the fact
that they *were* both remarkably like one another.
However, watching in the mirror as Maxine began to
comb her blonde hair, Tiffany gradually began to
notice the differences between them. Leaving aside the
colour of their hair, she could now see that Maxine's
teeth were a little more pointed than her own; that
the curve of her mouth when she smiled was a tighter,
more controlled version of her own broad grin. And
while it might be her imagination, of course, there
did seem to be a hard, somewhat speculative gleam
in Maxine's blue eyes, which were now regarding her
so intently in the mirror.

'Well, Tiffany, I guess this is a once-in-a-lifetime
experience, for us both!' Maxine gave another shrill,
high-pitched laugh. 'If you're not in a tearing hurry,
and since there's no one else in here,' she added, with
a quick glance around the changing-room, 'Why don't
you tell me something about yourself? Have you been
in Portugal long, for instance? It sounds as though
you've spent some time in America—but maybe
you're now a resident in this country?'

'No, I'm really just here in Lisbon for a short visit,'
Tiffany began hesitantly. However, the other girl appeared to be so interested and understanding that she
found herself telling Maxine all about her past, and

that she was now on her way back to England, where she hoped to start a new life.

'I don't blame you for giving your old aunts the heave-ho!' Maxine grinned. 'But surely you must have some other relatives in England? Or someone who's looking forward to seeing you again?'

However, when she'd learned that Tiffany had no other relatives at all, the other girl was very sympathetic. Explaining that she was also on her own in Portugal, staying in her husband's old family home in Sintra, Maxine urged Tiffany to come and spend the weekend with her.

'That's very kind of you, but I'm afraid that I've already booked into a nearby hotel,' Tiffany said, explaining how she'd been lucky to find even the small ground-floor room when the city seemed so full of visitors.

'Well, you'd better take good care of your passport. During the holiday, there's bound to be a lot of pickpockets on the streets,' Maxine warned her, nodding in approval when Tiffany replied that she'd left her passport, traveller's cheques and her plane ticket to England in the hotel safe.

A moment later, Maxine glanced up at a clock on the wall and gave a shriek of dismay. 'Heavens—I've got to go! I must make an important phone call, and then call at my bank. Since tomorrow is a bank holiday, there's no chance of it being open again until Monday,' she explained, hurriedly rising to her feet. 'Look, I don't know what you have in mind for the rest of the day—but why don't I come by your hotel, in a couple of hours' time, and we can go out for a drink and an evening meal?' she added, undoing her locker and quickly getting dressed.

'Yes—er—I'd like that,' Tiffany murmured politely, although she wasn't *entirely* sure that she wanted to spend too much time in Maxine's company.

The startling resemblance between them was having a slightly eerie, peculiar effect on her. Although Maxine had been very friendly, Tiffany instinctively felt that she had nothing in common with the older, far more sophisticated girl, who was apparently married to a Brazilian aristocrat—a man whom, it seemed, she actively disliked.

Very conscious of her own shortcomings during her brief marriage to Brian, and despite having travelled about the world on the tennis circuit, Tiffany had been shocked to hear the other girl's bald statement: that she'd only married her husband for his money.

'Actually, darling, I was in a bit of a hole at the time,' Maxine had drawled. 'So it seemed quite a good idea to marry one of the richest men in São Paulo. But it's all been a ghastly mistake,' and she'd shrugged her shoulders.

Tiffany, trying to disguise her discomfiture at what the other girl was saying, was even more shocked when Maxine revealed how she'd managed to trap her husband.

'I told him I was expecting his child—and he, poor fool, fell for the oldest trick in the book!' She gave a shrill laugh, brushing her blonde hair into a swirling cloud about her head. 'And since Zarco is stupid enough to believe in the sanctity of marriage—he's well and truly stuck, isn't he? So, we've come to an arrangement whereby he keeps me in the lap of luxury, and we hardly see anything of each other,' she added with another cruel, spiteful laugh.

It was obvious to Tiffany that this woman who so resembled her physically was not at all a nice person.

However, since she could hardly refuse to have a drink with her, she meekly agreed to meet Maxine some hours later, giving the other girl the name and address of her hotel.

Trying to overcome her natural distaste at the way Maxine had talked about her husband, Tiffany had almost made up her mind to find a convenient excuse to avoid the other girl. However, when she returned to her hotel after another swim in the heated pool, she rapidly changed her mind.

Her hotel bedroom had been *completely* ransacked!

Totally stunned at finding all her clothes piled in the middle of the floor, and covered with sticky blue paint, it wasn't until she heard the sounds of hysterical screams from the adjoining bedrooms that she realised she wasn't the only one to suffer such a misfortune.

It appeared that the hotel safe had also been broken into, and it wasn't long before Tiffany realised she was in deep, *deep* trouble. Not only had three ground-floor bedrooms been vandalised—but her passport, traveller's cheques and aeroplane ticket were missing from the safe!

Some of the other guests had also lost their travel documents, and the screams of rage and fury—not to mention a Spanish lady who immediately lapsed into raving hysterics—left Tiffany feeling mentally bruised and exhausted. It was at this point that Maxine had come to her rescue.

It was some moments before she recognised the girl standing in the hotel doorway. Why Maxine should be wearing a short black wig she had no idea, but she *did* know that she'd never been so relieved to see someone, in all her life.

'Thank God you've come!' Tiffany gasped, hurrying across the small foyer of the hotel to place a trembling hand on the other girl's arm. 'I didn't recognise you for a moment, but...'

Maxine grinned and patted the deep fringe of her false black hair. 'It was so peculiar, the two of us looking so alike,' she told Tiffany. 'So, I thought it might be easier if I changed my appearance. What on earth's going on?' she added, staring over at the noisy crowd of wildly gesticulating people by the reception desk.

'It's a total disaster,' Tiffany told her gloomily, sinking down in to a nearby chair, and burying her face in her hands.

'Oh, come on—it can't be that bad, surely?'

Tiffany shook her head disconsolately. 'It's worse!' she groaned. 'Not only has some sneak thief broken into three of the downstairs bedrooms—one of which was mine—but some of us have also been robbed of our passports and money. And that isn't all...' She brushed a distracted hand through her long gold hair. 'All my clothes have been vandalised. In fact, I've nothing but this tracksuit I'm wearing—and a small amount of money in my purse which, luckily, I had with me at the sauna.'

Tiffany didn't know what she would have done without Maxine's help. The other girl was simply marvellous, quickly appreciating the problems involved with the loss of her travel documents.

'You'll have to notify the police and the British Embassy too, of course. But there's no point in your hanging around here. You might as well come and sort out all your problems, in the comfort of my home,' she'd said firmly, leading the bewildered girl

out of the hotel towards a large chauffeur-driven car
which was waiting outside.

'But what about my underclothes and my make-up,
and——?'

'That's absolutely no problem,' Maxine assured
Tiffany as she helped her into the limousine. 'We can
come back and sort out everything after the weekend.
As far as clothes are concerned, you and I are just
about the same size, and I've got masses of things
which I've hardly worn,' she added persuasively,
giving Tiffany a warm, friendly smile as the vehicle
began moving off down the street.

'I really don't want to impose on you...'

'Believe me—it's definitely no imposition!' Maxine
laughed. 'I've been very lonely up at that old house
in Sintra, haven't I, Tony?' she asked the chauffeur.

'Yep—you sure have!' he replied, barely turning his
dark head surmounted by a grey cap, as he steered
the car through the busy streets.

Tiffany couldn't see much of the man who was
driving, but she was surprised to discover that he
clearly wasn't Portuguese. As far as she could tell, the
chauffeur came from somewhere not a million miles
from Brooklyn.

Seeing her surprise, Maxine gave one of her shrill
laughs. 'I wouldn't be without dear Tony for the
world! When I travel, he acts as my chauffeur and
general factotum. That's right, isn't it, Tony?' she
added with a giggle.

'You're the boss, lady!' he agreed in a nasal drawl.
'All the way to Sintra, huh?'

'You got it!' Maxine giggled again, the heavy
amusement in her voice and the slightly feverish,
sparkling glint in her blue eyes making Tiffany feel
rather uncomfortable.

Relax! Just be grateful for small mercies, she lectured herself sternly. Or large ones, in this case, she amended quickly, wondering what she would have done without Maxine's generous help. Settling back in the soft, luxurious leather seat, she tried to forget her worries as the vehicle left the city, speeding along the motorway towards Sintra.

The summer residence of the old Kings of Portugal, and of the Moorish rulers of Lisbon before them, Sintra seemed to be a magical place of romantic green, wooded ravines. As they approached the town, Tiffany's eyes widened at the sight of the ornate palaces and monasteries clinging to the sheer cliffs of the mountain range, with shady paths leading to wide green parks which, at this time of year, seemed to be filled with huge clumps of flowering camellias.

However, she hadn't realised that Sintra was so far away from the centre of Lisbon. When she mentioned as much to Maxine, her new friend pooh-poohed the idea that it might make difficulties in obtaining a new passport.

'With the public holiday tomorrow, which is a Friday, you haven't a hope of replacing all your documents until after the weekend,' Maxine assured her as the large limousine left the narrow streets of Sintra behind them. 'So, why don't we have a lazy weekend, possibly visiting one or two of the local sights, and then I'll get on the phone for you first thing on Monday morning?'

With a slight sigh, Tiffany realised that there was nothing she could do about the situation. And in fact, she reminded herself once again, she ought to be thanking her lucky stars that she'd been so fortunate to meet Maxine this morning.

When they arrived at the Quinta dos Santos, she could hardly believe her eyes. Maxine had referred to her house as a 'villa'—but she thought it looked more like a small palace!

'Hideous old pile!' Maxine grumbled as they got out of the car. And when Tiffany enthused about the pale faded apricot-coloured walls of the classical mansion, her new friend just shrugged her shoulders.

'Although my husband, Zarco, had a Brazilian father, his mother was Portuguese. This *Quinta* was her old family home, and when her husband died she returned to live here until her own death over five years ago. The house has been uninhabited ever since.' Maxine pulled a face as she opened the front door. 'So, I'd better warn you that it's a bit grim inside.'

'But it's fantastic!' Tiffany gasped as she stood in the centre of the hall, admiring an enormous tapestry, the colours of which seemed almost as bright today, as when it was woven many hundreds of years ago.

'Wait until you see the salon,' Maxine warned her, leading the way through wide double doors in to a much larger, if somewhat darker room. 'This place gives me the creeps,' she added over her shoulder as she went over to pull open the heavy, deep rich velvet curtains across the wide arched windows.

'Would you like me to remove the dust sheets from the furniture?' Tiffany asked, surprised that it hadn't already been done. 'That might help to make you feel more comfortable here.'

Maxine shrugged. 'I haven't bothered, mostly because I can't see anything making much difference to this dump. But removing those gloomy sheets might make it feel slightly more homely,' she agreed carelessly. 'Anyway, make yourself at home, and I'll fix us a drink in a few minutes. I've just got to put this away,' she added, indicating the large wicker basket which she'd been firmly clutching since they'd entered the house. 'I won't be a minute.'

Wandering idly around the room, Tiffany tried to understand the other girl's dislike of what was, for her, a truly lovely house. Everyone couldn't be expected to share the same tastes, and it was silly to feel disappointed at Maxine's jaundiced view of this charming room, she told herself firmly. By the time her new friend had rejoined her, Tiffany had swept away the sheeting from the elegant Portuguese furniture, and was idly studying a group of silver-framed photographs on a large table.

'I've made you a nice stiff gin and tonic—OK?' Maxine said, coming to a halt beside her with the two glasses in her hands. 'Oh, my God, just *look* at some of those old pictures—aren't they a hoot?' she said, handing Tiffany a drink.

'Some of the women's dresses do look a little old-fashioned,' Tiffany agreed. 'But who's this?' she asked, picking up a more recent photograph. 'I must say, he looks daunting!'

Maxine gave a shrill, caustic laugh. 'He does, doesn't he? And although they say the camera doesn't lie—I can assure you that Zarco is *far* worse in person! Yes,' she added as Tiffany turned to look at her in surprise, 'that's a picture of my *dear* husband. He must have given it to his old mother, just before she died.'

Having been thoroughly shocked by the other girl's cynical remarks about her peculiar-sounding marriage—how could anyone bring themselves to marry a man, just because he was extremely wealthy?— Tiffany didn't like to comment any further. But she couldn't prevent her eyes being drawn towards the

strong, handsome features of the man in the photograph. It was almost uncanny, the way that the photographer had managed to capture such force and
strength from his subject, and for the rest of the day
those dark fiery eyes seemed to follow her whenever
she was in the room.

Later that night, while drifting off to sleep in one
of the villa's palatial bedrooms, Tiffany tried to make
some sense of what was clearly a rather unusual
household.

First of all, there was this really very large and
beautiful house, which didn't seem to have any servants at all—other than the chauffeur, Tony, whom
Maxine had rather vaguely intimated she'd brought
with her from America. And there was no doubt of
Tony's nationality. If anyone had asked her, Tiffany
would have immediately said that he reminded her of
some Mafia hoodlum. In fact, if it weren't too ridiculous, she could easily imagine him making her 'an
offer she couldn't refuse'! However, since she'd had
no experience of chauffeurs, she was hardly in a position to judge, she told herself sleepily. Whatever her
reservations about Maxine herself, there was no doubt
that without the other girl's timely rescue from the
hotel in Lisbon goodness knows where she would have
spent tonight. Certainly not in this supremely
comfortable bed.

However, she felt distinctly ill when Maxine woke
her the next morning, at the late hour of eleven
o'clock.

'I feel *dreadful*!' Tiffany moaned, putting a trembling hand to her aching head, her mind feeling extraordinarily thick and sluggish, as if she'd been drugged,
or had drunk too much. Which was ridiculous, of
course, since she'd only had one glass of red wine at

supper. However, it took her some time to focus her eyes on the other girl, who was placing a steaming cup of coffee down on the bedside table.

Although her brain felt as if it were stuffed full of cotton wool, she couldn't help wondering why Maxine was still wearing that hideous black wig. However, as her new friend pointed out, it might help to make them feel less strange with one another.

And she was quite right, Tiffany acknowledged some hours later. Although she was still feeling faintly muzzy in the head, she'd welcomed Maxine's suggestion that a breath of fresh air would do them both some good.

'I thought you might like to see Cabo da Roca before we go back to the villa. There's a lighthouse on the edge of the cliff, overlooking the sea, where you can buy a certificate to say that you've been to the ''most Western point of Europe''!'

'That sounds fun.' Tiffany tore her eyes away from the passing scenery, watching as Maxine leaned forward to tap Tony on the shoulder—indicating that he should take the road lying between the vineyards of windswept sandy soil, rolling away towards the Atlantic Ocean. The awful wig, with its deep fringe hiding Maxine's wide brow, was very effective in removing the rather weird, uncanny feeling Tiffany had felt yesterday every time she'd gazed at the other girl's face.

It was yet another kind and thoughtful gesture on Maxine's part, she reminded herself—like the other girl's generous provision of one of her own dresses, and some costume jewellery, which Tiffany was wearing at this very minute.

Goodness knows, it was *years* since she'd worn a dress of this quality...not since her parents were alive.

Simply cut in a classic style, it was made from fine sapphire-blue silk which exactly matched her eyes. Relishing the feel of the soft material against her skin, Tiffany reminded herself once again of just how fortunate she was to have met Maxine. Even the elegant Ferragamo shoes fitted her feet to perfection. She knew that she wouldn't have been human if she hadn't revelled in the sheer luxury of such clothes, which she couldn't hope to be able to buy herself.

'Here we are—there's the lighthouse!' Maxine called out, her unnaturally tense, excited voice cutting into Tiffany's thoughts. 'Let's get out and take a walk along the cliff,' her new friend added as Tony brought the car to a halt.

'I'm...I'm not very good with heights, I'm afraid,' Tiffany muttered, shivering in the fresh sea breeze.

But it seemed her new friend was determined that she should view the sight of the ocean, pounding against the rocks many hundreds of feet below the cliff.

'Don't be so *stupid*!' Maxine exclaimed in a hard voice, her fingers tightening around Tiffany's slim arm as she practically dragged the girl's reluctant figure towards the edge of the cliff.

'Let me go!' Tiffany protested, suddenly gasping with fright as Tony materialised beside her, clasping hold of her other arm. 'What's going on? What are you doing?'

Tony gave an evil, spine-chilling laugh at her pathetic attempts to wriggle free of his hard grip. 'Don't worry, kid—I can guarantee you won't feel a thing!'

'Wait—*you fool*!' Maxine hissed urgently. 'We've got to change the wedding-rings—remember?'

But before her sluggish, drugged mind could even begin to understand what was happening to her,

Tiffany felt a sudden, heavy blow on the back of her head. And a brief fraction of a second later, she was falling . . . spinning down and down into an infinitely deep, dark void.

She was submerged—floating in a black swirling sea—living and breathing, but somehow protected from the world by a distant and hazy barrier of light and life.

A far-away light seemed to call to her, urging her up towards the surface of awareness. But as she became increasingly more buoyant there were many times when the encouraging light seemed to be blotted out by a dark presence. She had a strong sensation of menace and danger, which instinctively caused her to recoil, and once more sink back down into the comfortable darkness.

But eventually the light seemed to be pulling her through a long tunnel, and she rose up into a world of acute discomfort and pain.

The heat of the light seemed to be burning through her eyelids, which felt heavy as lead as she struggled to force them open. And yet, when she did so, her dazed and groggy vision saw that the space was illuminated by just one small lamp—the rest of the unfamiliar space hidden in shadowy darkness.

Trying to adjust her body into a more comfortable position, she gave a muffled groan at the sharp pain in her head, and she became aware not only of a throbbing, pounding ache in her brain—but that she was not alone in the dimly lit room.

'W-where . . . where am I? Who's there . . . ?' she mumbled fearfully, suddenly feeling frightened and threatened by an unknown, alien presence. There was a long silence before she heard the sound of a heavy sigh, her dazed blue eyes widening as a tall, dark figure emerged from the shadows and walked slowly towards her.

The man stood looking down at the girl, whose hair was completely hidden by the thick bandage wound about her head. His body seemed immensely tall—huge and threatening as he towered over her supine, trembling figure. Her first overriding impressions in the faint light were of a barely leashed force; of tautly controlled anger in the tanned face staring so sternly down at her, the dark eyes glinting with unmistakable scorn and contempt.

'Who...who are you? W-what do you want...?' she whispered fearfully, her body trembling and her eyelids fluttering with terror in the face of such obvious malevolence.

'You know very well who I am. Who better?' he growled savagely, before giving an abrupt bark of cruel laughter. 'God knows what you've been up to, Maxine. However, after such a long and tiring journey from Brazil, I am decidedly *not* in the mood to play games!'

Another quick, fleeting glance at the stranger did little to reassure her—nor did it dispel the formidable sense of intimidation and oppressively strong physical threat embodied in his powerful frame. The dim light from the lamp threw deep shadows over his hard, arrogant expression, highlighting the few silver threads amid the midnight-black colour of his hair; the deeply hooded lids over those terrifying dark eyes emphasising the high cheekbones of his tanned face, and the cruel curve of his sensual lips.

'P-please...please go away!' she whispered, certain that she had never felt so frightened in all her life. The deep throbbing in her head seemed to reach an almost unbearable crescendo, and as she saw him raise a threatening hand something seemed to snap in her injured brain. A low, helpless moan issued from her lips as she lapsed back into the welcoming darkness.

The man froze, his brows drawn together in a deep frown as he stood motionless for a moment. And then he lowered his hand, to carry out his original intention of straightening the rumpled sheet over the slender, deathly still figure of the girl, who was now lying unconscious in the narrow hospital bed.

CHAPTER TWO

WHEN Tiffany next opened her eyes, it was to find herself staring up at a white ceiling, dazzled by its reflection of the bright sunlight flooding into the room.

Her brief groan as she tried to adjust her eyes to the glare provoked an immediate response. She was aware of a soft murmur, and of cool fingers being placed over the pulse in her wrist. As her eyes became slowly acclimatised to the daylight, she gazed uncomprehendingly about her. Dazed and disorientated, she knew she didn't recognise the bare walls of the room, or the stark blinds at the windows. And then a sharp pain as she tried to move her head obliterated any other desire to explore her surroundings.

A few moments later, her vision was filled by the sight of an unknown man's face looming over her. He appeared to be saying something and she strained to catch his words. But she couldn't understand him—not even when he began speaking slowly.

'What . . . ? Where . . . ?' Her lips felt rubbery, too dry and stiff to pronounce the words properly. 'Water . . . ? Please can I have a glass of water?' she whispered helplessly.

'*Inglês* . . . ? You speak English?' The man, whom she now saw was wearing a white coat, gave a slight shrug and turned to speak to someone outside the range of her vision. 'Very well, *senhora*. You want a drink of water, yes?' he asked, in a thick foreign accent.

'Yes ... please,' she mumbled as, again speaking some incomprehensible language, he gestured to a white-clothed figure who materialised on the other side of the bed.

'But ... but where am I? What is this place?' she gasped as a woman held out a glass towards her.

Trying to lift her head to place her lips on the edge of the glass, she groaned at the sharp pain which zig-zagged cruelly through her aching brain. The blackness seemed to be threatening to close in on her once again, swirling mists of agony blanking out the sound of the man's voice, until the painful sledge-hammer in her head began to quieten down into a dull, pounding throb.

'You are in hospital, *senhora*,' the man told her. 'And you must lie still. Not to move—do you understand?'

'Yes,' she whispered. With closed eyes she lay back on the soft pillows, trying to think why she should be in a hospital.

Some moments later she opened her eyes again, focusing with difficulty on the features of the man who was still standing beside the bed. 'Are you a doctor?' she asked, not finding anything familiar about the dark-haired, slightly sallow face which was now gazing down at her so intently. 'And, if this is a hospital—what am I doing here?'

'You do not understand anything about the accident?' he queried, again speaking English with a heavy accent which she did not recognise.

'No—I don't—er—I don't seem to be able to remember anything about an accident,' she murmured helplessly. 'And ... and whereabouts *is* this hospital?'

'You are in Lisbon, of course.'

'*Lisbon*?' She winced as another agonising, jagged shaft of pain sliced through her head. 'Do you mean Lisbon—as in . . . in Portugal?'

The doctor frowned down at the pale, heart-shaped face of the girl in the bed, whose head was swathed with bandages. He flicked his fingers at the nurse, who hurriedly handed him a chart from the end of the bed.

'Ah, yes. I see that you were brought in by the Guarda Nacional Republicana, three days ago.' And when she continued to stare up at him uncomprehendingly, he added, 'The police—you understand? They are wishing to see you about the accident, up at Sintra. And your husband, also. He has been most . . .' The doctor paused, apparently hunting for a word from his limited English vocabulary. 'Most anxious . . . yes, your husband has been most anxious to talk to you.'

'My husband?'

The doctor smiled down at her. 'Senhor Marquês dos Santos has been most worried about you. Many, many times he has been here, while you have been unconscious. So, he will be pleased to hear that you are awake, yes?'

Slowly she raised a trembling hand towards her bandaged head, which was now throbbing with painful intensity.

'I don't understand. I don't remember. Why am I here?' she moaned. 'I'm sure I'm not married—at least I don't think I am . . . ?'

'*Esteja quieta*! Be still, *senhora*. There is no need to worry. You have been very ill—but soon you will see your husband, and all will be well. But for now,' he added, before turning to the nurse and giving rapid instructions in Portuguese, 'I think it is time you had a good sleep. Do not worry. You will feel much better when you wake up.'

She would have protested further, but, following the sharp prick of a hypodermic needle in her arm, all protest seemed to die on her lips, and she once again drifted back into the warm, comforting darkness.

When she awoke again, she realised it must be evening, since the room was only lit by two pale lamps, and the windows seemed shrouded in darkness beyond their half-closed blinds.

It was the bustling presence of a young, dark-haired nurse which had brought her back to full consciousness, she realised, and was grateful for the girl's gentle care as she helped to raise her sore head, so that she could drink some water. But when the nurse said something in a language she didn't understand, she realised that it hadn't been a dream. She really was lying in a hospital in Portugal. Although how she came to be here, she still had no idea.

'I do not understand. *Je ne comprends pas*,' she added, in the vain hope that the nurse might understand her schoolgirl French. But it was clearly no use, as they both stared blankly at one another. 'I want to see the doctor,' she said as slowly and clearly as she could.

'*Médico*?' the nurse queried, and, when she nodded carefully in agreement, so as not to increase the background throbbing in her head, the other girl nodded and hurried from the room.

However, when the nurse returned, she was not accompanied by the doctor whom she'd seen earlier in the day, but by a taller, somewhat older man in uniform.

'I hear you've been asking for the doctor, Dona dos Santos,' he said in English, with a slight accent. 'But if you feel well enough, there are one or two important questions I would like to ask you.'

'Thank goodness you can speak English!' she murmured, almost sagging with the relief of at last being able to find out what had happened. 'I've been so confused. I mean, I've no idea why I'm here, in this hospital—or what I'm doing in Portugal, for that matter.' She gave him a weak, tremulous smile and raised a hand to her aching brow. 'I think there must be some mistake. Maybe they've got the names muddled up? Because I don't know why everyone keeps calling me "Dona dos Santos". That isn't my name.'

The man regarded her with his head on one side for a moment. 'Very well,' he said patiently, as if to a rather dim-witted child. 'What *is* your name?'

'My name is...' She frowned, staring down at the sheet for a moment. Why did her mind seem to be like a completely blank piece of paper? Telling herself not to be silly, and that it was important for her to concentrate on this minor problem, she tried again.

'This is so stupid, because of course my name is... My name is...' She raised frightened blue eyes towards the man standing beside the bed. 'I... *I can't remember*,' she whispered, a rising tide of panic beginning to flow through her body. '*I can't remember—anything*!'

'Don't worry, I'm sure everything will start coming back to you, very soon,' he said soothingly, as he opened a breast pocket of his uniform to extract a pad and pencil. 'Maybe you can recall what happened, up at Sintra?'

'No.'

'Or why you were there?'

'No—I told you, I don't seem to be able to remember *anything*!' she cried breathlessly, her whole
body trembling with a numb sense of terror.

'Well—er—I will come back later,' he said hurriedly, looking up with relief as the door of the room
opened and the doctor entered, followed a few moments later by a very tall, broad-shouldered man.
There was a rapid conversation, in what she gathered
must be Portuguese, between the doctor and the
policeman, after which the white-coated doctor turned
to stare frowningly down at her.

'I understand you do not remember? Not even your
name . . . ?'

'No—no, I don't!' she cried fearfully, placing
shaking fingers at the side of her aching temples. 'I
just *know* that I'm not this "Dona dos Santos"—
whoever she might be.'

'*She* happens to be my wife!'

She tried to turn her head towards the tall figure
standing by the door—just on the periphery of her
vision. And then, as he moved slowly across the room,
she had her first clear sight of the menacing figure
who had caused her to feel such terror last night.

Now that she was able to view him more clearly,
the stranger's arrogant, tanned face and powerful
body did nothing to dispel her first nightmarish impression of the man. There was still the same physical
aura of spine-chilling menace about his tall figure,
and she knew with an absolute and total certainty that
she was not, and never had been, his wife.

Trying to shrink down beneath the covers, she gazed
fearfully up at the man. His dark, heavy-lidded eyes
were now empty of all expression as he viewed the
girl's pale, frightened face beneath the heavy mound

of bandages about her head; her slender figure now visibly shaking in the narrow hospital bed.

He seemed *so* tall! Although maybe it wasn't just his height and the width of his broad shoulders which made him appear to dwarf the other two men in the room. It was also something to do with the sheer force and power of his personality which, although he was still standing and regarding her in silence, seemed to radiate out to encompass them all. Even the policeman seemed to have shrunk a little, glancing deferentially at the man who appeared to so effortlessly dominate the room.

As her eyes flicked nervously over his hair, as dark as night and worn slightly long, curling over the pure silk collar of his immaculate white shirt, she found herself longing to be able to return to the peace and tranquillity of her unconscious state.

Everything about this man, from his obviously expensive, hand-tailored lightweight suit to the heavy gold cuff-links and the discreet glint of the diamonds on his equally heavy gold Rolex Oyster watch—clearly visible as he raised a tanned hand to check the time—appeared to shriek of wealth and privilege. What was such a man doing here in the hospital? He couldn't *seriously* be claiming that she was his wife...?

But it seemed that he was.

'Yes, this is indeed my wife.' The strange man's perfect English—clearly spoken for her benefit—sounded clipped and cool. Only a faint accent underlying the dark, rich tones of his voice betrayed his foreign origin.

The policeman turned towards her, raising a quizzical eyebrow. 'And do you, *senhora*, now wish to agree that this is your husband?'

'No... no, I don't!' she protested. 'I've never seen this man before in my life. Well, only very briefly, last night,' she added quickly. 'I can't possibly be married to someone and not know it, can I?' she begged the doctor tearfully. 'Especially not someone who's Portuguese——'

'Brazilian!' her so-called husband snapped irritably.

'But... but that's ridiculous!' she gasped. '*Brazil*? I know that I've never... I've never been to South America—and *certainly* not to Brazil. I mean... I don't even know what language they speak there or... or anything about the country,' she added lamely, flinching back against the pillows as the man who was claiming to be her husband threw her a scorching glance of contempt and dislike from beneath his heavy lids.

'I think it is time to call a halt to this farce!' he ground out angrily, before turning to the other two men. 'I can assure you that this *is* my wife. Unfortunately, while I do not know why she should deny the fact, I am sure that after I've had a few private words with her this simple matter can be sorted out,' he added dismissively with a shrug of his broad shoulders.

'Please help me!' she appealed to the doctor, helpless tears flooding her blue eyes as she realised that she was, somehow, trapped in what seemed to be a living nightmare.

'*Senhora* ...'

'I really *don't* know this man!' she wailed. 'I've never seen him before in my life, and... and if I could only just remember my *own* name, I'd be able to prove it!' she cried, wincing at the pain in her head, and unable to prevent the weak tears from trickling down her soft cheeks.

'*Manten-te descansada*... Don't worry, *senhora*...' the doctor murmured, before putting a hand on the tall man's arm, and drawing him away from the bed towards a corner of the room, where they were joined by the policeman.

Almost drowning in misery, she was barely aware of the low-voiced, rapid conversation between the three men. It was only when the man they all regarded as her husband gave an exclamation of anger, and was answered firmly and slowly by the doctor, that she could make a guess as to what he'd been saying.

The word 'amnesia' seemed to be the same in both languages, although it took her a few moments to understand just what the doctor meant. She must have hurt her head at some stage, she realised, slowly raising her hands to the crêpe bandages wound so tightly about her head. Did she *really* have amnesia? Could she have lost her memory? Was that why she didn't know this terrifying man? But if so, why was she totally certain that she wasn't married to him?

Her head was really aching with a vengeance, when the doctor broke away and came over to the bed.

'It is very likely that the blow on your head has given you what we call temporary amnesia,' he said, speaking slowly so that she could understand what he was saying. 'A patient with a head injury, such as yours, can lose their memory for a short time. But it will return,' he assured her earnestly.

'When? When will I get my memory back?'

He shrugged. 'That is difficult to say. Maybe soon— maybe a few weeks. Maybe longer,' he added with a frown. 'But yes, it will return.'

If it means being married to that awful, terrifying man, I hope it *never* comes back! she thought hysterically, only just beginning to comprehend what was happening to her. And then she panicked, thrown into increasing terror and confusion as the tall Brazilian announced that he wished to be alone with his wife for a moment.

'Please . . . please don't leave me!' she whispered, feverishly clutching at the sleeve of the doctor's white coat.

'Ah, *senhora*, there is no need to be afraid,' he murmured, giving her hand a kindly pat, before gently removing her fingers. 'Your husband just wishes to have some words with you. I am sure he will be kind and . . . how do you say? . . . he will be understanding, yes?'

She very much doubted whether that man had *ever* been kind or understanding in his whole life! He certainly didn't hold those sentiments towards *her*! Despite being ashamed of feeling so weak and helpless, there was nothing she could do to prevent the tears from falling again as the doctor and the policeman left the room.

There was a long silence before the Brazilian walked slowly towards the bed. As she glanced fearfully up at the man looming over her, she was surprised when he merely shook his head, and handed her a large clean white handkerchief.

'I have to hand it to you, Maxine. I never realised what a consummate actress you were!' His rich dark voice was heavy with contempt, echoing the gleaming scorn in his dark eyes. 'However, kindly dry your tears, because I think this foolishness has gone far enough, don't you?'

'I'm *not* Maxine,' she protested, noisily blowing her nose before drawing on her pathetically small reserves of strength to add, 'and I *really* don't know you. I'm quite sure that we've never met—let alone been married to one another. And . . . and it's no good jabbering away at me in a foreign language, either,' she wailed as he swore violently under his breath. 'I simply don't know what you are talking about!'

He stood staring grimly down at the tearful girl for some moments, his face darkening with anger as he clearly strove to contain his temper. And then, when he once again had himself under control, he gave a heavy sigh and shrugged his shoulders.

'Very well, Maxine. You can continue this farce as long as you like,' he told her bitterly. 'However, I think you'll find that you are making a grave mistake. The police want to know what *really* happened out at Cabo da Roca? You were very lucky that a visitor to the lighthouse saw you struggling with a man and woman, and sounded the alarm before they could throw you over the cliff. And, incidentally,' he drawled with silky menace, 'I'd be interested to know exactly what you were doing there, too.'

'I don't know!' she moaned helplessly. 'I've never heard of this Cabo da Roca—and I've no idea what you're talking about!'

'Well, that's a matter for you and the police to sort out, isn't it?' The dangerous, threatening tone in his dark voice sent shivers of apprehension fluttering down her spine as she gazed helplessly back at him.

'However,' he continued, 'what does concern me is, why you are here in Portugal? As you know, we have an arrangement that you will remain at my house in England during term-time, while Carlos is at school. So, why have you broken our agreement?'

'I keep telling you . . . I don't know what you're talking about,' she moaned. 'And who is Carlos, anyway?'

'Please stop this ridiculous nonsense!' he hissed angrily. 'You may have fooled the doctor with this so-called amnesia—but you certainly haven't fooled *me*! Besides my religion, you know very well that the only reason we stayed married—a marriage which enables you to retain your enviable lifestyle—is solely because of the arrangement regarding my son, Carlos!'

She looked at him in bewilderment. 'A son? We have a child?'

'Do not try my patience too far!' he warned, his voice heavy with menace. 'And do not insult my son— nor the memory of his mother, my first and most beloved wife!'

'I didn't mean . . . I didn't know . . .' she whispered tearfully.

He gave a harsh snort of contemptuous laughter. 'All that is in the past—it is the present that now concerns us. You can rest assured that, even if the police fail to discover *exactly* what you were doing in Portugal, I most surely shall not! And when I do,' he purred dangerously, turning away with a scathing, scornful glance from beneath his heavy lids, 'I have a feeling that you will be very, *very* sorry indeed!'

And then he was gone, the room suddenly still and silent as the door clicked quietly shut behind his departing figure.

The next few days seemed to pass in a blur as she was subjected to exhaustive tests. Physically she appeared to be in reasonably good shape. As the doctor had pointed out, other than the wound at the back of her head, which had required a number of stitches, and the bruises on her face—which had apparently occurred when she'd fallen forward to the ground—she appeared to be in very good health. The stitches in her head had required the removal of some of her long hair. 'But it will grow again,' the doctor had told her with a reassuring smile.

'I . . . I don't even know what I look like,' she told him helplessly. 'I mean . . . I'm trapped inside this person—about whom I know absolutely nothing! I think I ought to take a look at myself, don't you?' she added with a weak smile.

'Why not? I do not see it can do any harm,' he agreed, before leaving the room and returning a few moments later with a small mirror, obviously the possession of one of the nurses.

Despite having wanted to see what she *really* looked like, she hesitated fearfully for a moment, taking a deep breath before raising the mirror. The first thing she saw was the large gauze bandage about her head, and then the faint bruising near her mouth and across her nose.

Almost instinctively, she raised a hand to a thick tendril of hair, the rich colour of old gold. Well, at least she did have *some* hair left, she told herself, even if, on further examination, it looked as if someone had attacked it with a pair of garden shears.

Staring at her face for a long time didn't seem to help. Was this really her? The pale, heart-shaped face with its high cheekbones and wide brow didn't seem particularly familiar. As she studied herself further, it appeared that her eyebrows were a slightly darker shade than her hair, arching in a graceful sweep towards her temples over wide, clear blue eyes with thick brown lashes. But she couldn't help noticing the anxious tremble in her full lower lip.

With a heavy sigh, she let the mirror fall from her hands on to the sheet. It was no good. She *really* had no memory of that face. In fact, it might well have been a stranger staring back at her with such fear and nervous tension.

However, while the doctor and his colleagues were not worried about her physical health, they did seem to be concerned about the state of her mind. When it became clear that she had no knowledge of Portuguese, she received a visit from an eminent psychoanalyst, who informed her that he was attending the hospital on behalf of her husband.

'I am informed by Senhor Marquês dos Santos that you should have a good working knowledge of the Portuguese language,' the gentleman informed her, settling himself comfortably down on a chair beside the bed. 'Although with a Brazilian accent, of course,' he added with a twinkling smile.

She had at first been determined to have nothing to do with this man, especially since he'd been engaged by her so-called husband. But the kindly light in his eyes and the sympathetic, concerned way in which he treated the problem, softened her attitude towards him.

'I don't know any way to prove I *don't* know how to speak your language,' she told him with a helpless shrug. 'In fact, although nobody seems to believe me, I don't know anything about this woman "Maxine". All I *do* know is that I feel quite certain that's not my name. And... and if I'd been called that all my life—surely that's the one thing which *would* be familiar?' she added with a puzzled frown.

'Not necessarily, no. It is quite possible for someone to completely forget who she is, and all trace of her past life,' he told her, taking a large pad of paper from his briefcase. 'Do you mind if I make some notes?'

'Go ahead. Everyone else in this hospital seems to be having a field day, at my expense!' she told him bitterly.

Calmly disregarding her outburst, he merely gave her another sympathetic smile and made a note on the pad.

'Who am I?' she demanded with impatience. 'There's this terrifying man—who, incidentally, doesn't seem to like me one little bit!—insisting that I'm his wife. But if so, I don't know anything about her. I don't even know how old she—er—I am supposed to be,' she sighed heavily. 'You see the problem—it's all a complete blank!'

He hesitated for a moment. 'I do not know about your intimate married life, of course,' he informed her quietly, lifting another file from his briefcase. 'But I understand from your husband that you are twenty-seven years of age...'

'That old?'

'... and that you were born in England, where you lived for most of your young life before leaving home, and going to live in New York.'

'New York?' she frowned. 'What was I doing there?'

He consulted his notes again. 'It appears that you were a fashion model for some time before you married.'

She lay back on the pillows for a moment, considering the information she'd been given. 'It all sounds very unlikely to me,' she said at last. 'New York doesn't sound too strange—but I don't *feel* as if I've ever been a fashion model. Are you quite sure about all this?'

'Oh, yes. Your husband has even provided me with a birth certificate,' he assured her.

'And I married my husband in New York?' she asked, gradually becoming interested in the life of this strange woman, of whom she had absolutely no recollection.

He shook his head. 'No, *senhora*. Your first husband died, and it was then that you went to live temporarily with your father and stepmother in São Paulo, in Brazil,' he told her, adding that her father had been the manager of a large, prestigious English bank in Brazil. Now retired, he and his wife lived in Rio de Janeiro.

'And that's where I met my husband—in São Paulo?' she asked, and when he nodded she could only respond with a slow shake of her head. 'I don't even know what my husband does for a living. And why haven't I heard from my parents?'

'Your husband is a very—er—a very wealthy businessman,' he informed her. 'I understand that, due to the current financial situation in Brazil, he is transferring many of his assets over here, to Portugal. He has told me that he wishes to spend more time in this country, principally to modernise his very large estates in the Alentejo, which is a large province in the south of this country. As for your parents...' He paused. 'I believe that there has been some trouble in the past, with your stepmother. Maybe that is why...?' He didn't finish the sentence, but merely shrugged his shoulders.

'I don't think that I sound very nice,' she told him gloomily. 'Neither my husband nor my stepmother seems to like me very much.' She gave another heavy sigh. 'My husband mentioned his son, Carlos—but he's not *my* child, right?'

'Quite right. The boy, who is ten years of age, is the son of the Senhor Marquês's first wife, who died when the child was very young. He is at present in a boarding-school, in England.'

'Oh, the poor thing!' she exclaimed, suddenly having a fleeting vision of herself, clothed in a brand-new grey uniform far too large for her small skinny figure, sitting disconsolately by a classroom window as she watched the other girls being collected by their parents.

'I was always so lonely and...' Her voice trailed away as the brief vision faded, leaving her mind blank and void.

'Senhora...?' he probed gently as she stared blindly at him, her wide blue eyes filling with tears of frustration.

'I had a mental picture of myself at school—but it's gone! I can't seem to... I can't pull it back, if you see what I mean?' she told him in distress.

He nodded with understanding. 'It is quite normal,' he assured her. 'You'll have many more such "pictures" as your memory begins to return. But it is better if you do not try too hard. You must give your mind a chance to heal.'

When the psychoanalyst had gone, she tried to follow his advice. But she couldn't help striving to recall something—anything!—which would help to bring her closer to the mysterious woman, with whom she felt absolutely no affinity whatsoever.

Subsequent visits from both the doctor and the police officer, while not achieving any improvement in her memory, did at least provide some answers to the baffling question of how she came to be in hospital.

From the police officer she discovered that there was no question about her identity—certainly not as far as they were concerned. The man who had seen her struggling with two strangers, on the edge of the dangerous cliff overlooking the Atlantic Ocean, had fortunately disturbed the man and woman. They had left her lying on the ground, racing back to their car before driving swiftly away. And it seemed that they were still at large.

However, when the police and ambulance had arrived, her identity had been quickly established. The purse lying beside her body had contained not only her passport, but also her diary, charge cards and her first-class return plane ticket to London. And, if the police had needed any further identification, her husband had provided certain proof of her identity. He'd confirmed her appearance, and that the purse, her clothes, jewellery, *and* her wedding-ring, were all items belonging to his lawfully wedded wife.

So, it had rapidly become clear that no one had any doubts about her identity. As the policeman had pointed out: if she was *not* the wife of the Senhor Marquês Zarco dos Santos, who was she? And why had she been in possession of the other woman's belongings?

Her husband, on the other hand, clearly believed that, for some nefarious reason of her own, she was pretending to have lost her memory. And it wasn't until after another visit from the eminent psychoanalyst that Zarco—*very* reluctantly—began to accept the fact that she might not remember who she was.

'I suppose I *must* believe what the man says,' he told her grimly on one of his few, infrequent visits to the hospital. 'However, I know you, Maxine! Unlike the other credible fools in this place, I *know* that you are perfectly capable of pulling the wool over everyone's eyes. My only problem lies in wondering why. What you can possibly hope to gain?'

She *really* disliked this aristocratic arrogant man, to whom all the hospital appeared to be bowing and scraping whenever he deigned to visit her. In fact, if she really *was* Maxine—she couldn't think why she hadn't run away from the awful man, years ago! Every time he came anywhere near her, she found herself becoming suddenly breathless and sick with apprehension.

Even now, as she gazed at his tall figure in the formal suit, which seemed to emphasise the breadth of his shoulders, he was making her feel nervous. But she couldn't seem to tear her eyes away from the hard, firm line of his sensual lips, or the frosty glare from beneath the heavy eyelids—so sharply at variance with his cool, urbane stance as he lounged carelessly against the window-sill.

'Do you mean to say that the great Senhor Marquês Zarco dos Santos can't find an answer to such a small problem?' she retorted spitefully.

'Don't be impertinent!' he snapped, the only sign that she had managed to dent his iron control being the sight of a small muscle beating rapidly in his jaw.

'If you so obviously dislike your wife, why haven't you divorced?' she asked, still reluctant to accept that she could be a woman who, as far as she could see, was just about as nasty as Zarco himself.

'Because I have always taken my marriage vows seriously. *And* there is the fact that you have always refused to dissolve our union,' he ground out through clenched teeth. 'Also, as you well know, I have needed a mother-figure for my son, Carlos. Not that you have ever taken any interest in the boy, of course,' he added bitterly.

'Well, since you obviously wish that I was dead, maybe it was *you* who organised my "accident"...?'

she murmured, leaning wearily back on the pillows and closing her eyes. Life in a hospital was incredibly exhausting, and it seemed a very long day already, although Zarco had only been in her room for a few minutes.

'*Me* . . . ?'

She opened her eyes. 'Why not?' she muttered, gazing dully at the blank astonishment on his tanned, aristocratic face. 'From all you say, it would appear to be the perfect answer. Surely it would be easy, for a man of your wealth, to hire some thugs to push me off the cliff?'

'I would *never* do such a thing! It would be a mortal sin,' he retorted sternly, before pacing up and down the room. 'My code as a nobleman, and the pride I bear in my name—as a descendant of João Gonçalves Zarco, who with Henry the Navigator rediscovered Madeira in 1420—would forbid even the *thought* of such behaviour!' he added with resounding force and emphasis as he spun around to face her, his dark eyes flashing with rage.

Quailing beneath the onslaught of his fury, she dearly wished that she had never mentioned the subject. And as he advanced closer to her trembling figure, trapped in the narrow hospital bed, the raw force of his personality seemed to overwhelm her.

'Go away! Leave me alone!'

Her husky whisper seemed to hover in the air between them, her knuckles whitening with tension as she gripped the thin hospital sheet covering her trembling figure.

Zarco gave a harsh, sardonic laugh.

'"Leave me alone". . . ?' he mocked savagely. 'Have you really forgotten all those nights, when you tried to tempt me into your bed? The countless times you have endeavoured to entice me with the undoubted allure of your body?'

'*No*! That wasn't *me*!'

'And all to no avail!' he told her, ignoring her breathless denial as he leaned forward and whipped the sheet away from beneath her clenched hands. As she hastily tried to grab it back, their hands became entangled, his fingers becoming caught in the loose neck of her white hospital gown. There was a screeching sound as the thin, much laundered threads of the material gave way beneath the force of his action, and the garment was split open to her waist.

There was a long, stunned silence as she stared down in shocked disbelief at the display of her naked breasts. Numb with horror, she was unaware of Zarco's hooded eyes devouring the sheen of her pale body, the sight of her full breasts rising erotically between the torn fragments of thin cotton.

'Yes, you have a beautiful body. But it is not one that I have ever cared to possess. Not since I discovered how you trapped me into our mockery of a marriage,' he snarled, ignoring her frightened gasps of fear and panic.

Since she was desperately struggling to pull up the tattered fragments of the gown to cover herself, it was some moments before she became aware that it was a hopeless task. Colour flooded her pale cheeks, strangled moans breaking from her throat at the realisation there was nothing she could do; nothing to prevent the continued exposure of her naked breasts.

'Poor Maxine...!' he murmured sardonically, contemptuously brushing the long tanned fingers over her nipples, the rosy tips involuntarily swelling and hardening beneath his scornful touch. 'How you have ached for my caress...yes?'

'*No!*' she gasped helplessly, unable to control the sharp, quick-fire excitement surging through her trembling body at his intimate touch, the breath catching in her throat as she fought against his deliberate and remorseless arousal of her emotions.

'You may lie—but your body tells me the truth!' he pointed out softly, looking down at her with cold, merciless dark eyes.

She swallowed hard, helplessly praying for enough strength of will to prevent her body from reacting with sensual delight to his blatant arousal. 'Please...please, don't do this to me!' she begged huskily.

'There's no need to look so stricken,' he murmured sardonically, before swiftly pulling up the sheet to cover her nakedness. 'I was merely demonstrating that I am not to be influenced by your feminine wiles. That even now I have agents scouring the streets of Lisbon, tracking down your movements from the moment you first landed at the airport, two weeks ago.'

She shivered uncontrollably at the hard, spine-chilling menace in his voice.

'And when I *do* find out the truth behind your "accident"—as I most surely will,' he added grimly as he turned to leave the room, 'I have a feeling that you would be well advised to start saying your prayers!'

'But...but what am I going to do about my gown?' she wailed, her cheeks flushing scarlet with embarrassment at the thought of trying to explain how the garment came to be torn.

He gave a cruel laugh. 'I'm afraid that, my dear Maxine, is a problem you'll have to solve on your own!'

The sneering contempt in his voice seemed to echo around the small room long after he was gone.

Sagging back against the pillows, she trembled with exhaustion, not only from the shock of Zarco's insulting words and behaviour, but also from her own reaction. How *could* her body have responded with such breathless excitement to the degrading, offensive way in which he'd deliberately aroused her? A deep tide of crimson flooded her cheeks once more as she recalled the aching pleasure engendered by the touch of his fingers on her breasts.

She was sure that never before had she ever felt quite so demeaned and humiliated, while the realisation that she appeared to be married to a man who regarded her in such a loathsome, scornful light was almost more than she could bear.

CHAPTER THREE

MERCIFULLY, it was some days before Zarco came to visit her again. And during those lonely, unhappy hours Tiffany's low spirits were suddenly lifted by the completely unexpected appearance of Mrs Emily Pargeter.

An aged relic of the old British Raj, Mrs Pargeter was clearly one of those indomitable women who believed in 'doing good' to her fellow human beings—whether they wanted such aid or not.

'Hello, dear. The doctors tell me that you are just the tiniest bit lonely, and don't seem to have any visitors,' the elderly, grey-haired old lady said as she bustled into the room one afternoon. 'So, I've come to cheer you up!' she announced, throwing open the blinds, and letting the brilliant sunlight flood into the room.

'We can't have you lying here in doom and gloom, can we?' she continued brightly, coming over to sit down on the bed. 'Now, dear, what is your name?'

'I've no idea. *They* say that it's Maxine dos Santos,' she told the elderly woman, who was regarding her with bright, inquisitive eyes.

'And who do *you* think you are, dear?'

'I haven't a clue! That's the trouble, you see. I don't *feel* as though I know this person, Maxine, at all. And quite apart from anything else,' she added, her voice rising in a mixture of fear and overwhelming exasperation, 'I think she sounds *horrible*! Her husband obviously hates her and . . . and even her own father

50

and stepmother don't want to have anything to do with her!' she added, helpless tears of misery welling up in her blue eyes.

The older woman clicked her teeth sympathetically. 'Now come on, dear, have a good blow,' she said, handing the girl a handkerchief. 'There's no need to get in to such a tiff about something like this, is there? We must just try and see if we can't...'

'*What* did you say?'

Emily Pargeter looked at the young girl in surprise. 'I was just saying that you really ought not to get in such a tiff about——'

'Tiff...Tiff...?' She squeezed her eyes shut, desperately trying to catch the stray, brief thread of remembered sound which had suddenly illuminated the darkness in her mind.

'Well, of course I know it's a bit of an old-fashioned expression!' The elderly woman gave a laugh, which sounded like a horse neighing. 'My dear late husband, Brian, often used to tell me off for using slang words, like "tiff". Brian always said that——' She stopped abruptly as the young girl gave a strangled cry—and promptly burst into tears.

'Now really, dear! I can't believe that anything I've said could upset you like this?'

'No...no, you don't understand!' she sobbed. 'It was your words that triggered it off; I could suddenly hear and see my aunt Doris giving me one of her usual lectures. They always used to begin: "Really, Tiffany!" She and my Aunt Beatrice were always simply horrid to me, and——'

'Now do calm down, dear!'

'But don't you *see*? I've remembered something—at last!' She tried to smile through the tears streaming down her face. 'My name is Tiffany...Tiffany Harris.

And I'm married to Brian Harris—or I think I am...'
she added hesitantly. 'I keep seeing pictures of tennis
courts; always having to pack suitcases and staying in
hotels all over the world...' Her voice died away as
she lay exhausted back against the pillows.

'You've *no* idea—it's all such a relief!' she continued breathlessly. 'I mean...everyone, but *everyone*
has been telling me that I'm this awful woman,
Maxine. But I knew that I wasn't...I just *knew* it!
I'm quite certain that my name is Tiffany—and I
ought to know that, oughtn't I?' she begged, desperately catching hold of the other woman's elderly,
gnarled hand.

'Well, I think you're probably right, dear,' Emily
agreed soothingly. 'Now, dry these tears, and then you
can tell me all about the problem.'

Haltingly at first, and often breaking down into
fresh sobs of relief and exhaustion, Tiffany explained
what she knew of the events leading to her being in
the hospital. It was also a great relief to be able to
tell someone, especially another female, about her
shock in discovering that she was apparently married
to a Brazilian aristocrat, the Marquês Zarco dos
Santos.

'Goodness—how exciting!' Emily exclaimed.

'No, it's not! You've no idea how *awful* Zarco is!'
she told the elder woman. 'For one thing, he obviously hates his wife! And when I say *hate*—I promise
you that I'm definitely not putting it too strongly!'
she added with a shudder. 'Apparently his wife, the
woman he calls Maxine, shouldn't have been here in
Portugal in the first place—which is one of the things
he seems to be so cross about. And, just to make
things *really* complicated, while Zarco is totally convinced that I'm his real wife, *he* seems to believe that

I'm just pretending to have lost my memory!' she gulped. 'So...I seem to be caught up in the middle of a *very* complicated situation.'

'You poor girl!' the old lady murmured sympathetically. 'What are you going to do now?'

'I don't know...' Tiffany told her, her initial euphoria at the total certainty of her own real name draining away as she realised the problems that beset her. 'Everyone—except my beastly husband—is agreed that I'm suffering from amnesia. And, until I can *prove* that I am not Maxine, I don't see what I can do. But *you* believe me, don't you?' she begged the other woman.

'Certainly I do, Tiffany,' Emily Pargeter told her staunchly, but added with a frown, 'I do think you have a bit of a problem. From what you said earlier, it seems that you were found with a passport and documents all in the name of this other woman, Maxine dos Santos.'

'Yes, that's the trouble. I haven't got a shred of evidence that I'm really Tiffany Harris.' She lapsed into a gloomy silence. 'If only I could somehow get hold of my aunts,' she said at last. 'I know they were terribly angry when I married Brian—although I can't remember why. However, I'm sure they'd be able to back up what I say. But I can't do anything about it. Not while I'm stuck here in this hospital.'

'There is such a thing as a telephone, you know!' Emily told her with a grin. 'If you can remember your aunts' surname and their address—or better still their phone number—I can contact them for you, if you like.'

'Would you? Would you *really* do that for me?' Tiffany gasped, almost overcome with excitement at the thought of being rescued from the terrible situation in which she found herself. 'I'd be so grateful!'

However, she had to concentrate for a long time, lying back on the pillows with her eyes tightly closed, before she was able to recollect her aunts' surname, and their address in Eastbourne.

'I think that's right,' she told the old lady, who was busy writing the details in a small notebook. 'But I simply can't remember their telephone number, I'm afraid.'

'Don't worry, dear. I'm sure I will be able to get in contact with them,' Emily said, reassuringly patting the girl's hand. 'Now, I really must go. Keep your courage up, and I'll be back to see you tomorrow,' she added, before bustling from the room.

Despite all her excitement at having remembered her name, and the fact that Emily Pargeter was going to help to prove her identity, Tiffany found that she was extraordinarily tired and exhausted after the departure of her visitor.

Thinking about her talk with Emily, she realised that maybe she hadn't communicated forcibly enough *just* how formidable and menacing Zarco really was. How could she stand up to such a man? Especially someone so much older and obviously more experienced than herself. Not that he was really all that old, of course, she thought sleepily. It must be his ruthlessly arrogant, overpowering presence which made him appear so daunting...

Obviously far more tired than she'd realised, Tiffany slept heavily, not waking up until the next morning, when she found herself feeling immeasurably refreshed. Despite being slightly shaky on her legs, it was a relief to be able to leave her bed for the first time, and sit in a chair by the open window, savouring the bright sunshine and fresh spring breeze.

On waking up, Tiffany had been determined to assert her own real identity, refusing to be addressed by anything other than her own name. And, after some initial surprise and scepticism, the hospital staff agreed to her request, although she knew that they were merely humouring her—just as they might a spoilt, difficult child. All the same, it was one battle won...even if it was beginning to look as though she'd lost another.

As promised, Emily Pargeter had called to visit her, earlier that afternoon. But, after one quick glance at the older woman's face, Tiffany had known that she was the bearer of bad news.

'I'm sorry, dear. I did manage to obtain the telephone number, but, although the lady I spoke to confirmed that she *was* Miss Doris Kendall—she denied the fact that she had a niece called Tiffany.' Emily had looked at her with concern. 'The lady was very firm—almost unpleasant, in fact, I'm afraid.'

'Yes, she would be,' Tiffany had muttered with a heavy sigh. 'It's difficult to explain—but I can't remember things like phone numbers or the six-times-table. It's more . . . well, it's like seeing pictures in my head,' she had striven to explain. 'For instance, earlier today, I could *see* my aunt, absolutely furious with me for marrying Brian. I think he was a professional tennis player, although I'm not entirely sure.' She had shrugged unhappily. 'Anyway, my aunt kept saying, "We wash our hands of you! As far as we're concerned, you don't exist any more!" I can remember that she also said it was no good me running home, if my marriage ended in disaster—because they wouldn't want to know me any more.'

Emily had been very sympathetic. She had pointed out that it was only a minor set-back. It wouldn't be long before Tiffany was sure to remember more about her past life, and also the names of some friends who could substantiate her true identity.

Unfortunately, despite trying desperately hard, Tiffany's mind had obstinately refused to recall anything else. Maybe she was trying too hard? However, she found herself becoming increasingly nervous as she wondered how she was going to explain matters to her so-called husband.

With her aunts' denial of her existence, Zarco wasn't going to take a blind bit of notice of her, was he? Not when there was so much evidence stacked up against her. She hadn't just been wearing Maxine's clothes and jewellery—there was the matter of her passport as well. Above all, how could anyone—especially a hard, tough, confident man like Zarco—make such a mistake in identifying his own wife?

Going over these questions in her tired mind produced no answer—or not one that made any sense—and she was in a considerable state of nerves, when Zarco appeared unexpectedly in her hospital room that evening.

It was immediately apparent from the taut, tightly controlled expression on his face and the glinting sparks of rage in his dark eyes that he was almost beside himself with fury.

'Well, my dear wife—I now know *exactly* what you were doing here, in Lisbon!' he grated angrily, his tall figure looming over her as she shrank back against the cushions in her chair. 'Unfortunately, I have yet to discover the exact location of the jewels and the gold which you have stolen. So, I suggest that it would be *very* sensible of you to tell me where you have hidden them—*and as quickly as possible*!' he added menacingly through clenched teeth.

'Jewels? Gold . . . ?' She blinked up at him in bewilderment. 'The . . . the only jewellery I know about are the earrings and brooch which I was wearing when the police found me after the accident. And—er—this ring, of course,' she added nervously, glancing down at the gold wedding-band about her finger.

'Do not try my patience too far!' he hissed savagely. 'This farce about you having lost your memory must now *cease*! I want to know what you have done with my family's heirlooms—over two million English pounds' worth of emerald and diamond jewellery which, together with a large number of gold krugerrands, has been stolen from the safety deposit box in my bank, here in Lisbon?'

Tiffany stared up at him in open-mouthed astonishment. To say that he had obviously lost his temper was a complete understatement. Zarco was absolutely *livid*!

Since she was almost numb with terror as his wrath broke over her frightened figure, it seemed useless to try and explain that she knew nothing about any missing jewels or gold. She didn't even know what a krugerrand looked like, for heaven's sake!

Tiffany was totally bemused by Zarco's colossal and overwhelming loss of temper, and it was some time before she could make head or tail of his extraordinary accusation.

It wasn't easy to understand exactly what had happened—mostly because he kept breaking off to swear violently beneath his breath. However, by the time he began to simmer down, she'd managed to grasp most of the salient points. If only half of what he said was true, she could only be deeply thankful that she *wasn't* Maxine dos Santos!

It seemed that the agents, hired by Zarco, had produced clear evidence of his wife's involvement in the theft of both the gold coins and a fabulous, almost priceless collection of diamond and emerald jewellery, which had been in his family for generations. Zarco was also claiming that it had been a well-thought-out theft, which had required a considerable amount of forward planning.

'I will admit it was a clever scheme—what, I believe, the Americans would call a scam,' he growled through clenched teeth. And Tiffany had to admit that it sounded as if his wife had gone to some considerable lengths in order to steal the jewels.

While Zarco had been away on business in Brazil, Maxine had apparently left their house in England and flown secretly to Portugal. On arriving in Lisbon, she'd paid the first of many visits to Zarco's bank, in the Baixa area of the city, where she had opened an account in her own name. Maxine had also asked if she could have a safety deposit box, in which to keep some important documents—apparently for the purchase of a large house outside the city.

Making several visits to the bank vaults, to take out and replace the 'documents', Maxine had become well known and easily recognised by the official in charge. So, when she had arrived one afternoon just before the bank was due to close, and had asked the man if she could also transfer some of the 'documents' from her own safety deposit box to that of her husband, it had not occurred to the bank official to have any doubts about the wisdom of letting her do so. After all, the Senhor Marquês dos Santos was an old and valued client.

'The man does remember you carrying a large wicker shopping bag,' Zarco told her with a harsh bark of angry laughter. '*So* convenient—after you'd emptied *my* safety deposit box—for concealing within its depths all the antique jewellery and gold coins!'

And his wife had also, it seemed, planned the timing of her theft very carefully. Stealing the jewellery just before the bank closed on a Thursday afternoon—with the next day, Friday, being a bank holiday to celebrate the Day of Liberation—no one was likely to discover the robbery until well after the weekend.

'I have never denied that you are a clever and devious woman, Maxine,' he told her grimly. 'But in this case, I think you were perhaps just a little *too* clever for your own good! Was it a case of thieves falling out?' he demanded. 'Is that why you were seen struggling with a man and woman beside the cliff, only one day after you'd stolen the jewels? Is *that* why you received such a heavy blow to your head...?'

'I... I'm not even capable of planning such a complicated plot—let alone clever enough to carry it out!' she cried helplessly.

'You lie!'

The tension of the sudden silence which had fallen on the small hospital room was so thick and heavy that she could almost cut it with a knife, Tiffany thought faintly, her heart thudding and pounding like a heavy drum. The expression on Zarco's face as he paced up and down the floor sent frantic shivers of fear rippling down her spine; a dire warning—as if she needed any such reminder!—of the folly in continuing to defy this apparently invincible man.

Drawing on her pitiful reserves of strength, she made one last effort to convince him. 'I don't... I *really* don't know what your wife did, because I am quite certain that I am *not* Maxine. In fact I've now remembered . . . I now know that my name is Tiffany Harris, and——'

Zarco's heavy snort of anger cut across her words as she haltingly tried to protest her innocence.

'—and I don't know *anything* about any jewels—heirlooms or otherwise,' she added breathlessly as his harsh features grew dark with rage and fury.

'*Stop lying to me!*'

She cried out in alarm as he suddenly grabbed hold of her hands, swiftly pulling her trembling figure upright from the chair. Quickly clasping hold of both her wrists with one hand and taking hold of her chin with the other, he drew her closer as his tanned fingers forced her head up towards him.

She felt as though her mind was being probed by a viciously sharp laser. Standing so close, she was aware of the angry flush beneath the tanned skin covering his high cheekbones and formidable jawline; her eyes gazing helplessly at the cruel, sensual curve of his mouth.

'You are merely wasting my time,' he drawled with grim, silky menace. 'It is pointless to continue to deny that you stole the jewels and the gold—especially when I have such a large mountain of evidence to prove that you did!'

'Somebody...somebody may have raided your bank deposit box—but I promise you it wasn't *me*!' she wailed. 'I'm just not capable of doing something like that. You're making a *terrible* mistake!' she added in a tremulous whisper as his fingers tightened threateningly about her chin.

There was a long silence, her eyelashes fluttering nervously beneath his fierce gaze as he drew her tightly against his tall figure. She could feel his long, muscular thighs touching her own, and, despite her very real fear of this dangerous man, it was some moments before her bewildered mind was able to recognise the nervous, quivering response feathering through her trembling body.

Oh, *no*! Surely, she couldn't be *sexually* attracted to this man...? she asked herself wildly. It simply wasn't possible—she must have totally lost her mind! But then, of course, she *had* temporarily lost part of her mind, she quickly reminded herself. Although it seemed that Zarco, too, was beginning to doubt his own sanity.

'I must be losing my head!' he growled softly, gazing down into the wide blue eyes of the girl trapped within his arms.

Totally confused from the mental battering she had received over the past half-hour, and bemused by her inexplicable response to the dark attraction of this man whom she feared and hated, Tiffany was hardly prepared for what happened next.

Barely able to understand what was happening, she found herself crushed against his hard chest, his arms tightening like a vice about her slender body. The fingers gripping her jaw swiftly slipped down to clasp the back of her neck, holding her head firmly beneath him. His dark eyes flashed a glittering warning, and then his mouth came crushing down like a weapon against her lips, the relentless pressure almost paralysing her.

She was breathless, mentally stunned before the re-alisation of what was happening really hit her, so it was some seconds before she began to make a feeble effort to escape from his cruel embrace. She tried to cry out, but, even as she parted her lips, she realised that she was making a grave mistake as he took ad-

vantage of her foolishness, the hot exploration of his
tongue a savage invasion of her shattered senses.

Her first strangled cry had given way to an inaudible moan. She could hardly breathe, and, despite
her feeble attempts to struggle free, she knew that it
was hopeless. He was clearly possessed of a strength
she couldn't possibly combat. The arm clasping her
so tightly began to slide slowly down her body,
pressing her even closer to his hard frame, and she
was once again conscious of a strong tide of erotic,
sexual awareness within herself, which even his determined assault had not extinguished. It was even
more disturbing to realise that Zarco dos Santos was
also a victim of this inexplicable attraction between
them, the hard arousal of his own body clearly un-
derlining the fact.

And then she found herself released from her
torment. She lay limply in his arms, and it was some
moments before she could force her eyelids open,
blinking dazedly up at the man towering over her.

His dark glittering eyes were guarded, staring down
at her with a searching and watchful expression from
beneath his heavy eyelids.

'You . . . you've just assaulted me!' she gasped,
struggling to raise a hand to her bruised, swollen lips.

'It is hardly an assault if a man should decide to
kiss his wife,' Zarco told her dismissively. 'And maybe
it is something I should have done long ago, hmm?'

'But I'm *not* your wife!' she cried huskily.

'*Cale-se*. Be quiet!' he rasped, his temper almost
flaring up out of control once more. And then, after
a fierce internal struggle, he continued in a calmer
voice, 'I don't see how you can have it both ways.
Either you have *not* lost your memory—in which case
you must know perfectly well where you have hidden

the jewels, or you *have* temporarily lost your mind,' he drawled silkily, 'and it is, therefore, merely a question of my waiting until you have regained it, once again.'

He shrugged his broad shoulders when he saw that she wasn't capable of making any reply. 'In either case, I will soon have the answer. The doctors inform me that they are willing to let you leave the hospital tomorrow. And once we are back at my house in England...' He laughed. 'I do not foresee any difficulty in forcing you to tell me what I want to know!'

Her trembling legs gave way beneath her as his blood-curdling, evil laugh echoed around the small room. And she would have fallen if he hadn't tightened his grip on her slim figure.

'Let me go! Please—*please* let me go...!' she sobbed helplessly, ashamed to find herself losing all control, and crying out with terror as he quickly scooped her up in his arms.

Swearing violently under his breath, Zarco frowned down at the tearful, struggling girl in his arms. And then he spun around on his heel, walking swiftly over to place her surprisingly gently down on the bed.

'I'm not Maxine. I know I'm not!' she wept, still feeling totally shattered by his determined, fierce assault of only a few moments ago. 'My name is Tiffany Harris—and this is all a t-terrible, *terrible* m-mistake!'

Seemingly deaf to her tearful cry of protest, Zarco studied her in silence for a moment, before reaching over to press a bell for the nurse.

'See to my wife!' he demanded imperiously as the nurse swiftly responded to his call. 'And since I have permission to remove her from here, tomorrow,' he added, ignoring the presence of the sobbing girl on the bed as he strode towards the door, 'I expect her to be up and dressed when I collect her, tomorrow morning.'

She was shattered by her confrontation with Zarco, and her pathetic attempts to interest either the doctor, or the nurses, in what she feared was a clear case of kidnapping proved hopeless.

The nurses, although warm and caring girls, simply didn't have the clout to interfere with the doctor's decision—even if they had believed her story, which they clearly didn't. As for the doctor, while he was very kind and compassionate in his firm belief that she was indeed suffering from amnesia, he nevertheless felt that her best chance of recovery lay in accompanying her husband back home to England.

'O Senhor Marquês tells me that he has a *quinta* in England—a very large house and very quiet. It will be good for you to have peace and serenity, yes?'

No—it won't! she wanted to scream out loud. But, of course, she didn't. There was no point, she realised with dismay, in protesting any further. Not when the whole of the hospital seemed to be bowing and scraping before the Senhor Marquês.

She might have lost most of her memory, Tiffany thought glumly. But she had no difficulty in recalling the well-known saying, 'Everyone loves a lord!' It might be a republican country—but, as far as she could see, members of the aristocracy were still living high, wide and handsome in Portugal!

And, as if to complete her misery, even Emily Pargeter turned out to have feet of clay—falling a willing victim to Zarco's charm.

Calling in to see her the next morning, the elderly woman arrived just as Tiffany was being helped into the clothes for her journey.

'I didn't realise you were leaving us quite so soon, dear,' Emily murmured, raising an eyebrow as she viewed the ultra-smart white raw silk suit which the young girl was wearing.

When Tiffany explained that she was due to be collected by Zarco, and was being forced to return with him to his large house in England, Emily was most sympathetic.

'Although maybe it's for the best?' she concluded reassuringly. 'With lots of rest in the peaceful English countryside, I'm sure that you'll soon be able to remember far more about your past life.'

'I certainly hope so!' Tiffany said fervently, before telling her friend about the loss of the jewellery and gold from Zarco's bank—and how there was no way she could prove that she hadn't planned and carried out such an audacious robbery.

'Just as there's no way I can prove that I *know* I've never worn anything like this before,' she added, grimacing down at the *very* short skirt, which seemed to come halfway up her thighs. 'This outfit was apparently delivered here, for me to wear to the airport. And while it may well be the height of fashion, I'm quite certain that I've *never* possessed a garment made by Yves Saint Laurent. And I never wear white. With my pale skin, it makes me look totally washed out.'

The elderly woman smiled. 'Well, dear, I think you look very nice. Although I'd agree that maybe it's not a very practical colour in which to travel.'

'Thank you for trying to be tactful.' Tiffany gave a heavy sigh as she turned to look at herself in the mirror, raising a nervous hand to the thick bandage which was still wound about her head. 'Quite honestly, I don't need anyone to tell me that I look like an ad-

vertisement for keeping death off the roads!' she
muttered glumly.

'Come on, dear, cheer up!' Emily told her. 'And
what an exciting story you've just told me,' she added,
clearly more interested in the tangled web which the
young girl found herself than in the colour of her
clothing. 'I can't remember hearing about anything
so extraordinary before. And I hear from the nurses
that your husband is *such* a handsome man, too!'

Tiffany looked at her in astonishment. 'What does
it matter whether he's good-looking or not? The fact
is that he's a thoroughly awful, terrifying man who
scares me rigid. Quite honestly,' she added gloomily,
'I reckon he's *just* the sort of person who'd pull the
wings off poor little butterflies!'

Gaining considerable satisfaction at tearing the
character of her loathsome so-called husband to
pieces, Tiffany was distracted by the sound of a low
cough. Whirling round, she was startled to see the
tall, dominant figure of Zarco lounging casually in
the open doorway of her room.

How much had he heard? Tiffany felt quite sick
for a moment, her knees trembling weakly as he gave
her a tight, thin smile; a smile not reflected in his glittering dark eyes, which contained no amusement
whatsoever.

'I'm sorry to disappoint you—but it's a very long
time since I behaved in such a disgusting manner towards "poor little butterflies"—I certainly cannot remember ever doing so,' he drawled coolly, before
moving smoothly forward to greet Emily Pargeter.

'I understand that you have been kindness itself to
my dear wife,' he murmured, giving the elderly woman
a warm and engaging smile as he gallantly lifted her
hand to his lips. 'However, you may rest assured that

she will have the very best of care on our return to England.'

If she hadn't been feeling so furiously angry and upset, Tiffany might have laughed out loud at the glazed expression on Emily's face; an expression echoed by that of the young nurse. But if Tiffany had ever had a sense of humour, it had now completely deserted her. Fuming with rage, she found herself having to watch the dreadful man spinning a web of outrageous charm, in which he was clearly ensnaring her only friend in Lisbon.

Poor Emily seemed to have been totally swept off her feet, eagerly requesting details of exactly where Zarco's house was located, before eventually pulling herself together and declaring that it was time she went.

'Goodbye, dear,' the elderly woman murmured as she came over to give Tiffany a hug. 'He really *is* handsome—and *so* charming!' she whispered in the girl's ear, giving her a beaming smile before hurrying from her room.

Emily Pargeter had been quite right when she'd suggested that a white raw silk suit would be unsuitable for the rigours of everyday travel. However, after having been driven to the airport by Zarco's chauffeured limousine, speeding across the tarmac to where his private jet was waiting for take-off, Tiffany realised that for the seriously rich such details were irrelevant. Unfortunately, she was given little time for speculation about Zarco's wealth as, after handing her carefully out of the vehicle, he once again swept her off her feet.

'Put me down!' she gasped, trying to struggle free of his embrace as he carried her lightly up the steps and into the aircraft.

She hated being held so close to him. Strangely fearful of the strong, firm arms clasping her to his rock-hard body, she was acutely conscious of the same breathlessness—the very same *frisson* of excitement and longing which she'd felt yesterday, in the hospital.

Bewildered by her reaction to a man whom she was so certain she actively disliked, Tiffany found herself being lowered down into a comfortable seat. Leaning back and closing her eyes, she meekly allowed him to fasten her seatbelt. When she opened her eyes again, it was to see Zarco having a few brief words with his pilot, before moving towards a large executive-type desk, which seemed to be firmly secured in place.

Watching as he shrugged off the dark grey jacket of his expensively cut suit, to reveal the broad shoulders and strong, muscular shape of his tall body, Tiffany realised that she knew absolutely nothing about this man.

It was undoubtedly a waste of time, but as she studied the angular bones of his face, covered by a firm and deeply tanned skin, she had the distinct impression that such wealth as he possessed—and he was obviously as rich as Croesus—was not solely due to an aristocratic inheritance. Even if this particular man had been born a pauper, she was oddly certain that his sheer aggressiveness, his obvious ability to lead and command, would have taken him to the top of any company or international corporation.

Engaged in idle speculation on the forces which lay behind his powerful, ruthless personality, she suddenly realised that Zarco had turned his gaze in her direction. The searchlight of his glittering dark eyes bored into hers, as if searching for an elusive answer. For a moment it seemed as though the air were charged with electricity: a crackling tension that flashed between their still figures. But then the extraordinary sensation which had temporarily paralysed her body quickly drained away as he gave a slight shrug, and began to concentrate on the papers laid out on the desk before him.

Feeling extraordinarily tired and exhausted, Tiffany must have slept through most of the journey, moving like a sleep-walker through the formalities of London airport, before accompanying Zarco in yet another chauffeur-driven car to his country house by the Thames, in Berkshire.

As the vehicle came to a halt on the gravelled fore-court of Norton Manor, Tiffany realised how much she'd been subconsciously hoping that the house would seem familiar. But, as she was helped from the car and took a faltering step towards the front door, she was swept by a sudden wave of deep depression.

Against all common sense, she'd hoped to be able to discover *some* point of contact with Zarco's wife: how else could she have been found dressed in Maxine's clothes, and wearing the other woman's jewellery? But she had no recollection in her mind of this beautiful timber-framed medieval manor house, whose ancient diamond-shaped windows sparkled in the late afternoon sun. In fact, as she entered the large oak-panelled hall, fragrant with the smell of beeswax and bowls of fresh spring flowers, it all seemed desperately unfamiliar. As did the stranger, who bustled forth from the nether regions of the large house to greet Zarco with a beaming smile.

Weary and bewildered as she was, Tiffany instantly realised that the middle-aged woman—whom she subsequently learned was Amy Long, the house-keeper—was definitely no friend of hers. After ef-fusively welcoming the master of the house and informing him that tea was laid in the drawing-room, Amy Long's smile faded as she turned to coolly en-quire whether 'Madam would care to rest after the journey?'

Wilting beneath the chilly, hostile gaze of the other woman, Tiffany instinctively turned for protection to the tall figure standing beside her. After a swift glance at the frightened, nervous expression on the girl's pale face, Zarco smoothly informed the housekeeper that his wife was very tired, and would undoubtedly welcome a soothing cup of tea just as soon as he'd carried her upstairs to her bedroom.

Astounded to discover that Zarco was capable of being kind and considerate, Tiffany meekly allowed herself to be carried upstairs. Moving down a wide passage, Zarco entered a large, beautifully decorated room which was dominated by an elegant four-poster bed. As he lowered her gently down on to the thick pile of the pale cream carpet, Tiffany's eyes widened as she gazed about her. Through the open door of the en-suite bathroom, she could see the gleam of gold taps reflected in the shining mirrors which appeared to line the walls. Her stupefied gaze absorbed the shimmering pale green silk curtains edging the windows, the same material being used for the in-tricate drapery on the elegant pale satinwood columns of the bed, before she shook her head in disbelief.

'Are you feeling any pain?' he asked, still keeping an arm lightly about her slim, obviously drooping figure.

'No... I'm just feeling exhausted, that's all,' she muttered, her weary body filled with a deep longing to climb between the sheets of the wide, comfortable-looking bed. And then, as her weary brain absorbed the significant fact that it was a *double* bed, she could feel icy shivers of apprehension racing up and down her spine.

'Am I expected to...?' She gulped. 'I mean, do we—er——?' As she hesitated he gave a low rumble of sardonic laughter.

'No, my dear wife, we do *not* share the same bedroom,' he drawled, his sensual lips tightening as she visibly sagged with relief.

'If you really *are* suffering from amnesia,' he continued coldly, 'maybe I should inform you that we have not slept together since the date of our wedding.'

The harsh bitterness lying beneath his terse words seemed to reverberate around the room, almost battering her travel-weary body.

'I didn't know... I didn't realise...' she muttered, a flush stealing over her pale cheeks as she stared fixedly down at the carpet.

'Can it be that you are feeling some remorse?' he drawled sardonically, before turning to walk back across the room towards the open doorway. 'It is, of course, far too late for that. Especially, as you know very well, Maxine—or whatever name you now wish to call yourself—that I lead quite another—er—private life, in Brazil!'

As he closed the door quietly behind him, the only sound to disturb the deep silence of the large house was the fading echo of his wry, sardonic laughter.

CHAPTER FOUR

AFTER waving goodbye to Dr Granville, who'd been paying his weekly visit to see her, Tiffany was about to turn back into the house when she hesitated for a moment.

It was one of those rare, gloriously warm mornings in late May. And since it seemed almost a crime not to be outside enjoying the sunshine, she couldn't resist the temptation to explore the grounds of Norton Manor.

From what little information she'd been able to gather over the past two weeks, it appeared that the house had been built by a Richard Norton in the fifteenth century—mainly from the proceeds gained by lending money to both sides engaged in fighting the English War of the Roses. The timber-framed medieval house had continued to be owned by the Norton family through subsequent generations, remaining virtually untouched until it was inherited by the last member of the family, Charlotte Norton.

Strolling slowly past an ancient tithe barn and a large round dovecot, set in a red-bricked wall surrounding the garden, Tiffany found herself wishing that she knew more about Charlotte Norton. The English girl had been Zarco dos Santos's first wife—before dying at a tragically young age, shortly after the birth of her son.

It was no good asking Zarco, of course. During the first week following their return from Lisbon, he had barely been able to bring himself to be polite to her.

And, since he'd been away in Portugal on business for the last six days, her only source of information had been Amy Long, the far from friendly housekeeper at Norton Manor.

However, from what she had learned, it seemed that Charlotte had been an only child of elderly parents. After studying Spanish and Portuguese at university, she had decided to take a year off following her studies to visit Brazil. And it was there that she had met and married her husband—a marriage which had, apparently, been violently opposed by her mother and father. 'Miss Charlotte was always headstrong,' the housekeeper had told her with a wistful smile, explaining how Sir Richard and Lady Norton had eventually forgiven their daughter, travelling to Brazil to visit their new grandson and his mother shortly before she had died.

'And what about my—er—husband?' Tiffany had asked, having temporarily given up the unequal struggle to prove that she *wasn't* married to Zarco.

'Oh, he and Sir Richard got on like a house on fire! Which is why Miss Charlotte's father left him this house when he died—and then to be passed on in turn to young Carlos. Mind you, the Marquês being a real live aristocrat helped, of course,' Amy had laughed. 'Old Sir Richard always was a right snob! But my Miss Charlotte's marriage was a true love match—not like some "arrangements" I don't care to mention!' the housekeeper had added, giving Tiffany a scornful glance before bustling off about her duties.

With a heavy sigh, Tiffany sank down on to a carved stone bench, set against the warm brick wall surrounding the herb garden. The housekeeper, who had been at Norton Manor since she was a young girl, ran the house like clockwork. Assisted by three or four ladies from the nearby village, who came to dust and polish every day, Amy didn't tolerate any interference in the running of the manor house—and Tiffany's assurance that she was happy to leave everything to the older woman had been received in stony silence and with considerable scepticism. While Amy ran the house, her husband Tom acted as Zarco's chauffeur, general factotum and also as butler, when the need arose. The immaculate grounds surrounding the house seemed to have an army of gardeners constantly manicuring the lawns, making sure that no weed dared show its face in the flowerbeds. In fact, Tiffany told herself wryly, Zarco's annual bill for the upkeep of this house and grounds was probably as much as most people earned in a lifetime!

None of which, she quickly reminded herself, solved the problem of what on earth she was going to do about Amy Long. It was, of course, quite understandable that the housekeeper might resent Zarco's second wife—especially since the older woman had known and loved Charlotte Norton from childhood. However, it had become obvious that, although Maxine had lived in this house for some time, she had not succeeded in gaining the housekeeper's respect.

In fact, Tiffany thought gloomily, Maxine seemed to have had one really outstanding talent—that of upsetting and alienating *everyone* with whom she came into contact! It was deeply depressing to find herself trapped by a close physical resemblance to such a disagreeable and thoroughly unpleasant woman. And her own clear failure to recall any trace of her past life in this house—and how could she, when she'd never been here?—seemed to have Zarco and all the medical experts completely stumped.

She certainly had to give Zarco 'A' for effort, Tiffany thought grimly. In the week following her arrival at Norton Manor, at least four days had been spent going back and forth to London. Refusing to listen to her pleas that she wasn't Maxine, and that each passing day she was recalling more and more of her life as Tiffany Harris, Zarco had dragged her from the expensive consulting-rooms of one specialist to another.

At his insistence, she had been put through hypnosis, psychoanalysis and psychotherapy, until she was heartily sick of the sight of Harley Street! And all to no avail. In the beginning, she had thought it would be easy to convince the medical men of her true identity—especially since, as the doctor in Lisbon had promised, she was remembering more and more of her past life as Tiffany Harris. But, as soon as Zarco had followed her into the various consulting-rooms, his total and certain conviction that she was his wife put everything back to square one! After all, if a man didn't know his wife—who did? And Tiffany's increasingly desperate assertion that she *wasn't* Maxine had merely been put down to amnesia caused by the blow to her head.

Every expert seemed to have a different theory about why she couldn't recall her married life with her husband. A particularly ingenious explanation seemed to centre upon a famous case in America, where a woman was found to have at least three completely different personalities, and whose story had featured in a famous movie. However, it wasn't until her last visit to a surprisingly friendly psychiatrist that Zarco had finally begun to accept the truth: his wife really had no memory of their past life together.

'We have not achieved much success, I'm afraid,' Dr Watkins had told Zarco, when he'd entered the consulting-room after her visit. 'It's a very interesting story your wife has to tell, about her life as the wife of a professional tennis player, and——'

'Nonsense!' Zarco had snapped irritably. 'She knows nothing about tennis, and has always been completely uninterested in any form of sporting activity,' he'd added firmly. 'I wish to know when, in your professional opinion, my wife will recover her memory. And, in particular, how soon she may recall the events leading up to her injury.'

Dr Watkins had shrugged. 'I fully expect your wife to eventually recollect most of the details of her childhood, her adolescence and her marriage to you. However, I'm afraid that you must accept the fact that she may never remember what happened in the hours, or even days, before the accident.'

'*Never* ...?' A deep frown had creased Zarco's forehead, his lips tightening with annoyance and frustration. 'Surely there must be some way to extract that information from my wife? Some way of unlocking her memory?'

'There are plenty of other experts in London,' the doctor had told him. 'However, they will all tell you the same thing: your wife has temporary amnesia. While she *may* recollect what or who caused the blow to her head, I think you must face the fact that it is very likely that she won't be able to; that the details of what happened will be lost forever.'

Zarco had remained silent for most of the journey back to Norton Manor, his expression grim and forbidding as he steered the pearl-grey Aston Martin V8 down the motorway.

'It seems I *must* accept what the doctors say,' he'd grated, his harsh tones at last breaking the tense silence. 'But I am *not* abandoning the search to find out what happened in Portugal. My agents will continue to track down your movements during those weeks—and back through your past life, if necessary—until I discover the truth.'

'Good luck!' she'd muttered wearily, leaning back on the red leather head-rest. Nervously closing her eyes at the speed of the fast sports car—the one of Zarco's vehicles which he clearly preferred to drive himself—Tiffany had been just too tired to care *what* he did.

However, it had slowly become obvious, over the next few days, that Zarco had finally accepted her total inability to recall their life together. There had been no more visits to London to see various specialists, and she'd been left alone to recover her strength under the care of Dr Grenville, the local general practitioner.

Thanks to his no-nonsense approach, she was able to discard the heavy bandage, not even needing a plaster on her wound, which was apparently healing very well.

'Just relax, take it easy and I think you'll find that everything sorts itself out very soon,' he'd told her breezily this morning, before arranging to see her in his surgery in a week's time.

It wasn't the wound at the top of her head which had been worrying Tiffany so much as the fact that her hair had been looking such a mess. No wonder Zarco could hardly bear to look at her, his lips curling in distaste whenever his dark, glittering eyes glanced in her direction. And right up until the day after he'd left, on his business trip to Portugal, when she'd been at last able to throw away the hideous bandage, Tiffany had been miserably aware that, with her blonde hair having been roughly chopped into different lengths, she had indeed looked a perfect fright!

Determined to keep up a brave, defiant stance in front of Zarco—although it was clearly a waste of time, since he seemed determined to avoid her like the plague—Tiffany had, of course, spent many hours weeping disconsolately in the privacy of her bedroom. So it had been doubly mortifying when Zarco had appeared unexpectedly in her room the day before he'd left, and discovered her tearfully regarding herself in the mirror.

'Go away!' she'd howled, burying her face in her hands.

'What is wrong? Are you ill?'

'It's my hair—it looks *so* awful!' she'd sobbed through her fingers, desperately wishing that he would go away and leave her in peace.

But, expecting to hear the sound of the door closing behind him, she'd been startled to feel the light touch of his hand on her miserably hunched shoulder.

'I merely came to tell you that I will be going away for a few days to Lisbon, on business,' she'd heard him say quietly. 'As for your hair—that is a matter which can easily be remedied,' he'd added, giving her a surprisingly gentle pat on the shoulder before leaving the room.

Deciding that she must have imagined the note of kindness and concern in his voice, Tiffany had been astounded, on the day following his departure, to receive a visit from a man claiming to be Maxine's London hairdresser.

'Your husband asked me to call and see what I could do with your hair,' the willowy young man said, informing her that he was called Vernon. 'I told him it was going to cost a bomb—dragging me down from London, like this...' Vernon grumbled before giving a high, falsetto shriek of horror. 'Good heavens, ducky! What *have* you done to your hair?'

Stunned by the stranger's unexpected and bizarre appearance—she didn't recall ever having seen a man wearing a pair of long, dangling earrings before—Tiffany haltingly began to explain why her hair had been cut into different lengths.

'That *divine*, macho husband of yours mentioned that you had a cut on the head. But who's been dying your hair? Have you been a *naughty* girl, and visited another hairdresser?' he queried, mincing across the carpet towards her.

'No—I——'

'Hang about!' Vernon exclaimed, quickly dropping his camp tone of voice as he lifted a lock of her hair, running it through his fingers. 'What on earth is going on?' he frowned. 'This isn't your hair...or, to be more precise, it's not the hair *I've* been looking after for the past two years!'

Tiffany could have hugged him. Here—at last—was proof positive that she wasn't Maxine!

It took her some time to explain the complicated situation and how, incredible as it might seem, a terrible mistake had been made over her identity. And even if she wasn't Maxine, would Vernon *please* do something about her dreadful-looking hair?

Deciding that he was faced with an interesting challenge, the hairdresser said that he would see what he could do. And, well over an hour later, they were both happy to agree that he had done very well.

Fascinated to hear what details she could tell him about the blow to her head, Vernon revealed himself

to be a thoroughly sensible, down-to-earth Londoner.
'With a wife, two kids and several brothers and sisters
to support, I only do the "Hello, duckie!" bit because it's good for business,' he told her with a grin,
taking considerable care to achieve a style which would
go some way to disguising the wound on her head.

'Actually, I think you look rather good with short
hair,' he murmured, carefully brushing the now soft,
slightly wavy gold hair into a shining cap about her
head. 'It looks like you're in a real bind, although I
suppose there are worse fates in life than having to
live a life of luxury!' he added with a grin, stepping
back to view his new creation. 'All the same...I can't
help wondering what on earth has happened to
Maxine.'

Delighted by the dramatic improvement in her appearance, Tiffany hadn't taken too much notice of
Vernon's remark, at the time. But now, as she sat here
in the herb garden, relishing the warmth of the mid-
morning sun, Tiffany recalled his query. It was, she
realised, a question she should have asked herself long
before now. Because, if *she* was here at Norton
Manor—where on earth was Maxine?

Everyone who'd been in close contact with Zarco's
wife seemed to be in agreement that she was, or had
been, a deeply unpleasant woman. Moreover, it didn't
seem as though Maxine had any friends—certainly no
acquaintances had either called or phoned to say hello
during the past two weeks. All of which seemed very
strange.

Recalling Zarco's caustic, unhappy bark of laughter
about his wife, on the night of her arrival here at
Norton Manor, Tiffany totally failed to understand
what he could find amusing about a marriage which,
according to him, had been no marriage at all. And,

if it had been so awful, why hadn't Maxine run away years ago? Nothing, not even her dressing-room, which appeared to be filled to overflowing with *couture* garments, designer shoes and exquisite lingerie, could possibly compensate for what must have been a thoroughly miserable, desolate existence.

And what about Zarco? Every time she thought about the problem, Tiffany kept coming up against the same massive stumbling block. *Why* was Zarco so certain that she was Maxine?

Even if he didn't share his wife's bed, Zarco must have spent a great deal of time with her, right? But, although she might look like Maxine—and everyone seemed convinced that she did—Tiffany was certain that their character and personality must be very different. So, why hadn't he noticed that fact? After all, there was no one closer to a married woman, or who ought to know her better, than her husband.

As the arguments swayed back and forth in her brain, Tiffany gave a heartfelt sigh of despondency. She couldn't blame Zarco for not liking his wife—especially since everyone else seemed to detest the woman! But she had to admit that there were times when he had been surprisingly kind and considerate. The way he'd rescued her, when she'd first arrived at Norton Manor, and been upset by the housekeeper's chilly reception, had been really thoughtful. And his sympathetic understanding of her feminine despair and misery about the state of her hair had been equally unexpected. What was more, Zarco hadn't just taken pity on her obvious distress—he'd done something about the problem. Arranging the visit of a hairdresser had been a kind gesture, and one which she *must* try to remember the next time he was being particularly nasty or aggressive.

Tiffany gave a heavy sigh as she felt the light breeze rustling through her soft curls. As much as she might want to, it was no good trying to fool herself. Zarco was always going to be a hard, tough and ruthless man—a fierce, dangerous leopard who wasn't likely to ever change his spots!

As she recalled just how fierce and dangerous he could be, Tiffany could feel a deep flush spreading over her pale cheeks. Goodness knows, she'd done her best to forget the extraordinary, upsetting way in which he had treated her in the hospital.

Although she was remembering more and more every day, maybe it was because her memory was so blank that her brain seemed to have nothing else to do but run a constant, perpetual repetition of the embarrassing episodes. It was just as though someone had pushed the continuous play-back button on a video recorder. Unfortunately, whatever the reason, she couldn't seem to blot out of her memory the touch of his tanned fingers on her breasts, nor the heady warmth and sensual excitement of his mouth and tongue, when he'd clasped her so tightly in his arms.

Almost gasping at the intense, twisting pain which suddenly scorched through her body, Tiffany clenched her eyes tightly shut and tried to fill her lungs with a deep, steadying breath. What on earth was *wrong* with her? She didn't need to remind herself of how much she disliked Zarco dos Santos. Even with two casual acts of kindness to his credit, he was still someone who ought to carry a large, clearly visible warning: 'Beware! This Man is Dangerous!'

So, she must . . . she really *must* try to forget what had happened. It had obviously meant nothing to Zarco. He'd certainly never attempted to repeat the actions which, she was quite sure, had been meant as a calculated, deliberate punishment towards a wife he clearly hated. And, if she'd found the incidents profoundly devastating, it must have been due to her obviously weak state of mind and body, following the blow to her head.

Preoccupied with trying to rationalise and explain away her inexplicable, emotional response to Zarco, Tiffany hadn't realised that she was no longer alone in the herb garden.

Distracted by a slight sound, she looked up in surprise to see Amy Long picking some mint from a bed in the far corner of the garden. As she watched the plump middle-aged woman gathering a collection of herbs, Tiffany suddenly decided that this was a good opportunity to try and sort matters out with the housekeeper.

Amy had made it plain that she cordially detested Zarco's second wife, but Tiffany saw no reason why *she* should have to suffer just because the two women had loathed one another. And, with Zarco's departure for Portugal, she'd been left very much at the mercy of the housekeeper.

Tiffany felt sure that she'd never had to live with such enmity before: a cold hostility which was making her even more lonely and unhappy than she'd have believed possible. Every friendly approach had been firmly repulsed by the housekeeper, and she was feeling desperately in need of some warm, human companionship.

'Look,' she began, after telling Amy that she wanted a word with her, 'I don't know whether—er—my husband has told you about my accident, in Portugal . . . ?'

'I've heard very little, madam,' the housekeeper told her, in her usual prim and chilly tone of voice.

'Well, I'd like to talk to you about it, and . . . Oh—for heaven's sake, Amy! Won't you *please* sit down and relax?' Tiffany exclaimed with exasperation as the other woman remained standing stiffly in front of her.

'I don't bite. I haven't got an infectious disease. And, since we have to live together in this house, it seems absolutely *crazy* for us not to be friends. Right?'

Obviously startled by the girl's outburst, Amy hesitated for a moment. Then, with a slight shrug of her shoulders, she lowered herself silently down on to the bench.

'Well—that's a start, anyway,' Tiffany sighed, before taking her courage in both hands and launching forth into an explanation of all that had happened to her in Portugal. Nor did she omit the extraordinary story of the theft of Zarco's gold and jewellery from his bank in Lisbon.

'And, just to make the whole thing ten times worse, Amy,' she added helplessly, 'I can't seem to persuade anyone—not even my so-called husband—that there's been a really *terrible* mistake. That I'm *not* that simply awful woman, Maxine dos Santos!'

'Yes, well . . . if what you say is right, you do seem to have a problem!' Amy agreed slowly.

'I have remembered quite a bit about my past life as Tiffany Harris—when I was married to a not very successful professional tennis player, Brian Harris. We spent our life travelling around the world on the tennis circuit, but, unfortunately, I can't remember a thing about Portugal. I don't even know why I was in the country, in the first place. And as for being found up at Sintra . . . ?' She shrugged unhappily. 'I simply don't have a clue what I was doing there. And . . . and because I've lost my memory—there isn't a damned thing I c-can d-do about it!' she wailed, suddenly overcome by an avalanche of deep loneliness, and desperately ashamed at not being able to prevent the hot tears from flowing down her cheeks.

'Now, now. We can't have you crying like this,' the other woman murmured with concern, putting a comforting arm around Tiffany's bowed, quivering shoulders.

'I . . . I'm s-sorry.' The girl raised a trembling hand to brush the tears from her eyes. 'It just . . . well, it's all got on top of me, I suppose,' she muttered, gratefully accepting a handkerchief from Amy and quickly blowing her nose.

'See here,' the housekeeper said, when Tiffany had herself more under control, 'if it's any comfort, I can tell you that I've noticed you *are* very different, since you've returned from abroad. And if you really *aren't* Maxine . . . ?' She paused and frowned as she shook her head. 'Well, I don't know what to think—and that's a fact!'

Tiffany blew her nose again. 'Nor do I. Which is the whole trouble, you see.'

'Hmm . . . yes. I don't know why it never occurred to me that you might *not* be the Marquês's wife. I mean, although we've lived in the house together for some time, she was always very . . .'

'Very nasty and unpleasant?'

'You're not far wrong!' Amy gave a muffled snort of laughter. 'On the other hand, if the Marquês is convinced you really are his wife . . .' She hesitated and shrugged her shoulders.

'That's what has me stumped, too,' Tiffany admitted despondently. 'I've just been telling myself that a man *must* know the woman he's married to. I mean, you can't live *that* close to someone—not without knowing them really well, can you?'

To her horror, she couldn't do anything to stop the helpless tears from beginning to stream down her face once again.

'Now—come on, dear. This isn't going to help, is it?' the older woman said firmly, before suggesting that they go back to the house, and have a nice cup of tea in the kitchen.

Sitting at the large, scrubbed pine table and sipping the hot sweet liquid, Tiffany realised it was a tremendous relief to have been able to tell Amy about her problems. Even if the housekeeper found the situation difficult to understand, she was certainly being very kind and friendly.

'Thanks for listening to me, Amy,' Tiffany told her as she put down her cup. 'Quite honestly, I've been almost out of my mind over this business—except that I don't seem to have much of a mind to be out of!' she added with a wry, unhappy smile.

The housekeeper opened her mouth to say something, and then hesitated for a moment as she turned to take a saucepan off the ultra-modern kitchen range.

'I probably shouldn't say anything,' she muttered, turning back to face Tiffany, 'but you can't live in a house without knowing what's going on—if you see what I mean?'

Tiffany wasn't at all sure that she did see, but she gave the older woman an encouraging nod.

'Well...' The housekeeper hesitated again, her cheeks slightly pink as she said in a rush, 'I can tell you that, unlike most married couples, the Marquês and his wife didn't—er—they didn't share a bedroom.'

'Yes, I had gathered that,' Tiffany murmured, her cheeks flushed as she stared down at the table.

'Ah, but what you might *not* know is that they've hardly seen each other over the last few years.'

Tiffany raised her head. 'Really?'

'Madam hated having to live here at the manor; she much preferred her own small, modern apartment in London,' Amy said, pursing her lips in tight disapproval. 'Whenever the Marquês was due to come home after a business trip, that Maxine would skip off to London—quick as a flash!—and not come back here until he'd gone. If you ask me...' the housekeeper dropped her voice '...I'm sure it was an excuse to see that fancy man of hers!'

'A *fancy man*?' Tiffany looked at her with startled eyes. It was the first she'd heard about Maxine's apartment in London, and as for the other woman's boyfriend... 'Surely, with such an attractive husband, she couldn't possibly—er——' She broke off in confusion, a deep flush rising up over her cheeks.

Clearly relishing the opportunity to have a good gossip about a woman she actively disliked, Amy didn't appear to notice the girl's heightened colour.

'Oh, yes! She had the brass nerve to invite him here, once or twice, before the Marquês returned unexpectedly one day, and threw him out. Ooh...the Marquês didn't half lose his temper! I've *never* seen him so angry. "I'm not having that greasy hoodlum in *my* house!" he roared. And she took good care never to invite that Tony Silver to the house again. Mind you, she was always on the phone to him, and...'

Tiffany was only half listening as the housekeeper continued letting her hair down about Maxine's boyfriend.

At the first mention of his name, she'd had a fleeting image of a man turning to face her, his dark

swarthy features topped by black curly hair beneath
a grey peaked hat. 'You're the boss, lady! All the way
to Sintra, huh?' he'd been saying with a wide grin,
accompanied by a knowing wink and a slight laugh.
It was a brief image, which quickly began fading away
before Tiffany could grasp it. But, as she strained to
recall the sound of the man's voice, she realised her
fragile, shakily built house of cards had just collapsed.

'Mind you, both my husband Tom and I knew that
Tony Silver was up to no good—right from the first
moment we laid eyes on him!' Amy was saying as she
poured another cup of tea.

'What—er——?' Tiffany cleared her throat, which
seemed obstructed by a large painful lump. 'What did
Tony look like?' she asked breathlessly, unable to meet
the housekeeper's eyes, as she stared down at the nervously twisting hands in her lap.

'Well, he was sort of like those American gangsters
you see on TV. You know—sort of Italian-looking he
was, with lots of black curly hair. *Not* a nice man, at
all!' Amy added, her voice heavy with disapproval.

How she managed to finish her cup of tea, or go
through the polite motions of thanking the housekeeper, before slowly trailing upstairs to her bedroom,
Tiffany had no idea. It was, she realised as she threw
herself wearily on to the bed, one of the blackest days
of her life. Because, while she knew that she wasn't
Maxine, she also now had no doubts that she *had*
known Maxine's boyfriend. Although how or where
was still a complete mystery. Unfortunately, thanks
to the housekeeper's revelations, she could no longer
assume that there had been a simple mistake in identification. For her to have known Tony, it must mean
that she had also known Maxine. So—even if she
couldn't remember a thing about it—maybe she *had*

been involved in the theft of Zarco's gold and
jewellery, after all...?

Humming quietly to herself, Tiffany scattered a light
dusting of flour on to the large marble pastry board.
She wasn't going to be able to eat it all herself, of
course, but Amy had laughingly agreed to sample her
first attempt at salmon *en croute*, when the older
woman returned tomorrow from a visit to her married
daughter in Oxford.

The development of her new friendship with Amy,
and the peace and quiet of the old medieval house,
had helped Tiffany to come to terms with the fact that
somehow—somewhere—she'd met Maxine's boyfriend, Tony Silver. She still couldn't remember anything about how or why she had been in Portugal,
but over the last two days she'd been plagued by re-
curring visions of the man, the flickering images accompanied by frightening, strange feelings of fear and
alarm. However, whatever the true answer might prove
to be, there didn't seem to be anything she could do
at the present time—no alternative but to try and
accept this new life at Norton Manor until she had,
hopefully, regained her full memory.

However, her new relationship with Amy Long had
proved to be very successful. As had been Tiffany's
confession that she couldn't remember knowing how
to cook anything but very plain, simple meals—and
would the housekeeper please teach her how to
produce some interesting recipes? Apparently Maxine
had been quite a gourmet, and much given to criti-
cising Amy's efforts, so the older woman had been
only too pleased to take on the role of cookery in-
structor. Tiffany wasn't at all sure how her first solo
effort was going to turn out, but she was finding it

remarkably soothing to be alone, here in the kitchen, with just a large ginger cat for company.

'Well, if this turns out to be a mess, at least you'll be happy to eat the fish!' she told the cat who was lying curled up by the warm kitchen range. 'And that will make a nice change from the mice, which you keep leaving outside my bedroom door!' she added with a slight laugh, as she carefully rolled out the puff pastry.

'To be found talking to oneself is surely the first sign of madness?'

Tiffany gave a shriek, almost jumping out of her skin at the sudden, totally unexpected sound of the deep voice. Spinning around, she was amazed to see the tall, broad-shouldered figure of Zarco lounging casually in the doorway of the kitchen.

'Oh, my goodness! You gave me *such* a fright!' she gasped, clasping floury hands to her chest, where her heart was thumping and pounding like a kettledrum. 'And I wasn't . . . wasn't talking to myself. I was actually talking to the cat,' she muttered, before her cheeks flushed as she realised just how silly she must sound.

'Ah, yes. How is my friend the marmalade cat?' Zarco murmured, bending down to pick up the animal, who had raced across the floor to greet him, excitedly rubbing its back against the man's long legs.

'He's fine,' Tiffany muttered, backing nervously up against the table as Zarco walked slowly towards her, casually holding the cat against one shoulder of his expensive, dark grey suit.

Zarco smiled. 'And what do we have here?' he murmured, coming to a halt and gazing down at the pastry-covered board.

'I was just...I mean...Amy's been teaching
me...she's been very kind and...' Tiffany gabbled
breathlessly, confused by Zarco's sudden, unexpected
return from his business trip to Portugal—*and* his
close proximity to her nervous figure.

'I think that I approve of this surprisingly new
domestic side to your personality,' he drawled.

'You do...?' she murmured nervously, her attention distracted for a moment as she noticed the
ginger cat in his arms beginning to take a keen interest
in the salmon, lying on a plate beside the pastry.

'Yes, just as I most definitely approve of your new
hairstyle. The colour looks far more natural, too.'

Tiffany swallowed apprehensively, prevented by the
hard edge of the kitchen table from backing away any
further as he raised a hand to tuck a stray lock of
hair behind her ear.

'Yes, well...I've got to have a long talk to you
about that—and other things too,' she told him
huskily. The warm touch of his fingers on her skin
was having a disastrous effect on her nervous system,
not only leaving her breathless and with her legs
feeling as though they were made of jelly, but also
causing her to entirely forget what it was she'd been
going to say.

'I look forward to trying out this new recipe of
yours.'

'*What*...?' She gazed at him in confusion. The
glittering dark eyes beneath their heavy lids were regarding her with some amusement. 'You mean...do
you mean that you *actually* want to eat this?'

'Why not?' He raised a dark sardonic eyebrow.
'You aren't intending to poison me, are you?'

'No, of course not!' she retorted indignantly. 'It's
just that...well, I've never cooked this recipe before,

and so I can't guarantee that it's going to be a success,' she added, dearly wishing that she'd never had the bright idea of asking Amy to teach her *haute cuisine*. Although there wasn't going to be anything very *haute* about this particular piece of *cuisine*—not with the awful man looming over her, like this.

Almost as if he could read her mind, Zarco's mouth twitched in silent humour. 'I'm feeling somewhat travel-stained,' he told her blandly. 'So I think I would like to have a shower and change before we eat. That will not interfere with your—er—production of this dish?'

'No—not at all,' Tiffany told him hurriedly, suddenly finding the atmosphere in the large kitchen very claustrophobic. She couldn't help letting out a gasp of apprehension as he lifted a hand, flinching as if she had been stung when he brushed his fingers lightly across her breasts.

'I am merely removing the flour,' Zarco informed her coolly, ignoring her breathless and flustered protests as he calmly—and taking *far* too long about the job, in her opinion!—proceeded to brush her floury fingerprints from the bodice of her cotton blouse.

'There, that is better,' he murmured, after finishing the job to his satisfaction. 'Although, in future, I would suggest that you ought to wear an apron whenever you decide to do any cooking,' he drawled mockingly, before putting the cat back down on the floor and walking slowly away across the kitchen.

Patronising swine! Tiffany thought, her cheeks pink with embarrassment as she hurriedly turned back to complete her preparations for the meal.

After placing the pastry case containing the salmon into the oven, she quickly dashed upstairs to tidy herself before dinner.

A quick glance at her flour-streaked blouse was enough for Tiffany to know that she must find something else to wear. Slipping out of the garment, she pulled a face as she caught sight of her own reflection in the long, full-length mirror on the wall. Having no alternative to wearing the clothes in the wardrobe, she also had no choice but to clothe herself in Maxine's very expensive thin gauzy lingerie. So thin and transparent, indeed, that her hard, swollen nipples were only too evident through the fine silky material.

That dreadful man! Tiffany glowered at herself as she recalled the cool mockery with which he had viewed her embarrassment at his touch on her breasts. He *must* have known what he was doing to her, and the effect that his fingers would have on her body!

She blushed, turning away from the reflection of just how easily Zarco had aroused her weak flesh. Even now, there seemed little she could do to banish the strange, throbbing, sick excitement in the pit of her stomach. With a low moan she rushed into the bathroom, splashing her face with cold water and roughly towelling it dry, as she desperately tried to pull herself together. But, meeting her own blue eyes in the mirror above the basin, she couldn't escape the sight of their numb, apprehensive dread about the evening which lay ahead of her.

CHAPTER FIVE

TIFFANY took a deep breath and tried to relax her nervously rigid, tense figure. It looked such a peaceful scene—the sparkling crystal glasses and the gleam of the silver cutlery reflected in the glowing, highly polished surface of the antique oak refectory dining table. *But she knew better*!

Thanks to Zarco, she'd been in a state of total nervous exhaustion for the past hour, attempting to produce the sort of meal which Amy Long could easily have done with her eyes shut, and one hand tied behind her back! To add insult to injury, the dreadful man was now making her wait until he finished every scrap on his plate before expressing an opinion.

Why on earth had she wanted to learn to cook? It was obviously a completely exhausting pastime—and definitely not one she was in any hurry to repeat. In fact, as far as she was concerned, the sooner Amy took back full control of the kitchen, the better!

It was in the middle of changing her dress that Tiffany had suddenly realised she ought to serve a first course, before the salmon in its pastry case made an appearance. After a muffled shriek of dismay, she'd quickly jumped into the nearest garment in the wardrobe, before dashing back downstairs to the kitchen. And that hadn't been such a good idea, either, she told herself gloomily.

There was nothing wrong with the dress itself—a classically simple design in a shade of deep pink raw silk—but if she'd had more time, Tiffany wouldn't have chosen this particular garment. The thin material of the cross-over bodice clung tightly to her full breasts, and the way Zarco's deeply hooded eyes kept glancing towards the low V-shaped neckline was making her feel distinctly nervous.

Down in the kitchen and glassy-eyed with nerves, she'd stared at the packed shelves of the store cupboard, fervently praying for inspiration, before discovering some tins of beef consommé. After emptying them into a saucepan and adding a hefty slug of sherry, she belatedly realised she hadn't even begun to think about what vegetables to serve with the salmon. Or what they were going to eat for dessert.

Buzzing around like a demented housefly, she had more or less got things under control by the time Zarco had made an appearance.

Claiming that they must celebrate 'this auspicious occasion'—apparently, according to him, it was the first time that his wife had ever deigned to cook him a meal—Tiffany had found herself presented with a large glass of sparkling champagne.

Maybe it was the effect of alcohol on an empty stomach, but as she'd stood in the large, elegant drawing-room, with its french windows open to admit the soft evening air, Tiffany had suddenly felt sick with tension. And not just about the forthcoming meal.

Glancing nervously up through her eyelashes at Zarco's tall figure, she hadn't been able to help noting the length of his legs in the slim-fitting black cords. A matching black cashmere sweater worn over a casual, open-necked shirt seemed to emphasise his deeply tanned complexion. With his black hair still damp from the shower, and combed tightly to his well

shaped head, he looked formidable—and very, very
dangerous.

Unfortunately, Tiffany was also considerably
shaken to find herself thinking that he also looked
diabolically attractive! Although she did her best to
conceal her instinctive, quivering reaction to his aura
of dark sensuality, she wasn't at all sure that she'd
succeeded. The searchlight beam of those glittering
eyes seemed to be capable of invading her very soul.

How *could* she be so stupid as to feel this way—
especially about a man whom she both disliked and
distrusted? It was a question which had increasingly
dominated her mind throughout the meal, and one to
which she couldn't seem to find an answer.

'That was really very good indeed.' Zarco's voice
cut into her distraught thoughts now, as he placed his
knife and fork down on the empty plate.

'Oh—er—I'm glad you liked it,' she muttered, her
tense figure almost sagging with relief. 'Um...I
thought you might be tired after your journey. So I
decided we'd just finish the meal with fruit and
cheese,' she told him, trying to put a brave face on
the fact that she'd weakly chickened out of trying to
produce a glamorous dessert.

'That was very thoughtful of you,' he drawled,
rising from his chair at the end of the highly polished
table to pour her another glass of wine. 'And what
culinary masterpiece would you have produced, if I
hadn't been so—er—"tired"?'

After a quick, furtive glance up at the gleaming,
sardonic amusement in his eyes, Tiffany knew there
was no point in trying to fool him.

'I'm afraid that you'd have been out of luck!' she
admitted with a slightly nervous, rueful grin as he returned to the other end of the table. 'To tell you the

truth, my cooking hasn't progressed much further than learning how to boil an egg!'

Zarco studied her silently for a moment. Casually leaning back in his red-velvet-upholstered chair, he seemed to be absorbed in his own thoughts as he turned to stare blindly at the heavy crystal wine glass on the table in front of him, slowly revolving its slim stem between his long, tanned fingers.

Driven by her inner fear and anxiety of this daunting man, Tiffany quickly searched back through their previous conversation, seeking some clue to the sudden and oppressive silence which had fallen on the table. But she could think of nothing; nothing that could have upset him in the innocuous, harmless few words which they'd exchanged during the meal.

'I think...' Zarco murmured at last, slowly raising his gaze towards her '... I think that before we go any further with this interesting conversation I would like to get a few of the ground rules sorted out. Am I dining with my dear wife, Maxine, who appears to have forgotten that she did a part-time cordon bleu course, a few years ago?' he enquired smoothly. 'Or are you this apparently mythical creature, "Tiffany", who has just informed me—if I understood her correctly—that she wouldn't know an *oeuf mollet* from her elbow...?'

'My name *is* Tiffany Harris!' she retorted. 'Not only have I remembered a great deal more about my past life, but I'm now sure that I can now prove my true identity!' she added triumphantly. 'I was very grateful to you for sending the hairdresser, Vernon, down here to see me. And Vernon has said he's willing to swear that both the texture and the colour of my hair are *not* Maxine's!'

'Oh, really?' Zarco drawled, his voice heavy with scorn. 'I don't think that a statement by a mere hairdresser is likely to carry much weight, do you?'

Tiffany glared down the table at the handsome man who'd so lightly and cynically dismissed the only piece of hard evidence she'd managed to gather so far. How could she have possibly thought him attractive? In fact, Zarco was thoroughly *hateful*—and for two pins she'd tell him so, she raged silently, desperately trying not to give in to an overwhelming urge to shout and scream, and burst into tears of acute frustration.

'It would seem that I have upset you . . . ?'

'Yes—yes, you most certainly *have*!' she burst out angrily. 'I mean . . . how would *you* like it, if you woke up one day and discovered that you were married to a man who clearly hated you? That—although you couldn't remember a thing about it—you were being accused of theft and grand larceny? And that, all in all, you appeared to be Public Enemy Number One . . . ?' she demanded bleakly.

'Well, Maxine, I——'

'*Don't call me that*!' she stormed. 'If I've *got* to get used to this new life, I'm insisting that everyone calls me by my own true name!'

Zarco shrugged his broad shoulders. 'Very well, if that is what you wish—er—Tiffany. And yes, I will agree that if, as the doctors tell me, you really have no recollection of our past life together, it must indeed be a very trying circumstance.'

'"*A trying circumstance*"?' she exclaimed incredulously. 'Believe me—that's putting it mildly! You don't have *any* conception of the problem, do you?' She jumped to her feet, glowering down the table at him, her figure rigid with overwhelming rage and fury.

'Sit down,' he commanded brusquely. 'There's no need for any of this——'

'There's every need!' She waved her hands distractedly in the air. 'What do I have to do? How can I get it into your thick head that I'm Tiffany Harris? I can give you the names of my father and mother, and even the date on which I married my husband, Brian Harris. But will you listen? Will you—*hell*!' she yelled at him, her normally slow-to-rise temper by now well out of control.

'There is no need to shout at me,' Zarco said firmly. 'I am well aware that there are some facets of your behaviour which I find difficult to—er—match up with those of my wife.'

'Oh, *great*!' Tiffany raged, his cool, rational words merely adding fuel to her passionate anger and fury. 'The great Zarco dos Santos has *actually* noticed some differences between me and his foul wife? Wow! Big deal!'

His face darkened with anger. 'That's quite enough of this nonsense!'

'That's all it is to you—*nonsense*!' she lashed back huskily, the fierce storm of temper draining away from her trembling figure, almost as fast as it had arisen. 'For goodness' sake, Zarco—can't you admit that you've made a mistake . . . ? Do you *really* have to be s-so b-blind?' she begged tearfully, before taking to her heels and dashing out of the room, running up the long, curving staircase to seek refuge in her bedroom.

Tiffany sat up in the bath, wringing out her sponge to wipe away the last trace of her recent flood of tears. She really must pull herself together, she told herself firmly, leaning over the side of the bath to extract some tissues from her make-up bag, and blowing her nose fiercely. Lying back in the warm water, she stared blindly up through the clouds of steam as she tried to work out what on earth she was going to do.

She was sure that never before had she lost her temper quite so spectacularly. Quite certain that she was, normally, a quiet and reserved sort of person, which might be the reason why she was now feeling so exhausted and shattered at having made such an exhibition of herself, and for the storm of tears which had followed.

However, angry as she was with Zarco, she couldn't entirely blame him for what had happened. Because she had to admit that she'd been in a considerable state of nerves even before they had sat down to the meal. In fact, that meal had been positively her very last attempt to master the art of cooking. She had quite enough problems, without adding the strain and tension of trying to master an unfamiliar branch of science! However, while it was all very well to dismiss the idea of turning herself into a perfect little house-keeper—clearly an aim which she should never have attempted in the first place—there was no escaping the fact that she really must try and leave Norton Manor, as soon as possible.

Although she hadn't anywhere to go, Tiffany knew that she couldn't remain here any longer. For one thing, the thought of more rows and arguments was enough to make her feel ill. And those were bound to arise, since Zarco was obviously determined to continue trying to prove that she was his wife, Maxine. And, however futile it might be, she had no alternative but to continue insisting on her own identity. So... what choice had she? As much as she loved this old medieval house, she must leave and try to make a new life for herself—well away from the disturbing influence of Zarco dos Santos. But how she was going to do so, with no money or formal identification, she had absolutely no idea.

The rapidly cooling water of the bath intruded into her distracted thoughts, and, stepping out to envelop herself in a short, warm fleecy towel, she walked slowly through into the bedroom. Only to come to a startled, stumbling halt at the sight of Zarco, calmly sitting in a comfortable chair beside the bed.

'Ah, there you are—at last!' he drawled smoothly.

'Wh-what are you doing in here?' she breathed huskily, nervously clutching the towel around her naked body. 'What do you want?'

He ignored her breathless questions. 'I trust you are feeling somewhat better, and more relaxed after your bath?'

'Yes—er—yes, I'm sorry... I don't usually lose my temper,' Tiffany muttered, her cheeks flushed as she stared guiltily down at her bare feet, her toes curling with embarrassment into the thick pile of the carpet.

'That is exactly why I am here. I think that it's time you and I had a long talk,' he stated coolly.

'No, I really don't think... there doesn't seem to be any point in——'

'I have decided that we are going to have a long talk,' he repeated firmly. 'And, while I might agree that you look enchanting in that brief towel, I think you might feel more comfortable in something possibly less—er—revealing!' he added in a mocking drawl, his dark eyes glinting with amusement as he viewed her efforts to pull the towel more tightly about her slim figure.

Tiffany could feel a deep tide of crimson flooding over her face and body as she registered the sardonic,

cynical amusement in his deep voice. As she told
herself later, she really *would* have stood her ground
and ordered him out of the bedroom, if she hadn't
made the mistake of raising her head to give the
hateful man a scornful, withering glance.

Unfortunately, as soon as she viewed Zarco leaning
casually back in his chair, idly allowing his eyes to
conduct an analytical appraisal of her trembling
body—one that began at the top of her head and travelled insolently down over her slim figure to the pink
toenails of her bare feet—she was immediately thrown
into confusion. With no impulse other than to immediately escape from those insulting dark eyes, she
spun around and pulled open a drawer, swiftly
grabbing the nearest garment before whisking herself
back into the sanctuary of the bathroom.

The damned nerve of the man! she thought angrily,
banging the door shut loudly behind her. But her brief
spurt of defiance soon drained away as she took her
first good look at the garment she had so hastily seized
from her chest of drawers. Oh, lord! This thin, flimsy
nightgown was likely to be no better than the short
towel she was wearing.

In fact, she told herself gloomily a few moments
later, it was a good deal worse! Grimacing with
dismay, and unable to avoid the sight of herself in the
mirrors which lined the room, she desperately tried
to tug the edges of the minuscule bodice closer
together. Attempting to hide the deep creamy cleft between her breasts, Tiffany soon realised that she had
another, major problem.

A quick glance in the mirrored wall behind her confirmed her worst suspicions: the diaphanous black
nightgown was practically transparent! And, while
Maxine might well have fancied herself in this erotic-

looking négligé, Tiffany could only hope and pray that
a thunderbolt would strike down the dreadful man,
who was so calmly making himself at home in the
bedroom next door.

Unfortunately, she knew that her prayers had no
chance of being answered. After giving the thin,
shoelace straps of the garment another hopeless tug
upwards, she tried to brace herself for the forthcoming ordeal.

'I'm not coming out of here—not unless you
promise to close your eyes!' Tiffany announced tremulously as she opened the door a crack, only her
head visible as she glared across the bedroom at the
man who was, quite maddeningly, coolly reading one
of the books from her bedside table.

'I mean it!' she added tersely, her embarrassment
quickly turning to anger as Zarco gave a short bark
of sardonic laughter. 'If you don't close your eyes—
and stop laughing—I shall stay in here. All night, if
need be!'

Zarco shook his head and gave a heavy, impatient
sigh. 'This is clearly quite ridiculous. Especially since
I am a married man, and well used to the sight of my
wife in a négligé.'

'Not *this* wife, you're not!' Tiffany snapped, before
making good her threat and firmly closing the door.

She wasn't really going to stay in here all night, she
consoled herself as she leant wearily back against the
wooden panels of the small door. However, she was
at least safe in here for the time being. A comforting
thought, which was swiftly dispelled a moment later
when the door was violently thrown open, the force
of the blow propelling her across the room.

'Ouch . . . !' she moaned, wincing as she rubbed the
shin-bone of her leg where it had banged against the

edge of the bath. 'There was no need to barge in here like that,' she grumbled, turning to face the man whose tall figure filled the doorway.

'There was every need,' he grated forcefully. 'I want you out of here—*right now*!'

After a swift glance at his stern, angry expression, and the rigid stance of his tense body, Tiffany quickly decided there was little point in arguing any further. Raising her chin defiantly, she stalked past him, before throwing her dignity to the wind as she dashed across the room, quickly scrambling beneath the covers of the large four-poster bed.

'I have had quite enough of this nonsense!' Zarco stated flatly, advancing slowly across the room towards her. 'I have said I wish to talk to you—and that is exactly what I intend to do.'

He pulled the chair closer to the bed, before sitting down and regarding her with a hard, determined expression in his dark eyes.

Tiffany, anxious to cover as much of her semi-naked flesh as possible, nervously raised the sheet to her chin, inching as far back against the pillows as possible.

'Have I made myself clear?' he demanded, and, when she responded with an apprehensive nod, some of the rigid stiffness seemed to drain out of his long body.

'Very well,' he continued, leaning back in the comfortable chair. 'Earlier this evening you accused me of not only being blind—but also of not being able to admit that I might have made a mistake. And so, after giving the matter some considerable thought, I am prepared to listen to what you have to say.'

'And about time too!' she muttered under her breath.

Zarco blandly ignored her interruption. 'Let us assume, just for the moment, that you are who you say you are: that you are "Tiffany Harris". If so, I think that you should start by telling me everything you can remember about yourself.'

Tiffany gave a helpless shrug. 'Well, I'll try to do my best ... but I'm still having difficulty remembering *exact* dates and times,' she said, before staring down fixedly at the sheet as she tried to concentrate on the problem. This was clearly her best opportunity to try and open Zarco's eyes to the fact that she *wasn't* Maxine—and she must try to recall every single scrap of helpful information which had been slowly floating back into her mind during the past few days.

Slowly and hesitantly, she began to describe her life with the great-aunts who had brought her up following the death of her parents, Martin and Harriette Kendall. 'I expect I was a bit of a pain in the neck,' she admitted with a slight, rueful smile. 'But I missed my father and mother so much, and my life in that grim Victorian house was so awful that it's no wonder I took the first opportunity to run away from home!'

She was surprised to find that Zarco was surprisingly understanding when she confessed that there were still some large gaps in her life which she hadn't been able to fill. She could remember her runaway wedding to Brian Harris—and the fact that he was a not very successful professional tennis player.

'It's crazy, really.' She brushed a distracted hand through her short, wavy gold hair. 'I could draw you a complete layout of the courts at Wimbledon, Flushing Meadow and Forest Lawn. But ... but I don't ... I can't remember what's happened to Brian.' She gazed at Zarco in distress.

'Ah, yes—the elusive Brian Harris,' he drawled smoothly. 'Were you happy with your husband?'

Unfortunately, that was one part of her life which she could remember only too well. 'No, I...' She faltered, bitterly aware of a deep flush rising over her pale cheeks.

'Are you trying to say that you weren't happy—or that you cannot remember?' Zarco enquired drily.

Tiffany glared at him. Why couldn't the damned man mind his own business? 'No, I wasn't happy,' she snapped. 'And that's all I'm prepared to say on the subject!'

'Very well,' he murmured coolly. 'Leaving aside your unhappy marriage, what else can you remember about this life of yours?'

'Not much,' she admitted ruefully. 'I think...I think I remember packing our suitcases, and Brian telling me to hurry up, because we were going to be late for the flight to London, and...' Tiffany paused, closing her eyes as she tried to concentrate very hard on the faint thread of remembered sound. 'And...we *had* to catch the flight, to make our connection with the plane to...to Faro. Yes—*that's it*! Brian was being hired by a tennis club in the Algarve. That's in Portugal, isn't it?' she asked with a frown.

'Indeed it is,' Zarco drawled slowly. 'And how long ago was this trip to the Algarve?'

Tiffany shrugged. 'I don't feel that it was very long ago... but I really can't be sure about that,' she confessed unhappily.

Seeing that the girl was obviously distressed, Zarco decided to change the subject. 'We seem to have a brief outline of your life. However, I don't think I have asked how old you are.'

'Yes, well—that's one thing I *am* fairly sure about,' she told him, her spirits lifting at being able to be positive about one aspect of her life, at least. 'My birthday is on September the sixth. And I *know* that I am not yet twenty-five, because on my twenty-fifth birthday I'm due to inherit a considerable amount of money from a trust fund set up by my parents. I know that I haven't yet had the money, so I think I must be only about twenty-three or twenty-four years of age. No wonder I never felt that I was Maxine's age of twenty-seven—I knew I couldn't be *that* old!'

Zarco's shoulders shook with amusement. 'If twenty-seven is old, how do you think *I* feel at the ripe old age of thirty-eight?'

'Goodness—you don't look that ancient!' she exclaimed without thinking, before his snort of dry, cynical laughter made her realise that she might have put her foot in it. 'Oh—er—I didn't mean to be rude, or...'

'On the contrary—I rather think that I'm flattered by your reaction!' he said, giving her such a warm and infectious grin that she was amazed to find herself smiling tentatively back at him. And, since he appeared to be in a better mood, maybe this was the perfect moment for her to ask the sixty-four-thousand-dollar question.

'Have I... have I managed to convince you that I really am Tiffany Harris?' she asked him nervously, her shoulders drooping in dejection and despair as he gave a slight shake of his dark head.

'No, not one hundred per cent,' he told her quietly. 'You see, I have been married for some years to a woman whom I *know* to be a cheat and a liar. A very plausible and clever woman, who would be quite capable not only of convincing Harley Street specialists that she had completely lost her memory, but also able to concoct a completely new life for herself, such as you have just described.'

Zarco rose, pushing away the chair as he began to pace up and down the room. 'So, although I would like to accept what you say, believe me, I have been given good reasons in the past to be very cautious,' he added grimly.

Tiffany gave a heavy sigh. 'I believe you,' she muttered glumly. 'But what I *can't* understand is why you don't instinctively know that I'm not Maxine? I mean...' She frowned and shook her head as she tried to find the words. 'There's always more to someone than a...a physical presence, if you see what I mean? I know that I'm not expressing this very well, but if I was to see my parents again—even after all these years, and even if they looked completely different— I'm sure I would immediately recognise their individual personalities.'

'My wife and I lived very separate lives,' Zarco told her dismissively.

Tiffany sighed. 'You simply don't seem to understand,' she muttered. 'For instance, I *know* that I've never met you before. And that's not just because I don't recognise you—but also because the essential part of you, the personal aura you carry about with you, is totally unfamiliar. Surely you must see what I mean?' she added helplessly. 'Or is it that you are so fed up with Maxine, both for stealing your jewels and because you actively disliked her, that you can't see beyond the end of your nose?'

Zarco frowned as her voice rose in exasperation. 'Of course I understand what you are trying to say. But what *you* seem to fail to understand is the plain fact that every time I look at you—I see my wife!'

'Yes, I know,' she murmured gloomily. 'How on earth did you come to marry the awful woman in the first place?'

'It's a long story,' he told her curtly. 'And, unfortunately, not one which reflects any credit on myself.'

Tiffany gazed up at the man who had come to a halt beside the bed, and who was clearly buried in his own dark thoughts as he leaned against the carved bedpost. Watching as he pushed a hand through his dark hair, ruffling its normally sleek surface, and the heavy half-closed eyelids beneath which he was clearly retracing uncomfortable memories of his past, she was suddenly swept by a strong tide of deep compassion and sympathy for the unhappy man.

Totally confounded by such an unexpectedly strong emotional response towards a man whom she disliked and feared, she couldn't help giving a small gasp. The slight sound broke into his abstracted thoughts and he turned, his eyes narrowing thoughtfully as he viewed the unguarded expression on her face.

She could feel a deep flush spreading over her skin—an extraordinary sensation of white heat surging through her body. The room seemed to be shrinking about them, their two still figures caught in a time-warp, one in which she felt increasingly weak and light-headed. The strained silence seemed to last forever—beating loudly on her eardrums as her mind was filled with the disturbing sensual memories of the times when she'd found herself clasped in his arms.

As he slowly moved over to sit down on the bed beside her nervous, trembling figure, her heart began to pound like a heavy drum. The thudding beat against her ribs produced a swift surge of adrenalin throughout her body, leaving her breathless as though she'd just been running a race.

Her mouth was dry with fear and tension and, as she moistened her lips with her tongue, he seemed to stiffen, his low, tersely muttered oath cutting into the claustrophobic and oppressive silence.

She was unable to tear her eyes away from his hypnotic gaze, aware only of the strong, tanned column of his throat, the high angular cheekbones and the cruel, sensual curve of his mouth.

'I wonder why you appear to be so afraid of me?' he murmured slowly. 'Or, is it yourself—and your own emotions—of which you are frightened ... ?'

'I ... I'm not frightened of ... of anything,' she managed to gasp, so acutely aware of him that it was almost a physical agony. Why did this man have the power to upset and disturb her so easily?

Her brain a morass of chaotic thoughts and feelings, she was still gazing blindly up at him when she felt his warm hand touch her cheek, her body quivering and shaking almost uncontrollably in reply to the unmistakable darkening gleam in his eyes.

'No ... please!' she gasped as she felt his hand moving down her neck, his fingers slowly trailing over the fine bones and soft skin of her bare shoulders, lightly brushing aside the thin strap of her nightgown. 'Zarco—no ... !'

'I have told you before that you have a beautiful body,' he murmured, ignoring her strangled gasps of protest as he swept aside the other strap before impatiently pulling down her gown and the useless barrier of the sheet to cup his hands around her quivering flesh.

Tiffany knew she must stop him—right now! But when his tanned fingers moved enticingly over the hardening tips of her breasts she was unable to withstand the fiery excitement zigzagging through her body

as he lowered his dark head, his mouth closing possessively over one enlarged, swollen nipple.

'You may tell me no—but your body is saying *yes*!'
he breathed huskily against her skin, before his warm
lips trailed a scorching path over her quivering flesh
towards her other breast.

His fingers slipped down over her skin towards her
waist, and she shivered convulsively, her throat dry
and parched with the deep need and excitement she
could feel raging within her. She had a crazy desire
to slide her fingers through the thick, ruffled darkness
of his hair, to clasp his head against her throbbing
breasts, her trembling hands aching to caress the
strong male contours of his body. Embarrassment,
shame and fear mingled together into a tight knot in
her stomach as she desperately tried to control her
wild emotions, which seemed to be spinning dizzily
out of control.

She must do something! It was sheer madness to
allow him to continue to arouse her in this way!
Tiffany screamed silently at her weak body. But her
soft, yielding flesh resolutely refused to heed the
warning. She was only aware of the driving need to
surrender to the passionate desire racing through her
veins, her body melting helplessly beneath the dizzy,
spiralling excitement which she had never known
before.

'Your skin has the silky softness of velvet,' he murmured against her flesh, his mouth trailing a hot,
scorching path down to her navel. Heat flared and
burned through her veins. Half of her distraught and
bewildered mind wanted to escape from this delicious
torture, to flee as far away from him as she possibly
could. And yet…the other half of her confused brain
was strongly urging her towards an even closer in-

timacy; she felt a craving need and yearning to cast aside all her instinctive inhibitions and respond to such a wealth of rich, sensual delight.

Helpless beneath the masterly sureness of his touch, the breath catching in her throat as she felt his hands moving slowly down over her trembling thighs and the wet, moist caresses of his mouth and tongue, she gave a small unhappy moan as he slowly raised his head and stared down into her dazed eyes.

'It is obvious that you want me,' he stated flatly.

'No!' she cried, knowing that, despite her instinctive denial, he spoke nothing but the truth. She did want to touch Zarco as freely and openly as he was touching her, to taste the warm masculine scent of his skin, and to feel his hard, strong flesh come alive beneath her fingers.

'Don't try to fool yourself,' he told her roughly, his lips twisting as he gazed bleakly down at her flushed, naked body—the body that was obviously crying out for his touch, her nipples aching for the erotic, moist caress of his mouth and tongue.

'But, enticing as I may find you, I have no intention of being so foolish as to fall for this honey trap,' he added grimly. 'Until I am totally certain of who or what you are, I shall have to say "thanks—but no, thanks!"'

Completely dazed, and quite unable to believe that this was happening to her, Tiffany lay paralysed as he slowly rose to his feet. With a bitter, mocking expression he bent down to lightly toss the sheet over her nakedness, before turning to walk silently out of the room.

Later, lying alone in the darkness, Tiffany couldn't believe that she had ever felt such depths of humiliation, or such wretched unhappiness, as she did at this moment. Turning to bury her face in the soft pillows, there seemed nothing she could do to prevent herself from giving way to a storm of tears, her slender body convulsed by sobs of total desolation.

CHAPTER SIX

As the Aston Martin scorched down the motorway, Tiffany leaned back in her comfortable soft leather seat. The increasingly claustrophobic, oppressive silence within the vehicle was only escalating the strain felt by her tense, nervous body.

Zarco had remained totally silent so far, guiding the powerful car through the heavy traffic with consummate skill. She was vibrantly aware of the long fingers firmly grasping the steering-wheel, and the liberal sprinkling of black hair on his hard, muscular tanned arms beneath the short-sleeved silk shirt.

Stealing a fleeting glance through her eyelashes at his stern profile, the lines and planes of his handsome features highlighted by the strong sunlight flooding into the car, Tiffany clasped her hands tightly together. She must...she simply *must* try to stamp out this sick longing—a totally crazy urge to be clasped once again to his hard male chest—to rest her head against those strong shoulders. A small moan involuntarily broke from her lips, and she quickly tried to mask it with a cough.

'Are you feeling all right?' Zarco quickly turned his head to glance at the girl sitting so silently beside him. 'Would you care to listen to some music?'

She gave a slight shrug of her shoulders, turning her head to stare out of the car at the passing traffic, praying that he wouldn't notice the quick, hectic flush which she could feel sweeping over her face.

'Yes, maybe some music would be a good idea,' she muttered, trying to control the unnaturally husky, breathless tone in her voice.

A moment later, Tiffany found herself dearly wishing that she'd kept silent. Goodness knows what had prompted him to select this particular cassette. But, as the authentic strains of the Portuguese *Fado* singer filled the small space within the vehicle, the sad and melancholic tones of the haunting music reflected the desolation in her own heart.

The last few days seemed to have been quite the longest of her life. Tiffany was sure that she'd never felt quite so miserable. It was as though she inhabited a wretchedly lonely, alien planet, and nothing could seem to lift the heavy weight of her despair. Especially when it became obvious that Zarco had been deliberately avoiding her—almost as if she had some dreadful, infectious disease.

After the traumatic scene in her bedroom, she had slept fitfully, tossing and turning in the night as her weary mind and body were racked by painful dreams. Awaking the next morning, it took her a few moments to become aware of her surroundings, to realise that what she had imagined to be a fearful nightmare was an all too true reality. She was far too agitated to remain in bed, but it wasn't until she was gazing at her pale, listless face in the bathroom mirror that Tiffany suddenly realised part of her memory had returned.

It was...it was quite extraordinary and almost weird to discover how easily she could recall all the missing details of her life with Brian. As if, in some mysterious and strange manner, Zarco's lovemaking last night had unlocked part of her brain. Even if she had wanted to, there was nothing she could do to prevent her mind being filled with the flickering images of her marriage—up to and including Brian's tragic death.

Despite feeling totally washed out and listless after her sleepless night, and also hideously embarrassed at having to face Zarco so soon after his cruel, almost sadistic behaviour of the previous evening, she knew she had no choice. She must give him all the details of her past life which she had now recalled. Because, with this fresh information to corroborate her story, he could easily check out and confirm the details for himself.

Hurriedly getting dressed, Tiffany nervously checked her appearance in the mirror. Unfortunately, the aspirins she'd taken for the headache that throbbed and pounded in her head didn't seem to be working at all. She was still feeling like death warmed up, and there was nothing she could do to hide the dark circles beneath her shadowy blue eyes. However, after spending some time sorting through Maxine dos Santos's elaborate, expensive clothes, she had managed to find a simple sleeveless cotton blouse and matching blue skirt, in which she did at least feel reasonably comfortable.

Moving apprehensively through the empty house, she eventually tracked Zarco down in the kitchen, having a few words with Amy Long who'd just returned from visiting her married daughter in Oxford.

'I've been trying to find you,' she told him breathlessly. 'I . . . I've just remembered a whole lot more about Brian, and——'

'Can't you see that I'm busy talking to Mrs Long?' he demanded, lifting one dark brow as if astonished that she should have the temerity to interrupt his conversation. 'I will see you in the library in half an hour,' he added, his dark eyes sweeping scathingly over her nervous figure as he gave a brief, dismissive flick of his fingers before turning back to continue his conversation.

Furious at being treated as though she were something nasty that the cat had just dragged in, Tiffany nevertheless found herself obeying his terse instructions. Too much had happened to her lately—too many trials and tribulations—for her to be able to throw off her present downcast, forlorn state of mind. After she had trailed dejectedly into the library, it had seemed as though she'd been waiting for ages before Zarco condescended to join her.

'What is it you wish to say to me?' he demanded in a cold, hard voice as he entered the room, barely giving her a glance as he strode towards the large leather-topped mahogany desk in a far corner beneath the large mullioned windows. 'I am very busy— and have no time to waste on any female nonsense!'

Tiffany flushed at the harsh sarcasm in his voice. 'I . . . I have no intention of wasting your precious time!' she protested huskily, despising herself for still being so helplessly drawn towards this hateful man. 'I only wanted to tell you that, when I woke up this morning, I discovered that I could remember all about my life with my husband, Brian.'

'How convenient!' he sneered, not bothering to turn around as he sat down at the desk and pulled a file towards him. 'Am I supposed to congratulate you?'

She frowned in puzzlement. 'For what?'

'For realising that your story had as many holes as a leaky sieve!' He gave a harsh, bleak laugh. 'I imagine that you must have spent most of the night trying to remedy the damage, and in attempting to fill the gaps in your so-called past life.'

'That's not true!' she gasped.

'No...?'

'*No*! I promise you that what I am saying is the *truth*!' she insisted, her face paling beneath the scorn in those glittering dark eyes. 'I can now remember everything. All about my husband drinking too much, and his terrible car crash. Brian was in a coma for almost a year before he...he died without regaining consciousness. I really *am* telling the truth,' she assured the man continuing to sit with his back to her, apparently absorbed in the papers in front of him.

'I honestly don't know why I haven't recalled everything until now,' she continued in the face of his stony silence. 'Brian was in the hospital for such a long time that they're bound to have records to support what I say. And *that's* why I was in Lisbon,' she added, moving hesitantly across the carpet towards him. 'I had to stay down in the Algarve for some time, to earn enough money to pay for my plane fare back to England. And I only broke my journey in Lisbon, just to see something of the old city before going on to England.'

'A likely tale!'

Tiffany gazed at him, speechless for a moment. Did this man never give up? Was it totally impossible for him to accept that he could have been wrong?

'It's *not* a tale. I'm telling you the truth!' she reiterated firmly. 'And if I was going to tell a lie, I'd make up a better one than what happened when I arrived in Lisbon, because I was stupid enough not to know that it was a national holiday, and that it would be practically impossible to find anywhere to stay. I do remember travelling into the city in a taxi, but...I can't remember any more,' she added with a helpless shrug. 'Surely you must believe me?' she pleaded.

'Why should I?' he grated in a cold, hard voice as he turned slowly to face her. 'If you imagine that by attempting to entice me with your body you have succeeded in persuading me that you are not my wife, you are *very* much mistaken.'

Tiffany gasped, flinching under the cruel whiplash of his caustic words. 'I didn't...'

He gave a harsh, humourless laugh. 'I can assure you that I am not to be seduced from the truth quite so easily!'

'That's a rotten thing to say! It wasn't *me* who was doing the seducing last night!' Her voice wobbled dangerously as she fought to control the tears which were threatening to fall at any minute. 'I may have been married, but no one has ever...ever touched me like that before. And as an experienced man of the world, you ought to know that!' she sobbed, before fleeing out of the room, her eyes blind with tears.

And that was the last that Tiffany had seen of Zarco for the next three days.

It was unusually hot for the time of year, and she'd been plagued by tension headaches, which had grown increasingly severe as each day passed. There seemed nothing she could do to prevent herself from constantly thinking about the totally disastrous, cataclysmic scene in her bedroom, or her pathetically helpless response to Zarco's cynical lovemaking. How could he have used and abused her in such a way? Surely he must know, in his heart of hearts, that she *wasn't* his wife Maxine?

However, Zarco had provided no clue to his savage treatment of her. Mostly because she had hardly seen him during the last few days, she reminded herself bitterly, recalling how he had locked himself away in the library. There, with a battery of modern telecom-

munication aids at his disposal, he had apparently
been immersed in conducting his world-wide business
affairs. He'd even had all his meals in the solitary
grandeur of the book-lined room, with its sombre
decoration of dark red velvet curtains and the muted
glow of priceless Persian carpets.

Nothing had occurred to interrupt her desperately
lonely, melancholy existence. Even Amy Long—undoubtedly under the influence of her employer—had
reverted from her brief friendship to a cautious and
guarded manner, making it clear that Tiffany was no
longer welcome in her kitchen. In fact, it wasn't until
the unexpected appearance of Ralph Pargeter, after
breakfast this morning, that she'd had any hope of
escaping from her prison at Norton Manor.

The tall, fair-haired man, who had swept up the
drive in a black Porsche, had done much to restore
her damaged self-esteem. Announcing that he was
sorry not to have called to see her before now, but
his mother had only just contacted him on his return
from holiday, Ralph Pargeter had proved to be a
charming man.

'I can't tell you how glad I am that my mama asked
me to call,' he grinned as she led him into the large
drawing-room. 'I wonder why she never told me what
a stunningly pretty girl you are?'

'Probably because I was looking simply ghastly in
the hospital!' Tiffany told him with a smile before
asking Amy Long, who was hovering in the doorway,
if she would provide a pot of coffee for their visitor.

'I was so grateful for all the help and support your
mother gave me,' she told Ralph, as he came over to
sit down on the sofa beside her. 'I was nearly going
mad, trying to prove that I wasn't the wife of the man
who owns this house.' She shrugged unhappily. 'I still

haven't succeeded, of course, but I can't tell you what it meant to have someone actually *believe* what I said!'

'Have you managed to remember any more of your past life, since leaving Lisbon?' he asked.

'Yes, I have—practically everything. But it doesn't seem to have done me much good,' she sighed, her blue eyes shadowed with the pain and misery of the past few days.

Explaining to this friendly and handsome young man what she could recall of her past life, Tiffany told him how she still hadn't managed to remember what had happened after she'd arrived in Lisbon. 'And I don't seem to have found any way in which I can definitely prove that I'm not that awful woman Maxine dos Santos.'

'Well, I wouldn't worry about that,' Ralph told her breezily. 'By far the easiest option is for you to prove that you really *are* Tiffany Harris, right? And that's easy! All you have to do, is to toddle along to St Catherine's House.'

'Where...?' she was asking with a frown when Amy Long returned with a tray, containing a silver coffee-pot and some cups and saucers. Noting the older woman's stiff figure, rigid with disapproval, Tiffany was surprised when the housekeeper announced that Zarco was having a few words with the head gardener, but would be returning to the house shortly.

'I say—she looks a bit of an old dragon!' Ralph exclaimed when Amy, after giving him a freezing glance, had stalked stiffly out of the room. 'Are you finding life here a bit grim?'

Tiffany gave a slight shrug of her shoulders. 'It's not easy,' she admitted, surprised to find herself reluctant to blacken Zarco's character. 'And Amy has been very kind, really. It's just that she, and everyone

else who works in this house, is very much in awe of
my so-called husband. Actually...' She gave a nervous
giggle. 'It's just occurred to me—Amy probably thinks
that you're my "fancy man"!'

'Your *what* ... ?' Ralph looked at her in astonishment for a moment, before Tiffany quickly put him
in the picture regarding both Maxine's character, and
the housekeeper's suspicions about the other woman's
boyfriend.

Ralph laughed. 'Oh, I see—she thinks it's a case
of history repeating itself, does she? Well...' He
grinned wolfishly at the beautiful girl sitting beside
him. 'I'd be happy to join the list of *your* admirers!'

Tiffany blushed. Ralph was obviously a very nice,
kind man. However, she'd never been one of those
people who enjoyed carrying on a light flirtation—
and she certainly didn't intend to start doing so now.

'Thank you for the compliment,' she muttered,
hiding her embarrassment as she busied herself with
pouring him a cup of coffee. 'If we could—er—return
to what you were saying, before Amy came in ... ?'

'Oh, yes—I was telling you about St Catherine's
House, wasn't I?' Ralph said, taking both his cup of
coffee, and his rejection by the beautiful girl, with
equal aplomb. 'St Catherine's House in Kingsway,
London, is where they keep all the records for births,
marriages and deaths. So, if you can remember your
own birthday or when you were born, and the date
of your marriage, you shouldn't have any trouble in
being able to prove who you are.'

'Really... ?'

Ralph nodded. 'And driving over here, today, I had
one or two other ideas. For instance: it would be a
real help if you can remember the name and address
of a doctor who might have known you. And the real

cruncher—if you'll forgive the pun!—is if you can recall the name of your dentist. I don't know how long you've been abroad, but if you had your teeth seen to before you left this country the person you saw is very likely still to have your dental records.'

Tiffany's blue eyes sparkled. 'You are clever—that's a really brilliant idea!'

Ralph smiled, clearly pleased with himself for having come up with some helpful solutions to the girl's problem. 'I read somewhere that teeth are like fingerprints—because, apparently, no two person's teeth are exactly the same,' he told her. 'So, with your birth and marriage certificates, plus a doctor and dentist's verification, it will be easy to prove *exactly* who you are.'

'That's terrific!' she exclaimed, her eyes glowing with relief at the thought of at last being able to do something positive. 'So what you're saying is that I should forget the dreadful mistake everyone has made about Maxine? That I should just concentrate on establishing my own background?'

Ralph nodded. 'Absolutely! After all, once you've definitely proved that you're Tiffany Harris, it's going to be up to your "husband" to look elsewhere for his errant wife. And you...' Ralph leaned forward, putting a friendly arm around her shoulders '...*you* can just snap your fingers at Zarco dos Santos!'

'Do I hear my name being mentioned?'

The deep voice from the doorway behind them startled both Ralph and Tiffany.

'Enter the Demon King!' Ralph muttered under his breath, scrambling to his feet as Zarco strode into the room.

Tiffany, who'd felt a hysterical bubble of nervous laughter rising in her throat at Ralph's description—

Zarco *did* seem to carry around with him a frightening aura of brimstone and sulphur!—swallowed hard as she was subjected to a swift, crushing glance from Zarco's cold dark eyes.

'I don't believe I've had the pleasure of meeting you before?' he drawled, turning to smile blandly at the younger man.

'No. My mother, Mrs Emily Pargeter, asked me to call and see your wife,' Ralph told him quickly. 'My mother regularly visits patients at the hospital, in Lisbon, and...'

'Ah, yes. Who could forget Mrs Pargeter? An indomitable old lady! I trust she is well?' Zarco enquired smoothly.

As Zarco and Ralph continued their somewhat overpolite conversation, Tiffany was struck by the contrast between the two men. Ralph, who initially had appeared to be a confident, tall and handsome man, now seemed to be somehow insignificant when compared to the much taller, more dominant figure of Zarco, whose dark good looks completely eclipsed the pale, English colouring of the younger man.

'So, you're a foreign exchange dealer, are you? And how is business these days?' Zarco was asking in a clearly bored tone of voice, as Tiffany realised that she had been so absorbed in her thoughts that she'd missed some of their conversation.

'Oh, it's not too bad. It comes and goes,' Ralph told him cheerfully, obviously not too worried about losing his wealthy lifestyle.

Zarco gave him a bland, chilly smile. 'Well, you have come—but I'm afraid that we must go,' he drawled, smoothly turning to take hold of Tiffany's hand, which was lying on the arm of the sofa, and drawing her quickly to her feet. 'My wife and I are due to visit my son's school today, and I'm afraid that we have to leave straight away.'

Tiffany turned to look at him in astonishment. 'I don't remember you saying anything about...' she began, faltering as she felt his fingers biting like steel talons into the soft flesh of her arm.

'My dear wife has this small problem with her memory,' Zarco murmured sardonically to Ralph, still keeping a firm grip on her slim, trembling figure. 'So, if you will forgive us...'

'Oh, yes—of course. I only called in for a few minutes,' Ralph muttered, clearly caught between his years of upbringing as a polite Englishman, and the desire not to leave this obviously frightened girl alone; especially not in the threatening clutches of such an ominous-looking foreigner.

However, his ingrained national characteristics won the day. And, after giving Tiffany a faint hollow smile, he allowed himself to be issued out of the house by Zarco.

'I'm not having that spineless idiot calling here again!' Zarco growled as he returned to the sitting-room, where she had nervously collapsed down into a chair. 'If that silly young wimp thinks that he can just turn up, and flirt with my wife, he's *very* much mistaken!'

'Ralph wasn't doing anything of the sort!' she protested.

He gave a harsh, sardonic snort of laughter. 'Oh, no? If he was just making a neighbourly call, maybe you can tell me why his arm was around your shoulder?' he ground out angrily.

'He was being friendly and...and helpful, that's all!' she exclaimed helplessly, her cheeks flushing as Zarco gave another cynical bark of mirthless laughter.

Tiffany bit back the angry, bitter retort that hovered on her tongue, knowing that anything she had to say would only give him the opportunity to make yet another blistering comment about Emily's son.

There was no way he was going to believe her, she realised. Equally, there was no way she could tell him about Ralph's ideas to prove her identity. Any mention of her plans to obtain copies of her own birth and marriage certificates would merely give this dangerous man advance warning of her intentions. And besides, why should she have to explain herself, when she'd clearly been doing nothing wrong?

'Hurry up—we haven't much time,' Zarco's voice broke into her distracted thoughts. When she gazed at him in bewilderment, he added impatiently, 'We are going to see Carlos at his school—remember?'

'But I thought that was just an excuse you made, to get rid of Ralph Pargeter . . . ?'

Zarco lifted one dark, quizzical eyebrow. 'What an extraordinary idea. I wonder why you should think that?' he drawled coolly.

Tiffany wondered why, too. And, since those had been the last words he'd spoken to her, other than insisting that they must leave immediately, she had spent most of the journey so far trying to work out what was going on. Zarco had acted towards Ralph in a thoroughly peculiar manner. Just like a dog with a bone. In fact, if it weren't too ridiculous, she might think that he'd been behaving like a jealous husband!

Carlos dos Santos was proving to be an amusing young boy, and very different from what Tiffany had imagined.

'I say, Dad—this is absolutely terrific!' the boy mumbled, happily chomping his way through a third slice of Amy Long's Black Forest gâteau.

Tiffany, not used to the ravenous appetite of young boys, had watched with fascination and increasing awe as Zarco's son swiftly demolished most of the contents of a large, well stocked picnic basket. Surely, it wasn't possible for the child's thin frame to be able to absorb *quite* so many chicken drumsticks and cold sausages, as well as a mountain of ham sandwiches and four packets of crisps? Her sapphire-blue eyes had grown round with astonishment as he proceeded to tuck into the chocolate gâteau, while emptying at least three cans of fizzy orange!

'I think you've probably had sufficient, Carlos,' Zarco said at last, when even he, who must have been used to this boy's gargantuan appetite, clearly felt his son had eaten quite enough.

'For heaven's sake, Dad!' the boy grimaced, looking quickly over his shoulder to see if any of the other picnickers in the school grounds could hear what they were saying. '*Please* don't call me Carlos. All the other fellows call me Charlie—and I *much* prefer it,' he added, gazing anxiously at his father.

As Zarco frowned with irritation, Tiffany—who had immediately understood why his son should wish to change his name—instinctively found herself intervening on the boy's behalf.

'I know what you mean, Charlie,' she told him ruefully, being careful not to look in Zarco's direction. 'My full name is Tiffany Imogen Catherine Kendall, and until I was about fourteen years old everyone at school called me "Tick" or "Tick-Tock". I hated it—especially when the other girls used to call out, "Here comes Tick-Tock." I know it doesn't sound very bad,' she told Zarco hesitantly. 'But children can be very cruel, and it made my life an absolute misery.'

Charlie nodded vigorously in support. 'She—er—she's right, Dad,' the boy muttered, obviously confused as to what to call this woman, who was claiming that she wasn't his dreaded stepmother, Maxine dos Santos. 'It's just . . . well, I don't want to be different from the other boys, if you see what I mean?'

To Tiffany's complete surprise, Zarco responded by giving his son a warm smile, and holding up his hands in mock surrender. 'Very well—Charlie it shall be from now on. After all,' he added with a slight laugh, 'with the two of you in complete agreement, who am I to disagree?'

Zarco dos Santos—*that's who*! Tiffany thought grimly, still having considerable difficulty in accepting that this warm, humorous and relaxed man could be the same hard, menacing personality who'd so dominated her life over the past few weeks.

From the first moment they had arrived at Charlie's boarding-school, Tiffany had been struck by not only the obvious pride Zarco took in his son, but also his deep love and concern for the motherless boy. Charlie, too, clearly adored his father, greeting his arrival for the school's sports day with a wide, beaming smile. And although the young boy clearly had severe reservations, if not an active dislike of his stepmother, the few words he had addressed to her had been scrupulously polite. It wasn't until they had begun the picnic, under the shade of some old oak trees surrounding the cricket pitch, that Charlie had gradually become more relaxed towards her. And now, as Tiffany began to clear up the remnants of their picnic, she was surprised to hear Zarco suggest that, as he needed to have a few words with the headmaster, maybe Charlie would like to show her around the school?

'Maybe he would prefer to join his friends?' she told Zarco quickly, almost sure that the last thing Charlie wanted was to be lumbered with a step-mother. However, she was pleasantly surprised when the boy merely gave a casual nod, and agreed to his father's suggestion.

'This is my classroom,' Carlos told her some time later as they reached the end of the conducted tour. 'Are you all right?' he added, looking with concern at the woman as she leaned against the wall, obviously buried deep in thought.

'Yes, I'm fine.' Tiffany gave herself a mental shake. 'It's just…I'm finding it quite extraordinary how little schools have changed since my day. There's the same dusty smell of the chalk used on blackboards—and I bet if I opened your desk I would find it was in a thorough mess!' she grinned.

Charlie laughed. 'You're right!' he said, going to a small desk in the front row. Lifting the lid, he grinned sheepishly down at the clutter and confusion of exercise books, pens and pencils—and what looked suspiciously like a small jar of frog-spawn!

'You seem to be doing rather well in most of your subjects,' Tiffany said, studying a chart on the wall. 'Although it looks as though you've got problems with arithmetic.'

'Yes,' the boy sighed heavily. 'Dad's so clever at maths, but I seem to be absolutely hopeless.'

'When I was your age, I used to be quite good at the subject. Would you like to show me what you are doing at the moment? Maybe I could give you some help?' she offered hesitantly.

Charlie looked at her dubiously for a moment, before giving a slight shrug of his young shoulders. 'I don't suppose it will be much use. Especially since we've got a test tomorrow,' he told her, giving another sigh of despondency as he removed an exercise book from his desk ...

'So, if I put this here, and that there ... ? Hey—*it works*!' Charlie exclaimed some time later, giving her a smile that was so like his father's that Tiffany could almost feel her heart turn over.

'I can show you some more maths tricks, if you like?'

'I certainly *would*!' Charlie grinned, turning his head as Zarco entered the empty classroom.

'Ah, there you are,' he said as the boy scrambled to his feet and dashed across the room.

'She's a real whizzo genius at maths, Dad! I bet Old Barney will drop dead with shock when he sees how easily I can do those beastly sums!'

Zarco smiled fondly down at the boy. 'If you are referring to your teacher, Mr Barnard, I imagine that he probably will,' he told his son drily. 'I've just been hearing about your problems with mathematics.'

'Not any more!' Charlie told him gleefully, missing the hard, razor-sharp glance his father cast at Tiffany before following the boy out of the classroom.

For the rest of the afternoon, while watching the various games and races—and applauding Charlie, who was thrilled with himself for having come second in the one-hundred-metres race—Tiffany was aware of Zarco occasionally turning his dark, narrowed gaze in her direction. It was as if, like his son, he too was having difficulty in getting his sums right.

However, surrounded as they were by a milling crowd of parents, vigorously and noisily encouraging their sons during the various sports events, there was no opportunity for him to speak privately to her. A fact which, after their tense, stressful journey to the school, helped to soothe her battered spirits. Sitting quietly in the dappled shade of the trees surrounding the field, Tiffany was able, for almost the first time that day, to think about what Ralph Pargeter had said.

Although she was deeply grateful to Emily's son for suggesting several excellent, practical ways in which she could prove her identity, there were still some hard and tough facts of life which she had to overcome. If and when she managed to convince Zarco that he had indeed made a great mistake, what on earth was she going to do next?

Zarco *might* be kind enough to lend her some money, enabling her to rent a very small flat in London while she looked for a job—but she couldn't count on his being that generous, could she? Zarco was many things—but 'kind' or 'generous' weren't qualities which sprang instantly to mind when thinking of his hard, tough personality. Indeed, it was far more likely that he would be furious and extremely unhelpful! After all, once she'd proved that he *had* made a grave error, such proof was also going to make him look a complete fool. A man who didn't even know his own wife was likely to be an object of derision to his friends and acquaintances. In fact, the thought of Zarco's likely reaction in those circumstances was enough to make her shudder and tremble with fear.

However, that was only the first of her problems. It was almost overwhelmingly daunting to realise that she possessed absolutely *nothing* of her previous life. Why, even the wedding-ring she was wearing didn't belong to her!

Tiffany frowned as she stared down at her hand. For some days she'd been aware of a faint question mark in her mind regarding the slim gold band about her finger. And now, as she gazed down at the ring, set above the knuckle on the fourth finger of her left hand, she tried to concentrate on the problem. Come on! she urged herself roughly. You've got most of your mind back in working order now—so use it!

Ignoring the hustle and bustle of the crowd about her still figure, Tiffany gazed blindly down at her hand and tried to remember every scrap of information she'd been given, particularly about her original discovery by the police at Sintra. She, and everyone else, were agreed that this was *not* her own wedding-ring. In fact, according to the policeman who'd interviewed her in the hospital, Zarco had definitely identified the ring as one belonging to his wife Maxine. But, if that was so—how did it come to be on *her* finger? Looking at the problem from all angles, there could only be one answer: this thin gold band must have been *deliberately* substituted for her own wedding-ring!

For a brief moment it seemed as though the whole world was suddenly turned upside-down. Almost as though she was whirling through space and time as all the disjointed, separate pieces of the jigsaw re-formed themselves in her brain.

Although her own had been rather loose, wedding-rings were traditionally difficult to remove from their wearer's fingers. And therefore it must have been Maxine *herself* who had exchanged the rings! Although Tiffany couldn't yet see why—was it something to do with the theft of the gold and jewellery?— she now had no doubts that the other woman had been responsible for the substitution. However, in order to discover the reason which lay behind such a peculiar action, she was going to have to know more about Maxine—and the facts which lay behind her extraordinary-sounding marriage to Zarco.

'*Tiffany*!'

'Mmm . . . ?' She blinked up at the figure standing over her, his broad shoulders silhouetted against the fiery red ball of the setting sun.

'I've been looking for you for the past half-hour,' Zarco told her impatiently, bending down to grasp hold of her arm and drawing her up to her feet. 'It's time for us to go.'

'But I've just realised that——'

'Come along,' he commanded firmly, completely disregarding her muttered protests. 'My son wants to say goodbye to you. Although I can't think why,' he added curtly, striding so fast across the grass that she was almost forced to run to keep up with him.

'Maybe it's because he likes me,' she snapped, her brief spurt of defiance dying away as she saw Charlie standing beside his father's car, his face wreathed in a broad grin. She mustn't upset the boy by quarrelling with his father, she told herself quickly as Zarco's son ran towards her.

'Thanks for helping me with my sums,' he grinned, throwing his thin arms about her waist and giving her a hug. 'I'll write and let you know how I get on.'

She bent down to return the boy's hug. 'I'll look forward to hearing all about it,' she told him with a grin. 'Although I shall take it as a personal insult if you don't get ten out of ten!'

As Zarco steered the vehicle back down the gravelled drive of the school, she turned to wave at the solitary, rather forlorn-looking figure standing outside the school.

'He's such a nice boy. It does seem a pity he has to go to boarding-school,' she murmured. 'Wouldn't he be happier if he could live at home, and go to a nearby day school?'

'When I want your opinion about my son's education, I'll ask for it,' Zarco drawled coldly. 'Until then—why don't you mind your own business?'

Tiffany gasped, feeling as though she'd just had a bucket of cold water thrown over her. 'That's a totally unfair thing to say!' she exclaimed, turning to glare at him.

But Zarco ignored her protest. Clearly immersed in his own deep thoughts, he continued to remain brooding and silent, not uttering another word until he drove the Aston Martin off the main road and down a country lane, before bringing the car to a halt outside a large, ivy-covered restaurant. And even then, after switching off the engine, he continued to stare blindly straight ahead through the windscreen.

It seemed to Tiffany as if the ever increasing sense of menace and claustrophobia within the vehicle was almost tangible. But, just when it seemed to be practically beating on her eardrums, Zarco's hard voice suddenly broke into the oppressive silence.

'What is the square root of one hundred and sixty-nine?'

She frowned and turned to look at him. 'Why on earth do you want to know that?'

'Just answer the question!' he grated harshly.

'It's thirteen, of course.' She shrugged her shoulders. 'Now, do you mind telling me what this is all about?'

He gave a heavy sigh. 'My wife may have been a very clever, tricky woman—but she had one blind spot,' he said in a low, monotonous voice, empty of all expression. 'For some unknown reason, she was completely hopeless at any kind of mathematics.'

'I still don't see . . .'

'Maxine had the utmost difficulty with even simple multiplication and division. Anything more complicated would have been totally beyond her,' he replied flatly.

Tiffany gazed at his grim profile, her mind in turmoil. 'So, what you're saying . . . you mean that you're now prepared to accept the fact that I'm *not* your wife?' she asked breathlessly.

Zarco continued to stare straight ahead out of the car window, and it was some moments before he broke the tense silence.

'Yes, Tiffany . . .' he agreed with a sigh, slowly turning his head to face her. 'I rather think that I do.'

CHAPTER SEVEN

TIFFANY'S brain was still in a chaotic whirl as Zarco got out of the car, and came around to open the passenger door.

That he should have so swiftly capitulated—so quickly changed his mind about her—seemed almost unbelievable. And all because Maxine apparently couldn't add two and two without making five!

'I still don't understand,' she muttered as he bent down to help her from the vehicle. 'Why have you suddenly changed your tune? I've been telling you for weeks that I'm not Maxine, and now—all of a sudden...'

'It isn't all that sudden, of course,' he said, putting a hand on her arm as he led her towards the large building. 'I suppose I must have known the truth for some time. It just happened to be today that I finally realised there was no way you could possibly be Maxine.'

'Well, I suppose I ought to be glad that the penny has dropped at last!' she grumbled, still not really able to believe that her torment was at an end.

'I can understand that you might be justifiably annoyed with me...'

'I certainly am!'

'... and I clearly owe you a very deep and abject apology.'

'You most certainly do!' she snapped, before absorbing the quiet sincerity in his deep voice. Zarco—

actually apologising to her? She turned her head to gaze up at him in astonishment.

'There's no need to look *quite* so surprised!' he told her with a low, rueful laugh. 'I can occasionally admit to being in the wrong.'

It was a struggle, but Tiffany managed to bite back the extremely rude retort which had swiftly risen to her lips. And while she was still staring at him in open-mouthed exasperation he swiftly bent to brush his mouth across her lips.

'I think it might be a good idea to continue any further discussion over a meal, don't you?' he murmured, not giving her time to argue as he led her inside the large building.

It was hopeless. She was never going to understand this man, Tiffany told herself, striving to control the nervous fluttering in her stomach as they entered the restaurant. One moment he was deeply insulting, and then—in the twinkling of an eye—he could give her a kiss, and send her pulses racing out of control.

'But what are we going to do now?' she asked some minutes later, after they'd been shown to a secluded table in the beautifully decorated dining-room of the restaurant.

Zarco didn't reply immediately, and she waited with mounting impatience while he placed their order with the attentive head waiter. He was obviously a well known and valued customer, and there was some considerable discussion about which wines to have with their choice of cold watercress soup and chicken with a tarragon sauce.

She must be careful, Tiffany warned herself grimly. Not only did Zarco use his obvious charm like a weapon—even the waiter appeared to be bowled over by his warm, friendly smile—but it was a charm to which she was also extremely vulnerable. And she knew, only too well, just how this formidable man's dark, sinister attraction could affect her fragile emotions.

'Well . . . ?' Tiffany demanded as the waiter hurried away with their order. 'What am I going to do now? I mean, I haven't really had any time to think about it, but I ought to find myself somewhere to live—possibly in London?' She frowned, brushing a hand through her short, curly hair. 'I'd be grateful if I could borrow some money from you—just to start with, of course—then I ought to look for some kind of job, and——'

'No, I don't think so,' he drawled flatly.

She frowned across the table at him. 'What do you mean?'

'I mean that you aren't going anywhere. Not until we've solved the problem, and recovered my family's jewels, of course.'

'There's no ''of course'' about it!' she flashed back quickly. 'And it's *your* problem, not mine! I didn't ask to be hauled over here, like a badly wrapped parcel, and then treated by you as if I were some sort of criminal,' she added bitterly.

'Nevertheless, here you are and here you stay, until I find out *exactly* what happened in Lisbon,' he told her firmly.

'Oh—*great*!' She glared at him. 'So much for the abject apology!'

He leaned forward, putting his large brown hand over her fingers, which were toying nervously with her cutlery on the table in front of her. 'I think I would prefer to leave that until we return home,' he murmured, giving her a glinting glance from beneath his heavy eyelids which sent shivers quivering up and

down her backbone. 'In the meantime, I would
suggest that we concentrate on enjoying our meal.'

'Yes, well...' she muttered breathlessly, inching her
hand away from beneath his. 'Even if you haven't
recovered your beastly jewellery, there are still so many
questions which need answering.'

'Such as...?'

'Well—first and foremost is the question of your
wife Maxine. I still don't know what happened to me
in Lisbon, or why somebody hit me on the head on
that cliff-top, but she has to be behind it, doesn't she?'

'Possibly.' He shrugged his shoulders, as if the
whole question of his wife bored him rigid.

'There's no possibly about it,' she retorted. 'In fact,
I need to know everything you can tell me about that
awful woman Maxine dos Santos!'

Zarco's face darkened ominously. However, when
Tiffany quickly explained the conclusion she'd come
to earlier that afternoon, based on what must have
been a *deliberate* exchange of her and Maxine's
wedding-rings, he leaned back in his chair, regarding
her in a thoughtful silence.

'I know it must be difficult, and maybe even painful
for you to have to rehash your past life. But you're
the only one who can help to solve this mystery,' she
told him quietly. 'Quite apart from anything else, it
may also be helpful in locating the stolen gold and
jewellery.'

Zarco raised a dark eyebrow. 'I fail to see how a
discussion of my private life will aid the return of my
lost possessions.'

Relieved to see that he was at least prepared to listen
to her, Tiffany decided to place all her cards on the
table.

'I've had a lot of time to think about the problem,' she told him with a brief, wry smile. 'In fact, with the loss of part of my memory, I've had very little else to think about! And it seems to me that not only is your wife the central figure in this drama, but it's what you called the "scam"—the theft of your family's valuable jewellery—which lies at the core of the problem. You see,' she added with a shrug, 'I've always had one great advantage over you—I *knew* that I wasn't Maxine. And since *I* wasn't the mastermind behind the burglary, I really do need to know more about the woman who was!'

'And how would that help?' he enquired smoothly.

'Oh, for heaven's sake—surely it's obvious?' she exclaimed. 'There can't be many wives who deliberately set out to steal well over two million pounds' worth of jewellery from their husbands? So, the first question has to be, why should she do such a thing? I mean, even if you don't like each other—which is putting it mildly!—it does seem the most extraordinary thing to do, doesn't it? I don't know how wealthy you are, of course, but surely it would have been easier for her to have had a divorce, and settled for a large amount of alimony?'

Zarco stared silently at her for some moments, before giving a shrug of his broad shoulders.

'You are quite right,' he said at last. 'My wife would be very well off financially, following any divorce settlement.'

'There you are! Not only does the whole scam seem daft—but why should Maxine go to all the trouble of exchanging her wedding-ring for my own?'

He sighed and shook his head, but the arrival of the waiter with their first course prevented him from saying anything further. However, as they consumed the cold watercress soup, he remained buried in thought, until, laying his spoon down on the empty plate, he gave a resigned shrug of his shoulders.

'You are quite right. I do find it painful to think, let alone talk about my past life with my—er—wife,' he told her with a bitter, twisted smile. 'It is a story which reflects very little credit on myself, and absolutely none on Maxine. In fact, like Pandora, I think you will find this is a box that you'll wish you hadn't opened,' he warned grimly.

'I still need to know about her,' Tiffany said stubbornly.

He shrugged. 'What is it you wish to know?'

'I'm not entirely sure.' She gazed at him uncertainly. 'I just feel totally convinced that the answer to your wife's peculiar behaviour has to lie somewhere in the past. And, since we must have met at some time—how else would I have ended up wearing her clothes and her wedding-ring?—maybe something you say will help the missing part of my memory to return.'

'Very well—on your own head be it!' Zarco's jaw clenched and his lips tightened for a moment, as if bracing himself for an ordeal. 'I can give you very few details about Maxine's early life,' he began slowly, before relating part of the information which she'd been given by the psychoanalyst in the hospital in Lisbon.

'However,' he continued, 'Maxine's father—a most highly respected and respectable bank manager—has since told me that she was always very wild when young. Apparently, she ran away from boarding-school at the age of seventeen, her father and step-mother losing all track of her for some years—despite all their efforts to discover her whereabouts. It was only when her stepmother opened a magazine that they eventually discovered that she was a fashion model in New York.'

It really was the most extraordinary sensation, Tiffany decided, to listen to the story of a woman who was not only her double, but about whom she knew so little.

Maxine, it seemed, had by then already married her first husband—an American of Italian descent called Antonio Salvatore. Because it was shortly after contacting his daughter in New York that Maxine's father learned that she had become a widow.

'That is a period of my wife's life about which I know very little, and which my agents are investigating at this moment,' Zarco told her, not bothering to hide his clear conviction that Maxine's hitherto unknown life in New York would also turn out to be yet another discreditable can of worms.

'Surely Maxine must have done *something* decent in her life?'

'If she has, I have yet to hear about it!' he retorted curtly, before explaining that his wife had left America on the death of her first husband, flying down to Brazil to stay with her father in São Paulo, the business centre of that huge country.

Unfortunately, it seemed that the return of the prodigal daughter had not been a success. Certainly not as far as her father and stepmother were concerned. From what Tiffany could gather, there appeared to have been several unsavoury incidents, about which Zarco refused to give her any details, merely relating the fact that Maxine had led a thoroughly wild, dissipated life, which had horrified her respectable and somewhat strait-laced parents. However, he had known nothing of Maxine's debauched lifestyle. He'd only been aware that a business friend of his possessed a daughter—an attractive widow to whom he'd been briefly introduced at a large cocktail party.

'It was some years since my first wife, Charlotte, had died. And yet, pathetic as it may seem to you, I was still very much in love with her memory,' Zarco remarked flatly, before lapsing into a long and with-drawn silence.

'I don't think it sounds pathetic,' Tiffany assured him softly, her heart wrung by the deep note of past misery and unhappiness in his voice. 'I think that what you have just said must be just about the greatest compliment a man could pay his wife.'

'You think so?' he murmured, and for the first time that she could remember Zarco's hard and for-midable guard seemed to be momentarily lowered. His dark handsome features softened, and for a few brief seconds Tiffany glimpsed quite another and much softer personality.

But then his iron control reasserted itself as he slowly and with obvious discomfiture began to relate the events leading up to his marriage to Maxine—events which he clearly felt to be shameful and humiliating.

He was still mourning his dead wife, and, apart from burying himself in work, Zarco had been content to spend all his free time with his small son, who was cared for by a houseful of servants at his large home in São Paulo. However, his many friends were con-vinced that he was working too hard, and had per-suaded him to take a brief holiday in Rio de Janeiro, during the Carnival.

The holiday had not been a success. Mostly be-cause, as he explained, he had still felt very much alone, despite the frantic noise and spectacle of the celebrations. So it was perhaps inevitable that on his last night in Rio Zarco had taken refuge in the bar of his luxury hotel, drowning his sorrows in alcohol. When he had awoken the next morning, it was to find a girl sleeping beside him—a girl of whom he had absolutely no recollection whatsoever.

'I had dearly loved Charlotte, and felt sincere grief over her loss, but...' A faint flush tinged Zarco's high cheekbones as he confessed to not remaining celibate in the years following his first wife's death. 'I'm a mere mortal man—and certainly no monk!' he informed Tiffany, a wry smile touching his lips as he viewed her blush of embarrassment.

Emphasising that his brief affairs had been conducted with older, sophisticated women who were no more serious than he was, Zarco admitted that he'd been distressed and deeply ashamed to discover the girl beside him in the hotel bedroom. He truly didn't recollect ever having seen her before, and, suffering from a monumental hangover, he'd apologised to the girl for anything that might have happened, and sent her on her way.

It wasn't until some weeks after his return to São Paulo that the girl—who was, of course, Maxine—had contacted him. Revealing her identity, and claiming that she was pregnant with his child, she had demanded that he 'do the right thing' and marry her.

Zarco had realised that he'd no choice in the matter. Not only was Maxine the daughter of a *very* respectable English bank manager, but Zarco was also burdened by a deep sense of guilt at having ruined a girl's life by his careless, drunken behaviour. Moreover, as he firmly pointed out to Tiffany, his own personal code of honour as a gentleman had left him

no option: he must marry the young widow who was
expecting his child.

'We had just begun our honeymoon when my new
wife informed me that, just prior to our hastily arranged marriage, she'd arranged to have her pregnancy terminated.'

'But . . . but that's *terrible*! How could she do such
a dreadful thing?' Tiffany gasped, her soft heart
aching at the obvious pain behind Zarco's harsh words
and his bleak, stony expression.

'It has since occurred to me, of course, that she
might not have been pregnant at all. I did subsequently discover that she'd been on the look-out for
a rich husband, a fact underlined a year or two ago
when, in one of her violent rages, Maxine confessed
that she had deliberately followed me to Rio—with
the express intention of ending up in my bed.'

'Oh, Zarco—how awful! You must have been *so*
unhappy,' Tiffany breathed, appalled and horrified
by the story of his forced marriage.

'Yes, it is not a pretty story,' he sighed deeply. 'The
intolerable situation was not helped, of course, by the
realisation that I only had myself to blame. And when
I found myself locked into the prison of my marriage,
I buried myself in work and spent as much time
abroad as I could. My sole concern, of course, has
always been the welfare of my son. So, when I inherited Norton Manor a few years ago, I subsequently placed Carlos in his boarding-school, and have
virtually seen nothing of my wife—not until I received the news of her accident, in Lisbon.'

'You must have known that wasn't me!' she cried
huskily, oblivious of the other people in the dining-
room. 'I could never——'

'Hush! You must not raise your voice in here, like this,' he cautioned, clasping hold of her hand once more, and holding it firmly while signalling to a passing waiter.

'But I've never heard such a terrible story!' she exclaimed helplessly in a low voice, her cheeks flushing with embarrassment as she belatedly realised they were being regarded with some interest by the people dining at a nearby table. 'I could *never* have behaved in such a disgusting, foul way towards anyone—let alone trap them into such a dreadful travesty of a marriage!'

'Well, perhaps this is the right time to say that——' He was interrupted by the arrival of the waiter, who placed a large glass of brandy down on the table in front of her. 'Drink it up!' he commanded as she gazed dubiously down at the amber liquid in the balloon-shaped glass.

'I really don't think——'

'Do as I say!' he grated, frowning with concern as he viewed the girl's pale cheeks, and her visibly trembling figure.

The Aston Martin purred its way through the small country villages, its pearl-grey exterior shimmering ghostily in the light of the full moon. Having left the restaurant, Zarco had obviously decided to take a more winding route back to Norton Manor.

Tiffany turned to steal a quick, fleeting glance through her eyelashes at Zarco's stern profile, illuminated by the light from the streetlamps of a small village. He had been strangely silent and withdrawn since they had left the restaurant. Not unfriendly, but somehow distant and obviously preoccupied with his own thoughts. It was as though he had much to think about—as, indeed, had she.

As Tiffany leaned back on the comfortable leather seat of the fast car, speeding along the country roads, she had to admit that Zarco had been quite right. The consumption of such a large amount of brandy—especially since she wasn't used to strong drink—had definitely made her feel a good deal better. And, although nothing could diminish her basic revulsion at learning of Maxine's behaviour, she also had to admit that Zarco had done his best to soothe her lacerated feelings.

As he had pointed out, his marriage had taken place several years ago. 'I have had a long time to think things over, and to realise that my life wasn't a total tragedy—not when I had my much loved son to care for. I simply made the mistake of picking a rotten apple from the barrel of life. It could have happened to anyone,' he'd added with a rueful shrug of his broad shoulders, before deliberately changing the subject.

Refusing to discuss any further the vexed question of his wife, Zarco had proved to be an attentive and amusing companion during the remainder of their meal in the restaurant. Not drinking himself, because he was driving, he'd nevertheless made sure that her own wine glass was replenished. Which had not been a very good idea, if the fumes of alcohol now swirling around her brain were anything to go by! But, whether or not it was the effect of the wine and brandy which she'd consumed, there was no doubt that she had swiftly fallen a willing victim to the beguiling force of his overwhelming attraction.

In fact, you allowed him to charm the socks off you! Tiffany was telling herself with disgust as the car swept down over the gravelled drive towards the front door of Norton Manor. But even knowing how feebly

she'd caved in to his dark enchantment couldn't seem
to dent her extraordinary sense of happiness and euphoria as he led her inside the old house.

Luckily, Amy Long had left a tray containing a
Thermos of hot coffee in the drawing-room. And
while Zarco left her for a few minutes, to check on
some business matter in the library, Tiffany hurriedly
poured herself a cup of liquid caffeine.

Unfortunately, even with the assistance of black
coffee, her mind simply didn't seem to be responding
to the alarm bells which were ringing at the back of
her head. And telling herself that she was crazy—that
she was on a one-way ticket to disaster and deep unhappiness—couldn't seem to puncture her crazy mood
of elation and intoxication.

Intoxication was absolutely the right word! She
must sober up! Tiffany warned herself grimly.
Because, if she didn't watch out, it looked as if she
was in grave danger of losing her head—and her
heart—to the man who had so dominated her life over
the last month.

She ought to hate Zarco, especially when she remembered just how abominably he had behaved towards her. But no wise words or stern warnings seemed
to have any effect on the deep tide of sick excitement
which seemed to be flowing through her veins. Even
thinking about his broad shoulders and his long, lean
legs was enough to bring on a case of the hot flushes!
In fact, if strong liquor and a brief exposure to Zarco's
hypnotic charm could produce this sort of effect on
her, she was undoubtedly in *deep* trouble, she thought
wildly.

'Ah, is that for me?' Zarco said, coming into the
room and sitting down beside her. 'I've just been
checking my fax machine,' he told her, his eyes glinting

with amusement as he took the cup and saucer from her nervous, trembling hands.

A silence fell in the room as she stared down at her lap, trying to avoid looking at the man who was sitting so close to her. All the physical sensations she had come to associate with Zarco, whenever she was in close proximity to his tall figure, had returned with a vengeance: her pulse was racing out of control, her mouth was dry, and her skin was burning although she felt as cold as ice.

'And did baring my soul tonight, at dinner, give you any answers to the questions in your mind?' he enquired smoothly.

'No, I'm afraid it didn't,' she muttered huskily. 'But—er—I really ought to thank you for the lovely meal, although I'm afraid that I must have drunk far too much wine,' she added, turning to glance at him.

'Really?' he drawled mockingly, his voice heavy with amusement as he leaned back in the sofa and smiled at her.

With one of the inexplicable, violent mood swings which had been affecting her lately, Tiffany found herself glaring at his handsome, tanned face. It was just one of his usual megawatt smiles, she told herself furiously. It was hardly the end of the world! And why its mesmerising effect should be causing her to feel totally spaced-out she had absolutely no idea.

'I—er—I think it's time I went to bed,' she mumbled nervously, desperately trying to tear her gaze away from the disturbing gleam in his dark eyes, their brilliant glitter carrying a message that was making her head swim. She could feel a deep throbbing excitement in the pit of her stomach, and a disturbing mixture of emotions that swung wildly between fear and awareness, sending prickles of apprehension tingling down the length of her spine.

'What a good idea! I think I'll join you,' he drawled blandly, although he made no effort to rise from the sofa.

A sudden surge of panic caused her to snap, 'Not in my bed, you won't!' before a deep tide of crimson swamped her pale cheeks. 'What I meant was, I . . . I don't want to put up with any more of your nonsense!'

He gave a dry snort of laughter. 'My nonsense?'

'You know *exactly* what I mean,' she protested, making a valiant effort to close her mind to the memory of her helpless response to his cynical love-making only a few days ago. 'To put it bluntly, I don't want you anywhere near my bedroom.'

'Are you sure?' he murmured slowly, his mouth curving into a wide, sensual grin.

'Absolutely certain!' she lied firmly, clinging on to her feelings of anger about the way this man had used her as if to a lifebelt.

She should have heeded the warning gleam in his eyes. But Tiffany was far too pleased with herself for having, at last, been firm with the obnoxious man, and was caught unawares as Zarco's hand snaked out to grab hold of her wrist—and a moment later she found herself suddenly pulled into his arms.

Dazed to find her slender body trapped within his firm embrace, she couldn't prevent herself from trembling violently, her pulses throbbing wildly out of control. She stared into his eyes, her heightened senses overwhelmingly aware of the warm musky scent of his male body, the faint flush on his high cheek-bones beneath the smooth tanned skin, and the dark curly hair at the base of the strong brown column of his throat rising from his open-necked shirt.

And then his dark head came down towards her. 'You're such a little liar, Tiffany...!' The words whispered against her soft lips were tantalising, causing her to quiver and shake with a deep and urgent need as his lips gently traced the shape of her mouth. His ragged breath and the fast, irregular thudding of his heart was echoed by her own body, and she was shaken to the core as she realised he was right. It was far too late to warn herself against losing her head and her heart to this man. She was already fathoms deep in love with him.

With her last ounce of control, she tried to push him away, her panic and protest lost beneath his mouth as he stormed her defences, his deepening kiss sending waves of fire pulsating through her body. And then slowly, very slowly, the relentless pressure of his lips eased, and he raised his head to stare down at her in silence, lifting a hand to gently brush the soft wavy curls from her brow. There was a deep hunger in the eyes devouring her pale face, and in the fingers which shook slightly as they brushed across her soft skin.

'Please, Zarco—let me go!' she pleaded, her voice husky with desire. But when she saw the sensual mockery in his brief smile, and the glittering darkness of his eyes beneath their heavy lids, she knew there was about as much chance of her wish being granted as there was of an eagle releasing its prey. His next words confirmed it.

'You aren't going anywhere—except to my bed!' he growled, the hoarse determination in his voice causing sensual images to flood her mind. Pulsating waves of heat seemed to scorch through every part of her body as, with effortless ease, he rose from the sofa and carried her limp, trembling form out of the room,

across the hall and up the wide curving staircase to
his bedroom.

Never having dared approach this wing of the old
house, which was always firmly guarded by a heavy
carved oak door, Tiffany had a confused impression
of the large room as she found herself being lowered
down on to a wide bed. The soft light of the lamps
glowed warmly against the strong colours of deep red
and blue with which his bedroom was decorated. And
then her bemused vision was filled by his dark
handsome face as he leaned over her.

'*Deus*—I want you!' he groaned deep in his throat,
swiftly undoing his shirt and throwing it aside before
turning his attention to her blouse. Cursing under his
breath at having to deal with the tiny pearl buttons,
he impetuously ripped the garment apart, his action
causing her to tremble and shiver at the force which
lay behind his raging impatience.

'I can't...' she moaned, a muscle beating convulsively in her throat. 'Brian always said I was
hopeless...and I don't really know how to——'

'Hush, beloved,' Zarco murmured gently, gazing
down into the girl's bemused sapphire-blue eyes, and
the hectic flush now covering her cheeks. 'Your
husband...? He was not kind to you, in bed?'

She shook her head. 'No...' she whispered miserably. 'But it was all my fault, you see. I couldn't
relax...and then he always became so cross...so
angry, and...'

She clamped her eyes shut with embarrassment,
almost flinching as she waited for Zarco to reject her,
as Brian had done in the past. But then she felt his
warm arms tenderly enfolding her trembling body,
drawing her gently into his embrace.

'You have no need to worry, my sweet one,' he murmured, his voice husky with desire. 'Your late husband was obviously a foolish man—and it is now my good fortune to teach you the delights of the flesh, yes?' he breathed, before beginning to kiss her very softly, his lips seeming to carry a magic spell as they trailed slowly down over her face and throat to her breasts.

The feel of his warm mouth and hands on her bare flesh sent quivers of excitement dancing across her skin once more. Beneath the mastery of his touch she gradually lost all fear. She was swept by a need to feel his bare body against her, the tactile warmth of his skin pressed close to her own; to savour the mind-bending sensations of his hands and mouth on her flesh.

Gradually, the rising sexual tension began flooding through her stomach, swelling the soft curves of her full breasts, and causing her to move wantonly beneath him, in a silent plea to be freed of the remaining barriers between them.

Her emotions were spinning out of control—and she simply didn't care! She seemed to be held fast within the grip of a languid, yielding and timeless force which drove out all fear of the past and the future. The only hard reality was here and now; the urge to lift her trembling hands to the dark curly hair of his broad chest, to slide her fingertips over the tiny, damp beads of moisture on his skin, and to feel the warmth of the firm flesh over his hard, muscular torso. She revelled in his strength as her fingers explored the smooth length of his back, the sound of his husky groan at her touch as he swiftly removed the last barrier of her thin silk underwear, inciting her to press her quivering lips against the smooth column of his

throat, her mouth savouring the peppery male taste
and scent of his skin.

'*Deus . . . Deus*!' he breathed as he swiftly removed
the rest of his own clothing. 'I've wanted you for so
long,' he whispered, the deep, huskily sensual note in
his voice inflaming her desire.

She was totally seduced by his mouth, moving
without haste slowly down over her body, exploring
each soft curve and crevice, the heat of his tongue
flicking erotically over her tautly swollen nipples, exploring her navel with a teasing sensuality. Every nerve
in her body seemed to be throbbing in response to the
arousing, voluptuous touch of his lips as he kissed
each one of her pink toes, leisurely brushing his mouth
over her insteps and up over the soft, velvety skin
behind her knees and on towards her trembling thighs.

She felt as though she was drowning—drowning in
ecstasy as his hands, lips and tongue continued to
caress and arouse her body. Love for him seemed to
produce an overwhelming, surging passion in which
there could be no resistance, no holding back. She
wanted to express her joy, to cry out that she loved
him beyond anything in the world, but her dazed mind
seemed incapable of finding the words to express her
feelings. And then there was no time for conscious
thought as she writhed and moaned helplessly beneath his intimate touch.

His fingers and mouth were stroking her, leading
her upwards towards some hitherto unknown pin-
nacle of bliss and passion, a faint film of perspiration
covering her skin as she heard a voice she hardly recognised as her own calling out helplessly as the
rhythm increased to become a frenzy inside her, before
she was suddenly seized by an endless series of
mounting convulsions, soaring up into such a

transport of ecstasy and delight that she was certain
that she would faint or die at any moment.

It was only then that his tall figure swiftly covered
hers with a dynamic urgency, and she welcomed his
hard, powerful thrust and the devastating, forceful
rhythm of his vigorous body, lifting them both upwards to the stratosphere. The muscles in his arms
and throat were projecting tautly, straining like cords
of steel until at last he, too, groaned in the release
and ecstasy of their mutual fulfilment.

Later, as she lay happily wrapped in his embrace,
vibrantly aware that Zarco's lovemaking far tran-
scended anything she could ever have imagined,
Tiffany gave a small sigh of deep and total contentment, before slowly drifting into a dreamless sleep.

Hours later, when she awoke to find herself still
cradled in his arms, it was to see the grey fingers of
dawn stealing in through the window. She lay for a
time quietly listening to the strong, rhythmic beat of
his heart.

She hadn't realised that Zarco was also awake, not
until he whispered in her ear, 'Are you content, little
one?'

'Mmm . . .' she murmured, still in that blissful, delicious state of not being quite awake.

'I wanted you,' he whispered, his hands beginning
to move slowly and sensually over her body. 'From
the first moment I saw you in the hospital, I knew I
must have you!' he added, pressing his lips to the soft
flesh of her shoulders.

It was the word 'hospital' which broke through to
register in her sleepy mind. And even as she responded to the touch of his fingers, which were now
softly stroking the sensitive tips of her breasts, she

was suddenly swamped by a cold tidal wave of harsh reality.

'Oh, no—we can't . . . we mustn't do this!' she gasped, beginning to struggle in his arms. 'I'm not your wife, and——'

'I thank God that you are not!' he whispered against her skin, his fingers continuing to caress her body, which quivered at his sensual touch.

'But don't you see? We can't do this—it's quite wrong!' she cried, fear and misery lending her a strength she didn't know she possessed as she pushed him away from her. 'Maxine is still your wife! And so this . . . this is *adultery*!'

'Maxine has *never* been a true wife to me!' he growled bitterly. 'And, since you tell me that your husband is dead, how can our lovemaking be called adultery?' he demanded, sitting up and pushing a forceful, angry hand through his roughly tousled dark hair.

But Tiffany knew she mustn't listen to him; that she was far too vulnerable to the siren-song of his dark attraction. With an enormous effort, she forced herself to concentrate all her energies on scrambling quickly from the bed, because if she didn't do so immediately she knew it would be too late.

'No. No, we can't . . . we mustn't do this! It's quite, quite wrong,' she sobbed, running blindly towards the door, tears streaming down her face at the realisation that, however much she loved this man, they could never, ever have any future together.

CHAPTER EIGHT

THE early morning sun was beginning to rise up over the horizon.

Walking slowly over the wide green lawn, Tiffany's bare feet left clearly discernible footprints on the grass, which was still heavy with dew. But not as heavy as her heart, she told herself with a deep shuddering sigh, her tired and weary eyes barely able to absorb the tranquil scene of woodland and meadows stretching out before her.

It had, without a doubt, been, at one and the same time, quite the most wonderful and yet the very worst night of her life. She ought to be glad that Zarco had made no move to prevent her from leaving, or to follow her sobbing figure as she had fled from his bedroom. But, perversely, she'd desperately hoped that he would. His presence would at least have been proof that she meant something more to him than just a brief, fleeting desire for her body. But she couldn't fool herself. He had never, at any time, either said or intimated that he loved her.

For one brief moment, when she'd turned in the open doorway before leaving his room, she had seen his face illuminated by a grey shaft of early morning light stealing in through the open, mullioned windows of his room. His chiselled features, highlighted by the pale light of day, had looked drawn and haggard, and she could almost have deceived herself into believing that it was pain she'd seen in his eyes. But, of course, she quickly told herself, she must have been mistaken.

A sharp, agonising spasm gripped her stomach for a moment. It seemed impossible that she could ever be able to forget the total joy and ecstasy which she had experienced in Zarco's strong arms last night. And yet, having discovered the rapture and delight of his lovemaking, she now found herself burdened by a deep, heavy sense of wrongdoing. She didn't even have the excuse of not knowing that he was a married man. Who better than *she* to know the truth about his desperately unhappy state of wedlock?

And always in the forefront of her mind, and in every fibre of her trembling body, was the realisation—when it was now far too late—that she had fallen deeply and hopelessly in love, with a man who could never reciprocate her feelings—or make her his lawful wife.

Despite her lack of sleep, and the throbbing, pounding headache which was causing her to wince at the glare of the bright, early morning sun, Tiffany's brain was still capable of functioning normally. Totally sick at heart, she was torn between her common sense and her turbulent emotions. Although it was the last thing in the world that she wanted, she knew that she had no choice: she must leave Norton Manor as soon as she could—today, if possible. Because, if she'd wanted to run away before, to escape from the imprisonment forced on her by Zarco's mistaken identification, she was doubly determined to do so now.

There was nothing to keep her here. No excuse for Zarco to continue to maintain that she was his wife— a fact which she had always known to be false. And, now that he was firmly convinced that she was not

Maxine, Tiffany knew that she no longer had any reason to remain in this lovely old medieval manor house.

At the thought of Maxine, her mouth tightened. She felt a deep, simmering fury at having been so contemptuously used as a mere pawn by the other woman. And, although she still didn't know how or why, she was quite convinced that Zarco's wife had been the main force behind what was clearly a very complicated, well planned and well executed theft. If she should ever meet Maxine, she'd cheerfully plunge a knife into the other woman's black heart, Tiffany told herself with grim relish.

However, indulging in the fantasy of an extremely painful and clearly well deserved fate for the other woman wasn't going to achieve anything. In fact, even if the dreadful woman had never existed, and the meeting between her and Zarco had occurred in another time and place, he would still have been way out of her reach. Their relationship could never have had a happy ending—even if he'd been free and unencumbered by a wife. Because, if she was to be sensible and honest with herself, Zarco was totally out of her class.

What did she, who came from a very ordinary background and who'd been married to an unsuccessful tennis player, have in common with an extremely wealthy Brazilian aristocrat? Although they had both been swept by a sudden mutual passion for each other, it couldn't last. The white heat of overwhelming desire would soon have faded, and when it did—as it must inevitably—what would they have left between them? Tiffany knew nothing of his social world, or his business life, and would have found herself like a fish out of water. His smart friends would have looked at her askance, and she'd have been unhappy and uncomfortable in his obviously glamorous, sophisticated world.

So maybe his realisation that she was not his wife had come just in time to save them both from a dreadful mistake?

But, as Tiffany grimly acknowledged, it was one thing to give herself a stern, moral and sensible lecture—and quite another to try and force her wounded heart to accept the level-headed, practical good sense behind her reasoning. Instinctively she knew that Zarco was her first and only love. She would never be able to feel for anyone else the deep, overwhelming intensity of emotion that she felt for him; even when she was old and grey the thought of his tall, dark and handsome figure would always cause her heart to miss a beat.

As she was almost drowning in misery and despondency, it was some time before Tiffany registered the brief, jerky movements on the periphery of her vision. Frowning, she paused and peered through the early morning mist towards the dovecot. Surely... surely that had been the figure of a man which she'd just seen disappearing behind the ancient circular brick and stone structure?

However, as she moved slowly towards the dovecot, past the neatly clipped yew hedge, she realised that she must have been mistaken. There was no sign of anyone or anything—other than a frightened rabbit, which scampered quickly out of her way as she walked around the outside of the building.

She was just telling herself that it must have been a figment of her overheated imagination when a hand suddenly flashed through the half-open door of the dovecot, roughly grabbing her arm and dragging her inside.

Taken unawares, Tiffany gave a muffled shriek as she was spun around, and practically thrown against the rough brickwork inside the old structure. She was gasping with fright, and it was some time before her eyes became used to the murky darkness, barely pierced by the pale glimmer of daylight coming from the many small, round holes high up in the wall. She could only see the outline of a man silhouetted against the light from the open doorway, her legs trembling as her mind registered the threatening stance of the figure now moving slowly towards her.

'So, you thought you could dump me—huh?' the man growled. 'Well, I ain't being double-crossed—not by you, or by anyone else!'

Tiffany could feel her legs trembling. There was something about that voice that seemed familiar... The sound of the harsh, nasal twang was causing her to shiver and shake as if she had a fever.

'Yeah! It's me, honey!' The man gave an evil laugh as he came to a halt in front of her nervous, shaking figure. 'But I'm here to tell ya, Maxine, baby, that you don't get rid of your old man that easily!' He gave a snigger. 'Here I am—and here I stay, until I get what I've come for!'

As the man took another step forward, his squat, ugly figure was illuminated by pale shafts of light from the small openings, high above his head.

'T-Tony ...!' she gasped as a blinding flash seemed to zigzag through her brain like forked lightning. Once again she could see in her mind's eye the back of his curly head topped by a grey peaked cap as he sat in the front of a large limousine. 'I saw you...in Lisbon!'

'Yeah, yeah!' he muttered impatiently. 'I guess the fact that I'm here is one nasty surprise as far as you're concerned, right? Well, that's just your tough luck, Maxine, baby!'

'You're making a terrible mistake!' Tiffany protested breathlessly. 'I'm not Maxine. She's completely disappeared, and...' She faltered as he threw back his head and gave a peal of raucous laughter.

'Tell that to the Marines, honey!' he said, before the smile was wiped off his face as he took a menacing step towards her. 'I reckon it's time to stop fooling around, huh? I want my share of the loot—and I want it right now!'

'I don't know what you're talking about.' She flinched, cowering against the wall as he grimaced, and jabbed an angry finger towards her. 'I don't have any loot, and...and I promise you—I'm truly *not* Maxine!' she cried helplessly, her eyes skidding nervously about the empty building, looking in vain for some avenue of escape.

'Hey—you're really into this crazy act of yours, aren't you?' Tony shrugged. 'So—OK, I'm a reasonable sorta guy. All I'm saying is, a wife should share things with her husband, right? So, I'll guarantee to keep out of the way, and not to spoil your little game—but I ain't going anywhere, not without what's owing to me.'

'I don't understand...' Tiffany whimpered. 'You're not married to Maxine!'

'Oh, no?' Tony grinned wickedly at her. 'Well, I'd say that having two husbands is *definitely* one too many, honey! But I guess that's your problem—right?

So let's cut out all this nonsense. Just give me my share of the loot, and then I'll disappear like a good little boy.'

Tiffany had given up trying to understand what he was talking about. All she was concerned about was the burning question of how she could escape from this frightening, evil man. But as soon as she took even a small, sideways step, she saw that he was watching her like a hawk. Whoever Tony might be, he clearly had no intention of letting her go. But how was she to get out of here? He seemed totally obsessed by what he called 'the loot'. So, maybe...?

'I—er—I don't have the loot hidden in here,' she began tentatively.

He grinned. 'That's better. I thought I could get you to see sense. So, where is it?'

Tiffany stared at him blankly for a moment. How big was 'the loot' supposed to be? 'Er—it's in the house,' she muttered, 'and I'll have to go there to get your—er—share.'

'OK, I'll buy that,' Tony nodded slowly. 'Got the jewellery hidden away in a safe place, have you?'

Jewellery? Did that mean that Tony was also involved in the theft from Zarco's safety deposit box? But what had he got to do with Maxine?

'Well...?' Tony demanded impatiently.

'Oh—er—yes, it's in the house,' Tiffany agreed quickly.

'And the gold too?'

She nodded fervently. 'Yes—it's all there.'

'So—what are we waiting for? Let's you and me go and get it, honey!' he laughed, quickly reaching forward to grab hold of her arm and dragging her reluctant figure out of the dovecot, across the wide green lawns towards the house.

If *only* she could somehow attract Zarco's attention! Tiffany told herself desperately as she hung back, trying to delay their progress as long as possible. But it was no good. He would still be asleep in his bedroom, on the far side of the house, she realised with a sinking heart.

And then—quite miraculously!—as they neared the old building, she saw the front door being thrown open to disclose Zarco, a furious scowl on his face as he stood framed in the doorway, clothed only in a short towelling dressing-gown.

'Help! *Help me*!' she cried, wrenching her arm away from Tony's grip before taking to her heels and racing towards the security of that tall, dominant figure who had, surprisingly, made no movement towards her. 'It's Tony! He wants the jewellery that Maxine stole from you!' she yelled.

So intent on escaping from Tony, and reaching the safe haven of Zarco's arms, she had no thought or eyes for anyone else. As her bare feet sped across the soft, cushiony surface of the wet grass, she couldn't stop her rapid motion when she reached the gravelled drive.

She barely heard Zarco's shout of warning, nor the sound of the post office van, roaring up the drive to deliver that morning's letters.

The toot of the horn came too late for Tiffany to save herself. As her wet feet slid out from beneath her, she was struck a light, glancing blow by the wing of the vehicle, which tossed her backwards like a rag doll. A brief second later, her head hit the hard surface of the drive with a heavy thump, and as the world seemed to spin dizzily on its axis she was sucked down into a dark, swirling void.

She woke once, her confused mind having an impression of being inside a moving vehicle, and of bright lights slanting down into her dazed eyes, before she lapsed back into unconsciousness again.

When she awoke for a second time, Tiffany immediately knew where she was. It might not be Portugal—and from the sound of a high-pitched English voice next door it certainly wasn't—but hospitals seemed to be the same the world over.

And maybe it was the association with the hospital, in Lisbon, but she realised that she could now easily remember everything which had happened to her in the city—the meeting with Maxine; the destruction of her room in the hotel; her trip to the Quinta dos Santos in Sintra . . . even that desperate struggle on the edge of the cliff, when she'd been so nearly killed by Zarco's wife and Tony.

But *why*? The question seemed to be burning in her brain as she struggled to fit all the pieces of the complicated jigsaw together. But it was hopeless. She couldn't even remember why she was now lying here, in a hospital.

Raising a trembling hand to her head, she sighed with relief to find that she *wasn't* wearing a bandage. In fact, as her trembling fingers explored her head, she discovered that apart from a large, sore lump on her forehead, a splitting headache and a painful shoulder, she seemed to be all right.

The entry of a young, white-coated doctor, and his reassuring words, put her mind to rest.

'It seems you were in a collision with a post van,' he told her with a grin. 'And, although you've only had a mild concussion, your past history of a blow to your head, followed by temporary amnesia, means that we think you ought to have some tests. Just to make sure you're as fit as you look!' he added reassuringly, before his bleeper urgently called him to the aid of another patient.

The departure of the doctor seemed to set in train a series of flying trips around the various departments of the hospital. Checking her from tip to toe, all the various experts pronounced themselves satisfied, but she was left feeling desperately tired and exhausted.

'I'm going to give you a mild injection—just to help you to sleep,' the doctor told her as she was wheeled back into her room. 'You'll feel much better tomorrow morning.'

He was quite right, she realised, surfacing the next day as a pretty young nurse bustled into the room.

'And how are we feeling today, Mrs dos Santos?'

'All right, although my head and shoulder are still very sore,' Tiffany muttered, deciding that she really didn't feel strong enough to resume all the old arguments about the fact that she wasn't Maxine.

'I'm not surprised. You had a very nasty accident,' the nurse told her, coming over to take her pulse and temperature. 'Doctor says that you're going to have to stay here for another day, just until he's checked all the results of your tests.'

'I—er—I forgot to ask—exactly where am I?'

'This is the private wing of St Thomas's Hospital,' the nurse told her. 'And when you get out of bed you'll have a really wonderful view across the River Thames to the Houses of Parliament,' the girl added, going over to pull the curtains well clear of the large window.

'I wish I knew what I was doing here.' Tiffany frowned, unable to remember anything other than Tony's threatening behaviour in the dovecot, and her mad dash across the lawns of Norton Manor towards the safety of Zarco's tall figure.

'Your husband had you transferred up here by private ambulance from the casualty department of your local hospital. I'm sure he'll be pleased to hear that you're doing so well.'

Will he? Tiffany wondered, her fingers nervously winding themselves in the thin hospital blanket. 'I know I've been unconscious for a while, but I don't remember seeing him here, in the hospital...?' she murmured tentatively.

'Oh, well—I expect he's been busy at work. You know what men are like!' The nurse smiled at her comfortingly.

But the other girl's words had confirmed Tiffany's worst suspicions. Zarco *hadn't* been to see her. Was he already regretting their passionate lovemaking? Maybe this was the perfect opportunity for him to get rid of her, she thought miserably, the painful ache beginning to pound in her head once more.

When the doctor came to see her that evening, confirming that she'd been given a clean bill of health by the neurology department, she told him that she wanted to discharge herself.

'Oh, we can't have you doing that,' he told her firmly. 'I understand that arrangements have already been made to take you home tomorrow. So, just be a good girl, and take things easy for the next few days,' he murmured, before whisking himself out of the room to see to his other patients.

What home? she thought dismally. Norton Manor certainly wasn't her home. And, since Zarco hadn't bothered to visit her here in the hospital, it was obvious that he didn't want to have anything more to do with her.

Of all the trials and tribulations which she had suffered over the past month or so, Zarco's abandonment and desertion of her now—at a time when she desperately needed the warmth and comfort of his presence—seemed the unkindest cut of all. Surely he could have spared her just a few moments of his precious time? Even if only to say goodbye...?

The sleeping pill which Tiffany been given that night completely failed to send her to sleep.

Maybe it was her over-active brain which was to blame for her restless state, as she tossed and turned through the endless hours before dawn. Trying to think how she could escape from being taken back to Norton Manor, and having to suffer an emotionally fraught, humiliating farewell scene with Zarco, Tiffany kept coming up against the same obstacles: she had no money, no clothes and no personal identification. And, without any of those three important items, she was well and truly stuck!

The clothes question was temporarily solved the next morning, when a suitcase was delivered to her room containing a sapphire-blue summer dress and matching jacket. However, while resigned to her unhappy fate, Tiffany's spirits took a further dive when she looked at herself in the mirror. The sleepless night was reflected in her pale, chalky white cheeks and the dark shadows beneath her tired blue eyes. She looked

awful! But there was nothing she could do about it,
since whoever had packed her case—probably Amy
Long, now she came to think about it—had totally
failed to include any make-up.

Not that it mattered all that much, of course, but
if she was going to have to face an embarrassing scene
with Zarco she would have been grateful for at least
the help of some lipstick. The sight of her looking
like this was only going to confirm the wisdom of
Zarco's obvious decision to get rid of her as quickly
as possible.

With a heavy heart, Tiffany accompanied the nurse
down in the lift, and out through the main entrance
to the hospital.

Last night, she'd thought of a wild scheme of trying
to gain the nurse's help; of begging the other girl to
lend her some money, so that she could slip away to
a small hotel before getting a job, in London. But the
cold light of day had shown her the futility of such
an idea. Even her belated attempt to ask the doctor
to phone Zarco, and tell him not to bother to have
her picked up, had been greeted with a laugh—as
though she'd been attempting to be funny. Which was
a joke in itself, she thought gloomily. Humour was
just about the last thing one needed in any dealings
with that hard, dangerous man, Zarco dos Santos!

And she might have known her pathetic attempts
to escape their last meeting would be doomed to
failure. Because as the nurse led her across to a large
black limousine she saw Tom Long in his chauffeur's
uniform holding the rear door open for her.

Sitting in solitary magnificence in the back of the
large vehicle, she was grateful to Tom for not engaging her in conversation during the lonely journey

back to Norton Manor. She was feeling too distraught for social niceties, and by the time they rolled up the drive she was in a dire state of nervous tension.

At the sound of the vehicle, Amy came hurrying out on to the steps, anxious to welcome her home.

'The master is still away in Amsterdam, on business. However, I've faithfully promised that I'll look after you until his return,' she assured Tiffany, clucking her teeth with distress at the obvious strain on the girl's pale face.

'It's up to bed with you—and no arguments!' the housekeeper said crisply, leading the way slowly up the stairs, and along the passage towards Zarco's wing of the house.

'This isn't the right room!' Tiffany protested, as Amy took hold of her arm and steered her firmly into the large bedroom, whose rich jewel colours gleamed in the midday sun.

'It's the Marquês's orders. It's more than my life is worth not to do as he says!' Amy retorted, her cheeks reddening slightly as Tiffany gazed at her in astonishment. 'And not before time too, if you ask me!' the older woman muttered under her breath as she bustled off to run a bath for the clearly exhausted girl, who looked as if she was going to collapse at any minute.

'What is—er—the Marquês doing in Amsterdam?' Tiffany asked, when she was being helped into the comfortable bed by Amy.

After a swift look at the girl as she lay listlessly back against the pillows, Amy hesitated for a moment. 'I expect he'll tell you all about it when he gets home tomorrow,' she murmured, before drawing the curtains and advising Tiffany to try and have a good sleep.

And, despite her conviction that 'a good sleep' was quite beyond her, Tiffany realised that she must have drifted off, because it was many hours later when she opened her eyes—to find herself blinking dazedly up at the tall, commanding figure of Zarco.

Still not fully awake, she gazed sleepily at the man standing beside the bed; the arrogant Brazilian, who had totally dominated her life for the past month or so.

Dressed in a dark formal suit, his black tie starkly etched against the crisp white silk shirt, he looked particularly formidable. And yet, beneath the surface of his tanned complexion, his skin looked grey, with deep lines of strain etched on either side of his mouth and dark shadows beneath his eyes, which gave his handsome features a drawn, haggard appearance.

'How are you feeling?' he asked quietly.

She couldn't answer him immediately. Her heart was too overflowing with love and tenderness to be able to find the words to answer his polite enquiry.

'I'm much better,' she managed at last, careful to avoid his eyes as he helped her to sit up, holding the glass of water as she took a small sip. 'Did . . . did you have a good trip?'

'No, I didn't.' He frowned, as if her question was an unnecessary irrelevance, before grating, 'I hope Amy has been looking after you properly?'

'Yes, she's been very kind,' Tiffany whispered, staring down at her nervously twisting hands, and swallowing hard to keep her tears at bay. 'I don't mean to be a nuisance. I promise you that I'll leave—just as soon as I'm fit and well. I may have to borrow

some money, of course, but I'm sure that I can soon
find a job...' she babbled, suddenly frightened of this
tall, seemingly remote-looking stranger, who was now
gazing down at her with barely concealed anger in his
glittering eyes.

'That's *all* I need!' he exploded furiously. 'Don't
you realise just how much agony you've caused me?
You were only unconscious for a day—but, I swear
to God, it must have been quite the longest, most terrifying twenty-four hours of my life!'

She cringed back against the pillows as his rage
seemed to fill the large room.

'I didn't mean . . . it really was an accident!' she exclaimed helplessly. 'I was only trying to get away from
the awful man, Tony. He seemed convinced that I
knew where "the loot" was hidden. And he also
seemed totally convinced that I was Maxine! I was so
frightened . . . I couldn't think what to do . . . and then
I saw you, and . . .'

'Hush, my darling!' he murmured, swiftly casting
aside his anger and fury as he sat down on the bed,
gathering her shaking, trembling figure into his arms.
'It's all over now. You're quite safe, and there's
nothing more to worry about,' he murmured
soothingly.

Just my broken heart—that's all, she told herself
miserably, unable to prevent herself from savouring
the warmth and security of his strong embrace. It was
wrong for her to be leaning weakly against his broad
shoulders like this—and she'd never do it again, of
course. But surely she would be forgiven for seeking
the sanctuary of his arms . . . just this once?

'Please don't be cross with me,' she whispered tearfully against the soft cashmere of his suit jacket. 'I

know it was an idiotic thing to do—to run into a van, but——'

'*Deus*, Tiffany—are you mad? I'm not cross with *you*!' he exclaimed incredulously, his hands holding her away from him for a moment as he studied her pale face, and the tears welling up in her sapphire-blue eyes. 'It was the hideous danger you were in that I found so terrifying. When I saw you lying on the drive, like a limp rag doll,' he growled, his voice hoarse and grating, 'I nearly went berserk! I was convinced that you were dead, and I was almost out of my mind with shock. And, even when the doctors said you would live, I was so frightened that you would remain forever in a deep coma; that I would lose you—my heart's desire—forever!'

She had grown pale at the suppressed force behind his huskily voiced words, unable to believe what she was hearing.

'But Zarco, I don't understand...' she breathed, before he clasped her tightly in his arms once more, his lips possessing hers with a great hunger that said far more than mere words could possibly have conveyed.

Her slim arms wound themselves about his neck and she melted beneath the heat of his scorching kiss—desperately craving the touch of his lips on hers; a need and a desire so intense that she could almost die for it. And she couldn't bear for him to stop, because when he did she knew that she would have to be brave; to find some courage from goodness knows where, and force herself to bid a final, agonising farewell to the only man she had ever loved.

When Zarco reluctantly let her go some moments later, it was all she could do to open her eyes and look at him.

'The doctors tell me that I must take good care of you,' he said huskily, settling her carefully back against the pillows. 'Although, only the good lord knows how I am to keep my hands away from your delicious body!'

She shuddered at the sensual words, the hoarse note in his voice sending shivers feathering up and down her spine.

'Zarco—we really must be sensible!' she gasped, her own voice tremulous as she tried to find the right words which would finally put an end to their relationship.

'*Sensible* . . . ?' He gazed at her with incredulity, before giving a short bark of laughter. 'I never cease to be astonished by the English—or their use of the language! How can I possibly be *sensible* at such a time?' he added scathingly. 'I come from a Latin race—so kindly do not speak to me of sense and sensibility, when all *I* wish to talk about is my love for you!'

'But . . . but you can't!'

'No? And who is to tell me what I can and cannot do?' he demanded, with a return of his old arrogance.

'No—you misunderstood me. What I meant . . . what I was trying to say——' But she wasn't given a chance to finish the sentence, as Zarco leaned forward and kissed her.

This was madness! She *must* stop him! she told herself desperately. But the tender touch of his warm lips, and the moist excitement of his probing tongue as his kiss deepened, completely swept away all rational thought.

'I love you,' his murmured, his voice thick with a yearning hunger as he reluctantly raised his dark head. 'I love you, my dearest Tiffany, with all my heart!'

'And I love *you*!' she cried tearfully, caught up in a white-hot, feverish turmoil of thwarted desire and passion. 'But there's Maxine! We can't just behave as if she didn't exist, can we?'

If she had hoped that her words would bring him to his senses, it seemed that she had succeeded only too well. For one moment he stared at her with shocked, horrified eyes, and then sighed as he slowly rose to his feet.

'You cannot know, of course,' he said, as much to himself as to her, before walking slowly over to stare out of the window, which was open to the soft night air.

'Know what?' She gazed at his tall figure in bewilderment.

He didn't reply for a moment, continuing to stare blindly out of the window. 'I was not able to be with you when you were in the hospital in London,' he said at last. 'For the very good reason that I received a sudden call from Amsterdam to say that my wife had been killed in a car crash. It was a head-on collision with another vehicle, while she was being chased by the Dutch police. Luckily, the occupants of the other car escaped with their lives.'

Tiffany stared at him in horror. 'What . . . what was Maxine doing in Amsterdam?'

'It is the centre of the diamond trade, and it seems she was trying to sell my family's jewellery,' Zarco said, before giving a heavy sigh and pushing a tired hand through his dark hair. 'My agents had managed to track her down, at long last, and alerted the police. They were waiting for her in the shop, but she must have smelled a rat. Leaving the diamonds and emeralds behind her, she apparently ran out of the shop, jumped into a nearby car that had been foolishly parked with its keys still in the ignition, and must have been so intent on evading the police that she didn't look where she was going.' He gave a sad, weary shake of his head and sighed heavily once again.

'I think I should tell you that I've remembered what happened to me in Portugal. When I woke up in hospital, it was all there in my mind,' Tiffany said quietly, before giving him a brief outline of what had happened to her, following her meeting with his wife in the health club in Lisbon.

'Yes...Maxine was truly an evil woman—and what she did to you was unforgivable,' he said sorrowfully as he began to slowly remove his jacket. 'It all seems such a waste, somehow. Maxine was born with so many gifts: beauty, brains, courage...but they were all turned to corruption and wickedness by a twisted, vicious streak in her basic character.'

'What happens now?' Tiffany asked hesitantly. 'Do you have to go back to Amsterdam?'

He shook his head. 'No. The funeral was yesterday,' he said, taking off his black tie. 'It was a bit of an ordeal, breaking the news to her father over the phone. He took it very well, but I hadn't the heart to tell him about Tony Silver.'

'That awful man!' She shuddered. 'He was involved in the theft with Maxine, you know.'

'He was involved in far more than that!' Zarco told her grimly. 'While you and I have been going through the torments of hell, and agonising about my so-called "adultery", the agents I employed to dig up the details of Maxine's past have now come up with a pretty kettle of fish. It seems, my dear Tiffany, that I was never *legally* Maxine's husband...because she'd never obtained a divorce from her first husband, Antonio Salvatore—alias Tony Silver!'

'*What*?'

Zarco gave a short bark of rueful laughter. 'I really *was* a fool, wasn't I? I never thought to check out her background. But, if I had, I would have discovered that Tony Silver had fallen foul of the mob, in New York. Fearing for his life, he apparently arranged his fake death, and then escaped to Europe to lie low for a bit. In the meantime, Maxine—who had obviously been involved in Tony's arrangements—played the grieving widow to perfection. And her so-called marriage to me convinced Tony's bosses that he was indeed dead.'

'I can hardly believe this! You mean to say...?'

'Yes. Maxine's marriage to me was totally illegal. She was still Tony's wife—right up to the day she died. It's incredible, no?'

Tiffany stared at him with dazed eyes. 'So why did Tony turn up here, of all places?'

Zarco shrugged. 'It seems that Maxine had tried to double-cross him over the jewellery. Although I'm not totally certain about this, it appears that the original plan was for them both to carry out the theft, before disappearing together. But then...Maxine met you, my darling, and had a *much* better idea. If she could convince everyone that she had been killed, they wouldn't have been looking for her, would they? And with *all* the money from the sale of the jewels she could live very well for a number of years, with no fear that I would be trying to track her down.'

'But that's crazy!' Tiffany shook her head in helpless bewilderment. 'Ordinary people simply don't do that sort of thing!'

'You're quite right. But then, Maxine wasn't an ordinary person. And her plan wasn't so crazy—because it very nearly worked,' Zarco added, a note of grim savagery in his voice. 'If a stranger hadn't seen you struggling with Maxine and Tony on top of the cliff, and raised the alarm, this story would have had quite a different ending!'

'I simply can't seem to take all this in,' Tiffany muttered, her head spinning with confusion.

'I still find the whole business quite extraordinary—and I've had some days to absorb all the facts,' he agreed, coming over to sit down beside her, and gently brushing a small lock of hair from her brow.

'And you were *never* really married to Maxine?'

'No. I'm afraid that I have been made to look a complete fool.' He gave a rueful shake of his dark head.

'But... but I still don't understand why she went to all those lengths, and...'

'Two million pounds is a great deal of money,' Zarco told her quietly. 'And, since there was obviously a risk that divorcing me would have brought her dubious past to light, Maxine clearly decided to settle for what she could steal from my safety deposit box instead.'

'But why involve me?'

He sighed. 'My darling, I realise that you must have so many questions. But it has been a long day. So I'm going to have a shower, and then we'll ask Amy to serve us a meal, and then...' He leaned forward to give her a soft kiss on her forehead. 'Then we must make arrangements for a wedding. I am hoping that you will take pity on me—and make sure that I am *legally* married to someone, at long last!'

Tiffany gasped. 'You mean...?'

'I will leave you to work it out,' he grinned, giving her another swift kiss before rising from the bed and disappearing into his bathroom.

CHAPTER NINE

WHEN Zarco returned from having a shower, Tiffany, whose brain was still whirling in dazed confusion, could only stare helplessly at the man whom she loved with all her heart.

Wearing only a short white towel about the slim waist of his tall, lean body, his tanned skin still bearing tiny droplets of water from the shower, he looked impossibly handsome. Zarco *must* be every woman's dream hero, she told herself unhappily—quite unable to believe that he truly loved her.

'How is your poor head?' he murmured, coming over to sit down on the bed beside her.

In far better shape than my poor heart, she thought wildly, unable to tear her eyes away from the strong muscles of his bronze torso.

'There's nothing really wrong with me,' she told him huskily. 'The hospital were just worried because it was my second bout of unconsciousness.'

'Ah, yes.' He shook his dark head, sighing heavily as he clasped hold of her nervously trembling hands. 'They were quite right to be concerned. When I arrived at the hospital in Lisbon, I was warned that you might not survive your accident. You appeared to be in such a deep coma that I feared the worst.'

'But... but that was still when you thought that I was Maxine, so...'

'I cannot pretend that I felt anything for her, other than considerable repugnance and dislike,' Zarco said slowly. 'But I can promise you that I *never* wished her any physical harm—certainly not her recent and most shocking death. I hope you will believe what I say?' he added, looking at her with concern.

'Yes, of course I believe you,' she reassured him quickly. 'I can remember asking why you hadn't bumped her off years ago—and being surprised at just how forcefully you rejected the very idea of doing such a thing.'

He shook his head sorrowfully. 'I was not kind to you in Lisbon.'

'No—you certainly were not!' She gave a shaky laugh. 'I was simply *terrified* when I first saw you.' She shuddered. 'Not only did I think that you were the devil incarnate, but, quite honestly, I don't think I've *ever* been so frightened in all my life as when I woke up to find you looming menacingly over my bed!'

'But you must try to understand the situation in which I found myself,' he said quickly. 'I was very tired and full of jet lag after a long plane journey. And there was my wife—who had been no wife to me—lying unconscious in hospital. I could not understand why she was in Lisbon, or what she was doing there. Although, knowing her as I did, I knew that some trickery must lie behind her unexpected visit to that city. And yet...' He sighed deeply.

'I became desperately confused by your obvious fear of me, and of your sweet gentleness—both responses so completely unlike those of Maxine. And I must also confess...' He paused, his cheeks reddening slightly. 'I was also *very* confused and upset to find myself feeling a strong sexual urge and attraction to-

wards a woman whom I disliked; a woman I had never
touched since the day of our marriage.'

'Oh, Zarco—what a mess it all was!' Tiffany sighed.

He gave a low, rueful bark of laughter. 'That, my
darling, is a complete understatement! The situation
became even more complicated when I discovered the
theft from my safety deposit box. I was *so* angry and
furious—not so much at the loss of the gold and
valuable jewellery as at myself for having been careless
enough to let Maxine get away with such a plan—that
I couldn't see beyond the end of my nose. If I am to
be honest, I must confess that it was my pride that
was hurt most of all,' he added with a wry grimace.
'And, of course, I now realise that I had already begun
to fall in love with you. So I'm afraid that my frustrated desire only added more fuel to the flames of
my ever increasing rage and fury.'

'You always seemed to be in a blind rage with me,'
she agreed sadly. 'But surely you must have known
fairly soon—or at least suspected—that I wasn't
Maxine?'

'Yes, I think I did,' he muttered, letting go of her
hands to brush his fingers agitatedly through his damp
hair. 'But my emotions were in such a turmoil that
for some time I simply didn't know *what* to think. At
one point, I seriously feared that I was losing my
sanity. Especially since I could hardly manage to keep
my hands off you ...!' he breathed, leaning forward
to give her a long, ardent kiss.

'Don't!' she begged as his lips left hers to press but-
terfly-soft kisses over the soft contours of her face.

'Don't—what?' he murmured, trailing his warm
mouth down the long line of her throat.

'We shouldn't be doing this. I've only just come out of hospital, for heaven's sake!' she gasped, her voice barely audible as he pressed his moist lips to the swell of her breasts, rising above the bodice of her thin silk nightgown.

'Then you must just lie still—and do as you're told!' he teased gently as he slipped the thin straps of the gown from her shoulders, exposing her full breasts to his view.

The feel of his long tanned fingers on her burgeoning flesh seemed to trigger an instinctive response quite beyond her control. Gazing mistily down at his dark head as he caressed her breasts, tracing the outline of her nipples with his tongue, before drawing the hard peaks into his mouth, she couldn't help gasping with delight, a helpless victim of the sweet, urgent ache which seemed to possess her whole body.

Lost in a sweeping blur of overriding passion, she trembled beneath the waves of desire and longing crashing over her as he gently and carefully removed her gown, before he slowly and tantalisingly began to kiss his way down her slim figure. His lips seemed to be on fire, branding her flesh with the mark of his fervent possession and love as he sought and found every secret part of her body.

'*Zarco*!' she cried, writhing with ecstasy as he pressed his mouth to the heated centre of her flesh, the mounting excitement causing small helpless moans to break from the back of her throat as she shuddered convulsively beneath the erotic, sensual rasp of his tongue. And then he urgently tossed away the small towel he'd been wearing, and as his strong body covered hers she felt the hot, velvety thrust of his strong thighs.

'I love you, my sweet Tiffany,' he breathed thickly. 'I will always love and worship you . . . for the rest of my life.'

The sound of his husky vow seemed to fill her ears as the world faded away, leaving only their two bodies moving together in a delicious, exciting rhythm that was as old as time itself, before spiralling headlong into a whirling vortex of rapturous joy and total commitment.

Much later, as Tiffany lay drowsily cradled in his arms, he murmured, 'I know it was not wise to make love to you—not when you have yet to recover from your injuries. But, my sweet one, I *really* couldn't help myself! I was selfishly possessed of an overwhelming need and desire to demonstrate my total love for you,' he added with a sigh.

'Oh, Zarco . . .' she whispered, almost unable to believe her own happiness. 'Are you sure? Are you *quite* sure that you and I . . . that we . . . ?'

'I am certain that I love you,' he said firmly, the hard conviction in his voice allaying her numerous fears. 'I am also totally determined to make you my wife—as soon as possible. We will have a quiet wedding, here in the village church, and then I will take you away with me on the Orient Express to stay at the Cipriani Hotel in Venice.'

'Are you *always* going to make all the important decisions in our life?' she asked with a slight frown.

'Of course! Do you *seriously* believe that I am likely to change my character?' he grinned, softly kissing away the small crease from her brow.

'No, I'm afraid I don't!' she laughed. 'But why Venice?'

He gave a slight shrug of his powerful shoulders. 'Because you have never been there, and I am quite sure that you will be entranced by that lovely city. And also,' he added, the warm smile dying from his face, 'I don't wish to start my married life with you in Brazil, which holds far too many memories for me. And we will be spending much of our future life both here in England and on my large estate, in the south of Portugal. So...Venice seems a good choice, hmm?'

'Yes...it sounds marvellous,' she agreed, wondering how to frame her next and very important question. 'I—er—I've never talked to you about your first wife, Zarco. I don't want...I mean, I know you loved her very deeply, and...'

'That was a long time ago,' he said firmly. 'I was a much younger and quite different man when I was married to Charlotte. And, although I have grieved most sincerely for the tragic loss of her young life, she is now a warm and much loved memory in my heart. What I feel for you, Tiffany, is a totally different emotion. It is not that of the young, callow youth that I once was. It is a mature and adult passion; a desire not just for your body, lovely though it is, but for the kindness and sweetly caring nature of your soul.'

'Oh, *Zarco*!' she whispered, quite overcome by his words, and her total happiness in being in his arms. 'I will try to be a good stepmother to Charlie,' she promised.

'I have absolutely no doubt that you will succeed. The boy is clearly already very fond of you, and I'm sure that he will be thrilled to have some new sisters to play with.'

She gazed up at him in bewilderment. 'Sisters . . . ?'

'I would like some lovely daughters—just like their mother!' He smiled down into her dazed eyes.

'Oh—goodness! I hadn't thought about having a baby. I mean, everything has happened so fast, and...'

'You might even be carrying my child at this moment,' he murmured, placing a possessive hand on the bare flesh of her flat stomach.

'Well, I would like a little time for just the two of us—and Charlie as well, of course,' she told him firmly. 'I think you're going to be quite enough to deal with, before I have to cope with any more of the dos Santos family!'

'You will manage us all perfectly,' he told her with a slow smile, his fingers beginning to move sensually over her body.

'No, really Zarco—not again! You can't . . . !' she gasped as his touch became more urgent and determined.

'Are you seriously suggesting that I cannot be permitted to make love to my future wife?' he demanded imperiously.

'Who—me? I wouldn't *dream* of even mentioning such heresy!' she giggled, before happily surrendering to the overwhelming force of her love for that hard, arrogant man—Zarco dos Santos.

Next Month's Romances

Each month you can choose from a wide variety of romance with Mills & Boon. Below are the new titles to look out for next month, why not ask either Mills & Boon Reader Service or your Newsagent to reserve you a copy of the titles you want to buy — just tick the titles you would like and either post to Reader Service or take it to any Newsagent and ask them to order your books.

Please save me the following titles:	Please tick	√
BREAKING POINT	Emma Darcy	
SUCH DARK MAGIC	Robyn Donald	
AFTER THE BALL	Catherine George	
TWO-TIMING MAN	Roberta Leigh	
HOST OF RICHES	Elizabeth Power	
MASK OF DECEPTION	Sara Wood	
A SOLITARY HEART	Amanda Carpenter	
AFTER THE FIRE	Kay Gregory	
BITTERSWEET YESTERDAYS	Kate Proctor	
YESTERDAY'S PASSION	Catherine O'Connor	
NIGHT OF THE SCORPION	Rosemary Carter	
NO ESCAPING LOVE	Sharon Kendrick	
OUTBACK LEGACY	Elizabeth Duke	
RANSACKED HEART	Jayne Bauling	
STORMY REUNION	Sandra K. Rhoades	
A POINT OF PRIDE	Liz Fielding	

If you would like to order these books in addition to your regular subscription from Mills & Boon Reader Service please send £1.70 per title to: Mills & Boon Reader Service, P.O. Box 236, Croydon, Surrey, CR9 3RU, quote your Subscriber No:...
(If applicable) and complete the name and address details below. Alternatively, these books are available from many local Newsagents including W.H.Smith, J.Menzies, Martins and other paperback stockists from 12th March 1993.

Name:..

Address:...

....Post Code:.........................

To Retailer: If you would like to stock M&B books please contact your regular book/magazine wholesaler for details.

TORN BETWEEN
TWO WORLDS . . .

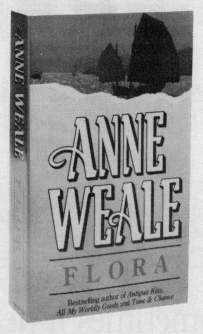

A delicate Eurasian beauty who moved between two worlds, but was shunned by both. An innocent whose unawakened fires could be ignited by only one man. This sensuous tale sweeps from remotest China to the decadence of old Shanghai, reaching its heart-stirring conclusion in the opulent Longwarden mansion and lush estates of Edwardian England.

Available now priced £3.99

W⬤RLDWIDE

4 FREE

Romances and 2 FREE gifts just for you!

You can enjoy all the heartwarming emotion of true love for FREE!
Discover the heartbreak and the happiness, the emotion and the tenderness of the modern relationships in Mills & Boon Romances.

We'll send you 4 captivating Romances as a special offer from Mills & Boon Reader Service, along with the chance to have 6 Romances delivered to your door each month.

Claim your FREE books and gifts overleaf...

An irresistible offer from Mills & Boon

Here's a personal invitation from Mills & Boon Reader Service, to become a regular reader of Romances. To welcome you, we'd like you to have 4 books, a CUDDLY TEDDY and a special MYSTERY GIFT absolutely FREE.

Then you could look forward each month to receiving 6 brand new Romances, delivered to your door, postage and packing free! Plus our free Newsletter featuring author news, competitions, special offers and much more.

This invitation comes with no strings attached. You may cancel or suspend your subscription at any time, and still keep your free books and gifts.

It's so easy. Send no money now. Simply fill in the coupon below and post it to -
**Reader Service, FREEPOST,
PO Box 236, Croydon, Surrey CR9 9EL.**

NO STAMP REQUIRED

Free Books Coupon

Yes! Please rush me 4 free Romances and 2 free gifts! Please also reserve me a Reader Service subscription. If I decide to subscribe I can look forward to receiving 6 brand new Romances each month for just £10.20, postage and packing free. If I choose not to subscribe I shall write to you within 10 days - I can keep the books and gifts whatever I decide. I may cancel or suspend my subscription at any time. I am over 18 years of age.

Ms/Mrs/Miss/Mr_____ EP31R

Address _____

_____

Postcode_____Signature _____